I AM ENGLAND began the magnificent saga of an English village from AD 70 to 1589.

THAT NEAR AND DISTANT PLACE continues the story of Furnace Green, which is also the story of England – of the ordinary people, of farmers and traders, witches, aristocrats and poachers whose lives were changed, challenged, and re-shaped by the history of the land.

THAT NEAR AND DISTANT PLACE is a huge and immensely satisfying novel that powerfully completes the story of a village community welded together by centuries of tradition, blood, passion and catastrophic change.

I AM ENGLAND was the winner of the 1987 Historical Novel Prize in memory of Georgette Heyer.

Also by Patricia Wright

I AM ENGLAND

and published by Corgi Books

THAT NEAR AND DISTANT PLACE

Patricia Wright

CORGI BOOKS

THAT NEAR AND DISTANT PLACE
A CORGI BOOK 0 552 13379 5

Originally published in Great Britain by
The Bodley Head Ltd.

PRINTING HISTORY
The Bodley Head edition published 1988
Corgi edition published 1989

This book is set in 10/11pt Linotron 202 Baskerville by
Rowland Phototypesetting Ltd, Bury St Edmunds, Suffolk

Corgi Books are published by Transworld Publishers Ltd,
61–63 Uxbridge Road, Ealing, London W5 5SA, in Australia by
Transworld Publishers (Australia) Pty Ltd, 15–23 Helles Avenue,
Moorebank, NSW 2170, and in New Zealand by Transworld Publishers
(N.Z.) Ltd, Cnr Moselle and Waipareira Avenues, Henderson,
Auckland.

Made and printed in Great Britain by
Hazell Watson & Viney Limited
Member of BPCC plc
Aylesbury, Bucks

CONTENTS

This book is dedicated to
CLIFFORD DEARDEN, Pilot Officer,
No 2 Squadron RAF
Killed in his Lysander defending the
beaches of Dunkirk, May 1940

. . . THE WITNESS:

Last night a great gale blew out one of Edenham's windows, showering my bed with glass. Fortunately the wind had dropped by morning although doors still slam, pictures rattle in the draught, and a couple of seagulls glide leisurely overhead. I hear them scream, and pretend I can see how gracefully they slant their wings this way and that, lazily playing with the wind.

Soon they will head back to join their quarrelsome kindred along the coast, some twenty-five miles from here as a hungry seagull flies, but for a morning they are content to use the ridge's updraughts as a holiday diversion. Now they are riding a strong gust northward to where the main road climbs up to Furnace Green, only to recoil from exhaust fumes and for the first time need some hasty flappings to reach a warm wet current which takes them across to the church tower. From there they study the whole village with their arrogant yellow stare: its single street of cottages and the green beyond; the blind turn by the churchyard wall, a legacy from monks a thousand years ago which gives frequent frights to motorists today; the house called Wyses, and beyond it the green where there used to be a pond. Beyond again and the rain-washed woods begin, on this autumn day alternately sodden dark and ablaze with gold and bronze and yellow.

A five-minute shower glittering with rainbows drifts out of the west and the gulls take off again, the call of the sea more insistent now. Indecisively they drift south-eastward towards the ruins of Ockham Abbey, the hedgerows beneath their wings exaggerated by shadow as if the vanished generations who wore those surfaces down still hurried about their business. Above Edenham the gulls wheel higher crying shrilly, and I come out on the doorstep, one hand on my stick. Though I cannot see them my ears remain sharp; my imagination, too, is more easily loosed in old age. The gulls clamour again, and in my mind I soar with them down the ridge towards Tisbury Hill. How very much I would like to see that distinctive shape like a woman's breast once more before I die, climb upward beneath its splendid trees until I reach the ancient banks where life first began hereabouts.

But I am being exasperating, indulging an old man's fancy and telling my tale as if all time was one. Instead I must grasp at time and distance, remember I have already told you about the first fifteen hundred years of Furnace Green. By the end of the sixteenth century, Sussex had lived through invasions, plague, a splendid flowering of abbeys and churches, also developed the first craft in which England became supreme: iron.

As the following century drew on, the Sussex ironworks began to exist precariously from year to year, fighting mud and foreign competition once small Wealden streams proved incapable of powering ever more ambitious processes. Privation threatened owners and craftsmen alike, made all the more bitter because for several generations this had been a place where life could be taken by the scruff and made to yield hope and opportunity.

It was as if events on the ridge, in however distorted a way, mirrored the catastrophe which began to overwhelm England itself during this time. As one by one the unspoken understandings, unwritten laws, ungodly compromises, snapped almost unperceived, until this very English way of forging strength for its government without overmuch repression was left resting on force alone. Here, the next four hundred years of Furnace Green's story begins.

1

An Oak Falls

1640–1657

The cart jolted unmercifully on unsprung wheels and its occupants realized soon after leaving Tonbridge how rash they had been to ignore advice to use oxen if they wanted to venture from Kent into Sussex. Rain fell in heavy, irregular showers. The road was often little more than a trough gathering wetness from a saturated land, its surface so pitted that their horses were in danger of drowning if they slipped.

The trio in the cart were ill-assorted. The driver was an old man so used to endurance that discomfort affected only his outermost rind; a woman lay on the boards behind him, less old, but so broken by the fatigues of her journey that the most shattering jolts no longer roused her, and alongside her sat a twelve-year-old boy. He looked about him eagerly, delighted by each fresh sight, and often scrambled down from the cart to investigate something which caught his fancy. He had a long nose and long narrow face; grey eyes, tousled straw-coloured hair and a narrow gangling body. Occasionally his tumbling curiosity reminded those who observed it of a heron poised above a particularly promising fish. His name was Daniel Gage.

Ten miles separated Tonbridge from Furnace Green, and during that autumn day they covered only seven of them; the easiest seven, a woman feeding geese assured them. '’Tis all steep from here, and the way like a river as you climb up to the ridge. The horses might swim up, but not pulling a cart full of traps.'

The old man shrugged. 'Us maun have a try.'

'Eh?' The goose-woman cupped her ear to the alien intonation of his voice. 'What heathen parts d'ye come from then?'

'Across the river in Essex, where land is land and no gurt sea o' mud and trees.'

'Stay there, then,' she retorted, and slammed her door in his face, leaving the geese honking disconsolately outside.

'There's a team of oxen coming,' said Daniel, standing up in the cart to see better. 'They aren't hitched to a load, so I expect they're on their way home. Shall I ask the drover if we could load our bundles on their backs? Oxen wouldn't notice even Mistress Coffey strapped on as well.'

The old man shrugged again, all he wanted was a completed task and payment in his belt. 'Do as 'ee likes, but I maun stay wi' the horses.'

Daniel lowered himself cautiously into the road, where mud reached nearly to his waist. Everything for miles around seemed to drain into this shallow valley where some huts surrounded an evil-smelling spring. After a struggle he hauled himself up a bank to await the oxen's arrival, quite certain that if he slipped their disagreeable old driver would never stir from his box in time to save him from drowning.

The ox drover was a powerful, gypsy-looking man who carried a twelve-foot goad, and two boys sitting on his lead pair jeered at Daniel as they came close. They were wild folk hereabouts, thought Daniel, who had never before left Theydon Magna in Essex. 'Hey, master,' he called to the drover, not knowing how else to address him. 'Are you going past Furnace Green?'

The man halted his team with a long-drawn 'Whoooup!' and pushed a leather hat back on his head. 'What if I am?'

'We would be grateful for a ride if you are indeed going there. It can't be far, but our horses are foundered.'

'Horses aren't any good for carrying burdens in the Weald.'

'No,' said Daniel patiently. 'We can see that now, but this country is new to us. We came from Essex and are bound for Furnace Green.'

'So you said. You must be the folk Lady Riffield took the corner cottage for.'

'Oh yes, we are, if you would only let us ride with you!' exclaimed Daniel hopefully. Mistress Coffey had not stirred under her coverings, and these hamlet people huddled around their reeking spring seemed as inhospitable as swine in a wallow.

''Tis all the same to me,' answered the drover, humming a tune and watching Daniel out of the corners of his eyes. 'If you shift yourselves, that is. I live at Corndown by Furnace Green, and have a fancy to be home before midnight.'

Daniel laughed politely, since it was not yet dark and midnight many hours away, but soon discovered that Alex Laffam never joked. Under a fitful moon the three miles between Tonbridge's Wells, as the reeking springs were called, and Furnace Green seemed endless. The oxen seldom stopped but zigzagged irregularly up a long slope to a ridge Daniel couldn't see, each leg deliberately pressed down a scant hoof-width from the last. Daniel rode perched on one of the oxen, a willing beast called Cheerful who did not require driving with the miniature goads wielded by the exhausted ox-boys. Mistress Coffey was strapped to one of the following pair, their packs slung haphazardly elsewhere on yokes and backs in exchange for a silver coin. Several fell off into the dark but Daniel did not notice this; Mistress Coffey had noticed nothing for a very long time.

Alex Laffam shouted often at his beasts and to keep his boys awake. Whenever they stopped to breathe the oxen he came wading up to question Daniel, each time beginning where he left off an hour or more before. 'Are you fearful?' he demanded once.

'No,' answered Daniel truthfully, although he had never imagined so dark and strange a place, where ancient forest met above his head and roots writhed underfoot like beasts from another age. 'I'm tired of tame flat fields. Three days ago we crossed the Thames by oyster-shallop and I saw ships for the first time; then at Chatham we passed the yards where they are made. There were carpenters' shops and ropewalks, sailmakers sewing cross-legged on their floors. One day I might like to go for a sailor, but just now I want a fire and a roof over my head again.'

'Why are you coming to Furnace Green?'

'Mistress Coffey was nurse and then tiring-woman to Lady Riffield until her eyes grew too dim for sewing, when she was given a cottage in Theydon Magna. Now milady has a fancy to bring her closer while her lord is away fighting for the king.'

'And you, young shaver?' Laffam poked Daniel experimentally. Boys were cheap to hire and this one seemed bright enough to be useful.

'I'm Mistress Coffey's sister's son. She took me to live with her after my mother died.' Daniel had grown up surrounded by consuming village curiosities, and did not resent interrogation.

'A slow life for a boy.'

But this Daniel refused to answer, because Laffam was right. He had indeed often felt stifled by the lack of interest in his days, but it seemed disloyal to say so while dull, well-meaning Mistress Coffey drooped soddenly from an ox's back, three parts dead from the chills.

They set off again, at last reaching a high open space where the noise of rain on trees faded and Daniel could see a blacker depth to his right, a few pricks of light on his left. By long instinct the team set off faster then, and Laffam had difficulty making them stop at a sharp corner where the wind droned against a church steeple upthrust into storm clouds. 'Stir yourself, boy!' he yelled. 'Pile off and collect your traps together. The beasts can smell their stall, d'you see, and if I let go the traces they won't stop before they reach Corndown. Untie the old woman and take her inside, Davey lad,' he added to one of the ox-boys.

Daniel was so cold and his thighs so chafed from unaccustomed riding that he could scarcely stand, and in the blackness he had to fumble with rain-swollen knots by touch alone. Since Alex Laffam had hauled them tight he had no chance of success, and when Davey came back from dumping Mistress Coffey over an unseen threshold he cuffed Daniel aside and slashed at the ropes until everything tumbled off in the mud. The boy then bawled that all was clear and the oxen instantly picked up stride again, leaving Daniel bowed under pelting rain, surrounded by packs he could not see and facing the dim bulk of an unlit and unheated cottage.

About five miles away to the west, Faith Scovell, Countess of Riffield, tossed restlessly in her wide bed, listening to the castle clock strike midnight. Even so late as this, Riffield Castle was seldom completely still. Faith had never counted how many people lived and worked there but it must have been over two hundred, and even a year of war had not greatly reduced the number. A few of the brawnier footmen, most of the grooms and perhaps a dozen outside servants had ridden off with Henry when he went to fight, but others had soon asked to take their place and it had never occurred to Faith that she might not need so many servants with her lord away.

Her father had been a London merchant who had built himself a mansion in the Suffolk countryside, and since he was both immensely rich and in a hurry to claim the place in society which riches and a better-born wife than himself could bring him, Faith had grown up in a household where everything, from a new colt to the lace for her dresses, had its own keeper and quite likely an underkeeper as well.

She listened now to horses stamping in the stables beyond the garden court, to feet on cobbles and soft, quick movement somewhere close followed by a smothered giggle; the call of a watchman from the stone tower which survived from the medieval castle was answered by a bellow from the gate-guard. But though Faith heard them, she did not notice these sounds of normality. Instead, her thoughts were on a boy she had never seen, who was coming to Furnace Green. Tomorrow, surely; he ought to be there tomorrow. But for appearances' sake, she mustn't seem over-eager to visit Mistress Coffey, her old nurse with whom he came, or tongues would certainly begin to wag.

She tossed again, her thoughts like spiderweb in a gale. What would Daniel look like? Like Gage? Like her? Please God, no, or this scheme to bring him closer would explode like a bombard in her face. She at least owed Henry her discretion, a loving husband whom she did not love. Like Gage, then. Her lips moved, smiling, against the quilt-edge. When she fell in love with Gage, one of her father's grooms, even in their time of glory she had never thought of him by his given name.

What a time it had been! A wild, impossible, crazy time when hitherto unremarkable Faith Littleton threw herself headlong into an affair with an under-groom, and so ensured his death. Gage hadn't cared any more than she about the risks they ran; Gage was fearless with men and horses, his insolence tolerated because of his way with Sir John's stallions. Nevertheless, he was often flogged for it, a magnificent young stallion himself who had filled Faith's body with mindless desire from the first day she rode out with him in liveried attendance.

To begin with he had mocked her when, too besotted for modesty, she whispered that she loved him. Then taunted her savagely, his dark arrogance like that of the peregrines tethered in their mews: the same expression of withdrawn violence, the same deadly curve of wing suggested by the edged bones of his face. His eyes too were almost golden; wild, malicious and uncaring. He had said quite frankly that he stayed at the manor only because he handled splendid horseflesh there, and when he had learned all he could, he would go. To join the Barbary pirates, the head groom said darkly, who each time Gage was thrashed was careful afterwards to watch the shadows behind his back.

Laughter, mockery and brutal indifference alike made no difference to Faith, when even pain was pleasure if it came from Gage. His strength, his flaying tongue, his unashamed male greeds, all mesmerised her and he, of course, never counted the cost of giving her what she craved. She was even more helpless after their first savage mating in a wood, snatched minutes as they waited for her mother to return from a social call, while Faith rode cross-country to meet her with Gage as attendant. Breeding, decorum, prudence, all were swept aside, and afterwards she thought only of next time . . . Next time he was rougher, his methods cruder, the risks they took more lunatic. But she remained like a drunkard who is satisfied only by ever rawer draughts. No wonder her memory blurred when she looked back. No wonder her body still quickened each time she allowed herself to remember.

Her senses returned two weeks later. They had grabbed a few minutes—because he never pretended to tenderness or consideration, Gage never needed long—as he escorted her from visiting a neighbour, but this time he threw her down across a root which drove into her back. Perhaps if the pain had come directly from Gage she would still have gloried in it. As it was she began to struggle, cried out and twisted under him until he could not have failed to know she was in agony. He simply forced her harder, until she thought her spine must snap and her mouth, impaled by his, could only shape the incoherent sounds of broken pride and revulsion.

He laughed when he finished, and invented a story about her horse throwing her, because she could scarcely walk.

Next day, he vanished. Although Faith was horribly stiff she went down to the stable yard, still fascinated, but with some of the joy fading from her love. A new man was strapping her mare and he gazed at her blankly when she asked for Gage.

Faith stamped her foot. 'Tell me at once! Where has he gone?'

He scratched his head. 'I dunno, mistress. Hired to look after your Firefly I be, not Gage.'

She bit her lip, frightened now. Of course Gage intended eventually to seek his fortune away from soft Suffolk, but it was unbelievable that he should simply go.

She heard herself muttering as she ran from stall to stall

in the yard. Truly, she had been crazed by Gage and the infection had raged too fiercely for her to outlive it in a single day. Then she heard the clatter of a horse ridden hard and raced out again, but it was her father dismounting by the hitching post. He looked as he might have done in his hard-bargaining days and not at all how his indulged younger daughter had ever seen him before. But, like any simpleton, she blurted out that Gage had gone. He swore aloud and turned to the head groom who had ridden in with him. 'Remember, Bull. You know nothing whatsoever of this.'

'No, Sir John,' said Bull woodenly, who had already been well rewarded for bringing this scandal to his master's notice. 'There'll be tattling, though. You maun blame me if—'

'I'll blame whoever I choose, so look you to it. Turn off anyone you must or start another scandal over someone else's daughter, I care not how you do it. Afterwards, you won't find me ungrateful.' He grasped Faith above the elbow. 'As for you, we'll talk elsewhere.'

Where they talked was another thing Faith did not remember, because he told her Gage was dead.

'You killed him,' she whispered unbelievingly.

'Don't be a fool,' he said impatiently. 'Although why I should say so I don't know, since fool is a compliment to how you've behaved. What in the devil's name possessed you?'

'Gage,' she answered simply.

He exclaimed aloud, but during the next few weeks Faith learned something of the abilities which had brought John Littleton a fortune trading in the City. When he told his wife about Faith's madness her first inclination had been to believe her husband was deranged, her second to retire to a darkened room. Instead Sir John made her give lavish entertainments, while he stirred up all the grosser infamies hidden beneath the surface of Suffolk society, until gossipings about Faith were lost in the most tantalisingly scandalous season the county had ever known. He also dealt unmercifully with Faith, since, as he said, she apparently had a taste for brutality.

This was not true. Faith Littleton was naturally gentle, a little stubborn perhaps, a beanstick of a girl with the kind of face which appealed to most men's protective instincts. Now Gage was gone she had the oddest feeling of being scarcely visible, as if every sensation her life was likely to hold had already been expended. Yet, in a way, Sir John's mastery slipped easily into the void where Gage had been. Inevitably, she was pregnant. She had never considered the possibility and indeed knew little about it, but her father was prepared: Gage, he said, was the kind of animal who could be relied on to quicken an out-of-season barren mare.

The high waistlines and flared stomachers of the time favoured concealment, and Faith was healthy and uncomplaining. Only Martha Coffey, her old nurse and now her tiring-woman, knew that she was nearly seven months gone with child before she was obliged to give up appearing at her mother's side, and by then the family had removed to London for a further round of entertainment. Gage's son, Daniel, was born in a hired house on Highgate Hill, swaddled and sent away with Martha Coffey before Faith woke to find her breasts bound and aching on the morning after her delivery. At first she wept, but was never given time to mope. Within a week she must be up and standing through a reception at Guildhall. Drabs worked the day after a birthing, said Sir John; if Faith behaved like a street-woman then she must be presumed to have their stamina as well.

Eventually she accepted that the boy would be best sent away into the country. She could not keep him and her father promised that if she did not make a fuss then Daniel would be well provided for. He also said quite plainly that if she refused to accept his arrangements, then the child would be farmed out for a London wet-nurse to rear, whose name she would never know. Any girl brought up even partly in the City as Faith had been, knew what that meant: few children kept in London's slums survived their first year, nor many born to richer parents either.

What Faith did not appreciate were the many retreats which would follow this first decisive defeat. Until after her father's death she was never able to discover where Martha Coffey had been sent to live, and Daniel became no more than an unseen pledge. If Faith did not welcome suitors . . . keep a still tongue . . . go wherever her parents wished in order to meet the sons of their friends . . . if she did not do all this and more, then Daniel would suffer whatever happened to be the likeliest threat at the time, the most potent of which became the threat to apprentice him at five years old, as foundlings were.

Long before then, Faith was married. Ironically enough not to anyone her father chose, the Earl of Riffield being far too grand for John Littleton to dream that Faith might become his wife. Henry Scovell, Earl of Riffield, was a scholar and thirty-eight years old, a widower for several years and childless. He needed to marry again since his ancient line had become thin-blooded and if he died then his inheritance, held in direct succession for six hundred years, would pass through a cousin to a pack of brawling Yorkshire squires.

Faith made not the smallest attempt to catch the Earl of Riffield's attention, nor did Lady Littleton introduce her daughter to him with any thought that he might be attracted by her. They met at a time when the king was squabbling with the London merchants over money, as well as with his Parliament over power, and the most unlikely acquaintances were struck up by such constitutional discords. Henry liked Faith's quiet gentleness and mistook her indifference for a placid and undemanding nature; he was also not above discovering that John Littleton was extremely rich as well as deeply committed to the Parliamentary interest. The Scovells, on the other hand, were king's men, although Henry was a born conciliator and recoiled from the idea that civil war might come: it didn't require much calculation to realize that John Littleton would be less strident in opposition if his daughter became the Countess of Riffield. Only after their marriage did Henry begin shyly and tenderly to love his wife, and Faith to discover her own impatience with caresses which seemed unendurably insipid after Gage's passions.

Matters weren't helped when Faith remained barren. She longed for children to take the place of Daniel, and, because she had conceived easily with Gage, when she failed to do so with her husband quite soon began to behave with subtle contempt towards him. The years dragged past but nothing seemed to get better. Faith detested the cold spaces of Riffield Castle, the belching ironworks spread across alien Sussex landscapes, and though she tried, was incapable of becoming interested in Henry's preoccupations. He was a scholar of some note and fascinated by the ancient documents in Riffield's muniment room; she shivered in the draughts blowing down stone-flagged passages, longed for the modern salons favoured by her father's trading friends and wrinkled her nose against the smell of rotting vellum. All the same, disloyalty towards a considerate husband made her feel wretched: Henry was so damnably kind that often she could have screamed.

The crisis of 1642 came on her unaware. King Charles had been quarrelling with his councillors, judges, Parliament men and tax-gatherers for as long as Faith could remember and she was used to her father's derisive comments about a monarch incapable of ruling his realm as had his ancestors, within a balance of interests. Though Henry often went to court, where Faith was surprised to discover that his opinion was respected by men whose names were household words, she could not make out what such heated wranglings were about, and he took so long to explain that she lost patience before he finished.

All the same, she loved to be back in London, where the streets boiled with excitement and courtiers spilled through Westminster's alleys in a great sprawl of silk and velvet and well-starched lace. Only here and there would dark-clad Puritans or a disapproving Parliament lawyer stalk through the cheerful throng, usually well jeered on their way and lucky not to be tumbled in the dust.

Then some crisis worse than the rest blew up and the Riffields left London in a hurry, much to Faith's disgust since she hated winter in Sussex. But once they returned to the castle, life quickly settled into its own routine; only the furnaces, though much reduced in recent years, were belching more smoke than Faith had ever seen, and at night the glow from Park Forge lit up the ceiling of her room.

Her first sense of real disquiet came in February 1642, when Parson Syke from Furnace Green rode over and remained with Henry for most of the morning. Faith disliked Syke, a self-important Puritan who saw the Devil everywhere, and eventually she decided it would be a kindness to rescue Henry from his clutches. The old Scovell barons would have set their hounds on such an irritating nobody, she reflected fretfully.

Henry looked up and smiled when she entered. 'Come in, my dear. I fear Parson Syke brings bad news.'

'Oh?' said Faith expectantly. Any news was better than none.

'He intends to blockade the track leading from Park Forge.'

Faith went into a peal of laughter. 'Wearing an owler's hat, no doubt!'

'I do not customarily joke about serious matters,' Syke said stiffly. Owlers, or Sussex smugglers, had short shrift from him. He had a bluff red face and looked more like a rollicking squire than an over-sober parson, a man of affairs who traded in iron at the same time as running his parish with unrelenting efficiency.

'Mr Syke is very hot for Parliament,' explained Henry.

Faith looked from one to the other, astonished. There could have been no greater contrast than between pudding-faced parson and ascetic earl; she wouldn't have believed her ears except neither was the type to join the other in jest. 'I remember Suffolk people as hot for Parliament, but it didn't lead them to blockade each other's tracks,' she said at last.

'Yet,' answered Henry drily.

'Aye, Suffolk is a godly county,' agreed Syke with satisfaction. 'Nor will His Majesty find many supporters here in Sussex. So we mean to make sure our cannon are kept out of his hands while this dispute lasts, since we cannot trust a tyrant not to use them against God's people.'

'Park Forge belongs to Riffield,' Faith said hotly. 'You can't—'

'There's no end to what Parson Syke has decided he can and cannot do.' Henry was leaning against some bookshelves and looked amused rather than infuriated. 'The law means nothing when set against his aims. Or so he says.'

Blood thickened in Syke's face, turning him an alarming mauve. 'When set against my conscience, no, my lord. I've watched your devil-furnaces working night and day to make guns for use against God's flock, don't you deny it. Well, enough's enough. If the king is to muster his followers in arms, then by my reckoning we also must protect our own. I myself have bought up Edenham Forge and plan to cast guns there again, a place which has been naught but a jobbing smithy since old Nick Wyse died close on forty years ago. Now we mean to see that Wealden cannon are made again to defend us.'

'I have no quarrel with that, Mr Syke.'

The parson's jaw dropped. 'You haven't?'

'I trust that all our weaponry will defend us, as one nation under our anointed king.'

'Aye, that's what we all pray for, but methinks only a godly realm can live in peace.'

'Oh, surely not,' said Henry gently. 'Englishmen have lived together in peace a long time now, but it would be a foolhardy man who said that most of us were godly. And the few that are, I'd say not often found in Sussex.'

'That will change, my lord. Meanwhile, your cannon stay at Park Forge.'

'Then let me propose a bargain. If I give you my word that no cannon will leave any manufactory of mine, nor any furnace hereabouts which is pledged to the king, so long as the situation remains in doubt, will you swear that none shall leave those bound to the Parliamentary interest?'

'All the great Wealden ironworks except yours are for Parliament.'

'Further south there are those which will cast for His Majesty, if it comes to war. Which God forbid.'

'I can answer only for Edenham, which isn't yet fired,' Syke answered sulkily.

'Indeed? My intelligence is otherwise.'

Faith listened in growing bewilderment. Henry Scovell might be a gentle husband and merciful landlord, but the blood of imperious ancestors ran in his veins and she had never before heard him deal with a trumpery parson as if he were an equal.

For the first time Syke looked disconcerted, and then thoughtful. 'It must be every man's hope that the fighting, if it comes, can be kept out of Sussex.'

'Then what say you to the bargain I propose?'

Syke hesitated, before thrusting out his hand. 'Aye, I accept. Let us try to keep peace between neighbours if we can.'

'No wish of ours will prevent great shedding of blood everywhere in the kingdom if war indeed should come. Remember that in your preachings, Mr Syke.'

'God and not I speaks through my mouth,' answered Syke, but as Henry remarked to Faith afterwards, one was never rid of Puritans without a final offering of cant.

'But why deal with him at all?' she asked. 'Your steward is paid to treat with petty parsons and their like.'

'When war comes—'

'When?'

'Yes, when. Even though I pretended that matters still rest in the balance. Once war comes, Parson Syke will be an important man: ironmaster, lender at interest and bigoted preacher all in one skin. God knows, he sets my teeth on edge but he's honest according to his lights, and might swallow some principles if it helped keep fighting out of the Weald. As I would, too.'

'Is it so very different if Englishmen fight each other elsewhere instead of Sussex?' Faith thought painfully of the wide pastures of her childhood.

'I tried and failed to counsel His Majesty and his ministers into prudence, so I'm not listened to any longer. Probably I never was. A Scovell who prefers compromise to a fight: what a pity, men will say, when the blood of an old line turns to milk. So now I protect my own people and lands as best I can, and if bargaining with Syke will help, so be it. Others already feel the same, and there will be more of us with each year of war. When there are enough, peace will come again. I fear that day is far removed.' He spoke jerkily, an accomplished pedant fumbling for words as Faith had never seen him do before.

She touched his arm. 'At least no one expects you to fight.'

He winced, and indeed she might have expressed her thought more felicitously to a husband sixteen years her senior. 'I shall ride to join the king when I must.'

'The king?' she echoed, truly astonished this time. 'You've opposed most of his policies for years, I heard my father say so! Why, we met in Guildhall because you came to conciliate traders quarrelling with the Privy Council over unjust taxes.'

'I opposed designs I believed would lead to disaster, but spoke and acted as a counsellor of His Majesty, not a rebel in the making. I'm too old to change my loyalties now.'

'Even though you know he has acted foolishly and unjustly?'

'Keeping a faith sometimes has little to do with either wisdom or justice. Not that my sword will greatly benefit His Majesty, supposing I can find one in the castle,' he added wryly.

After that, Faith took more interest in events, and yet it

remained very difficult to make sense of them all. News was scant and garbled, the countryside quiet, the prospects for hawking or harvest most people's main preoccupation. Henry subscribed to a circular letter which once a fortnight outlined the latest information, but it, too, remained as much filled with the price of cloth or wine as the long-winded sayings of people she had never met. One thing was clear, however: both king and Parliament were arming, while those of differing or torn loyalties eyed each other with new suspicion. Friendships grew colder and men began covertly to burnish such arms as they possessed.

As the harvest came in, the king raised his standard at Nottingham while Parliament began to gather its forces north of London, and so, without anything happening in Sussex to mark it, war began. A week later Henry led his personal following out of the courtyard of Riffield Castle to join the king.

He said farewell to Faith in the great hall, a public parting by intention. A man took his leave of a loving wife in private, but when he loved and all she felt was tepid affection, then formality was more bearable.

'Take care of your health and do not offend Parson Syke, who is likely to be our new taxmaster,' he said, smiling as he jammed his hands into ancient iron-studded gauntlets.

'And you take care in such unseasonable weather, my lord.'

He grunted, rain drumming on the hall roof like a doom-laden harbinger of war. Through the open door Faith could see the courtyard fetlock-deep in water, the men already mounted to keep their saddles dry. She went with him to the edge of the rain and stood, her hand raised to the door timbering while his groom whisked a cloth off his saddle and in the same motion threw his master up so hard that Henry had to struggle to keep his balance. He looked frail and old, huddled against the downpour. Regret and loneliness swept over Faith, tears unexpectedly blurring her sight. 'Come back safe, my dear.'

He looked at her, surprised. Then urged his horse across

to where she stood, bent and kissed her firmly on the lips. He did not speak, but she was glad to know she had sent him away happy.

It was six months after Henry left that Faith's father died, in February 1643, six months which had been filled with almost unbroken royalist success. Since there had been almost no fighting in Parliamentary East Anglia, Faith left almost at once to stay with her mother for a while. Although never a loving wife Lady Littleton was prostrated by grief, and Faith, who at first had been delighted to return to her own home, soon became exasperated with her. Of intent, she spent most afternoons working her way through her father's papers until eventually she found the docket she knew must be there somewhere. Sir John had been a methodical man and would not have lost track of a grandson, however unwelcome his parentage.

Faith discovered that Daniel Gage, now twelve years old, lived with Martha Coffey in the village of Theydon Magna in Essex, where Martha was paid to maintain him in the style of an artisan's orphan. Her first instinct was to order a coach and search the Essex backlands for Theydon, but fortunately her thoughts settled before she could commit such folly. Now she lived childless and alone in cold Riffield, she wanted Daniel close by for always, not kept hidden in Essex for an occasional visit.

Chin on her fist, she answered her mother's complaints at random while scowling through an evening at the fire, weaving her plots to bring Daniel into Sussex. Regretfully, she discarded the notion of employing him in the castle or on the Earl of Riffield's estates; she felt enough affection for Henry, wretchedly shivering through the discomforts of a hated war, to recoil from making him a laughing-stock while his back was turned. Certainly she would love Daniel too much to keep the relationship secret once he was established among the rampant curiosities of Scovell dependants, as she had loved Daniel's father too much to keep it secret from her father's servants.

Then she remembered Furnace Green, whose inhabitants kept as aloof from Riffield as they could. Like several of his ancestors, Henry had tried to buy the lordship of the manor of Furnace Green, and, five years before, when a certain Francis Bellwasher of Robertsbridge had died possessed of it, he believed the bargain struck. But in vain: Bellwasher's only daughter inherited and she refused to sell.

Furnace Green, then. Faith stopped scowling as she thought about the ridge, less than a morning's ride away across Riffield Park. She would send money to Martha Coffey as her father had done for years, but with the instruction that Martha and Daniel must leave Theydon for Sussex. Surely no one would think it odd if her ladyship's old nurse was rehoused near Riffield; the strains of war made everyone long to have friendly faces close.

It all took a great deal longer to arrange than Faith expected, inexperienced as she was in the ways of carriers, hired beasts and remitting coins in wartime. Nor did she want to send Martha more than just sufficient for the journey, lest she be tempted to take it and stay in Theydon. She must be old and set in her ways by now, Faith reflected, but without considering that she might also be too frail to travel so far by open cart. Nevertheless, although Faith was in a fever to see Daniel, the wait did not seem long. For the first time in her life she was forced to use her own wits to achieve what she wanted, without leaving any breath of suspicion behind, and the experience excited her. She was also helped by circumstances: Portnell, Henry's steward, continued to run the affairs of Riffield, but Faith must now ride about the estates as Henry once had done. To begin with, she did so because he had asked her to; later, the demands of war made it imperative. The Earl of Riffield was a known malignant, as Parliamentarians called supporters of the king, and the Puritan Sussex County Committee demanded increasingly punitive taxes as the months of war rolled on. Already Riffield was coming close to ruin. While Sir John Littleton lived these demands had been kept within reason, since he and his rich merchant friends were indispensable to Parliament. Once he died, Faith discovered how bleakly the wind was blowing on royalist supporters. So no one thought it strange when she bargained over a cottage lease through an attorney, or interviewed carriers alone, and at last here she was, tossing wakefully and following Daniel in her thoughts for every step of his journey from Theydon to Furnace Green.

Tomorrow or the day after, she would see him.

But, as her thoughts returned with a jolt to the present, surely there was more stir than usual in the night, even for Riffield? She sat up abruptly as she heard the suck of mud on horses' hoofs and voices calling at the gate. Perhaps Portnell was to be proved right, since he often said that one day Parliament would cease demanding tax and simply seize all the Scovell lands.

Faith leaped out of bed and ran over to the window, her heart hammering. A huddle of horses stood in the courtyard, their riders already dismounted, while a great many Riffield retainers were running to and fro. Hastily she began to fumble for her clothes; if Riffield was indeed to be seized then troopers could not be trusted to remember godliness if she was forced to appear in her wrapper. But boned cloth and layered skirts were impossible to manage, alone and in the dark. Becky, her dresser, was usually the first to bring fresh tidings, however bad.

Someone scratched at the door and her heart leaped. 'Who is it?'

'Henry. May I come in?'

Her thoughts whirled, readjusting everything in a dizzying instant. Henry, now of all times! She pulled open the door. 'My dear. Of course. Whatever brings you into Parliament's jaws?'

He grasped her shoulders. 'The roughest ride is worth it if I can see you for a single night.'

She flushed, absurdly embarrassed. After months of absence it was humiliating for ceremonious, diffident

Henry to find her in disarray, half into her petticoats. 'I thought you were Parliamentary troopers come to seize Riffield.'

'As they will, very soon.' He drew her to him and kissed her, but with kindness rather than the passion she had felt in him only a moment before. His face was stubbled and rain-wet. 'My dear, don't fret with your skirts. I'll scrub off a week of mud and come to join you if I may.'

Faith muttered something which was meant as welcome, but though she had often woken these past months with her body crying out for love, she failed him badly that first night of his return. He was exhausted yet unable to wait for a better time, a faithful husband through interminable months of war. If she had only been able to respond it might have been a fresh beginning for them both, as urgency swept his usual hesitant courtesy aside; indeed she did respond, but routinely, lacking love. As the sun rose and she watched his face beside her on their pillow, she felt overwhelming regret for what might have been, and pity too because he looked so old and ill. When he came to her in the night, still damp from hasty scrubbing, he had not felt old in the dark. Which meant that pity, that great destroyer of a woman's passions, could not be the only reason for her chilled responses, even if it flourished now.

Faith fumbled through her thoughts until she dragged the true reason from its hiding place. Daniel. Ever since she had discovered where Daniel was, she'd been dreaming of Gage again.

She left Henry to sleep and went downstairs alone, to find Portnell the steward waiting for her, wearing his gloomiest expression. 'Akehurst has been telling me his lordship rode here directly, after bargainings half way around Sussex for the king.' Akehurst was Henry's personal groom.

'Oh?' Faith was ashamed to reveal that in several hours alone she and Henry had hardly spoken.

'Aye, and his lordship ordered the castle gate to be

closed and everyone warned not to speak of his presence here.'

'Good,' answered Faith briskly. 'Parson Syke's friends would be happy to hear of so prominent a royalist under their thumb, so make sure the warning reaches down to the village. Depend on it, someone there will have seen his lordship pass.'

'Aye milady, but tell his lordship it isn't safe to stay here long.'

'Tell him yourself,' said Henry from the stairs. 'Good day to you, Portnell. Still a prophet of disaster, I hear.'

'Nor I'm not often wrong, my lord. But powerful glad to welcome your lordship back to Riffield all the same.'

Henry laughed and came over to stand beside Faith. He was wearing the comfortable velvets he favoured for a day spent in his library, as if he cherished each moment of respite from war. 'I mean to stay three days. Do you think the whisper of my presence will reach Parson Syke within so short a time?'

'Aye, I think so, my lord.'

For the first time Henry looked disconcerted. 'Surely not?'

Portnell pursed his lips. 'There's two Puritan families in Riffield village. Now I don't say they'd run tattling, being good folk like, but the war has changed many things, my lord.'

Faith saw Henry flicker a glance around the familiar timbered hall, and thought he was scarcely listening. 'Send Akehurst to fetch Fuller from Park Forge,' he said after a pause. 'I want to see him here as soon as possible.'

'You aren't well,' Faith said as soon as Portnell left. His clothes hung on him and his breathing sounded bad.

'I haven't time not to be well.'

She stared at him, baffled, as he fidgeted restlessly around the hall. He was at once completely familiar in brown velvet and utterly unfamiliar since today he refused to look at her. 'Why have you come?'

'If you loved me, you would know why.'

Well, there's no answer I can make to that, she thought. 'I don't think you came only to—to see me.'

He gave the ghost of a laugh. 'Let us say that I was glad of the excuse. I also intend to convey to His Majesty most of a year's production of cannon from the forges of eastern Sussex.'

'They're conveyed already to Parliament's use! Even Syke has set up two furnaces again at Edenham, as he said he would.'

'An efficient man, Syke. Well, we shall see.' He was straying from one piece of furniture to the next, touching familiarity. 'You have done well to keep Riffield out of his committee's claws for so long.'

'Oh, if only you knew what it has been like! Tax on everything that moves and on the land besides; corn seized from the threshing floor, carts and oxen signed for with papers which aren't paid. Our people will carry this year's harvest on their backs. Now, still more percentages are to be levied on malignants.'

'So I believe. It is war.'

She was so angry she wanted to drive her fingernails into his indifference. 'Do you remember how proudly you told me that your ancestors had held this place for six hundred years? Well, I can't be sure of holding it even six more months. Unless the king wins, and soon, you will be the last Scovell of Riffield.'

'That is a fact I've faced for a good few years. With or without a victory for the king, and I fear it is to be without.'

She flushed. 'I'm sorry, I didn't mean to taunt you.'

Nor I you . . . though he did not speak, Faith read the retort on his face. After the night they had just passed such restraint was merely infuriating. How she longed to shout that she bred easily, that only a man as unworldly as he would never have recognized the signs which showed she already had! Then, as she recollected Daniel, sympathy for her husband returned. She went over and stood tiptoe to kiss his cheek. 'I never said how glad I am to have you safely back.'

'Thank you, my dear. And yes, I know you can't hold Riffield much longer. I am indebted for all you've done to keep it this past year. When I said it is war, that was exactly what I meant. I have seen enough sacked houses to understand how fortunate Sussex has so far been, and pray it will so remain. Riffield—' he paused. 'You heard me tell Portnell to send for Fuller from Park Forge. Well, he has to account for each gun cast, yet under my orders has managed covertly to manufacture others and delay despatch of those destined for the Parliamentary armies. He can't delay much longer, nor hide for ever the store he holds for His Majesty, so I have come to seize them before it is too late. By force as it will appear, to save him from punishment. Park Forge isn't the only manufactory where such double-dealing has been successfully carried through, there will be a painful stock-taking among Parliament men once they discover how much has vanished from the Wealden ironworks. They will also discover my part in it all, since much comes from my planning. I haven't stayed at Riffield before, but twice came close enough to see your lamps glowing across the park.' He broke off, as if at painful memory. 'Once they discover who is to blame, they will also know who to punish. It won't be your fault when Riffield is lost, but mine. Which is also why I came here this last time.'

There was a long silence while Faith stared at him, astounded. Henry. Henry, of all people. An elderly scholar useless with a sword, and he had ridden all over hostile but familiar country, smuggling cannon for the king. Others could drive oxen and manhandle iron, but secret Sussex royalists and others less scrupulously seeking profit must have agreed to such enormous risks only because they knew and trusted the Earl of Riffield. 'You said the king would lose,' she said at last, being unable to think of anything else to say.

'Almost certainly.' He had settled at last with his back to the fire, as she so often remembered him.

'Yet in his cause you deliberately set out on a course

which was bound in the end to be discovered, and lead to the loss of everything you hold dear.'

He was silent, staring at the floor.

'Would you have done it if you'd had a son to succeed you?'

'I don't know. I hope so, if it had to be done, since I alone had a chance of doing it without destroying our supporters here in Sussex. Faith, I want you to go to your mother in Suffolk before the committee take over here. I made some provision for what might happen, you won't be penniless.'

'No!' she cried, her thoughts flying to Daniel, so carefully established in Furnace Green. 'Whatever happens, I stay here.'

'My dear, I thank you for your loyalty but doubt you will be able to. This time they will come with a writ of confiscation, not another demand for tax.'

'I'm staying,' she answered stubbornly, even while thanks for loyalty brought the blood into her face.

'I could give orders for you to be escorted to your mother.' He was alarmed and puzzled by her determination, but also touched, since this was the first time she had shown affection for the wet clearings of his inheritance.

'By force, my lord? I think it beyond your power, since you must ride to join the king. If you had only told me what you planned then matters might be different, but after so much effort given to preserving your estates I don't feel able simply to give them up.'

'Unlike me?' he suggested. He looked tired, so tired; sick and sucked dry of life.

'No,' she answered as gently as she could. 'You have done your duty, my lord. Leave me to mine.'

Those were almost the last words they spoke alone together before he left again two nights later and she felt deeply ashamed of them, since Daniel and not duty kept her at Riffield. Much of Henry's time between then and his leave-taking was spent in riding out unattended with an old cloak pulled about his ears, to meet ironfounders

Faith supposed, or closeted in his library with Jack Fuller and a crude ruffian called Alex Laffam from Furnace Green. An owler by repute, Henry said in answer to Faith's questions after Laffam left, and opened a window to rid his library of unwashed stench. An owler, or the roughest kind of smuggler: war forced the most unlikely partnerships indeed.

Then a quite different thought struck Faith and she picked up her skirts to run all the way to the stable yard, encountering many odd looks on her way. She caught Laffam as he mounted a surprisingly good horse. 'You come from Furnace Green, his lordship said. Do you know if my old nurse has arrived? I hired a cottage across from the church for her to live in when my father died, and she's on her way from Essex.'

'An old sick woman with a lad?' Laffam's grey-green eyes studied her speculatively.

'Yes.' Her heart thudded in her ears. Daniel. Daniel was already living on the ridge she could see from her closet window.

'She's arrived,' said Laffam briefly, and kicked his horse out of the yard when she neither answered nor offered him a coin. Bitch. He began to whistle a tavern ballad while considering a milady's eagerness over a mere nurse: there might be more than met the eye in the arrival of newcomers at the corner cottage.

After that, Faith became possessed by a wild restlessness, pacing the great hall of Riffield as if it was a cell and riding to see tenants at a reckless gallop, although no one expected her while the earl remained at Riffield. She no longer remembered that Henry was spending his last days as lord of his inheritance, but only wanted him to go. Go before rumour of his visit should reach Syke and the consequences of denunciation kept her countless more intolerable days in the castle, go so that she could visit Daniel. Wherever she rode the ridge seemed to mock her, bulked against the sky above Riffield Park. Gage's son was waiting for her there, and, perhaps because she was forced to wait yet again when he was now so close, he seemed to merge in her longings with Gage himself.

As Faith rode home on the third day after Henry came, she found her eyes drawn to the rightness of the castle's setting. A place so well chosen that each rebuilding flowed easily into the last. A single stone tower remained of the castle fortified by earlier Scovells to withstand siege and discontent, the rest an unplanned jumble of a building which combined most styles from the past two hundred years and in itself a kind of testimony to the slow civilisation of the Weald. Faith had simply accepted it before, and, anyway, ever since Laffam told her that Daniel and Martha had arrived all her thoughts had been directed towards Furnace Green. Now, as lamps began to glow from Riffield Castle's many sconces and mullions, her heart tightened with a sense of bitter loss. If Henry was right, then this place and all it represented would soon be part of her no longer.

And yet her loss was trifling compared to his.

She rode fast up the long ascent to the gate, and for once her mind was purged of Gage. The main courtyard was bustling, otherwise all remained peaceful: Portnell's pessimism so far had proved unjustified, and not one of the many persons of all degrees who by now must know that the earl was home had run to appraise the Parliamentary committee of the fact.

Faith found Henry alone in his library, a volume of Virgil open on his knees, and went in with a rush while her will to warmth burned brightly. 'How lucky to find you alone for once! I vow I despaired of it while so many owlers and ironmasters were tramping in and out!'

'What can I do for you, my dear?'

Faith flushed. 'I don't only seek you out when I desire a favour.'

He studied her, unsmiling. 'Then the fault was mine, I am sure.'

'No,' she said slowly. 'No fault either way perhaps,

except those made by circumstances. When do you leave, my lord?'

'Tonight. All is arranged and, God willing, we shall escort nearly a hundred cannon of all sizes to His Majesty in Oxford.'

'A hundred! Why, that must mean five or six hundred oxen yoked to pull them! Sweet Jesus, Henry! How will you ever carry such a quantity through a countryside held for Parliament?'

'By luck and the owlers' byways. Nor does Parliament hold strongly where its leaders believe themselves to be safe, since their armies in the field are desperate for men. We have teams and meeting points arranged all over the Weald tonight, and the rebels keep only a single troop of horse at Lewes.' He glanced at an old water-clock on the wall. 'In fact, everything is begun and my part finished, except for paying those of my accomplices who would commit murder for the bullion I carry.'

'And the others?'

'The ones I trust, either as honest traders or loyal subjects, are already paid.'

On impulse, Faith sat at his feet with her arm across his knee, but kept her head turned away as if she wanted only to watch flames leap on the hearth. Henry would soon be going out to the sodden discomfort of secret travellings, but his greatest burden would not be bullion but loss of everything he held dear. Her and Riffield, both.

He touched her hair before locking veined fingers on his lap. 'The Parliament men would have taken a rich haul if they had come here these past few days. The threads which would lead them to most of the king's supporters in Sussex, and bullion scraped from half a dozen reluctant towns.'

'And you. Yet you believed the risk worth taking.'

'I have known Wealdsmen all my life,' he answered, half-apologetically. 'They guard their own, even Portnell.'

'Portnell?'

'He's for Parliament, or didn't you know?'

'Portnell?' she repeated, dazed. 'You mean you came

here carrying the king's moneybags and stayed three days expecting to be safe, when you knew your own steward was for Parliament? Sweet Jesus, why didn't you turn him off when the war began?'

'Turn Portnell off, who has served me thirty years, and for no fault beyond a dissenting conscience? My dear, why ever should I? Portnell isn't the sort of man who would betray a friend for policy, and nor am I. I knew I should be as safe from him as he would be from me, and the king's bullion has nothing to do with it. Laffam, the owler of Corndown, now—' he shook his head, and laughed. 'He would kill me for it without a thought of policy in his head.'

Alex Laffam. Faith's mind switched abruptly to Daniel and the ridge again. 'When will you be back?'

He drew up his legs as if to stand, except she still leaned against his knees. 'After the war. Or never, I suppose. If we're successful the committeemen will learn how by my contriving six months' production of cannon found its way to the king, and they'll make very sure it doesn't happen again. I meant what I said, Faith. I want you safe in Suffolk.'

Faith stood. 'I should need an escort and coach, both of which will be seized if you are right.'

'I spoke to John Courthope of Whiligh. He invites you to stay and will see you safely bestowed afterwards.'

'Like cannon behind an ox!' she flashed, and then shrugged. 'Ah, what's the good?'

He bent, his lips just brushing her fingers. 'None, while men are fools enough to fight. You see, I believe Parliament won't just seize Riffield, they'll garrison it to make sure they can watch the Wealden furnaces in the future. I don't want you here when that happens. Thank God, neither side makes war on women yet, but angry troopers are unreliable at best.' For the first time his eyes held hers. 'My dear, this is a harsh world. As much for you as for me. I thank you for the kindness you have shown me, and trust one day you will do better.'

Her fingers tightened on his. 'Promise me to take care.'

'The time for care is past.'

'And also the desire?'

His eyes flickered. 'Perhaps.'

'So promise to take care.' She could not tell whether he was thinking of her or Riffield first.

He smiled then and kissed her on the lips. 'Promises are hard to keep in war. I will try. And you will promise me to leave immediately, for Whiligh and then Suffolk?'

'Yes,' she said, but with no intention of keeping a promise made only to set his mind at rest.

Henry, thirty-fourth Baron Scovell and fifth Earl of Riffield, rode away from his castle for the last time as dark fell, his following increased by two grooms and a villager who had asked to join him. The rule of committeemen dedicated to godly living and war taxation had not endeared their cause to Sussex. Each man rode with his weapon drawn, while the most trusted carried coin in their saddlebags, the splash of horses' hoofs fading slowly down the steep slope to the village and beyond.

Faith stood a long time after the last shape vanished. If there had been an ambush planned it would have been close to Riffield, where there was the best chance of catching both bullion and malignants.

'They are safe,' said Portnell quietly. 'I sent men out earlier to look. Come in, milady, before you take a fever.'

'Safe for how long?' Faith went over to the fire. She still found it difficult to visualise Henry riding by owlers' trails and bargaining with ruffians. At this very moment, oxen would be converging down quagmire hillsides, drawing cannon with agonising slowness towards the royal forces which must be riding in to cover them. Blood would be spilled, quarrels begun, feet crushed under unwieldy loads, reputations lost and gained, all because of one man who was happiest reading Virgil.

She turned back to where Portnell waited. 'If you had sent word to Parson Syke that the earl was here, then his lordship would have spent the rest of the war comfortably under guard. Riffield might have been spared confiscation and Parliament's cause advanced. In God's name, why did you not do it?'

Portnell eyed her warily, a bent pixie of a man who did not trust her. 'Milady?'

She tapped her foot impatiently on the flags. 'You heard me. His lordship told me you were for Parliament.'

But he refused to answer, taking refuge in a flurry of miladies, bringing wine for her to drink and making up the fire until she tired first, and sent him away.

Tomorrow she would ride to Furnace Green.

By that time, Daniel had lived in the corner cottage for four days. He had gathered enough sticks to kindle a fire on the hearthstone and hung their pot on a hook above; shaken out boxed coverlets, cut bracken for bedding and scraped the worst of the slime off the wet earth floor. Beyond this, he found it hard to decide what next he should do. The fire filled their one room with smoke, the bracken and coverlets were damp and the floor soon became fouled again because Mistress Coffey was ill and he did not know how to make her better. He sat on the doorstep to avoid seeing her but each time he came back inside her condition filled him with fright. If they had still been in Theydon Magna, neighbours would have shooed him into the fields while the women took charge of the sordid practicalities of a mortal fever.

Here he knew no one, and was too shy to beg for help from strangers. Those living along the street saw a boy fetching wood and smoke seeping through the tumbledown brick chimney, heard gossip from the Laffams and folded their arms to wait for whatever happened next. 'I'm sure I'm not one to push my nose in where I'm not wanted,' said Goodwife Oxley, and the rest agreed.

Parson Syke was the first to call, but by then he could only pray beside Martha's cooling body. When he had finished he threw open the shutters without regard for convention, and a cold wind poured into the small bare room so Daniel immediately began to shiver. 'Aye, boy, I daresay you would soonest frowst in the dark, but regrets never baked bread. When did you last eat?'

'This morning, sir.' Daniel found this plum-faced parson overwhelming, but preferable on the whole to solitary fear.

Syke sniffed in the pot. 'Mere pap, my boy.'

'I bought milk from a farm beyond the pool and mixed it with some meal we brought with us from Essex,' explained Daniel. 'I thought Mistress Coffey—'

'Milk may do for a sick woman, but it's no good to a lad. You'd best eat from my pot, and afterwards tell me about such skills as you have learned. Then I shall decide where you may best earn a living now this good soul has died.' Syke was heartily disliked by a great many persons throughout eastern Sussex, since his position as ironmaster, sheep-owner and Parliamentary committeeman as well as parson led him to meddle in everything, but his Christian charity was undoubted.

He hauled Daniel on to his horse's crupper without listening to his protests, urged it into a tooth-rattling trot down Furnace Green street (where, from long experience of his passion for interference, everyone had vanished inside shut doors) and on to the new house he was building outside the village. 'The parsonage is too poky to live in and Edenham too noisy.' He shouted information as if Daniel was half a field away. 'My new house, now, is exactly placed where I can keep an eye on all that goes forward hereabouts. If you turn your back on the Devil for an instant, boy, he'll snap up your soul. Remember that.'

'Yes, sir,' said Daniel obediently, looking about him. He had been attached to Mistress Coffey, but more by habit than affection, and now his future had been taken over by Parson Syke all he wanted was to forget the foulness of her death.

Parson Syke's new house was impressive. Foursquare like its master and of much the same rich colour, it boasted a small incongruous tower as if Syke was determined to proclaim himself no mere parson. There was even a herb garden where he told Daniel he experimented with distillations to help the sick. 'Never waste an instant, boy,' he added. 'Each is a gift from the Lord, and He didn't give them for us to waste.'

Daniel was fascinated by Parson Syke. He had never met anyone like him in his life. In Theydon Magna the elderly parson toiled on his glebe field like any peasant and seemed to care about little else, but Syke hurried everywhere, bellowing. He gulped his dinner standing up, and ordered Daniel to sweep the yard even before he had bolted the last morsel of an excellent stew, since he himself must go to some committee.

Daniel had not the remotest idea what a committee was, and he felt so weary after four terrifying nights and days of Mistress Coffey's illness, that all he wanted was to sprawl in the autumn sun and sleep, but such was Syke's force that he swept the yard three times from side to side rather than sit idle for a moment.

He slept in some stable straw once it grew dark, and was hauled out at daybreak to attend prayers with the rest of the household, from shepherd's boy to Mistress Syke herself. She was a thin wisp of a woman except for the bulge under her girdle. A serving maid whispered in Daniel's ear that the mistress had carried a child for each of the fifteen years of her marriage, and not one of them lived beyond six months.

Merciful Jesus, thought Daniel, peering through praying fingers at this wraith of unhappy maternity; he pitied the weak too easily and loved things he would have been wiser to disregard. Without warning, light cartwheeled behind his eyes as his head slammed against the wall; Syke could move softly when he chose and did not scruple to frustrate the practices of the Devil by a hearty buffet wherever it was needful, which included Daniel's wandering attention.

Daniel knelt through the remaining prayers almost semiconscious. His cheek swelled where Syke's blow had landed, and blood trickled under his hair. Tears of self-pity slipped through his fingers: Mistress Coffey had never so much as slapped him, nor was he certain what he had done wrong.

After prayers—which lasted a long time, since Parson Syke rose early in order to make sufficient time for prayer—he was informed exactly about the nature of his fault. 'Pray to God without ever allowing your wits to stray and He will give you the strength to resist Satan. Remember, boy, how constantly he prowls, seeking unready souls.' Syke thrust his face into Daniel's so he instinctively recoiled.

Daniel nodded and then wished he hadn't, as his brain seemed to slop against his skull.

'Very well then, we shall forgo a beating this time even though the Good Book bids us not to spare the rod.' Syke wondered whether he himself was about to sin through lenience, but in truth the boy looked green enough to spew. Godly labour would best set this soul to rights. 'Come, tell me your skills and I will set you to a master before the day is out,' he added briskly.

Daniel licked his lips. 'I—I have no skills, sir.'

'What? No skills? Come now, how can the good folk of Essex live without skills?'

'Mistress Coffey was nearly blind and received sufficient moneys to maintain herself from the family where she once worked. I think—I think she was unwilling for me to labour in the fields, and since we had enough—' Daniel's voice trailed away. Martha had told him he was her sister's son and that she'd wanted him softly reared, yet all Martha recollected of how gentry raised their children was that they didn't toil with their hands. Consequently, she never considered how dull and unprovided with companionship this left Daniel, once other boys his age worked from dawn to dusk.

Syke stared at him, aghast. No skills, and brought up to despise godly labour! 'Boy, you came to Furnace Green only just in time to save your soul from burning in force-draught. Do you know what a force-draught is?'

'No, sir.' Daniel was careful not to shake his head.

'It is what we use to melt metal out of earth, so you can see how easily a soul would be shrivelled into nothing.' He snapped his fingers under Daniel's nose. 'The Devil is as a roaring lion, seeking whom he may devour. No skills, then. Let me see. Master Carpenter of Danesdell will need a boy come hop-harvest time, I'll speak to him for you this very day.'

'A man called Laffam brought us the last part of our way from Essex. He did say . . . I think he thought he might use me with his oxen.' After his one glimpse of the world, Daniel already yearned to discover more.

'No.' Syke's face mottled alarmingly. 'God forbid I should send you into such a blasphemous family as the Laffams. Go now and help in the byre until I'm ready to bury Mistress Coffey, by then I shall have spoken for you to Will Carpenter.'

Helplessly, Daniel watched Syke ride out of the yard and was promptly cuffed again by a groom for not running at once to the byre. At least he must be thankful the parson showed no inclination to hire an unskilled boy for his ironworks, Daniel reflected.

He felt depressed and resentful, although by nature he was neither; he also found it difficult to think when so much had happened to him in a short time. There were, he knew, a few coins left from their journey among Mistress Coffey's bundles, and if his head hadn't ached so he would have been tempted to search for them straightaway, and leave before Syke disposed of his life.

Daniel fingered his swollen cheek reflectively. Those coins were his, surely. Mistress Coffey had never spoken of any other kin. Nevertheless, he decided it would be better to ask Syke about them first; Daniel had once seen a thief half blinded by a branding on the cheek, and had no desire to suffer a like fate.

The only time he found to ask Syke about the coins was after long prayings beside an open grave, where burying his one link with a peaceful past made him feel unexpectedly wretched.

'Coins?' said Syke, as he strode to the church gate. 'I have them safe, you may be sure. But until I hear from Theydon I cannot be certain to whom they should belong. I shall write to the parson there this very night.'

'I doubt if he can read a letter,' said Daniel timidly.

'Not read? Not read, hey? Now that is the kind of slackness in God's ministry we are fighting this war to end! Once we have won, all ministers will be learned men.'

'But the coins? I swear Mistress Coffey has no kin.'

'You are kin yourself, are you not? What if there are others, or debts to be paid where you came from? No, no, boy! Besides, coins given to the young only encourage idleness. Why, you said yourself you had no skills!' He shook his head, still amazed by such a thing in a boy of twelve. 'Accept this chance to work and be thankful.' He flung Daniel up behind him and this time some of the street folk failed to scuttle inside fast enough to avoid a shower of admonition as he rode by.

'That's Wyses,' Syke roared at Daniel as they passed the only brick-built house among timbered, reed-thatched cottages. 'Caught fire last year. I told those slothful Browns who live there a dozen times to build a brick chimney before the rafters smouldered through, but would they? No! Not until the Devil set his spark to their rafters. A fine blaze we had, I can tell you, and all a consequence of idleness. There's more people tossed into Hell for that cause than any other, and don't you forget it.'

Since Daniel had already decided that idleness away from Parson Syke was infinitely preferable to activity near him, he didn't consider argument worthwhile.

Beyond Wyses and a paddock full of decaying sheep-pens, the street abruptly became a foot-trail through long grass, the old thoroughfare which generations of ridge people had trodden from church to pool and back again, but now almost unused since Nicholas Wyse had caused a new deep well to be dug. *Though I have no children to follow me, at least let Furnace Green remember the name of Wyse*, he had written, and so it was. Griped bellies became less commonplace once sweet clean water could be drawn from Old Nick's Well in the driest season, and the old mired pool closed in on itself again. Though the great trees had long ago vanished from around it, except for the broken trunk of a single mighty oak, a grove of hazel now framed water which had again become deep and black. Beetles darted across its surface and a chilly wind scudded fallen leaves into the shallows; to Daniel the whole place seemed oddly secret, a coiled, primeval being dreaming of a world he couldn't see. At the far side of the pool the banks were trampled where some of the Danesdell beasts still came to drink, but not a single hovel remained to tell of all the pool folk who once had lived here. With the Wealden furnaces and pastures hard at work for the armouries of war, no one needed to rot on scraps of common-land except by choice, and Parson Syke of Furnace Green so hectored anyone who idled in his parish that those who were inclined towards ease preferred to find it elsewhere.

Will Carpenter's Danesdell Farm lay across some ploughland beyond the pool, a huddle of timber buildings in a hollow. Daniel had come here before to buy milk for Mistress Coffey, and even then he had thought how foolish a man must be to build a farm in an undrained hollow. If anyone had told him that seven hundred years before it had been chosen because a woman lay here with her lover amid agrimony, periwinkle and trailing vetch on a day when the ridge was new, then being Daniel he would have seen it change before his eyes. As it was, he lowered himself gingerly from Parson Syke's horse and felt slime squelch into the gapped stitching of his boots.

Syke's bargaining with Will Carpenter was soon done, the deed of Daniel's indenture could be drawn up later. Which did not mean that Daniel was any the less bound from this moment. 'There, boy, you are settled,' he said, kindly enough, but with one foot already in the stirrup.

Daniel's eyes shifted to his new master, a man whose face filled easily with anger or suspicion. 'I—I . . . Sir, what am I to do?'

'Do, boy? Why work as Master Carpenter directs, of course.' Syke hauled himself into the saddle with a grunt.

'But—' Daniel had watched boys at Theydon being sold to a master when they were left without anyone to speak for them, and the terms were always harsher than a bargain made between kin. 'I don't want to work for Master Carpenter.'

'You don't, hey? Would you sooner run into the forest for the Devil to catch, with the winter coming? In all my years, I never before found a boy past the age of eight who had not been bound to his labour, and you are near thirteen years old! We don't harbour vagrants here, whatever the custom is in Essex.'

Daniel stared at him helplessly. What else indeed was he to do? If he left Furnace Green, then he could be whipped and branded in every parish where he was caught without means of support, Theydon being the only place in England where he had a right to settle. Syke, indeed, was generous to arrange this hiring, because the poor-rate payers of Furnace Green would thenceforward be obliged to support him if sickness or ill fortune struck. Daniel's gaze sank to the mud which hid his feet: Ah, what's the good, he thought. The truth was, he knew too little even to imagine what he wanted, except it wasn't this.

'There is one thing I wanted to mention, Parson,' said Carpenter, after a pause. 'Have you heard the earl's come home?'

'The malignant Scovell?' exclaimed Syke, immediately forgetting Daniel. 'Nay, he's with the king.'

'He's been at Riffield these past three days. So says my wife's sister's lass, who works in the bakehouse there.'

'Alone?'

'Aye, except for some grooms who rode away with him last year. He's off again soon, the lass said, but went up straightway to his woman's bedchamber with muddy boots still on his legs, so mayhap war has made him ruttish. No matter, eh, Parson? Once God's people have their victory, 'twill be easier for a camel to go through a needle's eye than the rich to enter heaven, so then he can go prick himself.'

But before he was fairly finished, Syke let out a roar of rage and spurred his horse forward, sending both Daniel and his new master sprawling in the mud. 'How dare you smear filth on God's victory? The tongue is a fire that runneth abroad seeking whom it may destroy, and behold what great matters a little fire kindleth! The Earl of Riffield is a man like any other and his wife a remedy for sin.'

Carpenter floundered to his feet, spitting rage, a freeholder on his own land and unused to humiliation. 'I spoke of a malignant strutting on his dungheap under your committee's nose!'

'Then you could have spoken it more fairly. Let your words be aye and nay, without adornment. I will inform the committee that the earl is thought to be in Riffield again, although a man visiting his own home for a couple of nights will scarcely affect the outcome of God's war. As for you, Will Carpenter, repent on your knees with groanings of the spirit, and remember that the dealer in hogs at Tonbridge Market is a friend of mine. If I bid him not to buy from a backslider, you will find yourself without a profitable sale for your autumn beasts.' And with this threat, whereby Syke showed himself a shrewd judge of character rather than a spiritual man of God, he spurred out of Danesdell.

He was so angry he shouted aloud all the way across the fields to Edenham, outraged to discover a parishioner with evil flourishing in his heart. 'Give light to them that sit in darkness!' he thundered as he set his horse at a hedge. 'Quench the fiery darts of the wicked!' echoed across his pastures as he galloped down the slope beyond, so his shepherds grinned at one another and were thankful his rage was directed elsewhere.

By the time Syke reached Edenham the heat in him had dulled. He grappled with sin daily and would have been defeated long ago if he allowed each setback to rankle. But while he ran a ruthless eye over his furnaces, sending men sprinting hither and thither in a lather of anxiety, his mind remained busy with the problem of the Earl of Riffield. His duty as a committeeman was clear. He ought to round up some militia and arrest him at once. On the other hand . . . Syke would have been loath to admit it, but he respected Henry Scovell, malignant though he was. This had nothing to do with his title or estates which it would be sin to envy, but came rather from the knowledge that responsibilities were best borne by men who could be trusted to administer them fairly. The earl was such a man, who had kept his word during the difficult months before war came, when they both had tried to keep faction and ill-neighbourliness out of eastern Sussex. If he had indeed ridden all the way from Oxford through enemy-held territory to spend a few nights with his wife, then probably it was because he refused to sleep with whores. And if he should beget a son at last, then the Weald would be the better for it.

With this thought Syke's own calvary of childlessness opened again before him, and in the end it was very human feeling for Henry Scovell which caused him merely to send a belated note to the Parliamentary committee, informing them that the Earl of Riffield had come home again.

In this strange manner Parson Syke made the worst error of judgement in his life. If he had gone at once with some militia to Riffield, he and the earl would probably have met, silver and all, in the castle entry. And even if he failed to arrest him (militia not being renowned for skill at arms) then Syke was quite intelligent enough to recognize the signs which should have told him that more had happened at Riffield than a man's visit to his wife. A messenger could then have galloped to the garrison at Lewes, or westward to the Parliamentary forces on the Hampshire border. Only thus could the route from the Weald to Surrey, where a royalist covering force was waiting, have been blocked in time. Oxen moved slowly enough, God knows.

As it was, he did nothing for two days except write a routine despatch and attend to his most pressing affairs. Then, slowly, as happens with the choicest gossip, the tide of laughter began to flow. He became aware first of whispers, then barbed words, and finally of joyful belly-laughs from people recently and perfunctorily converted to sober industry. The Weald might have chosen, probably would still choose, God's Parliamentary cause, but felt even less affection for its new rulers than it had for the old. And less again because they were new, when Wealdsmen preferred known ways and, insofar as they fought at all, they fought to restore what they saw as their liberties of the past.

It took a week for the full import of the joke to roll from Ashburnham ironworks in south Sussex to Furnace Green in the north, as men began to realize just how many cannon had vanished from under the Parliamentary committee-men's noses. Only furnaces like Edenham which were owned by Puritans were immune, and even there the forgemen chuckled out of sight. Too late, a messenger raced to call up cavalry from Chichester, the distance was too great. A few foundered oxen were discovered and cannon spilled on awkward slopes, but the main haul was safely into the Surrey hills. Long before then, Syke understood how much he was to blame for this disaster, since it is often easier to prise secrets loose with laughter than with torments. If Henry Scovell had not been well known as a studious and introspective man perhaps his coup would not have appeared so exquisitely funny, but, as Roly French, a puddler at Edenham, confided to his furnaceman: 'His lordship be a Wealdsman for all he mazed hisself wi' books, and they committeemen nobbut gurt prating fools.'

The Laffams, that owling breed who thrived on unlawful contrivings, were also missing from Corndown. When Syke called there six days after Will Carpenter first told him the earl was home, he found only children under ten and gaffers grinning by the hearth. Even the younger women had vanished, although they would soon be back, or so the gaffers said.

Syke ground his teeth in fury and so far forgot himself as to swear, which brought a night of contrite prayer on his knees. Next day was committee day, when he would have to confess that he had known the earl was home a full day before he leisurely sent the information on.

After a rip-roaring meeting, the Parliamentary committee responsible for the Rape of Pevensey in the county of Sussex decided unanimously to sequestrate all property belonging to the malignant, Henry Scovell, and also to billet a riding garrison at Riffield which would patrol the ironworks of the Weald.

They then drew up a list of those they suspected of undermining the Parliamentary cause in eastern Sussex: most were merchants, ironmasters and hirers of draught beasts, but among the ungodly appeared the name of Parson Syke.

Daniel disliked Will Carpenter from the moment he was made to work for him. He would have disliked anyone who forced him to labour from before sunrise until after dark, but when Syke sent Will sprawling in the mud for reasons Daniel did not understand, a sharp hatred was born between master and hireling. Henceforward, Carpenter needed to reassure himself that a boy who had witnessed his humiliation wasn't still sniggering up his sleeve at him, and his rancour made Daniel's life more wretched still.

Time became meaningless as monotony took hold of him. His hands cracked and bled, his back ached and, as the sun blazed out of a clear September sky, his head was often throbbing by midday. He had to wrestle hop plants off their poles, dig out ditches ready for winter and shovel yellow-green hops from trough to cart to barn, and then up to the drying floor by rope hoist. Hops, hops and more hops. Will Carpenter was the only man in Furnace Green who grew this new crop and he prospered in consequence, but their musty, sweetish smell became to Daniel a badge of servitude. Mostly, the fault was his. Because he had never worked before, each day seemed immensely long, and since he had caught that single glimpse of the outside world on his way from Essex, he fancied himself on fire to discover more. But so far as he could see nothing further would ever happen to him, except Parson Syke might eventually give him Mistress Coffey's few coins: enough to buy a pair of boots which did not leak perhaps, or clothes in which he would not feel ashamed to walk to church on Sundays. When he worked alone it was not so bad, he could think and dream and imagine things; worst of all were the days spent under Will Carpenter's censorious eye. Will loved his hops and treated them as he would delicate and capricious animals. Hops failed easily and the expense of cultivation was such that if they did, from being moderately prosperous, Will would immediately come close to ruin. Consequently, nothing concerning them was too trifling for his attention, and Daniel was harried even more unmercifully.

Will seldom swore, since Syke had denounced profanity from his pulpit for more than thirty years, but sarcasm cut more deeply into Daniel than oaths, deeper even than Will's ash cane cut into his flesh. Otherwise Will spoke little, considering pleasantries a waste of time and gossip contrary to the word of God. Mistress Carpenter on the other hand, loved gossip. When Will was there his family moved briskly and silently about their business, but at other times the big Danesdell kitchen was a cosy place and full of chatter. Only Jane, Will's eight-year-old daughter, was too guileless to remember to alter her conduct in her father's presence, and was always suffering chastisement as a consequence.

Daniel slept in the byre and each day was kicked awake while it was still dark, the stars drawing away as he pattered barefooted across the yard, mud squelching icily through his toes. And it was only September yet! He couldn't imagine what it would be like with leaking boots in winter. His first job was to milk the household cow, the rich swish of milk and warmth from her flank making this the best time of the day. When he took the milk across the farmyard, Mistress Carpenter gave him a hunk of yesterday's bread to chew, together with some fat and ale, another good time this. Then he must bring in wood for her fire and carry water all the way from Old Nick's Well, six journeys across the common pasture now called the green.

The worst part of these journeys was when he staggered under the weight of full pails hanging from a yoke across his shoulders, half running in haste because by then the sky was showing streaks of colour. Mistress Carpenter was a worrier, and also frightened of displeasing her husband. Hurry up, she would say to him each time he reached her kitchen; hurry up, the master's nearly finished eating. You know what he'll say if you aren't ready as soon as he has finished. Oh, hurry, pray!

This flustered Daniel still further. Not only did he know what Will would say, but the whippy cuts his stick inflicted oozed painfully in the wet. Every day, immediately after breaking his fast, Will Carpenter walked every one of his fields, and usually Daniel had to follow carrying a bag of corn for the sheep. If he wasn't ready, Will would rush round the yard pretending his whole day was disarranged by the delay and striking out with his stick. When they reached the sheep, Daniel always had to catch at least one for closer inspection, making a dash for whichever beast Will indicated. Since most of these were tough and cunning, his quarry often got away after delivering the kind of kick Daniel never learned to dodge, or else would trample him as it fled. Then Will would dance around calling him a gurt mooney unfit to wipe snot from a baby's cheek, while poor Daniel had to chase all over the pasture snatching at greasy wool.

After that it was usually hops.

The slap and rattle of harness on Danesdell's single horse, the smell of sweat as beast and men warmed to their work, the uneven suck and squeal of wheels and undergreased axles, the clouds of insects dislodged from the hop bines; for a while Daniel's heart would steady down as he did whatever he was told. He was gentle with animals and they worked well for him; had he been left alone probably he would have managed satisfactorily. But something would happen which made Will start to shout and throw clods of earth, so that Daniel and the horse both became confused. Then matters generally went from bad to worse. Harness tangled, sacks split, hops spilled. If Will had just shouted and threatened it wouldn't have mattered so much: somehow Daniel would have learned to manage better. But the blows always seemed to land wherever he was most sensitive: on his head the day it ached or where a water-bucket had gashed his leg, the taunts so exactly judged that he forgot each day the little he had learned before. The men working on the farm saw nothing out of the ordinary in the way their master behaved. Boys starting work were usually run witless for a while, and Daniel was simply despised because he came late and unhandily to his trimming. The men knew that hops needed cosseting and, like Will, they enjoyed Furnace Green's interest in their doings. All Daniel thought was, what a stupid fuss about cartloads of green leaves.

An unreasonable loathing of Will Carpenter began to take hold of him. Even when curled up in his straw at night, it seemed no time at all before the same round began again. He was so much alone that, sometimes, tears seemed his only company, although he was ashamed to weep. Indeed, so swift had been the disintegration of his world that Mistress Coffey would scarcely have recognized the boy who had managed quite handily for the two of them on their journey, and then tended her while she lay dying.

The only relief came when those Danesdell hirelings who lodged at the farm walked behind their master and mistress to church. Not talking, because chatter was frivolous on the Sabbath, answering greetings with a mere inclination of the head. And after the service, Will Carpenter whisked his household away from what many secretly regarded as the main business of the day: gossiping and illicit trading in the street. Syke railed against money-making on the Sabbath, but having suffered him for nearly thirty years as their parson, the ungodly of Furnace Green had grown adept in such matters. As he prowled down the street with his black clothes flapping in suspicion, behind his back traders would slip from group to group, chatter re-form in a different pattern and hands be struck in rapid bids for crops and beasts and wives.

But at least work was kept to a minimum on Sunday, and at Danesdell they ate even better than usual. Meat and curd cheese were served on pewter plates, warm flat loaves piled high on the hearth and a fresh butt of home-brewed would be broached. Will prided himself on his hop-strengthened beer, and did not consider it a sin to drink deeply. He was always best-natured on Sabbath afternoon, the younger members of his household encouraged to scatter on their own affairs while he and his wife dozed by the hearth.

Unfortunately, this was a time when Parson Syke had succeeded in closing Furnace Green up tight. Doors were expected to be kept shut so people could read the Bible undisturbed, children be set to learn the psalms by rote; woe betide the young man who was caught sneaking out to meet his sweetheart. They would both be forced to stand by the church door next Sabbath, she in a puritanical shift and he in sacking drape. The only exception to the general gloom was the Laffams, who worked, whored or danced as they pleased. They set great starving hounds on Syke if he came to denounce them, and blocked their lane with burning undergrowth when the committee came with constables to arrest them. Once the war eased enough for him to be able to borrow some cavalry from the army, Syke planned a reckoning with the Laffams.

The Carpenter sons vanished after Sabbath dinner, but Daniel never guessed that they, like many others, sneaked off to Corndown for cocking or merry-makings in the barn.

So Daniel was left to moon disconsolately alone in his one free time, although even he had sense enough to keep away from Syke's angry pouncings in the street. Usually he lay watching the life of the pool through half-closed eyes, dozing sometimes if it was warm. He loved the pool and found his only comfort there. White cress, blue brooklure, tangled brambles and hazel were reflected from its surface, together with the clouds. Insects curved ripples from bank to bank, and the occasional duck gave back stare for stare. One evening towards the end of September, he climbed into the remains of a great dead oak which must once have towered high above the water and from it gained a quite different view; the stump was enormous, far larger than he had thought from below, its heart eaten out and only the disbarked rind left behind, silver-grey and as hard as stone. Daniel gazed down at the pool from where he was perched, dreaming he was on board one of the ships he had seen on the Thames, but somehow the zest was vanishing from his longing. Fear sprouted in its place, and all he could think of was how a ship might be even more brutal than Will Carpenter's petty tyrannies. So, searching instinctively for relief, he began to wonder what this tree had seen and how many centuries old it possibly might be. A hundred years at least for such a great trunk to rot into almost nothing, he thought. Perhaps five hundred more for it to grow from an acorn into the giant this dead trunk suggested. Just thinking about so much time made him feel happier, and after a while two nightingales began to sing in the sunset sky above his head, pouring their music across the ridge and into the misted depths beyond.

But soon, in the black hour before dawn, he would again be stumbling across to the well with his water pails. An old woman often came there as early as he did, and was almost his only contact with life outside Danesdell. She spoke disjointedly but each day told him something new, as if she spent the time in between thinking which titbit to offer him next. She had no kin remaining in Furnace Green and lived on poor relief in a leaking hut. Once, she said, she had had five strong sons, but two of them had gone to work in the larger ironworks in south Sussex, because before the war those in Furnace Green were dying and would again when the fighting ended. Her other three sons? Well, one died and one wed a weaver's daughter and left. 'T'other? Well, maybe he'll be back one day. He rides wi' Parliament for the Cause. The Cause, young minikin. No, I dunno why they call it that, but 'tis right, you see. The cause of men being men, and the Weald ruled according to good custom. What custom? Why, all men know the good when they see it.'

This explanation of Parliament's war aims seemed logical but not entirely satisfactory to Daniel, since Will Carpenter was also for Parliament and very far from good. He did not argue with her, though, in case she refused to talk to him any more.

Her name was Meg Parleben, and she was as bowed and creaky as an old roof. Daniel would have liked to carry her water for her, but with Will shouting for him at Danesdell he didn't dare.

One morning she told him a lady had come to Parson Syke, asking for Daniel Gage.

'A lady?' asked Daniel, astonished.

'Aye, t'Scovell lady, so they say. I dunno. I can't see like I used to, and her soon rode on again.'

'But she asked for me? Me, by name?' Hope beat loudly as Daniel remembered how he and Mistress Coffey had come here so she could live near her old employer. Perhaps this lady might give him coins or—hope of hopes!—offer him a place in her stables. The only warmth in Daniel's present life came from affection for Danesdell's old horse, and he could not imagine a greater joy than working in a stable.

Daniel was agog all that day and the next, expecting to see a fine lady ride across the green towards him, but nothing happened and nothing again the day after that.

Although he questioned Old Meg closely, she could not tell him any more. The lady had come, found the corner cottage deserted and Mistress Coffey buried, had asked Mistress Syke about Daniel and gone again.

Where had she gone? Meg shrugged and would not answer. She spoke of what she saw and heard, and lacked the habit of considering what other folk might do. So Daniel tried to practise patience and began to tell her about the oak; how last Sabbath he had imagined great branches spread above his head and wondered about the times when an acorn sprouted into a mighty tree. 'Sometimes I can imagine the people then,' he said, without pausing in his task of winding up water. 'Great ladies perhaps, resting in the oak's shade while their men hunted.'

But Meg only exclaimed in alarm, crossed her fingers and spat to fend off witchcraft.

'But just think!' he said eagerly. 'If another oak was to be planted there, that too might last five hundred years!'

But, unlike other Parleben kin around the parish who would have had no difficulty in imagining it, Meg could not, although for his sake she tried. Only little Jane Carpenter, who had followed him across the green seemed properly impressed. 'Why don't you and I plant an acorn?' she demanded, swinging on his arm.

But her swinging spilled some water, which made him cross, and he didn't trust any Carpenter not to spoil the only place he liked in Furnace Green. So he refused to answer, which Jane thought rude; at eight years old she was already sensitive enough to notice Daniel's wretchedness and feel sorry for him, but was unused to being ignored. So she stuck out her tongue and stumped off to view Goody Apps's new calf.

The next week saw the end of hop-harvest and not a moment too soon, as a great storm rode out of the west. Daniel found it hard to believe he had only worked for Will Carpenter for the time between three Sabbaths: three weeks out of a future piled like a numbing wall in front of him. Insidiously, his will to escape into a wider world had been sapped by exhaustion and fear, the black Wealden forest closing in around him like a trap rather than beckoning him into flight. Legitimate work away from Danesdell was out of his reach until the seven years of his apprenticeship expired, runaways every man's prey, to be flogged and returned to their masters when caught, and with winter so close he would starve alone.

Once the harvest was finished, Daniel was luckier than he realized, late autumn work at Danesdell being largely made up of drying, bagging, brewing and selling hops, all tasks carried out in the dry. Will Carpenter had experimented through several seasons to discover how best to work his kiln: if hops were dried too sharply or too long, their flavour became unpleasant; if too slowly or with too little air, they soured and could not be used at all. Only if everything went exactly right would they help produce a rich brown brew which kept fresh for weeks, as unlike the old thin ales as venison from rabbit.

The hops to be dried must be spread each day on a horsecloth laid across the barn's upper beams and it seemed to Daniel that he spent each day racing down ladder rungs to stoke or damp the fire, only to be chased up again to toss the hops. One morning when the wind was stronger than Daniel realized, he used the bellows too vigorously: if he managed to make the charcoal glow white, then he could linger out of sight for a few minutes on the drying floor. He never knew quite how it happened, but the bellows must have sucked in sparks instead of air and his next stroke drove a long tongue of fire from the vent, which set light to a chimney made only from laths plastered with mud and dung: adequate to withstand steady heat but not flame projected from a bellows. After a horrified moment of indecision, Daniel dashed for the water-trough which stood in a corner for just such an emergency.

Will Carpenter fairly capered with rage when he saw his soaked charcoal and a whole chimney needing to be remade, and for the first time thrashed Daniel with a long-thonged driving whip, and left him bound to the hitching post until dinnertime.

It was October and blustery wet, but his suffering

seemed to draw a circle around Daniel until everything inside it became unnaturally distinct. He wasn't cold nor did he notice much pain, though blood-tinted rain dribbled to where his bare mauve toes curled against the cobbles. Rather, he felt hot and filled with strength. The grain of wood against his cheek fascinated him, and exultant plans spun dizzily where despair had been because, within his circle of immunity, at last Daniel had decided on his escape. He would kill Will Carpenter. This resolution, though sudden and unexpected, had a solid, satisfactory feel to it. Now he had learned so much about blood, the idea that Will's should join his own on the cobbles seemed almost matter-of-fact.

Pain became real again when suppertime brought release, and under its impact this latest of Daniel's many dreams began in its turn to disintegrate. He hated blood and foulness, felt quite as helpless under the violence boiling inside himself as before his master's unconsidered rages. Perhaps he and not Carpenter was better dead. He turned that thought over through a nightmare-ridden night, walled away as he was from the last flicker of hope by a rising fever, loneliness and despair. Yes, it would be better. He wondered why he hadn't thought of it before.

It had been days now since he had last wondered whether Meg Parlben's lady would come again to ask for him, and he didn't think about her now. Exhausted, he dozed intermittently, and as he did so the idea of finishing his misery curled deeper into his mind. Very late, he got up to bid farewell to his only friend, the horse. It was lying down in its stall and when he stroked the old grey muzzle, the creature rested its head on his shoulder as if in sympathy. Daniel laughed and scratched under its jaw. 'You're tired too, old fellow, aren't you? I've spoiled your rest while dawn's still far away.' The horse sighed and wiped its nose delicately down his front. The stable was warm and, comforted, Daniel slept at last, curled against the horse's flank.

When he woke everyone was yelling for him and he

tumbled, aching, out of straw, everything except terrified haste wiped from his mind. Later, while shovelling hops, he remembered the escape he had decided on in the night and a sense of relief spread all the way from his raw back to his confused, underslept mind.

By his own choice, this would be his last day of servitude.

Immediately, a kind of courage returned to him and he paused in his work, stood straddle-legged and deliberately urinated over Will Carpenter's drying hops. Then, covertly, he began to look for rope and a likely beam.

Faith rode to Furnace Green only two days after Daniel began his labours for Will Carpenter. She found the corner cottage deserted except for the unpleasant smells of decay, and at first thought Alex Laffam must have been mistaken when he told her the travellers had arrived. She stood on the step, completely at a loss, while a great many eyes watched her from along the street. Her disappointment was so enormous that temporarily it shook rational thought out of reach; she had come to find Gage's son as a bride might seek her lover. So she simply rode away again, and her groom, who was used to the many errands his mistress undertook to keep Riffield running and their monthly tax paid, never so much as wondered at her headlong pace.

For a night and a day Faith behaved like a harridan, throwing things at the servants and riding her horses so they came home with their heads hanging. In the castle they thought she was worried about the earl and some crude jokes were cracked, since everyone knew that until he came home this last time they had lived together more in courtesy than affection.

Eventually Faith decided to seek out Laffam. He had said that Daniel had arrived in Furnace Green, let him tell her where the boy had gone. With decision reached her madness left her, and she saw how demented she must have been not to ask along Furnace Green street whether Daniel had indeed arrived, and, if so, where he and Mistress Coffey had gone. She paused. No, perhaps instinct had saved her from disaster when to greedy outside eyes all she must show was cool interest in her old nurse. She wanted to keep Daniel close, not send him away again as the only way to silence tattling tongues.

After her first sound sleep since Henry left, she woke late and her plans immediately received a setback. When she said casually to Portnell that she must ride to settle a reckoning with Alex Laffam, he pulled his lip and reminded her that Laffam would be away. 'His oxen were hired by his lordship to pull cannon, like most others hereabouts.'

'When will he be back?' Her impatience caught fire again.

But Portnell did not know. 'Once they're rid of the cannon, Parliament won't be able to prove anything on beasts returning home. He'll be back fast enough then.'

Faith hesitated for two more days, torn between prudence and fear over what calamity might have whisked Daniel and Mistress Coffey away from the corner cottage. At the end of that time she decided to discover whether the Laffams had returned, and if not then to visit Parson Syke. She detested Syke, who had once denounced orris powder on a woman's face and silk on her body as tantamount to harlotry when Faith had been wearing both, but he wasn't a gossip. Even if she had to tell him that Daniel was her son, then he would belabour her with prayers but not tattle to anyone else about her sins.

Faith had never been to Corndown before, the Laffam farm being situated just off the Furnace Green to Edenham track. She noticed the burned woods alongside their lane and exchanged a laugh with her groom: the tale of how the committeemen had been sent away well scorched had spread across the Weald. Fowls fled squawking from under her horse's hoofs, as if swift escapes were a condition of survival in the Laffam household, but Faith was surprised by the extent of the outbuildings, all more or less dilapidated but stretching around three nettle-filled yards.

'They need gurt many beasts for hauling all manner of trade,' observed her groom.

Indeed, all manner of trade was lying about: wagons, yokes, fleeces, timber, iron and barrel-strakes all tumbled together with rootling pigs. A handsome, heavily pregnant woman came out of a house which must have been two cottages tipped into one. 'What'll you be wanting, mistress?'

'Alex,' said Faith baldly. 'Is he at home?'

The woman shook her head.

'Do you know when he will be back?'

'What's that to thee?'

'I—my husband asked me to transact some business with him.'

'The lord'll be doing his own business with Alex, I reckon,' the woman said drily, thereby revealing that she recognized Faith and was disrespectful by choice.

So that was that, thought Faith. If she wanted to learn about Daniel, she would have to endure Syke's hectorings.

The parson's new house wasn't far, on the other side of the track from Corndown, and Faith was aware of nervousness as she dismounted on his step. Riffield's incumbent put reverence for the Scovells at least on the same level as his religion and Faith went along very comfortably with him in consequence, even if Henry complained that his sermons were infernally dull. Syke was different, and owed reverence only to his puritanical God.

Mistress Syke was roused from her bed and came down looking as heavily pregnant as the Laffam wench, but where the other had glowed with health she strained wretchedly against the burden in her belly. 'Oh, milady! If only you had warned me you were coming! All I have in the house is a cheek of pork!'

'I don't want anything, thank you,' Faith said hastily. 'Only to see Parson Syke for a few minutes if he is in the house.'

'No, milady, he's not here. There's been so much trouble with the committee lately I wonder sometimes whether I'm on my head or my heels! Haven't you heard they've turned him out? I never expected to find the Devil's work in a Parliamentary committee, did you?'

Faith resisted the temptation to say yes, she had long suspected it. Though by upbringing Parliamentarian, actually she cared not a jot why the war was fought, only that every month came more demands for tax. 'Why is he turned out?' she asked instead. 'I believed him very hot for the cause.'

'Oh, he is! That's what is so unfair. They blame him for this worry over cannon, although I confess I don't understand why! Nor dare I ask when he's in such a rage and who can wonder at it?'

Faith realized with a jolt that in her anxiety about Daniel she had completely forgotten Henry's conviction that Riffield would be sequestrated, and her promise to leave before it happened. 'I daresay your trouble will blow over, since I cannot believe Parson Syke was ever disloyal by intention,' she said briskly, rising to depart before Mistress Syke's lamentations could flow again. 'I wonder—have you heard anything of a woman and a boy who were to have come to live in the cottage opposite Furnace Green church?'

'Oh yes, the woman died! Of an inflammation, I believe. She was buried . . . now let me see. More than a sennight past.'

'The boy? What happened to the boy?'

'He was called Daniel, I remember. A strange lad who allowed his attention to wander during prayer. John had to chastise him for it.'

'John? Who . . . oh!' Somehow it was difficult to imagine Syke having a Christian name. Like Gage. No, not in the least like Gage. 'Did you take him in when Mistress Coffey died? That was kind. She was my nurse, you know. Where is he now?'

'I'm sure I don't know,' said Mistress Syke vaguely. 'We always have strays about the place. John brings them in and feeds them and finds them a godly place to go. He's such a truly good man, and now the committee have turned him out!'

'Try to remember where he went. It can't be more than days ago.' Faith kept her voice steady.

'I can't, really I can't. Why, we've had a younger boy and a fouled old vagrant since—a Christian soul, I'm sure, but not in my kitchen with all his lice, I'm sure milady will agree.'

'Think,' Faith said fiercely. 'Sweet Jesus, you must remember something.'

Mistress Syke goggled at her, horrified by blasphemy. 'Milady,' she whispered. 'Repent. If John heard you take the Lord's name in vain—'

'Oh, fiddle-de-de! He didn't hear, and if you had listened where Daniel went, I wouldn't have said it. Please bid Parson Syke to call at Riffield as soon as he returns.'

Faith was so furious that she rode the shortest way back to Riffield, which meant slipping and sliding down the steep bank from ridge to park. Thus she passed between the pool and Danesdell, within a hundred paces of where Daniel carted hops.

Syke did not come next day to Riffield, nor the one after, being involved in arguing his way out of a punitive fine imposed on him by his erstwhile colleagues. The parson of Furnace Green drew a modest stipend of eight pounds a year, but as Master of Edenham, Syke was a rich prize to hard-pressed committeemen always behindhand on their tax collections.

Faith chafed and fretted at the delay, but really there was little she could do about it. Daniel was somewhere close and apparently well; Syke knew where he was. It would be madness to start enquiring around the neighbourhood for a boy she would only recognize because he looked like Gage. Or, more dangerously still, because he looked like her.

She slept badly again, tossing under her goosefeather coverlet until the September night, seemed stifling. On the third night after her visit to Mistress Syke when still the parson had not come, Faith climbed out of the great bed as the watchman struck three, the deadest hour of night, and padded across to the window. Moonlight lay tranquilly across the landscape, the trough of the park silvered over, the dark hills glinting where pale light reflected from wind-tossed leaves.

How beautiful Riffield really was, its stones silvered too, gardens and courtyards laid out like some astrologer's chart. Faith sat a long time in the oriel, soothed by stillness and with her thoughts set comfortably adrift. How strange that Henry should be the descendant of men who had seized and begun to tame this wilderness, a task as yet unfinished. Gage, surely, had been closer to the kind of men the old Scovells must have been, his son a worthier heir than any Henry could have begotten. Well, she couldn't give Daniel any part of Riffield, but would scrape an inheritance for him out of somewhere, even if it meant short-changing Parliament on their tax. Still, the implications of possible sequestration meant nothing to her.

Out of the corner of her eye she saw something move; when she turned her head it was gone. The great hall roof hid whoever was riding up the slope. By the time they emerged into sight again, the troop of Parliamentary horse was less than two hundred yards from the castle gate. Faith stood frozen, hearing the lookout (who must have been dozing) call a challenge which was answered with a brisk: 'By order of the Two Houses!'

Then they were riding into the courtyard, pair after pair of them, clattering steel. A moment later Faith heard something—a sword scabbard probably—hammer on the door, then heavy footsteps in the house. Riffield had long ago become a castle in name only and armed men with the law behind them would splinter the windows if the porter refused to answer their call.

'Milady, oh milady! There's troopers muddying everything with their boots and an officer demanding Lady Riffield on the instant!' Becky, her tiring-maid, came scuttling into Faith's room like a flushed stoat, teeth bared in terror.

This at last was reality. A reality Henry had warned her about, and she had dismissed as unthinkable. Reality come so swiftly that Faith was left strangely calm. 'Help me dress and stop squawking,' she said sharply. 'I don't intend to meet the Two Houses of Parliament in my shift.'

The troopers showed no sign of scattering upstairs, but Faith could smell the rankness from their clothes as soon as she left her room. The great hall was full of them, milling about and staring at Riffield's treasures in avaricious calculation. The trinkets on the dresser had already vanished and Faith railed at herself for being so wilfully blinkered that she hadn't even considered what might be hidden.

The officer in charge was young and hollow-shouldered; though he wore a sword he looked more like a clerk than a soldier. He also clearly detested the task he had been given. 'Milady of Riffield?'

'Yes. I'm afraid that if you are looking for my husband, he is away with the king.'

'Aye, I know. Madam, I have a writ of sequestration to serve on you, issued the fourth day of October, 1643.'

Faith did not move to take the official paper he held out. 'I will appeal against it.'

'To the committee which issued it? Come, madam. Take it and hand me your keys.' He spoke with the flat London twang she remembered in her father's associates.

Faith put her hands behind her back; it was childish, but she refused to be party to the seizure of Riffield even by a gesture. 'I am sure there isn't any law in England which allows armed men to take another's property at dead of night without cause shown, or redress.'

He flushed, then placed the paper on the mantle. 'There is the law of the Two Houses, I assure you, madam.'

'Which is something rather different, or don't you agree?'

'Not different for you,' he answered grimly, and jerked his head at a sergeant. 'Send the maidservants here for their safety and then make a thorough search of the house, stables and outbuildings. Break down locked doors, but preserve any account books you find for me.'

Faith saw the tough faces around her slacken into satisfaction; only account books had been mentioned. Everything else in the house was at their mercy. 'Wait. Portnell, bring your household keys and also those for the stables.'

In silence Portnell bowed and went to fetch them, his face like dry seamed timber.

'It's too late, you know,' the officer's fingers were fidgeting with the orange sash at his waist. 'I have orders to send your horses to the army, billet troops here for as long as may be necessary and impound your records so the committee may learn about the estate. From this day on, all income due to the Scovells must be paid to Parliament.'

Faith swallowed. 'The house?'

He stared at the floor and did not answer. The keys might prevent a few doors being splintered, but mostly the soldiers would be too impatient to try each one for size. County committees knew that if they billeted men in confiscated property, then they were powerless to prevent most things in it from being smashed or looted. Better for discipline to take the opportunity of throwing a morsel of reward to men brought close to disaffection by a bloody and fruitless war.

This shamefaced boy was certainly incapable of controlling men withdrawn in haste from fighting in the west when the tale of vanished cannon spread. He and Faith, together with a huddle of terrified maidservants, stood together in the high-raftered hall and listened to the sound of booted feet hurtling from room to room, tearing wood, breaking furniture, the beginnings of merriment when the first of many kegs was broached; heard the screech of a maidservant who had not reached the hall in time.

'For God's sake,' said Faith through stiff lips, 'you'll never keep watch over the Weald with a pack of drunken swine.'

He stared at her out of wretched, apologetic eyes. 'I'm sorry, madam. If troops rather than a magistrate are sent to a sequestered house, they know everything in it is theirs. It's best if they purge their greeds in one coup, however foul. I shall stave in the remaining casks while they sleep, and bring an end to the worst. They know better than to break windows or let in the weather when they must live here through the winter.'

'Another rule is that they may rape a maidservant so long as the mistress goes free, in case she has relatives in Parliament?' demanded Faith scornfully. She was too angry to feel afraid.

He drew himself up. 'I did my best to protect you all, and regret it if I failed. The women who wanted to come here had time, I believe.' He hesitated and then blurted out, 'I was a military clerk to the committee until this very day, when they ordered me to bring troops here.'

'I hope they discover someone more fitted to command them through the winter then, or Riffield will turn into a freebooters' den,' Faith said cruelly, and after that they waited in silence.

The old building shook to the bite of axes and pound of predatory feet. Merciful Christ, Henry could never have imagined what the murder of his home would be like. Crowhurst Manor nearby had been sequestered the previous summer and there the family had been coldly dispossessed and the rents gathered into Parliament's coffers, nothing more. This was the revenge of petty men made to look like numbskulls: committeemen mostly came fresh to a power undreamed-of even a year before, and the laughter of half a county had caught them on the raw.

Faith would never forget how that dawn broke, the sky set fair and birdsong the only sound. 'You'll be safe now while I go to stave in the unbroached kegs.' The lieutenant spoke into the stillness. 'Tell your steward to show me where every single one is kept. All your inside servants must leave within the hour for their homes, those outside will be needed. You may keep your personal woman and with her make a room habitable for your use.'

'My use?'

'You stay here until the committee is satisfied they have mastered the Scovell affairs. You have been overseeing the land in the earl's absence, have you not? I think there will be many queries to be answered before I finish my reckonings.'

'Portnell is my husband's steward.'

'You are better surety than any steward if my accountings are to tally. Or so the committee says. Choose a room I may keep under my eye, which has a door with an unburst lock.'

Faith shrugged without answering, since argument was clearly a waste of breath.

'And, madam . . . I left a trustworthy guard in your stable and another on the gate. If you thought to leave while my back is turned, you would have to go on foot. I assure you my men are not so drunk that some could not be kicked awake to hunt a woman down. But once my work here is finished I will make sure that horses and moneys for your journey are left aside.'

'Thank you,' said Faith stiffly. 'What is your name?'

'Hosmer, madam, a lawyer's scribe from London. My master was one of the judges who resigned rather than carry out royal orders which he believed infringed the liberties of England. Until last night I thought I knew what I fought for and loved what I knew.'

'Until last night I scarcely thought of the war at all except to curse the tax-gatherers,' Faith said with venom. 'Now I shan't be satisfied until every lawbreaker in the realm is gibbeted.'

It was as well she had not seen for herself the destruction which lay beyond the great hall before she replied so defiantly, because defiance vanished before the scene which met her eyes. Panelling hung in strips from the walls, there was vomit in Henry's library and his books tumbled into it from the shelves; hangings were torn, trinkets had vanished, furniture was thrown into hearths for firewood; store-shelves were swept bare of preserves, some to be trampled wantonly underfoot.

No one spoke but tears ran down the cheeks of men and maidservants alike, most of whom had served the Scovells since childhood, and their ancestors before them. Only Portnell and Faith stood dry-eyed amid the wreckage, though they wept too, but secretly; which is the hardest grief of all to bear.

Faith chose Henry's library for her prison and grimly she and Becky cleaned out foulness, stepping over snoring bodies to boil water in the kitchen. The library was small enough to be snug, the hearth did not smoke and the entry formed part of an older stone wall, the door ironbound and very strong.

Lieutenant Hosmer approved her choice, helped them to throw broken furniture through the window and carried in whatever she chose of the pieces which had escaped destruction. 'You needn't worry,' he repeated. 'When the men's heads have cleared they'll be under control again and I shall keep them busy on patrol.'

Certainly he tried. Or so Becky said, although Faith heard little in her lair. The castle was scoured bleakly clean and from her window she saw when patrols rode out, which wasn't very often. Sometimes there were crashes and laughter in the night but the sounds were not particularly menacing and after a while she began to suffer extremes of boredom, as Hosmer's visits with the Riffield rent rolls became the only variation in her day. He had put a guard on her door, a phlegmatic individual who did what he was told; Becky came back flustered sometimes from her trips to the kitchen, but her eyes sparkled with excitement too. Now Portnell had left and the soldiers were merely behaving as soldiers might be expected to behave, Becky was enjoying some of the choices they offered. It's no use worrying, Faith thought, and truly she did not care. All she wanted was to get away from Riffield.

She was delighted when Hosmer at last brought Parson Syke to see her, being in the state of mind where she welcomed any visitor, but Syke above all because Daniel was again her main preoccupation. She had been pacing restlessly for hours, raging to get out, but when she saw Syke standing in the doorway suddenly she could not speak. He knew where Daniel was; how he looked and the timbre of his voice.

'Milady,' he said, and bowed. 'I regret to see you in so sad a case.'

Riffield; of course, he referred to Riffield. But Faith was beyond pretence. 'I believe you cared for a boy called Daniel Gage and hired him out when—when Mistress Coffey died in Furnace Green. She was once my tiring-woman and wet-nurse.'

Syke hugged his hat across his belly. 'Aye, that is so.'

'Where did you hire him?'

'What is a parish orphan to you, milady?' Ever since his wife's disjointed account of Lady Riffield's visit, unwelcome speculation had refused to be dislodged from Syke's sharp mind, but he had never expected so brazen an approach.

Faith took a deep breath. 'He is my son.'

No amount of thought had suggested how she could obtain information from a man like Syke, except by telling the truth.

'God have mercy!' He looked around the narrow room. 'Though it seems some retribution has already been visited on you.'

'Retribution began the day after Daniel was born, and I woke up to find him gone. As for the sack of Riffield, that must be retribution on the earl rather than me. And if you can explain how he deserves such punishment from a God who calls himself just, then I think you must be the cleverest man in Sussex.'

'Vengeance is mine, I will repay, saith the Lord.'

'That is no answer, since you can't answer when I ask for what his lordship is being repaid. Beyond making fools of you all, I suppose, and that is a fortune of war. Now tell me quickly where Daniel is.'

'Oh, do not speak with Satan's voice!' Syke steepled his hands as a gesture towards prayer, but his face had flushed mauve with anger. 'My daughter, listen to admonition, bow your neck to chastisement and beg mercy for your soul.'

'I might, if you could truthfully tell me this: why should you of all men call a sinner your daughter?'

Syke had never been so flabbergasted in his life, all the sinners in his experience having been fearful or defiant, never coldly enquiring. 'I am the Lord's servant. Man goeth forth to his labours, yea until his last hour.'

'So, both duty and charity cause you to entreat for me?'

'Fervent in spirit, praising the Lord.' Syke eyed her warily, aware that a snare was being set for him.

'Then if God bids you to call me daughter although I am not, neither would He deny me the chance to name Daniel as my son. Since he is mine by blood, and a great deal more than duty or charity draws me to him.'

Syke fingered his hat. 'What will you do if I tell you?'

Faith knew then that she had won and cared about nothing else. 'As soon as Lieutenant Hosmer releases me I will go and offer Daniel employment, and compensation to his master, I suppose. With Riffield taken I shall have to return to my mother in Suffolk, and it wouldn't seem too unlikely for you to beg me to convey a stray youth back to his birthplace, which should not be too far aside from my journey. So I keep the earl's name free of scandal and win time to gain Daniel's trust before disclosing the truth to him.' She lifted her head and stared into Syke's bloodshot eyes. 'I intend to tell him frankly that he is my son by a man I loved.'

'You said you owed this ignorant boy more than duty or charity. What then of the earl your husband in the future, who, a few minutes past, you also said did not deserve retribution?'

Faith inclined her head; when he stopped mouthing texts Parson Syke was worthy of respect. But her mind was made up. 'I have bitterly wronged him, and expect to pay for it. If I could spare him by any means other than by leaving Daniel unacknowledged I would do it. But I cannot, and once I have returned to Suffolk I never expect to live with him again.'

Unknown to Faith, Syke immediately thought of his own wife, whose premature labour had delayed this visit for several days. Yesterday he had buried his seventeenth child, and he understood a little of how Faith must feel after years of barren marriage. Though how very shocking it all was, to be sure! When God's war was won there would be such great purgings of sin that wives would never again deceive their husbands.

'Well?' Faith looked at him with the same narrow-lidded eyes as Daniel. The same fair skin and thin features; strange he had not seen the likeness before.

'He is apprenticed to Will Carpenter at Danesdell,' he said reluctantly, at last. 'Where he will learn the skills he lacks. You would do better to leave him there, so he may serve the Lord in the station of life to which he has been called.'

'You should know all about that,' said Faith bitingly. 'Since I understand your godly labours have been rewarded by a fine from your committee. Good day to you, sir.'

Syke was enraged by this conversation, and all the rejoinders he would have liked to make came back to him in the night. After all, the real reason for his original misjudgement had been charity towards the earl. He writhed in his bedstraw with fury and eventually reached for his wife, but she just whimpered and lay slackly under him, leaving his rage unslaked, her miscarriage being only a few days past. Women. Adam had something to answer for when he provoked God into creating them as an entirely unsatisfactory remedy for sin.

Next day he wrote a letter to the Sussex County Committee, sucking his quill often while he wrote:

. . . wish to inform you that the garrison at Riffield Castle does not appear to me well ordered, Lieutenant Hosmer being too inexperienced for the task. I would advise appointing a commander

the men will respect, under orders to restore discipline by any means which may be necessary. Only then will the district be securely kept and the malignant Scovell's wife sent away as soon as may be. So long as she remains, contumacious persons will remember how the Scovells once ruled in Riffield . . . written by your servant to command this twenty-eighth day of October 1643, John Syke.

He shook sand over the paper, smiling. The committee must learn that they could not manage this part of the county without Parson Syke, then would he make terms with them over the matter of his fine. Meanwhile, the sooner he was rid of an unrepentant daughter of Babylon, the better. If she managed to claim her brat and be gone without setting every tongue wagging for miles, then he for one would be very much surprised, and a fine day for harlotry that would be.

Thus was made the last of a great many mistakes, which began with a girl's infatuation thirteen years before.

The first Faith knew of the consequences of Syke's letter was a sense of tension in the castle. Feet beat in the passages, laughter stopped, the trooper outside her door refused to answer the simplest questions. No less than three well-burnished patrols went out within a day, one of them led by Lieutenant Hosmer himself, sitting very stiffly in his saddle. There could scarcely be enough men left to guard the gate, thought Faith, as she counted the mounted figures. The owlers of the Weald would need to watch out for themselves tonight.

Becky told her that a new commander had come, which Faith had already surmised, a captain of dragoons who had all the men and horses turned out into the courtyard within an hour of his arrival. 'He kept them standing in the rain all morning, daring anyone to offer an insolent look. Well, you know how they've been, milady.' Becky rolled her eyes. ''Twasn't long before one said his belly griped and another pretended his horse was too lame to stand still. While that were going on a few began to snigger like, an' a couple in the back rank slipped away into the stable while the new captain's attention were took up.'

'What happened?' demanded Faith eagerly. A new man must mean that events had begun to move again at last.

'Ah, he's a devil, that captain. He'd seen the men slip off, no matter his back were turned. He ordered three troopers to arrest them and once they were seized he charged them with desertion then and there. Drew and cocked his pistol while everyone stood mumchance, with a smile on his face which made every man understand he'd be pleased to see blood on the cobbles.'

'Desertion?' Faith said slowly. 'A soldier is hanged for that. They'd only dodged an overlong muster, surely. Which deserved a flogging, I suppose.'

'Aye, they'll be hanged, or so the whisper runs. Then everyone will know they've got a master now.'

'What happened to Lieutenant Hosmer?' demanded Faith. Hosmer had done the best he could, and only in war was it held against a man if he was incapable of shooting anyone who defied him.

'I don't know,' said Becky regretfully. 'He were given a rare old trimming, but in the great hall with the doors closed.'

After this Faith was agog to meet the tyrant come among them, since even the Devil himself in buff and steel might help to pass the time. But the new commander did not come, and when Becky went to fetch the evening meal, she failed to return. Faith lit a candle and sat on the window-seat, with nothing to distract her from hunger. The patrols had not come back and, she guessed, were unlikely to do so until the morrow at the earliest; even the guard outside her door seemed to have been removed, as if to emphasise that a return to discipline made the precaution unnecessary. 'Oh God,' she said, to shelved books in languages which mostly she could not read, 'let me get out of here soon.'

It must have been hours later, when the candle had

guttered out and an owl hooted in the trees outside her window, that she heard heels on flagstones, then the key turned in her door and Gage stood in the entry.

There couldn't be any mistake; as if the harsh directness which now ruled Riffield had already conditioned her to recognize little more than a silhouette in reflected moonlight. Neither spoke, as if speaking first was a battle lost. This improbable battle, while the owl still keened like a demented soul.

The next Faith knew, she was seated with her head against her knees and nausea in her throat.

'I thought you were going to puke,' remarked Gage, and threw open the casement to admit raw air.

Faith shook her head, the movement setting her senses loose. 'My father told me you were dead.'

'Did you believe him?'

'When I made him tell . . . what he had done . . . yes. After a while. Indentured servants sent under hatches to the West Indian plantations don't live more than months, he said, and I understood that he must know.'

'Aye, and I'd have killed him for it if I'd got back before. I shipped into Plymouth six months after the war began and rode at once for Suffolk, only to discover that John Littleton had recently died. More's the pity.' Gage's voice was harsher, his body thicker, the golden eyes black pits in dimness. Faith did not need to be told that he had changed very much for the worse, and when she had known him before he'd been a violent man.

But, Gage. Gage here, and alive.

She stood, trembling, and went over to stand close, her face raised to his. 'I remembered you.'

He laughed. 'How tender. How sweet of you to remember my rotting corpse each silk-lined day of your ladyship's life.'

'No. I remembered how much I had loved you.'

'Aye, I daresay you did long for some lust in your life again. Once a mare's been mounted, she misses the stallion.' His kiss took her by surprise, his hands as hard as his armour crushed against her breasts, his mouth a trap of steel.

'Take off your clothes,' he said, and stood back unbuckling straps.

'I can't, not without help.'

He gave a grunt which might have been laughter or derision, and unconcernedly finished his own business of undressing. Faith had never seen a naked man before. Henry came shamefaced in a night robe to her bed, and doused the candles before climbing in beside her; her previous times with Gage had been so hastily snatched that each occasion was a matter of open breeches and thrown-up skirts. The moon came out as she watched, showing her thick muscles, black hair from chest to thighs, and private parts like those of the stallion he accused her of desiring. Then he took her by the shoulders, turned her round and tore ribbons, tapes and lacings one from the other.

Instinctively, she tried to cover herself with her hands.

'You look remarkably foolish bobbing there with your eyes squeezed closed and God knows what twice-rotted cravings in your belly.' His voice was harder than his discarded breastplate on the floor. 'Stand up straight, milady Riffield.'

Her eyes flew open; terror and desire congealed by stupefaction. He had moved back again by the door, his nakedness grotesquely exaggerated by the moon-shadows.

Why strip her, if he immediately stood back to jeer?

Because every step of this revenge was a step he meant her to take alone: Faith made mistakes, but understood Gage too well to make them easily with him.

Gropingly, she picked her way clear of fallen skirts while he remained silent, detached, encased in hatred. And under the weight of shame and silence, her instincts suddenly shifted and she faced him, hands defiantly behind her back.

He looked her over critically. 'Turn round.'

She turned, gladly; it was easier then to imagine he might want her for other reasons than revenge.

'Lie on the bed.'

She did not move. 'You have commanded men for too long. I can't be chained up for a flogging.'

'No? On the gallows beside your precious father would be a fitter end. Lie on the bed.'

So she went and lay, wanting him very much now. Ashamed to want him, while all the time the clamour from her body grew. Only hunger left from all the barren years, when Henry's apologetic fumblings made her yearn for Gage. He took her as brutally as he knew how, and there wasn't much he hadn't learned about brutality in the years since he first discovered how much soft Faith Littleton desired his harshness.

He also left her the instant he was finished, as if to underscore that lust was all he felt for her.

'Did you know I was here?' Faith tasted blood on her lips and lay very still; sated to a kind of dreadful satisfaction, confused and humiliated into tears and out again.

He pulled on his boots. 'I don't believe in chance. Chance didn't batten me into a stinking hulk bound for the Indies, nor would it have led me here. When I rode into Suffolk seeking to kill John Littleton, I found a great many people only too willing to tell me about the splendid marriage Mistress Faith had made. So I sold my sword to Parliament and eventually came into Sussex. If the committeemen hadn't wanted to replace that gutless fool Hosmer, I should have reached here some different way.' He turned in the entry. 'I will be back later tonight.'

Not again tonight. Even Faith's shameful cravings couldn't endure him again tonight. But he had already gone, the bolt shot into wood. Nor would he have listened to any pleadings.

She mustn't tell him about Daniel. That was her first thought after he had gone. Gage was no longer, probably never had been, a fit father for any son to have. He was—just sometimes—a fitting lover for the trollop who inhabited the darker spaces of her body. But could it be so very wicked, sometimes to need such mastery?

Then, as days and nights slid into a single whole, even the trollop in her could less often welcome the crude force which was Gage, dreaded the thought of him coming whether she wanted him or not. Yet slowly, slowly her tremblings would change from dread to desire again, from pain to craving and on again, until craving became a desperate greed for surfeit in this one extraordinary time away from tediously similar embraces.

After that first night Gage was never again quite so vengefully brutal; merely insatiably inconsiderate because he knew no other way to take a woman. He made no effort to rouse her, although in truth it was scarcely necessary, handled her as he chose and went away immediately afterwards. Sometimes he came two or three times in a night and sometimes left her forty-eight hours alone. Then she wept with relief. And wept for loss again before the time was finished.

Faith Scovell, milady of Riffield, was as bewitched as Faith Littleton had been all those years ago. She seldom bothered any more to dress, but, though exhausted by patternless time so avidly filled, she knew she would rather have Gage like this than never to have experienced Gage at all. Indeed, there was no other way to experience a man like Gage; he had lived like a brute for so long that he wouldn't have understood if she'd tried to speak of love. Nor did she love him. She desired him and was made frenzied by his power; hated and feared him even while she continued to savour both hate and fear.

Then, gradually, the heat of such obsessive lust began to char her spirit. His unconcern settled like grit to chafe her emotions raw, until all she wanted was for him to go before only hate was left, although she accepted that for a man like Gage revenge was a necessity. His skin was puckered from whippings, chainings and toiling under a burning sun, but in a strange way she came to believe that so long as hatred was not left to stand alone, then after this frantic time both their sufferings would be allowed to rest.

If only he would go.

Faith began to feel very old and tired, wishing he would go. Becky must be shut out of reach, she never saw her now. Gage himself brought food for her when he came, carelessly, as one might feed a puppy, and sent in a wooden-faced woman Faith had never seen with buckets and hot water. Riffield's garrison must know what was happening, but Gage's superiors would have some difficulty in proving anything against him.

If only he would go.

Faith began trying to reckon time again, in an effort to stop herself from growing crazed with this longing for him to go. How long really since he came? Ten days? Fifteen? Sweet Jesus, he could have been sent to command Riffield for the whole winter, and long before such a length of time was over she would hate him utterly and he be sated by such passions. She did not dare think what Gage would do once his passion died.

That night he came as he always did, boot-heels drumming down the passage, the lock drawn as if struck by a mallet, back and breastplate tossed wordlessly on the floor; sash, boots and breeches. He came and stood beside the bed this time instead of taking her at once. 'Kiss me.'

She kissed the part of him she had always known best, and felt him shudder under her lips. He joined her swiftly then, but for the first time stayed after he finished. Faith lay watching his darkness asleep beside her, for that was how he was: a Lucifer of darkness. Dark hair, dark passions, dark needs; the only light about him those dangerous eyes, which told of a pride Lucifer also knew.

He stirred after a while and reached for her at once. 'I'm going in the morning.'

'Where?' A great rush of thanksgiving in her heart. Jesu, she must not show her thankfulness.

'I am sent to Waller's Horse in the west. That weasel Hosmer ran off to the committee and told them—' She felt a grunt which this time was certainly laughter. 'Christ, I don't know what he told them. A boy stuffed full with romantic gallantry wouldn't want to dirty the name of Lady Riffield, would he? Anyway, he said enough to have me sent away, so God have mercy on Lieutenant Hosmer if ever he joins the real army. I'll spill his guts in the first fight where we ride side by side.' Probably he meant it, from habit if nothing else. But his tone was light and Faith could tell he was glad to return to fighting. Despite himself Gage had ceased to think of her as an enemy, but then, the moment revenge lost its savour, Riffield would become a routine duty and she a wench the same as any other.

They would be parted only just in time.

If he had stayed confined with her through a winter, then one of them must have turned killer and Faith could not have sworn, cross her heart, that she would not have sickened first. And yet . . . and yet . . . she felt desolate when he left her and began to dress. She watched him in the cold grey dawn, the last time she would see strapped steel buckled impatiently tight. 'Can I leave here once you have gone?'

'How do I know? I'll leave the door unbarred if you like.'

'Thank you,' Faith said drily. 'I think I also need a pass for the journey; money, a coach, horses and a groom.'

'Come follow the armies and travel light,' he answered carelessly. 'I find it better so. But I daresay your romantic weasel will come scuttling back as soon as I am gone, so all will end merrily after all.'

'I don't expect a merry ending. Do you?'

'God, no. I shall cough my blood up in a muddy field somewhere, I expect.' He jerked the coverlet off her and stood looking down. 'You never told me you had birthed a brat.'

Her heart froze and through a confusion of darkened eyes and drumming ears his shape seemed poised again to crush her. Then the mist cleared and she heard her voice say yes, indeed. She had borne her husband a stillborn son, but, like all else in her marriage, it was nothing to do with him.

Gage flicked the silvery lines on her belly with his fingers. 'Then perhaps his lordship should be grateful if I've left him something to remember me by. Either way, I wish good fortune on your explanations.'

He bent, leather, steel and sword-hilt crammed heedlessly against her nakedness, his mouth as demanding as it had ever been; but Faith sensed that just for a moment he did not want to leave her. A kind of victory perhaps, and the only one she would ever win over Gage.

Then he was rapping away down the passage, and not long after she heard a single set of hoofs beating across the park and into the distance. She knew she would never see him again.

Faith lay all that day dozing memory away, her memory like hounds baying the moon, maddening each other with their barking.

Becky came back that evening with the supper, her eyes sliding from the unlocked door to the change in Faith. Quite what this change was Faith herself could not have said; except she felt tired, which was scarcely surprising. She also felt more in charity with the world and less inclined to carp. Mercifully, though clearly agog with curiosity, Becky only dared to hint at her many questions and these Faith ignored.

So Faith ate and then slept again, deeply this time, to wake just before dawn. The same owl was calling from the trees below her window as if nothing at all had happened since the time she last noticed it. She leaped out of bed, stretching like a cat and feeling agreeably content. Lucifer possessed every vice except one: he left his women satisfied. And now Gage had gone, Faith was pleased to discover that all trace of hate had vanished with him. She was glad he had gone, glad also that he had come.

She opened the casement and took deep breaths of woodland air. Even if she had to walk, today she would fetch Daniel.

In fact, Lieutenant Hosmer came to the rescue, as Gage

had predicted. He was embarrassed by what he considered the shameless seduction of a prisoner but brought a bag of coin as well as an order from the Sussex committee which allowed her to leave for Essex.

'I will escort you myself as far as Whiligh, where Sir John Courthope has stood surety for your release. He said the earl arranged for you to leave Riffield in good time before sequestration and he had been expecting you from day to day.' Hosmer's tone was reproachful. 'He will arrange your journey into Suffolk. I am sorry that today I have only a riding horse for you; all your draught beasts are taken for the army.'

'A ride is just what I should like. You can't imagine how I long to be out from these four walls!' answered Faith.

'Indeed I can, milady.' His tone was so heartfelt that Faith nearly giggled. 'I hope you don't mind my escorting you but I thought it better if the Courthopes—any of your acquaintance—did not come where they might hear unwelcome tales.'

'No, indeed,' Faith answered gravely. 'Oh dear me, no.'

They rode side by side down the slope from the gate to Riffield village, but Faith reined in as they reached the first cottage, her wood-mouthed army remount standing with its head drooping while she looked back at Henry's castle. At long grey walls and single tower, faceted windows and snapping Parliamentary flags. 'I wonder whether he'll ever get it back.' She wasn't aware she had spoken aloud until Hosmer answered.

'The earl? Once Parliament has won and provided he will take the covenant. Aye, perhaps.'

'But the king is winning.' Gage had told her that a royal army was advancing on London.

'Well, he will certainly get it back if that is so.'

'But you don't think so?'

'That the king will win? No. In spite of . . .' He flushed and then continued steadily, 'In spite of some crimes committed in Parliament's name, our cause is England's liberty.'

'So you say.'

He nodded. 'We do. And so we shall win. One day.'

'Then I hope that if Riffield must have a new master, he will love it as the Scovells did.' As she and Hosmer rode across the park to Furnace Green, Faith did not look back again. Riffield had fallen and, win or lose, she could not believe that Henry would have the heart to attempt to get it back.

Late autumn sun rioted through the bracken as they rode, a brisk wind stinging Faith's uplifted face. Blue sky, huge trees spraying bronze and gold: she was seeing the Weald at its best on this last day. Her horse was blown by the time they scrambled up from the park to the ridge, and while she and Hosmer waited before riding the short distance on to Danesdell she explained that she wanted to visit Farmer Carpenter on her way to Whiligh. Ah, how tedious were explanations.

Even so, she owed Henry such decency as she could contrive, when whispers must be rife about the happenings at Riffield. 'There is a boy living at this farm who came from Essex. Now he is orphaned and when Parson Syke came to see me he asked if I would offer him the chance to return with me to his own country.'

'Yes, of course,' said Hosmer, thinking how truly good she was. And that brute Gage—

'Strange how a clutch of freeholders have clung to this one ridge,' added Faith musingly. She had been wild with impatience to see Daniel; now she was so close to him a strange reluctance held her back. 'My husband tried twice to buy them out, and his father before him, so he said. Scovells hated to look across at land they did not own. Yet in the end it is they who lost while these lesser folk survive.'

'Perhaps we all have to learn how to look without envy at what others own.'

'Perhaps.' Faith had had more than enough preaching from Syke and urged her horse on again. 'God help the Parliamentary army if beasts such as this are all it has left.'

Danesdell was not at all as Faith expected it. Eroded

banks formed the trough in which it lay and bare poles sticking skywards gave the fields around it a forlorn appearance now the hop-harvest was finished, hops not yet being a familiar crop in Sussex. There was also a surprising number of people standing about: children, two smocked labourers, a woman, a man in a cloth jerkin leaning on an ashplant.

'Are you Master Carpenter?' Faith asked him.

'Aye.'

'Parson Syke told me he hired a parish orphan out to you.'

'Aye.'

Faith moistened her lips, as excitement came flooding back. 'Daniel Gage.'

Hosmer moved sharply behind her back but she never noticed, had forgotten he would know the name.

This time Carpenter simply nodded.

'He came from Essex.' Her voice drumming against her skull, like Gage's heels on stone. 'I am returning to Suffolk through that county and Parson Syke suggested I should give him the chance to accompany me. Will you let me speak to him and offer a position as my horse-boy? I'll pay . . . I'll compensate for your loss.' By the time she finished she might have been speaking to a row of gargoyle faces on a gutter. Utter silence, staring eyes, mumchance mouths.

Will rubbed his cheek on his sleeve, bristles scraping on rough cloth. 'Nay.'

Faith recoiled. '*No?* Why, what is it to you? Most farmers are glad to rid themselves of a labourer for the winter.'

'Aye, but I'm already rid of him. He's dead.'

Her lips slipped one against the other. 'When?'

'Yestere'en.'

Yesterday. Oh Christ. She could have been in time. Even allowing for the wasted weeks which weren't her fault, she could have been in time. 'How?'

Will looked at her, and knew. Furnace Green had been awash in rumour ever since the buffcoats garrisoned Riffield, and Alex Laffam when boisterously drunk one night, had said that he was minded to buy Daniel off Danesdell and see what he was worth to the earl when next he came home. This remark had puzzled Will Carpenter, but now he knew. With her face emptied of all but anguish Faith looked remarkably like Daniel when he, too, was brought to nothing by despair. Useless, thin-blooded creatures both of them, in Will Carpenter's opinion. Really, he was surprised by the rumour that a Parliamentary captain of dragoons had thought her worth tumbling in the straw.

He whacked his stick against his gaiter. 'He hanged himself. Once they're forced, dullards and bad-doers like him either learn better ways or weary of the effort, see? He wearied.'

Faith came anyhow from the saddle, her knees softer than curd. 'I want to see him.'

'Aye, if you wish. I don't know what to do with him and that's God's truth. Parson won't want him in the churchyard, I'm sure.' Will wasn't consciously cruel to Faith any more than he had been to Daniel, merely a blunt man who spoke few words and those exactly what he thought.

The childish body sprawled in an ox-stall was little more than bone and skin, the face discoloured and afraid. Fair hair like straw, sharp narrow cheeks and jaw, eyes closed with pennies which gave him the look of drilled stone. Faith stared at him, feeling nothing except horror. He did not look like Gage at all, and because she had come expecting Gage's son she felt no kinship with this pitiful, muddied boy, a raw welt cut sinew-deep into his neck showing how he died. A dullard, a poor doer and her son.

Hesitantly she reached out and touched him. Cold, stiff; not anything any more. What had he been? Had he thought of anything beyond byres and hops and tasks too heavy for his frailty? She would never know, and so this horror was all she felt. A horror which changed shape even while she stood staring, and became a haunting guilt.

She bent and curled her fingers into his, lifted his grimed knuckles to kiss them. She could at least give him a scrap of softness to take with him into the dark. And as her lips touched coldness she saw the likeness, not to Gage but to herself. How much of a dullard and poor doer would she have been, shorn of everything which made life endurable?

Well, she thought, I shall find out. God knows there is not much left to make me want to face the years ahead.

She went outside, knowing that if she stayed she would howl like a woman hired to mourn at funerals. Lieutenant Hosmer was waiting for her in the yard, a child standing beside him. 'Madam, this is Jane, Master Carpenter's daughter. She says the boy . . . she says the only place Daniel liked was the pool yonder. She thinks he would be happy lying there.'

Faith stared at him and then at the child, about nine years old and stained with blackberry juice from mouth to ears. 'By the pool?'

'He would be best buried where he was content.' Hosmer avoided her eyes.

Suicide. Her son was a suicide; Will Carpenter would only be waiting for Parson Syke's permission to tumble Daniel into a hole by the roadway with a stake driven through his greenstick ribs, as a warning to others not to join him in damnation.

'Does she know—' Faith stopped. Her fault with Daniel had been wanting him because he was Gage's son, never for himself. She crouched beside the little girl. 'Tell me, Jane. Do you know which was Daniel's most favourite place by this pool?'

She nodded vigorously. 'The rotted oak.'

Faith was taken aback, having expected something better. Poor Daniel, even in death he was dogged by squalor.

'You take the lady,' said Hosmer, and at once the child dragged her off; up the muddy bank, across wet grass to the pool and then through a hazel thicket where Faith found difficulty in following. Beyond lay a stretch of turf ravined by mighty roots, which supported the remnants of a trunk which must once have spread a cathedral growth of green boughs.

'He used to come here on Sundays.' Jane was still holding her hand.

'You watched him?'

'Weren't nothing else to do, Sundays.'

What was he like? The question died on Faith's lips. It seemed mere prying to ask once it could do no good. She looked around her. 'I'd like to think of him here.'

'My mam said parson'd make us put him by the cross-roads wi' a stick through his belly.' Tears trickled through the purple stains on the child's face.

Faith's mind set abruptly. 'No. I won't leave him to that. We'll bury him here between us, and once it's done I'll go and see Parson Syke. I believe he might understand.'

She discovered that Hosmer had sent her away with Jane on purpose: while Faith was still comforting Jane, he appeared carrying Daniel's body wrapped in a cloth, went away again without a word to fetch an axe and spade. A sensitive young man, he had anticipated Faith's decision and silenced Will Carpenter with his authority as a Parliamentary officer.

The digging was hard, between roots which only occasionally crumbled to the touch. Faith, who had never handled spade or mattock in her life, would never have managed it on her own. By the time they finished she and Hosmer were dirtier than Jane, but at least some part of her guilt rested with Daniel, in the one place he had liked.

'Would you bring flowers sometimes?' Faith said to Jane when the last turf was patted back into place.

'My mam says flowers is for Christ, greenery for Tiw.' The child repeated the saying sing-song, without comprehension. 'I won't bring hops, though, Daniel hated hops. I'll plant an acorn if you like. He'd be pleased by a new tree watching over him.'

Faith thought of the fields filled with hops around Danesdell and her mind gave the first sharp twinge of understanding for how Daniel had really been, as if her son's barren pain had fused at last with her own.

Lieutenant Hosmer said a prayer over the mound but

Faith scarcely listened. Prayers and sermons had always bored her, and a god who willed a stake to be driven through a child's heart because he was unable to sustain the life which she and Gage had so negligently given him couldn't ease her grief, now or ever.

Faith wrote to Henry three weeks later, by which time she was living with her mother at Littleton Manor. She said nothing of Riffield nor what had happened there, but simply thanked him for his provision for her journey and said she was safe arrived. She knew he loved her, and had taken some uncharacteristic risks this past year because she was incapable of loving him; so when she wrote she mentioned nothing which really mattered to either of them, since in her heart she knew that Henry as well as Gage would be killed before this hateful war ended.

Oddly enough, once she was settled back at Littleton Manor, what Faith remembered best out of the weeks since Henry rode away from Riffield was Lieutenant Hosmer's kindness. Not Gage; not Daniel's death or Syke's condemnation, but simple human kindness. England would have need of kindness when peace returned at last.

During the following year of 1644 it seemed as if the war never would be over. The king's advance of the previous autumn had been stopped after a fiercely contested fight at Newbury. Now bloody skirmishes and battles followed each other without apparent end: Arundel, Newark, Lincoln, Lostwithiel, York, Marston Moor. There were many mourning families in Suffolk after Marston Moor, where the army of the Eastern Association carried the day for Parliament after it was nearly lost and so—eventually—made sure the war was won. Ludlow, Inverlochy, Bristol, Taunton; the pattern still seemed purposeless. But at Marston Moor the king lost his best troops and though the war dragged on, each month now brought his armies closer to disaster.

The countryside was mutinous, too. Peasants and freeholders alike began to arm themselves with anything from clubs to cannon in order to fight impartially against those who took their sons, then taxed and robbed them beyond endurance. It had ceased to matter whether these intruders were royalist or Parliamentarian.

And, as a consequence, the generals gradually became alarmed. If peasants dared rise against both armies, any army, what must their leaders fear for property once the war was over? Even Cromwell, who could beat a rabble in arms every day before he shaved, thought England's liberties sat dangerously on a peasant's pike. But still the king refused to see it so. Another bloody battle at Naseby, the loss of Bristol and two more winters of murderous raiding and counter-raiding were necessary before Hosmer's prediction came true and Parliament won. That is to say, the king surrendered, prevaricated, was kidnapped, sold and ultimately executed, which, two years later, triggered another war.

In August 1651, when the fighting in this second war reached its climax at Worcester far away to the west, Faith was sitting in the orchard at Littleton Manor, trimming lace. Suffolk was a long way from this latest fighting. On the wall behind her plums and apricots ripened, the purposeful drone of wasps making the day seem hotter than it was.

She looked up, enjoying the sun against her skin, and suddenly she was shaking so uncontrollably that her teeth rattled like old bones. Henry was walking towards her across scythed turf. His hair was quite grey and he was wearing the plain clothes which would please Puritans; otherwise he looked much as he had when she last saw him eight years before.

During that instant of unreason she very nearly fled. Instead she stood, wondering what on earth she could say to him. She had been so certain he would be killed or kept in exile out of England that she had never seriously considered how she would face him if, one day, he returned.

He bowed with the elaboration of a different age and

kissed her fingers. 'My dear, I am happy to see you looking so well.'

'And you, Henry? I expected to hear next that you were at Worcester fight.'

'No. Oh no.' He was unexpectedly vehement. 'I have done what I felt bound to do. I am not murdering any more of my countrymen for no purpose. I also find that both exile and exiles stick in my throat, so I have made my composition with Parliament and mean to live in my own land from now on.'

'You have taken the covenant?' demanded Faith, astonished.

'Well, not quite,' he admitted, and touched his clothes, smiling. 'I don't mind sober colours, though, and desire only to live peaceably with all men. It was mostly a matter of pledges and payment in the end.'

'Riffield?'

He shook his head. 'I could not raise a tenth of the amount they would ask for releasing it from sequestration, and what is the point, after all? When I am dead it would go to kin I scarcely know. Such moneys as I have left are better used to restore Merivale, whose tenants are sorely distressed by destruction from the war.' Merivale was a Scovell manor in Oxfordshire, previously used chiefly as a hunting lodge.

Faith hesitated and then said deliberately, emphasising the first word, 'You will live there?'

His eyes flickered, mouth tightened. Henry Scovell was no fool. 'I had thought of it, unless you think it too remote.'

'Sit down,' Faith said suddenly. 'For heaven's sake, what are we doing after eight years, standing as if I bargained with a pedlar for his stuffs?'

He gave a kind of gasping laugh and handed her to the stone seat where she had been sitting. He also left his arm along the carved stone behind her as if for the first time he began to hope, so she sat bolt upright and said baldly, 'Henry, I have treated you so badly, my dear. Yet I'm not sure I could have done better. I thought I would never see you again . . . you always wrote from wherever the fighting was and then I heard nothing for so long while the king was taken. Afterwards it was Hamburg, Amsterdam, The Hague . . . I hoped I would be spared having to tell you this, I suppose. I cannot live with you.'

When he did not answer, she added desperately, 'You will be happier without me.'

'I'm afraid that isn't so.' His eyes were fixed on the grass between his feet. 'You'll have to tell me why, Faith.'

No wonder she had shied from thinking about this moment. 'We are too different. I do not love you.'

'You must think me a romantic fool,' he said contemptuously. 'We were always unlike and you never loved me. What difference does it make? We would do better together than apart.'

'You know, don't you? Not what happened, perhaps, but that something did happen those last days at Riffield . . . I think I always knew you were bound to hear anything which happened in the Weald. However garbled the rumour.'

'I shouldn't have believed it, had you not told me yourself.'

'I?'

'Your letters. If you recall, I used to spend a great deal of my time studying manuscripts. Which led me sometimes to understand things the writer thought but did not say.'

'It—it wasn't how you must have supposed.'

'There cannot have been many things I left unimagined in eight years. But I understood well enough that you did not want to see me, or I would somehow have come before.'

'Why did you come now?'

He looked up at last. 'I am too old to wait much longer. I hoped that after so long there might still be something left for us, since you now live as much alone as I.'

There was a long silence, cut across by the sharp clatter of hoofs coming into the stable yard. 'My dear. How much I would like to have it otherwise, but I cannot change my mind. I don't live alone, but with my son.'

'There are men from Suffolk in exile in The Hague. Several have congratulated me on conceiving a son during the last nights I was ever to spend at Riffield, and told me he did well.'

Faith looked at him measuringly. Not once in his letters had Henry ever mentioned a child; of course he knew it wasn't his. 'I had no choice except to give him your name.'

'Of course. You are my wife. I spent those nights with you.'

'I expected you to be killed,' she said harshly. 'You and Luke's father, both. I never heard any more of him so I suppose he was.' Her voice faltered for an instant. She still found it difficult to imagine Gage dead, and, remembering Gage, could not possibly live again with Henry. 'Anyway, I shall never see him again, except Luke is very like him. A child scarce seven years old, and I know already the kind of man he will become, unless somehow I can put affection amongst the devils in his heart.' She had called him Luke because the name carried an echo of Lucifer.

'A hard task for a woman alone.' Henry's voice was muffled, his eyes fixed on the ground again.

'My dear . . . my dear. You would hate him.' There were times when Faith herself came close to hating Luke, and there would be more as he grew older.

'And he me, I am sure. No boy of spirit could believe for long that I was his father.'

'I wish to God you were,' Faith cried. Henry's son would surely be generous, civilised and considerate, whereas Luke —if they lived together, Luke would delight in making Henry's life intolerable. Luke was Gage, yet even Gage had softened—surely he had softened—when she showed him what softness was. Faith felt exhausted just thinking about the endless tally of years she must spend in trying to show Luke what softness was. She stood, shaking out her skirts. 'Farewell, my dear. I should be best helped if I was able to think of you happy at Merivale.'

He stood too, and she wanted to weep for the defeat she saw in his face. Luke and Gage were winners; Daniel and

Henry losers born. In her present mood she found life's defeated infinitely preferable to its arrogant victors.

At Worcester the royalist cause suffered its final defeat in arms, and in the years which followed, the generals and secretaries of Parliament embarked on a quarrelsome search for legality. This was made more difficult by an English preference for traditional ways, and by almost universal detestation of new and opinionated rulers who attempted simultaneously to enforce killjoy bigotry and raise large sums by taxation from a nation already infuriated by extortion. At least order returned, and victory abroad, which was some compensation. But victories were soon forgotten, while men grumbled even more loudly against an order which seemed to rest more on their rulers' whim than within a framework of laws they understood. If anyone had asked the English, quite soon a surprising number would have answered that the king had best return to his place again, because only thus could their ancient rights be re-established, too. They had beaten Charles Stuart, hadn't they? Any king would watch what he did more carefully than the plague of fanatics presently squabbling over power. As a consequence of such sentiments, of which he was well aware, Cromwell no longer asked the English their opinion, which made the royal loser's son appear even more acceptable to the changed temper of the nation.

This change was by no means so well understood by lesser fry riding high in the counties, bloated with their new power and enjoying every minute of it. In Sussex, as elsewhere, the mood was sullen but quiet. Taverns kept a close watch for prying presbyters; Mayings and mummings were forbidden, the churches stripped of decorations and humiliating punishments forced on those dubbed sinners; hop-strengthened beer was railed against from the pulpit but here the preachers met their match. The new brewings continued to thrive, though consumed behind closed doors for a while, if needs must.

One spring morning in 1657, two men were strolling through the rooms of Riffield Castle, one taking notes and the other poking into corners with his stick. This latter was much the older of the two, but still upright and alert, and looking about him with some dissatisfaction. 'There is so much to be done, to attempt the task will be like pouring money down a conduit.'

'You would be pouring it into the loveliest house and park in the Sussex Weald, Sir Amyas. And during all my travels in the war I saw no country I thought equalled this.'

'The Weald also stretches into Kent, I believe.'

'Oh, Kent,' said London-born Benaiah Hosmer disparagingly. ''Tis well enough in its way, but not Sussex after all.'

The other laughed. 'There's naught like a convert, so they say. I shall look forward to meeting your wife, she must be an excellent woman to have dug you deep into clay within two years.'

'Aye, she is. When I saw her first she had gapped teeth and blackberry stains from ear to ear, but now there's no luckier man than I.' Ben Hosmer had lost his taste for clerking once it meant squeezing Riffield for the benefit of a distant war, and rode instead to join Cromwell's Ironsides, where he saved his pay and resigned as soon as the fighting finished. He carried one shoulder higher than the other, its ache a reminder of the musket ball lodged there during the second battle of Naseby, and remained obstinately unmilitary in temperament.

When he left the army, he had been unable to resist riding leisurely from Cornwall, where for him the fighting ended, all the way to Sussex, a journey which eventually took him to Riffield and Furnace Green. There he encountered Jane Carpenter again, seventeen years old and glowing with the generosities of youth. Ben Hosmer was so sickened by war that in his eyes she immediately appeared very beautiful, a belief from which he never wavered, although in truth she was comely and little more. She was warm and merry, though, she bred easily and they were very happy. Ben obtained an ill-paid position as clerk at Ockham ironworks because they both liked Furnace Green and wanted to stay there, but when he heard a rumour that the Sussex committee were behindhand with their remittances to the treasury, and consequently planned to sell Riffield for what it would fetch, he had seen the opportunity of a lifetime. As soon as he and Jane had scraped the necessary pence together, he wrote off to the master he had served before the war began, Sir Amyas Dyer. The ironworks of the Weald were dying; war had brought them back from the brink once but, God willing, there would never again be civil war in England and so the scattered Wealden furnaces, linked by their precipitous and frequently impassible tracks, were doomed. Already Ben earned too little to keep his wife and babe, which meant they had to live in one of old Will Carpenter's leaking shacks. Ben cordially disliked Jane's father and was chafed by such dependence, but there was no employment outside the ironworks for a clerk: Park Forge and Edenham were already closed, which meant that Ockham could recruit at half the wage paid ten years before. And so, like many others whose livelihood depended on iron, he and Jane would have to leave Furnace Green unless . . . unless . . .

Amyas Dyer looked about him reflectively. God have mercy, this place was a ruin. He poked his stick where panelling had been ripped off and plaster fell in soft wet flakes on sodden boards. Once the need to patrol the Weald had passed, Riffield Castle had been abandoned to rot. Tiles and glass vanished, no doubt greatly to the benefit of cottages round about; the weather had broken in and part of the roof collapsed.

'I didn't realize it had become so bad,' Ben said into the silence. 'It was still garrisoned when I left in the spring of '44, the house well-looted but weathertight.'

'At least no one could load its situation on an ox cart and remove that in the night.' Dyer stepped over to a gaping casement. The ground dropped away below and the ancient hunting park of the Scovells rolled to the further hills like a sea broken up by shallows. Wind combed spraying colours as he watched, turning spring green to yellow and back again, while larks spiralled song into puff-ball clouds. It wasn't Wiltshire, of course, but still . . . Sussex was convenient, and Amyas Dyer had affairs in London which required his frequent attention. He turned away from the window. 'We'd best look at the outbuildings then, although I expect there's even less left of them than there is of the house.'

'You like it, sir?' Ben could not keep delight out of his voice.

'Perhaps I am vain enough to think a ruin will give me more chance to try my eye at the new styles of building. Yes, I like it, and believe it may be no bad thing to live more obscurely for a while. I should not like the royalists to remember me when they return, filled with rancour about the past.'

'You think we will have a king again?' Ben said slowly.

'How does it look to you?'

'I fought for—well, for the Republic, I suppose.'

'Did you? Come, I trained you better as a clerk than that.'

'"Search out the truth before you make up your mind, not after," that's what you used to tell us. Aye, we're all weary of long-nosed prying into our lives. We didn't fight for that, nor for Noll Cromwell to reign in place of the king.' He paused. 'There is a family in Furnace Green—a tribe more like—called Laffam. I'm told that when the war began they were mighty hot for Parliament, being rogues who covet other men's possessions. Now they call themselves king's men and do not care who hears.' He grinned. 'Even the most zealous sectary being unequal to the task of controlling Laffams.'

Dyer looked at him thoughtfully. 'If you mean what I think you mean, then the war has made a shrewder man of you.'

'We need to learn something from our lives, besides how best to kill,' answered Ben with sudden rage.

'Well, your Laffams may indeed grasp at essentials faster than most. You know as I do that rogues flourish best when left in peace to follow their own desires, and since all of us are partly rogues, not only your Laffams are wearied by interference and uproar, high-minded though it be. But we have taught both king and Parliament that England is not minded to be mastered by a tyrant, no matter what his name, which is some kind of gain. A gain less glorious than you supposed when you rode out to war, but worth fighting for in the end, or so I trust. Now, where are those stables?'

Amyas Dyer was exactly what his name suggested: the son of a long line of dyers of woollen cloth. Dyers were usually the richest among the trades connected with cloth manufacture, and Amyas's ancestors had prospered both in their native Wiltshire and, later, elsewhere. Younger sons became dealers, attorneys-at-law and stewards of other men's property; older sons engrossed the trade of their locality, invested their profits, and wedded well-dowered wives. Daughters contributed to their kindred's well-being by marrying into similar families wherever the wool trade reached, which meant that by the time England's greatest mediaeval industry declined, there were few places in the kingdom where the Wiltshire Dyers could not call on the help of cousins to forward their endeavours. The occasional ineffectual son, or daughter who wed unwisely, was regarded with contempt. Yet Amyas, fifth son of a Marlborough merchant struggling against the effects of a depression of the cloth trade, was the first of them to perceive the glittering prospects offered by the corrupt state of England's courts. As the Stuart kings began to use their judges to squeeze ever larger sums from their subjects, Amyas considered his situation carefully and at the age of seventeen took himself off to London. There were, he reckoned, too many Dyers attempting to live off reduced pickings in Wiltshire for a fifth son to grow rich there without offending most of his close-knit but quarrelsome kindred in the process.

Soon, he was working for a rising exchequer clerk, who found his ability and lack of scruple extremely useful. Before many years had passed Amyas Dyer was rising too, and letters began to flash from one Dyer cousin to another, with the consequence that a great many of them came to occupy minor positions in the royal administration, where they became extremely useful to their ambitious relative. As Amyas was to them.

In 1635 he was appointed a justice of common pleas, and thereafter became the richest of all the Dyers. Unless a litigant was quite exceptionally stupid, he invariably offered his judge a bribe and Amyas would have been astounded if anyone had suggested he should refuse it. Nevertheless, complaints about Mr Justice Dyer were not long in coming, when those who paid him to favour their cause discovered that this made little difference to his interpretation of the law. But as Judge Dyer pointed out, men paid in the hope of receiving his favour, not because they were certain of obtaining it.

He purchased his knighthood as any sensible man might, as a gesture towards rank and a contribution to His Majesty's funds, and all went well until King Charles himself found occasion to complain about Judge Dyer's behaviour. This happened when John Hampden challenged the Crown's right to raise arbitrary taxes and cited a number of legal precedents in his own defence, some technical and some more generally directed against overbearing and capricious government. His appeal was heard before a panel of twelve judges, of whom five dissented from the majority verdict recorded in favour of the king, two of them on grounds of principle: one being Amyas Dyer.

Quite why he did this no one ever established, and his Dyer relatives generally considered that he had been the victim of a brainstorm. He himself merely observed that he had customarily spoken his mind and was now rich enough to speak it to the king as well. His rashness lost him his seat on the judges' bench and shortly afterwards he was imprisoned, although he soon eased himself out of this latter discomfort.

When the Civil War broke out, and especially when it became apparent that Parliament was likely to win, his family perceived the method in his madness; Sir Amyas returned to the judges' bench in 1642 and became even richer than before. In 1648 he left it again, after an obscure quarrel with the Council of State, and went into trade in the City of London. Again the Dyers despaired, and again congratulated themselves on possessing so astute a relative when, not long afterwards, the king was put on trial and ultimately executed without any blame for so questionable a deed attaching to their name.

Since then Sir Amyas had been most excellently placed. Trade under the English Republic was buoyant and the City of London one corporation with which even Cromwell hesitated to interfere. Dyer knew most government officials who might be useful to him, his wealth made him readily acceptable in the City and his cousins remained attentive to his wishes. He resisted pressure to return to an official position, yet profited from the fact that his advice in matters of law and trade was frequently sought by a hard-pressed Exchequer.

However, in this year of 1657 his unerring sense of circumstance had led Sir Amyas to the conclusion that this happy balance would not operate to his benefit for much longer. He needed to distance himself from a government he considered ultimately doomed, and so preserve his gains for a better and more lasting day. Hence Ben Hosmer's letter giving details of the castle and park at Riffield, soon to be sold by the Republic for what it would fetch, had come at an auspicious moment. A tactical retirement into countryside not too remote from London would suit him very well. It was a pity that only a small portion of the former Scovell lands was included in the sale, but, given time, Sir Amyas Dyer was confident of buying on favourable terms as much of these as he desired, from officials whose weaknesses were well known to him.

'I think it would do very well,' he commented, after a tour of rubbish-strewn courtyards which once had been surrounded by stables, falconries, brewhouses, and workshops of every description. 'Especially as the site will have to be cleared and much of the house rebuilt. Even Cromwell himself could not expect my cousin to offer more than ground value for it.'

Ben's jaw dropped. 'Your cousin? I thought—I hoped —you might be interested yourself, Sir Amyas.'

'I am,' said Dyer blandly. 'But I should dislike very much to be told in a few years' time that because I had bought sequestered property, I must return it, gratis, to the Earl of Riffield. The old earl is dead, but I understand he left a son, a boy now thirteen years of age who, unlike his father, is no gentleman and already making an ill reputation for himself. He would not have scruples over the means he used to grab an inheritance back, I fancy. So I will buy, but only after passing the property through other hands than mine. The law of England will doubtless be restored along with His Majesty, a law which protects a *de facto* owner very well, provided he is innocent of previous theft. As by that time I shall be innocent, you may be sure.'

Ben swallowed, such doings were too deep for him. Instead, he found he was adding up time in his head and thinking about this new Earl of Riffield: a boy who was no gentleman, thirteen years of age. Trust Amyas Dyer to have spied out such matters before he came into Sussex.

'I shall have to send down a man from London to take charge of rebuilding,' remarked Dyer a little later, while they stood together beneath the gate. 'There is a great deal to be done, especially once I have bought back the land.' He looked sideways at Hosmer as he spoke. He liked the younger man's enterprise in writing to appraise his former employer of Riffield's imminent sale, and, whatever Dyer's own shortcomings might be, he valued honesty in his servants. But if Hosmer wanted a good position he must ask for it; a man who had not learned to assert himself during ten years in the army would be useless, except as a quill-biting scribe.

He turned away and prepared to mount; he would have to become used to riding horseback in all weathers again if he came to live in Sussex. A coach was out of the question unless he chose to drain a great many miles of road. He settled himself in the saddle and gathered up the reins; well, he wasn't so old that he could not ride when it suited him.

'Sir,' said Ben, very red in the face. 'Sir Amyas. I would be honoured if you would consider me for employment in your affairs here.'

'What do you know of building a great house, or renting lands?'

'Precious little, I daresay. But I have learned something about Wealdsmen in two years of living here, and it is they who will do the building and pay the rents. I believe I could see you were not cheated.' He paused. 'Well, not *excessively* cheated, anyway. There are a great many rogues hereabouts.'

'I will hold you to that, at least until your Wealdsmen discover I am an ill man to defraud.' Dyer brought a fistful of coins out of his pocket. 'Start by repairing the gatehouse so you have somewhere close by to live. I will send to inform you as soon as I have obtained clear title and we can begin to level the site for rebuilding.' He pointed with his stick at the Tudor hall, whose massive timbers remained undamaged by a mere few years of rain. 'I like that, and the old tower at the end. Use your wits and I will use mine. When I come again I expect to see set out such ideas as you may have in matters of design.'

Ben watched him out of sight. He had been little more than a child when he went to learn clerking under Amyas Dyer, and remembered him merely as an exacting but humane taskmaster. Now, he understood that he was going to enjoy himself very much, serving a deviously skilful man of intermittent principle.

Ben Hosmer walked back across the park to Furnace Green, looking about him with new eyes. All this would soon be in his care, with blame to carry if he failed to administer it efficiently. He pulled a slate out of his pocket and began to jot down some of the things he saw: overgrown rides, boundary palings which needed to be re-staked, the evidence of poaching.

He paused at the top of the steep bank to the ridge, remembering that distant day when milady Riffield had ridden an army horse beside him, looked back and wished without rancour that Riffield's new masters would love it as the Scovells had. Ben could not tell whether Amyas Dyer was capable of love, but he would undoubtedly care well for anything he owned. He'd need to, Ben reflected, and use his cunning to keep it, too. If, as he suspected, the young Earl of Riffield was indeed Gage's son, then the Dyers would have to watch their backs for many years to come.

He turned and saw Jane running towards him across the green, baby Sally jouncing wildly on her hip. She knew how much Ben had hoped for from this day, and must have been looking out for him. He ran to meet her, and kissed her so she knew at once from the triumphant feel of him that all was well.

'We shall have to live at Riffield,' he said.

She tossed her head. 'Riffield, that's not far. I thought yestere'en how it would be London if this failed.'

He tickled his daughter's cheek. 'One day, when the new Riffield is built and Sir Amyas safely in possession, I'd like to come back to live in Furnace Green. I could run his lands as well from here as there, and find I'm still enough of a Parliament man to want to own my home, and with it my soul.'

'That's good news,' said Jane cheerfully. 'Furnace Green folk are used to Riffield trying to buy them out. You'll be useful to us if these Dyers are as covetous as Scovells.'

'I don't think I could do that.' Ben looked so appalled by the prospect of divided loyalty that she laughed and punched him in the ribs. 'Silly to worry about it now. Come instead and tell Father we don't need his hateful hovel any more.'

His arm was about her waist they went together, young Sally slung in her shawl between them. They passed the pool, open again now as men left workless by the decline of iron tried to feed their families by stocking any common ground with sheep.

As she had promised, Jane had planted a sprouted acorn on Daniel's grave in the spring after he died. As a child she had felt a proprietorial pleasure in its growth and tended it rather too lovingly for its health, so that for a while it had looked sickly. She forgot it as she grew older and next thing she knew its branches were on a level with her nose, such rapid growth being due perhaps to its predecessor's goodness rotted into the soil. Thus did the first eight centuries of human life on the ridge blend with the next, and Jane's oak become a vigorous sapling just in time to be safe from nibbling sheep.

'Our oak,' she said as they passed it, because Ben was the only other person who knew why, in a land of forest, this one tree mattered to her. Jane still said a prayer there sometimes, for a boy whose features she'd forgotten and the lady who had wept there thirteen years before.

Ben touched its leaves covertly for luck, and was promptly ashamed of himself for superstition. Furnace Green oak, he thought. And dear God, he also thought, I wonder what this one will see before it, too, rots into earth.

He shivered, uncertain whether this was an uncanny or a comforting thought to take away with him to Riffield.

'You're cold,' said his wife. 'Come, I'll race you round the pool.'

They ran together with Sally bumping and shrieking between them, laughing boisterously because this was their happy day.

. . . THE WITNESS:

When the Countess of Riffield and Lieutenant Hosmer of the Parliamentary army buried Daniel Gage beside Furnace Green's pool, they discovered that oak roots take even longer to decay than the trunk, and as a result his body was only shallowly covered by earth. Had they been able to dig deeper, they would have come upon the scraps of bone which were the remains of earlier dwellers on the ridge, whose lives and deaths in seemingly trivial ways had also shaped its future. So in his death Daniel was no longer alone. Moles and rabbits burrowed past his nose, sheep eventually uncovered his crossed hands and children paddled close by; foxes also came that way to raid the village's hen-runs.

Once the acorn which Jane Carpenter had planted grew into a tree, lovers often whispered in its shadow. As a boy, I remember Granny Paley—the last of a long, long line of Furnace Green storytellers—saying that when she was young a few betrothed couples still met secretly by the pool before they wed. Then they would wade into its shallows when the moon was full and lie afterwards under the oak —just once. More than once made a woman wanton. If the mating went well, they married; if not, not. Nothing was ever said, of course, but everyone knew the reason if the expected banns weren't called, and your guess is as good as mine how far this superstition stretched back.

I suppose it must have been March 1937 when Audrey and I walked across to stand beside the pool in an icy wind. By then I don't think anyone besides myself still remembered the generations of lovers in whose footsteps we followed, and I should have been happier if Granny Paley had left me unaware.

'I love you so very much, my dearest,' Audrey said.

'As I love you with all my heart,' I answered.

She sighed. 'How I've longed for you to say it. Now I'm glad you waited until you're back in your own place again.'

I drew her close, her soft silk hair blowing across our lips as we kissed; and even while we did so the pool of Ferenthe Ridge worked its last enchantment and my heart nearly broke for love of Chris.

I call it a last enchantment quite deliberately, because by then the pool was near the end of its life. It began to leak during the dry summer of 1911. I suppose that a thousand years after it had been tramped into place, the clay base must at last have cracked. Everyone knew it needed digging out again but by then we had heard that mains water might be on the way, and nobody wanted to waste good working time on a pond which still held water for most of the year. So, gradually, it dried out, and in 1952 earth was bulldozed into the smelly puddle which was all that remained. Nowadays children play on swings and a roundabout there, but though it may seem otherwise, I've never hankered for a return to the past. I know better than most how hard that past was, and enjoy hearing the children laugh.

All I want is to pass on some little understanding of the long laborious task and dense pattern we call inheritance, together with a warning: inherited virtues by their nature are very fragile, whereas prejudice, violence and greed are most readily transmitted. Either each generation struggles to build on the best their past can offer, or through negligence and vanity exploits its weaknesses. Then their inheritance works against instead of for them, putting at risk the future too.

Once upon a time in Furnace Green, this lesson was most harshly taught.

2

Dark Winds Blowing

1748–1749

The pack-train straggled along a couple of miles of track, as horses and ponies stumbled with weariness under heavy loads. Perhaps a hundred and fifty beasts and twice as many men and boys strung like blasphemous knots along a tenuous cord. The boys each led an animal while the men were bowed under loads, except for a chosen few who acted as guards and were armed with flails or long ash clubs.

The track led in a long zigzag down through trees to a stream surrounded by bog, before winding up again through tangled scrub to the end of this particular journey. The goods would travel on, of course, while these men and creatures returned to their normal tasks for a while.

Until next time the smugglers called them out.

Surrounded by weary companions, Bartholomew Laffam alone strode out as proudly as he had when the pack-train left Hawkhurst early the previous evening. For years he had led packhorses on the smugglers' runs, a boy disregarded among many others, but tonight for the first time he was a guard, a swingler, as flail-carriers were called to distinguish them from batmen, who carried clubs. A man's task for which Bart would be paid ten times a labourer's weekly wage. And he just eighteen years old! Though, of course, the Laffams of Corndown had been so long entangled in the smuggling trade it was easier for him to make the step from menial carrier to prestigious guard.

'Close up!' he hissed at the beasts and men slithering in darkness. The last slope after a night's journey by black-dark paths was always the worst, but at least this way into Furnace Green was less sheer than if they had approached it from the west.

'How much further, Bart?' Bart recognized Tam Sleech's

voice, a boy on his first run who greatly admired Bart Laffam.

'Not far, little 'un,' answered Bart grandly. 'We're down below Edenham here, and the track for Ockham away to our right. But smugglers have their own ways, see? Cut your throat if you ever tell.'

'Of course I wouldn't.'

'You'd better not.' Christ, little 'uns were as coddled as eggs sometimes.

And just at that moment Bart heard a sound he didn't like. Panic needled in his veins and then away again when it wasn't repeated; no one else seemed to hear.

Bart hesitated, fingering the oak grip of his flail and straining his ears into darkness. All the Laffams could hear like bats at night, but he could only pick up the sounds of horses jouncing kegs, of other swinglers and batmen coming up behind him. All the same, he didn't feel easy after that. He had enjoyed every moment of his first run as a swingler but now he wanted it to end. His legs ached in tall, unaccustomed boots and unease lay like a knife against his skin.

Only moments later and a horse whickered somewhere up ahead, and another answered where no horse ought to be.

Instantly, hideously loud after a night of painstaking silence, shouts followed, and a great deal of noise in dense undergrowth; shots, screams and a huge explosion that must have come from Josh Smith's duck gun, which needed a strut under the barrel before it could be safely fired. Nevertheless, he always brought it on a run, balanced across a pack-saddle; the smugglers always said he'd blow off his horse's head before he hit a riding officer. As soon as he heard that explosion Bart ran up the path towards the growing racket, his boots tripping him on the slope. Boys were pulling packhorses aside into cover but he was a swingler and must run towards trouble when it struck.

Soon he was swearing with such breath as he could

spare, because the noise was nearly finished and he had done nothing to help. If this was an ambush by riding officers then they must be crazy to intercept so large a convoy in a place where all the advantages lay with their adversaries. Horses were back-haunched everywhere, teeth snapping and eyes flashing in the moonlight, steam rising from their flanks. At last Bart caught up with more swinglers, all of them racing towards the noise, but by the time they reached the scene of attempted ambush everything was over and three bodies lay sprawled on their faces, another floundered among drifted leaves. The smugglers themselves had done all that was needed. Villagers like Bart carried clubs and flails and added to a gang leader's consequence; professional smugglers carried pistols, killed their enemies on sight and were as drunk as nightjars by the finish of every run.

The swinglers muttered and shuffled their feet, discontented that they had missed out on a fight. Fights didn't happen often, since the smugglers had come close to controlling eastern Sussex. 'They were a rash lot and no mistake,' someone remarked to Bart.

'Aye, I disremember when I last heard of riding officers attacking in the forest.' He felt ashamed because he'd heard a sound yet failed to raise the alarm.

'We attacked them,' someone answered, overhearing, and Bart recognized Abel Grey, the leader of this gang. He organised whole pack-trains and ruled his territory like a king. In daylight his eyes reminded Bart of dulled wax balls; a shrewd, ugly and ferocious man.

'I heard—' began Bart.

'Aye, one of their horses whickered or we wouldn't have known they were there.' Grey stuffed his pistol back in his belt. 'Give me your flail, young 'un.'

Bart handed it over, feeling absolved from blame once Abel Grey refused to listen when he attempted to confess failure. After all, it hadn't mattered; the riding officers were dead or run off, the convoy safe. All the same, he couldn't imagine what Abel wanted with his flail, nor could he afford to lose it. So Bart stayed behind when the other swinglers went to get the horses moving again, making himself as inconspicuous as possible while half a dozen men from Grey's gang stood swilling spirits out of a puncheon one of them carried on his saddle-bow, the three dead men at their feet. A handful of long-noses against the smugglers' hundreds; usually riding officers tried only to watch and learn until, one night when they thought they had discovered the smugglers' plans, they would borrow a troop of cavalry and hope to surprise a convoy.

Grey wiped his mouth on one wrist, Bart's flail held in his other hand, and turned. '. . . doesn't matter a curse. It'll give the buggers something to think on. Now . . .' He strode to where the wounded man had dragged himself to the cover of a bush, and brought down the flail across his trailing bloodied leg.

Taken unaware, the man squealed but then sucked in his breath and for a while did not cry out again. All Bart saw was his own familiar oak-gripped flail, whining and thudding into a grotesquely jerking shape. Behind his back the convoy was moving again, the horses snorting as they caught the scent of blood, boys and guards staring in fear or satisfaction as they passed. None would forget the dreadful lesson they saw dealt out by Abel Grey to a man caught interfering with his trade.

After the flailing had gone on some time, Bart was sick. By then the riding officer was incapable of staying silent any longer, and moaned or gulped with each blow of chain. Scraps of flesh flicked past Bart's face each time Grey drew back his arm, until eventually the sounds of suffering wavered and mercifully died as his victim lay mashed into the leaves of the forest floor. Then Grey spat on the body and threw the flail back to Bart. 'No call to puke. The likes of them's the enemy of any Sussex man who earns good money from our trade.'

Some boys on the track heard this and cheered, although without seeing what had gone before. If they had, probably it wouldn't have made any difference: you seldom went on a run without seeing some kind of violence, since most grown smugglers ended each night drunk.

You did not often see cold-blooded torment, that was the point. You saw a riding officer spilled out of his saddle by a musket ball, an informer taken away never to return; slashed hands or faces after a brawl. And you tramped past like these boys were doing. Riding officers deserved a bullet up the backside for trying to cheat poor Sussex men out of their only chance to earn good money.

Only for Bart was this time different, because he had stood watching while an injured man was flailed to death. As he walked, head down, into Edenham's farmyard he could feel pieces of skin and sinew clogging the iron links he held and his throat still burned from the alcohol he'd vomited.

As the convoy arrived, the next part of the operation swung smoothly into place. Fresh beasts, drovers and guards waited; pack-saddles were swiftly transferred as Abel Grey moved among the throng with bags of coin paying off those whose tasks were finished. The incomers dropped wearily on the ground, beer and spirits flowed freely, bread and cheese laid out on a trestle for those who wanted it. The new drovers were still reasonably sober, most others well-drunk and becoming drunker. This was when the fights began, and men lost their pay in hasty wagers. But a pox on a few squandered coins! The smugglers would soon call for help again. Noise was recklessly loud, but that didn't matter either; Edenham was a regular hand-over point and Grey had his watchers out, although with most of the countryside against them the riding officers had little chance of achieving surprise on a cleared ridge like Furnace Green.

Bart felt too sick to drink, and went instead to search for other Laffams, instinctively craving the comfort of his own blood kin. He soon found several: Jug Laffam, so called from his thirst, was sprawled drunk by a fire; Duck-ears Laffam transferring packs, while Bart's father, Trapper Laffam, stood with his hands on his hips doing nothing particular and being paid for it. For some reason, this was an age when nearly everyone in Furnace Green was known by a nickname.

'Da,' said Bart, and went over to stand close; usually he called his father Trapper like everyone else.

'You aren't hurt, are you?' asked Trapper.

'No.'

'Heard you had trouble up the front end.'

'There were riding officers watching, but one of their horses whickered.'

'Any get away?'

'I'm not sure. Three, no four, were killed. Abel Grey finished off the fourth after he was hurt.'

'Well,' said Trapper reasonably. 'What else would you do with a wounded riding officer? Tuck him up at Corndown and wait for the swine to lay evidence against you?'

'No, but—' Already the flesh on Bart's flail felt crisp to the touch.

'Look, boy. You were a swingler tonight so you must get used to man's work or stay a pack-bearer all your days, eh? Don't think on things you don't want to think on, that's all.'

'I can't help thinking.' Bart felt even more miserable because he didn't feel as a swingler should.

'Then I'll tell you what to do.' Trapper ruled the Laffams, but by cunning since they did not take kindly to orders. 'You take up the parsonage and Black Bear kegs instead of Jug, and by the time you've off-loaded you'll be too weary for aught else than sleep. Tomorrow, all you'll remember is coins clinking in your pocket.'

Bart shrugged and turned away, he might as well take the Furnace Green kegs as not. Unless he stopped himself thinking soon, he'd go the way of a smuggler he'd seen fall off a cliff at Hastings once, because his mind wasn't on his job.

Even caught up in his own concerns as he was, Bart looked back at Edenham as he left, to him simply a place where the inland gangs met those who ran contraband from the coast; half way to London, and convenient for supplying the gentry who were beginning to visit the sulphur springs at Tunbridge Wells. Squatters now lived at Edenham, a family nicknamed Rabbit because of their breeding rate, who ran in and out of the old millhouse offering ale and broth and receiving thrown coins in return. When the Rabbits played host to a large run, they earned enough in a single night to keep their clan through weeks of enjoyable idleness. Torches streamed sparks into the night, horses whinnied, men joked and quarrelled beside the fires, outgoers jostled to be gone. Once a musket exploded by accident and everyone merely laughed; in the middle of Sussex where Sir Jonas Dyer, Justice of the Peace, lived only eight miles away at Riffield surrounded by dozens of grooms and retainers he could call out in the name of law and order, smugglers who had just committed a multiple murder felt completely safe.

Somewhat comforted by the bustle and normality of it all, Bart turned back to his packhorses. Tam Sleech was leading them, asleep on his feet. He lived in Furnace Green village and might as well lead horses on his way home as not, so Trapper Laffam said. But after he fell twice from sheer weariness, Bart slung him up on top of a keg and led them himself. The child—Christ, he was a scrawny brat! —smiled sleepily. 'Thank you, Bart. I lasted, though, didn't I? All the way from Hawkhurst in a single night.'

'Aye, you did.'

'I'll be a swingler too, one day.'

'Go to sleep,' Bart said roughly. 'I'll tip you off on your doorstep as I pass. The horses'll find their own way from there, I reckon.'

The splash of hoofs along the familiar track which led from Edenham to the village blurred Bart's thoughts at last; kegs slopping, ropes creaking, muffled harness rubbing tired backs. The sky was softening in the east, birds beginning to sing as he reached Old Nick's Well where the track forked, one trail leading to pool and green, another to the street. Nowadays folk imagined Old Nick as the devil and weren't surprised his water tasted bad; a larger population than ever before scouring it to the dregs. The lane here was sunk between steep banks, worn down by so many centuries of ox-sledges, restless feet and toiling women that the banks reached above Bart Laffam's head, hiding the open green on his left, the well on his right.

Head down, he gave none of it any thought; everything about Furnace Green was so familiar that it never occurred to him to think about it. He left Tam on his doorstep and a keg on Parson Brookland's, no need to conceal it. Parson was a Kent man from Romney Marsh and a drunkard who associated openly with the smugglers. Bart's legs were dragging now, his feet burning. He was proud of his new long boots but more usually walked barefoot.

The old Black Bear inn had changed in the past hundred years, too, as old timbers rotted and were replaced by brick; nowadays, fashionable swells sometimes drove out to Furnace Green from Tunbridge Wells, so there was a parlour as well as a taproom, a snug stable yard and barn. Reed thatch had been replaced by tiles and, most astonishing innovation of all, the Dyers of Riffield had paid to have cells constructed beneath the tap. These were useful nowadays for storing contraband, but there had been a time when the Dyers were uncomfortably zealous in upholding the law, insisting that even the freeholders of Ferenthe Ridge did not flout it openly. Which wasn't surprising, when Bart's own grandmother could remember one of old Sir Amyas Dyer's sons being murdered by a rogue who called himself the rightful Earl of Riffield.

The packhorses shambled into the inn yard and stood shuddering with exhaustion, this journey too short for it to have been worth harnessing up fresh animals. 'Is that yourself, Jug?' a voice called cautiously. Ned Oxley, the landlord.

'No. Bart.'

'Where's Jug?'

'Drunk. You know Jug.'

Oxley laughed, a sound like ale swishing in a tankard.

'Aye, I know Jug. I'll help you myself then, if you've come all the way from Hawkhurst. A true swingler at last, eh, Bart lad?'

And Bart felt his pride return, like moonlight across dark hills. 'Aye. We had some trouble, too.'

'What kind of trouble?'

Bart told him, briefly, and was pleased to discover that vomit stayed in his belly where it belonged. He did not realize that, in this instant, just because he was pleased no longer to feel badly about what had happened, his life divided. From this peaceful dawn in the Black Bear stable yard, one thing would lead to another all the way to the day he died. Later he wondered sometimes why things happened as they did—tried to bring out more shades of colour from his life which might help to explain cause and consequence, but he never managed to straighten either in his head. Yet this moment when he ceased to feel revulsion over the tale he told, was when the greens and browns of everyday life began to change into the red of blood and purple of gibbeted faces.

But almost as he told Oxley what had happened Bart was asleep, pitched into oblivion like a stone dropped off a cliff, so that Oxley had to stack his kegs himself, stow packs of tea and silk in his barn. No concealment here either, so safe did he, too, feel in his trade. Tomorrow he would send an ostler to Riffield with the brandy Sir Jonas Dyer had ordered.

When Bart woke, Rose was standing over him as Trapper Laffam in his wisdom had known she would be, laughing heartily with her hands on her hips. Rose Oxley always drew her lips back when she laughed, showing strong white teeth and healthy gums. Everything about Rose was strong and healthy: brown plentiful hair, red cheeks, bright eyes and square ripe body which several boys in Furnace Green already knew better than Bart did. Bart thought Rose the most enticing woman in Sussex, which meant the most enticing anywhere, and as a consequence had so far admired her with yearning rather than lust. This was in direct contradiction to his deserved reputation outside Furnace Green as a skilled seducer of women.

'Rose,' he said, and smiled, drowsily content.

She tossed her head. 'You slept all day.'

'I walked all night. And the night before, as well as spending most of the day in between fetching and loading horses.'

'And are you still tired clean through, Bart Laffam, lying there like a block of wood?'

'No.' He reached for her ankle. Jerked it, so she fell beside him in the straw all sleek and warm and pretending to be angry. Surprised too, because Bart had behaved so respectfully before that she had begun to disbelieve the tales she heard about him. But because Bart had wakened knowing he must never again think about Abel Grey flailing a man into bloodied strips, he also knew that the easiest way to forget would be with Rose.

In fact he was so eager to untie her linsey-woolsey dress, yet then began smoothing her breasts more like a babe wanting milk than a lover, that even Rose wondered a little at the difference in him. No difference she could name, though she felt urgency, panic and power all in him at once. Then she simply enjoyed the difference, which completed Rose Oxley's conquest of Bart Laffam.

'Rose,' he said a long time after, 'will you come back to Corndown with me?'

'Ah, get on with you! What do you take me for? Everyone knows Corndown is no place for respectable women.' She began shrugging back into her dress.

Oddly enough, it did not occur to either of them that she could scarcely be described as a respectable woman. And it was true that females at Corndown were sometimes shared among the Laffam clan. 'I'd kill my own brother if he laid a finger on you,' Bart answered hotly, and meant it.

She laughed.

'I would so.' He knew he sounded like a ninny.

'Ah well, medear. I'll think about it if you like.' Rose

customarily returned encouraging answers to most questions she was asked, and on this occasion had so much enjoyed Bart's lovemaking that she was genuinely tempted by his offer.

Bart followed her across the yard and into the taproom, without caring if everyone knew that he and Rose had enjoyed each other in the straw. He had made his choice and she had promised to think about it; the evening after a run was always particularly wild at the Black Bear and, one way or another, Bart had already decided that he would have more than a promise from Rose before it ended.

The taproom was crowded and already noisy. Nearly everyone in Furnace Green was involved in the smuggling trade, if only to lend draught animals, so even those who had run no risk felt triumphant after a cargo had gone through, a feeling very much encouraged by the smugglers' liberality in rewarding the slightest service.

Parson Brookland was there, drunk on his own new-tapped spirits before he ever reached the Black Bear. Half a dozen Laffams leaned on the keg-top bar; each considered Rose calmly and knowingly when she came in with Bart, as if they realized that she was different from his other women and would soon join them at Corndown. Arthur Brown, late of Fawkners and now living at Wyses, was there too: he organised the local distribution of contraband with Ned Oxley, and intended to use his profits to build new cottages in the square formed by the tumbledown old Fawkners site. Bruiser Bywood, the Furnace Green blacksmith, was bragging in a corner, a lazy bully of a man, but respected for his strength. Next to him were some Rabbits, whose individual names no one bothered to learn; Roger Frenchman of New House, Billy Parleben and Wat Smith who lived in some recently thrown-together huts by the pool, as immemorially ill-kempt as pool folk had always been; ancient Jack Carpenter of Danesdell who looked as if he had lain in his grave for years. There was even a Dyer; Giles, a young scoundrel who, being possessed of a short-fused temper as well as powerful relations, was more dangerous to know than any smuggler. Ever since Sir Amyas made his fortune, the Sussex Dyers had retained a streak of acquisitive duplicity in their natures, though soft living weakened them; nevertheless, his family was ashamed of Giles, a tavern-drunkard and a duellist who picked quarrels with his inferiors in skill.

'Ah, Bart.' Trapper ran an experienced eye over his son. 'Abel Grey gave me your pay with the rest. 'Tis back at Corndown and double a swingler's normal rate. He said he'd spoiled your flail and you'd have to buy another.'

Bart swallowed ale so hastily that he spluttered. Don't think, don't remember; better to drown in ale than remember. 'It was nearly wore out anyhow.'

The disagreeable feeling Bart experienced just thinking about the flail made him realize even more clearly how badly he would need a woman as soft as Rose beside him every night of the coming winter. After swallowing the rest of his beer he pushed his way over to where Oxley stood behind his kegs. 'Could I speak to you, master?'

Younger men still called all those who owned their own land or trade 'master', until an undefined moment when they themselves, with luck, became of sufficient worth to discard respect.

'You're speaking to me.' Ned slapped a fresh tankard down in front of Bart. Customers bought heavily and often in his tap or stayed away, an attitude which was not resented in these times of plenty but produced a great many drunkards in Furnace Green.

'I asked Rose to set up with me and she agreed.' As soon as Bart said this the two men smiled into each other's eyes, each understanding the nature of Rose's answers and Laffam habits, which only rarely included church blessings on their relationships. On the other hand, once a woman went to Corndown she seldom complained of neglect and, if she wished, in a higgledy-piggledy way she was supported for life.

'Aye? Well, young Bart, 'tis between you and she, I

reckon. Rose has always been too fond of following her own way.'

'You agree?' cried Bart joyfully.

'Why wouldn't I? I've told Rose and told her this last year since her mother died, it's time she settled.' Ned studied Bart from beneath lowered lids, wondering whether the boy could be as guileless as he seemed. Almost immediately he decided that he wasn't, merely besotted. Any Laffam knew from the cradle how faithless some women were, and solved the problem by not allowing it to worry them. Ned suspected that Bart might not like this solution so far as Rose was concerned, which would lead to some rare old ring-outs between them, but that wasn't his affair; Rose at the moment was. The girl was itchy and unlikely to be respectably wed; soon, she would be no use for anything except conceiving disowned brats. 'Aye,' Oxley repeated. 'If she's willing then take her as soon as you wish. I can hire a wench to help in the tap.'

'Shame on you, landlord, to speak of taking a wench when you've a parson right under your nose.' Giles Dyer spun his tankard of brandy across a keg-top so it struck the rim and spilled into Parson Brookland's lap.

Brookland dabbed tipsily at the wetness, muttering about waste and believing the fault to be his own.

Giles's hand closed over his, squeezing until he yelped. 'Why not wed them here and now?'

'Wed who?'

'Does it matter? Mumble your words, drink and be merry! Who cares if tomorrow you discover you've married a pig to a cow?'

'A pig to a cow? Nay, I couldn't do that,' said Brookland, shocked.

By then nearly everyone in the tap was more fuddled than a midday owl; tallow dips guttered in dregs of fat, men staggered about and sang, beating time with their tankards. Smoke from the fire and contraband tobacco mingled with the stench of sweat, jerkins torn open in the heat left several men nearly naked. Under Giles Dyer's orders a couple of these roisterers hoisted the nearly comatose parson up on a keg, where he promptly collapsed again under the effort of trying to concentrate on instructions roared at him from every side.

'Martin!' Giles Dyer's drawl pierced the racket like a rapier. 'Listen to me, you drunken scum. I wager fifty guineas you'll be laid out colder than a gutted mackerel before you can croak your way through joining this pair of yokels in a form of sinful wedlock worth the hearing.'

Fifty guineas! The shout of approval at so handsome a wager – and blasphemy would salt the jest—hit the beams and rebounded in a floodtide of noise. Those sober enough to do so screamed at the parson to stand straight and gabble his way through any words sufficiently outrageous to satisfy Giles Dyer; the rest joined in the hubbub without understanding what it was about.

Ned Oxley, not drunk at all and bent on handsome profits, promptly tapped another keg of spirits. If Rose was going to Corndown then it was better some form of words were spoken over her by the parson than none at all. Besides, talk of scandalous doings at the Black Bear brought in custom from the kind of people who nowadays had most to spend: the smugglers and the smugglers' men of business.

Giles became steadier with drink, coldly dangerous rather than wildly so. Now he organised the rest with swift efficiency. Kegs were piled together below a dead rat nailed to the wall in parody of an altar, Bart and Rose forced to their knees by staggering friends, Rose screeching like a corncrake and at the same time giggling with scandalised enjoyment.

By then Martin Brookland had disappeared, and was discovered maudlin in a corner.

'Come, after all these years you should be able to repeat even sacrilege by rote.' Giles heaved the parson up on his keg again.

'Light candles, more candles.' Brookland rolled his head

and sketched the sign of the cross, entering with a rush into the spirit of the jest.

''Tis all a very shady to-do. You want I should try to rouse some of the lads?' Trapper Laffam was also drunk but insufficiently so to be unmindful that his son was being made to look a fool. He also knew that fifty guineas staked on what promised to be rare entertainment meant the Laffams would be heavily outnumbered if they tried to come to Bart's aid.

Bart shook his head. He didn't mind swearing oaths to Rose. Since temperamentally he was as unfaithful as a tom-cat, and pagan with it, the fact that these would be spoken under the blessing of a rat worried him as little as it worried Ned Oxley. Black Sussex. Once, long ago, Mother Earth was cherished here, then Tiw. Each in their turn held something of the best in man and also pandered to his darkness. Christ, too, was necessarily served by as many sinners as saints, intermittent conscience the best most of his followers could muster. Now conscience had fled from Furnace Green.

A great laugh was roused when Bruiser Bywood, the smith, tripped over old Jack Carpenter and sent him tumbling among the embers in the hearth. 'Don't forget you're up the steeple tomorrow, Bruiser!' yelled Wat Smith.

'Oh, Master Bywood, would you be so obliging as to climb my steeple in the morning?' Brookland flung wide his arms.

'Not me, your holiness. I thought I'd pay the Hosmers to take my place.' Bywood was enormous, muscles rippling all the way from his cheekbones to his calves.

Everyone laughed afresh at that, thumping their neighbours on the back until the weaker collapsed among those already snoring on the floor. The Hosmer family kept the single shop in Furnace Green, the only inhabitants who openly disapproved of smuggling. In consequence they were poor and becoming poorer, their stock often raided by mocking gangs of children, the shop itself occasionally wrecked when men reeled out of the Black Bear on the lookout for mischief.

'Get on, get on!' Brookland was clamouring for attention now, and when he caught it he gabbled, very fast and clear: 'The Devil my father who in hell doth dwell, renowned be thy name. Thy kingdom last from now to aye, thy will in Furnace Green be done. Thou givest us drink as well as bread, and sin never to be forgiven. Revenge and profit are the coin in which thou dealest, temptation the way to find them. Lead thou thy followers into evil, and Bart Laffam and Rose especially; while we here present pursue our calling, of daily murder and plunder. For thine is the kingdom the power and the glory, which lasts for ever and ever, Amen.'

The shout when he finished made the flames in the hearth flicker, a wave of delight which sustained Brookland just long enough for him to gallop through a further medley of prayer and incoherence parodied from the wedding ceremony, while Bart and Rose knelt clasp-handed with someone's cloak flung around their shoulders in place of the nuptial mantle.

The moment he finished, Brookland collapsed across Ned Oxley's feet and began to snore.

'Well, I have to admit church-mouthings were never more handsomely spoken, so damme if I won't give my guineas to those still on their feet.' Giles pitched a fistful of coins in the air, so they bounced off keg-tops, lodged in sprawled bodies and vanished into dirt underfoot. Everyone capable of grasping the fact that gold guineas were there for the finding scrambled after them, heads thudding together and miniature battles being fought on hands and knees, like crazed dwarfs duelling.

Giles himself flung down on a bench, laughing. 'Well, my fine young boar. I trust Parson Brookland's Devil will bless your wedded life.'

Bart shook his spinning head, uncertain whether he wanted to reply aye or nay to that. It had been a merry night he supposed, but he felt resentful to discover that it had already joined those other things he did not want to remember. Rose's breasts had come loose from her bodice and she was still giggling, this time over the antics of men fighting on their knees. Just as if she wasn't tied at all, Bart thought irritably. Because no matter what strangeness Parson had said, Bart now regarded Rose as exclusively his for as long as he desired her.

'Get you gone straightaway to Corndown, the pair of you!' Oxley possessed an infallible nose for trouble—real trouble of the kind it might be difficult afterwards to tidy away.

'Ah, don't spoil sport, landlord. The night is yet young and the wench willing.' Giles reached for Rose, his other hand close to his sword-hilt. 'I've had her before and I know.'

Dark colour suffused Bart's face. His sight dimmed and he threw himself at Giles. And, being heedless of danger, he was quicker than a sword which needed to be unsheathed. His hands fastened around flesh and bone, and the pair of them went sprawling on the floor, whence almost immediately came a satisfying crunch. Giles thrashed only once before falling back slack-limbed in Bart's grip.

'Get you away to Corndown with Rose,' repeated Oxley without any change of tone, and threw a pitcher of water in Bart's face. 'Leave me to clear up here.'

Bart spluttered and dashed wetness out of his eyes. 'Christ. Is he dead?'

'What did you think he'd be, if you broke his neck?'

In truth he hadn't thought at all. 'Where's Trapper?'

'Gutted like a fish.' Oxley jerked his head at a stertorously unconscious Trapper. 'You're a swingler now, eh? You can't run to your da each time you meet a spot of trouble.'

'Rose—'

'I'll come with you to Corndown, Bart. I said I would, didn't I?' Fright had turned Rose's giggles into panic, and she tugged at Bart's hand as if she wanted to tumble him headlong out of the door.

'What will you do?' Bart asked Oxley, hanging back.

Oxley shrugged. Now trouble had come he began methodically to strike off in his mind the best sequence to follow to protect them all. 'He isn't the first man to be finished off in a fight at the Black Bear.'

'He's a Dyer.' Bart was suddenly and fearfully sober, stunned by the realization of what he had done.

'A Dyer was murdered once before in these parts, and no one hanged for it. They're come-latelies, aren't they? A Scovell, now, they'd have had their ways of finding out what really happened, I daresay. As for Mr Giles, his kin may be glad he's dead and won't look too close into whys and wherefores. I'll make it seem as if a branch swept him off his horse as he rode home drunken, don't you fret.'

'They'll know. You can't make it look like that, not nohow.' Bart stared at the bruises on Giles's throat.

'By the time they find his body in the forest, he won't be a sight any kin would want to look upon,' answered Oxley indifferently, and pushed Bart and Rose out of the inn door without more ado.

Bart was astonished by how easily everything worked out over the next few weeks. The Weald as usual contracted like a salted snail under questioning; there were coroner's officers poking their noses where they weren't wanted and Sir Jonas Dyer rode over from Riffield to hold a sworn inquest in the taproom of the Black Bear, scrupulously scrubbed out for the occasion. Twelve freeholders of Furnace Green gave and heard evidence that Giles Dyer, gentleman, had left the Black Bear in his cups to ride, he said, to a tavern better suited to his quality in Tunbridge Wells. No blame to anyone if his body weren't found until five days had passed, your honour. By then, 'twas mortal hard to recognize the young gentleman after so long, and animals finding him first, like.

Twelve good men and true gazed honestly into Sir Jonas Dyer's eyes and sighed. What a waste of a young life, your honour.

Dyer glared back at them, aware that they lied but uncertain what to do about it. Giles was better dead and evidence altogether lacking. Sir Jonas Dyer was a shrewd but lazy man intent on his own concerns, and, almost inevitably, he eventually decided it simply wasn't worth while to pursue the endless threatful questionings which might have ferreted out a whisper of what had really happened.

Amos and Clemency Hosmer were God-fearing people, a credit to Amos's ancestor, Benaiah, the one-time Parliamentary captain. They lived in the same corner cottage where Daniel Gage once watched Mistress Coffey die of fever, which now the Hosmers had opened up as Furnace Green's first shop. For some years their trade had prospered to such an extent that the weekly market ceased to be regularly held: for those who craved choice or luxury in their purchases, Tunbridge Wells was only a few miles away—rough downhill miles, to be sure, but the town was growing fast and a journey there made a pleasant change. At all other times the Hosmers' new shop became a necessity the parish took for granted. Did Widow Apps find weevils in her flour? She could hobble to buy a ha'p'orth of fresh-ground for her baking. Did Mistress Bywood wish to placate her chancy-tempered spouse with molasses on his dumplings, or Mistress Brown's maidservant need a twist of thread for mending? All these requirements could be satisfied out of the sacks and bundles in Hosmers' shop, the time of day passed, an agreeable gossip enjoyed beside their wide hearth.

The family prayed together before the shop opened, ate well, traded sharply and gave charity to the unfortunate. The trouble was that Amos lacked grace in his giving, although it must be said that in these expansive years his strictures against the indigent were often justified. No one able to work need fail to find it, and the infirm could be easily supported out of their children's plenty. However, Furnace Green people disliked Amos Hosmer preaching at them if they were improvident, and human frailty meant that even in these prosperous times, ill health and thriftlessness took their toll. Large families were a drain on resources, while greed or spite sometimes split those who needed care from those who should have provided it. Contraband spirits also mingled with beer to such an extent that men became more quarrelsome with each year that passed, while easy money offered ever more scope to indulge in sin.

Eventually Amos Hosmer felt he had to make a stand, and he refused to sell any more goods which had been handled by the smugglers. At first Furnace Green could not believe it. Everyone had become used to being able to buy a handful of smuggled tea or a length of good-quality cloth at the shop, in the same way as they bought pitchers of spirits at the back door of the Black Bear.

'No,' said Amos Hosmer, gazing virtuously down his nose. 'No more. I serve Christ and not the Devil, henceforth only taxed goods will cross my threshold.'

A year went past in growing exasperation on either side. Perhaps Amos's stand might have been accepted if he hadn't been so intolerably (and intolerantly) sermonising about it. After all, Ned Oxley was quite happy to sell whatever smuggled goods people wanted to buy at the Black Bear.

But when Martin Brookland came as parson the Hosmers lost their last support. Brookland openly sneered at Amos's righteousness and a month after he was inducted as priest, their shop was broken into for the first time, its contents strewed in the street and a bag of smuggled tea left triumphantly on the counter.

Amos's second son, Joseph, was twelve at the time and never forgot helping his father to save what he could of his stock. 'I swear I won't ever ask to lead the smugglers' ponies or act as swingler,' he had said, squatting to pick dried beans out of the gutter.

'You would defy Christ and my wishes if you did,' answered his father, and that was all. Never a word of understanding for the ostracism Joseph was to suffer at the hands of other Furnace Green children, the jibes when younger boys than he ran risks on wet dark nights. Tribal gatherings of the village young threw stones at him and even men who did not usually deign to notice the antics of children, jeered when he was forced to peddle spoiled goods from door to door. The shop was broken into again and again after that first time, until the Hosmers became poor instead of prosperous. Amos tried to guard it but often the gangs were too insolent or too drunk to be withstood. Once, Joseph's older brother, Isaac, was so badly beaten he died two years afterwards, but when Amos sent Joseph running for Bruiser Bywood, who happened that year to be constable, he simply laughed and went back to hammering iron.

Next time the shop was broken into, Bruiser led the rabble.

'We shall have to leave while we've still a few guineas hidden and can start up elsewhere,' said Joseph, surveying the wreckage with glum satisfaction. Sacks split and the counter smashed this time; they would have to go and he was glad.

'Leave Furnace Green? This is our home, of course we couldn't leave.' Amos was astonished a son of his could even consider such a bizarre idea.

'I don't make my home where I'm not welcome,' answered Joseph. Nor did he. When a map-maker came through Furnace Green not long after, Joseph went to the parlour of the Black Bear and offered to work for his food alone if the man would teach him some part of his trade, and since he was able to read and write (having been reared on the Bible and penning texts) the map-maker was pleased to agree. In the years since then Joseph had journeyed all over southern England, measuring estates and fields and roads, before settling down in Lewes to pursue on his own account the new and booming trade of map-making.

He returned only rarely to Furnace Green, but made

sure that when he did, he rode the kind of horse the villagers would envy. In fact, only his filial duty to bring money to beleagered Amos, Clemency and young Tobias, the last son of their old age, brought Joseph there at all, and then he preferred to come by night. Apart from Tobias all the other Hosmer children had fled, like Joseph, from isolation: two daughters into service in London, another son as far as the new colonies in America. Only Amos and Clemency struggled on, refusing to leave or change their stand; awkward, irritating, obstinate.

So it happened that on the night after the smugglers had been making a run to Edenham, Joseph Hosmer was riding to reach Furnace Green before daybreak. He was sensitive about the way he preferred to slink home unseen, but somehow his courage seemed to have vanished during the years when he could not cross the street without running the gauntlet of taunts and bullying. He loved his present trade, with all its precise and delicate disciplines, its finely crafted instruments and mathematical exactitude. He liked comfort and was delighted by his own success, which recently had allowed him to buy his own tiny house in Lewes; he was also contemplating marriage with a widow whose possessions included a scrap of paper which named her ancestors as lords of the manor of Furnace Green. Obscurely, he felt that possession of this meaningless paper would offer some revenge on the place which had made him so wretched.

This prospect had finally convinced Joseph that a man of affairs like himself need not brave derision for the sake of it, and on this occasion he had again spent the previous day at a tavern and ridden for Furnace Green at dusk.

When first he saw a dark shape on the Ockham road he thought it was a pothole, but the pothole moaned as he came level with it and his horse shied from the smell of blood.

'Who is it?' he demanded sharply.

No answer, only another shuddering moan.

Joseph hesitated, peering into bushes which crowded

either side of a track scarcely wide enough to accept a farm cart. If this unfortunate had met with an accident then offering help was safe enough, but if he had been set on by footpads they might still be close by, waiting to rob a would-be rescuer.

When nothing moved, reluctantly, he dismounted. Although it was years since he left home, Amos's Bible-readings had so engraved the story of the Good Samaritan on Joseph's mind that it seemed impossible simply to ride on. His tinder must have been damp and failed to ignite, so he had to feel the fallen man for broken bones. Immediately, he snatched back, shocked by what he discovered. Blood everywhere, torn flesh, splintered bone; this moaning thing was scarcely recognizable as a man.

Joseph's heart drummed loudly in his ears. He had not stumbled on an accident, nor the result of an attack by footpads, who stunned or possibly killed a man but were uninterested in flaying him alive. Only the smugglers, who prospered because they balanced generosity towards their many helpers with brutality towards the few who angered them, could possibly have turned a man into little more than flayed skin and broken bones.

Joseph was already preparing to remount when the thing in the road moaned again.

Amos Hosmer always woke early, in fact he rarely slept for more than minutes at a time. Night and day he strained to hear the sounds which signalled another destructive break-in to his shop, although roistering gangs came less frequently now he owned so little worth spoiling.

The night before he had heard Bart trudge past with a keg for the parson and a load for the Black Bear; tonight he listened to the distant uproar from the tavern tap. It was nearly dawn when he heard the hoofbeats of a single horseman coming through the churchyard, from which direction the corner cottage was the first dwelling he would reach. And surely only the Devil rode through a graveyard in the dark.

Amos crawled out of his bedstraw, leaving Clemency snuffling lightly in her sleep. His bones ached and now he was old he was often frightened. Afraid of sickness, since their neighbours would not help a Hosmer; afraid of hunger if Joseph was late in bringing money; afraid of not selling the few petty goods which enabled him to face the world as an independent master who owned his own trade. Afraid he would call and Christ fail to answer, unsure of everything once faith seemed so ill rewarded.

'Is it trouble?' Tobias rolled out of his bedding by the hearth as his father scuttled past.

'What else do we ever have but trouble? The Devil, the Devil rides to steal souls from their grave.' Amos's skinny body trembled as he stood listening to those hoofbeats coming closer.

'It's only one man.' Tobias brushed his father aside and shot back the yard-door bolts. He was growing up bold and brash, often bloody-nosed after encounters with other village boys, who consequently respected him more than other Hosmers. 'Joseph! Why, Father thought you were the Devil come to Furnace Green.'

'He has come indeed,' answered Joseph harshly. 'Help me down with this and watch where you put your hands.'

'How . . . Oh, Christ!' Tobias stared at the body on Joseph's saddle-bow.

'Pull yourself together and take his weight while I dismount,' snapped Joseph. He was too poor a horseman easily to manage the showy hacks which pride made him choose when he returned to Furnace Green.

Teeth gritted, Tobias did as he was bid, and Amos too came hurrying forward, only to recoil in his turn. 'God have mercy, what happened to him?'

'Smugglers, as I would guess. I found him crawled out of undergrowth on the Ockham road. God knows how he managed to reach it with such injuries, when the smugglers' way runs down in the valley.' Joseph slid his hands under the inert shape, then he and Tobias edged with their burden through the door and up the stair.

By the time they reached the top Clemency was awake, a small weak-looking woman bundling into her petticoats. She twittered over the invasion of her bedchamber, but none of her menfolk took any notice. The injured man once laid on the bed, Joseph kindled tinder and candles, all his movements as precise as when he handled a traverse, light for the first time filling in the detail of all that his touch had told him.

'How can any man in such a state still live?' Tobias whispered, a normal voice unthinkable. A normal anything unthinkable.

'It's certain he can't live much longer,' answered Amos peevishly. 'It was unchristian to inflict more suffering by bringing him so far on horseback.'

Joseph flushed. 'I suppose you would have had me ride past on the other side.'

Amos pressed his lips together, feeling that life was very unjust. It was all very well for Joseph to quote holy writ back at him, but the Good Samaritan had not been forced to live in the robbers' den after he tended their victim.

'Did anyone see you bring him here?' asked Tobias.

'No. I came through the churchyard.'

'Someone may have been stirring. A woman most like, since their menfolk will be stale drunk.'

'It isn't yet full light, and misty with it. They are used to me riding in at night, and would not have seen the nature of any burden I carried.'

Clemency shuffled into the room carrying a bucket of water. 'There you all be, argufying while he bleeds. He's here, isn't he? We can't throw him out with the rubbish, so here he has to stay until the smugglers hear of it. You've finished us this time with your goings-on, Joseph.'

'I don't see why the smugglers should hear.' Because he had only with difficulty overcome his own terror of defying the smugglers, Joseph felt vexed to discover his kin mirroring his cowardice rather than his eventual resolution.

Amos gave a small derisive sniff. 'They'll hear. You don't live here any more, so 'tis all very well for you to—'

He broke off as a fist pounded on the door downstairs, freezing argument. Into the silence came a faint breathy moan, the first sound the man on the bed had made since Joseph hauled him across his saddle.

'D'you mean to tell me the saintly Hosmers drank a keg with the best of us last night? Or are you at your prayers?' yelled a voice from the street, followed by more pounding on timber.

'Bruiser Bywood,' breathed Tobias.

'Let him in,' Joseph said. 'Perhaps he only wants to buy something in the shop.'

'I'll go.' Tobias scampered down the stairs, thankful to be away from a horrific bedside. The injured man moaned again, shudderingly, and Joseph closed his hand across the pulped lips to stifle sound, jerked his head at his father. 'You'd best go down too. We don't want Tobias beaten up for insolence as well.'

Amos hesitated, then shrugged and went. It was all too much for him. Though he had woken that morning frightened, it had been the same fear he had lived with for years. Now he was conscious that a calamitous happening had begun and nothing would stop it until all the Hosmers tumbled to disaster.

Bruiser Bywood was planted squarely in the middle of the shop, his massive blacksmith's arms folded across his leather working apron, iron-shod boots clinking impatiently on bricks. 'I enjoyed good sport at the Bear last night and still reached my work earlier than God-snivelling Hosmers.'

'Joseph arrived early and we were exchanging our tidings together.' Tobias clattered shutters briskly, his tone dangerously disrespectful. Alone of the Hosmers he was excited rather than alarmed by this morning's crisis, largely because he had long hankered for a taste of danger, which everyone else enjoyed whenever they went with the smugglers.

Bruiser took a step forward on his clinking boots, then changed his mind and laughed. 'Listen how offal squeaks once it's well rotted. But look'ee, I've a task for Hosmers. I came to tell you I'm casting nails and metal strapping in my forge today. Parson Brookland wants his steeple mended and I reckon you need the chance to earn good wages more than most, eh?'

Amos gaped at him. 'What has the steeple to do with me?'

'It's likely to fall down, isn't it?'

Tobias squinted to where the steeple threw its shadow almost across their doorstep. 'It's been falling down for years. Drunkards must have built it all those years ago.'

'Well, Parson don't want it to fall while he's responsible, see? So he tells me to tighten a strap where it'll hold all together until after he's dead. Then it can go and welcome, he says, but he don't want no bishop bothering him meanwhile. So I'm making a gurt iron chain and I want help to fix it.'

Amos licked his lips. 'Not me. I couldn't climb the steeple.'

'You're God-fearing, aren't you? Be nearer heaven up there than mouthing prayers.' Bruiser gave another bellow of laughter and marched out.

Amos sat limply on a sack of beans. 'God have mercy.'

'I'll go! I'd like to show Bruiser—' Tobias kicked joyfully at a block of salt. 'Christ, I'll show the swine a thing or two before we're finished up that steeple.'

'Don't blaspheme.'

'Joseph says—'

'Your brother's speech is naught to do with you, although I admonish him about it.' Then, reluctantly, Amos added, 'I am afraid of heights.'

'Of course you couldn't climb up there!' Tobias's tone was half contemptuous, half concerned.

'Nor you.'

'Why not? Heights don't frighten me.'

Amos winced. 'Because you don't understand a man like Bywood. If you go you'll be lucky to come down alive. That is why he taunts you into wanting to climb with him.'

'Perhaps it'll be him, not me, who won't come down alive.'

'Tobias, you mustn't even think such sin!'

But Tobias shrugged and refused to listen, often neglecting his work that morning to stand with his eyes fixed on the steeple, while more customers came into the shop than usual, each one agog with the rumour sweeping Furnace Green.

'I hear you hired yourself to Master Bywood for the task of patching our steeple, Amos. He told us you believed the task would prosper best with the help of a prayerful man.' That was Mistress Brown from Wyses, who came herself to purchase pins instead of sending a maidservant.

'You make sure Bruiser agrees a fair wage before you goes up and not a stingy one after,' declared Widow Apps, whose husband had been the last Apps to own the Black Bear.

'Holy, holy Hosmer, climbing up to heaven,
Atishoo! Atishoo! He will fall down!'

A clutch of children sang outside, dancing in a circle until Tobias pounced on them wielding a broom. They scattered, screeching with delight, and within minutes were back again, just out of reach.

Up in the bedroom under the eaves, Joseph and Clemency ignored the commotion until their task of tending Riding Officer Stephen Larkworthy was finished: Joseph had found bloodied papers in his pocket which gave his name, together with instructions *'To keepe watch on the doinges of Abel Grey's gengge'*. By the time their splintings and bandagings were done at last, Larkworthy's moans had ceased again and Joseph thought he was dead.

Clemency shook her head. 'His heart beats strongly. If he lives through the fever which will come, and the inflammations afterwards, he may recover. But he'll be raving by tonight for all the street to hear. And recover to what, when we daren't even call a 'pothecary? 'Tis certain he'll never walk again.' She went out, muttering. In her opinion the Hosmers' lives depended on Riding Officer Larkworthy dying without fuss inside the next few hours. She had tended him with such skill as she possessed, which after a lifetime of dealing in herbs was considerable, because that was her duty and Clemency saw her duty clearly. Which didn't alter the fact that if God had Christian folk's interests at heart, He would save Stephen Larkworthy further pain by taking him to heaven without delay.

After she had gone Joseph glanced around the bedchamber, and a fearsome sight met his eyes. Pitchers of bloody water stood on the floor, stained cloth and dirty straw were thrown in corners, while over everything lay the stench of suffering. But he didn't regret not being able to fetch an apothecary. On his travels he had learned that apothecaries and chirurgeons killed more often than they cured, whereas the precision and cleanliness a map-maker brought to his trade could occasionally cure hurts without fuss.

But this man had not been crushed by a runaway cart or bitten by a dog; he had been systematically flayed close to death. The extent of his injuries had been revealed by cleansing, though now, coated with Clemency's ointments and wrapped in fresh linen, he appeared almost comfortable. Drained dry of blood but eased for the moment. Joseph shrugged and turned away. Clemency was right. If Stephen Larkworthy lived he would be maimed for life. There had been a bullet in his leg and although that was out, the flesh was pulped from thigh to ankle, two bones fractured. Face, arms and hands lacerated, a flap of skin hanging from his scalp: he might easily waken crazed.

Clemency came back to the doorway, breathing hard. 'Amos has to climb the steeple tomorrow.'

'Climb the steeple?'

'Bruiser Bywood came. He said Amos had to help him tomorrow up the steeple.' She began to weep.

Joseph thrust her aside and went down to where Tobias was weighing beans behind the counter. The two brothers' eyes met, twenty years between them and a gulf of experience: Joseph portly, prosperous and exhausted by crisis, Tobias barefoot still and excited by change come at last into his life. But only one glance and each understood the other. Tobias felt Joseph's incensed desire to be quit of Furnace Green for ever, and Joseph knew that nothing he said, no threat he offered Bywood nor plea to Tobias, would prevent him from gleefully taking his father's place up the steeple on the morrow.

Rose, meanwhile, was enjoying her first day at Corndown.

There was, she supposed, a main house because Trapper lived in the middle section of three interconnecting cottages, and where Trapper lived was the nub of the Laffam clan. Not that Trapper was the eldest Laffam. There was an old man as twisted and bewhiskered as a gorse bush who, Bart told her, was over ninety years old, although Rose didn't really believe him. But whatever his precise age, he was clearly incapable of exercising authority over his sprawling kin.

Trapper lived with a young-old woman called Sarah, who gleamed with desire one moment and was as querulous as a harridan the next. Wife, cousin or grand-daughter, what does it matter so long as Trapper's kept mellow? said Bart, when Rose enquired about their relationship. Despite her easy nature, Rose felt a shiver of shock at this last suggestion, until eventually she decided that Bart was prone to exaggeration.

Apart from the three cottages and a ramshackle farmhouse, the Corndown homestead was made up of a huddle of outhouses shared by people and beasts together, a large cobbled yard, several barns stacked with contraband, as well as a great many paddocks and enclosures full of horses, oxen and carts. The Laffams were great carriers of goods, most but not all of them illegal.

A community of only intermittently active people suited Rose exactly. In between smugglers' runs the Laffams lived idly, intemperately and violently. They were brutal towards weakness but relatively obedient to the will of whoever fought his way into being master (or mistress) of the clan, aware that they needed a common front against the world. For the moment that was Trapper, his lusty roaring voice an inescapable accompaniment to the life of everyone who lived at Corndown.

On the day after Rose arrived Trapper was suffering from his intake of alcohol the previous night, and also a sense that while he lay drunk the Laffams had been made fools of at the Black Bear. Only when Bart told him that he had killed Giles Dyer did Trapper allow himself to be consoled, after knocking the boy down to teach him caution.

Rose did not mind intemperance or violence, being well used to both. What she enjoyed at Corndown was freedom from restraint, and the reckless bounty which meant she had only to express a wish for it to be granted. Beer, spirits, meat, perfume, fine cloths, good horseflesh: all were tumbled together in barn and store and paddock. Fortunately, Rose had no more idea than the Laffams what else money might buy, and like them was satisfied by prodigal quantities of everyday goods. Like them, she also preferred to work only when the returns were immediate. Consequently, the fields of Corndown were indifferently farmed, the cottages dirty and the hedgerows cluttered with broken carts. However, when the smugglers wanted to run goods the Laffams would toil mightily together and think nothing of their exertions.

Oh yes, Rose liked Corndown very much, even when her first night there was spent on old straw. She also liked Bart, and wondered whether she might not come to love him.

'I'll put up some planking and a brick chimney to make a space here of our own,' he said carelessly, while they lay together.

'That will be lovely.' Rose wasn't in the least put out by the idea of a home planked-off from one end of a barn.

'Oh, Rose, just think of the summer I've wasted wondering—'

'Wondering what?' she mumbled, coiled into him like a cat.

He laughed. 'Wondering about the answers I found with you since last night in Ned Oxley's barn.'

But in spite of Rose, Bart started awake in a sweat of terror much later that same night. His shivers woke her and she reached for him sleepily, only to come fully awake when she felt fright slithering on his skin. 'What's the matter?'

'I don't want to speak about it.'

'If something's troubling you we'll have to speak of it soon or late.'

He sighed and lay back. 'Maybe, but just now I don't want to. I want to forget.'

'Forget what?'

'God damme, leave it will you? I'm forgetting, like I said.'

'Like I can feel,' she answered coldly, her hands on gooseflesh.

After that, he began thinking about Rose instead of a nightmare about swingling injured men, because her hands were teasing him the way he sometimes teased trout in Edenham's stream. He didn't want to rise to her teasing, nor let the impudent bitch drag thought out of him so soon, but, like the fish, he was quickly caught by soothing yet tantalising holds. A fool he'd been, that's what, not to have her in his life before.

'You know I killed Giles Dyer last night,' he said softly.

'Of course I know. I wasn't sotted like the rest.'

A pause for other enjoyments while he thought about that. She didn't mind. He didn't mind. But then, he hadn't woken sweating about Giles Dyer, over whose death he felt no remorse at all.

'Rose.' He began twisting her hair over and over in his fingers. 'You ever seen a man killed before?'

'Once. There was a fight and we didn't rightly know

who did it, but this pedlar was cold meat when it finished. My da got rid of him, too.'

'I've seen others too, but . . . on our last run I saw . . . you know Abel Grey?'

'He comes to the Black Bear sometimes and puts his head together with Arthur Brown of Wyses.'

And so Bart told her, haltingly and leaving time between for her fingers to stroke his skin.

'Now that doesn't seem right,' she said when he finished. But she said it calmly, because her main concern was Bart and he would be helped by calmness. Such a death clearly wasn't right and she disapproved of it, but Rose did not believe in wasting effort over things past helping.

'No, it wasn't right,' he answered.

And strangely enough, after that Bart hardly ever thought about the riding officer's death again, or if he did it seemed to matter less and less.

Next day they drove one of Corndown's carts to pick up a bed from the Black Bear, since Rose refused to sleep on a straw pile only with winter coming on. She sat up on the bench flourishing a whip, while Bart lolled in the back, laughing as they spanked along at a pace which threatened to land them in the ditch. Rose's hair flew in the wind and the earth was so thick with harvest scents you could taste them on the tongue.

'Something's up,' called Rose. 'Look, everyone's in the street.'

'Likely they've come to cheer an unbroke mare called Rose, driving a Corndown cart.' Bart tumbled on the bottom boards to avoid the whip she flashed at him, laughing more heartily than before. Only when he had disentangled himself sufficiently to stand, did he see that Rose was right. Something was up in Furnace Green that morning, since nearly everyone seemed to have found a reason to watch two black figures cling to timber high on the church steeple.

When pegs had first been hammered into turf behind a mouldering Saxon chapel three hundred years before, they had marked out a rectangular stone church with a tower at its western end. Solid, compact and unassuming, the kind of structure devotion and patience could construct in the frequent absence of skilled craftsmen, and which, once built, should stand through the centuries. Then the priest who had conceived and driven through this project fell from scaffolding before the upper stonework was finished, or the tower more than a dug ditch to take foundations. In consequence, Furnace Green church remained thatched for nearly another fifty years, and when a tiled roof was ultimately completed it had been built by men who had never covered such a span in their lives, and sagged almost as soon as it was finished. More serious still was the tower. Furnace Green people had soon wearied of jests about their 'rotted tooth', which was a fair description of the jagged courses of stone they had piled on the original foundations. Riffield, on the other hand, possessed a fine perpendicular church filled with Scovell tombs and topped by an elegant spire, which looked like the spirit of man pointed up to heaven.

So, in the early years of the sixteenth century, the ridge's inhabitants decided to build a steeple taller than that of Riffield. Ten years passed while the tower was slowly re-mortared and completed, then above it began to grow a steeple framed in oak. Furnace Green craftsmen understood oak and by then iron was being produced in the parish, which helped scarf beams together. They guessed the height of Riffield, added another oak trunk for luck and erected a steeple eighty feet tall and clad in split beech shingles. In 1527, seven years before King Henry seized the abbey at Ockham, all was finally complete and a single bell triumphantly rang out across the ridge so that (in a favourable wind) Riffield folk could hear and grind their teeth in envy.

The weight of the steeple was prodigious. Oak trunks, adzed square, formed its spine; more oak strutting was added to take a cladding of battens and shingles. After less than twenty years some cracks appeared in the stonework supporting this structure, but then, inexplicably, the timbers seemed to settle together and nothing further happened for a long time.

Everyone became used to a cracked church tower and not until the year 1662 when a mighty gale blew out of the west, was it noticed that the steeple was slightly askew and the cracks wider. All kinds of remedies were suggested but nothing was done until Sir Amyas Dyer came past one day, sitting like a gnome on his horse and said they ought to make an iron strap and strain it around the tower, so preventing it from cracking further. He even offered to pay, remarking that Riffield could afford not to crow when other men's ambitions overleaped themselves. So, although everyone in Furnace Green felt sulky about it, they accepted his offer. The Dyers weren't really Riffield, after all. Merely rich, and in the Weald it was considered criminal to refuse a bargain.

So the ridge ironsmiths wrought a massive strap in two parts and bound the stone tower together, so that it and the timber steeple above stood for another eighty years.

Unless something was done, it wouldn't stand for many more. For years, the steeple had moved whenever a storm blew out of the west, wearing down the stone on which its timbers rested, flexing the tower, flaking mortar. Shingles fell and the steeple began to tilt more visibly from the vertical. All of which was particularly upsetting when Furnace Green church was a symbol of the ridge's pride, and likely to be expensive too, since the bishop had warned Parson Brookland that the parish freeholders would have to pay for any damage to their church.

After much head-scratching, oaths and contemplative silence around tankards in the Black Bear, a plan had been devised to deal with the situation. Bywood would make another strap, this time a chain which could be tightened around the octagonal steeple by means of a bar, and so prevent the timbers from working any further apart. Specially forged spikes would be driven in to support this chain and secure the timbers still further; the fallen shingles could then be replaced and all would be well for another eighty years.

They were not particularly sober at the time, and failed to grasp the difference between stiffening a square stone tower and attempting the same task on the sloping sides of a steeple. Also, Bruiser had boasted that he was willing to climb up himself and place the chain in position.

Brute though Bywood was, he possessed the kind of courage which comes from a complete lack of sensitivity. He knew the chain he had forged was strong, and the bar would tighten it. There were footholds in plenty where the shingles had slipped, and he liked swaggering in front of a crowd; he also balanced as easily a hundred feet up as on his own forge floor.

He and Tobias started their climb about mid-morning: Amos had begun by ordering Tobias not to go and ended by begging, to all of which his son affected a maddening deafness.

'Shut your prate, old man,' Bywood said at last, exasperated. 'If he didn't come willing, I'd have taken him by the scruff, see? Me needing help and Hosmers being around to offer it free.'

'For a wage, you said,' snapped Tobias.

'I must have been thinking of someone else. It seems to me that Hosmers can't need money like the rest of us, since they're too fine to earn their keep with the smugglers.'

'Today I'm earning it up the steeple.'

'Oh no, you're not, my lad. You're going up out of the goodness of your heart, that's what.' Bywood fastened a hand on Tobias's neck and shook him until his senses swam. Then he force-marched him to the base of the tower and dealt him a hefty kick on the rump. 'Get started, you mule's bastard.'

Without a word, Tobias started up the small circular stair inside the tower. He was scowling, his eyes slitted and considering. He had never intended to back away from climbing the steeple, relished the chance of proving it wasn't lack of courage which kept Hosmers from following the smugglers. Now Bywood made him seem a snivelling faintheart again: if the smith could have seen his expression he would have known he needed to watch out for himself on the dangerous toeholds of the steeple.

The air had seemed still in the street, but on the catwalk at the top of the tower a strong breeze blew. Tobias had never been so high before and, fascinated, he looked out over the cleared ridge and its meandering trails. Even their own corner cottage looked quite different from above: fleetingly he wondered how Joseph was keeping Riding Officer Larkworthy's ravings quiet when so many people were gathered under the bedchamber casement. The parsonage just to the west of the tower looked as ill-kempt as the parson himself, while the Black Bear flaunted richness like a banner, nestling among new outbuildings, yard and barn. From where Tobias stood, Furnace Green looked disconcertingly small and threatened by the forest, which centuries of effort had still not thrust so very far away. Cottage roofs were revealed as patched, the gravestones in the churchyard leaning towards each other like so many squabbling crones, and the Dyers' great possessions as lapping at the very threshold of the village.

But at least when viewed from above the yellow stonecrop flowers growing in most cottage thatches glowed even more brilliantly than they did from the street; because these hung in clumps from most eaves, Furnace Green nicknamed it the welcome-home-husband-though-never-so-drunk flower. Otherwise the village was drab compared to the surrounding hedgerows. Vegetables grew in neat patches, but only the occasional honeysuckle or dog-rose softened brick and timber, since fowls pecked each dropped seed and pigs grubbed up most bushes which struggled into leaf.

Still . . . it was home and prosperous. Tobias had never known anywhere else and he was simply interested to see it from above. He didn't feel dizzy looking down, and was filled with anticipation when he turned to face Bywood as he emerged from the stair. Between them they soon rigged a pulley and hauled up Bruiser's chain, twisting bar, clamps and spikes, until the narrow walkway at the top of the tower was so filled with clutter they could scarcely move.

'How are we going to do it?' demanded Tobias, studying the steeple which slanted from his toes up into the sky.

Bywood stared at him. 'You go up first. I'm not leaving you to play tricks between me and the ground.'

'All right. What do you want me to do?'

'Climb until I tell you to stop and then hammer in a fresh fixing for the pulley. Here, put the mallet in your belt.'

Testing each step as he went, Tobias began to pull himself up. Occasionally he needed to kick out rotten shingles to achieve a secure grip but otherwise, for an active boy lacking any fear of heights, the climb was easy. The only problem was kicking out the few shingles which remained securely fixed in order to reach a foothold on the battens underneath.

Kick, pause, heave up another step. Kick.

When Tobias reached up next his fingers encountered only paper-thin planks crumbling to the touch. 'The steeple isn't battened up here.'

'Aye? No matter, you're high enough. Hammer in the pulley.' Bywood sounded brisk and businesslike now the job was begun.

Silence closed in around Tobias as he had to use first one hand to reach the mallet in his belt, then the other to take spikes from a pouch. The breeze was even stronger up here, plucking at him as he leaned into the slope of the steeple. By the time he had the pulley shackle fixed, his muscles were trembling and a sharp pain stabbed from groin to knee. He paused, holding on tightly with both hands.

'Get on with it,' said Bywood, and just for a moment, Tobias's senses spun. He hadn't known the blacksmith had climbed up close behind him. Instead of Bywood just below his boots, he saw those faces in the street, far below and shifting sickly with his loss of balance. The wind blustered against his skin and the whole steeple seemed to move, flowing very slowly, tilting with his senses.

'Look up! *Look up*, you bitch's bastard,' spat Bywood. 'Get on with hammering and don't waste time.'

Rage helped Tobias to wrench his eyes back to the shingles under his nose, which immediately settled ground and sky back into their rightful places.

After that, everything became a misery he had not expected and wouldn't have been able to sustain, had it not been for the anger which possessed him. Bywood made him do all the most dangerous tasks, by means of oaths, taunts and the promise that he would let him rest once all the gear was hauled up. First Tobias had to thread the rope through the pulley while only the friction of his knees kept his body crouched inward against the steeple, then he must hold more spikes for hammering, tighten clamps a handsbreadth at a time.

In the street below, for a while everyone watched those two black-beetle figures in silence, until eventually interest began to flag and tongues to gossip when there was so little to see beyond slow movement against eye-dazzling sky. Only when Arthur Brown came shouldering through the crowd braying out odds on whether the boy would fall, did everyone again fall silent. At first a stir of shame followed in his wake as people idling away a working morning realized that the possibility of tragedy was indeed their real reason for lingering. Then Wat Smith took up the offer of odds, yelling a wager of his own, and subtly but quickly the mood of the watchers changed. In place of stillness there was avid speculation, instead of shame a lust for something to happen soon. Covert sympathy for Amos, wringing his hands at the bottom of the tower, was replaced by sniggers over the pitiable buffoon he was making of himself.

As the noise grew, Joseph went upstairs to stand beside Riding Officer Larkworthy in the bedchamber, whose casement was directly above the crowd. Every time the suffering wretch had tried to screech or babble he had forced raw spirits between his teeth. No other way to keep him quiet, and Larkworthy had for some time been deeply unconscious: breathing badly but in too much of a stupor to be a danger for the moment.

'You ought to have stopped Tobias,' said Clemency, on her knees beside the bed. She had prayed all morning, unable to watch her son's life dangling on a whim of Bruiser Bywood.

'I couldn't have stopped him.'

'You ought to have tried.'

'He wouldn't have listened to me! Any lad of spirit who has been forbidden to take the same risks as everyone else in his daily life would seize the first chance he has to prove himself! You should offer thanks he hasn't shamed you by running off to join the smugglers one night while you slept.' He flung out of the room, slamming the plank door behind him, wretchedly aware that he himself had merely run away from Furnace Green.

Downstairs he found a child shamelessly pilfering from a keg of molasses and sent him off howling with a blow on the ear. Matters were come to a pretty pass when brats reckoned they could filch anything that took their fancy. Joseph went to stand on the doorstep, hands thrust under the skirts of his bottle-green coat; he was short-sighted and saw the steeple as a blur, but Arthur Brown soon came thrusting through the crowd. 'I'm offering odds on the boy falling. You're a man of affairs these days, so what about a wager worth the taking?'

Joseph stared across the crowd to where, short-sighted though he was, he could just discern the broken bank and ruinous buildings of Fawkners, still owned by Arthur Brown of Wyses. 'I will wager with a promise, if you like. Before you have built the new cottages you plan inside the square of Fawkners, out of profits amassed by dealing with Abel Grey, those who have corrupted Furnace Green will have been destroyed.' Bart Laffam, handsome scoundrel that he was, was standing up in a cart with his arm round a giggling wench and bellowing encouragement to Bywood up the steeple.

Brown laughed in his face. Stamped and spluttered in great hoots of mirth. 'Pray how will you make such a rash promise good, when a word sent to Grey will see your throat cut before you have ridden a mile? And suppose you should reach a magistrate, what will you tell him? Sir Jonas Dyer having my kegs in his cellar, like.'

'I draw maps for a living and at the moment am engaged in surveying the Duke of Richmond's estates. You'll have heard of him, I daresay, the scourge of smugglers in West Sussex. The Dyers may not be so hot for justice as once they were, but should Grey choose to kill me, then he'll find His Grace of Richmond an enemy to be reckoned with.'

This was bluff. Almost alone among the great landlords of Sussex the duke was indeed a scourge of smugglers, but Joseph's acquaintance with him was limited to drawing a few sketch plans of his land purchases. In the surge of panic which followed his rash words to Brown, however, Joseph was ready to grab at straws. He couldn't imagine what had possessed him to abandon the habit of a lifetime and reject prudence just this once. He was also tired after two nights of strain, revulsion and fright. He knew he ought to get out of Furnace Green at once but couldn't seem to bring himself to it, when all he really wanted was to lie down and sleep.

So he let defiance stand, which for Joseph was a most unusual action, and after a while Brown finished cursing and went off, leaving Joseph to scan the crowd for any indication which might tell him what was happening beyond the limits of his sight. Bart Laffam was bellowing still, while the girl he held fumbled shamelessly under his dirty jerkin, but suddenly Joseph saw him freeze, mouth open and tongue flapping. Talk stopped abruptly and a sigh ran through the crowd like wind through reeds.

Joseph grasped the nearest arm. 'Tell me what is happening.'

'Damme, look for yourself.' The man tried to shake him off.

'I can't see so far.'

'He's going to fall!' bellowed Bart.

'Who? Jesus, tell me which one is falling!' Joseph's fingers dug into his neighbour's sleeve.

But the man stood rooted without answering, everyone rooted in utter stillness, the only sound a scream of pure terror.

Bruiser Bywood and Tobias had succeeded some time before in heaving the chain about a third of the way up the steeple where, for some reason, the blacksmith declared it would best hold the structure together. The next problem was how they could carry one end around the eight facets of the steeple and, having done so, fasten the whole together. After that it would only be a matter of winding everything up tight: difficult enough some seventy feet above the ground, but not to be compared with scrambling around an unsafe structure dragging ponderous chain.

'You'd best drive a spike into each face first, and rest the chain on each as you go,' said Bywood, while he and Tobias rested after they had hauled up everything they expected to need.

'It's your turn.' Tobias had left that one moment of dizziness behind by performing prodigies of recklessness, and felt insolently triumphant in consequence. He looked at Bywood, calculating his chances of forcing a wary adversary into error without the onlookers below perceiving what he had done.

'Nay, 'tis a lad's work. I'm twice your weight and on an outside face that makes a difference.'

'Aye, gutless tremblings could rock even oak beams apart, I daresay,' jeered Tobias. 'I'll enjoy telling how Abel Grey's chief swingler lacked nerve to climb where a Hosmer went.'

He swung himself off the catwalk without waiting for an answer and climbed up even quicker than before, each foothold already kicked clear. He felt nothing beyond excitement stinging in his veins; not the wind blustering against his back, nor the dangerous weariness which lurked beneath elation.

Today he had shown a pack of bullies what courage was.

Tobias quickly reached the place where a double hank of chain hung waiting for him, swinging slightly in the wind. Bywood was right, unless he drove a spike into each face of the steeple first, he would never be able to drag such a weight with him.

'Send up some spikes and the mallet,' he called.

When Bywood hauled them up without argument, Tobias wanted to shout with delight. He had won . . . won . . . won, after a lifetime of losing. Bruiser Bywood was following the youngest Hosmer's bidding, and all that remained was to lure him into error. Or if that failed, then so to rub his pride in Hosmer daring that it would be deformed for life.

Tobias finished five out of the eight steeple faces surprisingly quickly. He drove a spike into each, then looped the chain over while Bywood fed across more slack. I hope they can see in the street how he is working as my apprentice, Tobias thought. The most difficult face had been the fourth where the steeple's lean from the vertical, although only a matter of inches, made it seem like an undershot cliff. Probably Bruiser had been right, his extra weight there could have added unnecessary danger, but Tobias discarded that unwelcome reflection instantly.

Two more faces to go and then the eighth, where Bywood stood well-braced beside the pulley.

The oak framing of the steeple was so tough that Tobias needed each time to find a fissure before he could drive home a spike. On the sixth face the timber was as smooth as in the year it was adzed; twice Tobias tried to place a spike so it would stay wedged long enough for him to drive it home while keeping one hand to hold himself safe. Twice the spike fell into the graveyard below before he could reach for the mallet in his belt. He cursed and put out his hand, being just in reaching distance of Bywood again. 'Give me another spike.'

'It's the last one, I didn't reckon on you a-throwing them all over the place.'

'I'll get it in somehow. We can tighten the chain between us without worrying about spiking the last face.'

After the perils of that outside face where the ground seemed to reach up behind his back, Tobias's confidence was like a weapon freshly honed. He balanced easily and used both hands to force that last spike home. Even so, it was a difficult task, the oak as unyielding as Bywood's iron.

'That will do, I think.' He tossed the mallet over his shoulder so it soared down to vanish in rank graveyard grass.

'You young braggart! Watch what you do for once,' exclaimed Bywood angrily. 'There's folks down there.'

'More fool them,' answered Tobias coolly. He rested a moment before beginning to manoeuvre more chain from spike to spike until just enough remained to reach where Bywood waited to splice the two ends together. And as he rested that last time, Tobias again became aware of the wind. Its hollow moan around the tapered steeple seemed to vibrate the air and a gust struck at him, followed after a few moments by another. 'We'll have to be quick.'

'Mayhap we'd best finish tomorrow,' answered Bywood uneasily.

Tobias laughed. 'You go down if you're afraid.'

'It'll take both of us to tighten the chain.'

'The chain doesn't matter.'

'The chain doesn't matter?' shouted Bywood. 'Why have I been risking my life if it doesn't matter?'

Tobias stared at him across the remaining facet of the steeple: not much time left to lure Bruiser into error. 'I don't know why you risked yours, but I risked mine for the pleasure of watching you scuttle for safety first. If the steeple is ready to fall in the next gale, then it'll fall, and a chain won't stop it. So run off home and welcome, king of the swinglers.'

Bywood fingered the chain, each hammermark a record of his sweat. Of course the steeple would be safe again once it was spliced up and taut. Then a gust stronger than the last forced him to hold on tightly until it passed, and he, too, felt the thrum of the steeple, low and menacing beneath the sound of the wind. But there was Tobias's mocking face, and for him Bywood felt a grudging respect. Courage was courage, wherever you found it. Blindly he reached out. 'Pass me your end.'

'You're afraid,' said Tobias, smiling.

'No!'

'Not many men like listening to the truth.'

Surely any man in his senses would be afraid, part way up a steeple ripe to fall, when his only companion was a brat drunk on his own foolhardiness.

Tobias grasped his end of chain and heaved. It required all his strength to lift it across that last, unspiked, face towards Bywood's outstretched hand and between them they bungled it. As Tobias leaned further away from his handhold, he could hear his sinews crackle with the strain; a boy of only moderate strength whose normal work was in a shop. The smith's hand reached out towards him . . . still an inch too far away. A vast blackened paw unsteadied by fear. If Bywood hadn't been afraid, he could have achieved that extra inch of reach; a thought which made Tobias throw back his head and laugh.

As he laughed another gust of wind reached out of the west and the loose end of chain he was holding swayed, taking his body with it. Instantly, panic swept thought aside. Knees jammed anyhow against timber but that no longer helped, his heart stampeding as the earth spiralled terrifyingly out of reach. Then his scruff was seized and Tobias looked up into Bywood's eyes. 'Drop that chain, you fool, and kick another foothold.'

Tobias's face scraped painfully across shingles as he

dropped the chain and scrambled for a hold. He was hanging from his own left hand and the blacksmith's choking grip, Bywood himself spreadeagled away from safety, huge muscles straining.

But hanging as he was, Tobias could not kick through even rotten timber, nor was there any other grip on this unspiked face. His hand and leg were shuddering from the strain of supporting most of his weight, his free fingers slithering helplessly across lichened shingles. He felt his foot begin to slide on his single remaining toehold, the upward pull on his clothing as Bywood's arm was dragged inexorably downward by his weight. His ears roared, drowning the sound of the wind and Bruiser's panting effort.

For half a dozen heartbeats, Tobias hung, staring up at the blacksmith out of bulging eyes. He didn't believe this was happening. It wasn't happening, it couldn't be. When his muscles relaxed at last all he felt was relief, then rage as Bywood's grip at his neck became suffocation. Already, he was incapable of realizing that this alone kept him from falling . . . Then Bywood, steeple and tower were turning, spinning away from him, and he screamed in agony as his back struck the parapet of the tower, screamed again as an immense and painshot terror filled the last curve of his life.

Tobias hit the tower edge and tumbled legs over head to fall on the flagstones near the church door. He was dead before Amos reached him from a few paces away. The watchers ran too from where they had waited in the street, but a glimpse told them all they needed to know. So they stood in a knot whispering amongst themselves before beginning to drift away, leaving Amos still on his knees in the dust with Joseph standing beside him. The women mostly went no further than their doorsteps, whence they could continue to watch events, the men walked to the Black Bear to await the return of Bruiser Bywood.

'Look at it how you will, he's come out of this better

than he went in,' observed Bart Laffam over ale in the taproom.

'Aye, he gave a lesson they pious Hosmers won't forget, and all served up as accident too. No magistrate can say different, us being witness to what happened,' agreed Roger Frenchman.

'A warning more than a lesson. Do you know, Joseph Hosmer tried to threaten me? You Laffams too, as well as Abel Grey.' Arthur Brown shook his head at such folly.

Bart spluttered in his ale with laughter. 'A squinty clerk threaten half a hundred Laffams! He piddles in his breeches if we so much as give him the time of day.'

'There's naught like quill-driving for making a man uppity.' Brown turned to Oxley. 'Ned, why are we drinking stuff like Joseph's piddle? We need brandy to toast Bruiser when he comes, or are you drunk dry already?'

Since the cells below Oxley's tap were stacked with kegs and Brown's pockets clinked coins from all the wagers he had collected over the matter of Tobias falling from the steeple, this query was hailed as an offer to unlimited free spirits. Which, as Brown intended, soon dispelled any tendency for some of the company to retire behind their tankards of home-brewed and reflect with some unease on the events of the day.

When the din at the Black Bear returned to its usual pitch, the women up in the street knew this would be another night when the welcome-home-husband-though-never-so-drunk flower would live up to its name. By then, Joseph and his father had carried Tobias into the shop, there to lay him out across barrels hastily dragged together. While Amos and Clemency prayed beside their son's shattered body, Joseph closed the shutters, a task he had carried out easier at twelve years old than he did as a man unused to the weight of planks and iron bars.

As he stooped to fasten the last bolt he saw a heavy shadow thrown against the woodwork, dismayingly recognizable as Bruiser Bywood, fresh from a killing. 'Open up!'

Joseph hesitated, glancing to where Amos and Clemency

apparently remained oblivious of everything except their grief. If Bywood put his weight to a plank door it would tear out, bolts and all. So, his throat abjectly dry with fear, Joseph stood aside to let the smith past. Yet once inside, Bywood seemed undecided over what to do next.

'I tried to save him,' he said roughly, at last.

'You killed him.' Christ, why must his tongue persist in senseless bravado?

'Didn't you see how it was? The brat was like a crazed viper up that steeple! . . . Once before, I saw a man made drunk by playing catchpenny with death and that's how Tobias was. I tried to save him, I tell you.'

Joseph scratched his head, his ideas upset by a man like Bywood attempting to justify himself. 'You planned to take Tobias up that steeple. Thought the Hosmers were due for some fresh tauntings, I daresay,' he said querulously.

'I didn't kill him,' repeated Bywood. 'You weren't up there, Master pringling quill-biter. You don't know how it was. What if I did take him with me to offer help I needed? The lad fell because he was a fool.'

He clinked on his iron soles to where Amos and Clemency knelt, and almost admiringly touched Tobias's cold cheek with his finger. 'Almighty God, what a fool he was, but shall I tell you something? I'm glad I tried to save him.'

All this happened on a Friday, and the following Sunday for only the second time since a chapel was rebuilt on Ferenthe Ridge after a Viking raid nearly nine hundred years before, there was no act of worship in Furnace Green, Parson Brookland being too sotted to recollect the day or time. At first, church-going folk muttered amongst themselves but after three Sundays had passed the empty church ceased to seem so strange. Some families held their own Bible-readings or said prayers each day, a few farmers like old Jack Carpenter of Danesdell complained that God's curse on Sussex was smugglers instead of locusts, the rest shrugged and went their way. When all Jack Carpenter's hayricks burned into ash soon after he likened the smugglers to a biblical curse, no one helped carry water from the pool. Those who complained about the smugglers' grip were lucky to escape with only a few burnt ricks.

Joseph Hosmer was still in Furnace Green when this happened, chafing against the delay. Amos had not recovered from the shock of Tobias's death and crept around like a man in a cloister, whilst Clemency fumbled among her pots and applied potions to Riding Officer Larkworthy's hurts but showed no other sign of sense.

Much as he yearned to go, Joseph felt unable to leave them in such a state, alone except for a sick fugitive in their bed. Yet as each day passed he had to reckon another commission as lost, and the thought of his drawing tables gathering dust while clients beat unanswered on his smartly painted door in Lewes, made him want to howl with frustration.

'Why won't you let me find lodgings for you somewhere away from here?' he kept demanding, but every time he did so Amos and Clemency stared dumbly back at him, like half-crazed dogs.

'You'll have to take them away by force, or not at all.' Joseph had jumped the first time a voice answered him from the bed, having grown used to thinking of Riding Officer Larkworthy as no more than a hunk of ill-smelling meat. Now they spoke quite often, using the short sentences which were all Larkworthy could manage in his weakness.

'I can't drag them from their home at a cart's tail,' answered Joseph now.

'Then you'll be caught here until both of them die.'

'By God, that I will not!'

Larkworthy croaked a laugh. 'Then walk out tonight and don't come back.'

'If I did, you'd starve as well as they.'

'Aye, of course.'

'A fine choice you offer, I must say,' Joseph said indignantly.

'It is the choice you have. So take it, or not, and cease complaining.'

Joseph sat on the sagging bed, feeling very ill-used. Larkworthy had thanked him once, brusquely, for his life, but otherwise was a disagreeable guest: uncomplaining although clearly in great pain, but offhand, guarded and arrogant. 'It's all very well for you. You're lucky to be alive, but I had a trade freshly won which I cannot afford to leave untended, as well as a snug widow who seemed willing to join her fate to mine.'

'And your eye on her snug jointure too, no doubt.'

'Well . . . she had this paper, d'you see. That's what brought us together first of all, me coming from Furnace Green.'

'What paper was that?' Shrewd blue eyes watched Joseph struggle out of the coils of indignation, only to fall into those of pride and ambition.

'A paper to do with Furnace Green. The spelling of it was mortal strange but she was told many years ago that this was the place her paper related to, and I am sufficiently familiar with old writings to see that indeed it was. From my maps, you see. I know not how this deed came into Widow Toogood's family, but she told me her grandfather's name was Bellwasher, and when I was a boy an old crone of that name still lived in the almshouse here. A feckless, undeserving woman she was too, quite unlike Widow Toogood, who is monstrous fine,' he added. 'The paper relates to manor rights in Furnace Green. Why, if I wed Widow Toogood I should be lord of the ridge! It doesn't mean much nowadays, but just think of that!'

'Just think of it, indeed. May I guess that your widow is somewhat above you in age?'

'What if she is?'

'Compared to a paper which makes you lord of the manor, less than nothing, I am sure.'

'Why, so say I! You see how I must be back in Lewes soon?'

Larkworthy closed his eyes. 'Go tonight before the fetters

of mercy bind you tight, or stay and make the best you can of it.'

Though Joseph continued for some while to bemoan such impossible alternatives, not one further word could he squeeze out of this most infuriating of the encumbrances which had come to dominate his life. 'I've a good mind to order a cart from the Laffams and send you in it to Tunbridge Wells,' he exclaimed at last. 'Even the smugglers wouldn't dare to murder you over so short a distance.'

'Distance has nothing to do with it. And those same Laffams would be very interested if they heard how the Hosmers had sheltered a riding officer all this time.' His eyes did not open. Only when Joseph had flung out of the bedroom in a fury did Stephen Larkworthy stir, helplessly beating on the bedstraw with the one arm he could move. Here he was, turned into nothing for the rest of his days, and that prissy clerk expected him to be grateful for his life! An object of pity whose sole purpose was to blab thanks, when he had always prided himself on not being beholden.

At least, beholden only to pretty Nancy, the childhood sweetheart he had wanted to wed from the age of ten. Whom he had indeed wed, though at the time she was only a lass, as soon as he was old enough to leave their Devon village and support her by becoming a riding officer. Nancy and their baby Stevie waiting for him now in Lambeth, a squalid pesthole where she was frightened to go out alone.

He groaned aloud as pain burned in his twisted legs. The Hosmers had not dared send for a bonesetter, which meant that any faint chance he might have had of walking again was lost, and the worst pain of all was looking down the useless years ahead of him. God strangle all smugglers with their own plaited tripes! God curse all bumbling fools like Joseph Hosmer, who possessed two whole legs yet spent their days bewailing circumstance.

The door latch snicked and, such was his weakness, Stephen was thrown into a fit of coughing as, too late, he tried to grab at his moans and kennel them away from pity.

When his sight cleared, the room was empty again.

Angrily, he wiped the tears from his cheeks. Someone had stood beside his bed he was sure. Not Joseph but a much heavier presence, clicking on ironshod boots; he had felt its menace even through the agony of coughing against crumpled bones.

He lay very still after that, yet in a way he was glad if his enemies had found him again. Or would have been, except his moans might have betrayed the Hosmers, too. For himself, Stephen Larkworthy wanted very much to die.

Downstairs, Bruiser Bywood faced Joseph across the oak counter. 'Who is he?'

'What business is it of yours? What do you mean by climbing to our bedchamber without so much as by-your-leave?' Joseph tried to bluster but his voice squawked awkwardly in fear.

'Anything which threatens the smugglers hereabouts is my business, so when I hear groans I can't account for I take a look, see? And what do I find? An injured stranger, the snivelling Hosmers have kept secret from their neighbours.' Bywood grasped Joseph by the neckband. 'Tell-me-who-he-is!'

Joseph tried not to tell. He blubbered and whined and lied, while Bruiser slapped his face with hands like rock each time he spoke, crammed his nose into a fresh honeycomb and held him there until he nearly suffocated, before throwing him across the room. If he had not fallen against a pile of sacks Joseph knew he would have broken more bones than Stephen Larkworthy.

'He's a riding officer!' he screeched as Bywood came striding towards him again.

'I don't believe you. Not even Hosmers could be such fools as to hide a long-nose here in Furnace Green.' He hauled Joseph back on his feet. 'Tell me the truth and so long as there's nothing for us to fear I'll say naught about it. Me owing you something for Tobias, like.' If Bywood had promised as much even seconds before, Joseph was sure he could have thought up a convincing lie. But he was now so confused and frightened by what he had already admitted that he could only babble everything he knew and hope Bruiser would be satisfied.

When he finished, Bywood stared at him in disbelief. 'He really is a riding officer? You saw a nearly-corpsed long-nose and did not bid your horse step on his face?'

Joseph nodded, utterly crushed. 'You have nothing to fear, I swear. He-he . . . one leg's flayed down to bone and the other will never knit so he can use it.'

'Don't you know long-noses are always dangerous, tied by the leg or no? What if he sends word to his fellows, and afterwards swears evidence against Abel Grey and the rest of us?' Bywood flung Joseph aside and blundered up the stairs again.

The bedchamber door crashed open so violently this time that one of the leather hinges snapped, but Riding Officer Larkworthy was prepared, lying relaxed and almost eager once remorse over the Hosmers could not affect matters one way or the other. Bruiser saw matted hair, fouled bandages and bright blue contemptuous eyes. The room stank since the single casement was tight shut. 'That runt downstairs said you were a long-nose.'

'Who are you?'

'You want to know who's come to finish you? Well, why not? I'm the blacksmith of this place, and well able to strangle you with one arm tied behind my back.'

'Ah, that's easy for a brave fellow like yourself. Were you the smugglers' leader on the night I was beaten?'

'Once a long-nose always a long-nose, snuffling after evidence. But evidence won't help you this time. I heard Abel Grey brag about how he'd flayed a long-nose on last month's run so I suppose you must be he?'

'Aye.'

Bywood stared at the man on the bed, nonplussed. His previous killings had been in tavern brawls or smuggling affrays in the dark, the idea of strangling a mocking, helpless carcass in cold blood quite alien to his temperament. He opened and closed his fists, hearing the wind moan in the eaves.

'Get on with it, man,' said Larkworthy, for all the world as if he was a farmer discussing when to cut a crop.

Bywood took a step which brought him from the doorway to the bedside, and grabbed Larkworthy's neck. Blue eyes on his: calm, uncaring, glad, even if calm quickly turned into the instinctive thrashings of suffocation. The bed, foetid room and his own strangling hand, began to spin around the edges of Bruiser's vision; swung, steadied, swung again. A few moments longer and the long-nose would be dead, while all the time Bruiser was panting, sobbing, his fingers sunk deep into flesh, only the final twitch of muscle lacking which would finish this.

The wind shuddered heavily, beating against thin cottage walls.

Transfixed, Bywood stared down to where his hand, as if of its own volition, was beginning to slacken instead of grasp for the remnants of Larkworthy's life. Slowly the knuckles smoothed, black hairs lay flat again, thick fingers lifted. He staggered over to the tiny casement and slammed it open with his fist, so the green glass shattered into the street below.

Downstairs, Amos, Clemency and Joseph heard only the sounds of struggle followed by silence. Then a considerable time passed before Bruiser brushed past where Joseph was standing at the counter, and went away up the street like a man in a trance. Yet another hour passed before Joseph nerved himself to venture up to the bedroom; as he kept telling himself, there was no reason to hurry now Larkworthy was dead. Half-guiltily, he was relieved that one of his burdens was removed—an awkward ungrateful burden, too. He was shocked by a killing, of course he was shocked, and ashamed he had babbled the truth so easily, but Joseph had never considered himself courageous, merely as someone who worked hard and tried to do his best. In the matter of Stephen Larkworthy he had done exactly that; it wasn't his fault if a brute like Bywood forced failure on him. More immediate was his fear of retribution, once Bywood told Abel Grey that the Hosmers had sheltered a riding officer. In the face of this final disaster, Amos and Clemency refused to budge at all, staying hunched either side of the hearth as if willing death to release them, too.

When Joseph crept upstairs at last, carrying a lantern against the dark, he found wind blasting through the broken casement. The flame in his lamp blew out and what with the noise of the wind and groanings of timber all around him, at first Joseph took no notice of the whisper. Then he stood absolutely still, straining to hear that thread of sound again. A ghost was his first thought. A spirit come to strangle him with remorse, for the life he had not done enough to save.

'I tried!' he screamed into the wind. 'I brought you here and nursed your stinking carcass! What more did you expect?'

And for a moment the wind died, leaving only that threadlike whisper, which uttered words quite unlike those to be expected from a vengeful spirit. 'You gutless sheep, I'm freezing cold, not dead. More's the pity. Come and cover me up.'

Instantly, all Joseph's shame and fear left him in a great gust of honest rage. God, what a fool he had been made to look! The kind of fool who betrayed an injured fugitive and then gibbered with fear when faced by his ghost. 'You deserve I should leave you for the gale to finish off,' he snapped, and stalked over to jerk coverlets back in place.

He was standing beside the bed when the wind came again, a roaring gust of it which snatched reeds out of the roof. The casement flapped and from somewhere very close came a noise like pebbles down a shute.

'It's tearing shingles off the steeple,' he said aloud, thinking of the chain which no one had attempted to secure after Tobias fell, beating against timber up there in the gale. 'It's going to be a right proper ridge storm this time.'

'May it sink some smugglers, then. You know Bywood will send word to Abel Grey in the morning?' Larkworthy was left with only the faintest of croaks for a voice.

'Why should he, when he let you live?'

'He didn't dare kill me himself, that's all. He wanted to. After a night to think about it, he'll send for someone with more nerve than himself.'

Outside, another gust threw itself across Furnace Green's single street and a tree crashed in Fawkners farmyard opposite.

'Then he only need go as far as Corndown. Plenty of Laffams would think nothing of a killing.'

'He'll send for Grey. I'm his meat, don't you see? Bywood knows that now.'

Joseph felt bewildered, and didn't know what to answer.

'I asked who flailed me, and Bywood answered: Abel Grey. He'll reckon Grey should be the one to finish what he began.'

'I'll hide you somewhere.' But who in Furnace Green would hide a bedridden man the smugglers meant to kill, thought Joseph despairingly. Anyway, he knew his own weakness now. Under Abel Grey's torments he would tell at once where Larkworthy was.

A hand clutched at his sleeve. 'I don't want to hide. Do you think I care to live like this? But if Grey comes himself to kill me, then everyone will know who did it and one day he'll hang. But you can't wait for that because the smugglers will kill you too, for helping a riding officer.'

'I know,' said Joseph bleakly, and remembered how he'd answered Arthur Brown taunt for taunt while Tobias was up the steeple. He had almost forgotten the certainty he felt then, now it stole over him again. Alone, he could do little to beat the evil strangling the ridge, but understood quite clearly that it must and would one day be beaten. He sighed. 'The village is solid for the smugglers, except perhaps Jack Carpenter since they fired his ricks. We're the only family to refuse a keg, who won't turn out to help a run.'

'I'm a Devon man myself, where wreckers are our curse, so am well placed to judge how Sussex has sold its soul for kegs and coin. To a breed like Abel Grey, cruel braggarts who kill for pleasure. I believe this time they'll be driven into a deed so terrible this place at least will turn against them.'

At these words Joseph felt vomit fill his throat, because he knew Larkworthy spoke of his own death, and Joseph's too, perhaps. If afterwards Furnace Green should be shocked enough to turn against Abel Grey, it would be too late for them.

Sometime in the black middle of the night the church steeple began to fall. Most of the shingles were already blown off, and from where, by then, Joseph lay huddled under Stephen's quilt trying to keep him warm in a gale-filled room, he could hear the swinging thud as the chain worked loose. The first timber to shake free from its jointing crashed through the nave roof, although the night was too dark for this to be seen. For a while afterwards the wind seemed to drop, then it shifted and leaped unexpectedly out of the north, tearing into weakened strutting, hurling iron straps and oak crosspieces into the graveyard far below.

The night Joseph spent huddled against Stephen Larkworthy affected him strangely. He knew Larkworthy only considered himself reprieved in order to face another and worse death, and that he, Joseph, ought to run for safety this very night, but now he felt those knobbled bones against his own well-fleshed limbs he became perversely determined to save him if he could. They did not speak much, but when Joseph climbed out of bedstraw in the dawn, for the first time Larkworthy seemed to soften. 'If you survive all this, will you send to tell my Nancy what happened? I've only five sovereigns saved so she'll find life very hard, but she'd want to be able to tell our lad the truth of what happened to me, one day.'

'I'm going to try and get you into hiding.'

'She lives in Lambeth now, the lane just past the Cock. Second door on the right. Repeat it.'

'The lane past the Cock. Second door on the right.' Joseph snapped, annoyed. It wasn't his business to start worrying about Nancy in Lambeth, nor did he believe that Bruiser would allow his forge to grow cold just so he could jaunter twenty miles to explain to Abel Grey how he'd failed to kill a long-nose. They had time to plan, if only they used it wisely.

Meanwhile, there was the church steeple to marvel about.

Joseph Hosmer, sketcher of oddities in the margins of his maps, scuttled out into the street first thing in the morning quite as eagerly as the rest of the village, there to gape at the fangs of timber sticking out of the tower-top, the hole torn in the nave roof, the debris hurled everywhere by the gale.

'A good storm, I call it.' Widow Apps leaned on her stick and surveyed the changed landscape with satisfaction.

'Maybe all right for those who don't have to clear up afterwards,' retorted Tom Rabbit. Among other casual works, the Rabbit family earned pence by scything the graveyard.

'Lor' love you, there won't be much clearing to do. Folks'll take good timber and shingles as soon as they're certain Parson's sotted,' Widow Apps said scornfully. ''Twas a good storm, say I, and did you ever see such a rare old morning to follow it?'

It was indeed a rare morning, the sun brilliant on wet grass and splintering light from puddles in the roadway. Widow Apps's judgement proved accurate in another matter, too. As soon as everyone realized that Brookland was indeed far too sotted to worry about casual thefts, they scuttled hither and thither until there was scarcely a fallen timber or shingle anywhere to be seen. Seasoned, squared timber was valuable, and a great many households had leaking roofs after the storm.

Widow Apps cackled as she watched from her doorstep, and about midday she hobbled to buy a handful of beans at Hosmers' shop. As she emerged again she saw a group of men coming down the street, smugglers from the look of their showy catskin waistcoats, but unknown to her, except for Bruiser Bywood and Bart Laffam. She was not much interested; nowadays, strangers often came to Furnace Green. Though she coveted the brandy and good wages brought by the smugglers, being old and poor she depended on the generosity of others for her share. She sighed, crooked knuckles clutched on her stick. Ah, if only she had still been Alex Apps's sweetheart, the new-wed mistress of the Black Bear! What times she would have seen with the smugglers then. When she'd been young the smuggling trade hadn't grown into the riotous monster it had since become, and six weeks after she married him, her husband was stricken by a gripe in his belly and died.

So Ned Oxley bought their tavern after three hundred years of Apps ownership, and it was he who grew rich with the smugglers while she withered into childless old age and earned pence by laundering.

The group of smugglers Widow Apps saw were shoving and shouting among themselves, taking up the whole width of roadway although there were less than a dozen of them. She kept her eyes down and paused by the Hosmers' fence to let them past. Great pesky lads, she thought, but without resentment. I wonder why they're in Furnace Green today?

'Heh, old woman!' called one of them, who was clearly drunk. 'I'm Jim Blake from Hawkhurst, and who are you?'

'Ah, get on with you. If you're drunk by day as well as night the long-noses will take you for sure.' Perhaps because she seldom shared the smugglers' bounty Widow Apps did not fear these bumptious louts, merely coveted the coins in their pockets.

'You hear that?' shouted Blake, astonished. 'Bruiser, this is your home and you let old women answer smugglers so?'

'Sows grunt all the time,' answered Bruiser uneasily. He had been in his forge when Bart came in with half a dozen others to discuss details of a run arranged for the following week; after they had drunk together for a while, and without considering the consequences, he had blurted out about Riding Officer Larkworthy. They were at first incredulous, but agreed with him the best thing now would be to tell Abel Grey. Only as they became drunker did the idea of an immediate expedition to Hosmers' shop take hold. At first Bruiser dissented from the general motion, having hoped that Larkworthy's throat would be cut without him, but he was overruled. Another tankard of neat brandy passed from hand to hand, fuelling decision, and then they roistered off through the village, to encounter Widow Apps on their way.

'Old women should step aside when smugglers pass,' shouted Blake, although this was what she had done.

'How old are you, hag?' A second thick-bellied, sour-faced stranger breathed spirits in her face.

Bewildered, she shook her head. 'My mam said I were born ten years before the century changed.'

'Born before the century, old woman? Then truly you have lived long enough by now!' He snatched the stick from her hand and without warning struck her over the head with it, again and again as his frenzy mounted, knocking her to her knees and striking aside the arm she flung up to protect her head, continuing long after she lay like rags flung on a midden.

When he threw the stick down beside her, the knob-end had cracked where it had long been polished by her hand. 'What good are old women anyway, creeping like witches from post to post?'

'Once they can't warm a bed they're better dead,' agreed Blake. 'Did you bring a flask with you, Bruiser?'

'There'll have to be an inquest,' said Bruiser blankly. He had neither liked nor disliked Widow Apps but she wasn't just any old woman. She was part of his own place. Bart was staring, too; not interfering because that was something he'd learned not to do, although he himself would never have contemplated killing an old woman for no better reason than the pleasure of it.

'An inquest? Christ's blood, why should there be? Old

crones die every day and are tipped into a pauper's grave. Your parson's with us, isn't he?'

'Aye, but—'

'Bid him scavenge her out of sight, then. Now—' Blake wiped his mouth on the back of his hand. 'Let's be finishing with Bruiser's long-nose, eh?'

Laughing uproariously, they swept without more ado into the shop, upending Joseph into a trough of pickling salt as they passed and hurling Clemency and Amos neck and crop into the yard. Plenty of time to deal with them later.

Bruiser Bywood's forge was a small building on the edge of the green between Wyses and the Black Bear. In one corner stood the hearth with its great bellows made from cowhide, and heaped all around were broken ploughshares, wheels needing new rims, scythes, sickles and the massive household pots peculiar to the Weald: made from such prodigal quantities of iron that they had lasted from the time when most villages possessed their own furnace, now nearly two hundred years past.

Usually it was blazing hot inside the forge, but that night Bywood sat alone beside a chilling hearth, wringing his great hands together without noticing the pain he inflicted on himself. Some time before dawn, he stood up and went outside, walked up the slope to the end of the street near Wyses and on towards church and shop. Moonlight lay over shut doors and the scuffed dust where Widow Apps had died. Bruiser wondered who had taken her body away and whether Parson had been hauled out of fuddlement long enough to mouth some words beside her grave. But though he thought these things, he quickly forgot them again.

The shop's door lay splintered in the gutter and when he went inside Bywood's boots crackled on debris underfoot. Everything he blundered into seemed torn in pieces. Then he touched something soft which whimpered and he darted back to the doorway, panting like a baited dog. Very slowly the moon touched in the details of chaos, while still hiding other things he had come to discover. Eventually Bruiser decided that the creature he had touched was only Clemency, snivelling and loose-minded. He left her where she was, being a guilt-ridden rather than a merciful man, and climbed up the stair which was nearly steep enough to be called a ladder. Blood was everywhere, and stinking bandages flung in a corner as if Stephen Larkworthy's killers had gloated over his injuries before they finished their work. Otherwise the room under the eaves was empty.

Bywood blundered downstairs again and shook Clemency, roughly. 'Where are Amos and Joseph?'

But she scuttled away from him, crab-like across the floor and he swore aloud. Crazed women ill-wished those who caused their wits to scatter. He tramped back through the shop and stood irresolutely on the step. Dawn was just beginning to touch the trees behind the church and doors were opening along the street. Young Tam Sleech came out from the cottage next door, knuckling sleep from his eyes and humping a yoke of buckets on his way to the well.

'Hey, where's Joseph?' called Bywood.

The child hesitated. 'I dunno.'

'Oh yes, you do.' Bywood grabbed at him but Tam jinked out of his grasp with the ease of long practice, wooden buckets flying. 'Look, I don't want to hurt him.'

'Mam said not to tell.'

'She didn't say not to tell me. Christ, boy. You come to the forge often enough, begging to lead horses on a run.'

Tam hitched the yoke on his shoulders and didn't answer.

'You just leave my Tam alone.' Mistress Sleech came out on her step, arms crossed under her shawl.

'I only asked . . . what happened yestere'en, mistress?'

'You were there.'

'I went off after Widow Apps was killed. I want to know what happened next.'

'Why?' Sue Sleech was red cheeked and hefty. Bruiser had always liked her hard-headedness, but today she looked at him as if he was a slug to be crushed.

'I—' He turned and aimed a kick at Tam so he scampered out of earshot. 'Listen here, Sue. I been around smugglers a long time, like the rest of us, but I haven't ever killed an old woman just because she was old nor I don't aim to start. If that's the kind Abel Grey has in his gang nowadays, then I reckon the time has come to keep them out of Furnace Green.'

'And wait for them to kill us too?' she jeered, sharp eyes snapping, elbows hugged tight.

'Not if we band together, like. Together we let them come here, together we can turn them out. If we wants to, or so it seems to me.'

'Well, Bruiser Bywood.' She stared at him. 'You mean it, don't you?'

He spat and set his foot on spittle, without answering. Bruiser knew nothing of Tiw or Mother Earth (and precious little about Christ, for that matter) but the earliest hill-people on the ridge would have recognized this gesture of a mind made up.

'Come in if you like then, Joseph be out the back.' Sue jerked her head.

'Amos?'

'Dead. Of fright mayhap, there weren't a mark on him, and Clemency is gibbering.'

'The long-nose?'

She snorted. 'What do you think?'

'For God's sake!' He sat on a stool and put his aching head in his hands. 'Just tell me, will you.'

'They squeezed him through that minikin window of the room where he lay hid, and a dreadful to-do it did make. Him being a big man and needing to be skinned like a rabbit to get him through so small a space. He were bad hurt before, but you know that, don't you? Much worse hurt after they'd a-done with pushing and a-shoving of him through and then let him fall down in the street, spine broke, I think. He lay there moaning like a gutted pig while they smashed up the shop, and just before they went he died.' She slapped down a bowl of gruel in front of Bruiser. 'I don't hold with long-noses, but 'twas a terrible thing. Though they stripped him down to broken bones to get him through that window, not one of us dared squeak a word. Me, I just hoped they'd leave me and mine alone if we kept quiet. Other folk did the same. Not many here feel proud of themselves today.'

'They're devils,' said Bruiser dully.

'They're men, rotted by spirits and accursed by riding roughshod over Sussex these many years. They're us, Bruiser. Bart Laffam of Corndown was one of them, wasn't he?'

'Aye. They came to the forge first and we drank together. Young Bart, he were boasting about his Rosie, making us drink toasts to her, like, and as he grew wilder—you know how wild Bart can get.'

'Laffams have always been wild. 'Twas Abel Grey made 'em vicious.'

Bruiser pushed the gruel aside. 'Unless we clear off Grey's gang soon, we'll all turn into wolves.' Only yesterday he would have stayed a chief swingler all his days and been proud of it. Could have stomached even such a brutal murder as Larkworthy's, since he was a stranger. It was Widow Apps's blood which had made the difference; an innocent, and bred in Furnace Green. Also Bart's senseless laughing as he followed the rest inside the shop.

Tam sidled back inside the cottage, slopping water out of his buckets. 'Everyone's talking at the well.'

'They would be, wouldn't they, after such goings-on?' Sue ladled more gruel for him.

'Rare tittle-tattle talking. Like saying they ought to burn out the pack of rascals at Corndown.'

Sue exchanged glances with Bruiser. 'You've got your following, then. All you need is to harness them away from talk.'

'Attacking Corndown wasn't what I had in mind. You said Joseph's here. Is he bad hurt?'

'He's blind. For the moment, anyway. They tumbled him in the brine-trough like a flitch put to cure. Here, I'll take you through, or he'll think you've come for him again.'

Joseph was lying under a deerskin coverlet, his face layered with wet linen which Sue wrung out in the fresh water Tam had brought. Bruiser glimpsed inflamed red lids and oozing eye-rims edging darkened slits; raw lips, and the rest of Joseph's flesh like dirtied snow.

'Christ,' he said, and it was closer to prayer than an oath.

'Bywood?' mumbled Joseph. 'Larkworthy didn't care when you came for him and I don't either. I shan't ever draw another map. I don't want to live.'

Bruiser fumbled with a skein of unfamiliar feelings, wishing he had never come. Fat pompous Joseph whom he'd never liked; sanctimonious Amos, stupid Clemency. These were his victims too.

'Go on,' Sue said ruthlessly. 'Tell him why you came.'

Bruiser rubbed his nose. 'I'm sorry. I wanted to tell you that. And to say Abel Grey and his gang are no longer welcome here. We'll keep them out by force if that's the only way.'

There, it was done. Bruiser might bluff his way out of a rash promise made to Sue Sleech, but could never retract a pledge made to a gutless porker he despised, who nevertheless had come out of these past disastrous days with more credit than himself. But, infuriatingly, Joseph wasn't interested. He simply went on muttering about not drawing maps and turned his cloth-covered face to the wall like a sulky child.

'Hosmers were only ever good for ladling out piety with their wares,' Bruiser said disgustedly, although secretly he was pleased that Joseph was now behaving badly.

'They've done their part, and been punished for it. Now it's up to us.' Sue led the way back to her kitchen. 'I dunno about maps but blind folk are always badly placed, and him without anyone to care for him. Of course he thinks only of his plight.'

'He'll nest like a cuckoo by your hearth if you let him, so beware.' Bruiser's thoughts came back to the present with a rush, as, for the first, time he perceived the full extent of his folly. Too late. He had sworn in front of Joseph. 'I'd best call everyone together, I suppose. Abel sent last night to say he planned to bring his next run this way in four days' time.'

'Tam can pass the word. Say when and where.'

'Christ, I don't know. We always meet at the Black Bear to discuss a run.'

'This time you need everyone on the ridge to come, the Bear's not big enough. Anyway, Ned Oxley won't turn against Grey. Not fattened on profits like he is.'

'I know that,' Bruiser said irritably. Women always carped just when a man needed to turn things over quietly for a while.

'Well, it's no good leaving things in the air now you've decided what we ought to do,' Sue said unsympathetically. If it was up to her she would have called everyone together that same morning, but the men would need a lump of brawn like Bruiser to lead them if they were to stand against Abel Grey. Jesu save us, she thought, we'll need more than brawn.

'The smithy is too small,' he said slowly.

'Aye. The church then?'

'No!'

'Why not? You want everyone to come in from the farms as well, don't you? They can't be here before dark. You'll need space to talk where torches don't blow out in the wind.'

But Bruiser was adamant. He would not feel easy in the church. 'We'll meet by the oak. In Gaffer Parleben's tales the oak was always Furnace Green's meeting place.'

Sue snorted. 'You won't persuade many to come if it rains.'

'We'll meet at the oak,' he repeated, feeling reassured now he had thought of it.

Oddly enough, although Sue remained scornful over the notion of meeting under a tree in the dark, other people seemed to share Bruiser's sense of rightness. In winter, tales were told around most hearths, in which only the trimmings changed from one generation to the next: occasionally someone would possess enough imagination to tell a completely new story, but young and old alike usually preferred tales so familiar that they could anticipate every twist and horror. 'Alice's Hair Tree' was still a favourite, drawing the same squeals of laughter when the princess became completely bald as it had three centuries before. And so, through stories told and retold, most inhabitants of the ridge retained a fanciful notion of their history even if any sense of time had long ago been lost. They knew the spirits of their ancestors haunted the Meeting Oak, friendly guardians who could be propitiated if you circled the trunk three times and pressed the ball of your thumb against the bark. They accepted that the pool foretold the future for newly betrothed couples, and generations of children had shivered with fear to hear how wicked Queen Mary had piled up a pyre with her own hands and burned their ironmaster for all to see.

Almost by accident, Bruiser Bywood had struck on the right place to meet at such a pinching moment and people came as much because they knew that this night's gathering would add its mite to legend as because the smugglers had finally outstripped indulgence.

Among those missing was Sir Jonas Dyer who, although he did not live on the ridge, was the justice responsible for its conduct. Which only went to prove that after close on a hundred years at Riffield, the Dyers still weren't accepted as Wealdsmen, since he had heard nothing of wild doings at Furnace Green. The Laffams too were absent, and by design. Tam and the other messengers had been told not to go to Corndown, and also to warn everyone not to tell the Laffams about this meeting. Since the Laffams were Wealden to the marrow they would hear what was afoot within hours, but for a single night the stratagem worked.

The pool, which by day appeared little more than a green-scummed drinking place, at night became mysterious again. The sound of the wind always seemed more frightening there and the screech of owls more mournful. On the night after Widow Apps was killed the moon was hidden by cloud, and at first the oak seemed to stretch out threatening arms towards the early-comers, so their teeth fairly chattered with fright. But then more lanterns bobbed across the green, and everyone began to fill with a sense of great matters brewing. They shouted greetings as if at a wassail, broke into loud laughter and yelled encouragement when Bruiser climbed on a branch of the oak where everyone could see him. Nearly a century after Daniel Gage died and Jane Carpenter tended an acorn on his outcast grave, the Meeting Oak of Furnace Green had grown into a tough strong tree though still far from mature.

Once up on his branch, Bruiser suddenly became tongue-tied. Perhaps he half-expected the oak to put words in his mouth; certainly he had lacked the forethought to prepare the words he needed. 'Eh, neighbours . . .' he began, it seemed as good a beginning as any to him and the bobbing lanterns were a marvellous sight from above. 'Eh, good neighbours . . .'

'Eh, good blacksmith,' mimicked a voice from the back of the crowd and everyone laughed.

One of those cheeky Rabbits, Bywood thought, annoyed. He scowled, but still the words would not come, so he began again. 'Eh, good neighbours—'

This time the howl of mirth hit the wind and bounced, men and women alike sobbing with the drollery of a joke you had to be at a secret night-time meeting to appreciate.

Bruiser's fury shook the branch he stood on. 'Shut your teeth, you bag-puddings, and listen to me. We've finished with Abel Grey and his gang. They killed Widow Apps and she a harmless body buying beans for her pot. We've finished with 'em and so I'll send to tell all smugglers who behave like Grey.'

The lanterns steadied behind their smoky horn-eyes and everyone stopped laughing. 'About time too,' said old Jack Carpenter, tapping with his stick. 'If you'd listened to me you'd have finished with them a long time past.'

'They shouldn't a-killed Widow Apps but—'

'Aye 'tis all very well for Bruiser to talk bold, but how—'

A babble of voices made it clear that outrage at last spoke louder than coins or kegs of spirits; it was equally clear that fear of the smugglers would soon overwhelm the desire to break with them unless a plan of defiance was instantly decided, which everyone would subsequently be ashamed to disavow.

Bruiser understood this, having felt exactly the same himself, and immediately bellowed them into silence. 'Listen, all of you! There's a run planned for four days' time. The smugglers came yesterday to tell me the number of swinglers and leading-boys they wanted, and where. I say we send word that this time we won't be at the staging-point, nor do we want Abel Grey's runs through here again. Other runs of course, if the gang behaves itself decent. But not Grey, ever again.'

'They'll kill you if you send such a message, and hang your flayed pelt where the rest of us can see,' said Arthur Brown, thus becoming the first person to refer even obliquely to Riding Officer Larkworthy's swingling and death. An outsider and a long-nose, he was not their direct concern. Nevertheless, the dreadful details of his torment had contributed to the general sense of revulsion, nor would Widow Apps have been unlucky enough to encounter smugglers in a killing mood if they had not set out, drunk, to finish off Stephen Larkworthy.

Only to Arthur Brown was Larkworthy more important than Widow Apps, and so he made the mistake of reminding the listening crowd about his murder. Brown was

Grey's partner for onward distribution from Furnace Green, and knew that however lax and distant the government might be, the death of a Crown employee such as Larkworthy could never pass unremarked.

There was an angry growl as he spoke, and also a sense of satisfaction because Brown at least was under their thumb—an unlikeable man and easy game. 'I'd hang out their pelts instead!' yelled back Bruiser instantly. 'We're going to fight 'em, don't you see? If they try to come through Furnace Green—and they will—then we'll fight.' He understood fighting and was no longer at a loss for words.

'Do you know how many men Grey commands? Hundreds, if he calls out his followers from Rye and beyond.' Brown was beginning to edge away from the crowd.

'Rye! Now that's a powerful long way for anyone to bring his toadies. We breed the men we need right here on the ridge! Smugglers want to earn gold, not waste time wrangling with those determined to keep them out. If we're sure and stay sure, we'll win; and I say it'll be a right good fight.'

Everyone yelled back at Bruiser then, fists and faces slicked over with light from lanterns set swinging by the wind. 'We fight! We fight!'

The pool beyond glittered darkly too, as along its edge shadows pranced and gestured. Bruiser came down from his branch with a rush and led everyone in procession twice around its waters before they scattered back to their homes, although why such a ritual seemed fitting he could not have said.

In this manner Furnace Green went to war with Abel Grey's all-powerful gang.

Tomorrow Tam Sleech would be sent to Corndown with a message from the ridge: warn Grey to come this way no more. And if you Laffams wish to stay at Corndown, then you, too, must brawl elsewhere.

* * *

Everyone plodded to their work as usual in the following dawn.

Young men like Walt and Roger Frenchman of Newhouse Farm sang as they harnessed oxen in the shadow of Parson Syke's strange old tower, while their sires whistled or hummed, since dignity had to be preserved. Their wives were more thoughtful, as they studied their store cupboards and counted the cost of defying the smugglers, not just in immediate danger but in scanter living afterwards. 'But I'm that pleased the men will be drinking home-brewed for a while in place of they pesky spirits, I reckon 'tis worth it,' observed Matty Smith over a washing-slat to Sue Sleech. 'I'm fair weary of my John reeling home so late there's naught but the welcome-home flower awake to greet him.' So she, too, hummed a tune as she slapped at wet laundry.

Across the green at Danesdell, Master Carpenter neither whistled, sang nor hummed. He was cast in the dour Carpenter mould and had never been known to indulge in such trivialities. Instead he stumped about with the nearest approach to a spring in his step that had been seen for thirty years or more, and swore with less venom than usual when he caught some feckless Rabbits illegally gleaning his crops. Once Furnace Green was cut off from the smugglers' bounty—and a battle with Abel Grey would frighten all smugglers away for a while—a farmer would again be able to rule his domain how he liked, without fearing that his men could afford to throw curses back in his teeth and earn what they needed carrying kegs.

So he tapped a rhythm with his stick, a faint sour smile on his lips. Ah, the pity of it, he thought. No kin to follow me at Danesdell, just as a new time dawns when a man might rule his own again.

Further beyond Danesdell, on the track which led to Twisbury Hill, a considerable swathe of forest had been cleared during the harsh century while the ironworks declined and everyone scraped a living as best they could. Here ownership had long been disputed between the occupants of the ancient freehold of Ferenthe Ridge and the barony of Riffield. Masterless men and rogues took advantage of this uncertainty to live more or less out of sight until they established a dubious right to minute clearings of their own, pigs helped root up saplings, snuffle and chew out roots; their manure made poor soil richer, the earth piled up by their snouts went easier under the plough. Pigs were the husbandman's friend. The poor squatter clearing his patches and patiently burning away at the boles of immemorial oak most often survived on flitches of bacon and fresh-killed pork, two litters a year out of creatures which needed little to make them thrive, while also helping him in his task. Pigs or no, such work was very hard. The men who toiled in Pigpasture Woods, as this disputed area came to be called, were the toughest on the ridge, their women worn out by the time they were thirty.

William Locock, a footman, came there after he was dismissed for theft by Sir Amyas Dyer, and his descendants had put together a steep wet holding on which it was just possible to live. Later comers scrabbled a starveling subsistence alongside the Lococks and relied on the smugglers for the extra guineas they needed to keep their children fed. Most of these others carried the surname Pigg, since Furnace Green folk scarcely distinguished one from another; squatters came and went in such places almost unperceived, though the edge of Pigpasture Woods lay only half a mile from Furnace Green church. At this particular time, when new opportunities lured the footloose away to London and beyond, there were only six Piggs left in the woods, four men who originally were unrelated and two women. There were also children but until they survived long enough to help, only the women bothered with them. These six Piggs owned a few small enclosures and worked to clear more; they possessed pigs, an ox between them, and lived in leaking hovels. It was nothing unusual for them to sing as they worked, loud bawdy ditties which rang through the trees in time to the chink of their axes. They needed to sing when every day was so hard, but though they felt glum about Furnace Green deciding to give Grey's smugglers their come-uppance, on the morning following the gathering at the meeting oak they sang louder than ever.

The Piggs loved a fight.

They held clog-kicking bouts among themselves because they loved fighting so much, but regretfully had to allow their women to pull them apart just when the blood began to flow since they could not afford broken shins. They set badgers against each other in a pit, stole cocks if they could and trained even barnyard fowls to battle to the death; robbed passers-by and earned pence in bare-fisted fights on Riffield fairday. They scarcely knew how to wait now a proper battle was brewing; the dread of starveling winters to come when they would lack earnings from the smugglers was quite crowded out by excitement.

Swatch Locock of Pigpasture Farm was cast in a different mould. Despite his poor land and tiny fields, he was proud of his larger holding and ambitious to increase it. His wilier, more sophisticated mind, as well as his undisputed leadership of the Piggs, normally prevented him from joining their cruder pastimes which he might otherwise have enjoyed. He was, all the same, a skilled and entirely unsuspected poacher of Dyer deer. His philanderings on the other hand he did not trouble to disguise. As a widower Swatch considered all women his legitimate quarry, although he had not been noticeably less warm towards them when wed, but no matter how badly he behaved no woman had ever been heard to speak against him. A sinewy man, personable and proud, Swatch Locock on market day might have been mistaken for the master of much more than some illegal forest clearings.

And a fight, a proper fight, was something he, too, could enjoy without feeling he demeaned himself.

So one and all, at Pigpasture they sang.

'Bruiser said . . . there'd be a run . . . come four days,' chanted Swatch in time to the pitch of his hayfork.

'Four days to a fight,' sang Digger, his son.

'I'll be a-sharpening my axe,' bawled Snotty Pigg.

'I'll be stringing a bow.' Bows might be out of date, but for poachers like the Lococks and Piggs they remained a tool of their trade, the yew opposite Bruiser Bywood's smithy unanimously agreed to provide the whippiest, most desirable weapons for miles around.

'T'smugglers a-tole Bruiser this run's a-coming thisaway.'

'The run will come long-oh the ridge.'

'The fight will start long-oh my slope.'

'The blood will flow long-oh my ditch.'

Lococks and Piggs alike possessed simple tastes, although Swatch at least soon tired of ever more bloodthirsty and obscene variations of this chant. Everyone else was vastly pleased with it and choruses continued to echo through the trees for much of the next four days; the children squealed their own versions and covertly sharpened skinning knives, while Curly Peg and Annie Potdropper, the two Pigg women, stamped in time to the beat.

A fight—a praaper tur'ble fight—was luck beyond the dreams of avarice.

The rest of the village no longer felt so carefree.

Tam had not returned from his mission to Corndown, and when Sue went searching for him she encountered Bart, lounging against the bank where the Laffam trail left the main Ockham track. 'Have you seen my Tam? He should have reached Corndown near midday but he's not come home for his supper.'

'Aye, I've seen the brat.'

'Where did he go?'

'Nowhere,' Bart negligently picked his teeth. 'He's in our barn.'

'Eh, the pesky lad! He must a-known I'd be worried if he weren't home as the sun went down. You just wait until I take my washing paddle to him,' said Sue indignantly.

'Abel Grey took his whip to him, so there's no need to waste your strength, mistress.'

She paled. 'What is it you're saying, Bart Laffam? Abel Grey was at Corndown?'

'Aye.'

'But—but even a devil like him couldn't . . . Tam scampers messages for everyone, earning pence.'

'Not messages to Abel which tell him his gang isn't welcome at Furnace Green.'

But Sue was already overwhelmed by panic and mouthing disjointed words about the brat being only ten years old. As if age mattered, thought Bart, disgusted. Actually, remembering Tam's admiration of himself, Bart had tried to tell Abel the boy was only young; until Grey had pointed out that defiance, not age, was what mattered, and the insolence which tried to tell Laffams how they ought to live. So Bart threw Sue off, sending her sprawling. 'Go back to Furnace Green, woman. Tell them Grey will take a flail instead of a whip to the next person who disobeys him.'

She wept, her face slobbered with dust. 'Let me past. I have to reach Tam.'

'Stop jabbering and listen. If you try to go past now, Abel will thrash you like he thrashed the boy.'

'I don't care! Let me past!'

Bart swore. He hadn't enjoyed watching a squealing child beaten bloody, but beatings were commonplace after all. Nothing really, compared to a swingling, or skinning a crippled man through an upper window like meat through a mincer. Furnace Green needed a quick lesson, or rebellion against Grey's methods might spread like an infection through all of east Sussex. Then he, Bart, would hang. Soon, Sue's sobs rasped at his restraint and he kicked her where she snivelled; the ferocious edge smugglers like Grey put on a man's temper became sharper with each day Bart spent in his company. 'Go home, I say. Tell everyone the next run comes through like we planned, and if the packmen, boys and swinglers we need aren't waiting, why, Tam'll be thrashed again and I reckon Abel won't stop afore he's dead.'

Sue wept afresh and began to plead with him, but this made Bart so uneasy that he left her. He knew she retained enough sense not to try and reach Corndown now he'd made clear Tam's position as a hostage, and as for himself —why, womanish qualms vanished the moment he was back among like-minded Laffams.

The whole village was thrown into confusion when Sue Sleech ran keening up the street. For a while everyone's wits were scattered by yet another unimaginable happening, and they hurried about quite aimlessly. Although Riding Officer Larkworthy and Widow Apps had already been killed by the smugglers, few Sussex people felt much sympathy towards riding officers and everyone accepted that Meggie Apps's murderers had been drunk. Drunken deeds might be wicked, but they were explicable. Furnace Green had made its stand because enough was enough of anything, not because they perceived the nature of the monster which had grown up in their midst. Now, suddenly, they saw the monster clearly: with blood on its muzzle and crouched to devour them.

Their heads and knees swam, their bellies turned to gall as they stared back into its demented eyes; stark terror the name of what they felt. He's mad, they said. Abel Grey's a madman run loose who's started killing children. But really they knew he wasn't mad. It was their ridge of Sussex soil, with its single street of cottages and handful of familiar faces which had run mad without them noticing, because they had allowed vileness to become commonplace. Their own sane workaday world which was revealed as supping heedlessly with the Devil.

'We could go to Sir Jonas Dyer, he's the magistrate and ought to know what to do,' suggested Roger Frenchman, brought from Newhouse by the tidings of disaster.

'No.' Sue lifted a tear-bloated face. 'Grey'd kill Tam the moment he heard we'd laid information against him.'

'What could a bladder of lard like Sir Jonas do, anyway?' Will Sleech, Sue's husband, was a shepherd and often did not return to Furnace Green for weeks on end, but one of the Rabbits had given him the news of his son's whipping.

'He'd bring his grooms and suchlike, and trample everywhere without seeing a smuggler,' Bruiser answered glumly for them all. Furnace Green had never become used to running off to either the Scovells or the Dyers whenever they needed help.

'Ned Oxley,' mumbled Joseph Hosmer. His lips were still raw and his eyes swathed in linen, but he had stumbled down to the smithy when the rest of the village gathered there. 'He could visit Rose at Corndown as a matter of course, and spy out our chances of getting Tam away. The smugglers won't mind him, they'd reckon he's one of their own.'

'Isn't he?' demanded Swatch Locock sceptically.

'I'll go and ask.' Bruiser stood up. 'I reckon Ned will help Tam if he can.'

'Arthur Brown said that the oftener brats were thrashed the better, what's all the fuss about? Maybe Oxley feels the same.'

'They don't get thrashed in revenge by the likes of Abel Grey,' answered Joseph, which summed it up. Bart had implied to Sue that Tam was still alive, but he might easily be dead. And all of them here had sent him to Corndown without ever dreaming of danger, like the simpletons they were, that was the rub.

Bruiser found Ned Oxley swabbing his plank bar. He knew there was a great hubbub going on from which he had so far been excluded as a smugglers' man, and was philosophic about it. When he learned that the village had told the smugglers to keep out he had been astonished, but on reflection decided that such foolhardiness would neither last nor be successful. The Black Bear could afford a wait to recover its custom, when everyone would be back with a thirst and their tails between their legs.

He threw down his cloth as Bruiser entered. A convivial man, he was glad of any company. 'So you're the first to recover your wits, then. Have a daffy on the house.'

'Ah, and don't I need it!' Bruiser drank the neat spirits thirstily. 'You seen Rose lately?'

'A week gone, it must be. The lass is grown as lazy as a cat.'

'Then it wouldn't seem strange if you went to see her?'

'Me tramp to Corndown and leave every no-good in Furnace Green to help himself out of my kegs? Not likely. There's naught wrong with Rose, except she's growing slatternly with Corndown ways.'

'But you could go,' persisted Bruiser. 'You see—' He plunged into an account of Tam and Abel Grey and Sue howling like a hound, which became even more confused when Ned forgetfully refilled both Bruiser's tankard and his own.

In the smithy they waited anxiously for Bruiser's return. Every corner was crammed with people, while their children slept on the grass outside.

'Do you think Ned's gone directly to Corndown?' asked Sue, her voice nearly washed out with weeping.

I hope not, thought Joseph. Damned fools, the pair of them. If Ned went pelting over to Corndown in the middle of the night, then Grey would know for sure that he didn't come to visit Rose.

Joseph fiddled ceaselessly, irritatingly, with his bandage. His face felt stiff and puckered-up, his eyes like dried plums in grit-filled sockets. But when Sue changed his linen strips before she went off looking for Tam, he had seen misty shapes floating in a junket of curdled vision and he longed to peep again. Shapes, however opaque, meant he wasn't blind. Shapes were hope, the chance of not living the rest of his life as a pauper away from maps. He tried hard to think about Tam, but found it impossible to keep his mind away from his own hurts for very long. If he wasn't blind then he could go calling on Widow Toogood again, bask in her admiration perhaps when he let slip how brave he'd been in opposing Abel Grey.

Almost simultaneously, they all heard the noise of voices

singing, quarrelling raucously and then singing again as they came closer.

'It's Bruiser and Ned,' Sue said furiously, and shot off the plough beam where she had been sitting. When the two men appeared in the doorway, she dealt them such a couple of buffets that both fell down and began to fight, each thinking the other had attacked him. 'Sober them up!' screeched Sue. 'Jesu, throw them in the pond and let them drown!'

Really, no one knew whether to laugh or join their fury to hers. They wanted to laugh when it was so droll to see niffy-naffy Ned Oxley thrown in the forge pond beside Bruiser, whom no one normally dared to touch no matter what he did. They were also truly sorry for Sue and would have hated to increase her anguish by laughing. Only the Rabbits did not gather round the pond to watch two wet and shamefaced men struggle out of the water, though they were usually the first to waste time enjoying any sight, the last to mind their own affairs. Now they stood in a gaggle, heads together and whispering.

'Missus.' A Rabbit tugged at Sue's sleeve.

'Leave me be!' she snapped, and Bruiser leapt howling as she kicked him while he spat out duckweed.

'Nay, missus, listen. Your boy be safe at Edenham.'

She swung round, shook the Rabbit until his teeth rattled. 'I-am-not—'

'Nay, missus. 'Tis no have-on. T'old gaffer hobbled all the way from there to tell us. Rose brought the boy out. They're by our hearth, being the nearest place to Corndown, like.'

Sue broke into another wail, this time of relief, and hugged him until his ribs creaked; undersized Rabbit kicking his boots up in her grip until this time everyone did laugh as word spread that Tam was out. Then they all surged away from the pond, some to stand talking excitedly under the yew while the rest ran after Sue and Will Sleech, already on their way to Edenham.

Clearly it wasn't safe to let them go alone, when for all

anyone knew the smugglers might already be searching for Tam.

'We're a-going to have our fight!' shouted young Digger Locock.

'The fight will start long-oh my slope,' yelled Mingy Pigg.

'The smugglers will turn tail upalong the ridge.'

'And we'll be a-chasing after!' panted Roger Frenchman. 'Sue, for pity's sake don't caper off so fast. It's a long time since I had to run, a-following oxen.'

But Sue's massive body was weightless with relief, and she maintained a lunging headlong rhythm all the way to Edenham which left her escort strung out along the track like so many coins counted out of a miser's purse. She burst into the old millhouse kitchen apparently not even out of breath. 'Where's my Tam?'

A gypsy-looking Rabbit woman tilted her hand in a graceful gesture of succour. 'By our hearth, mistress.'

Sue immediately became brisk again. She was not really demonstrative and before Tam vanished if anyone had asked her whether she loved her youngest son she would have been hard put to answer; children died so easily it was unwise to become too fond of them. Only the barbaric and unimagined nature of Tam's fate had overset her, and in her relief she began at once to scold him.

Then she paused, pursing her lips like a witch, because the moment she touched him she knew Tam was close to death. Immediately, she swallowed her scoldings and began to croon a lullaby he might recognize in his fever. The gypsy Rabbit nodded approval. 'I dressed his hurts as best I could. Keep him quiet and his senses may come back in time.'

'Why's he so sick?' demanded Will, his father.

'Rose said he was whipped by Abel Grey.' Her warm moist lips shaped the words indifferently: Rabbits accepted life as it came.

'But how badly hurt is he?'

'As badly as anyone but a fool would expect, when Abel

Grey whips a child. Rose said he didn't intend to kill, but then Grey isn't familiar enough with brats to know when to stop.'

A short fleshy Rabbit man, reeking of sweat and onions, smacked a girl on the bottom and bade her offer broth from the pot. Stirred ashes in the hearth revealed a handsome fireback and brick-patterning but both were so splashed, sooted and ash-covered that any detail had gone unseen for generations. Rush lights flickered in clay blobs pressed to the oak hearth-beam, which charred spoon-shaped hollows year by year from its surface at the same time as layers of greasy deposit were laid down everywhere else. Edenham's kitchen was also too small for all the people now crammed into it, drinking the Rabbits' broth. Sue screeched whenever boots trampled too close to Tam, the atmosphere was stifling and everyone began to scratch. Fleas were commonplace, but the Rabbits bred insects in swarms, each jabbing like a worker-bee.

Swatch Locock was the first to leave, and Bruiser followed him. 'Christ, what a pit. I never knew before how many Rabbits there were, teeming like maggots on a carcass.'

Swatch grinned. 'They look the same, that's why. Dark and dirty.'

'They say Rose has gone back to Corndown.'

'Aye, why not? Grey's left, they also say, or she'd never have been able to get the boy out. Bart won't hurt her, no matter what she's done.'

'I wouldn't be too sure of that, but it's his business.'

Locock shrugged. If Bruiser couldn't see that Rose was very well able to flaunt her ripe body until Bart cared for nothing else, then it wasn't worth explaining. 'Grey will have left because of the run. It's due on the third night from now.'

'I know,' said Bruiser irritably.

'What will you do? Grey's certain to stick to his plan of bringing it this way, just to spite us.'

'Fight, I suppose.'

'Damme, of course we're going to fight! That's agreed. Did the Rabbits tell you what else Rose said?'

'Aye. Unless we let Grey through, help his gang as willingly as we've always done, he'll burn every house in Furnace Green.'

'Well?'

'So we've a choice,' said Bruiser belligerently.

'We chose already. To fight. I'm not aiming to change my mind just because Grey's whipped Tam Sleech and threatens more. We knew why we had to fight after Widow Apps.'

'But burning Furnace Green—'

'If we lose. But I don't fight to lose and I disremember you ever did, neither.' Locock smiled as he felt Bywood straighten in the dark.

'Nay, I never did. But everyone will have heard what Abel's said by now, those cursed Rabbits repeated it often enough. We mayn't find so many willing to fight any more.'

'We've said we'll fight and we shall. Don't you start thinking different, and no one else will either.'

Swatch knew that Furnace Green would not follow him as they would Bruiser. For one thing, he was still regarded as little better than a squatter and people had their sense of what was proper. For another he lacked Bruiser's fighting reputation, although he could already see quite clearly how they ought to set about overthrowing the smugglers. Ah well, he would just have to work through Bruiser, that was all. 'You said the run was coming up past Twisbury this time,' he added.

'Aye, and Grey'll keep it that way, just to rub our noses in his power. Bring his pack-trains along the street itself, I daresay, instead of transferring packs at Edenham. Then no one could pretend afterwards that he hadn't won.'

'All the better. There's a heap of secret trails through the forest but only one way along the ridge. If we don't provide the swinglers and leaders Grey will need, even if he brings more smugglers than usual they'll have their hands full with strings of mules and horses. We lay for them above Pigpasture and run the bastards off.'

As soon as he considered carefully what Locock had said, Bruiser began to feel more cheerful. It hadn't previously occurred to him that without the ridge's willing help the smugglers would be handicapped by their goods, their defensive strength considerably reduced. 'We'll talk again tomorrow, you know the ground at Pigpasture better than anyone,' he promised as they parted, which set Swatch whistling as he strode home, past the dark waters of the pool and quietly rustling oak.

The next day Tam seemed better, his fever fading and his torn flesh less puffy than before. Then something happened. Quite what, Sue wasn't sure; you seldom did know why people sickened or why those expected to die sometimes recovered. Perhaps a child lacked strength to replace lost blood, or to sustain the pain he suffered. Whatever the cause, on the following night Tam weakened rapidly and in the morning he was dead.

Word of his death spread rapidly in the wake of scuttering Rabbits. Bruiser heard it by his anvil, where he was working like a man possessed to sharpen spikes and ancient blades; Ned Oxley heard it in his taproom and forgave the village for his ducking. Instead he began lovingly to scour and grease a musket his great-great-grandfather had brought back from the Civil War nearly a hundred years before, which had the reputation of breaking the shoulder of any man courageous enough to fire it. Arthur Brown heard about Tam when one of Wyses' windows was shattered by a stone, and two of his own labourers stood idly by while clods of filth followed it into his parlour. He bolted doors up tight, cursing as loudly as everyone else, but in his case at the threatened break-up of a prosperous trade.

Rose Laffam (Rose Oxley still to those who set store by church marryings) heard of it at Corndown, and when Bart came in to bid her farewell before he went to join Grey's run, he found her pulling dough in angry jerks. 'What's the upset, sweeting?'

'Tam Sleech died.'

'Oh aye, I heard. Didn't you think he would when Abel held the whip? As well for you he did, or we'd have a fine time explaining how he escaped. Now Grey need never know.'

Rose lifted a desolate face to his, her soft cheeks slack, mouth pinched. 'Don't you see? One way or t'other, it's finished for us. Before, if the village won they'd have left Corndown alone. Laffams have as much right on the ridge as anyone and once Grey's gang went elsewhere, few would have cared whether you followed him or not.'

'Ah, don't worry.' He kissed her, groping as always for her breasts. 'How can they win? Abel will make sure no one takes him by surprise. Christ, we'll be with him and there isn't a hiding place anywhere around Furnace Green the Laffams don't know. If Bruiser and his mob don't run when they hear us coming, they will at the first shot. I never heard of anyone owning so much as a pistol at Furnace Green, did you?'

'My da has a gun.'

Bart hooted with laughter. 'That old cannon! Sweeting, are you run mad? Ned will be with us.'

Rose merely looked at him remotely and with pity. 'It don't matter who fights nor wins. The Laffams are finished here.'

But Bart was becoming angered by such obtuseness. 'You'll swallow your words when I come back in the morning, with gossip enough to fill a dozen winters. Christ, I shall puke up laughing, to see the likes of old Jack Carpenter leaping out of ambush with his blackthorn, and at his side Joe Hosmer wi' his face tied up! Nor I've never met a Rabbit yet who didn't run at the first sniff of trouble. We'll win, never fear.'

'So then you watch Abel burn the village. Your village. Everyone you were reared with driven into the forest to starve through the winter; see then how you like living at Corndown. How long could even Laffams last with only hatred for a neighbour?' Rose went back to her dough.

Bart eyed her back in baffled scorn. He wanted Rose to kiss fortune into him before he went, a ritual which had begun as a joke but assumed unexpected importance now it was lacking. Then the kitchen door was kicked open and a gathering of other Laffams bellowed impatiently at him from the yard. With a sound between a curse and an entreaty he turned and plunged out to join them.

The sound seemed to release Rose from self-absorption. Blood rushed suddenly into her face, and she ran out after him. 'Don't go!' She hugged him fiercely, without caring about good-natured jeering from the other men. Most had pistols in their belts and were filled with anticipation over the prospect of a real fight to break the monotony of a run.

Bart smacked great hungry kisses back at her. 'I knew you wouldn't let me down, Rosie! You gurt fine bitch, you.'

'Don't go.'

'Of course I'm going! What kind of booby do you think I am?' He squeezed her belly affectionately; only a week ago they had decided she must be breeding. 'Take care of the little 'un now, and I'll be back in the morning.'

Rose turned to Trapper, undisputed king of the Laffams. 'You could keep them all here.'

Trapper stared back at her sombrely. 'I'm sworn up. Laffams been with the owlers since before my da's da was born, and then afore again. They're our living and that's how it'll always be.'

'You can live off Corndown.' He's naught but a toad, she thought. Standing there all pouched into wrinkles and greed.

He chuckled. 'Give over, lass. There's a deal too many of us for one holding, and can you see Laffams a-following oxen all the weary days until we die?' He hitched a bag of home-cast bullets higher on his shoulder and strode out of the yard, all the other grown male Laffams trailing after him. 'Women have their fancies when they're breeding their first brat,' he said aside to Bart, so the boy would not feel ashamed. 'Don't worry your head about it.'

'Give a few years and if it's a boy he'll be coming with

us,' agreed Bart, and began to whistle. Rose had kissed luck into him, that was what mattered.

Up in Pigpasture Woods most things were in chaos, Furnace Green being a great place for windy grumbles as well as resolution. Only Swatch Locock stayed minding his own business while everyone else ran with their complaints to Bruiser: Will Sleech wanted to strike the first blow; Ned Oxley demanded that someone be ordered to help fire his gun; the Rabbits turned somersaults from excitement and a desire to avoid hard work; the Piggs infuriated everyone by digging their own personal traps for the smugglers to fall into without so much as mentioning what they were doing.

Locock watched the swarming figures with an indulgent eye and late in the afternoon sauntered up the hill towards them, carrying a well-honed sickle. 'You all ready?' he enquired.

Bruiser glared at him. 'As ready as we'll ever be, and precious little you've done to help.'

'There seemed enough help for whatever you had in mind,' Swatch answered blandly.

'Aye . . . well. D'you realize those damned Piggs have dug a trap right across the path for us all to fall into unless we watch our feet a sight more smartly than the smugglers?'

'Then maybe we'd better take up position away back from their pits. Let the smugglers past and attack them part-way along the line.'

'They'll see the pits, don't you realize? Those accursed Laffams know every bracken clump on the ridge even if Grey doesn't! Some of them will be out in front and it's no good the Piggs saying they can cover up what they've done; any Laffam can smell dug earth as easily as a hound.'

'Then like I said, take up your position nearer Twisbury. The smugglers be less likely to expect us away from the village, surely, and when a warning comes back about the pits they'll have to stop. It won't matter then whether they fall in or not; we attack while they're all mixed up with a couple of hundred horses on a narrow path.'

Grudgingly, Bruiser agreed, since during a long day's arguing he had decided on no clear plan of action, and by dusk everyone was coaxed into position, including Sue Sleech who lay with a skinning knife in her hand. Signals were agreed and instructions dinned into the thickest head. All this was Bruiser's doing while Swatch Locock hung about looking inconspicuous and throwing in occasional suggestions; in reality the dispositions were Locock's, communicated by a variety of means.

When everyone was in place, Swatch chose a moss-lined hollow for his hide and promptly went to sleep. He felt satisfied by his success in getting everyone settled before the smugglers, a slipshod bunch grown careless with success, sent spies ahead of their convoy, and until their approach there was no more he could do. He had also taken care that he could keep an eye on both Bruiser and the Piggs from his chosen hollow, who struck him as the most irrational elements in the ridge's fighting force.

Joseph lay further back, his bandages removed in case the glint of linen gave away the ambush. His heart beat so uncomfortably fast he needed to swallow often and kept licking his lips. Of all those behind bushes and up trees, he was the one who most heartily disliked fighting in any form, although only the Piggs and Will Sleech looked forward to the night with unclouded relish. His eyes now ached rather than hurt and he could see quite well in the dark; in daylight they still watered too persistently for him to be certain that his sight would ever be of much use again. He laid his face on his arm dejectedly. How could he ever repair his fortunes when this was over, one way or the other, which only a short time before had looked so hopeful?

A long time passed in such dreary speculations before Joseph became aware of sounds drifting down the track from Twisbury Hill, making his flesh leap on his bones.

These soon hardened into the thud of hoofs and creak of rope, also indefinable stirrings as wild creatures bolted through the undergowth. Terror made his eyes water even more than bright daylight and by the time the first shape passed his hiding place, Joseph could not tell whether it was man or beast. Charlie Portnell at his side whispered that it was a group of four men loping easily along, their heads turning at each stride. Laffams all, set to spy out the way ahead. But neither Joseph nor Charlie stirred, all the people of Furnace Green lying as still as veterans. We attack together and achieve complete surprise, or we lose, Swatch had said to Bruiser. So Bruiser cuffed and swore and cajoled until each man understood that his family's lives and home depended on a plan which, by then, had become Bruiser's own.

The Laffam scouts passed the Piggs (Snotty kept face down by Swatch's fist on his scruff); passed the place where Will and Sue Sleech lay quite literally licking their lips over the imminent chance of vengeance for Tam, and they saw nothing.

They saw the Piggs' pits though.

A nightjar's call whirred back in warning through the trees and a short time afterwards a figure ran back light-footed, presumably to report what they had found.

By then a line of pack-beasts was strung out all the way from Twisbury Hill to Pigpasture Woods: Bruiser had lost count of how many had passed him. Too many, and a great number of smugglers. 'Now,' he heard Swatch whisper as soft as the airs inside the wood.

But faced by the smugglers' strength, Bruiser hesitated, incapable of committing the fate of everyone in Furnace Green to the chance result of a scrimmage in the dark.

Locock spat on his hands for luck, and stood. He knew in his bones that this was the moment, before the smugglers abandoned their led beasts and gathered into fighting groups. Let Bruiser take the credit if all went well, and he the infamy if not, but they mustn't wait another instant. Putting his fingers in his mouth, Swatch pealed out the triple call agreed on as a signal of attack, while Bruiser still clawed unavailingly at his arm.

From behind bushes and out of gullies men sprang, clutching the weapons of husbandry. Charlie Portnell's brother Jem dropped out of an oak and struck a smuggler on the neck with his massive boots; Will Sleech cut a throat almost before anyone else had moved. Within seconds a tumultuous hand-to-hand fight developed along nearly half a mile of path, pack-beasts panicking among swearing men and ill-aimed blows.

Each inhabitant of the ridge fought in a pair as Swatch had earlier suggested, maintaining a surprising discipline considering that this was the first fight to the death any of them had known. The second man in each pair was the older or less skilful of the two, but protected his partner's back, and Swatch had also said to cut as many pack-girths as they could reach. Most remembered this and snatched dangerous seconds to slash at rope and leather: kegs slipped and banged against unwary legs, making the animals bolt in fear, chance cuts terrifying them still further. Instinctively, the smugglers tried to stop their cargo from vanishing into the forest, turned backs and split attention offering easier targets for attack.

Abel Grey himself was bellowing further up the track, cut off from the fighting by a press of men and beasts, which was fortunate or a pity depending on how badly you wanted a chance to put a sickle in his guts.

Swatch Locock fought fast and cunningly, reckoning it was better to send men screeching out of the fight than worry overmuch about killing them. He was forced forward by the pressure of that roaring throng, jostled by headstrong mules, his head nearly blown off when Ned Oxley fired his gun with a boom like the last trump. Sweat streamed down his face, dripped into his mouth; even a life spent clearing forest did not prepare a man for this.

A shape loomed up in the dark and he slashed at its legs as he had before, checked and snatched back when he recognized Trapper Laffam.

The power behind his blade was lost just in time, the edge turned harmlessly by leather; for an instant the two men stared at each other, mouths open with the incoherent shouts of battle. Then Trapper drew back his lips in a hangman's smile and lunged, quick as a stoat. Laffams lived by self-interest, not sentiment.

Locock dodged, knowing he could not dodge fast enough, and saw Will Sleech appear behind Trapper's back; Trapper's face turning earthly even before he fell, because Will had driven a pitchfork so hard into his back that the tines sprouted from his chest and impaled him, thrashing, to the ground.

Will scarcely stopped to look but plunged off at once, yelling, 'For Tam! For Tam!' Soon others took up his call as a kind of battle cry, the Piggs chanting it, the Rabbits humming contentedly as they scavenged on the debris of battle.

Another enormous roar echoed through the trees as Ned Oxley succeeded in loading and firing his gun a second time; twigs flew overhead and the remaining pack-beasts bolted, upending everyone in their path.

Like a prudent man, Swatch dived for cover and discovered he was sharing a gorse bush with two kegs and a pack-saddle. He thrust them thriftily further out of sight before coming to his feet again, to encounter Joseph staring vaguely at an empty stretch of track. 'Where's everyone gone?'

Locock began to laugh. 'We ran them off.'

'Did we?' He sighed. 'Thank God for that. Do you know I was surprised how much I could see in the dark? Perhaps if I shaded a lantern I might be able to draw out part of a map each night.'

'Aye, why not? Should I tell you what I'd do now if I was you? Go as fast as I could back to your shop and fetch a cart. Then come back here to pick up kegs and contraband before anyone else thinks of it. Like that, you'll have good stock to sell while you discover how much map-making you can manage.'

Joseph blinked. 'The smugglers took our horse when they killed Larkworthy.'

'God damme!' said Locock in exasperation. 'How many horses are there swilling around the ridge tonight? Here, I'll catch you one.'

He plunged into the undergrowth and returned with a nag too footsore to enjoy bolting far, without a ceremony heaved Joseph up and gave the beast a slap on the rump. He considered that Joseph was owed a few months' living by the ridge, but could not guarantee to keep his temper with such a nodcock for long.

Once the smugglers began to retreat they gave ground fast, having nothing to fight for except a cargo which was now dispersed. Abel Grey howled at them and fired his pistol indiscriminately at anyone who ran past him, but this had the effect of scattering his force still further and retreat became a rout. There were plenty of excuses a prudent smuggler could offer later, and plead that their first task was surely to scour the forest for dozens of horses and their burdens.

The villagers of Furnace Green, except Swatch Locock, his son Digger and the Rabbits, who were industriously recovering scattered contraband for themselves, panted in pursuit until the lower slopes of Twisbury Hill finally snatched the breath out of them, then they dropped where they stood in exultant sweat-soaked heaps.

'We did it,' said Bruiser, awed, when he was able to lift his head from his knees.

'By Christ, we did it,' agreed Will Sleech savagely. 'My pitchfork is still caught in Trapper's chest.'

Bruiser shivered. Trapper was Furnace Green, and before tonight they had been trading colleagues. 'You didn't have to kill our own.'

'My Tam were whipped to death at Corndown, weren't he?' Will lunged to his feet. 'Who's coming there with me?'

'Where?'

'To Corndown, and burn out a nest of rats. We ran off

the smugglers, now we'll rid ourselves of Laffams for good and all.'

'You killed Trapper, isn't that enough?' Bruiser grabbed at him.

Will shook him off. 'No, it isn't. They would have burned our homes if they'd won, wouldn't they? Killed Tam, didn't they? So I killed them and now I be going to burn them.'

The Piggs hailed this with delight and trotted along behind Will, breathily composing a new chant. A handful of others followed, boys mostly, who didn't want the only night of real excitement in their lives to end. The rest shrugged and walked back down the track talking boisterously among themselves, inflating each deed and moment of the fight until, astonishingly quickly, no one was quite sure what had really happened.

Meanwhile, Will Sleech led his little following cross-country down the wide gulley which lay below Pigpasture Wood and then up the other side, cutting across Danesdell land towards Corndown.

The first Rose knew of the outcome of the fight was a leap of flame from Corndown old barn. All around the house and cottages which formed the core of Laffam settlement were barns and yards, the oldest nearest to the house. So the crackle of flames was immediately audible and burning strands of straw soon began to settle in the houses' thatch.

Most of the Laffam women and children had gathered to wait in Trapper's kitchen: drinking spirits mixed with hot water, talking desultorily but lapsing often into silence, only a few of the more hardened sleeping as the night wore on. They knew tonight was different from a normal run and for once idleness was no pleasure. Indeed, Laffam perfunctoriness over household tasks contributed to sudden shrill quarrels, slapped faces and children howling underfoot. By the hour before dawn, even those who remained wakeful had fallen silent.

'I can smell smoke,' said Sarah, Trapper's woman, suddenly.

By now Rose heard crackles, too. 'So Furnace Green won.'

'Hold your tongue!' snapped Sarah, and threw open the door so they all saw the flames at once, brilliantly yellow against paling sky. She let out a screech and ran acoss the yard, but even as she ran more flame exploded from a different direction: in a new barn this time, where kegs were stored for sale in the booming settlement of Tunbridge Wells. Smoke and sparks burst almost instantly through the barn's tiled roof, a roar of heat rocking the ground as burning spirits and barrel-staves gave the fire a white-hot heart which put it out of control within seconds. The women stood still, stricken by such a sight, and the small space between cottages and pig byre where they sheltered was suddenly filled with fear—fear for their men and fear, too, for Corndown which held all of their lives, as well as for themselves.

'We have to try and save our homes. The barns are lost.' Sarah ran back to the well. The other women grabbed the empty kegs and pitchers which always lay discarded in odd corners at Corndown, while Rose wound frantically at the well pulley. Behind her another stack of casks exploded and she felt the wind blow more sharply as heat sucked in air to feed the flames. Burning wood flew up through collapsing roofs and spilled spirit flared eerily across a yard to ignite a stable and ricks beyond.

Some of the women were running about looking for missing children or belongings: impossible to tell who might be lost when women, old men, children and untethered beasts swirled in the press together. Sarah yelled curses at them until a line formed between the well and cottages, whose roofs were already giving off clouds of smoke and steam from embers embedded out of sight in thatch. A gable-end began to bulge, the timber dairy to show tiny glowing lines of light.

'Leave it,' Rose ran to where Sarah stood nearest to the flames, splashing water wherever she could reach. 'It's too dangerous.'

'Danger!' Sarah spat, hair stuck by sweat to her face. ''Tis my place.'

'All you're doing is make a show of yourself. If you looked like beating the flames they'd stop you fast enough,' Rose answered coldly. She was seething with anger and felt no pity at all. The Laffams had behaved like clodpates, and because of it her happiness was destroyed.

Sarah looked over her shoulder and for the first time saw the group of motionless figures outlined against the flames, torches still smouldering in their hands.

As Rose finished speaking there was a blinding flash and a report which snapped their ears as a whole shed full of kegs blew up at once. One of the watching men squealed as a gob of flame arched out of the sky and momentarily engulfed him: Rose recognized Sammy Smith whose fondlings she had enjoyed before she followed Bart to Corndown. His jerkin and hair were instantly set on fire, and he began capering like a demented soul instead of rolling in the slop underfoot, while everyone else stared dumbfounded at so terrible a sight. Will Sleech was the first to move, grabbing a bucket from one of the women and throwing water over him. By then it was too late. Sammy's screams became moans as he spun around and round snapping at himself like a dog, before collapsing in a blackened heap on which ghost-like flames still flickered.

'Go. Get out of Corndown and never come back.' Will's voice was hoarse when he turned back to the women, but his stare remained implacable.

Sarah sat down on the well parapet. 'This is my home and here I stay.'

Will simply caught her by the shoulders and heaved her round to face the cottages and farmhouse. During the lost moments while everyone stared at Sammy Smith's death, bricks had begun to glow, the timbers to crumble. The roof was burning, the great stone casement which long ago had been stolen from Ockham Abbey dropped outwards on the ground, leaving the oak settles and the table by the hearth, where only that afternoon Rose had kneaded dough, obscenely revealed. For an instant the familiar kitchen looked unchanged, as if Trapper might come roaring in to demand his soup at any moment. Then the wind blew flame from one side of the room to the other and familiarity vanished.

A moan rippled through the women, because by now the other cottages were burning too. Only Sarah tossed her head and smiled, lips drawn back. 'A pox on you, Will Sleech. May the Devil rot thy bowels and consume thy prick before thine eyes. May thy children die and thy women scorn thee in thy misery.'

'My son, Tam, is dead already at the hand of Grey and the Laffams,' answered Will stonily, and struck her across the mouth. 'Get out, the pack of you, or I'll throw you down the well with Sam.' While everyone stood rooted, he picked up Sammy Smith's blackened body and heaved it down the well, the sole water supply for Corndown steading. Then he cut the bucket loose, kicked in the pulley, tore down the timber supports around the well shaft in a kind of berserk fury and threw these, too, down the well, thus preventing anyone from being able to fetch up Sammy's body before the spring was fouled.

As soon as this was done he turned and left at a half-run, as if the Devil already hunted him, his followers trailing shamefacedly after and apparently forgetful that they had been told to make sure the women left.

Dawn had come by then, the suck of fire-driven wind dying away as the last timbers burned. A few bewildered animals stood on their own long shadows thrown by the rising sun; ill-cultivated fields showed silver through smoke clinging like thick mist to the ground, the sky a luminous shade between blue and grey which promised a hot day to come. Birds circled and swooped in a nearby stand of beech, the snap of cooling brick a counterpoint to their song.

In the farmyard one of the children began to wail, swiftly followed by others who until then had been held dumb by wonder.

‘What can we do?’ a hushed voice asked.

‘Where are our men?’ demanded another.

But Sarah scorned to answer such foolishness and while they watched walked slowly across to Corndown’s blackened doorstep, now lacking a door or wall behind it. There she sat down and threw her apron over her head.

Rose went over and snatched the apron down. ‘We can’t stay here. Even if we wanted to, no one on the ridge would help us to set up again.’

Sarah’s face never flickered and her eyes stayed closed. ‘I were born here and here I die.’

‘There’s no call to die unless you try to stay through the winter without so much as a bin of corn or a roof for shelter.’

‘Trapper’s dead.’

‘You can’t know that!’ To Rose, Trapper seemed immortal.

The eyes opened at last, pits which no longer reflected light. ‘I know. You go and leave me be.’

It was the following day before the last of the Laffams left, but in all that time Sarah never stirred: head down on her knees and hidden by her apron she stayed sitting on the doorstep, soot-blackened hands clasped around her knees. Children tiptoed past her as they scavenged for anything worth saving; women whispered fearfully that Sarah was willing her spirit to enter one of Tiw’s own black hounds a-ravening after Will Sleech. One by one their men had slipped out of the trees, bringing with them the tale of more disaster; Trapper indeed was dead, and another Laffam badly hurt.

The remainder, which included Bart who had suffered a slashed face, looked at the still smoking ruin of Corndown, spat superstitiously each time their glance slid over Sarah, and agreed they would have to move south for a while, into Abel Grey’s own country.

They could have rebuilt shelters of a kind before winter, dug out the well, felled timber for a barn, but somehow they lacked the heart for it. The labour would be harsh now all their trade-goods, stores and most of their beasts were gone, and Laffams had long been unaccustomed to the disciplines of axe and adze. Also, Corndown's fields were insufficient in themselves to support the tribe the Laffams had become, even supposing they could bring themselves to trudge in furrows behind an ox. Sarah's brooding presence with the curse it promised, as well as the memory of defeat, also discouraged them.

Quite apart from the fact that magistrates must even now be on the ridge, and this time the Laffams, alone, could not rely on their neighbours to lie on their behalf.

They would recover their pride more easily living elsewhere for a while, and return when—if—it suited them.

Only Bart looked back as the Laffams trudged away down their lane, driving their remaining beasts ahead of them. He wasn't imaginative but the stark timbers of Corndown old barn seemed like the skeleton of all the Laffams who had lived before him in this place, Sarah the dead spirit of his kin. He let his eyes linger on what remained of his home, then turned away down the lane.

Rose didn't look back at all, instead she sniffed at the breeze blowing out of the south-east, which was Abel Grey's country, as if she already detected the smell of carrion. In reality, the air was filled with the scents of the ridge: bracken, sheep and leaf-mould. When the straggle of Laffams reached the Ockham lane, without hesitation they turned left. No time this for the bravado of using the ridge road past Furnace Green pool and then on again past the Piggs' dug trap which was all that remained to mark a lost fight.

'I'm not coming any further, Bart,' Rose said, when they reached the curve just above Edenham.

'Is your belly griping? Why, it's months before the brat is due!' Bart caught her arm in alarm. He looked an ugly sight with moss bound across his slashed cheek.

'Oh no! I expect I'll birth as easily as a sow,' she answered carelessly. 'I'm not leaving Furnace Green, that's all.'

'We have to leave for a while! We'll be back I daresay, after a season or two of trading with the smugglers.'

Rose shrugged. 'Maybe. The ridge will be too hot to hold Laffams for a good while yet, and you may lose your taste for living here after a time with Abel Grey. I'm staying now.'

'We can't,' said Bart flatly. 'Parson Brookland may have buried Widow Apps without anyone thinking twice about an old hag dying, and even a riding officer—well, no one knew he was here, did they? But the whole Weald will hear about a battle which left a dozen dead, especially when Abel Grey's gang was beaten by a pack of yokels.' Bart bore a bitter grudge towards Furnace Green over the destruction of Corndown, but at the same time felt proud that it was his village which had dared take on and beat the smugglers. 'Sir Jonas Dyer will be holding his court at the Black Bear this very moment, I expect. If I stay, I'll hang.'

'Aye, I know.'

Bart stared at her; baffled, hurt and angry. 'You said you'd be mine, and my little 'un's in your belly.'

'My child will be born where it belongs, in Furnace Green. If you go to Abel Grey, sooner or later you'll hang anyway and I don't choose to watch it happen. As for being your woman, I reckon you had your chance. Aye, we were happy and swore oaths before a drunken parson, but 'tis over, Bart-love. We wouldn't be happy away with Abel Grey.'

Bart swallowed. He couldn't have described what he felt for Rose, but facing her on the track above Edenham, it grew again into a thudding desire. 'You come with me.'

'No.'

'They'll hound you out of Furnace Green if you try to stay.'

'Why should they? Ned will have fought with the village and I tried to save Tam, didn't I? The Rabbits will let me bide by their hearth while I wait for affairs to settle out.' She picked up the bundle containing her share of the fragments saved from Corndown. An iron trivet, a pot, some harness buckles and a handsome iron latch decorated with cornstooks from off the parlour door.

'You've got to come. I'll make you.' Bart swallowed again and Rose saw that his eyes were bright with tears.

She looked away, ashamed for both herself and him. 'If you force me to go with you, I'd run off the first time you looked the other way. You've had your chance and threw it away, although I begged you not to. I'm staying here.'

A stillness came to his face. 'Then I won't ever come back.'

'You'll always be welcome. Come alone, and you'd be safe enough once a few months have passed.'

'As you're welcome to come with me now.'

She shook her head, but as he turned away she felt she could scarcely breathe. And, afraid that her resolve would crumble, she ran as fast as she could down the bank to Edenham.

At Corndown, only Sarah remained after the last sound of the Laffams died away down the lane which bore their name and the dust of their departing settled. Greatly daring, one of the Portnell boys crept soft-footed out of the woods two days later, intending to boast to his fellows how he had visited ruined Corndown: he saw Sarah still sitting witch-like on her doorstep and fled screeching about evil-eyes. When Will Sleech fell ill scarcely a month later, then developed a twisting in his belly and vomited bile until he died, everyone spoke openly about the Devil's curse, and years afterwards scarcely anyone ventured near Corndown's gutted buildings. So, to the boastful tales of Pigpasture fight were added others about the haunting of Corndown, and generations of naughty children were threatened with a gurt black devil-hound which would eat their bowels unless they changed their ways.

Only when the winter gales began to blow across the ridge did Sarah's clothes shred away from rotted flesh, her bowed head sink lower with each gust until the bundle of bones she had become finally overbalanced and sprawled face down in mud.

The following spring grasses sprouted all over Corndown yard. Vetch, cow-parsley, dog's mercury and periwinkle followed, covering Sarah's bones and the bones of barn and house; the fields sprouted saplings and the only sound was the guttural call of rooks nesting in the grove of beech which over many centuries had sheltered the Laffam steading.

A few days spent with the Rabbits at filthy, ramshackle Edenham had been quite enough to send Rose back to Furnace Green where, as she expected, beyond a great many sly remarks, no one made her feel unwelcome. Nevertheless, she soon found living at the Black Bear again almost equally intolerable. Each night she ached for Bart and each night pot-valiant braggings in the taproom made her loss seem worse: a great many kegs of spirits remained hidden around the village and disorderly celebrations would continue until every one of them was finished.

Rose found these celebrations unexpectedly painful, and infuriated Ned by dawdling around the village instead of helping him during the last rip-roaringly profitable time the Black Bear was likely to enjoy for a long time to come. Yet the more he complained, the more pertly she answered back. About a week after her return to the village she was sitting on the church wall, shredding dog-rose petals idly into the wind, when she saw Joseph trip outside his shop and sprawl in the gutter.

He blinked at her gratefully when she helped him to his feet. 'It's the sun, you know. I can't see when it's bright.'

'It'll soon be winter,' Rose answered unsympathetically. Everyone had their own troubles, after all.

'I'm looking forward to grey days,' agreed Joseph. 'I've sent to Lewes for my chest of instruments and will try then to draw again.'

'You're staying in Furnace Green?'

He looked about him uncertainly. 'I can earn a little at

the shop and though I shall try map-making again, I doubt I'll find a living in it. Could I trouble you to measure out a smock-length for Mistress French before you go? There's a bolt of linen somewhere.'

Rose enjoyed measuring and fingering stock, and soon drifted into helping Joseph. Most particularly she enjoyed deciding who she would cheat and how. Those whom she liked, like good-natured Annie Portnell or Swatch Locock, received full measure. Others, whom she imagined slighted her or to whom she bore a grudge for what had happened at Corndown, were astonished by how little their ha'p'orths bought. Not that they caught her giving short measure. That was the part Rose liked best: outwitting those she disliked. From hollowed weights and false measuring marks, she moved on to double-skinned sacks and air inserted by means of a reed into pies she baked on Joseph's hearth.

But despite all Rose's tricks, under her direction the shop soon thrived even more than in the Hosmers' early days. Her hot pies were a novelty, her scrubbed counter and saucy smile much admired, while the grace with which she included a few extra raisins or finger-width of cloth with an order became a kind of accolade to the few customers who received it. She bullied Joseph for his own good and he was grateful, occasionally stole coins from his takings while preventing others from doing so, seldom bothered with any task she disliked, and charmed Bruiser Bywood into fixing the old wrought iron Corndown lock on the shop's yard door.

For two such dissimilar people she and Joseph managed surprisingly well together until, about a month after Sir Jonas Dyer had finished using the Black Bear's parlour to hear evidence about the deaths at Pigpasture fight, a heavy coach muddied to the axles drew up outside the shop-place.

Rose was outside in a flash, hoping to profit from a wrong turn taken: the few coaches that came through Furnace Green used the highway which ran from Tunbridge Wells, up the steep ridge-end and past the Black

Bear, where Ned Oxley paid a boy to run out and try to drag blown horses into his yard.

The coach was old and unsprung, but large enough to keep Rose's hopes alive. A sag-faced woman poked her face past leather curtains. 'Have you a Master Hosmer within?'

Rose curtsied. 'Yes, mistress. Shall I call him to you?'

'No, no! I shall alight.' The face disappeared and under Rose's startled gaze an enormously fat rump emerged backwards from the coach, clad in cherry, white and green striped silk. The lady turned, her face puce with effort under a feather-trimmed wig eighteen inches tall. 'Really, I am vexed! The way is so bad all my feathers are broke.'

'They're still beautiful,' Rose said enviously.

The lady wagged her fan playfully. 'I fear you are a flatterer but no matter, compliments never come amiss.' She gave a hearty laugh. 'Now take me to Master Hosmer, if you please.'

'Be careful to mind your head, ma'am,' said Rose nervously. The shop door was low even for broken feathers on top of such a wig.

'Oh la! How like my Joseph to hide himself in such a place. I declare I couldn't believe my ears when my maid came in with a tale that his trunks were packed to leave Lewes for good.'

'He—he has suffered an accident with his sight and thought he might stay quiet for a while,' Rose answered. But if the lady heard she took no notice, standing and looking about her with little darting glances so that Rose immediately saw the corner cottage through her eyes: small, mean and grimy.

'Where is he then?'

Rose squeezed past her and darted up the breakneck stair to the bedroom, where Joseph was lying on stale straw staring disconsolately at the ceiling. 'Master, there's a fine lady asking for you downstairs. She wears a wig so high it sweeps the cobwebs, and a dress I never saw the like of in my life.'

'A fine lady and asking for me?'

'Aye, it seems she came all the way from Lewes.'

Joseph sat up with a jerk. 'Did you ask her name?'

'I didn't think of it,' Rose said frankly. 'Come on with you now, you can't keep her waiting.' She straightened his coat with quick excited jerks and fairly thrust him downstairs, keeping her palm in his back when he seemed inclined to panic.

'My dear Mr Hosmer,' said the lady archly. 'Never did I expect to have to come so far to call on you.'

Joseph ran a finger nervously inside his neckcloth. 'I never asked—'

She laughed—very high and jangling it was too. 'Dear Mr Hosmer! As if I would not come when in the note you sent to bid farewell, you said you wished events had turned out otherwise! Did you think I would abandon you the moment trouble struck?'

'Yes—I mean, no! You are too good for that,' said Joseph fervently. 'But you see—'

'Because that's the kind of trick I don't hold with and never have! If you thought Abigail Toogood was a twicer then I'm fair ashamed, and don't know what I've done to deserve such a low opinion from you!'

Rose listened, fascinated, while the majestic spate of words swept over Joseph, leaving him bobbing tongue-tied in their wake. Mistress Abigail Toogood must be twice his age and poundage, but Rose instantly recognized wrought-iron determination not to allow even so helpless a male as Joseph to escape from whatever attentions he had paid her. Surely only Joseph could have been unwise enough to pay her any attentions at all.

Nothing would satisfy the lady until Rose was sent hot-foot to the Black Bear to bespeak a chamber for her, and when Joseph went out to the coachman he discovered she had brought his trunks as well as her own instead of leaving them to the mercies of the common carrier. She even tried to prevent him from unloading them, insisting she would be afraid to enter a bush-tavern like the Black Bear unescorted.

'Of course I will come to see you settled, but—'

'Not only to see me settled, when I have told that foolish girl a chamber must be prepared for you as well! A lady cannot stay at an inn alone, I always say.'

Joseph had a notion that ladies did not stay at inns accompanied only by male acquaintances either, but was too timid to say so. 'I will sup with you and return home afterwards. Ned Oxley is a good fellow and will look after you, and I have to mind my pence nowadays. I shan't be far if you need assistance.'

She tapped his knuckles with her fan. 'Not assistance. Support. I doubt you could offer that in the middle of the night from down a dark and muddy lane.'

She was well pleased by the Black Bear, however, Ned Oxley quite entering into the spirit of the affair after Rose's gasped account of Joseph's sweetheart. He bowed until his nose nearly touched his knee and called Mistress Toogood a ladyship despite her half-hearted disclaimers. 'Although she's no lady and far less a ladyship,' he confided to Rose. 'Why, Lady Dyer's as unlike this old sow as geneva spirits is to home-brewed!'

'She'll wed him all the same and he not know what's happening until Parson hiccups the blessing.'

Ned sniffed. 'Some folks never see when money isn't worth the price of being locked in a cell worse than Newgate. Joseph must have some of the smugglers' goods still left to sell, which Sir Jonas's grooms won't find no matter how they search. Not to mention the trade you're working up for him at the shop. He'd do best to lay easy at nights and be satisfied with leaner living than dance the jig that woman will lead him.'

But Rose only laughed, having recognized from her first encounter with Mistress Toogood that Joseph's fate was settled.

After the fight in Pigpasture Wood rumour had swept

through East Sussex, and had indeed brought Sir Jonas riding in at the head of a troop of grooms. The village was searched, the men cross-questioned, a jury sworn to discover what they knew about eight persons wickedly killed: not to mention arson at Corndown and Samuel Smith accidentally burned to a cinder. No contraband goods had been discovered and everyone enjoyed outdoing their neighbour in block-headedness under questioning; eventually the jury swore to a sequence of events which reflected the maximum credit on the inhabitants of the ridge. Only the Laffams, safely decamped or dead, emerged with comprehensively blackened characters.

'And surely Furnace Green must be the bravest, most praiseworthy village in all England,' declared Mistress Toogood when she sallied across the green on the morning after her arrival. 'To think of all those bloodthirsty rascals sent packing because this one place would not join in a dastardly trade! Of course, my ancestors came from here and I've a paper to prove it, but I never considered it a matter to boast about before! Nor did I think a fusty old paper scarcely worth keeping since a lawyer told me the rights in it weren't worth pence any more. Now I declare I feel quite reconciled to living here.'

'Living here?' echoed Joseph, trotting beside her and stumbling over tussocks. 'Mistress, I thought you would return soon to Lewes.'

'When you tell me now that you will never return there? Shame on you, sir! The moment I heard your lodging in Fisher Street was quite sold up, Abigail, I said to myself, it's Furnace Green for you, if that's where he wants to live. Tunbridge Wells is becoming quite fashionable or so I hear, and that's not far. It's not as if I must move quite into a wilderness.'

'I couldn't come back to Lewes. I may work on maps again but never enough to earn my keep. The shop—'

'You may pay Rose to work in the shop.' Income was income after all, providing her Joseph didn't measure beans and cloth himself. She stared across the green. 'What is that house?'

'Which? Mistress, you do understand I can see very little now?'

'Phooh! A man is wed for better or bad is he not? Mr Toogood, my first, now he was a foul-swearing, drinking man, though he cut up quite rich in the end, so I daresay I shouldn't complain. What is poor eyesight compared to that?'

'You're very good,' said Joseph humbly. 'I think the house you mean must be Danesdell. Old Jack Carpenter farms a good hop-holding there.'

'Will he sell?'

'Sell?'

'If I am to live in Furnace Green then I fancy a house away from the village but not remote. That one would suit me very well once we do away with all those pesky beams and rebuild the front in the latest style.'

'The Carpenters have been at Danesdell since I disremember when,' Joseph said, dumbfounded.

'My dear Mr Hosmer, what has that to do with anything? A farmer is always glad of an opportunity to build spanking new buildings in the middle of his holding, take my word for it! Let us go at once and ask how much he requires to sell the house and a paddock.'

'I don't think we could just go and—' Joseph's voice trailed away as he thought of Jack Carpenter's hastiness with his blackthorn stick.

'Nonsense! Once I know my mind I don't believe in flim-flamming about! Folk who are afraid to ask for what they want never get it, or so say I.'

It came as no surprise to the inhabitants of Furnace Green when, four weeks later, Mistress Toogood and Joseph Hosmer were wed. The church was packed for the occasion, and though rain dripped through where timbers from the spire had torn a hole, and Parson Brookland was so foul-tempered from having drunk his last keg of smuggled brandy the week before that he bellowed the prayers as if he was reprimanding a regiment, nothing could spoil everyone else's rollicking good spirits. Abigail, particularly, beamed about her with expansive pride and was heard to observe quite audibly during the benediction that what she liked was a spanking service, no mealy-mouthed whisperings about it.

'Well!' said Rose, looking after the trap in which the nuptial pair drove to Tunbridge Wells for, as the new Mrs Hosmer put it, a fine shake-in together while their house was made fit for Christian folks to live in. 'I don't know which will cause us more trouble in the future now, Abel Grey or Abigail Hosmer.'

'No wonder Jack curled up his toes,' agreed Sue Sleech, for so it had happened. The exertions of the fight at Pigpasture, where Jack Carpenter split a smuggler's skull, had left him blue-mouthed and gasping for breath; after a week of shouting down Abigail's determination to buy Danesdale farmhouse, he took a seizure and died. Since Jack was the last known Carpenter of all those who had lived in Furnace Green, before his body was cold Abigail told her man of affairs to buy the entire holding, apparently quite undaunted by the task of managing a farm whose main crop was hops, which, as she said bracingly, was something she had never clapped eyes on in her life.

Soon, Danesdell was echoing with activity, the speed of Abigail's dealings greatly helped by a fragile deed she possessed, hung with the great seal of Elizabeth I, which confirmed a grant of *'All wasteland and commons within the Manor of Ferenthe, together with the rents customs and services belonging therewith . . . to Nicholas Wyse of Edenham Forge, Ironmaster & Gunstonemaker to the Fleet'*, together with various crabbed clerks' writings which proved that Abigail's great-grandfather was a Francis Bellwasher of Robertsbridge, to whom the grant had been willed by his great-uncle, Nicholas Wyse.

As Abigail explained to Joseph, 'There was never a time when the Dyers or the Scovells before them weren't after this piece of writing, so we swore to it regular. Not that it's worth a cow's spit now, so I'm told. I were that disappointed when my man of affairs explained how people were accounted freeholders once they hadn't paid manor rights for so long, I nearly wrapped my rubbish in it! But I never believe what I'm told and besides, old Nick Wyse might curse me if I sold out what he left us. A right old devil he were by all accounts, so his curse would raise a few blisters, I daresay. You can imagine how I pricked up my ears when you came visiting in Lewes and said this was the place where you was raised, and now just see how matters have turned out! Jack Carpenter may have fancied himself a freeholder, but this paper stopped a great deal of work being made out of nothing when I bought Danesdell, I can tell you.'

'I was interested, too, when you spoke of a paper giving you grants in Furnace Green,' confessed Joseph.

'Very right, too! I've no patience with those who don't know how to help themselves to what the good Lord offers, when it's as plain as a pikestaff He wouldn't offer what He didn't expect us to take. But there, I'm not as young as I was and I've a fancy to live where my forefathers did—though rare rascals I should think them, I don't doubt. The two of us will be well suited here once that tumbledown old house is fit to live in, especially since I'm told them nasty Tunbridge Wells waters clear out the bowels better than a purge.'

Making Danesdell fit for Abigail to live in took longer than expected, her ideas becoming more ambitious with each new-laid brick. Fortunately she was not as rich as she liked to put about, and the purchase of Danesdell had made considerable inroads into her competence: sober letters from her man of affairs eventually modified her plans and brought her scurrying back from Tunbridge Wells to lodge for the winter at the Black Bear, where she could oversee John and Matthew Portnell the Furnace Green carpenters, and plague the life out of bricklayers, plasterers and painters by urging on the one hand more elegant workmanship than anything they were used to, and on the other the most nonsensical economies.

One day in early spring, Swatch Locock came to call on her in Ned Oxley's parlour, which she had appropriated as her own. Rain and wind slashed against the windows which, since these were small and the glass clouded, created an outlook similar to that encountered by an embryo tadpole floating in its jelly.

Swatch wiped his face and smiled. 'A better tomorrow to you, ma'am, since I wouldn't wish this one on my worst enemy.'

Abigail chuckled; even under the present circumstances her spirits remained high. 'It's my poor building-men who have to work in the rain, not me, so why should I worry? What can I do for you, my man?'

'Put me in as tenant of Danesdell Farm, ma'am.'

Joseph looked up from a table in the corner, where he was squinting against the light of a lamp while slowly shading in scrollwork around the border of a map. 'My dear, this is John Locock of Pigpasture.'

'As if I didn't know that! There aren't many Furnace Green faces I can't recognize now I've struggled four months across that dratted green, fair weather and foul! A tenant for Danesdell? What makes you think I would put a wood-clearing squatter into as fine a holding as you'd find anywhere? Didn't you hear I sent Roger Frenchman of Newhouse off with a flea in his ear when he asked for the tenancy?'

'Quite right too,' agreed Swatch. 'Roger hasn't the will to work in him his father had. A share of Newhouse is enough for the likes of him.'

'*And* I turned away an uppity young fellow from Riffield who brought a recommendation signed by Sir Jonas Dyer himself,' added Abigail triumphantly. All she knew of the Dyers was that they were great people hereabouts, who coveted the paper she owned; either consideration quite sufficient to make her rejoice at the chance of turning away their protégé.

'I'm not uppity, nor on the nid-nod with the Dyers.' Swatch looked at her out of teasing blue eyes.

'Oh yes, you are,' she said with relish. 'About the Dyers I don't know, but you're uppity, clear enough.'

He laughed. 'I'm also a good farmer and no mere squatter, my holding having been fenced these ten years past. Since last autumn it's well-stocked too, me having sold a tidy pile of contraband the smugglers left scattered when they ran. I'd make good profits for both of us out of Danesdell.'

'You think so, hey? How many acres have you in this Pigpasture of yours?'

'Two small enclosures and one larger. That has nothing to do with it, except as the reason I want a tenancy at Danesdell. If you give me the chance to show what can be done there, neither of us will regret it.'

'What do you know of these—these hops?'

'I've lived next door to hops all my life and coveted land which could grow them. Enough to understand that Jack Carpenter had lived past the time when he grew them well.'

Abigail stared at him, pulling at her lip. Like every other woman whom Swatch set out to please, she warmed to his mix of assurance and charm. She also remembered that Joseph had named him as the man who in reality had led the villagers' fight against the smugglers. Even more important to Abigail's way of thinking, was that he had retained the common sense to profit out of victory, by secreting contraband as soon as the rascals were beaten. 'How much would you offer?'

'Twenty pounds a year, and five pounds down in return for a licence to build a cottage and buildings on the pasture.'

'Forty.'

Swatch smiled. 'I'd be a ruined man inside the year, without any profit to either of us.'

'Roger Frenchman offered thirty-five.'

'Ah, but like you said, you turned the fool away.'

'I'm sure it's worth more than twenty,' Abigail said peevishly. Really, she hadn't the slightest notion what a hop farm was worth and had so far disliked all aspiring tenants. 'I shall have to send and ask my man in Lewes.'

'He won't know about hops, they're a Wealden crop. Ma'am, I'll tell you a way out of our difficulty. I'll offer twenty guineas instead of pounds, and for no cost build you that wall I heard you wanted to keep beasts out of your new garden.'

Another hour passed before the bargain was struck, at twenty-four guineas and a finer wall than any Furnace Green had ever seen, in stone, no less. As Swatch well knew, Abigail had been crestfallen when her mason named such an outrageous price for building the grandiose stone wall she fancied around her new property, that she had had to shelve the notion altogether. As for Swatch himself, he had obtained a run-down farm at a rent which would enable him to profit hugely once several years of labour brought it back to what it ought to be. Of course, now Danesdell House was separate, the land would lack buildings of its own, as well as stock since Carpenter's death, but no one leapt from scratching a living on a forest patch to being tenant of a ridge-top farm without taking risks.

After leaving Abigail, Swatch went directly to the churchyard, where he had already reckoned up the fallen stone which lay in drifts around the tower. The village scavenged shingles and timber but had less interest in stone, although each gale brought down more, while Parson Brookland continued to sprawl in front of his hearth without making the least push to do anything except snarl about his lost supply of spirits. If only a few more courses of the tower could be induced to fall in a hurry—Swatch turned on his heel and walked over to the shop. 'Rosie, has Joseph kept his father's cart?'

'Aye. A misery of an old day, isn't it? Have a pie while you're here, they're proper spoiling for want of customers.'

He bit into thick crust systematically, licking each scrap of gravy off his fingers. 'Joseph was a lucky man to find you to run this place for him.'

'Poor Joseph! Do you know, when he came here yestere'en that woman sent Billy Portnell around scarce five minutes later, commanding him back because she couldn't find her shawl?'

'I daresay he was happy enough to go,' said Locock cynically. 'Joseph will always prefer idling over his maps to aught else, and if finding a shawl is the price he has to pay, I reckon he won't mind too much.'

'She's a bitch.' Actually, having Abigail in the village was like enjoying a fair every day of the week.

Swatch grinned but didn't answer; he felt singularly in charity with Abigail at that moment. 'That cart now, can I borrow it tonight?'

'Tonight! It'll rain like a waterfall until dawn, I'm sure.'

'So much the better.'

Rose shrugged. 'If you like. Do you expect the smugglers back, or what?'

'Not yet at any rate, and never Abel Grey again. Have you any news of Bart?'

Unexpectedly her eyes filled with tears. Furnace Green might accept her as part of its community, but Swatch was the first person to mention Bart or any of the Laffams in her hearing. 'A whisper, that's all. A packman from Rye said Grey's men had gone west to recover a cargo the long-noses caught, and put in the Customs House at Poole. West! What did he want to go away west for? I made sure that when our baby was born he'd come secretly one night to see her.'

'You sent word?'

'Oh yes, I sent him word,' she said bitterly. 'To Rye, Hawkhurst or wherever. How should I know where Laffams go once Corndown is lost? And now they say he's travelled west! Sometimes—' she stopped.

There was a long silence and then Swatch leaned forward and kissed her gently, tasting salt on her lips. 'Nay, lass. Don't you go a-following him, wondering whether you might have been wrong after all when you chose to stay. He took the infection off Abel Grey and it's only a matter of time before it kills him. Which you knew then, and nothing has changed since.'

Swatch returned as darkness fell, this time bringing his sons and four Piggs with him, as well as his own cart and the half-team of oxen they owned between them. First he went to the parsonage, carrying the last of the kegs he had secreted after the fight.

'What do you want?' demanded Brookland roughly when Locock was shown into his parlour.

'Naught. I came to bring a gift since I know you miss the smugglers' visits.'

Brookland started up, his eyes glittering with need. 'Locock, I'll never forget this! A whole keg for me?'

'Aye.' Swatch thumped it down on the table and before he reached the door, Brookland was already fumbling with the bung. 'By the way, d'you mind if I pick up the stones lying underfoot in the churchyard? Some more of the tower is ready to fall.'

Brookland scarcely heard the question, tongue flicking in an agony of impatience while he waited for Locock to go. 'Aye . . . aye, I'd be glad if you would tidy around a little. One day we must do something about that tower.' He reached for a tankard as Swatch thumped the latch shut behind him.

That's Parson out of the way for some time to come, thought Swatch cheerfully. By the time he's recovered from swallowing a whole keg by himself, 'twill be half way to spring again, I reckon. Almost certainly Brookland would remember nothing about permission to gather stone, but Swatch had long ago learned the art of insuring against most kinds of trouble.

All that night it rained unmercifully, while the Lococks and Piggs transported stone from the churchyard to Danesdell. Swatch had taken the tower key from its hook on the parsonage wall, and while the Piggs drove the first load away he unlocked the tower door and climbed up into the wind carrying a crowbar. The tower was alive with the noises of wetness, a makeshift capping over the space where the steeple had once been, and it took only minutes for him to prise loose some rafters and begin driving his crowbar into the crumbling upper courses of stonework. Before the Piggs returned he had several blocks loosened, and others already tipped into the graveyard ready for them to take. It would take several nights' work to transport the amount he needed for Danesdell's wall but such a storm was too good to waste. The gale, of course, was no more than another of Swatch's insurances, the villagers would know how the tower's decay had been speeded up. The only people who failed to share this knowledge would be those most closely concerned: Parson Brookland and Abigail Hosmer.

It was weeks before Brookland emerged white-faced and trembling from his drinking bout, and some time after that before he noticed how much more of the tower had vanished, how completely the graveyard was swept clear of fallen stone. But he had long ago given up the habit of visiting around the parish and never did discover where it went. Soon, he ceased to worry about it, his intellect being well pickled even before Swatch Locock's keg.

Abigail, likewise, never learned the origins of her wall. Swatch stored the stone behind Danesdell and went back to the church for more each night of the time Brookland spent drinking. By day he and his sons dug and mortared industriously, their progress helped by ready-cut stone, and it never occurred to Abigail to wonder how he kept his stock topped-up. He even put aside shaped pieces for the coping, these last from the tower crenellations. The finial which had once capped the steeple he found in some long grass, and placed triumphantly on one gatepost.

'Hm,' said Abigail, examining this. ''Tis all very fine, I must say, but lop-sided, don't you see? You'll have to carve another like it for the other gatepost.'

'That is kept clear for your escutcheon, ma'am,' answered Swatch respectfully. He was so exhausted by concentrated larceny that even supposing he possessed the skill, he could scarcely have set a chisel into stone. 'The

Dyers have theirs carved into the entry at Riffield, and though the Hosmers are folk like us I made sure you would possess a design you wanted to display as they do.'

'Hm,' said Abigail again, but this time thoughtfully, at the same time casting a suspicious glance at Locock's guileless expression. 'If you're as good at growing hops as you are at flattering your way out of trouble, then twenty-four guineas a year for Danesdell fields is too cheap.'

'There's a story we tell our children hereabouts,' answered Swatch, smiling. 'It's called "Alice's Hair Tree" and tells how a clever fellow made his fortune by bringing hair seeds from a secret tree when the queen went bald. You see, he didn't make it by flattering the queen into thinking she looked prettier bald, but because he knew the secret of the tree. It's the same for hops, I reckon. Either you know how they grow and are willing to give your lifeblood to tending them, or you don't. 'Tis the knowing and the tending which makes my part of our bargain.'

Which satisfied Abigail perfectly, since beneath her many layers of whalebone and leather she possessed a romantic heart, and was easier convinced by an irrelevant tale than any amount of protestation. She entered on the task of modelling her escutcheon with enthusiasm, and decided that Queen Elizabeth's time-chipped seal on Ferenthe's manorial deed was as good a model as any other; his wall completed, Swatch Locock slept for two days without stirring and woke to receive his tenancy at twenty-five pounds and four shillings a year.

Abigail and Joseph moved into Danesdell House just as the first cuckoos began to call out that summer was on the way. The old wet hollow where it stood had been drained into an ornamental pond around which Abigail intended to plant a herb garden, and the timber farmhouse had vanished behind a brick façade with eight symmetrical sash windows. A panelled door and gleaming brass knocker, a high tiled roof behind a parapet which hid the servants' attic completed the change. Seen from behind, the house remained much as it had always been: a straggle of dairies, stables and outbuildings. But when a traveller entered between the two stone gateposts in the front (one topped by a strange-looking spike and the other decorated with Mistress Abigail's understanding of the Tudor arms of England) he saw a residence in the latest style, the first truly non-village house that Furnace Green had known.

Unfortunately, Abigail and Joseph possessed few acquaintances amongst those who might be expected to pay formal calls, and their first visitor came to the kitchen door.

When Molly Twort looked up from scrubbing the Danesdell scullery floor she nearly screamed when she saw a creature she took for a ghost leaning against the passage wall. Molly was twelve years old and impressionable, the first member of her family to work away from their woodcutters' hut in Greggs Wood.

'Wayfaring folk will often call at such a grand house as this, hoping for milk and bread,' said Leah, Abigail's tiring-maid, briskly when Molly ran to her for help. Leah's consequence was well-served by her mistress's fancy to inhabit the one large house in a village rather than live unmarked among many grander people in Lewes. 'The mistress will be happy to offer charity, but you make sure they keep their fleas out in the yard.'

Molly shuddered. 'It were a witch I saw. I'd be frighted to go close.'

Leah clicked her tongue in annoyance. Raw country girls were cheap but more trouble than they were worth. She bustled downstairs, noting approvingly how well her mistress's furniture fitted into the square front rooms, to find the female already sagged down on the floor, a brat mewling in her arms. 'Eh, get you away from our clean kitchen and I'll send bread to the barn and milk for the babe.'

The woman shuffled obediently out, to slump on straw in the first shed she reached, where the baby immediately began to squall more loudly than before. Leah poured soup into a pitcher from the pot kept on a chain above the hearth, intending to thrust Molly outside with it willy-nilly: mercy was one thing, lowering her dignity to wait on a beggar woman something else again.

But Molly adamantly refused to budge, wailing about witches and eventually bolting into the cellar when Leah boxed her ears. Consequently, when Leah stalked across the yard to slap down pitcher, milk and bread beside the woman she felt both virtuous and affronted. She intended to leave at once, and would have, except she saw the babe's pinched face. A belly on it as dry as leather, I'll be bound! thought Leah indignantly; in her view any woman feckless enough to be tramping the roads deserved to starve, but a child . . . Leah was childless and once had yearned so much for a mouth at her breast that she stole a neighbour's babe, only escaping a whipping by running for refuge to the miller's daughter, who had married well and lived away in Lewes. She had served Abigail ever since.

'You'd best sleep the night here,' she said gruffly.

'Thank you.' A whisper in reply, no more.

'But don't you start thinking that because you stay one night here, you can stay for ever.'

The woman's head flicked back, revealing eyes as fierce as a polecat's. 'They told me in the village this is Joseph Hosmer's place. I'm staying until he shows where my man died.'

Her accent was strange enough for Leah to need time to grasp her meaning. When she did, she stared back speechless. Then the baby wailed again and the woman bent over it, hiding anger beneath her hair.

Leah left the stable as fast as her dignity allowed, then ran in search of her mistress. Abigail would know what to do. Though she could rage and box ears when it suited her, Leah had never seen her mistress caught off-balance by the unexpected.

'Is this female threatening?' she asked as soon as Leah had tumbled out her tale.

Leah shrugged; she wasn't sure. 'She said she wasn't leaving until the master showed where her man died.'

Abigal frowned. 'At Danesdell? Is she demented?'

'I think—perhaps. Ma'am, should I send to Master Locock to ask for one of the farm men to come up and restrain her?'

Abigail remembered the cells beneath the Black Bear: dark, wet and stinking. 'She has a child with her, you said.'

'I could look after the child.'

'I will see this woman myself and decide.' Abigail heaved out of her chair. There was nothing she enjoyed so much as interfering in other people's lives and besides, Leah was untrustworthy where children were concerned. She could be making a mystery simply in the hope of borrowing a baby for a while.

On their way down the new-planked stairs they encountered Joseph, just returned from a visit to his shop. Abigail hesitated, in two minds whether to tell him about the wench and her child. Really, it would be more enjoyable to ferret matters out for herself. Then Leah coughed and she saw how demeaning it would appear if she seemed to keep a matter concerning him from her husband. 'Ah, Mr Hosmer, I am glad you have come in. There is a woman in our stable who asks for you.'

'For me?' said Joseph, surprised. 'I don't think that can be right.'

'She has a child with her.'

He flushed. 'Then there is most certainly a mistake.'

'My dear Mr Hosmer, I merely mentioned that she carried a child with her, which is nothing to the matter after all.' Abigail was not displeased by the result of her words; she did not suspect her timid Joseph of seducing beggar women but believed that everyone should occasionally be made to feel uncomfortable. 'We are about to visit her in the stable yard. Perhaps you would care to accompany us.'

'Certainly, if she asked for me.' Joseph did not query the need for them to go out to the woman. Only fools let beggars bring infections, vermin and dreams of theft into their houses.

Both woman and child were asleep when they reached the stable, but Abigail dug her slippered toe unsympathetically into the woman's ribs. 'Get up, wench.'

One tawny eye opened and then the other, sharpening almost instantly out of exhaustion. 'Is that him?'

Joseph peered short-sightedly at her face. 'I'm Joseph Hosmer, but fear I have never met you in my life.'

'And I am Mistress Larkworthy.'

He recoiled. 'I'm sorry. I didn't know. When I received no answer to my letter, I'm afraid—'

'You forgot all about my Stephen being murdered and me left with a child to keep. Aye, well, I was ill with grief and then little Stevie here caught a fever. We've begged all the way from Lambeth to this place I never heard of, nor knew where it was. It took a while.' She stood and faced them, yellow eyes disquietingly fragmented by the light. 'Where did he die?'

'Not here. When I wrote to you I lived at my shop-place still. He asked me to tell . . . He thought you might find things easier if one day you could tell your son how—' Joseph's voice trailed away as he glanced at the baby's hunger-pinched face.

'Nothing will be easy for me, ever again. Except telling my son to avenge his father's death.'

'I told you when I wrote how Riding Officer Larkworthy's death helped cause the smugglers' defeat.'

'You told me it was the murder of Widow Apps and that boy Tam which stung the village into a fight,' interrupted Abigail, who possessed no tact at all.

'Aye.' This time Mistress Larkworthy's voice was soft as a worm on a leaf. 'That's why I came. A dozen folk, a dozen different tales of what happened. I got a tapster to read me your letter, master, but I don't believe in writings. So I came to find out for myself how my man died.'

Abigail and Joseph gaped at her, as if each expected their throat to be cut the moment complicity was proved. 'I'd best take you over to my shop,' said Joseph feebly, after a moment.

'If that's where you say Stephen died, then I'm suited to begin there.' She settled the sleeping child on her hip.

They crossed the green in silence, and only when Joseph saw Rose behind the counter did he remember Bart's part in Stephen Larkworthy's murder. 'I didn't expect you back again today, master,' Rose exclaimed, as she saw him in the doorway.

'I didn't expect to be back. Rose, this is Mistress Nancy Larkworthy.'

'Oh?' Only the name, so foreign to Sussex, eventually triggered Rose's recollection of who this woman must be. 'You are welcome, mistress, although this is a sad place for you to come.'

Then her voice, too, trailed into silence as she encountered the violence shimmering behind her visitor's eyes.

Joseph groped for words to fill the void. 'Mistress Larkworthy has—has spent some weeks on the road and—'

'Eight months since my Stephen was murdered and each day I've been planning for this moment.'

'Planning what?' Instinctively, Rose already knew.

'To find out what happened, and to punish.'

But this time her mouth quivered, because she was looking around the dim place where her man had died, and pity replaced Rose's instinctive fear. 'You'd best stay then, and I'll answer what you want to know tomorrow. Your babe looks fair chowsed with the journey.'

'Rose—' Joseph wished fervently he had never kept his promise to write to Larkworthy's wife, and so brought this alien avenger down to Furnace Green.

'You leave everything until tomorrow, too, master. It'll do no one any good to be starting fresh quarrels when Mistress Larkworthy is asleep where she stands.'

'So long as you think everything will be all right, Rose,' said Joseph with typical naivety, because of course nothing was all right; he felt masculine relief too, at being spared a disagreeable scene. 'I'll go back to Danesdell then, and leave you to become acquainted. I know Mistress

Larkworthy will find everything very different from her imaginings once you've explained matters to her.'

And I know she won't, thought Rose as Joseph trotted away with more haste than dignity. Those eyes weren't made for understanding. Neither woman spoke as Rose notched the shutters into place and stirred up embers on the hearth. She lifted little Emily out of her crib and began to suckle her as she moved about, in the hope that Nancy Larkworthy might be appeased, however slightly, by some sense of fellow-feeling. 'Is yours a boy?' she asked over her shoulder.

'Aye.'

'How old?'

'Fourteen months.'

Astonishment spun Rose round. 'Fourteen months! Why—'

'You thought him new born like yours, didn't you? But Lambeth's not much better than a plague pit and we've both come close to starving since Stephen was killed.'

'Then you'd have done better to forget revenge and think first of your son. Tramping the roads in all weathers suits only gypsy brats,' snapped Rose. 'Here, give him to me. I've milk enough for two.'

'No.'

'Because I'm Furnace Green?'

'Because I don't choose to be beholden.'

Menace sprang out of darkness and Rose felt gooseflesh prickle her uncovered breast. Nancy did not want to be beholden in case revenge should be weakened by humanity. Abruptly, Emily dropped off her nipple and began to wail. 'So you'd let your child starve while my breasts dribble milk,' she said sharply.

'You don't understand.'

'Oh, yes, I do. I hated everyone after I was left alone, and most especially my man, Bart. I loved him, you see.' Rose teased Emily's mouth open with her finger and pressed her nipple back into place.

'My Stephen was murdered.'

Rose stared at the dulling embers; she had not lighted any dips and the hearth gave out the only light in the shop. 'I wait each day to hear that Bart has been taken and will hang.'

Silence closed in on them.

'You'll have to tell me what you mean,' the other said wearily at last.

'Bart was—is—a smuggler. He left after the fight here. I haven't seen him since.'

Rose heard the rustle as the other moved, saw a shape between herself and the hearth. 'When Mr Hosmer wrote he said my Stephen was killed by smugglers, but before the fight.'

'Aye. He and a woman called Apps. And Tam Sleech, a boy aged ten. Bart—' She swallowed. 'He isn't a bad man.'

Rose had sensed violence in the other, but the blow across her face caught her by surprise; attack by one woman on another when each held a child in her arms, something which had not crossed her mind. She jumped up, her nose bleeding all over Emily. 'Keep your hands to yourself, curse you! What good can blood on both our babes do now?' She blundered over to the crib and wrapped Emily back in her covers. 'Here, give me yours.'

'No.'

'Give him to me. There's been enough killing for no purpose. I've plenty of milk and you haven't, that's the only difference between us which matters now.'

No answer. No sound except breathing, ragged as if Nancy had run that moment up the hill which led to Furnace Green.

'All right, don't answer. Listen. I'll tell you how it was and then see if you still want to kill another innocent afterwards. We'll begin upstairs.'

Rose went up the steep stair without a backward glance to see if she was followed. And Nancy came, dragging her feet from weariness and awkward because of the child she still held in her arms.

Rose turned by the bedroom window, where deep gouges still spoke of the agonised struggle which had taken place when Stephen Larkworthy's broken bones were forced through a space too small for them. Anger had faded again, its place taken by the despair she always felt in this chamber; herself, Rose preferred to sleep by the hearth below. Quietly, she told all she knew of what had happened: how heedless, vigorous Bart had caught the sickness of violence from Abel Grey; how Joseph had found Stephen Larkworthy injured and brought him to the only place which might shelter a riding officer. How the infuriating piety of the Hosmers had inflamed their neighbours into tauntings which became more mindless as drink eroded common decencies, the manner of Tobias's death dividing the village still more deeply, until Stephen Larkworthy's fate was sealed along with that of Clemency and Amos Hosmer. She told how Widow Apps and Tam Sleech had died, Corndown and the Laffams were destroyed.

'I was destroyed as well,' Rose added bleakly. 'People say how lucky I've been that Master Hosmer wanted me to mind his shop, but like you I'm left the rest of my life to lie in empty straw. I've seen how some folk spit and cross their fingers as I pass, as if I was some kind of witch. Like Corndown, I'll be cursed long after everyone's forgot exactly what happened.'

'Stephen lay in this room? Couldn't anyone have got him away? Both his legs broke so he couldn't move even when they devils came for him?' The dreadful questions went on and on. Frenzied, Nancy began making little dashes from one tell-tale sign of the pain which had filled this room to the other: from window to bed and back to the broken door hinge.

This time Rose watched her unsympathetically. She wasn't afraid any longer, only disdainful that any creature should allow herself to become crazed by adverse circumstances. Things happened and you had to make the best you could of them. 'Here, give me your son,' she said again after a while, and without waiting for an answer snatched him away as Nancy passed. 'Did I hear you call him Stevie? Poor thing, he's like a bundle of sticks.'

Nancy did not answer, seemed not to notice, so Rose tiptoed carefully past her and down the stair. It was enough to curdle anyone's milk to share a room with a jack o'lantern nursing spite, she thought, as she sat by the warm hearth nursing the child of a man Bart had helped to murder.

The shop seemed very quiet, so quiet that Rose could hear the bubble of milk in the child's dry stomach. At least he seems able to swallow, she reflected, although so feeble she would have to be careful not to drown him during his first few sucklings.

Gradually she became conscious of the quiet in a different way, began to listen for such fleeting comforts as a mouse scuttering or voices in the street outside. And as she listened, there came a kind of stealthy creak on the stair. Her heart jumped. There were always noises in a timber house at night, she told herself; Bart would laugh if I could tell him I was afraid of a starveling wraith.

Carefully, she eased her breast out of the baby's mouth and laid him beside Emily in the crib, stood in the dark corner behind it straining her ears. The creak was repeated, and quietly Rose stepped further away from the glow of the hearth. Moonlight fingered through cracks in the shutters, and she saw a shape move into and out of this uncertain light.

The shop was rectangular; a hearth against the back wall, a counter close to the front, the small space where Daniel had once tried to save Mistress Coffey from dying of a fever cluttered with sacks, boxes and bins. Rose waited until she sensed that Nancy had moved nearer to the shuttered front door, before tiptoeing towards the back stable entry. Her fingers felt corn-stooks outlined on the splendid lockplate she had brought from Corndown, then fastened on the key. But, Emily! she thought. I can't leave her for a madwoman to find.

It was as if this one place in Furnace Green was cursed, destined to fill again and again with terror and despair.

Daniel first, then the ostracised Hosmers and tormented Stephen Larkworthy, now Rose. As she hesitated Rose heard Nancy go past her with a rush, muttering to herself, then a click of wood she recognized as the crib rocking to a touch.

'Leave the children alone.' Rose moved immediately, before her voice could betray her position.

She heard an answering sob of breath. 'Who are you?'

'Rose. I fed your babe, and now you should rest yourself.' She moved again, but Nancy was between her and the door.

'I can't rest. I thought I'd go home to Devon, but first I had to come—where was it I had to come?'

The words tumbled out so that Rose found the West Country accent even more difficult to comprehend than Leah had done: the rhythm quite different from Sussex speech. 'You told me you came from Lambeth, which is London, I suppose,' she answered cautiously at last; if Nancy had forgotten why she travelled to Furnace Green then Rose had no intention of reminding her.

'Aye, Lambeth. How I hated Lambeth. I begged Stephen to take me back to Devon. Be a long-nose if you must, I said, but let us live where I'm not afeared to set foot outside my door. Do you know what it was like? Me waiting weeks for him to come home wi' my pennies running out, then his step on the boards and bounty for a day, a week if I was lucky, before he'd be off again. Never content to walk each day to the fields like other men, he weren't. To stay home wi' his lass and babe. So I was left to count the days in a stinking pit, waiting . . . Oh God, waiting until I heard he wouldn't come again.' Rose felt breath touch the skin of her face, and flinched. 'You're afraid of me, aren't you? I had a husband and this place killed him; you know I've come to tear the throat out from the lot of you. You most of all, because you still say your man wasn't bad. But I say he must have been rotten bad, like last year's taties stinking in the bin. I want to see you starve like Stevie and me have done, except it'd be too good for you. Too good! Oh God, I had a husband and I loved him. You killed him here and I'll never know a happy day again.'

She began to moan, a grotesque sound tearing through the dark.

Rose cried out then, since the Sleeches' cottage next door possessed a common wall with the shop, but before she could draw breath a second time Nancy threw her arms tight about her, butting with her head and sinking her teeth into Rose's cheek.

Nancy was shouting too, the western burr this time too strong for comprehension, and as she did so Rose threw her violently off; reached frantically among the bins and boxes in search of a weapon before the creature came after her again. Rose never remembered quite what happened next since she seemed to be fighting something quite inhuman; given time to think she might easily have been paralysed by fright. Her opponent bit, scratched, clawed, sobbed and kicked, Rose's life saved only because the attack was so mindless. When she fell, a teetering, pouncing thing tried only to grind her deeper into the dirt, and it was then that Rose was able at last with all her strength to drive a billet of wood her desperate, scrabbling fingers had found into the darkness above.

Rose felt the wood strike softness, but the only reaction from Nancy was a louder screech and more frenzy; so she struck again and again with the strength of desperation, pulling herself to her feet as Nancy weakened, until the screeches bit off and weight slumped on the floor. Only then did she become aware of fists pounding on the shutters outside, and voices calling. Slowly Rose fumbled over to the hearth, groped there until she found an ember hot enough to kindle a wick. She could feel one of her eyes already closed and blood pounding in the swollen bite on her cheek. When flame grew in a dip at last, the first thing she saw was Nancy Larkworthy sprawled face up with a splinter of wood protruding from her eye.

* * *

Sir Jonas Dyer regarded himself as a patient man, but when both the sheriff's officer from Lewes and the constable of Furnace Green brought him ill-tidings in a single day, he felt he had a right to be out of humour. Especially when the sheriff's writ also concerned Furnace Green, a nest of ruffians already stirred into a dangerous state of excitement.

Old Sir Amyas would have felt small regard for most of his descendants who lived after him at Riffield Castle, since all but a few of them lacked the industry which had brought previous conniving Dyers their success. Perhaps the times were too easy. Amyas left a comfortable rather than an enormous fortune after his purchase of the Scovell estate; but the elegant, mellow-brick house he built on the foundations of the castle was far easier to keep up than the previous centuries-old maze of stone and timber. Only a single tower and the old great hall, tacked on to one end of his Stuart mansion in fine disregard for architectural taste, remained from earlier times. He had also only lived long enough to buy half of the land previously owned by the Scovells, that is to say about fourteen thousand acres almost equally divided between unproductive park or forest, and moderate quality farmland. This supported his descendants in style without the need to work; on the other hand there was insufficient surplus to indulge in fashionable flights of fancy. Nor did the Dyers enjoy an automatic right of entry into the political élite of England, as the Scovells had done before them. Consequently, most stayed at Riffield to hunt and farm and judge their fellows but did little else of note: Sir Amyas would have been extremely rude about the self-satisfaction and lack of enterprise which seemed the most lasting result of the Dyers' move into Sussex.

Then two things happened which changed the mould of their existence again. In 1711 Sir Gregory Dyer married an eccentric and accomplished woman who birthed ten eccentric and accomplished children, and ten years later the family lost most of its unentailed wealth when the banking speculation known as the South Sea Bubble burst. Giles Dyer, whom Bart Laffam had killed almost (but not quite) by accident in the taproom of the Black Bear, was the youngest son of this marriage and an example of the unsteady Dyers who were to recur thenceforward in several following generations. Jonas was the eldest, a shrewd and avaricious man who watched London's explosive growth for a while and then embarked on a series of risky land purchases which had already more than repaired his family's fortunes, all without bestirring himself very much.

And now he was constrained to ride to Furnace Green yet again, and take his grooms away from their proper tasks as well, in case he required force to back up his authority as magistrate. 'Damme, that place is enough to sour the belly of a saint. Stuck on its ridge in front of my eyes yet owning no man as master, it's the worst nest of scoundrels in all Sussex!' he said irritably to his wife, Sophie; Jonas possessed an eye for young girls and so far had worn out two wives and this, his third, was twenty years his junior.

'I think it's pretty, set up on the skyline all framed in bracken and trees,' she answered absently. Sophie was four months pregnant and all fluffy prettiness, yet in reality as obstinate and self-centred as a butcher's mule.

'I'd wager my best mare that Giles was killed up there, for all they found his body half way across the park.'

Sophie sighed. She had been fond of scapegrace Giles and was sorry the child she carried couldn't possibly be his. 'You weren't sorry when they fought the smugglers.'

'And not a drop of good brandy left in my stables since!' snapped Jonas. It was one thing to fight a brute like Abel Grey, quite another to frighten smugglers out of the district altogether.

'They'll be back when it suits them. Nowhere in Sussex manages long without the smugglers.'

'I daresay so, but meanwhile here's another fuss in Furnace Green. A woman found dead, or so they say, but killed for some reason or another I've no doubt. And I with a sheriff's writ which orders me to meet a troop of dragoons there tomorrow and hang a felon's corpse where everyone can watch it rot.'

Sophie opened her pouting little mouth and blew him a kiss. 'Dragoons and a corpse to be exhibited at Furnace Green! Why, I'm half in a mind to come with you to watch such sport, Sir Jonas! Will you be back for dinner this even?'

'No,' said Jonas morosely. He had doubts about Sophie, sometimes. 'I shall have to stay at the Black Bear: empanel a jury and hear evidence on the woman's death today, wait for the dragoons tomorrow.'

He rode to Furnace Green at his usual sober pace. Jonas disliked hey-go-merry gallops and besides, his bulk required a horse better suited to the plough than acquiring fine paces. He also needed time to think. Hanging up a felon's corpse in his own home village was rare; an exemplary punishment invoked when the need to demonstrate the law's power overrode all other considerations. In this case, Sir Jonas would have objected strongly to such a course since Furnace Green had, after all, opposed the smugglers, but he had been given no time to do so, probably deliberately. The felon's carcass was already on its way, two weeks after a hanging in Southampton so the writ informed him, and no doubt stinking worse than a tannery.

Jonas grunted and looked around him. Instead of taking the shorter route across the park and climbing the steep ridge-side, he had chosen to ride the easy way between Riffield and Furnace Green which skirted Twisbury Hill, and here the forest was almost untouched: vast brooding trees in gently misting rain. Soon he would pass the place where the villagers had fought their brawl with the smugglers: Jonas had already cleared that mess up without anyone in Furnace Green appreciating quite how lucky they had been. The village could have been torn apart in a witch-hunt if Dyer had decided, as magistrate, that the blood of Widow Apps, Riding Officer Larkworthy, Samuel Smith and Tam Sleech—not to mention half a dozen smugglers—required him to arraign a great many aiders-

and-abettors in the dock. But he had calculated that a very rough justice had more or less been done and further probings would benefit no one except perhaps Abel Grey, who might ride back in triumph on the wash of resentment which any arrests would cause.

Jonas Dyer's skills in double-dealing had been tested to the uttermost in his carefully specious reports to London, as well as in his handling of lying witnesses, but eventually he convinced his superiors that in spite of unflagging zeal he could find insufficient evidence of felony against anyone except Grey's gang. Which did not mean that by the time he was finished, Jonas himself had not acquired a very shrewd notion of who was to blame for what, and why.

Probably he had not quite succeeded in hoodwinking London as thoroughly as he hoped, which might be one reason why a corpse was to be strung up in Furnace Green tomorrow. Governments were a distant matter for subject and magistrate alike, but just occasionally not quite as distant as the counties would have liked.

'And damn my guts,' Jonas exclaimed aloud. 'Now the oafs needs must kill another woman.'

He dismounted in the yard of the Black Bear, maintaining the kind of overtly incensed silence which made Ned Oxley order a tankard drawn from his best cask of brandy even before he took Sir Jonas to view Nancy Larkworthy's body lying in his barn.

Jonas considered the corpse carefully before turning it over with his boot. 'What happened to her face?'

'She must have fallen in the dark and then perhaps a cart ran over her.' Ned stared at the flattened mess which had been the best the village could contrive to hide the splinter-wound which had killed Nancy Larkworthy.

'Why didn't you send for me at once?'

'Your honour?'

'She's at least two days' dead, isn't she? D'you think I'm an idiot, man?'

'No indeed, your honour.' Most of the village did, in fact, consider Sir Jonas soft, because of the ease with which they had hoodwinked the law after Pigpasture fight; Ned Oxley made no such mistake when all the jury sittings had taken place in his parlour.

Dyer grunted. 'What's her name?'

'We don't know, your honour. Finding her on the hill like we did, she could be anyone.'

'She could have been lying for a while before she was found, I suppose. Which would account for the two days since she died.'

'Aye, that it could, your honour,' Oxley agreed, much relieved.

'Now you listen to me, Ned Oxley.' Dyer's florid face was thrust out like a toad's. 'I'll be swearing in a jury in your parlour and this time damme if I don't indict someone for this murder. At Furnace Green you begin to think you can kill whomsoever displeases you and the law will listen to a pack of lies. Sometimes lies make up a kind of justice, but not often. If this should be part of your feuding with Abel Grey, then you have to convince me first.'

'I don't know who she is, like I told your honour. She could have laid out in a ditch—'

'That she did not or you'd have told me such a promising tale before I pretended to guess it for myself.' Dyer bent down and pressed the mess where Nancy's face had been. 'Nor did she die of a flattened face. You have half an hour to think up a more convincing tale, or I'll tie up that jury in such knots they'll accuse you to save themselves.'

Oxley rubbed his hands nervously on his breeches. 'Mayhap they will, at that. Me being the culprit, d'you see.'

'You damned blithering fool! Stop playing games with me!'

'It's God's truth, your honour, and since you noticed something strange-like I'd sooner confess to what I've done, rather than be swore against by a jury of my neighbours.'

A long silence followed, during which Oxley found himself unable to look away from little bloodshot eyes glaring at him out of folds of fat. 'I never trust anyone who says he speaks God's truth,' Dyer observed at last. 'You are a widower, are you not?'

'Aye,' said Oxley, bewildered.

'You have sons?'

'No, your honour.'

'What other kin?'

'A daughter, Rose, your honour.' Too late, Oxley saw the trap in front of him.

'Ah, I remember. My brother Giles bragged about fair Rose at the Black Bear.'

Oxley reddened. 'She is wed now, with a child.'

'Giles,' repeated Dyer thoughtfully, and drank from Oxley's tankard of brandy. 'If you are so touchy about your loose-skirt daughter, then maybe Giles also died in the Black Bear instead of in my park. Him being partial to wenches like your daughter, as I recall clear enough.'

'No . . . no, it weren't that way at all, I swear it!'

Oxley bit his lip as Jonas smiled derisively. 'I warned you to beware of swearings. So, like this woman, he died somewhere here, as I always thought most likely. The next question I ask myself is why the landlord of the Black Bear, who has a great deal to lose by lying to a justice, should be so concerned to cover up such matters. And each time the answer is the same. To protect someone else. When Giles died I thought the smugglers might have killed him and could not blame men overmuch if they feared to lay evidence against Abel Grey, but the smugglers have gone for the moment. They cannot have killed this woman.'

'I killed her,' Oxley repeated stubbornly.

Dyer left him and strode across the yard, shouldered open the taproom door with a crash which made everyone inside spring to their feet. Twelve good men and true, he thought sardonically; each sitting according to age and only age distinguishing one from the other.

He ordered more brandy and drank it slowly, watching Furnace Green's jurors fidget under his stare. Oxley cleared his throat. 'Your honour, shall we remove to the parlour?'

'No.'

Oxley opened his mouth, closed it, went behind his bar and made a great to-do of swabbing with a cloth, only to find that Dyer had turned to face him. 'I don't intend to let you nod and wink behind my back, nor offer the chance for whisperings on the way into your parlour. Tell me, you said your daughter was wed now. Who did she wed?'

Oxley's eyes shifted but he did not answer.

'Come, man. I can send to ask the parson, I suppose.'

One of the jurymen, Roger Frenchman, snickered, the sound cut off abruptly. My instinct hasn't led me astray, reflected Dyer. This dead woman whom Oxley knows but says is a stranger; his daughter, whom Giles bedded I'll be bound and whose wedded name her father will not tell me: somehow they are connected. The connection still escaped him, however.

'Laffam,' said Oxley reluctantly, at last.

'Which Laffam?'

'Bartholomew.'

'His carcass is to be hung up here tomorrow.' A rustle and clink of boots behind his back, but Dyer did not turn.

'So he's dead,' said Oxley stupidly.

'Since his fourteen-day corpse is to be hung up here in chains, so it would appear. I received a proclamation from the Sussex sheriff this morning. Grey's gang had the cursed effrontery to storm the Customs House at Poole and recover a cargo they had lost. They were taken two days later, in arms against the king. Most were killed or hanged, the rest hunted.' His voice hardened. 'Which means Bartholomew Laffam's widow loses everything and could be delivered to gaol if I suspect her of complicity in her husband's felonies.'

Oxley licked his lips, a prosaic man trapped by the weakness of affection. 'Rose was never mixed up with the smugglers.'

'She must have been if she lived at Corndown.'

'Aye, she did live there, but . . . it was she who tried to save Tam Sleech. She wasn't mixed up in nothing, like I said.'

'She works in my shop now, a good trustworthy girl.' A voice from behind Dyer this time: Joseph Hosmer. From his investigations the previous year, Dyer remembered him as softer-skinned than a bark-grub. He swung round abruptly. 'A good girl? That wasn't how my brother, Giles, described the landlord's daughter at the Black Bear.'

'Oh, but she is,' said Joseph earnestly. 'Why, she's suckling—' he broke off with a gulp as eleven boots hacked his shins under the table.

Dyer bellowed for one of his grooms and when the man came running, ordered him to fetch Mistress Laffam from the shop.

'Now see here,' said Oxley angrily. 'Rose hasn't done anything to bring her in front of a jury.'

'And I told you I didn't believe your swearings,' answered Dyer coldly. 'Stay silent and sit where I can watch you.'

Until Rose came to the taproom door Dyer had not supposed for a moment that she might actually have killed the woman whose body lay in the barn. He knew Oxley was lying and believed his daughter was the lever he could use to prise loose the truth, but as soon as he saw Rose's swollen and bitten face he knew that if he wished to indict a murderer then here was the felon he must take. Her figure was good, though; Dyer's lusts continued to judge women for such qualities as they possessed even in the most unfavourable of circumstances. 'Mistress Laffam?'

She shrugged. 'If you like.'

'I have to tell you that your husband Bartholomew's body is to be publicly hanged in chains until he rots, in this his birthplace. The dragoons bring it here tomorrow.'

She stood as still as stone, everyone in the taproom as still as stone.

'This woman who died two days—or perhaps two nights—ago. What was her name?'

Rose's lips moved but no sound came.

'Don't answer!' Oxley leapt to his feet, and behind Dyer's back oak squealed on the sanded floor as men pushed back benches in consternation, looked at each other and sank back again. A magistrate was a magistrate, there was nothing they could do against him.

'The woman who died, I said.' Dyer slammed his tankard against a keg. 'God's bowels, what kind of dolts are you? I haven't yet phrased accusation how I ought, but I will if you force me into it.'

'Nancy Larkworthy,' said Joseph suddenly. 'She came here, half-crazed and looking for her husband's killers. He was the riding officer murdered by smugglers, as you will recall, Sir Jonas. I took her over to my shop, since Larkworthy died there and she had a right to understand the truth. She seemed quite harmless then. Later she became frantic and there was a fight in which she died; I blame myself for leaving Rose alone with her. Rose is now suckling Larkworthy's babe as well as her own.'

'Bartholomew Laffam helped to kill Riding Officer Larkworthy,' Dyer said flatly.

No one answered. They had not grasped before how much he understood of what had happened the previous autumn in Furnace Green. Twelve faces stared back at Dyer like furrows in the soil, and the woman too, who still had not moved.

Great black guts of hell, thought Dyer violently. Accuse her and half the village will end up at Quarter Sessions, all the loose ends from last year I've just tidied out of sight be unravelled in open court. More lying reports to write and a pack of trouble before I am quit of this; I shall have earned the right to buy up Ferenthe Ridge by the time I get my hands on it, as get my hands on it I will. Sir Jonas Dyer's desire to keep Furnace Green out of the clutch of both the law and the Crown sequestrators was by no means entirely unselfish.

A half-squadron of dragoons rode out of the trees and across the green in mid-afternoon the following day, nearly seven centuries after armed troops had last enforced their will there. Ungreased wheels squealed in their midst and when the two lines of horsemen peeled apart a cart could be seen, driven by a hangman clad in black leather from head to toe.

Sir Jonas was waiting for them, seated on his horse near Bywood's smithy. 'You have had a disagreeable journey, I fear.'

The young cornet in charge nodded, took off his tricorn hat and bowed; indeed the stink from the cart was terrible. 'This is one year when I would have preferred less sun. You have all the inhabitants of this parish assembled?'

'So far as I can tell without searching the fields myself.'

The cornet grinned. 'Curiosity brings 'em, if nothing else. Where shall we string him up?'

'Anywhere, so long as it's away from the well and out of sight of the church.'

'That yew, then.' He shouted some orders, and his men rode over to where a crowd of villagers stood at the end of the street, began to herd them closer to the smithy and yew. The cart bumped over tussocks at the edge of the green and the driver climbed down, charnel house stench more powerful than ever.

'God in heaven!' cried Bruiser from his doorway. 'I'm not having that reek on my doorstep for weeks, driving good customers away. I fought the smugglers, didn't I? Why should I have Bart rotting under my nose?'

'Work harder over your hearth than ever you did before, and you won't smell aught else,' answered Dyer curtly. He wouldn't insult them or himself by suggesting they ought to feel glad when a neighbour was hung up in chains, member of Grey's gang though he'd been. Dyer glared at the shuffling, muttering crowd and shook open the proclamation he had been sent to read: '*George the Second by the Grace of God, King . . . Whereas Bartholomew Laffam has been taken in arms against His Majesty . . . and for the most pernicious and wicked deeds in the Counties of Sussex, Kent and Dorsetshire . . . condemned to hang by the neck until he is dead and his carcass exhibited in the place from whence he came . . . In the name of His Majesty this seventeenth day of May, 1749.*'

Dyer sat, heavy and unmoving, daring anyone else to move, while the hangman lifted liquescent flesh encased in iron and chain out of his cart and dragged it across to a yew previously best known for the quality of bow made from its branches.

The cornet held his tricorn across his nose. 'Will you bid whichever villager you most desire not to forget this day, to climb up with the end of chain, sir?'

'No, this is your business. See you to it.'

'It is hangman's, not a soldier's work!'

'Precisely. These people fought the smugglers fairly, and won. I will not bid them haul corpses into trees.'

'The Laffams were murderous swine of smugglers, and came from here.'

'And this Laffam will leave again in your cart unless one of your men does what he is paid to do.' He saw the cornet's mouth open to shout, and added softly, 'Without me, you have no power here to order anyone except your dragoons.'

So the dark and horrible thing which had been Bart Laffam was hauled up into the branches of the yew by the Lewes hangman and a puking trooper, while the people of Furnace Green watched; some in disgust or sadness, others with thrilled and avid horror.

Most people watched, that is.

Even had Sir Jonas felt so inclined, his six grooms were insufficient to sweep all the inhabitants of the ridge where they did not want to go, though some came willingly to witness a rare spectacle. Joseph and Abigail stayed inside Danesdell House: Abigail peering through an upper window and regretting that dignity forbade her to gape with the rest. Swatch Locock, too, considered a fine day better spent in his fields than gawping over bones, and so cheated his sons and labourers of a holiday.

Ned Oxley did not go, but walked up instead to the shop, only to find the door barred against him. Rose did not answer when he called out, although, as Oxley well knew, she was inside and alone except for the crib shared head-to-toe by Emily Laffam and Stevie Larkworthy.

Strange how alike they look, she thought dully. If Nancy could be believed then Stevie was nearly a year older than Emily, but no one would have guessed it from their size. Both were brown-haired, soft-skinned, unformed. Yet formed already by what had happened, fate squatting like a cuckoo beside them in the crib.

Bart, Rose thought, and shuddered.

Oh God, I had a husband and I loved him. That's what Nancy said and I despised her for being overset. Bart, oh Bart, why must you have caught an infection from Abel Grey? And by the hearth Rose wept, while caged stench and bones were hauled into the branches of the yew.

Across the street from the shop Arthur Brown, too, had not gone to see the son of an old accomplice hung up. He hated idleness, however, too much to stay prudently indoors at Wyses. Instead he used the unwonted emptiness of the street to stake out the site of some cottages he planned to build inside the almost vanished banks of Fawkners. Brown didn't believe in vain regret: the smugglers would be back but in Furnace Green the wolfpack days were probably gone for ever, and with them his share of the profit. Instead he was already making tidy sums by paying others to produce fat poultry and other delicacies for the rich gentry beginning to visit Tunbridge Wells's foul-smelling springs. Over the coming years, his past gains and these more modest schemes would enable him to build several cottages in this hitherto open side of Furnace Green's street, and then to rent them out for extortionate sums.

When the dragoons at last had finished their grisly business, Sir Jonas Dyer rode home to his child-wife with his mind almost entirely filled by calculation. All Laffam property would be forfeit to the Crown, which meant there would be land on Ferenthe Ridge for sale at last. A pity he would have to deal with the Exchequer for Corndown, but it could have been worse. Once he gained a foothold on the ridge then damme if he didn't find other parcels of land to buy after such an upheaval as there had been this past year. Joseph Hosmer was the last of his name to live in Furnace Green and unlikely to get issue on his old sow of a wife; the Carpenters were finished after centuries of amassing one enclosure with another, the church glebe held by a drunken sot of a parson. Oxley, too, would discover that he was unable to deed the Black Bear to a woman tainted by the name of Laffam, without first agreeing a deal with Sir Jonas; justices of the peace were concerned for the good name of any tavern in their locality. The possibilities kept unfolding while he considered them.

There and then, Dyer decided to offer for the site of Corndown's burned buildings without delay, while leaving the fields another season to deteriorate. It would be cheaper to clear a few saplings than pay an inflated price. There was also Greggs Wood and Edenham, Pigpasture too; Dyer would wager that neither Tworts, Piggs nor Rabbits would be able to prove title to the scratchings they inhabited. He had placed good money on loan to the Africa trade and expected fat profits there; give these a year or so to mature, and he would start buying up the ridge in earnest.

Jonas knew that the people here now accepted him as a Wealdsman; yesterday, once they understood that he would protect them from the consequences of what had happened, they had accepted him. Because not one of them had ever imagined that fighting Abel Grey would bring such varied and bewildering results, already they were wearied by complexity, felt threatened by an uncertain future. A brief conjuncture of events, which at the time had seemed a victory, instead made Furnace Green's independence seem a burden, a wily protector desirable rather than a despot to be resisted. Sir Jonas Dyer smacked his hand on his thigh. How very agreeable to succeed where even the Scovells had failed, and engross Ferenthe Ridge into the Riffield estate at last.

Some villagers, on the other hand, far from seeking security, were unsettled by the excitement of so many happenings and would not stay much longer on the ridge. After Swatch Locock left to take up the tenancy of Danesdell, most of the Piggs abandoned their clearings to tramp off to London, where they lived by thieving in its unlit alleys. Bruiser Bywood, who had come to believe that he had won the battle with the smugglers almost single-handed, threw his hammer into the forge pond on the same night Bart's corpse was hauled up into the yew and strode away to follow the dragoons, leaving a wife and daughter unprovided for behind him. He was well suited by a military life and died courageously ten years later, in the battle which won French Canada for the British Empire on the Heights of Abraham.

As for Ned Oxley, he was finally delivered into Sir Jonas's hands when he told him that Rose had only married Bart in a blasphemous ceremony suggested by Giles Dyer. Ned hoped this would shield her from some of the consequences of being a felon's relict, but Dyer promptly complained to the bishop about Furnace Green's parson and shook his head over the need to call Rose as a witness of Brookland's sacrilege. Since the likely consequence of this was Rose's indictment, too, for blasphemy, not long afterwards Ned gratefully accepted Sir Jonas's offer to intercede on her behalf. Somehow, after that, it wasn't long before Oxley became Dyer's tenant rather than a freeholder, but at least Sir Jonas kept his part of the unspoken bargain. The case against Brookland collapsed for lack of evidence.

I suppose Giles must have been killed in that same blasphemous brawl, reflected Sir Jonas as he again rode home in high good humour after completing this latest among his Furnace Green deals. Not that it matters now; scoundrels all of them, up on the ridge.

Jonas did not consider that he had finally become accepted there precisely because of the kind of scoundrel he was too, nor would it have worried him if it had. Black Sussex. A hundred years after the Dyers came to the Weald, they had finally become absorbed into its life.

. . . THE WITNESS

And so I reach a time when people who were still remembered in Furnace Green when I was a boy begin to enter these stories. The tale I am about to tell concerns, among others, Mark Smith, who was my great-grandfather. My own father remembered sitting on his knee. He said great-grandfather always wore a brindled calfskin waistcoat and liked to boast that his nose was as beaked as Old Hookey's, meaning the Duke of Wellington, in whose army he had served against Napoleon. 'Aye, and I remember Grandfer spanking me, too, when I said his nose looked to me more like a barnyard rooster's than a duke's,' Dad liked to add reminiscently. 'A powerful spank he had and no mistake, for an old 'un. Whiskers that struck out every whichway, white flaky skin on his face and cheekbones like a shelf.'

So I know what Mark Smith looked like, and some of the others, too, who lived here a hundred and fifty years ago. Village memories used to be very long, and faithfully recalled exciting events and personalities for several generations.

My father's mother was a Locock, my own mother born Eliza Larkworthy, which means she must have been descended from Stevie, the baby Rose Oxley suckled. Mum's grandad died only five years before I was born, and he was Liddy's brother Pete, who as you will hear, was the one Larkworthy who chose to return to Furnace Green after . . . but I am confusing you again, with the names of people you have still to meet. Of course, Liddy played quite a part in the wild doings of the year 1830 on the ridge, the year of Captain Swing, when Davey Portnell went out seeking justice. No direct descendant of his ever lived in Furnace Green, but once upon a time I loved a girl called Christian Portnell. As I love her still, never the past tense for Chris. 'I think Davey was just a great big fool,' she used to say and toss her plaits, but even Chris spoke as if Davey had only that moment walked away down the street.

Then there were the Braybons. Uppity newcomers in 1830 but accepted afterwards, because of the way General Braybon behaved in a time of crisis. When he died the family moved away, time speeding up, people coming and going more quickly now, but in his will the general left a sum of money to help deserving boys and girls from Furnace Green to set up in a trade. At a crucial time in my life, I was to become a beneficiary of this fund.

And so, in a trifling way, the tales Granny Paley told me and my own are beginning to overlap at last.

As soon as I say it, I see this as a false distinction, because, in places like Furnace Green, the link of blood is seldom completely lost. Once settlement began and monks dug the first sod of their chapel, inheritance flowed deviously but uninterrupted until the present, when all the English rural certainties and rhythms quite suddenly vanished within the space of a single lifetime. Consider the Paleys, for instance: minstrels, pedlars and tricksters by inclination. The first Parleybien stayed only two days in Ferenthe, as it then was called, and most of his descendants chased will-o'-the-wisps off the ridge and disappeared for ever from its story. And yet, for four hundred and fifty years some of them also stayed. Only in 1925 did the last Parleybien of Furnace Green die, whom we called Granny Paley, and she lives on in the tales she told.

When Granny was a girl in the middle of the last century, nearly everyone who took part in the events I am about to relate was still alive, although it has been interesting to discover that, even so, her sense of time remained erratic. In Granny's memory the iron industry still roared and clanged encouragement to Captain Swing, when in reality its fires had cooled long before; the Scovells and Dyers were interchangeable in her stories, Parson Syke a force constantly to be reckoned with. My part in resolving the riddle of time and distance has been to research what ended where, the why and how of what happened, to tease out puzzles and browse through crumbling documents. I made slow progress until my friends stepped out of their past to keep me company and show me which way to go, at a time when my need for them was very great.

As Granny Paley would have put it, 'Look'ee, my purty. Y'oim queered ter tellit taalses lik em shod be tellit, surelye. 'Tis tur'ble orkerd ter twiddle em tergidder praaper. T'ough nary a one among em be gallus taalses an boco be vaaliant foine.'

I offer my memory of Granny speaking as explanation for the way I have written my version of stories from the ridge. I'm proud of the Sussex in my own voice still, but even in my boyhood, when most of the village kept the broad vowels and slurred speech of their ancestors, Granny spoke an older dialect. The common word 'boco', meaning many, probably came from refugee French ironworkers; 'gallus', an adjective or adverb meaning wretched or mean, may have echoed the centuries when gallows were a common feature in the countryside.

It would be a weary business to read any book made up of such speech, and pointless too, since even such recognizable English as this did not emerge in the Weald until around the fifteenth century. I also have another motive for writing simple standard words, for in their own eyes this was what the village spoke. Nowadays people often laugh at dialect, as if speaking it turned their fellows into clowns. Nor can I understand why the country poor all over the world are often made out to be stupid, sly or squalid. My parents were poor enough, God knows, but they fought every day of their lives for self respect, and very often won. 'Don't you crawl to nobody,' Mum would say to us children. 'Work as you should and don't short-change, but never let a master wipe his shoes on you. People won't respect you if you do. If you can't get on by honest means, don't ever start trying no short cuts. The Lord won't give his blessing on that.'

Mum knew that only pride and religion made lives like ours endurable. Pride which allowed us to hold up our heads among our neighbours, and God's promise that the poor were people too. My father possessed the kind of courage which quietly endured everything put on him, Mum's came from the spirit and was more vulnerable to suffering. Both of them seemed good people to me, as good as any people could be. Others were bad, of course, like Abel Grey. Above all, they were individual, not lumps of earth seen from a carriage window. Which is why I tell their story in English everyone will respect: I would hate to think that anything I wrote helped to hide how they and their neighbours really were, just because it is easy to mock or weary of the way they spoke.

3

Reaching Out

1830–1838

In the heat of a July afternoon a girl walked up the lane which led from Edenham Mill to Furnace Green. Overgrown hedgerows cast some welcome shade, since laying and trimming was winter work, but all the same Liddy Larkworthy was hot. She felt anxious because she was hot. It would never do to arrive at Greenview House red-faced and sticky.

She was dressed in an undyed calico smock, and carried a small bundle tied up in a cloth. When she reached the beginnings of the village, where the lane cut deeply between high banks, she paused, shifting the weight of this bundle from hand to hand. Opposite her was the house called Wyses, its soft brick and uneven roof looking as if they had been there for ever, but in the paddock adjoining it a much larger house, called Greenview, had recently been constructed in plain but modish style. Bright green shutters hung each side of sash windows, the walls were stuccoed and a verandah ran along the front of the house. A carefully tended gravel drive swept up to the front door, and the garden was enclosed by a high brick wall.

On Liddy's right was the street and church, where cottages now lined the eastern as well as the older, western side. These street cottages looked pleasant enough, but Liddy knew that far too many people were crammed inside. Furnace Green held twice as many inhabitants as it had only a couple of generations before, and yet there was less work. Organised smuggling had finally been defeated a few years previously, many of the old crafts had migrated to the towns, and the farms could not absorb the surplus. Consequently, poverty was everywhere in evidence.

But Liddy wasn't looking at the street, everything there too familiar to attract her interest. Instead she was looking at Greenview House with its intimidating stretch of gravel leading to whitened, brass-bound steps. A gardener was raking scythed grass, and on either side of the drive stood ornamental urns sprouting spiky greenery.

Nervously, she turned aside to walk across the stable yard. Today, if only all went well, the whole of her life would change and Greenview House become her home. Liddy took a deep breath, shifted her bundle one last time, and pulled the iron knob beside the scullery door, holding her breath when she heard it jangle alarmingly far away.

A red-nosed girl opened the door. 'Who are you, a-pulling the bell like the Devil himself hung on to it by his tail?'

'I'm sorry. I wasn't sure how hard to pull it,' said Liddy nervously. 'Mr Hooke told me I could ask for a position in the household.'

The girl put her hands on her hips. ''Tis mortal hard work being 'tweenmaid here, the mistress is that particular.'

'I'm not afraid of hard work.' Dear knew, she had worked ever since she was old enough to be of use.

'Come in, then.' The girl led the way along a stone-floored passage. 'There's three children in the nursery so we could do with another pair of hands. The parlour-maid will tell Mrs Braybon you're here.'

The kitchen was the largest room Liddy had ever seen. A coal range stretched along one wall, the rest of the room —huge as it seemed—taken up by a scrubbed table, chairs, shelves, polished pans, tubs of provisions, knives, bowls, a tabby cat. On her way from the back door Liddy had already passed half a dozen smaller rooms where she glimpsed crocks and churns, stone sinks, slate shelves, wooden bootjacks, a hundred things she could not name.

A stout grey-haired woman snored beside the range. 'Cook,' whispered the scullery-maid. 'She always sleeps in the afternoon and mind you take care not to wake her.' She vanished upstairs.

Liddy couldn't stop staring at that kitchen while she waited, and the comforts it contained. Until today she had lived all her life at Edenham, which she had considered large compared to the cottages in the street, but the whole house would nearly be swallowed up in this kitchen. The old mill had been converted to grind flour soon after Sir Jonas Dyer turned out all the Rabbits, and as Dyer tenants the Larkworthys had been millers there for nearly twenty years. Partly because their rent had been set in more prosperous times, they only fed really well in exceptional seasons, but on the other hand they never actually starved. The cottagers did. Which was one reason why Liddy cherished high hopes of her chances now she was to be interviewed for the post of 'tweenmaid at Greenview House, since most employers disliked having servants who suffered from the ailments and scrawny looks which came from poverty.

'You're to go up,' said the scullery-maid, reappearing. 'May will meet you at the stairhead. She's the upstairs-maid.'

Liddy's heart beat hard as she climbed the back stairway. She was eighteen, which was old to be entering service for the first time, but this made it all the more difficult to strike away from everything she knew. Her new boots hurt and she couldn't yet put her hair up tidily into braids.

May met her in the pantry, a sharp-faced girl with an accent Liddy later discovered to be London. She wore a grey and white-striped dress, a high starched collar and cuffs, an apron and an elaborately ruffled cap; Liddy couldn't imagine herself looking so strange. She grinned encouragingly though. 'Don't worry. If you're decent and mind what you're told, they'll treat you fair.' She opened a door. 'The new girl to see you, mam.'

Millicent Braybon was stitching cambric by the window. Against the light her capped head and ivory silk dress offered an impression of solid severity and Liddy gulped, unable to move.

Mrs Braybon looked up. 'Come where I can see you.'

Liddy advanced timidly across unfamiliar carpeting.

'Mr Hooke recommended you as willing and used to children. I hope that is right?'

'Yes, mam.' Samuel Hooke was the schoolmaster and poor law overseer, a good friend to the Larkworthy household in ways Liddy did not quite understand.

'I realize a household like this is new to you, but you know how to clean, of course?'

'Oh yes, mam.'

'And wash baby clothes and starch and iron? Naturally you will be shown exactly how I like things to be done.'

'Yes, mam,' said Liddy again.

'Good. You will also help in the kitchen with the dishes, carry up the nursery meals and take care of the schoolroom wing. Do you think you can learn to do all that properly?'

'I'll try, mam.' Liddy's voice trembled.

'You must not feel frightened. What is your name?'

'Liddy, mam. Liddy Larkworthy.'

'Oh yes, I remember now. Your baptismal name is Elizabeth, I believe?'

'I've always been Liddy, mam.' And, after a few half-hearted attempts to call her Elizabeth or Eliza, Liddy she remained.

Without more questions, the position of 'tweenmaid apparently was hers, but it was some while before Liddy realized that even by the standards of rich folk, the Braybon household was unusual. Mrs Braybon seemed cold and disciplined, but she was not. Quite the contrary, in fact. Without warning she would fly into furious rages, when she threw ornaments at the wall or ripped up sewing over which she had laboured for weeks. She was careful never to indulge in such fits in front of strangers, but within the household she could change within seconds from being completely calm into a harridan shouting at everyone to leave the room. As soon as they had, they would hear the sounds of frenzy through the solid mahogany doors, but providing she was left alone no one suffered more than inconvenience as a result. An hour later Mrs Braybon would be quite collected again, and industriously attempting to mend whatever objects she had torn or broken.

Her husband, General Braybon, reminded Liddy of the vases either side of the gravel drive. Tall, dramatic, and finished by a great many bristles at the top: whiskers, hair and eyebrows. He had lived for many years in India, and married quite late in life when he retired to England. His skin was yellow and he spoke in an enormously loud voice, although Liddy soon understood that his roars meant nothing in particular beyond good spirits. He was lean and straight, and his moustaches extended outwards in two sharp points which could be seen quite easily from behind, like the horns of ploughing oxen. These weren't waxed but sustained by their own strength; likewise the hairs which sprouted from his nose, eyebrows and ears. Even so, his eyes were his most remarkable feature, Liddy decided. Set deep, and very dark and glittering. Occasionally the glitter was of rage but much more often of devilment; and when his eyes laughed the eyebrows seemed to join in merrily on their own. In anger, they stood as stiffly as soldiers grasping lances.

Just sometimes Liddy heard General Braybon being astonishingly rude, and disbelieved her ears because everyone else she knew was rude to inferiors and polite where it suited them. But General Braybon addressed children, servants and labourers with such exquisite courtesy that they found it hard to believe he wasn't in fact insulting them; everyone else he treated on their merits and was rude exactly where he chose. He read a great many books which May said were in heathen languages, and wrote trenchant monographs on new farming methods which he believed would help support the swelling British population. He had also bought Corndown fields from the Dyers, where he experimented in such matters as leather pumps for muck-spreading. As a diversion from these activities he carried on a perpetual sniping warfare with Mr Aitchison, who lived across the green at Danesdell House, on subjects which made no sense at all. Mr Aitchison, an antiquary and a magistrate who fancied his power, squirmed under the thunderbolts hurled at him over such matters as the Peloponnesian Wars and the iniquities of English common law.

Three children, Jasper, Tessie and a baby, completed the family, the servants required to run Greenview House greatly outnumbering their employers, which was fortunate when work was so short. There was Hester and a wet-nurse who looked after the children; May and Annie, the two upstairs-maids, and Liddy the 'tweenmaid; Cook, Milly and Hetty who spent their lives in the kitchen; William the footman; Banks, Twort and Billy Rabbit in the garden; Akehurst the groom; Johnny the boot- and saddle-boy; Mrs Sleech and Mrs Baker who came in to scrub. Mrs Paley across the green took in the heavy laundry, while Mrs Smith employed three girls in Pigpasture Farm hayloft, sewing for the larger houses beginning to appear around Furnace Green.

At first, Liddy's head reeled with the complication of such a household, but she was by nature quick and adaptable as well as thrustingly anxious to better herself by working hard. Every time she went up to the attic room she shared with Hetty she contrasted it with cramped and dusty Edenham. There, she shared a bed with her sister, Kate, and baby Dick, and no matter how hard they cleaned the house dust flew everywhere from the grindings at the mill. At Greenview House three solid meals were served each day and she and Hetty each possessed a bed and dresser of their own; at Edenham, fear became tangible when any of the circumstances which threatened crops meant grinding might slow or stop. By gaining employment at Greenview, Liddy had won free from all that. Her sister, Kate, now inherited the task of looking after the younger children, while it became Liddy's duty to take home five out of the six sovereigns she would earn in a year.

Altogether, Liddy was too happy to remain frightened very long, too excited to feel tired even though she worked from before dawn until after dark each day, besides learning a great many things she had never dreamed existed before. Because there were limitless quantities of good things to eat, never in her life had she felt so full of energy. Barley broth, meat stews and pies, oat cakes, cheese, ale, bread and jam for the staff, while the family and their friends ate exotic mixtures out of vast dishes which Liddy was afraid of dropping when she climbed with them up the backstairs to the pantry. There, William, May and Annie took over to serve the dining room.

Long before then Liddy would have carried trays up to Master Jasper, Miss Tessie and the schoolroom staff, and it was there she had her rare encounters with General Braybon. The nursery door would slam and in he would stride wearing his evening dress of black-striped trousers, cutaway coat and embroidered waistcoat, everything set into a commotion by his arrival.

One day he encountered her climbing the last flight of stairs carrying a particularly heavy tray, and had to wait because she failed to realize he was there.

'Beg pardon, sir.' Liddy squeezed against the wall as soon as she heard his step.

'Allow me.' He took the tray out of her hands.

'Oh no, sir! You can't carry the nursery tray,' Liddy said, scandalised, and so far forgot herself as to try to grab it back.

'Of course I can carry a tray, don't be foolish, child. What's that? What did you say?' And he answered himself as if Liddy had replied, another disconcerting habit. 'Oh yes, how entirely I agree! It is only right I should carry this devilish heavy tray for you. We do not desire to break the camel's back, do we? Lead on then, Liddy, and we will surprise them all.'

This they certainly did.

Liddy nearly fell through the schoolroom door in her anxiety to perform the service of opening it for her master, and the general arrived on her heels, having needed to travel faster and faster along the passage to prevent the dishes from sliding over the tray's further edge.

The nurse leaped to her feet, all her double chins flapping

with astonishment, Tessie and Jasper squealing with delight as their father bellowed at them to catch cruets, cutlery and spilling plates. 'Oh, Papa, will you bring our supper every night?' demanded Tessie.

The general shook out a silk handkerchief and mopped his face. 'Without Liddy's ministrations you would starve to death up here, Miss Tessie. Let us be quite clear about that. It is she who sustains your and Master Jasper's gluttony. Make sure you always thank her nicely when she comes.'

'We could live on the first floor,' said Jasper. 'I'd like that. Then I'd see everything that's going on without people being able to tell me fusses are none of my business. I like fusses.' He cast a darkling look at Nurse.

'I like fusses too,' agreed the general with relish, his eyebrows prancing.

'Please, sir, it's no trouble to carry trays up three flights of stairs.' Liddy couldn't help laughing inwardly at the consternation which would be caused if the general lightheartedly agreed that the children should inhabit the lower floors.

However it soon emerged that he was too wily to be caught either carrying trays as a habit or suffering his children permanently underfoot. 'It would be ungentlemanly of me to upset your mother's arrangements, you do see that, Master Jasper, do you not? Good. I am detestable in many ways but I do try not to be ungentlemanly. Tessie, if you pick up the tray and give it to Liddy, then you both may stack the empty dishes thereupon.'

This was much more difficult to accomplish than if Liddy had stacked them for herself and between them they broke a dish, but Liddy considered this a small price to pay for preventing the general from carrying her tray down to the kitchen. He bowed to her ceremoniously when everything was in place and told Jasper to hold open the door. 'We are all sinners, Master Jasper. In this world the best we can hope for is to be gentlemanly.'

The general found the notion that he was a sinner

extremely useful, since he preferred being gentlemanly to aspiring to virtue. On Sundays, he would marshal his household for the short walk to where a new church was almost completed at the end of the street as if he was commanding a division to the charge. His malacca cane prodded the tardy into line, and when everyone was paired to his satisfaction he would march ahead of them as far as the gate. There he would stop. 'As a sinner, I must now bid you farewell. I do not presume to enter where I am not worthy, but in my absence make sure you comport yourselves as if this Sabbath was your last. You hear me, Miss Tessie? Do not kill wasps inside your psalter today.'

'I really think occasionally you should accompany us, Humphrey,' hissed Mrs Braybon. Notwithstanding her discretion these last-minute urgings were always audible.

Sadly, the general would shake his head. 'You think so? You really think I might be forgiven? But no, I fear that at my age I must be presumed to know where I am likely to be blackballed, and find it preferable to attempt a few noble thoughts of my own on a Sunday morning. Lead on, Master Jasper. Make sure you bow to each lady of our acquaintance.'

'Really, all he does is smoke a cigar and read his journal with never two noble thoughts to rub together!' said Liddy, laughing, to Davey when he met her at the stable gate. Greenview House servants had every other Sunday afternoon off after the dishes were finished, and this was her first after two and a half weeks in the Braybon household.

'If Parson hadn't threatened I might lose my 'prenticeship if I didn't attend church each Sunday, I'd be off myself. At Ockham there's a different kind of meeting on Sundays, where men talk about our wrongs, which I'd like far better to attend,' Davey answered, scowling.

'Then I'm glad Parson did threaten you! You're best away from such troublemakers! I heard the general telling —' Liddy wrinkled her brow. 'I think he said the magistrates were listening out for dangerous talk.'

'I've more important things to trouble my head about

than what your general thinks. You and me will quarrel if you can't talk about anything except what goes on inside Greenview House.'

'Why shouldn't I talk about the only things I know?' Liddy exclaimed hotly. 'You tell me fast enough about your doings.'

His hand tightened about her waist. 'I'm sorry. But I've never been able to talk before about the kind of things those Ockham fellows talk about. I've thought them, I suppose. Felt angry and wanted to believe there might be something different to how things are. Now I know there is.'

Liddy nodded. She had felt like that when she had wanted to believe there was a better life for her if only she could reach it; but whilst her dreams had taken shape at Greenview House, Davey seemed unsettled by whatever it was that he'd discovered. 'Don't let's spoil our afternoon,' she said after a pause.

'Must you go home to Edenham?'

She nodded. 'They'll want to hear everything that's happened, and just fancy! Cook gave me a meat pudding to take home! The little ones will never have tasted anything so good.'

But that wasn't right either, because Davey scowled afresh and refused to answer.

'Whatever's the matter now?' cried Liddy in exasperation.

'Well,' he said deliberately. 'I'll tell you since you've asked. It isn't right for us to drool over scraps from the rich man's table. Like it isn't right for Sarah Pigg to feed her five brats on peelings she digs out of Greenview House waste pit, secretly at night.'

'Cook's meat pudding isn't scraps! She made it special as a surprise after I said grinding was bad this year, now there's so little water in the stream.'

Davey shrugged. 'I thought you might understand, but you don't.'

'I do!'

'If you did, you'd see why I'd like to drop your meat pudding in the dirt.'

'Don't you dare!' Davey had walked out with Liddy for nearly six months and until today she had never seen a single thing wrong in him; three years older than herself and in the last year of apprenticeship to Lavender the mason, he was at present engaged on rebuilding Furnace Green church. Davey's eyes were level and clear, his mouth and shoulders wide, his boy's bones filling out with the muscle of a man. There wasn't a girl in Furnace Green who didn't envy Liddy her catch.

'Of course I wouldn't drop it unless you said I could,' he answered stiffly. 'But I must say, Liddy, I do think you might.'

'Might what?'

'Tell me to throw it in the ditch.'

For the life of her, Liddy couldn't see why she should be addled enough to bid Davey throw Cook's meat pudding in the ditch. A pudding she had felt such pride in taking home, a token of her new status as a provider. 'Well, I shan't. I've a right to that pudding. Cook *gave* it to me. How could I go back tonight and tell her I threw it in a ditch?'

'All right, don't then. But one day you'll understand how charity insults a man who cannot feed his family no matter how many hours he works.'

'I suppose you would sooner Mrs Braybon didn't send soup to Mrs Paley when she was brought low by a fever, nor subscribe to the clothing fund and send a shawl to each new-born babe on the ridge?' said Liddy, stung.

'I'd sooner the farmers paid their men a decent living.'

Liddy pounced. 'The general pays his men at Corndown even when it rains.'

'Locock doesn't. Nor most other farmers neither. As for your father and his dealings—' Davey closed his lips and strode on so fast that Liddy was forced to take little skipping steps to keep up.

'David Portnell!' She tugged loose from his arm about

her waist. 'You're always hinting things against my da. You finish what you begun this time or I'll go on from here alone.'

He turned to face her and slowly his expression softened, long mouth lifting at the corners. 'Sometimes I like you best when you're angry. Your hair is coming down and your bonnet is over your eyes.'

She stamped her foot. 'Tell me this instant! What has Da done that you can't abide? And give me that pudding back before you begin, in case you forget what you promised and throw it in a ditch.'

He grinned and handed it over. She was like a sparrow, he thought, perched on those damned button boots, head on one side so the sun lit the freckles on her nose. No one could have described Liddy Larkworthy as pretty, but the clear outline of cheek and jaw, her small straight nose, the hair and eyes which Davey privately thought the colour of fawn's hide, all conveyed eagerness and warmth.

'Now tell me,' she commanded.

'What about sitting beside me while I do?'

Liddy considered. 'Only for a minute, and right here on the bank. Then after you've explained, *if* I still want to sit with you, I just might walk a little way by the stream.'

'Promise?'

She nodded. By immemorial custom, Furnace Green girls walked along the ridge lanes with their young men on Sunday afternoons, and sat whispering together at the limit of their walk. The further away they went the faster gossiping tongues clacked. But sitting together out of sight was a different matter altogether. If they were seen, tongues would do more than clack; Liddy could lose her position if Mrs Braybon heard rumours which suggested that Liddy Larkworthy was no better than she ought to be.

Davey sat beside her on the hedgerow bank and frowned at his square-fingered craftsman's hands. 'You know how Hooke reckons up poor relief at the meanest amount which will keep a family from starving?' Liddy nodded again. Everyone knew how Samuel Hooke, schoolmaster, overseer of the poor and churchwarden as he was, pryer into every corner of the village, delighted in his power. 'Then, instead of giving out the miserly few pence they're owed, he gives tokens for flour at Edenham Mill.'

'It's flour the paupers want, isn't it?' said Liddy, puzzled.

'And most things else. Ever since Hooke has taken to giving tokens instead of pence, they not only have to grovel for his charity but also waste time tramping out to Edenham, there to be paid in sweepings. Short measure, of course, so your father and Hooke can split the profit between them. But that's not the end of it. Next they must trade their handfuls of flour for the other things they need, while each trader in turn profits from their desperation. At the shop—' He broke off and then added, each word dropped like a stone. 'At the shop my accursed Portnell cousins refuse to accept flour in payment. So a poor woman who needs a scoop of salt or sugar loses twice. First when she changes flour sweepings somehow into pence, and then pence into scrapings from the stalest goods in the shop.'

'You're sure?' asked Liddy quietly, and bit her lip. She wasn't really surprised, because what Davey had said explained a great many things she hadn't understood about two men as unlike as her father and Hooke, often with their heads together at the mill. It explained nothing at all about the hard-working father whom she loved.

'I'm sure. It's a way of life in the village, after all.'

'Then I do understand why you'd like to throw my pie in the ditch.' Liddy held Cook's knotted cloth tightly between her hands. 'I can't do it, though. Like my da can't stop what he's begun, I reckon. Dear knows, he needs any pence he can get if he's to pay his rent to the Dyers in a season as dry as this one.'

'That's wicked.'

'I know it's wicked! Don't you dare preach at me, Davey Portnell, just because you listen to hot talk at Ockham! I expect Da decided he'd rather be wicked than be turned out with his rent unpaid, and watch us starve.'

She jumped to her feet, trembling violently, turned and

slapped Davey's face with all her strength. As she did so the meat pie slipped from her grasp and fell between their feet. The cloth burst and rich meat filling flooded into the dust.

Liddy blinked, unwilling to believe her eyes. Her hand stung and her lips moved, trying to form words.

'You said you would come with me by the stream.' Davey slipped his hand under her elbow.

She shook her head.

'You promised.' He forced a passage through the hedgerow for them both. 'Liddy, we mustn't quarrel. We won't talk about it any more, that's all.'

'Where's the good in that, if we can't talk about what matters most?' she cried.

'You matter, don't you?'

'Oh, thank you very much.' She scrubbed her face on the sleeve of her dress. 'But I think that today neither of us matters too much to the other. I'm thinking about dropping Cook's meat pie and how my da swindles scraps out of our neighbours' mouths. You've got your head packed full of talk you've heard at Ockham tavern.'

'Heads are made to hold more than one thing at a time.'

'Who are these troublemakers at Ockham anyway? A gang come to build a fancy house for gentry among the abbey ruins. They'll be gone again soon and leave you facing all the quarrels they've stirred up.'

'It's those who refuse to pay their labourers a living wage who are the troublemakers! Farmers like Locock with his new threshing machine, which will cheat ten men out of their winter hire. Why, Caleb Hankin says—'

Liddy clapped her hands over her ears. 'I don't want to hear what he says, nor any other of they Ockham men. I'm fair sick of you braying other men's thoughts!'

'They're my thoughts, too. The only difference is, I haven't learned how to put them into words. But I will, you just wait.'

She stared at him, shrewd enough to see the obstinacy and also the wistful dreaming in his face. Davey listened and was led; one day, he might lead others. She also saw the red mark where she had struck him, a blow which many men would have repaid by thumping her in return. 'Meanwhile, there's my pie in the dust,' she said after a pause.

He laughed. 'Oh, Liddy. Would you . . . could I kiss you?'

Liddy shut her eyes and turned her cheek, thus indicating that he could; all the same, she realized that he could afford to kiss and make up since he had gained his point: the meat pie was irreparably lost.

Davey left her on the slope above Edenham, promising he would return to walk her back up the lane in the dark. Previously, it had upset and mystified Liddy when Davey refused to come into her home; today she was relieved when he turned away.

She was unprepared, though, for how small and poky Edenham looked, how deeply crouched into rampant undergrowth. Nettles, ivy and willow-herb thrived where furnaces had once poured out molten iron, the house almost hidden behind climbing honeysuckle and convolvulus. Such a short time spent away, and on her return Liddy saw unkempt poverty rather than her home. Did not her mother scrub the floor every day, and had not she herself slaved to keep the children clean, damped down flour-dust so it could be swept up? Before, Liddy had been part of the battle against want and dirt, today she saw only how hopeless the struggle was.

Her brothers and sisters came running all the same, from baby Dick who wobbled up the slope to throw his arms around her knees, to Kate, eagerly listening to everything Liddy had to tell, because soon it would be her turn to try and find a position—and Liddy's duty to help her discover it.

'Aw, come on Liddy! Tell us again how the general carried your tray!' Pete begged, as they ate supper.

'Strange to think how he prides himself on being a

gentleman and then carries a tray for all the world like a varmint,' observed Mrs Larkworthy, polishing a mug on her apron.

'He is a gentleman,' insisted Liddy, everything forgotten except the pleasure of imparting and receiving news. 'Tell me, has Mrs French had her baby yet?'

'Twins! And both as merry as fleas.'

Liddy broke into a delighted laugh, demanding instantly to hear more. Her mother often acted as the parish midwife, and the Frenches of Newhouse were two miserable old grouches who had been trying to birth a son for years. But, strangely, in spite of her chatter, Liddy could only nibble at her food.

The children clamoured to hear exactly what the Braybons ate and how much was served in the kitchen at Greenview House, their eyes as round as millwheels when Liddy said that when her mistress entertained the meal lasted at least two hours.

'I do think you might have smuggled us a taste,' said Jane, disgusted. 'Imagine, a—a marchpane cake as high as a sack of flour! What is marchpane, Liddy?'

As for her older brother Alec, leaning against the door jamb all white with flour from head to toe, he muttered something under his breath which sounded like bitch.

'Of course Liddy couldn't bring anything. If she was caught stealing 'twould be the end of her place,' said Mrs Larkworthy firmly. 'Later, when she's become more valued I daresay there will be things she can bring home. Why, I remember when I worked for Parson Nash, he threw away more in a day than my father took to the fields for his lunch in a week! But after a while when I learned my way around, I was able to take some home and no one thought twice about it even if they knew.'

Liddy pushed her platter of bread and preserve aside, feeling as if Cook's succulent meat pudding was stuck between her ribs.

'You watch what you say, mother, and leave the girl to make the best she can for herself,' Liddy's father answered roughly. 'Start her on that road and she'll lose out, certain sure. 'Tweenmaid, isn't she, with no call to go near the storeroom? You begin her thieving and there's no knowing where she'll end.'

'Oh, Da.' Liddy touched his hand in an agony of compassion. Let Davey say what he wanted about wickedness, she understood easier than he did how affection could betray anyone into doing wicked things. Then, even if you wished to, you couldn't change the road you'd chosen.

As Liddy watched, her father's shoulders straightened and he stood. 'I must get back to the mill. Farmer Locock's fetching away his load to Tonbridge market in the morning, and a penalty for us to pay if it's not milled in time.'

Liddy went to say goodbye to her father before she left. There was so little water in the mill pond that the wheel was hardly turning, the air thick with white dust.

'Behave yourself, Liddy.' Her father spat spittle as thick as dough, and coughed. 'See you again in two weeks, is it?'

Liddy hugged him, although when she arrived she had scarcely known how to wait before pouring out the shame and indignation she had felt when Davey explained what went on at Edenham. 'Aye, two weeks. I'll bring you all something next time.'

'A drop of rain will see us right. I meant what I said. Don't you go risking nothing.'

Alec brushed past them carrying a sack, which he left by the door without speaking to her. 'Da,' said Liddy quietly. 'Those sacks you keep by the entry. They're the sweepings, aren't they?'

'Dust and straws mostly, aye. What of it?'

'Is that what Ma uses for her baking?'

'You know it isn't. You wouldn't expect a miller to scour his belly by eating bread made out of chaff, now would you, lass?'

'So why keep it, if it isn't fit to eat?'

'It's fit for them as hasn't a choice. See here, what's this about?'

Liddy could feel the millwheel shuddering the floor under her feet, saw the sun setting through a pinkish haze of flour dust. 'I've heard things said about Edenham and I wondered if they were true.'

There was a pause before he said angrily, 'I thought better of you than listening to gossip in the street.'

Liddy shook her head. 'I can't help listening. Blame's something else again.'

'It's that young stir-up David Portnell, isn't it? I've had just about enough of him chawing about me and Sam Hooke to anyone who would listen, without him starting on you. We'll make him swallow his vomit one day soon, you see if we don't.'

Guilt and humiliation spoke through his bluster, leaving Liddy torn more than ever between affection, disgust and understanding. So, instead of answering, she stood tiptoe and kissed him on the cheek, the taste of sweat and flour remaining on her lips as she hurried up the slope to the lane.

Clear as clear, Davey was right when he accused Da of robbing the poorest folk on the ridge. But could he help himself? That was a puzzle too hard for Liddy to answer.

Davey Portnell whistled as he worked next day at grooving stone, a deft workman who did what he was told while allowing his mind to rove elsewhere. As an apprentice his labours were mundane and Furnace Green's new church of uninspired design. No carving, no stone vaults. Even the pillars were cast iron, sent ready-made from the Midlands as if in calculated insult to a place which had pioneered the ironsmith's trade, and now was left without a single furnace to help support its people.

In reality, economy was the reason for both iron shafts and plain design. Furnace Green's ever-swelling numbers struggling for subsistence on land whose produce seemed inexplicably to fall in value, meant that their landlord, Sir Maurice Dyer, must himself bear most of the costs of rebuilding the church. The old freeholdings of the ridge were lost or beleaguered, the Frenches struggling at Newhouse, the Locucks as miserly as cockroaches while they scrimped to buy their freehold. Mark Smith at Pigpasture Farm was a Dyer tenant, the unfelled forest between there and Riffield a Dyer preserve where the villagers were no longer allowed to trap game or gather wood.

So, when the old church finally became too dilapidated to be worth patching any longer, the Dyers failed to see why they should waste money on ornament for yokels. Ungrateful yokels, too, who scowled whenever their landlord came to inspect his property. By all means let them have a building in which they might worship God and remember their place, but ornament was for those who might appreciate it.

Occasionally, while he worked, Davey would come across fragments from the old church, although it had become so ramshackle that even the walls were pulled down. Davey liked those old fragments, because he never knew what he might find. A capital from a pillar showed tendrils so delicate he could scarcely believe they were stone, and once he found some painted plaster on which a merry angel seemed to dance a jig. He wished he could have seen the picture whole.

On the day after he had walked Liddy to Edenham on her first day out, Davey found his best treasure yet, the figure of a man being tormented by the devil. He very nearly shovelled it into filling for a wall, but glimpsed carved shapes and grabbed it back; he hid it behind a tombstone to look at later, the master-mason being a man who beat apprentices caught slacking on the job. In the summer Davey worked fourteen hours a day, broken at noon by just sufficient time to eat bread and ale. Consequently he had to wait several hours for dinnertime before looking at his trophy; when he did, he nearly choked on his mouthful.

Himself a solid worker in stone rather than an artist, Davey possessed more than enough imagination to recognize artistry when he saw it. 'It's beautiful,' he breathed, as if what he saw required acknowledgement in words, no matter what. The fragment must have been some kind of decorative boss, representing . . . Unexpectedly, Davey felt his admiration begin to chill as he sensed the subtle way in which consummate skill had been corrupted. How had a man understood that a pinprick in stone just there would give an expression of such hate? A pared edge here a feel of malevolence that reached across the centuries to lay a finger on his heart?

When he stood to go back to work, Davey almost threw the fragment into the bushes, no matter how marvellous the carving. And yet, somehow he could not bear simply to toss such splendid craftsmanship aside, and all the long afternoon while he laboured under a hot harvest sun, for once Davey's thoughts were on the past rather than the future, as he puzzled over a genius who left as his memorial a gloating paean of praise to human torment.

Just as the men working on the church were packing up for the night, the vicar came over from his new vicarage which, like the church, was solid, spacious and with no damned flummery about it. He, too, was a Dyer, an impoverished uncle appointed through Sir Maurice's patronage and in temperament one of the unsteady Dyers. As a young man he had dissipated a comfortable competence almost without noticing it, by dabbling in improbable inventions. As a way out of scandalous debts, his family had bought him a captaincy in the artillery (which was both cheaper than the cavalry, and more likely to accommodate an irresistible itch to dabble in unreliable contraptions), in which position he acquitted himself creditably during the Peninsular Campaign, acquiring in the process a liking for the trappings of discipline. As a result, when he sold up from the army he was attracted by the hierarchy of holy orders, and only the fact of being already married kept him from the authoritarian splendours of the Catholic Church. Dyer patronage brought him to Furnace Green, and there he recommenced his experiments, this time with gunpowder and the production of electricity from innumerable jars, rotating balls and sheets of glass. Untroubled himself by considerations of order, economy or religion, he was a stickler for these virtues in others.

The moment Davey saw the vicar coming, his instinct was to follow the usual village practice of slipping away before the reverend's fault-finding kept him kicking his heels. Then he remembered the questions which had nagged at him during the afternoon, hesitated, and was lost.

'It is early to be finishing work, is it not, master-mason?' Dyer called the moment he saw the men trudging off.

'No, Vicar. Finish an hour before dusk this time of year, sir.' Mr Lavender stood no nonsense from anybody.

Dyer did not answer, but stood looking silently about him. Davey shuffled his feet. 'Please, sir, could you tell me about the old church?'

'About the old church? It fell down because of slack workmanship. Mortar each joint as if your life depended on it, young fellow! That's the lesson to learn from our old church.'

'I wondered who worked on it, sir. Who carved the bosses on the pillars, like?'

'Do you have any idea how long ago that church was built?'

'No,' said Davey, annoyed. 'That was why I asked you, sir.'

'Too long ago for you to worry your head over the names of men no history book remembers. Mortar each joint as if your life depended on it, that's the way to be a workman your master will rely on.' He turned. 'Look here, Lavender, I'm not at all satisfied with the way you are getting on with this work. Not enough is being done each day, not by a long chalk.'

Although Lavender had become used to the vicar's homilies and the finishing date for the church was set in his contract, he still looked very black. As for Davey, he was beside himself with rage. Now the master would take out his ill-humour by driving everyone longer hours, probably single out Davey for the most unpleasant labour, too. And all for no better reason than him asking a civil question.

'I'd have liked to slosh the bastard with my mallet, the bloody psalm-singing swine,' he said savagely to his friends, the Ockham builders, after he had walked there that evening. 'Who the hell does he think he is, a vicar an' all, treating me as no more than a pair of hands?'

'That kind make you feel more like a convict than a man,' agreed Hankin. He was frail and pale-faced, looking as unlike a gang foreman as it was possible to look. Nevertheless, he was tougher than most men twice his size and kept order by a combination of oratory and a kind of violent cunning.

'We'll teach them, though, won't we, Hankin? Tell them straight not to take what's ours or it'll be the worse for them.' The speaker this time was a slater; this particular building gang had kept together for several years while moving from one new mansion to the next.

'Aye, but telling won't do much good. You can't alter human nature and the masters have got everything, so they'll keep it, see? Unless we sweep out the lot of them and change the way things are.'

'Human nature's human nature, you can't get away from that,' agreed a plasterer.

'You can if you smash up everything that is, and get something different,' insisted Hankin, pale eyes flashing. 'That would end poverty and nothing less will do it.'

'Oh, curse the end of poverty! That's chaw-bacon talk with naught ever likely to show for it. Give me something I can get my teeth into, like another shillin' on my wages.'

Everyone shouted at once then, which was how tavern-talk at Ockham usually ended, since some of Hankin's gang had long ago become bored with views expressed nightly for several years. Only Davey sat wishing they would all be quiet and let Hankin explain. Smash everything that is and get something which would end poverty for ever; smash up some vicars too, who talked as if everyone else was an idiot. That was more like it.

He gripped his hand on the stone carving he'd put inside his shirt; perhaps the reverend had been right in one thing. Names did not matter. It was what men did that mattered.

When Davey walked home that night his head was spinning from the effects of exhaustion and Hankin's words. Smash up everything and get something different. That wasn't talk which needed puzzling out, unlike some other things Hankin said, which might suit wandering builders but were meaningless in Furnace Green.

There was certainly a great deal which needed smashing on the ridge; things which made life much harder than the older villagers remembered it in the past. Like Sam Hooke and James Larkworthy, the miller, cheating on the poor rate, and bread costing more each year; like the Dyers buying up freeholds and Farmer Locock bringing in a threshing-machine which beat winter work into nothing with its hateful dust and clatter.

It was midnight by the time Davey reeled into the cottage next to the shop, where he lived with his mother. She had been born a Sleech and so inherited this tiny freehold, where Davey was lucky enough to have a room of his own once his father died and his three sisters married. He was unlucky, however, in that his mother would depend on his earnings alone as she aged. For the moment, three guineas remained of the seven she and her husband had saved through many abstemious years, more than enough with her wages as sewing-woman at the vicarage to see them through until Davey's apprenticeship ended in six months' time.

He was doubly unlucky too, because his mother spun webs of dependence over him like a spider trapping flies, waited up when he was late and drove him crazy with her curiosity.

'A good mother takes an interest in her children, and Davey's all I've got,' she explained to Cousin Portnell at the shop. 'Take an interest and they won't stray, that's what I always say.'

'Poke your nose where you're not wanted and they'll tell you a pack of lies,' retorted Jenny Portnell, a mother of eight.

'Oh no, Davey never tells lies.'

But Jenny only laughed and teased Davey about how cleverly he lied, since he was never found out.

'Oh, Ma,' said Davey, exasperated, when he came in and saw her dozing at the kitchen table. 'I've told you and told you there's no purpose to sitting up when I go to Ockham. I always come back too late to talk.'

'Too late for your own good when you have to be at work by six. Nor I wouldn't sleep sound unless I knew you were safely up that nasty dark old lane. Why you can't drink at the Bear like a Christian, I don't know.'

'I told you. They have better talk at Ockham tavern and though I trip over Dyers everywhere on the ridge nowadays, I refuse to drink under the Dyer arms.' He had never disclosed the nature of the talk he listened to at Ockham.

'What's in a sign? Everyone still calls it the Bear. Davey, I do wish you wouldn't walk more miles on top of a day's work just to drink in a hedge tavern. It's too much for you and like I told Mistress Jenny, you've been looking right moithered these past weeks. A boy your age needs his sleep.'

'Then let me past so I can reach my bed. I'm sorry, Ma. I'm not drinking in the Bear while that damned sign creaks overhead, and that's that.'

Davey stumbled up the steep stair while she still clucked concern. Walter Keyes, the hireling landlord of the Black Bear, had changed the inn name to the Dyer Arms only the year before, a brash new sign flaunting chevrons and a sheep-fleece in place of the dim old bear everyone knew. This nearly everyone interpreted as another badge of servitude, and resented accordingly.

Davey half-fell on his bed, expecting to plunge instantly

into sleep. After a day's work and five miles there and back to Ockham he always dropped like stone off a ladder into insensibility.

But late though it was, tonight he could not rest.

Couldn't sleep. Couldn't.

Smash up everything that is and get something different; his mind swung in time to Hankin's words. There are more of us than there are of them, Hankin had also said, much later. Reach out and take what's your due because if one thing's certain sure, no one will give it to you.

Davey thrashed again, willing himself to sleep, and sharp edges jabbed his ribs. He yelped and sat up, pulled chiselled stone out of the shirt he had been too tired to strip off. Dawn was breaking, birds rousing. Soon he must be off to work again.

Too late to be worth trying to sleep any more.

Davey stared at the carving out of gummy eyes. The stone had flaked off a larger piece, but each chisel and mallet stroke was as clear as on the day the carver finished his work. Hatred, malice and all uncharitableness sprang out at him, rejoicing in its triumph over humankind. And this time as he stared, the carving seemed to symbolise all that he'd felt during the night. Somewhere, some time in his life he meant to smash out at evil and help reach for the rights which common folk had lost. Only when he knew in his heart that his part, no matter how small, in the long process of retrieving justice was accomplished, would he throw this carving in the midden where it belonged.

Samuel Hooke knew when he was on to a good thing. He had come as a child to Furnace Green when his father set up there as a cobbler, and ever since had been amassing coins like a magpie. He began by stealing hobnails, twine and patches off his father's bench to sell to labourers who mended their own boots. Next he sold potions to the credulous, and turned shillings into pounds once he learned how to lend fractional sums at interest to desperate men. His appearance helped this progress towards respectability, since in a cold way he was very handsome. Neat grey hair was parted precisely across the crown of his head, his cheeks were well barbered, his whiskers trimmed. In youth his mouth might have been sensual, although a lifetime of extortion had set it into an expression of sarcastic determination which made the bravest suppliant quail. The vicar considered Hooke an example of diligence rewarded and had appointed him some years before as schoolmaster, on a small stipend from the church: beyond doubt, those parents able to squeeze the money for their children to learn pothooks and numbering in Hooke's cottage half way down the street were seldom disappointed by their sacrifice. Pupils who would have cared little about a beating cringed under Hooke's cruel tongue and learned diligently; he was also a genuinely able teacher. Having risen from very little himself, he believed in the power of words, and, most especially, figures.

Not long after Hooke became schoolmaster, the vicar was so delighted by his protégé's abilities that he appointed him church warden as well, a position which enabled Hooke to handle the offertory bags, and thereafter his secret cache of coins grew much faster than before. It was only natural that when the post of overseer of the poor also became vacant, Sir Maurice Dyer's agent should consult the Reverend Dyer and then appoint Hooke to the office, after which his bleakly supercilious bearing occasionally became almost genial. Unless, that is, you happened to be an inmate of the parish poor-barn or a labourer entitled to supplement miserly wages from the poor rate. Then, a visit to the window Hooke cut through the wall of his cottage just above his counting-table was an ordeal which left the suppliant ashen-faced with humiliation and defrauded of his due.

One day Hooke encounted Liddy Larkworthy on her return from an errand to the shop for Mrs Braybon. 'Well, Liddy. You are very fine these days.'

She curtsied; no one taught by Hooke failed to offer him the same formalities as they would to Sir Maurice Dyer himself. 'I am very happy at Greenview House, thank you, Mr Hooke.'

'You recall, I hope, that my recommendation obtained the position for you there?'

'I think Mrs Braybon engages who she chooses.' The retort slipped out before she stopped to think.

Hook smiled thinly. 'Your father owes me half a sovereign for my introduction. You may inform him next time you are home, that because of your impertinence the sack of flour he supplies to the poor-barn, this week must also be delivered free of charge.'

'You can't . . . Da agreed to pay the half-sovereign out of my wages because of the word you spoke for me to Mrs Braybon, although as for—' Liddy closed her lips tight, not daring to continue. As for me, I'd refuse to engage anyone you recommended, she had wanted to say. Probably Hooke had done no more than mention her name, and for so little they owed him half a sovereign! 'You can't ask Da to deliver your flour free,' she finished lamely.

'He'll do whatever I say! Another sideways word from you and it will be two sacks instead of one.'

To Liddy's astonishment, when she went home the following week, this was indeed the case. 'You little fool, for God's sake mind what you say to Hooke,' exclaimed Alec, snapping his fingers in vexation, while her father swore under his breath.

'Why not tell him to take his threats elsewhere? Why should we send him even bad flour free?'

'He most often accepts it well priced-up, that's why.'

'I still don't see—' began Liddy, mystified, but at once her father became very bluff and hearty, pinching her cheeks, tweaking her hair and exclaiming that he had never imagined life at Greenview House would make her look so pretty, until the moment for asking questions passed. Liddy would have liked to ask Davey what he made of all this, but unease held her back. He had walked nearly to Edenham with her again, as merry as she ever remembered him and without once mentioning Caleb Hankin or the tavern at Ockham; he even laughed when she described how General Braybon was putting his head together with the vicar to devise a cylinder driven by gunpowder which might take the labour out of pumping muck. If she mentioned Hooke or sacks of sweepings masquerading as flour, the whole day would be spoiled. But rack her brains as she would, Liddy could not see why her father should be forced to deliver flour free to Hooke.

She soon forgot her worry, because next day Greenview House was set in an uproar when Annie, the second upstairs-maid, was caught in the stable straw with William the footman. Not that the general took too serious a view of the matter, as Liddy could not help hearing on her way up to the nursery. 'What of it, my dear, when straw is made to be slept in?' He spoke loudly enough to be heard up two flights of stairs. 'Anyway, William is our best slow bowler and we can't spare him from the team.'

'Really, Humphrey! Whatever importance has cricket compared to loose morals? Which I most certainly shall not overlook in my household, as you seem to expect. I told them both to be gone within the hour.'

'Of course, if you believe in human sacrifice—'

'Human sacrifice, fiddle-de-de! I did it for their own good and the good of the other servants entrusted to my care. It's no good trying to interrupt, my mind is quite made up.' Her voice rose, always the warning of a tantrum when ornaments might be thrown.

'I suppose you remember we have guests for luncheon tomorrow?'

'You leave me to manage my household and we shall proceed very well. Now, get out . . . get out! My head aches dreadfully.'

There was a squeal of wood as she thrust back her chair, and the general skipped nimbly into the hall before Liddy could scuttle out of sight. 'A very good afternoon to you, Liddy.'

'Good afternoon, sir,' said Liddy primly, quite as if neither of them could hear china tinkling in the hearth.

His eyebrows twitched, eyes glinted. 'Good indeed for everyone except miscreants in the straw. Would you be so good as to request William to see me before he leaves? We cannot send him and Annie out on the world without so much as a guinea in their pockets, can we? Thank you, I was sure you would agree. I hope you are able to help May wait at table?'

'Me, sir?'

'If you would be so good, Liddy. You understand our difficulty, do you not? Five guests to luncheon tomorrow and both William and Annie on their way to search elsewhere for their fortune. If Mrs Braybon should ask, I do hope you will see your way to assist us.'

Liddy was more than willing to assist in any way she could. She was nervous of course, but thrilled by such an unexpected chance to fly up two whole rungs in the household ladder within six weeks of arriving at Greenview House. No one could blame her if she didn't manage everything exactly right, and should she do most things very nearly right, then perhaps—just perhaps—she could ask to be considered for Annie's place. Even in her dreams, she had never imagined she might better herself quite so fast.

The following day, when the Braybons filed into the dining room with their guests, May and Liddy stood at either end of a sideboard covered with silver chafing dishes. Normally, Liddy would have brought these up the backstairs and handed them through a hatch to May as each course was served, but on being appealed to, Mrs Braybon had agreed that if the meal was to pass without disaster, then the scullery-maid could not be trusted to bring up the dishes in Liddy's place. So everything was put in place before the meal began, since, as the general pointed out, their guests would be too well-bred to mention that the later courses were served half cold, whereas a tray dropped from the top of the backstairs to the bottom was bound to cause remark.

Grace was said by the vicar, a guest with his wife, together with Mr Aitchison of Danesdell House and Major and Mrs Boyd of Hill House. Then everyone sat down with the deliberation of people who have a great deal of time to spend over the business of eating.

Not that Liddy was taking much notice. She was giving such close attention to handing an enormous and blisteringly hot tureen of soup that she hardly dared raise her eyes. She was also wearing her first-ever black satin dress, the mark of an upstairs-servant, and, trembling from pride and anxiety, was only concerned not to become confused as she handed round and cleared away a bewildering display of dishes, plates, finger bowls, four different kinds of glasses and innumerable coasters, cruets and kickshaws.

In her experience, meal-times meant seeing there was enough bread and cheese to go round, the children washed and a kettle put on the hob in time to boil. At Edenham, talk was sparse until the pot was scraped and every crumb eaten. Only then would the men light their clay pipes—the tiny bowls fashioned to take mere pinches of tobacco—and the day's doings be discussed. But the Braybons and their friends talked all the way through a meal, seeming hardly to notice what they ate.

'Do none of them have appetites like ordinary folk?' hissed Liddy to May, when they carried the next course out.

'The general's a big eater usually, but it's ill-mannered to guzzle in front of guests,' answered May.

What a sad waste of food, thought Liddy, although only when a spun-honey cake was served did she at last have time to listen to the talk.

'. . . all off to Canada soon,' Major Boyd was saying. 'Letty insists on coming with me.'

'Oh Letty, my dear, whatever will you do with your girls?'

'They'll come to Canada with us, of course. John says it may be years before he completes this canal he is being sent to build, so naturally we shall stay together.' Mrs Boyd was dowdy but distinguished, an heiress wed to a husband so unsuitable that after their marriage they left her native Gloucestershire to settle in Sussex. As a soldier on half pay since the wars, Boyd was clearly delighted by any assignment, even to build a wilderness canal. Florid, clever and loud-mouthed, he had been born the son of a Thames waterman, yet during the Napoleonic Wars he had obtained a commission in the Royal Engineers, and by sheer ability had risen to divisional Engineer-Major. Mrs Braybon complained about his habit of spraying the table with food whilst talking, but the general found him interesting and gleefully egged him into swearing in order to watch his wife fine him on the spot.

Liddy did not hear much more about Canada because she had to change the dishes yet again, but she couldn't help thinking how strange it was that here around one table were the general and Major Boyd who talked about living in India or Canada as if it were commonplace, Mr Aitchison who admitted that he knew Greece better than Sussex, and the reverend who had fought all over Europe before he settled down to blow himself up in a shed behind the vicarage.

And Liddy herself had never been outside Furnace Green!

'. . . He's nothing but a rogue. You just wait until next week's meeting and then you'll see some sparks,' bawled the general, so loudly that Liddy nearly dropped a bowl of sweetmeats.

'Hooke's very far from being a rogue,' answered the vicar stiffly. 'I'm surprised to find a villager so accomplished.'

'Accomplished at what, pray? Swindling the rate and bloating like a tick on the heartsblood of all paupers. Him and that scoundrel Larkworthy, there's nothing to choose between them.'

Liddy gasped and clutched at the edge of the sideboard. Felt May's eyes swivel to where she stood and then quickly away again, as shock sent blood drumming in her ears. By the time she could hear again she had missed whatever was said in reply.

'Good God, man—' the general was bellowing.

'Humphrey!'

'I'm sorry, my dear, but did I hear aright? You called Hooke accomplished and did not mean to infer that he was accomplished in one thing only, namely in pandering to callous greed?'

'I cannot accept such a scandalous untruth for an instant.' The vicar went red above his whiskers. 'I do not know how I would manage without Hooke, when there is so much settling up to be done with the builders of our new church, and more idlers come each month to demand a share in the poor rate.'

The general laughed scornfully. 'How you waste Sir Maurice Dyer's money by allowing Hooke to settle your accounts is no affair of mine. He can afford to be swindled, I daresay. The poor of Furnace Green cannot.'

'This is outrageous. Swindled? How dare you say such a thing? It is slander, no less.'

'Then bid Hooke take me to the lawyers. Let me tell you, sir, I learned in India what corruption means and can see better than most men what is going on under my nose. By God, sir—'

'Humphrey!'

'It's not a jot of good thinking you can fine me for a word out of place the way Letty fines Boyd,' shouted the general unrepentantly. 'Hooke and Larkworthy deserve that I should inform the Almighty of their misdeeds. Not that I would dream of leaving retribution to Him, which is a shuffling, improper thing for one gentleman to do to another. If you come to the parish meeting you will hear me denounce those ruffians to their face.'

'Humphrey, I beg of you! When have you ever attended a parish meeting, of all things? They are not for people like us.' Mrs Braybon kept her voice steady but no one in the household was in the least doubt that had there been no guests, the porcelain would have been in danger.

'What is that to the matter? Why should anyone go to a parish meeting until they wished to stir something up?'

'I think you are very wrong to arouse feeling against a respectable man like Hooke, appointed to his offices by Sir Maurice and our vicar,' said Mr Aitchison. 'That way you only encourage the lower orders to feel discontented, and who knows then what might happen? There are tales of unrest in Kent this very moment, and as a magistrate I have been forewarned to act most strictly against any such sentiment in the Weald.' He drew down his lips as if sitting that very moment on his bench. 'Why, you will recall that when the Roman Empire was threatened by plebeians—'

'I trust you will never advocate that British rulers should follow the example of fellows I always thought little better than savages,' said the general, bristling.

Aitchison's jaw dropped. 'Savages? *The Romans?* My dear general—'

'Some kind of Italian, weren't they? What would you say, I'd like to know, if the Duke of Wellington began behaving like that fellow Nero? Well, we all know our present majesty wouldn't make an agreeable dinner guest, drunk more often than not from what I hear and inclined to spit on the carpet, but you wouldn't expect him to throw his bishops to the lions, now would you, sir?' the general sat as straight as a cricket bat in his chair, with the air of one who has proved his point.

'What have lions to do with Samuel Hooke?' asked Mrs Boyd, bewildered.

The general considered. 'I daresay there are a good few people in Furnace Green who would not object if Hooke was served up to well-starved lions as a treat. Which is why I shall attend the parish meeting next week.'

Mrs Braybon caught the ladies' eyes with a very speaking look and rose, while Liddy whisked cruets and crumbs off the table before leaving the gentlemen to their port. As she left she heard the reverend say quite clearly, 'You will have all the gentry and farmers against you, Braybon.'

'Pity I'll have left for Canada,' observed Boyd. 'I'm not a gentleman and I'd be for you.'

'I don't give a curse who is against me. I'll prove Hooke ought to be in gaol, and see then if you dare confirm him as overseer for another term.'

'Good God, you'll be laughed out of the meeting! Lived in Furnace Green little more than a year, haven't you? If I wasn't your guest I'd tell you what everyone is likely to think about a stranger interfering in our ways. Sussex don't take kindly to meddlers in other folk's affairs.'

'Pray do not allow being my guest to discommode you in the least,' the general answered genially. 'As I shall not allow my recent residence to obstruct me. Swindling is swindling wherever I find it, after all.'

'But it isn't your business here, whatever it may have been in India!'

'Indeed? Perhaps you are right.' He put his head on one side to consider this. 'No, I fear you are not. The poor cannot easily defend themselves against such as Hooke and Larkworthy, whereas I shall find my time agreeably enlivened by exposing them as they deserve.'

Liddy shut the door hastily, her cheeks burning from another mention of her father's name.

May pounced on her the moment they reached the pantry. 'Fancy them not knowing you are a Larkworthy!'

'Mrs Braybon knew when she interviewed me 'cos she asked my name, but I'm just Liddy to them since I came.' The parish meeting was next week, thought Liddy feverishly, and she not due home again before it happened.

'I wonder sometimes whether they think servants are deaf except for hearing orders. What are you going to do?'

'I don't know.'

'Is it true your da's a twister like this Hooke?'

'I don't know.' Liddy wrung her hands.

'The master seems sure enough. Fancy him telling the reverend the Dyers could afford to be swindled! It's awkward for you, all the same, or will you keep quiet and hope they never do remember you're a Larkworthy?'

'I don't know,' Liddy repeated desperately, tongue stuck in her mouth, brain stiff with fear. The Larkworthys of Edenham to be named by her own master as scoundrels in an open parish meeting! After what had been said at table today, rumours of General Braybon's intentions were bound to fly about and everyone be there to hear.

Liddy cleared the dishes, polished the table, turned down beds in a daze, lay wakeful while the scullery-maid snored the hours away. Eventually she couldn't stay in bed any longer, and when the new church clock struck one in the morning she picked her clothes off the chair and crept out of the room. Dressed hastily in ill-buttoned layers, she tiptoed downstairs. Her footsteps made no sound on stairs or kitchen floor; the back door bolt slid easily in a well-greased socket.

She would have to leave the door on the latch, and the yard gate too, but that ought to be safe enough providing she was back before anyone began to stir. Strong moonlight made the street look as if giant cobwebs had been spun between the sleeping cottages; impossible to imagine that behind those doors people lay lusting on straw, women felt the pangs of childbirth, children whimpered with hunger made worse by Edenham's chaff-filled flour. Better to look at the sleeping hills instead, sloping away from the lane which ran from Furnace Green to Edenham. There, moonlight made the landscape look immense, but simple. Hill folded into hill, remnants of forest into fields; everything black and silver, fragrant and motionless in the September night.

Liddy lifted her skirts and ran as fast as she could all the way to Edenham. When she reached it, the mill was dark, the millwheel silent. She stood for a moment looking at it while sadness sapped at her courage, before her shoulders straightened and she went down the slope to pull the latch-string. In the kitchen Alec and Pete lay asleep in their usual place by the hearth; her parents, Kate and the younger children slept upstairs.

'Alec!' Liddy shook him. 'Alec, wake up.'

He grunted, sodden with tiredness. 'What—'

'Ssh, come outside. I have to talk to you alone.' Pete was stirring too.

Already Liddy was conscious of time sliding past; in another hour the early milkers would begin tramping sleepily from their cottages to byre and pasture. If anyone saw her slipping back to Greenview House in the dawn—anyone at all—the tale would spread that Liddy Larkworthy was up to no good at nights. A tale Davey would hear within a day, and that she could not bear.

She began to think she would never succeed in getting Alec on his own outside. When she did, he sat blearily on the step and seemed scarcely to listen to what she said.

'I don't know what you can do,' she finished. 'But I had to tell what I heard. The general will do as he said, I'm sure.'

'All you can talk of nowadays is this bloody general,' Alec snapped back then. 'Curse the general, say I, and let me sleep.'

'All right, sleep like a hog no matter what, and be held up like Aunt Sally for the village to throw things at, I'm sure I don't care. I've warned you as I thought I must, the rest is for you and Da to worry over.'

'No, you wouldn't care any more. All you're good for is prinking and prancing at Greenview House while we sweat in the mill.'

'I came to warn you,' she said helplessly.

'Aye, so you did. Now you'd better get back before anyone stirs.' He knuckled his eyes and stood. 'That's how it is , Liddy. You there, us here. I'll tell Da what you said in the morning.'

She stamped her foot. 'You do just as you please. As for me, I feel here as well as there and don't you forget it.'

He laughed. 'You always could make a fellow feel like dirt. But whatever we'd like, there's naught we can do to change. Part of our living depends on our cut from Hooke, and with prices so low we must stand by him or be ruined.

He'll outsmart this general of yours, never fear. A right downy fellow, Hooke. Your warning will give him time to make sure he's reappointed overseer by one means or another.'

'I wish he didn't have to be,' said Liddy. 'Paupers oughtn't to be paid in dirty flour instead of pennies.'

'There's no ought or oughtn't about it, so don't worry your head about things you can't understand. Paupers need flour, dirty or otherwise, don't they? Like we need Sam Hooke.' He gave her a push. 'And Liddy—thanks. But the village can't do aught against us. What if they do jeer at a parish meeting? Next day we'll be grinding corn again and them bringing poor-law tokens to change for whatever we choose to give them.'

Somehow Alec's softer manner made his acceptance of extortion worse. At least her father seemed ashamed of what he did; Alec was merely used to it. Liddy felt even more wretched than before as she started back up the lane, because by coming here tonight she had helped Hooke hold on to power. How cheerfully she would have helped duck him in Furnace Green pool, yet all she'd done was warn him! As anger gradually distilled out of confusion, Liddy pelted faster and faster up the lane, past Old Nick's well and into black shadow between steep banks. Luckily it was there and not in full moonlight that she nearly ran slap into Tom Rabbit.

As feckless as most of his ancestors, Tom was one of the poorest of Furnace Green's poor. He lived in a hovel on waste ground together with a wife and five children, and because he was so poor he was always the man least likely to be hired, the most frequently bullied by impatient masters. Fortunately for Liddy he shambled past without seeing her, but to her he seemed an accusing ghost of those she had betrayed to Hooke by running to Edenham in the night.

Parish meetings were usually dull affairs. In earlier days they had often been hurried through in the taproom of the Black Bear, nowadays, in deference to the Reverend Dyer's views on the tendency of the lower orders to become distracted by drink, they were more formal and held in the vicarage dining room.

In this September of 1830 the sole business of the meeting was to appoint a parish overseer of the poor, a formality which could have been completed within a few minutes by those few ratepayers who bothered to turn up. However, the Reverend Dyer had experienced some misgivings since the conversation at Greenview House the previous week, and took the precaution of intimating to everyone who could be expected to support the Dyer interest that their presence was obligatory on this occasion. Only at the last minute did a certain air of expectancy in Furnace Green, and some panicky conferences with Hooke, make him decide that the church nave would be a more strategic place to conduct this particular meeting.

As he observed to his wife, 'Then any inclination towards rowdiness on the part of the common people will be overawed by the majesty of God's house. Heathen though Braybon is, he has at least been trained in the discipline of respect.'

The vicar's calculation proved less happy than he had hoped. He was cheered to find the street deserted when he crossed to the church at the appointed time, a feeling which changed to outrage when he discovered its new nave to be packed with people. There were some faces he had never even seen before, but most were familiar; a good scattering of women amongst them too, he thought indignantly. He would give them a good homily next Sunday for poking their noses where they had no business to be.

At least the front pews were occupied by people who knew where their duty lay. Aitchison of Danesdell House and his tenant Locock; the Frenches of Newhouse and Walter Keyes, the landlord of the Dyer Arms, the Larkworthys of Edenham. These were the men who had appointed Hooke in the past and pride in their judgement, as well as a sense that it was both perilous and demeaning to make concessions under threat, would make them wish to re-appoint him.

And damn me, the vicar thought, measuring his foe more as an old soldier than a man of God, Hooke *is* the right man for the task. A weakling would not do as overseer, especially now rumours of unrest are coming out of Kent.

He wished he could spot Braybon. Or was it too much to hope, that such a born troublemaker might have had second thoughts?

The vicar took his stand on the chancel steps and cleared his throat. 'I shall address my remarks to those qualified to vote, namely the freeholders of this parish and those tenants whose land is assessed for poor rate. Samuel Hooke has served us faithfully in a number of capacities over the years and due to his efforts, many who would otherwise be ignorant can read the word of God. As church warden he has been my right hand during this time of rebuilding—' Dyer glanced around limewashed walls and foundry-moulded pillars, barely repressing a shudder. 'Mr Hooke is not to blame for the plain design, which arises from lack of prosperity in the countryside. If such difficulties are encountered in building a house of worship, how much greater would they be if the poor rate was not kept within bounds! Hard work, thrift and sobriety are the cure for our ills, not recklessness with other men's money, and all these virtues are to be found in Samuel Hooke. Unremitting in his labours, thrifty over discharging many duties, sober in his daily life. I have no hesitation in commending to you his reappointment as overseer of our poor. Are we agreed? Thank you.'

Hooke stood up three rows back and bowed, looking very distinguished in a new broadcloth jacket piped with grey to match his hair. 'Thank you, thank you, Reverend. It is always a pleasure to do my duty for my neighbours.'

The vicar rubbed his hands. This whole affair was going to brush through without any trouble after all.

'No, we are not agreed. I pay poor rate on my property at Greenview House and on Corndown fields, and I consider Samuel Hooke unsuited to the post of overseer. Or to any other post for that matter, since he is a liar, a thief and a cheat.' General Braybon had been hidden by the brawny figure of Charlie Twort but now he stood to face Hooke across the aisle.

'I disagree,' said the vicar, breathing heavily. 'Nor can I allow raised voices in the house of God. There is a majority for Hooke, and I declare him reappointed.'

'Why should he be, if there is a doubt? You spoke for him and I stayed quiet, do you the same while I speak and there will be no raised voices.'

A kind of collective grunt came from the seated villagers; hands tightened on knees and faces tilted as if to make sure of hearing every syllable.

'You have the right to speak as a freeholder, I suppose,' said Dyer grudgingly. 'Pray remember that Mr Hooke has protection under the law if you dare to bandy accusations against him.'

The general's spurred eyebrows thrust outward in mock surprise. 'Well, bless my soul. Thrifty, sober, hard-working Mr Hooke. But for whom are these virtues engaged, I ask myself? Certainly not for the poor.' He threw out an arm dramatically. 'Imagine I am a pauper!'

'I do not see how play-acting will help conclude this matter,' interrupted the vicar. 'Sit down sir, and let us finish.'

'I am a pauper,' repeated the general, and before their eyes his shoulders slouched, his clothes hung on suppliant bones. 'I detail to Mr Hooke—' a trembling hand stretched out—'those pitiful wages on which my wife and children depend, and beg for his help. Help to which I am entitled as a resident of this parish, mark you. And what happens?' He straightened sharply, every whisker quivering condescension. 'Hooke bids me be more thrifty. Hooke moralises on the evils of extravagance, though I cannot remember when I last owned ha'pence for any luxury.' Head stabbing forward, he caricatured contempt like a long disjointed cat about to pounce, eyes fixed on Hooke, who stared back mesmerised by such remorseless mime. 'At length this man the parish pays to succour its poor has extracted sufficient pleasure out of misfortune and condescends to throw a tally at his suppliant's feet.' A tally-stick skidded across the aisle. 'Not the pence to which he is entitled, but a tally which can only be exchanged for dirty, mildewed flour at Edenham Mill. So this poor man who needs to work each hour of daylight, must next waste time fetching this filth, but at least he now has food for his family, has he not?' The general courteously inclined his head, as if to listen. 'You are quite right, of course. No, he has not. Children cannot live on dirty flour alone. Nor is a man capable of labouring fourteen hours a day with naught else in his belly. So his wife must carry half this flour to the shop, to the inn, to a market stall, in an attempt to barter it for the other things she has to have. Milk, if she is fortunate; soap, just occasionally; a pinch of tea or sugar. Salt perhaps. Boots? Ah no, those are luxury indeed. Save up flour for boots and you would need to save two years and what would Mr Larkworthy's mildewed flour exchange for at the end of such a time? So, no boots. Yet if a man lacks boots he cannot indulge in the toil Mr Hooke enjoins on him, therefore, twice perhaps in a lifetime, he must buy boots. His family starves for boots; a single pair of boots becomes the most enormous, most unimaginable achievement of his life. One of his children could even die, a sacrifice to boots. And Mr Hooke? He waxes richer every year, a monument to thrift.'

'By God, sir—'

'Yes, in this place God may listen too.' The general's voice clashed with Hooke's and bore it down. 'Are you about to enquire how I will prove all this? Thank you, I felt sure—'

'I ask nothing of the sort!' shouted Hooke. 'I refuse to allow my good name to be trampled before—'

'Before so great a cloud of witness? But it was the vicar who was thoughtful enough to suggest we should discuss these differences where everyone may judge how much of the truth is spoken. I was very grateful to him.'

Another rustle swept through the church, this time of

amusement, and Dyer scowled more blackly than before. 'I put it to the meeting—' he began.

'In a moment, my good vicar, in a moment.' The general studied Hooke from under drooping lids until amusement died and tension wadded into every cranny of the nave. 'For each two shillings Hooke draws from the parish to disburse in relief, I estimate he keeps sixpence for himself. A quarter of the rate, when sixpence is the difference between sufficiency and starvation for desperate men. Nor is that all. In partnership with Mr Larkworthy of Edenham Mill he accounts for good flour to the parish and forces poor men to accept sweepings. The good flour thus saved they sell on their own behalf, further profiting by as much as a hundred pounds a year between them. Ladies and gentlemen! We are no longer speaking of pence, but of *one hundred pounds a year*. A ploughman perhaps receives thirty. And yet, if that same ploughman should fall on evil days it is Mr Hooke who despises his lack of thrift and forces him to grovel for relief.' He turned to the vicar. 'Now, sir, I beg you to take your vote.'

At the back of the church, Davey Portnell leaped to his feet with such violence that his oak pew rocked. 'Every word is God's truth, and a cartload more which hasn't been spoke. I say we run Hooke out of the parish and never let him back!'

Immediately, people who had remained silent while the general spoke began to shout, more pews were pushed back and, hidden in the recesses of the nave, Tom Rabbit picked up a prayer book and threw it with a poacher's accuracy so it hit Hooke on the ear.

'Be silent! Sit down in your places and do not move.' The general's voice, trained in Indian cantonments, rose easily above the din but the damage was done. Hands hesitated on missiles, bodies settled back watchfully on the edge of seats, but the two vital rows of voting ratepayers, some of whom had begun to look thoughtful while the general spoke, were now anxious to finish a thoroughly unfortunate business before worse happened. The vicar was right. Only Hooke could be trusted to keep their labourers respectful; God knew what might happen if they won even a trivial victory by force.

Almost simultaneously, Sir Maurice Dyer's agent, Ward, Mr Aitchison and the rest transferred their gaze from the assembled throng to the nave ceiling, their minds made up.

George Dyer was not a coward. He had stayed on the aisle steps and now seized his moment. 'I do not accept unsubstantiated accusations against any man, especially when calumny is directed against someone whose probity I have been in a position to judge. I have proposed Samuel Hooke for a further term of office in the post of overseer of the poor. All those in favour.'

Everyone in the front two pews stood up, except, rather surprisingly, Locock. Since he was renowned for tight-fistedness, probably he had been impressed by the accusation that Hooke cheated the ratepayers as well as the poor.

'I have the vote of Sir Maurice Dyer in respect of all the lands he holds in this parish,' said Ward, his agent.

The vicar nodded. 'Sir Maurice pays just under half the rate, so the majority is not in doubt. Those against?'

Five people stood: Mark Smith of Pigpasture Farm, old Miss Brown who lived alone at Wyses, Charlie Twort who farmed a tiny freehold near Greggs Wood, John Locock and General Braybon.

An odd silence fell. It was late; long past the time when men who had laboured since dawn should have been fed. They and their wives felt exhausted by unaccustomed tension, argument, disappointment. It was as if a keg of gunpowder had exploded but left the barrel strakes intact. Then General Braybon rapped his cane sharply on his pew. 'I do not indulge in unsubstantiated accusations, and will prove everything I said here today. Then I shall demand that this vote is taken again.'

'The vote has been taken,' said Dyer with finality. 'Thank you for again undertaking such onerous duties, Mr Hooke.'

'Damn you all to Hell,' a voice said clearly from the back of the church; Davey Portnell again, though only those who knew him well were sure. 'We'll be rid of him in our own way, then.'

But Hooke just smiled, and smiled; he knew his power as overseer. He was also one of those who recognized Davey's voice, and would take his own revenge when the opportunity offered. As for that sod of a general . . . He turned and bowed in a parody of Braybon's style, savouring his triumph.

Liddy of course had not attended the meeting. Torn as she was between shame and apprehension over what might happen there, she never even considered asking Mrs Braybon for permission to leave Greenview House. Nevertheless, everyone from the mistress to the boot-boy was on edge as they waited for the general to return, and most discovered excellent reasons for being in the hallway when his figure was seen coming down the street.

'Good evening, Frederick.' Impossible to tell anything from his face as he handed over hat and cane to the new footman.

Mrs Braybon darted out of the drawing room. 'Well?'

'I lost. The scoundrel was reappointed.'

'Humphrey, no!'

'Oh, Humphrey, yes. I had put doubt in their minds when an idiot boy began shouting threats and all was lost in an instant.'

'An idiot boy?' asked Mrs Braybon, bewildered.

'Unfortunately he reminded those with votes that they had reason to fear for their property in this time of unrest. Ah well. I may be in the twilight of my life, but I am not yet ready to be beaten by a rogue like Hooke. When is the cricket match against Riffield, Frederick?'

'I—I will enquire, sir,' answered the footman, flustered.

'I hope you were not mistaken when you told me you could bowl well pitched-up. I expect my footman to be able to help out the village team.'

'Now why in tarnation should he mix cricket with the parish meeting?' demanded May during kitchen supper. 'He lost, or so he said, and mighty set he was on winning. But I never see a man so little put about by being beat.'

In this May was mistaken. General Braybon detested losing, sheer cold rage at losing hidden behind determination not to lose for long.

The immediate result of the parish meeting was that Samuel Hooke rode higher than ever. Too vindictive to learn discretion from his fright at the meeting, too domineering not to use his authority to hit back at hostility, he soon ensured that even fewer people than before came to his window asking for relief.

But when Davey met Liddy on her next Sunday off, he soon told her that Tom Rabbit was an exception. 'He fell down Farmer Locock's hophouse steps last week and gashed his leg. He hasn't any choice except to beg at Hooke's damned window until it's healed. His wife and eldest boy earn pence, otherwise . . . well, the family relies on what Tom poaches, I suppose. He don't earn more than the odd shilling outside harvest and threshing times, I reckon.'

Liddy gazed at a distant cart creaking up the hill. 'The sickles are nearly thrown on this year's harvest, there'll be many more men laid off in the next week or so.'

'Aye, God knows what the winter will bring. Locock isn't the only farmer who has bought a threshing-machine. There'll be less work than ever to share out until spring.'

The traditional ridge way of ending each farm's harvest was for the men to stand in a circle and throw a sickle at the last stand of corn. As recently as fifty years before, this ceremonial killing of the spirit of fruitfulness had marked a season of feasts and bargaining; nowadays casting sickles had become a sign of doom. A death of work, an end to warmth and full bellies for another year.

'What happened about Tom?' asked Liddy after they had walked a short way in silence.

'Hooke gave him a half-tally for flour after a morning's pleading. Why anyone was fool enough to listen to your accursed general when he told them to sit down and be good, I'll never know. If they'd followed me, we'd have run Hooke out of the parish there and then.'

'It was you who called out?' Liddy remembered the general's scathing reference to an idiot boy who had frightened the ratepayers into backing Hooke.

'Yes, as Hooke knows only too well. He's after Master Lavender to cancel my indentures.'

'Surely he couldn't?'

'He could make it so he hasn't much choice, since Hooke is settling for all the work we do on the church. And me with only six months more of apprenticeship to run!'

Liddy slipped her hand under his arm. 'What would you do if Hooke did succeed in having them cancelled?'

'Hankin says I can join his gang if I want.'

'Davey, no!'

'Why not? I've a fancy to see more than Furnace Green in my life. Hankin stirs things too, and I like that. Smash up everything he says, and fashion what we want from the ruins. The trouble is, I'd be a labourer for always once I joined his gang. Me with my indentures broke, like.'

'Nor you wouldn't ever come back,' said Liddy flatly. She was wearing a walking-out dress for the first time in her life, an out-of-fashion dimity given her by Mrs Braybon. She had waited for Davey to notice but he hadn't; wanted to skip down the lane for sheer pleasure in her day off when there was a handsome young man by her side, and on every side the fields blazed gold, the sky sparkled blue above. Instead they had spoken only of dearth and misery, seen beauty as a threat. Of course she couldn't expect Davey to feel light-hearted when he was so upset about the dreadful things which kept happening, but it did seem a pity he couldn't stop worrying about everything just occasionally.

Oblivious to Liddy's disappointment, Davey kicked angrily at a stone. 'Once you're on the travelling gangs you go from job to job. 'Tis a rough life and the women who follow, well, I wouldn't want you to be one of them. Hankin says—'

'Who cares what Hankin says! If I wanted to follow you, I would.'

He stopped. 'And would you want to, Liddy?'

'Oh Davey, I don't know! Of course I'd never forget you, but—'

'But what?'

She put her head on one side and smiled, freckled nose crinkling in self-derision. 'You're born for trouble, Davey. It's part of why I like you, I suppose. But I couldn't bear trouble all my days. Day in, day out, never a look for me but always a-worriting about other folk's wrongs and reaching out for what you couldn't have. I'd weary of that in the end. Besides, I want to better myself if I can.'

He drew her to him and kissed her, gently at first and then quite roughly, her back curved under his hands. All in the middle of Edenham lane, she thought indignantly, before indignation vanished and she began to kiss him in return. They stood closely together for a long time in the singing sun; kissing inexpertly and staring at each other, half-smiling and half-astonished by how much a kissing changed. The whole of them echoing with joy and wanting, wanting more; yet also satisfied and not wanting more so soon, in the humming summer quiet of Edenham lane on the day when both of them came freshly to the touch of love. 'How sure are you now you wouldn't follow if I had to go?' he said softly.

'I don't know what I'd do.' But this time she said it like a promise, quite differently from before.

He laughed and stroked her nose with his. 'Liddy?'

'Mm?'

'You look awful pretty in that dress.'

She jumped, so their noses jarred together. 'David Portnell! You gurt tease, you! You noticed right away.'

'I always notice you,' he said simply, and then they had to jump apart because someone was coming up the lane.

It was Tom Rabbit, shambling more than ever with his gashed leg and carrying a knotted package. Miniature explosions of flour puffed out of tears in the cloth with each step he took, and a scarecrow hound followed at his heels.

'How's your leg, Tom?' asked Davey.

'How d'you think?' He was probably less than a dozen years older than Davey but already as snaggle-toothed and wrinkled as a gaffer. Black shifting eyes, black smeary beard and hair, washed-out clothes wearing everywhere into holes.

'I hope it heals quickly,' Liddy said after an awkward pause.

'You can shove your hope where I'd like to shove your da, him and his rotten flour. Look at this.' He shook the cloth in Liddy's face, more flour escaping with each flourish. 'A nest for bloody maggots. Maggots is meat, eh? Meat fit for bloody Rabbits, eh? You won't find bread made from the like of this on Edenham's table when your da sits down to guzzle, will you?'

The worst thing was that even while he fumbled to express his rage, Tom's eyes kept flickering towards the basket Liddy carried, not as if he might seize the scones and jam she had brought from Greenview House, but wistfully, like a child.

'Here,' Liddy thrust the basket at him. 'I'd like you to take this home for your children.'

He grabbed it and fled as fast as his leg would carry him up the lane, immediately frantic in case she changed her mind. No thanks nor thought of thanks, which made Liddy feel resentful until she began wondering what, in all of his life, Tom Rabbit could have learned about gratitude. Except from his dog perhaps. Anyone else would have found a lurcher to assist in his poacher's forays; Tom found a useless crossbred pup and kept it alive by sharing whatever he ate himself, an extra mouth in a destitute household.

After that encounter, Davey was back in one of his towering dark moods, and he left Liddy above the slope to Edenham as if their kiss had happened to someone else. But this time she understood how anger could set so hard that nothing else managed to squeeze past; as for herself, distress and love, pity and new delight in her own body were all mixed together in such confusion that she didn't know which mattered most. She sighed and walked alone down the bank to Edenham. Perhaps it was easier only to feel one thing at a time.

'Liddy's back! Liddy's back! Liddy, what've you brought us this time?' Baby Dick raced out of the house to hug her legs.

'I gave the scones and jam I brought to poor Tom Rabbit, which serves you right for asking.' She scooped him up in her arms. 'We'll go and look for mushrooms instead, shall we?'

And somehow, romping with Dick and Pete, Liddy forgot Tom Rabbit. To her, it seemed that once in a while you did yourself a lot of good by shutting your eyes and ears to certain things; they came back quick enough afterwards on their own. And, naturally, these particular things came back as soon as she and the boys returned for tea and her father asked what General Braybon intended to do next.

'Something to do with a cricket match, I think,' said Liddy.

'A *cricket match*? Look here, lass, I meant about Hooke. Braybon swore in church he wouldn't accept defeat and I've a feeling he's the kind to mean it.'

'He is.'

'Well?'

'Like I said, he plans something to do with the match against Riffield next Saturday, but no one knows what. If anyone asks, he just rubs his hands and says the Riffield match is the last of the season.'

'Aye, but whatever could he mean to do there?'

'Da,' said Liddy carefully, 'couldn't you break loose

from Hooke? Tell him you refuse to give the likes of Tom Rabbit rotten flour any more?'

'Liddy gave Tom the scones and jam she brought for us,' announced Dick, kicking at the table discontentedly. 'And then we only found two mushrooms.'

Mrs Larkworthy sighed. 'Oh Liddy, the children were so looking forward to something special for their supper today.'

'Tom needed it,' said Liddy briefly, gazing at her father.

'Tom is a thieving no-good who's never saved aught against a rainy day! Too thick-witted to work, too idle to poach more than rabbits. His ills aren't any fault of mine!'

'He's got a bad leg, so he can't work or poach just now.'

'And I had a fever last week!' shouted her father suddenly, slamming his fist against the wall. 'A-shaking and a-shivering so I could scarcely lift the sluice, but I still had to pay my poor rate to the likes of Tom Rabbit, didn't I? Still had to keep on my feet to earn a living! How do you think I save for a rainy day, eh? Not by stopping work for a gash or feeding a worthless hound wi' food my children need! Nor yet by questioning good bargains when they come along, let me tell you!'

He wiped his hand across his lips and then gripped it tightly on his knee, the only sound in Edenham that of leaves blowing in the wind outside, as around the table the children's mouths dropped open in alarm, their elders discomforted not so much by anger as by the pain beneath it.

'I'd best go now,' Liddy said at last, and climbed out from her place on the bench. 'It's no good coming home to quarrel.'

'We'll see you in two weeks!' her mother cried out sharply.

Slowly Liddy shook her head. 'We'd only fratch again. And by then General Braybon will have done whatever it is he means to do, and if he wins . . . this time I'll be glad.'

* * *

General Braybon was briskly busy duri
between Hooke's reappointment as overs
cricket match. He was aware of eyes follo
swung his cane more vigorously in conse
as upright as a drill sergeant and enjoyec
drama he could wring from the situation. H
that his movements were sufficiently erratic to baffle Hooke into saying that he had always considered military men as addled as poacher's eggs.

One move which he made could not be disguised. He visited Larkworthy's mill at Edenham and, as a ratepayer, demanded to see the receipts for flour supplied during the previous year to the paupers of Furnace Green.

'I had to show him,' James Larkworthy said to Hooke, that same evening in the schoolhouse parlour. 'He paying poor rate and spouting all manner of laws which he vowed gave him the right to pry. When I said I hadn't heard of suchlike laws, he swore he'd ride to fetch a magistrate if I wanted.'

'Bluff,' said Hooke positively. 'You should have told him to ride and be damned.'

'Aye, perhaps. But magistrates hereabouts are all in Sir Maurice Dyer's pocket. I don't want any of them suspicioning against me.'

Hooke sipped his beer. 'Suspicion don't matter, if Braybon hadn't the right to look at your books in the first place.'

'He'd make a right, wouldn't he? Stands to reason. Spin a tale as if . . . as if . . . Well, I dunno, but nobs stick together, don't they? Then the magistrate would look in my books as well, and the end of that would most likely be another rise in rent.'

'So you let nosy Braybon look?' said Hooke reflectively.

'Aye.'

'Not much to see though, was there? Even supposing he could figure out that vile fist of yours, which I doubt. I'd have beaten you for it every week if you'd come to me for schooling.'

…iller stared at his beer. He wanted a drink badly …as afraid his hands would tremble on the tankard. … sat down at my kitchen table and copied every figure … could find. What he couldn't read, he asked, and if I disremembered a jotting, then he came over to check my mill-marks, saying he could work things out for himself. And all the while talking and a-putting mealy words in my mouth, until I didn't know which way I stood.'

'Where has he learned to read mill-marks, I'd like to know!' exclaimed Hooke, outraged. 'They're nothing to do with poor rate neither, you could have stopped him there.'

Larkworthy shrugged. Like most older craftsmen he could only spell and reckon with some difficulty, and preferred to keep his accounts by means of marks cut into the millhouse beams.

'You could have stopped him there,' repeated Hooke, his voice rising.

'If you think that, then all I can say is you don't know how it feels to house a bloody general for the day. By the end of it I only wanted to be rid of him.' And Larkworthy coughed, a miller's phlegm-filled cough.

'Well,' murmured Hooke, after a pause, 'I don't see what he can make of a dozen beams full of marks, which tell of grinding done for farms over most of the ridge, as well as for the parish.'

Hooke wished he could be certain of it all the same, apprehension for the first time tempering his complacency. Generals weren't like ordinary men, but could afford entirely to please themselves. Even Sir Maurice Dyer was more controlled by precedent. How bitterly unfair it was that one of these irrational beings should come to live in Furnace Green, and then for no good reason decide to dabble in Samuel Hooke's affairs.

The Riffield cricket match was always the last of the season and then usually had to be postponed because everyone was busy harvesting. Quite often it finished in the dark, or a change in the weather found one side gleefully skittling out the other in a downpour; but, no matter what, the match was completed. In this particular fixture, luck was exploited to the hilt.

Because of such chancy circumstances, and the fact that Furnace Green cherished a grudge against Riffield (which, in their opinion, was inhabited by milksops fit only to be owned by Dyers), this match alone out of all the contests of the season was played by two sides hellbent on winning. To add further spice to the occasion, Sir Maurice himself usually played for Riffield, possibly in the vain hope of conciliating the only disaffected portion of his estates. There was undeniable attraction to hurling a missile legitimately at a resented landlord, and Furnace Green invariably played Bert Wicks, the butcher, whose bowling was so erratically lethal that where other parishes were concerned, they generally refrained.

On this particular Saturday, the Riffield team arrived punctually at midday by wagonette except for Sir Maurice, who rode. Their numbers were made up largely from the castle household: footmen, grooms and gamekeepers, all neatly dressed in high stovepipe hats and green livery waistcoats. This in itself made a difference between the sides, since those from Furnace Green wore anything from Wicks's striped butcher's smock to working corduroys.

The general was umpire, a rare choice since he was considered too indulgent towards opponents, but the word had gone round that this was something he particularly desired today. Agog, the village conceded that if his request had anything to do with discomfiting Hooke, then umpire he should be.

Furnace Green won the toss and chose to bat, a handsome advantage in a match which began after midday on an autumn afternoon, and several Riffield players were heard to remark that Furnace Green always won when their own coin was used in a toss.

Greenview House wall marked one boundary, the pool and roadways the others. Seats were set for the gentry beneath the oak which by this time was in the full majesty of its growth, nearly two hundred years after Jane Carpenter planted an acorn on a suicide's grave. The sloping green, some limes and beeches scattered behind the cottages along the street, a distant glimpse of the new church tower, all gave the look of peaceful abundance to a reality which was quite otherwise.

Furnace Green started well, accumulating thirty runs for three wickets, considered good on a pitch from which the sheep had only been removed an hour before. Then the son of Sir Maurice's head groom began to bowl and the ball fairly spurted off the edge of drying hoof-prints. Eight for fifty-one.

'Step down the wicket and you'll find his length is suspect,' called the general, his umpire's neutrality forgotten as Frederick the footman passed on his way to the wicket.

Frederick slammed the first ball into the pool, which was always considered a five, stepped back from the second and fell on his wicket.

Furnace Green was all out for fifty-eight shortly afterwards.

'And to think Alec Larkworthy hit twenty against Mayfield and today was out for two,' lamented the general, when everyone gathered under the oak between innings.

Alec, overhearing, swore under his breath. What did the old viper expect, when everyone at Edenham now lived in dread over what the future held?

Jugs of ale were passed round the teams, Riffield tossing it down with the abandon of men who received half a firkin of beer each a week as part of their wages, while Furnace Green sipped with the parsimony of habit. Except for David Portnell that is, who swallowed faster than the fastest Riffield drinker, just to show them he was as good as they.

The servants from Greenview House brought out the refreshments then, great hunks of bread and cheese for the onlookers and the Furnace Green team, plates of cakes decorated with marchpane for their guests.

'A speciality of Furnace Green which I thought you would like to try,' explained the general. 'Except for the marchpane of course, which my cook insisted on adding for her honour's sake, and who am I to argue when it comes to a lady's honour?'

'Quite so.' Sir Maurice Dyer was unused to hearing a cook described as a lady, and covered his confusion by putting one of the cakes into his mouth whole. He had inherited young, and promised to become one of the steady Dyers: medium fair, medium height, medium clever and meaning no particular good or ill to anyone. The cake was just small enough to make a single mouthful, but the instant he began to chew his expression changed from mild to acute embarrassment, head turning instinctively to seek a place where he might discreetly rid himself of so vile a taste.

'You need to chew well to obtain the flavour, which is quite exceptional,' said the general, swallowing with enthusiasm.

By then all the Riffield men were desperate to rid themselves of a substance which combined the texture of pigeon droppings with the taste of metal, while their instincts of service remained sufficiently ingrained for each to overcome his need to spit so long as Sir Maurice retained his mouthful.

'I find the recipe particularly unusual when cooked in my own ovens,' added the general blandly. 'Although I am bound to say that in the village they have become accustomed to a more liquid texture, brought about by lower temperatures. Since our woodlands have been fenced off to preserve your gamebirds, Sir Maurice, the villagers cannot fetch wood for burning as they used. Of course, now you have savoured our speciality you may feel this is all for the best: a softer centre preserves some of the maggots alive as my hotter ovens failed to do.'

With a valiant effort, Sir Maurice had just swallowed his mouthful. 'Maggots?' he said, aghast.

By then, every soul in Furnace Green who was close

enough to hear was grinning, even Alec Larkworthy, but no one laughed. As if one and all they were drawn into the general's charade, while still aware that they comprehended only enough of it to be terrified of spoiling whatever he had in mind.

Dyer snatched his bat from a groom. 'If we were not bound to finish the match I would leave at once, for never have I met a host who offered a joke in such excessively bad taste.'

'A joke? Nothing could be further from my mind, I assure you, sir. As for bad taste, I was but anxious to introduce you to a delicacy even more piquant than the dish I had previously regarded as in a class of its own—the staple of those outcast by society in south India. I believe they mix their dough with excrement. You must agree that Furnace Green is to be congratulated over outdoing such a flavour with mere maggots.'

You could have heard an ant move on the grass beneath the oak.

It took a moment for Sir Maurice to grasp that he was being deliberately insulted, most especially by the word excrement, which no gentleman would use in mixed company. His expression froze and he strode without answering to the wicket, St George about to slaughter a particularly ill-bred dragon.

The general followed him, chuckling. 'I would like to offer a wager, Sir Maurice, since this has become a match both sides wish to win rather more than is usual. A meal against my new colt.'

Dyer blenched. 'A meal?'

'You to attend a Furnace Green special in my house if Riffield loses, against my new colt if you win. Since we have scored but fifty-eight runs, it is a fair gamble unless you lead a side of good-for-nothings.'

'They are worth twice your scarecrows!'

'You agree then?'

'I've never refused a wager yet. Yes, I agree.' Dyer

reflected that even if he lost, the terms proposed did not bind him to consume any of the filth which might be set before him. Really, it was only mannerly to humour a drivelling dotard. India must have stewed out Braybon's wits long ago.

Rumour of the wager flashed instantly across the green. 'I can't see it'll do aught but harm to make an enemy of Sir Maurice, but maybe the old gentleman has a trick up his sleeve,' observed Mark Smith.

'Ah, crafty as a tinker's monkey, he is,' agreed Charlie Twort. 'Now, Bert, no bowling barred today, eh? Make Riffield howl and no one will worry how you do it. We have to win now there's a wager on it.'

Bert Wicks spat on his palms and was understood to agree, although not much given to words as a rule.

The scoring was slow at first, but steady. Maurice Dyer, unlike most village whackers of the ball, was an elegant bat who usually considered it badly bred to score too many runs off those less well taught than himself. Today he was concentrating as never before and, once he had played himself in, began to show signs of taking command of essentially indifferent bowling.

Twenty-three for no wicket.

Then the Riffield saddler was caught close in, and two grooms walked back to the oak in quick succession after trying to hook loose balls to the boundary.

'Time for us to put Bert on, I fancy, or Sir Maurice will win on his own,' said Locock, as they waited for the next man in. Tough, precise and possessing hands like hay-rakes, Locock had kept Furnace Green's wicket for twenty years.

'He'll find the job even easier if Bert can't keep 'em straight. We haven't many runs to play with.' If Wicks's lack of accuracy terrorised batsmen, it could also concede vital runs.

Locock shook his head, and his great-grandfather, Swatch, would have applauded inherited calculation. 'You watch. This time Bert knows we don't care what the complaints are afterwards, so long as we win. He'll be out to enjoy himself.'

Wicks soon showed that Locock's expectations were correct. He went for Riffield's batsmen like a demon, protruding his tongue and pounding up to the wicket from an immense distance before delivering a low-arm missile which lifted like a snipe. The only answer to Bert reaching a length was to throw caution to the winds and try to drive the ball straight back whence it came. It was then a matter of who first disabled whom.

Sir Maurice, however, had been taught rules rather than ruthlessness on the cricket field, and also believed he was good enough to score runs off the fastest ball when bowled to an obviously fragile length. The fifth time Bert came bucketing out of the distance, he opened his shoulders and hit a six over Greenview wall.

He dodged the next two deliveries, then Davey Portnell had the task of bowling his best to save runs at the other end: after he had managed to deliver three runless balls to one of the castle under-gardeners, the next was slammed for what looked like a certain three. Both batsmen ran, but whether from the effects of maggoty flour or not, the gardener was still yards away from his wicket when Tom Rabbit threw with his usual deadly aim from the boundary and flattened his stumps.

'Well played!' bawled the general, hopping from one foot to the other. 'Now we have them on thc run.'

'I thought you were the umpire sir, not captain of the side,' commented Sir Maurice coldly.

'You are right, right indeed, but a trifle of encouragement never came amiss.' To make this point clear, the general applauded the next Riffield man all the way to the wicket. He applauded more loudly still when the new batsman failed to take the single which would have offered his employer the chance to annihilate Davey. Forty-six for five.

Wicks wetted his palms again, measured his distance and delivered the first ball of his next over to Sir Maurice, only to find one of his most unplayable deliveries despatched to the boundary. Unnerved, his next ball was a wide, to Riffield's frantic applause from beneath the oak.

'Get the bastard, for God's sake,' said Huggett, the saddler. 'What's the matter, can't you see the wicket or something?'

'He's good,' answered Wicks succinctly.

Sir Maurice needed all his skill to keep the next ball from hitting him behind the ear, stonewalled the next two and contrived to hook the last to leg for a single.

'Christ, that leaves him with the bowling. Davey—'

'I won't let him get a single run if I can help it,' said Davey between his teeth.

By now most of the Furnace Green team were enjoying the best game of cricket they could remember, and only to Davey did Sir Maurice still figure exclusively as the Enemy rather than a stroke-player to admire. Even so, he was forced to concede four more runs before Tom Rabbit's throwing again sent Sir Maurice's partner back to the oak and brought out Riffield's blacksmith to face Bert Wicks in the gathering dusk.

He stepped out to the first ball, flinched, and was clean bowled by a delivery which made him hug his shin with a yell of pain.

Fifty-five for seven, and five balls of Wicks's over still left, while Sir Maurice stood helplessly at the other end.

The next man in decided to hit his way out of trouble and came galloping back to the oak quicker than he went out.

He was followed by the castle steward, who took guard holding an ancient curved bat over his shoulder and lofted the first ball he received straight into the hands of Locock behind the wicket, having failed to see it from the moment it left Wicks's hand. By then everyone around the ground was yelling themselves hoarse, although as soon as Wicks went to begin his run for the final ball of the over, the silence was such that it was still remembered fifty years later. The last man in for Riffield was a dour gamekeeper who stood foursquare to face the bowling with the air of a man who has faced worse in the woods at night.

'Just keep it out of your wicket, and we'll win,' called Sir Maurice.

'Cocky bastard,' muttered Charlie Twort under his breath.

'I fear he is right, though,' said the general, overhearing. 'Do you move in a trifle and it may help to unnerve him.'

'Christ,' said Charlie, and moved where the umpire's covertly flapped hand told him. 'I never reckoned to field Bert's balls with my nose before.'

Bert Wicks turned and pounded across the turf, knees kicking at his smock, to pitch a skidding delivery exactly where the sheep had cut the wicket most. It kicked up vertically, the gamekeeper recoiled but not fast enough, just snicking the ball as it whizzed past. Charlie dived to his right in a flurry of hobnailed boots, and a roar of delight from all around the green marked the victory of Furnace Green. 'Well played, well played indeed! I haven't enjoyed myself so much for years.' The general wiped his face with a bright red handkerchief and turned to Maurice Dyer. 'Which day would it suit you to take luncheon with us?'

Liddy had not attempted to warn her family of danger when Cook was given a sack of Edenham's worst sweepings and instructed to make cakes of it for the cricket match. Like everyone else, she was baffled by what the general's purpose could be, and anyway, the uproar at Greenview House was such that she scarcely knew which way to turn when Cook flatly refused to demean herself by using ingredients she described as fit only to poison gallows-bait. 'And lawks-a-mercy, I never thought I'd be asked to cook with such, nor I don't intend to start!'

Consequently, Liddy and the scullery-maid had to struggle somehow to turn maggoted, rancid flour sweepings into cakes, while Cook drowned her outrage in several mugs of porter. Unskilful and disastrous though their efforts were, General Braybon insisted on sampling these himself, ruthlessly rejecting batch after batch until a sufficiently nauseous balance of taste and texture was achieved.

'Though why I didn't throw them in the midden the moment you finished, I'll never know!' Cook exclaimed when Liddy returned hotfoot from all the happenings at the match. In fact, after drinking such an unaccustomed quantity of porter she retained only an indistinct recollection of the previous day's events. 'Fancy the master making Sir Maurice eat one of they dreadful things! I might as well cut my throat right away as hope I'll ever outlive the shame.'

Liddy laughed. 'The master wagered Sir Maurice that Furnace Green would win. Him to eat a luncheon here against the master's new colt. You should have seen Sir Maurice's face after he lost, quite peaked up he was with wondering what manner of muck he'd have to eat.'

Cook plumped down in her chair and threw her apron over her aching head. 'Never did I think I'd see the day when a gentleman would dread eating a meal from my kitchen! But now Sir Maurice is coming here, let the master order what he will, I'll prepare the finest luncheon you ever did see.'

Apparently, however, nothing could have been further from the general's intention than an attempt to insist on serving muck. Instead, he merely remarked that by the time he finished with young Dyer he'd need a good meal to restore his humour.

'No, that is too much! I won't allow you to quarrel with a guest in our own house,' exclaimed Mrs Braybon.

'I do not intend to quarrel with him.'

'I insist you tell me what you do intend, because plain as plain you're up to your tricks again. Really, I can't stand any more.' She clutched imploringly at his sleeve.

'Don't do that,' said the general testily, disengaging himself. 'Dyer's a fool if he thinks I'd treat a guest dishonourably, and so are you. I've brought him here in a mood to listen, haven't I? That's all I wanted and there's an end to it.'

'But why such a rigmarole? Why not simply call on him at Riffield Castle, in the ordinary way?'

'And be received all devilish polite no doubt, a glass of wine for my thirst and half an ear for my grumbles. Poor Braybon, one of those old India hands you know, and a trifle touched by the sun.' He snorted. 'I tell you one thing, my dear. Never in his life will young Dyer forget the taste of poor-law flour.'

'I still think—'

'No, no! It's no good thinking! Let me tell you what happened when I called on the good vicar with my poor-rate investigation tucked under my arm. A Dyer, like his nephew.' The general's voice changed to a fair imitation of the vicar's preaching tones. '"You may have a point, my dear Braybon, a point indeed. But I ask you, what would happen if we gave way to the lower orders each time they found a grievance? I daresay Hooke may commit a few small peccadilloes, but he's the kind of overseer we need at this time, you take my word for it."' The general shook his fists in the air. 'A few peccadilloes, by God! I say Hooke and Larkworthy are pocketing some two hundred pounds a year out of the thousand disbursed in relief.'

'Two hundred pounds?' exclaimed Mrs Braybon. 'Why, that's more than all the wages of our servants here. You must be mistaken.'

And: 'Two hundred a year?' echoed Sir Maurice Dyer. 'What kind of hoax is this?'

'*I* am not in the habit of assembling fraudulent accounts, I assure you,' answered the general, bristling.

Dyer had come to Greenview House torn between apprehension at what he foresaw as an embarrassing meal, and curiosity over a situation which in retrospect seemed bizarre. He was quite unsure what to expect but when his reception was entirely humdrum, insensibly he relaxed.

The only oddity was to be whisked immediately into

General Braybon's study and sat down in front of a pile of pamphlets.

'Printed in London at my own expense,' announced the general, twirling his moustaches so that the words he wanted to emphasise became precisely the same length as the longest whisker. 'I could have had them done locally, but wanted to keep my intentions secret. Look at the figures I have detailed and tell me what you think.'

Dyer reflected that since he had come expecting eccentricity, pamphlets were preferable to an inedible meal. In fact, the smells wafting from the kitchen were very agreeable. 'I'm afraid I'm not very good at figures,' he said apologetically.

'You can add and subtract, can you not? Very well then, apply those elementary skills to the columns on the right-hand page and note down the difference.'

'Two hundred and sixteen,' replied Dyer after a pause. Really, military men were intolerable.

'Which is the amount I can prove that Furnace Green's overseer of the poor has put in his own pocket, and the pocket of his accomplice Larkworthy, this past year. It does not include some smaller swindles less easy to establish.'

'*Two hundred a year?*'

'That is what I said. The man should be in gaol, should he not?'

'How can I tell without hearing what he—'

'He would deny everything, of course,' said the general with contempt.

'Then why stir up resentment without hope of remedy? It is just the kind of thing which causes trouble.' There must be three hundred pamphlets here, smelling of printer's ink.

'I have every intention of seeking a remedy. Tomorrow these will be distributed to every poor-rate payer in this and the neighbouring parishes.'

'Good God, you can't do that! These are unproven statements based on gossip.'

'I can and will. Hooke cannot refute my findings because

they are true and he is quite sensible enough not to try, in the expectation that no matter what my allegations, within a week any stir I cause will already be dying down. And why? Because at heart, neither the gentry nor the farmers truly care whether they pay to keep their paupers fed, or into the pocket of Samuel Hooke to ensure their labourers stay cowed. Farmers and gentry not being forced to eat weeviled flour, you see.'

There was a long silence, while Dyer remembered the taste of weeviled flour.

Then his eyes dropped to the pamphlet in his hands and he began to read, this time with his full attention. Several minutes passed before he finished, checking back occasionally to a figure. 'You are quite sure of what you say?'

'On my honour, and there is more besides.'

Dyer drummed his fingers on the table. 'I will tell Ward to look into it.'

'As your agent, his vote did more than the rest together to put Hooke where he is. Only your direct order will force him to undo what he has set in place, since he must consider his repute as engaged along with Hooke's. Your uncle the vicar likewise.'

'Then you cannot expect me to go against their judgement, most especially in a place where my authority as landlord is less well accepted than it should be.'

The general hummed a tune, bouncing on small gaitered feet. 'There have been reports of unrest in Kent, I believe.'

'Rick-burning and cattle-maiming, yes. Quite disgraceful.'

'Life must be desperate indeed, don't you agree, before men can bring themselves to destroy the fruit of their own labour?' The general inhaled a pinch of snuff and sneezed violently. 'If you do not take this last chance to dissociate yourself from Hooke, then I predict that before this winter ends he will be run off by force, even murdered perhaps, and where will you be then? You say your authority is less respected here than it should be. Well, let me inform you that once violence comes to this parish it will no longer be a matter of disrespect, but of hate which will last a generation.'

'And you seriously suppose that my authority would be better set up if I dismissed a man my agent and my uncle had appointed to his office?'

'I am certain of it.'

'By God, I will not do it! The flour perhaps, it is wrong to pay poor men in bad goods. I will tell Ward that the paupers of Furnace Green must receive the relief they are owed in shillings and pence. The full amount, as calculated at Quarter Sessions. Then, if Hooke has juggled the tallies he will be prevented from being led astray in future, but he remains as overseer.'

The general stood, head bent, and did not answer.

'I am grateful you brought an abuse to my notice,' Dyer added. 'But under the present circumstances particularly, anyone appointed with my authority must remain appointed. Later, a convenient moment may occur to set this man, Hooke, aside.'

'You can rely on Furnace Green for that, and sooner rather than later I fancy. Come, sir. Let us go and enjoy the unweeviled repast with which my cook seeks to retrieve her reputation.'

Just for a moment Maurice Dyer's skin flushed pink, as if he was shamed at last, then he bowed and laid the pamphlet he was holding back among the rest before preceding his host out of the room.

'Will he keep his word?' asked Mrs Braybon, some days later, which was the first occasion she had found her husband prepared to discuss the partial nature of his victory.

'Oh, yes, henceforth the poor rate will be paid in coins. Men like Dyer play straight bats and keep their word.'

'If I was him and accepted what you said about Hooke—and I must say I find it hard to credit that such a presentable man is a rogue—then I, too, would decide as he has done. Giving way to threats is what I don't approve of and never shall. What Sir Maurice must think about your conduct towards him I don't know!'

The general was standing by the hearth, one arm along the mantel. 'I'll tell you exactly what he thinks. Generals should know their place. Everyone should know their place. It's easier to hold his damned bat straight when tenants are grateful to their landlord, labourers for their pittances and generals stay in barracks out of sight. I tricked him into understanding why men ought to be paid in coin rather than bad flour and once this simple fact was thrust down his gullet, to his credit he undertook to see the abuse was stopped. Unfortunately, even I cannot think of any way short of insurrection to make him realize that some injuries must be cauterised before they cease to fester. By dismissing Hooke, for instance. Cautery hurts, and Dyers aren't used to being hurt.'

'What's cautery got to do with it? It seems to me that you have been a great deal too busy about the whole affair, I am not surprised that the dear vicar's Sunday sermon . . . Well, he preached about not interfering with God's purposes, and anyone with a grain of sense understood that he meant you.'

'Then you should have walked out, and I will go straightway to tell the nincompoop what I think of him. I may be at a loss over how to proceed further against Hooke, but I haven't reached the point yet where I accept the reproofs of a mere parson with humility. I'm nowhere near it, in fact, when within a few weeks everyone will see who is right.'

'That is exactly the attitude the dear vicar felt impelled to denounce. Spiritual pride he called it,' Mrs Braybon retorted triumphantly. 'What is it, Liddy? The tea table? Thank you.'

The general stood fuming while Liddy bustled about, prevented by her presence from retaliating as he wished.

Liddy bobbed a curtsey when she finished. 'Excuse me, mam. Might I have tomorrow afternoon to visit home?'

'Tomorrow? Oh Liddy, no. I expect Mrs Silcott to call

and take tea. You have every other Sunday afternoon, do you not?'

'Yes, mam. But last Sunday I never went, Cook being took bad over the cakes for the cricket match.'

'And I'm sure we're grateful for your loyalty, Liddy, but I can't spare you tomorrow, I'm afraid. Next Sunday perhaps . . . No, now I come to think of it that will be May's day off. There's nothing for it but to wait until your turn comes again.'

'Please, mam,' said Liddy desperately. 'I can't wait. My family are leaving and will be gone before the Sunday after next. I have to say goodbye.'

'I'm very sorry to hear that, Liddy. When they are settled elsewhere, then perhaps I will try to spare you for a whole day, so you may visit them. At the moment it is out of the question.'

'Why are they leaving?' asked the general, momentarily diverted from brooding on the iniquities of the vicar.

'Never mind that,' said Mrs Braybon hastily. 'That will do, Liddy.' She waited until the door closed. 'I only remembered the other day and then I thought it would make matters dreadfully awkward if I told you. Now you've done what you felt you must, there's an end to it. Liddy's father is the miller at Edenham.'

'Liddy's a Larkworthy? No, I didn't know. Of course she must have the afternoon to go home tomorrow.'

'Oh, you are impossible! Go away at once, and don't come near me for *hours*. It's just plain wicked the way you interfere everywhere and think no one except yourself knows one thing from another.' Mrs Braybon leapt out of her chair and hammered her fist on the mantel an inch from his face.

'Hours you have asked for and hours you shall have.' The general disliked being called wicked even more than being preached over by a parson. Once out in the hall, however, he paused and then put his head round the dining room door, where May was laying cutlery. 'Will you ask Liddy to come to me, please?'

'I think she just slipped to the shop on an errand, sir.' May stared guilelessly over his shoulder.

'Thought there was time to reach Edenham and back before dinner if she ran both ways, did she? Very well, we shall say nothing of this to anyone, but will you convey to Miss Liddy my profound regrets about the way this whole matter has turned out so far as she is concerned?'

'I'll tell her, sir,' said May, round-eyed. 'Sir Maurice only gave the Larkworthys one week's notice, for fraud on the paupers so he said.'

The general did not answer; courteous he might be to his servants, but he did not believe in bandying opinions with them. Naturally, Maurice Dyer had taken the easiest way of ensuring that the fraud in flour was stopped, and Larkworthy was certainly guilty of cruel exploitation of his weakest neighbours; which only made it additionally unjust that Hooke, who was even more to blame, should continue in his offices while the miller lost both trade and tenement.

General Braybon blinked wet eyes, swallowed heavily and felt for his pocket handkerchief. He was as easily overcome by sentiment as by more robust emotions.

At Edenham it was a time of dull, speechless misery for most, but not all, of its inhabitants. Despair pressed heaviest on Peter, little Dick and their mother, because each understood that this was the end of life as they knew it. Ten-year-old Freddie never seemed to think about anything for long, and for Kate and Alec, as for James Larkworthy, their father, there was a great deal more besides misery to think about.

Ward, Sir Maurice Dyer's agent, had brought the notice to quit two mornings ago. 'Count yourselves lucky not to be gaoled after being caught thieving,' he added, holding a copy of General Braybon's pamphlet in his hand.

Suddenly, everyone seemed to have a copy of that damned pamphlet. Just thinking about it made James Larkworthy clench his fists when he was milling the last load of grain he would ever mill in his life. Lord above, he must have been crazed to listen when Hooke first hinted how he could profit from the poor-tallies.

And yet . . . What else could he have done? At the time he had been supporting eight children under twelve years old, of whom two had subsequently died, and prices were so low that farmers could pay only pence for each grinding. And then they kept the miller waiting for his money, whereas his own rent remained at the high level reached during the war against Napoleon. If he hadn't listened to Hooke, he would have lost Edenham long ago. That was the curse of tenancy; rent must be paid though everything else was lacking. As for the likes of Tom Rabbit, James had long ago stopped worrying about the unfortunates who suffered once he and Hooke put their heads together. Dimly he remembered a time when he used to worry, but he had soon realized that ill fortune came to everyone. The only remedy was to save for a rainy day and mind your own affairs. God knew, he'd been lucky to make thirty extra pounds a year; Hooke kept the rest.

'Da?'

He turned and saw Liddy in the doorway. 'I wondered if you would come.'

'I had to.'

'But you're all right? The Braybons will let you stay?' he said, alarmed.

'I'm all right.' In fact, she might easily be dismissed, not because her name was Larkworthy but for running off without leave. 'Where will you go?'

He shook his head; he did not know. Where did elderly millers go when they lost their mill? 'I've got a little money saved. Alec plans to go right away to Canada. When Major Boyd left to dig that canal there for the government, he said any Furnace Green lad would be welcome at his camp.'

'Alec means to leave you and Ma alone to manage for the children?' cried Liddy.

'He said he'd send for Pete once he's settled. Kate's old enough to start in service, which only leaves Freddie and

Dick. If there really is a better life in Canada they might go out too, one day when Alec's doing well.'

'Alec shouldn't leave until you're settled somewhere again.'

'Aye, he should. I want him to. Reach for his chance while there's time, for better or ill. Like I reached for mine when I became tenant at Edenham all those years ago, during the wars. Corn prices were sky-high then and the rent didn't seem too bad. I never wanted to be a cowman like my da, was always sure that whatever I could reach, I'd hold. But it's been rags to rags with me, and I'd like to think Alec might do better.'

'But where will you and Ma and the children go next week?' Liddy couldn't imagine Edenham empty, her family broken into fragments.

'Would you be able to ask Mistress Braybon if she knows of a place around here for Kate?'

'I'll try,' she answered gently. After such a great scandal as this, surely it would be impossible to place any Larkworthy in service hereabouts for a long time to come. 'I'd have to know where to write if I succeeded.'

'London. It has to be London, don't you see? 'Tis the only place where no one cares who you are or where you've come from, so long as you earn your way. I've a year or two of earning left in me, I reckon. Do my cough good to be away from milling flour.' He smiled painfully.

But London was a distant vastness Liddy couldn't grasp, a menacing word in itself which sounded like stamping feet.

'It isn't fair!' she exclaimed. 'There's Mr Hooke still strutting about as if nothing had happened, and you must leave for London! Alec and Pete off to this Canada and none of us to meet again, I daresay. It's cruel, that's what it is.'

Her father held her then, as he had not since she was a child, the flour dust on his clothes tickling her nose. 'It's going to happen, Liddy, that's all there is about it. I've long ago given over trying to unravel rights and wrongs.

Do the best you can for yourself like I hope Alec will, so don't reproach him for what he's decided is best for him. Now my bit of deciding has gone sour, it'll make me feel better to think the next lot of you may bob up higher.' He turned back to bagging corn from the spout and after a few moments of watching him, Liddy went over to the house.

Then began the worst time of all, because her mother had just called everyone to supper. Liddy ought to have run as fast as she could back to Greenview House, though grand people like the Braybons ate later than cottagers; instead she slipped into her familiar place intent on scoring each moment into her mind.

She glanced around the snug kitchen, lingeringly. Soft brick, smoke-black beams and cinders crumbling on a chequered-brick hearth, all these were woven into her life, like the sizzle of water in the kettle, the sighs of hunger satisfied. Bustle, bustle went Ma, serving everyone with mighty sploshings from the pot. 'No good leaving aught behind,' she said briskly. 'Eat up until you bust, the lot of you.'

Kate smiled, but with a look in her eyes which meant that she at least was glad to be going. 'How many days will it take to walk to London, do you think?'

'Nearly as many as me on a ship to Canada,' answered Alec, laughing. 'Christ, Pete, by the time you come, I'll have milk and honey poured off my own land waiting for you.'

'I don't like milk or honey,' muttered Pete.

'Aw, rubbish! If there was honeycomb on the table, you'd be the first to dig in when our backs were turned. A land of milk and honey, that's what Major Boyd called Canada and it sounds good to me. Christ, I could tell you—'

'Grown man you may be, but I'll belt you if you swear,' said Da, but absently. On any other day Alec wouldn't have dared swear at all.

Liddy saw Da's eyes swivelling around the kitchen too,

and Ma watching him. All of them thinking, thinking: last time all together in our own place, last time. 'I wonder how many people have sat here since Edenham was built, and known that tomorrow they must walk away for ever?' she burst out suddenly.

'Why waste time wondering?' answered Alec, chewing hard.

But perhaps because Alec said it was a waste of time, everyone else looked over their shoulder as if expecting an apparition to answer. Ma shivered. 'I never thought before how this place might be haunted.'

'Why should hauntings always be bad? Why, I'd like to meet every single person who ever lived here before us.' Liddy blew a kiss towards the hearth. 'Greetings, ghost!'

Everyone laughed, but uneasily. Ghosts were capricious and it didn't do to tease them.

'I don't want to go. Not to London nor Canada, neither. I want to stay here. Janey Locock and me have built our very own house in a tree, why can't I live there?' Pete had always been more interested in fields and wild creatures than the mill.

'You'll do as you're told, now eat up and don't dare say another word.'

Liddy saw Ma's eyes on Da, as if she knew he couldn't bear much more. Time pelting past now and no excuses left to linger any longer. 'I have to go,' she blurted out. 'Pete, I've just thought. If you still don't like London in . . . well, three years say, you ask Da to write and I'll try to find you a place.' Three years was the least time she could imagine in which the shame of being a Larkworthy might be overlooked.

'Pete's following me to Canada,' said Alec brusquely. 'Major Boyd said there was land for the taking, no landlords, no nothing to stop you. Stay here and you'll always be fleeced for other men's profit, with naught at the end of it to call your own.'

Kate winked at Liddy over the rim of her tankard. 'If

this Canada was as easy as you say, there'd be no one left in Sussex.'

Liddy scrambled out between table and bench while Kate and Alec quarrelled, as they had done ever since Kate left her crib. Better to go while things were how they had always been.

'Remember,' she whispered as she kissed Pete, 'if you still want to come back later, then I'll do what I can to help.'

Baby Dick was the worst, clinging to her legs and begging her to stay. Babes didn't live long in London, so it was said.

No, Ma was the worst, weeping without restraint at last. Yet even now, Liddy couldn't grasp that she might never see Ma again.

But in the end Da was the worst, because she loved him best. Because he loved her best, although neither of them ever spoke such a thing aloud. She was ashamed of what Da had done, almost disbelieved it still, yet at the time of parting only their love seemed to matter.

Liddy's last glimpse of them all was of black figures outlined against the lamp, light spilling between them as she climbed away up the slope. As soon as she reached the lane, she began to run. Hedgerows and trees reeled past; fright at being so long away from Greenview House surfacing like scum on the grief which had previously filled her mind. If she lost her place with the Braybons now, then far from bettering herself, she, too, would be rags to rags inside a single life.

'Oh Liddy, what an age you've been!' May pounced on her the moment she clattered down the passage to the kitchen. 'An hour you said, and it's been more than two. The mistress asked where you were when I fetched the tea things, and then again when she caught me turning down the beds.'

'She knows I've been out?'

May nodded. 'You're to go up to her this instant. The general—I'll tell you later what he said. If it had been only him, I think he'd have taken care not to notice you had gone.'

Liddy seized a fresh-starched apron and ran up the backstairs still tying the strings behind her back, telling herself that it was no good regretting things you couldn't help.

She knocked. 'You wished to see me, mam?'

'Oh . . . Liddy.' Mrs Braybon looked up, uncharacteristically hesitant. Her eyes were angry, though. 'Have you seen my fan?'

'No, mam. Would you like me to look in your bedroom?' Liddy was almost too taken aback to answer, having expected instant dismissal.

'Since you are here at last, you might as well make yourself useful,' she snapped, thus making her displeasure clear as well as a decision to overlook it.

On the other side of the hearth the general removed a cigar from his mouth and contemplated the glowing end. Perhaps it was just the smoke which made him look uncommonly smug, but General Braybon was a man who liked to pay his debts.

There'll be some china broke before this evening's done, thought Liddy gleefully as she ran upstairs. Now I wonder just how he made her keep me?

It was especially pleasant to be living in Greenview House for a few weeks after that, as a cold brown October followed on the heels of harvest. Outside Greenview House was a different matter, the dread of winter along the street almost as visible as the autumn mists. Because most employers only paid wages when a full tally of work could be accomplished, a single wet day could lay off a quarter of the village men, while a long wet spell made life wretched for nearly everyone. Winters killed off children and the old, sent fevers seeping down the street, left strong men demoralised by their own helplessness. Already this year threatened to be worse than any which had gone before, Farmer Locock having shown the way when he bought one of the new threshing-machines, which manufactured paupers almost as fast as they spat grain into heaps. In winter, a great many families depended on casual earnings, which during the snowy weeks after Christmas mostly meant threshing.

Take Tom Rabbit: he, his wife, his dog and children could not survive the cold time of the year on the chancy results of moderately skilful poaching. And strangely enough, Tom delighted in the labour which most men hated: threshing out corn with a flail. Farmer Locock had always been glad to hire Tom for two months in the winter because from dawn until after dusk he was quite happy to stand pounding away with a flail, speaking only to his dog, taking no food except for a piece of bread and a pinch of salt. Then, an hour after everyone else had finished, he would put on his coat, drink a tankard of ale at the farmhouse door and tramp back across the green, proudly carrying two crusty hot loaves of bread and his one-and-sixpence wages. This year there would be no work for Tom, no one-and-sixpence, no task in which his endurance was respected. No two months when the remarks thrown at him were admiring instead of contemptuous.

But, even after all that had happened, the dread and resentment along the street still barely touched Greenview House. The Braybons had come too recently to Furnace Green for them to know the villagers except to nod greetings if they passed; the general's efforts to reduce Hooke's swindlings were appreciated, as was his habit of paying his men at Corndown when it rained, but that did not make him part of the daily struggle for existence.

As Davey said, while sitting beside Liddy on the churchyard wall, 'What do I care if your general pays men as he ought or his wife sends food to Moll Huggett, who has no milk for her third? That is between them and their conscience, not mine. All I know is that Moll's milk failed because she has only scraps to eat, while your cursed general sits down to three meals a day.'

'I eat three meals a day and so do you. Tell me, what

would Moll do if you went running to give her your supper every night?'

'Box my ears,' he answered, grinning. 'Ah Liddy, give over, will you? Moll ought to have what she needs to live without begging for charity. God knows, there's enough in Sussex for everyone, if only it was fairly split.'

'Farmer Locock says prices are too low, rent and tithes too high, for him to hire as many men as he used.'

'God cripple Farmer Locock, blood-sucking devil that he is!' shouted Davey, his legs fairly swinging with rage. They were sitting on the churchyard wall because, on Liddy's Sunday afternoon off, they had nowhere else to go. The wind was cold, the sun setting in winter pinks and greys.

'Don't you start talking foul or you'll be sorry.' Liddy put her nose in the air. If Davey thought she came to listen to him cursing, then it was time his mind was changed. In her opinion, things were how they were and you did the best you could with them. Which included David Portnell, whom she wished was less clearly marked out for trouble.

'Go to hell,' he said, laughing now.

'Go there yourself if that is how you are,' she snapped, and jumped off the wall.

He jumped down too, and caught her by the waist. 'Liddy, do you know why I'm still in Furnace Green?'

'No,' she said, although she hoped she knew.

'I'd quite decided to go with Hankin's gang when they moved from Ockham, only . . . only—'

'You'd be a fool to run out on your apprenticeship once Mr Lavender refused to cancel your indentures.'

'But then, I am a fool, as you well know, my sweetheart. The Devil curse my indentures, when what I really want—'

'Yes,' she whispered. 'What is it you do want, Davey?'

To him she looked very beautiful then, her face half turned away and with redness whipped into her cheeks by raw October air.

'You,' he said.

'Now be honest, will you!'

'All right,' he said doggedly. 'I want you, and also a scrap of justice in this world. I also want to help in the fight to get it.'

She turned to look at him directly. 'Eh, but I like you best when you're honest. So I'll ask another question. Are your wantings that way around?'

From where they stood the churchyard looked out on the slope which led north off the ridge, where a winking light marked a carriage on its way to Tunbridge Wells. A dog fox barked in the dusk and a vixen answered, sounds snatched from the blowing wind. 'I don't know,' he said, reluctantly, at last. 'That isn't a question I can answer. Nor would you ask it if you understood how I am at all. I can tell you this, though, 'tis you I love. So you answer me truly too, who or what do you love best?'

Liddy tossed her head just as if this wasn't the most important question of her life, while, inside, unhappiness and uncertainty churned her stomach close to sickness. Nothing but heartbreak waited for her with a man who didn't know which came first, love or trouble. Whereas in Greenview House lay safety and bettering herself, like she and Da both wanted. 'If you aren't sure of your mind then I'm not either.'

'But I am sure. Sure of you and justice. What's wrong in that?' He kissed her then, but lightly, so it didn't help in making up her mind. 'Why, I reckon you're just afraid of being forced to choose between me and your old general!'

'Don't you dare say dirty things to me, Davey Portnell!' But in the sense he meant it, he was of course completely right, which only helped to sharpen her temper.

'Answer what I asked then. Who or what do you really love, Liddy?'

There was a long silence before, grudgingly, she answered, 'A boy from Furnace Green street and I wish to God I didn't.'

'Tell me his name,' he whispered.

'. . . David Portnell.'

'And I thee, Elizabeth Larkworthy. By my heart I swear it.' And he kissed her three times, which made a pledge well-omened.

Her thoughts spinning under those kisses, Liddy felt a new trembling spread from him to her and was ashamed. Ashamed of desire which threatened to spill her on wet grass like a wanton, ashamed because she had only spoken of her love, not sworn to it as Davey had. Then the shock of his hand on her breast, his lips stronger than a witch's spell on hers, wrenched her back to the present. 'No,' she said clearly, and drew away. In the space between them their breath mingled and steamed in the chill.

'Oh Liddy, what a lass you are for no's. We swore, didn't we, so why not yes for a change?'

'I didn't swear. I said I loved you, which God knows is true.' And God knew, too, how much she wanted to say yes to his wanting hands, that wildness in her growing with his touch, wildness she could never have imagined while she went dutifully about her tasks at Greenview House.

'Then if you love me—'

'I love you, but I have my own way to go.'

'I've been too quick for you, is that it? Liddy . . . I'd never force you, you know that.'

'Yes, I know that,' she answered gently. 'It's just that I don't want my mind forced either, don't you see?'

She saw his face change and set. 'If you won't let me give what you want to take, what then? All of your life wasted while you run to please rich pigs in their wallow, is that it?'

'I don't know what I want yet, and I won't let you call the Braybons pigs, neither,' she said desperately. There was so much she did not know. So much she would never know, unless she went her own way for a while. 'Davey, please, don't you see? I can't face being tied down yet without a choice, when here I am, only three months away from my own home hearth.'

'So you're the same as your da after all, pretending one

thing and then offering sweepings in its place,' he said cruelly, tossing her hands aside as if discarding them on a heap.

The wind pounced at Liddy around the corners of the church as she pelted away from him across the graveyard. Davey was right and she was wrong, he wrong and she most certainly right. But why must desire be such a demented thing, which shouted that only in Davey's arms could she gain the one thing she really wanted?

'Liddy.' Somehow he had raced ahead, and was waiting by the back entry to Greenview House. All along the street people must have been peeking out of their cottages to watch them chasing past. 'Liddy, I didn't mean it. You told me straight whatever I asked, it was the truth you offered and not sweepings.'

'Oh Davey. You devil, you,' she said, and held him tight.

He laughed and kissed her, but this time without the asking edge to his mouth she had felt earlier; a devil indeed he was, and understood very well that for certain purposes tenderness is best. 'Three years at least before I've saved enough to tie you down for good,' he whispered against her cheek. 'By then you'll know the way your choice has to settle.'

After he'd watched her through the gate, Davey walked away down the street, whistling. Very pleased with himself he was, too, the promise in Liddy taking such a swing at his senses that he knew she couldn't feel much different. He'd win her round, and with luck not have to wait three years, either.

Greenview House kitchen was warm and dark when Liddy let herself inside; she fetched some milk from the larder and sat in Cook's chair by the hearth while she waited for it to warm. A few sounds drifted down from upstairs as the family went to bed, a creak on the stair, the rasp of bolts on the front door. The general always locked up himself, a legacy of his years in the East. The house was alive, sheltering, homelike. Safe. Beyond its walls the times were desperately hard and likely to get harder, especially for women who had to bear children and make mean wages spin into a sufficiency. Bitterly hard for any woman pledged to a man who must forever be kicking against everything in his path; a man who also knew how to mix hot blood with caresses, rages against circumstance with the promise of passion in dark places.

The milk fizzed sharply on hot cinders and Liddy jumped up, then paused with the skillet in her hand. Davey is like this milk, she thought. Where else among the furrows of the ridge would she ever find a husband who, instead of being dulled by hardships, was made by them to fizz with anger, love and dreams?

All the same, she had done well in a three short months at Greenview House, begun to realize what vast hierarchies of servants existed everywhere in which she could make her way. Why, the housekeeper at Riffield Castle was said to reign like royalty over a household counted in hundreds! Not only had Liddy very quickly appreciated comfort and order, but her ambitions had continued to unfold under the influence of prospects she had not before been able to imagine. She knew she was quicker than Cook, nimbler than May, more hard-working than dismissed William or cricketing Frederick. She was already relied on by the household. Surely, once she was trained, she would be able to enter some grander establishment and rise to dizzying heights?

But . . . Davey, Davey.

Liddy had no idea—how could she have?—that she would only see Davey twice more, and those times fleetingly, in the next eight years.

Trouble came down on the Weald from the east, and with very little warning. First of all the rumours began, whispers from lip to lip telling of disturbances in Kent. It was said that if you climbed high enough at night you could see the glow of burning ricks, but Jim Huggett sneaked up the church tower when the vicar's back was turned and reported the horizon clear, so no one knew what to think. Then came the mutterings. Where they began was impossible to guess, but wherever people met, these muttered rumours grew like a storm building against the wind. It was said some villages were already demanding an end to tithes, or had turned out hated overseers; barns were reported on fire around Maidstone, threshing-machines broken at Canterbury, revolutionary flags hoisted at Sittingbourne. When this last rumour reached Furnace Green, mouths were pulled down disapprovingly: trust Kent to become infected by French bobberies like flags. In Sussex they weren't interested in suchlike, and most especially not in French suchlike. Fire and muscle were the weapons they understood.

Then, quite suddenly, Furnace Green street was no longer populated only by children and women during the daylight hours; old 'uns stood in the wind instead of staying by the hearth, the younger men idled aimlessly while work went begging in the fields.

The Friday after Liddy and Davey had sat on the church wall together, General Braybon returned to the stable yard only minutes after he had left it to inspect the progress of his agricultural experiments at Corndown. 'Told me to bar the outer gates at once, then go to order more doorbolts from the blacksmith,' reported Akehurst, the groom, when the servants gathered for their mid-morning ale. 'A mob went on the rampage in Battle yesternight, and began a-burning and a-pothering all around.'

'That's in Sussex,' said May, awed.

'Rye too,' added Akehurst with relish. 'There's smoke blowing over Rye as well, so they say.'

You could smell trouble after that. The tang of violence, whether real or imagined, came in like smoke on the air and sent farmers and householders scurrying to watch over their possessions. Soon, in Furnace Green street men began to fuse into drifting groups, and the mutterings grew into shouts.

Mr Aitchison walked across early that same evening, and was immediately closeted with the general in his study. Then the male servants were summoned to join them, an unheard-of occurrence.

Liddy was upstairs drawing the curtains when they trooped out again together: she had been trying to catch a glimpse of Davey among the men in the street, but her view was restricted by a corner of Wyses and Greenview House garden wall.

When she heard the men clatter back to the kitchen, she abandoned the remaining curtains and raced down the backstairs to hear what extraordinary happenings they must have to tell. Never since the Braybons came to Greenview House had any of the outside staff previously been summoned into the house.

'. . . I told him I couldn't see my way to it.' Akehurst's voice, as she arrived breathless at the bottom of the stairs.

'Well, I don't see why we shouldn't, when it promises good sport.' Fred-footman stripped off his waistcoat as if ready for instant action. 'Riding hey-go-merry over the countryside after rioters, now that'll be even better than a cricket match!'

'They may be rioters to you, who comes from outside the Weald, to me they're neighbours fallen on ill times,' retorted Akehurst. 'As for hunting them down, like I said, I can't see my way to it.'

'Doing what, for mercy's sakes?' shrieked Cook. 'Upon my soul, are we all to be murdered in our beds without you lifting a finger to help?'

'Hold your screeching and talk sense, woman. We're speaking of men we know and not a pack of Frenchies, which is why I'll have naught to do wi' it.' Akehurst stalked out, very slow and dignified in his polished gaiters.

'Will someone just tell me what's to-do?' Cook appealed to Frederick.

'The master wanted to enrol us all as special constables because of the fires and riot, and swear the oath in front of Mr Aitchison. Him being the magistrate, hereabouts.'

Frederick looked well pleased by such an exciting turn in events. The gardeners—Banks, Bob Twort and Billy Rabbit—were all local like Akehurst.

'Mercy me!' Cook plumped down in her chair. 'You never mean Mr Akehurst refused?'

'Yes, I do. And because he wouldn't swear, the rest of 'em wouldn't either. Except for me, of course. But never you mind, Mrs Cary, I'll make sure no one chases after you with a pitchfork.' He began to nibble a fragment of pastry.

'Well, of all the cowards! You just wait until I give Mr Akehurst a piece of my mind! I wouldn't have thought it of him, that I wouldn't.'

Banks, Bob Twort and Billy Rabbit exchanged shifty glances, none of them used to bandying words in the kitchen, although Banks, the head gardener, was a martinet in his own domain. Far less were they used to defying the master, and in his own study at that. 'It were like this, see,' said Banks apologetically. 'We didn't want to get ourselves swore in against our own. Special constables now, I reckon they have to do whatever they're told. Be hung if they don't, for all I know. Mr Akehurst said he weren't willing to ketch those he'd known since he was a nipper, good law-abiding men driven beside themselves by not knowing how to feed their children. We felt the same, Bob and Billy and me.'

'And me,' said Johnny the boot-boy pertly.

'You keep your mouth shut, my lad, and do what you're told,' said Banks, by which he did not mean doing what Johnny's master ordered. Some loyalties could be taken for granted, even in ten-year-old boys; in most of the ways that mattered Furnace Green remained a tribal community, almost a thousand years after Saxons first settled there.

Cook pulled at her lip. 'I'm Hartfield born myself.'

'There's been fires at Hartfield, too. Their overseer drove out at a cart's tail, so I hear, and a good job too. I reckon Hooke must be a-trembling in his boots by now.'

On this agreeable thought the gathering in the kitchen broke up, and Liddy flew upstairs to finish her tasks. Later, Frederick and May reported that dinner had been consumed almost in total silence. 'The mistress is frightened more about the children than herself, now there's all these tales of fire and riot. With the dessert she said maybe they should all stay in Tunbridge Wells until the dragoons come,' May said to Liddy afterwards. 'I thought the general were going to burst he went such a dreadful colour. "I shall not run from an enemy in my declining years any more than as a soldier, and these people here are not our enemies," he said, all bristling like a breeches-brush. "As for those dastardly servants of mine, I'll show them where their duty lies."'

Liddy giggled. 'I wonder how. Does he really expect the likes of Tom Rabbit to come forcing their way in here?'

'Don't you think they just might? Once they start thinking about all the food in our larder, just waiting to be stolen?'

Liddy could not visualise it. Not boys and men she knew, trampling in where they weren't welcome, smashing and stealing and yelling dirty words like Mark Smith said the Frenchies did in their revolution. Mark had been a sergeant in Wellington's army, he and the general often smoked a pipe together while discussing old campaigns. Liddy had been surprised when she glimpsed Mark among the men idling in the street; but as the tenant of poor wet land at Pigpasture Farm, probably he had almost as hard a struggle as anyone else to make ends meet.

Nothing changed next day. Men still drifted back and forth, arguing when they ought to have been at work, though the women were beginning to get restive over no money coming in. And Liddy still found it as hard as ever to imagine anyone she knew running wild. Except perhaps Davey. He wasn't like the rest, who were made desperate by hungry-bellied families and wretched wages interminably pledged to redeem old debts. He actually wanted to whip up wildness for purposes of his own.

Liddy glimpsed him midway through the afternoon, in an eddy of men which burst away from Mr Wicks's butchery shop and flowed past Greenview House at a different pace to the aimless turbulence of the past two days, crossing the green at a run and only stopping when they reached the great oak beside the pool.

She raced up another flight of stairs to the nursery passage window, but all she could see was shifting figures and once a spark of metal when the sun edged through a break in grey and scudding mist.

It was that glitter which at last made Liddy no longer sure what men she knew might do, once they goaded each other on. A single flash off a naked blade enough to make her previous confidence seem absurd.

Underneath the Meeting Oak there was complete confusion. Half a dozen men had been arguing in Bert Wicks's shop, no different from all the other arguments which had been raging for the past two days, when the butcher suddenly grasped his knife and began to shout that it was about time they left off talking and marched to demand their rights.

Except on the cricket field Bert was regarded as a slowtop, but by chance he struck precisely on a time when everyone had wearied of talk. The more sober were becoming alarmed by so much waste of working time, while the courageous yearned to emulate deeds which had set their world alight. Battle, Robertsbridge, Hartfield, Mayfield; all were astir, and rumours of burned ricks, smashed threshing-machines, assaulted overseers and besieged parsons blew like a windstorm down Furnace Green street.

Quite why Bert grasping his knife should make everyone jostle out of Wicks's shop was uncertain, but, almost without their own volition, the group there did run outside with him in their midst. Other idling men were scooped up from the street, their pace quickening as they reached the green.

Once a substantial number were gathered under the

oak, others drifted across to increase the crowd still further; everyone still knew the oak as a magic place which kept the ridge's spirits, the why and how of this belief quite unimportant once fable and truth intermingled. Because the oak existed, it drew its people back as soon as a crisis broke.

Bert Wicks was thrust forward first to speak, perhaps because he held a knife.

'Say again what you said in your shop, Bert,' called a voice.

'I said 'twas time to stop argufying and march to demand our rights,' he replied, as if it was the simplest thing in the world.

A nonplussed silence fell, while everyone began at once to realize the enormity of this aim when put into words. Then Jim Huggett snickered. 'Where should we march then, Bert?'

Because the question was clearly jocular, everyone laughed, as if glad of the chance to draw back before it was too late.

'We'll march where we want, in the name of King George,' Bert answered stoutly.

'There isn't a King George,' objected Mark Smith. An old soldier knew to whom oaths should be sworn, even if his neighbours seldom troubled about which king or minister was which.

'In the name of King William then,' Davcy Portnell called, as the meeting showed signs of breaking apart as fast as it had come together. 'If kings really offer justice to all their people, we've a right to march against thieves who took what once was ours.'

'March where?' demanded Mark. Forty-five hard years old, he still held himself as straight as a staff; his hair and beard bleached rather than grey, his face all angled bone.

'To Riffield, where else?' Davey shouted. 'It's our rights we want! The Dyers took them and only they can give them back.'

'I say a pox on Riffield, what's Riffield to we? 'Tis the

threshers that'll squeeze us dry this winter. Let's smash up Farmer Locock's bloody machine afore anyone can stop us!' Tom Rabbit yelled from the outskirts of the crowd, where his words struck an immediate response.

'Aye, the threshers!'

'Farmer French has ordered one as well, he'd soon have another think if we smash up Locock's!'

'To Lococks!'

Davey joined in the rush; any action was better than none, although he was annoyed that his first attempt at agitation had fallen flat. On the other hand, the first step into disorder must be the hardest for law-abiding men to take. Once they tasted violence, their appetite might grow.

The way from the oak to Lococks Farm led past Danesdell House, whose tenant Locock was. The wrought-iron gates of Danesdell House were padlocked shut between their twin gateposts, one surmounted by a spike and the other by a coat of arms which, in a lop-sided way, resembled the Tudor arms of England. The present owner, Mr Aitchison, that enthusiastic antiquary, was inclined to the theory that Queen Elizabeth must once have slept there. Today, however, he was not thinking about any such thing, as he peered between chinks in drawn curtains at a mob streaming past his walls. As a magistrate who enjoyed the consequence of his office, he knew his duty was to confront and disperse them if he could. As a timid and panic-stricken individual he desired nothing so much as to remain out of sight.

His wife was away on a visit, but never before had it occurred to Benjamin Aitchison that he lived alone in a wilderness; that the whole government of England could within a morning vanish out of reach. Now he peered out from his darkened room, trembling with solitary fears, and saw only bellowing mouths and raised fists, a clash of steel which made Aitchison's belly quake, beating feet and wolf-pack howls.

When everything was quiet again he opened his study door and tiptoed down the kitchen passage. There had been no answering face when he pulled a bell, and the kitchen proved completely empty; every soul in his employ had apparently run off, if not to join the mob, then to relish the excitement.

He stood in Abigail Hosmer's handsome panelled hallway for quite a long time before somehow wringing a kind of resolution out of the silences surrounding him, although it would have been hard to decide whether a longing for company or a sense of duty ultimately took him out to the stable. Once there, he saddled his horse and, keeping as much under cover as possible, set out to ride across the park to Riffield.

John Locock was in his farmyard when the mob came in, where his threshing-machine happened to be standing idle, a consequence of good ploughing weather rather than the unsettled times. The advantage of the new threshers was that time lost could be made up, often without any need to employ the gangs of flailmen and winnowers which previously had been necessary.

No one particularly liked Farmer Locock. They thought him hard because wasted moments were rare on his farm. His workers feared him, his sons respected but did not love him. He had no patience with slackness or inefficiency, since his main ambition was to own the land he rented. Because he never spared himself he saw no reason why he should spare others, nor was he displeased to be respected rather than held in affection. Indeed, it gave him satisfaction to feel he kept everyone up to the mark. John Locock had no intention of joining the growing numbers of farmers who had been bankrupted by failing to trade keenly during a time of chancy prices.

Locock had heard noises approaching down the lane from Danesdell House, and when the crowd of villagers came round the corner of his barn its leaders found themselves face to face with him, a droving whip in his hand.

'Good day to you,' he said coolly, a glance sufficient to

tell him that rumour and grievance had fused at last in Furnace Green.

'Good day to you, Master.' Ted Sleech, one of his own labourers, was the only one to answer, and he shamefaced.

'There's enough of that,' shouted Davey. 'We've come for our rights, Mr Locock.'

'What rights are those?' enquired Locock. 'I did not know I'd taken anything which was yours.'

'Not mine,' Davey waved his hand. 'These men's here. Your damned machine has taken away their livelihood.'

'And we want to be paid on wet days as well as dry! Two-and-threepence a day in winter, two-and-six in summer,' called Ted Sleech. He was afraid of his master, but now he had come he knew he had nothing more to lose by being bold.

Locock tapped his leg with his whip. 'I pay what a man is worth to me, and you are worth one-and-ten in winter and two shillings the rest of the year.'

'That be damned! You with your snug farm and me with a wife and five children to keep!'

'Another man's children are not my concern.'

'Ah, curse your guts, is it not any Christian man's concern if he waxes fat while others starve?'

'As to that, you'd be worse fed, not better, if I was forced to sell up. And now, by God, I will ask you all to leave my land.'

'It's true, what he says,' called Mark Smith. In his heart he was ashamed of being caught up in a mob of labourers when, as a smallholder, he liked to consider himself Locock's equal. Only, prices were so depressed, Pigpasture land so cold and wet, that somehow he always lived hand to mouth.

Locock looked at him reflectively but did not answer. By now his three sons had come running and stood at his back, fingering billets of wood.

Mark flushed violently under that cold scrutiny. 'Me, I can't pay a penny over one-and-six at any season, tithe and taxes being what they are. But a prosperous man like you now, you could afford more and to employ your men through the winter. Then there would be less poor rate for the likes of I to scrape for.'

'That I cannot, when the rate I pay is already increased to make up for the lower wage your men are forced to accept. As for being rid of tithe, you should go bid that Christian man, our parson, to manage his affairs without it.'

This cunning stratagem very nearly worked. Immediately several voices were raised, and none of them louder than Mark Smith's, demanding that the vicarage should instantly be besieged until such time as Parson Dyer swore to cease collecting tithe. Tithe was hated by everyone, perhaps the only common cause between labourers and their employers, since neither saw why a tenth of all profits from the earth should go to a church which gradually had ceased to use this income for their benefit.

Davey swore and shouted at the faces nearest him, trying to make them see how Locock planned to send them on a fresh chase away from his farm, but as the noise grew so his arguments went unheeded. Everyone had become jostling and uncertain, only Ted Sleech unexpectedly willing to start breaking things up unless Locock was humbled without more ado.

A yell from across the yard rallied them. Tom Rabbit was dancing on top of the threshing-machine, a mattock in his hand. 'Watch me! Watch me! See how easy these devil-machines smash up!' He whacked his mattock into a flywheel. ''Tis easier than breaking fresh-turned clods!' Whack again, and metal clanged.

One of Locock's sons hurled his wood billet at Tom, and he jerked up his leg with a howl as it hit him on the thigh. This caused him to lose his balance and he only saved himself by hooking his mattock into canvas belting. As he fell, this too jerked free and he tumbled head over heels into the opening where, when the machine was working, a drum revolved to thrash grain out of corn-stalks. The drum, Tom's hob-nailed boots and pieces of canvas all rotated with a clatter, Tom's yells changing to pure terror as his hand spiked between drum and casing.

'Lie still, you dolt,' shouted Locock, and moved to free him.

'You stay where you are and we'll free our own.' Davey shoved him violently aside. 'Once you get your hands on Tom, he'll be locked up for the magistrates to hang.'

A general fight instantly erupted as the Locock boys struggled to reach their father before he was trampled underfoot and Davey led a surge of men towards the thresher, where Tom Rabbit's screams were sufficient in themselves to addle thought. Incapable of keeping still, his struggles were continuing to rotate the drum, shredding his hand as it did so.

Davey was the first to climb the high timber sides of the thresher, without realizing that the one thing he needed to know, and did not, was how to brake and then reverse the drum. Canvas belting, blood and iron castings bewildered him by their complexity. Tom's shrieks jangled in his ears, everything he tried to do seemed only to make matters worse.

'We'll have to knock the drum off its mounting,' shouted Ted Sleech, and ran for an axe which he knew was kept in the barn.

'For God's sake stay away from that flywheel,' Davey screamed at the rest; he could see that the drum was rotated by the wheel, although solid engineering hid most other secrets of the thresher. He seized Mark Smith's arm. 'We have to stop Tom struggling!'

Because of his age Mark had taken his time about climbing to the top of the thresher, now he leaned over quite calmly and took Tom by the throat. Squeezed until his face turned purple and his tongue protruded, until at last his struggles ceased. Mark Smith had seen men gutted in battle and knew how to make them still. By then Ted Sleech had climbed back carrying an axe. 'I'll soon have the casing split away.'

The axe swung and swung again.

Chips of wood flew, sparks too when the axe struck metal. A plank split from the frame with a crash and the men gathered around the thresher cheered. After that, no one could have said whether freeing Tom or breaking the thresher mattered most, Tom's mangled hand and arm no more than part of how their lives had been maimed.

When they had him free at last, and the machine was so solidly made that by then he had lost a great deal of blood, they finished the work Ted's axe had begun. Smashed plank from plank, tore canvas, fractured iron. And when they had finished, set fire to what remained.

'No more starveling wages in winter,' called Bert Wicks, and cheered.

'Now we'll go tell Parson he must swear away his tithes!'

'No more machines to cheat us of what we're owed!' Cheers swirled through mist-laden air as flames reflected redly in the murk.

'You blockheads, after this morning's work some hangings outside Lewes gaol are what will happen next,' said Locock coldly. He grasped a glowering son in each hand, like hounds held back from a kill, the third looking quite as furious just behind his back. Locock himself was muddied but not apparently much hurt, nor did he look as angry as his sons. His eyes flickered to where Tom Rabbit lay moaning on the ground. 'If you had let me, I could have braked the drum and had him out with only his fingers torn. As for my thresher, it was insured. I shall have a better model here within the month.'

'That you will not, now we're the ones to say what happens in Furnace Green,' exclaimed Jim Huggett.

Locock smiled his tight, annoying smile and did not answer.

'He means it,' cried Ted Sleech. 'What the master says, he means. Christ, what a pass I been a-brought to, hustling and bustling into losing my hiring over a morning's madness!'

'No,' said Davey swiftly, sure again of his purpose. 'We broke a machine to show we mean business, but we've still to take back our rights. Once we have them, there'll be justice like there used to be. Hirings for all and good wages even in the winter. All you have to do is follow me.'

Nearly everyone was still jubilant enough over destroying the thresher to shout their agreement, but this time no one asked where they had to follow, as if they feared to hear the answer.

Waving their arms and shouting excitedly to each other, the men of Furnace Green began their march to Riffield, sending farmers along their way scurrying to protect their ricks. 'This is the day!' chanted Davey at their head. 'This is the day we take our justice back. Listen all you out there!'

And they listened to him, young as he was. Old men, sober men, desperate men, all torn between terror and triumph over what they had already done. Not that Davey was afraid, far from it, that was part of the spell he spun. He knew that now the dispossessed had risen, they had nothing more to fear. The men who followed him were different: they were quite simply drunk on new-found power, while at the same time a small shrivelled nut of fear remained at the back of their minds, waiting to strike root. Of course Davey had to be right when he said that once ordinary men took back their rights, the farmers would be the same as everyone else, but just for a moment Locock's self-confidence had opened a chasm at their feet. A chasm where all their pitifully few possessions would plummet into the darkness labelled failure, their families, hoarded pence and inherited scraps of furniture, the familiarity of fields and daily toil.

The long tramp to Riffield did not help. Trees dripped and boots leaked, most of the men felt oddly tired. They were used to working from dawn to dusk, but had never before experienced such a tumult of emotions as this day held.

Already Davey had decided they had best go by way of Tisbury Hill rather than directly across the park, where it would be easy for some of the more cautious souls to slip away once their fervour cooled. Already their numbers were considerably reduced from the fifty or so who had gone to Lococks Farm. Some had simply vanished, while the graziers and smallholders had mostly followed Mark Smith, when he announced that instead of marching on

Riffield he intended to go tell the vicar he must forswear tithes. They reckoned the vicarage would be easier game than Riffield Castle, thought Davey angrily.

No matter, those who came with him were the most determined, and by choosing to go the Tisbury way he gathered more followers out of the fields along the ridge. He had the luck, too, to fall in with a band of Wadhurst men who had also hit on the notion of shaking their anger at the Dyers. When the two groups met, everyone immediately realized that such an encounter could not happen by chance: the whole Weald must be on the march, and their cheers knocked moisture off the trees. Boys turned cartwheels for joy, strangers thumped each other on the shoulder and without a pause they all swept on to Riffield with doubled numbers.

Mr Aitchison rode directly across the park to Riffield imagining that ruffians lay in wait for him under every bush. Despite such fears he had an uneventful journey, which did not prevent him from arriving at the castle gateway in a great lather of alarm.

As it happened, Sir Maurice Dyer was about to set out with his groom to shoot rabbits, all his friends having cried off from the house-party normally held at this season. The Weald was not the only part of the country to become unsettled, and most landowners had decided that they preferred to reside in their own homes at such a time, to make sure their property was well guarded.

'You seem to have taken a deal too much out of your horse, Aitchison,' said Maurice Dyer disapprovingly. 'Those banks between here and Furnace Green are the devil on an unfit animal.'

'I had no choice, Sir Maurice. If I could have a word with you alone—'

'I haven't many secrets from Crittle,' Dyer answered. He disliked Aitchison, with whom he shared a magistrate's bench, and didn't intend to spoil an afternoon's sport over some petty complaint.

'No, no, a trustworthy man I'm sure, but the news I bring is for your ear alone!'

'Oh, very well. Ride on, Crittle, and I'll join you.'

The groom touched his hat, but even before he was out of earshot Aitchison began on his tale of marauding mobs. 'They must have decided to march on Lococks Farm,' he ended. 'I daresay they will have fired everything about his ears by now! But when they gathered on the green I heard some of the men shout about coming to Riffield. Danesdell House is not far from the pool, and my hearing most acute. I thought it my duty to ride immediately to warn you, no matter what dangers I might encounter on the way.'

'As for dangers in my park—' began Dyer scornfully. 'D'you mean you left Locock without support to face a mob of fifty men or more?'

'What else could I do?'

'You are a magistrate, are you not?'

'Which was why I felt it my duty—'

'Your duty was to read the Act to rioters you believed to be on their way to destroy property scarcely two hundred yards from your doorstep. What else is authority for, except to nip unrest before it spreads?' Maurice Dyer was seldom troubled by doubts, one way or the other.

'But Riffield—I thought you would be relieved to receive warning of attack,' said Aitchison, flabbergasted.

Dyer glanced to where Sir Amyas's mansion blended with the older tower and great hall. 'Good God, man, I can look after Riffield. Enrol as many special constables as I need to guard the place while I send for the dragoons. Quickest way to catch rioters, pinch 'em between defended walls and a squadron of dragoons.'

'Oh no,' said Aitchison earnestly. 'That is what most particularly alarmed me. These Wealden men stick together. I could not get a single one of my servants to swear the oath as constable, and only General Braybon's footman out of his. This is a conspiracy, with every man's hand against those who own property.'

Dyer laughed. 'Whatever may be the case with your

servants, I assure you I shall have no difficulty with mine.'

When this indeed proved to be the case, Aitchison found his feelings almost equally divided between resentment and relief. Within the hour no fewer than forty constables were sworn in from among the grooms, footmen, gardeners and gamekeepers of the Dyer estate, a great many more mustered to help as needed. Feudal loyalty was not so different from the loyalties of a tribe; and in the Weald both remained most vigorously alive.

The men of Furnace Green and Wadhurst turned into a buffeting wind as they left Tisbury Hill behind. Rain was beginning to spit out of the west and soon Davey was moving up and down the line, encouraging everyone to whistle and shout to keep up their spirits; but these were people used to steady labour and once excitement settled back into a rhythm they felt ashamed to shout. None of them slipped off home, though; they had already travelled too far from safety to abandon their purpose now. Here and there eyes gleamed with hope, a few faces lifted to the rain-filled clouds as if they saw their rights waiting there, the rest tramped on and answered Davey's encouragement with grunts.

'Why did you come on this chase?' a man from Wadhurst called Robin Butler asked Davey, as they passed the fingerpost which pointed the last mile to Riffield.

'For our rights, of course. Why did you, if not for them?'

'For my children,' Butler answered, and smiled. 'Even if we lose, I reckon enough might be changed afterwards for them to have a mite of hope.'

'We won't lose!'

'Perhaps, perhaps not. But it makes me feel good to know they'll win, no matter what, because I chose to fight.'

It was dusk by the time they reached Riffield, a disadvantage Davey had not considered. He sensed that if he allowed his following to scatter into shelter then the heart would have gone out of them by the morning; they must go forward without delay. Some of the men had chopped pineknots to act as torches as they trudged through the forest; red light and sparks made Bert Wicks's knife look as if he had cut a dozen throats, increased the number of pitchforks, flails and scythes by throwing their black shadows on faces and upstretched arms. To the men themselves the torchlight also relentlessly exposed how tiny was their host, enclosed by soft fog walls. Six dozen at most, thought Davey, and for the first time felt his belly hang heavily beneath his ribs. He was cold and so famished that the smells of wet leather and hot resin nauseated him, but as they reached Riffield he straightened his shoulders and tossed his hair out of his eyes. High above rain and mud were stars and stars without end; he would think of them. Of the rights poor folk needed so desperately and had lost, he knew not how or why.

Immediately he felt cheered and stepped out briskly again, although, perhaps because dread refused entirely to be banished, his heart unexpectedly became filled with tenderness and desire for Liddy, of whom he had not thought all day.

Riffield village straggled up a slope towards a fine avenue of oaks which led to the castle gates. A few onlookers had gathered by the lower cottages, drawn by the lit torches perhaps; others watched from behind half-closed doors and windows. The whole place had a look of greater prosperity than Furnace Green, the cottage roofs watertight and gardens trim behind painted fences. Here, the proximity of the castle meant there was work for all.

'Come on Riffield and join us! We've come to demand our rights,' Davey shouted as soon as they were close enough to be heard.

No one answered him. The children sucked their thumbs, the old men poked the roadway with their sticks. There seemed to be no young men among the watchers at all.

'We are Wadhurst and Furnace Green together, so what about Riffield to make it three for luck? Then we'll never starve through another winter, and that's a promise.' Davey tried again.

‘The Dyers be fair to those as is fair to them. What need have we to follow madmen into the hangman’s noose?’ an old gaffer answered this time, and spat.

‘Why march around the country, when you can go to the Devil quicker by staying on your godforsaken ridge?’ called another voice, and laughter rippled from face to face.

‘To hell with you for a pack of cowards! Riffield always was a nest of boot-lickers,’ cried Davey furiously. ‘If I should hang, then by God I’ll hang in better company than I’d find here.’

This was the very first time any thought of hanging had crossed his mind, and even now he did not consider it, shouting at once to his followers that they had better hurry, since the castle was the best place for them to demand shelter for the night. A few laughed at this sally, just to show the Riffield people what they thought of them, but laughter wasn’t much to hold against a silence which lasted from one end of the village to the other.

They left the cottages behind at last and the avenue of oaks leaned over them. ‘Look, we’re nearly there and no one around to stop us,’ called Davey. The rain was gusting heavily now, dribbling from his neck all the way into his boots.

At the avenue’s end, chained and locked iron gates were set into a barbican, where the escutcheon of the Scovells was carved into stonework to mark an earlier rule. ‘We’ll soon have those down,’ said Robin Butler. ‘Heave, all of us together now.’

They heaved; once, twice, and then, packed together, brought the gates down with a crash.

Davey shouted, Butler shouted, the crowd about them shouted and began to run up the long driveway, fanning out to trample shrubs and flower-beds.

When Sir Amyas Dyer rebuilt Riffield Castle, his design enclosed three sides of a square which roughly marked the line of the old castle bailey. On one side was his new brick mansion, where salons, tall casements and lightwood panelling were in the Stuart style, on the next the old Scovell great hall and tower, the third containing a straggle of stables, kitchens and servants' quarters, reached through an ancient stone arch. None of this had been planned with an eye to defence, Sir Amyas being of the opinion that the English had learned their lesson during the blood-letting he had lived through, and would not fight among themselves again. For nearly two hundred years his judgement had proved sound, now, this later Riffield Castle was far from ideal for outfacing riots. Gardens and terraces sloped elegantly to vantage points over the surrounding Weald without a defensive position anywhere to be seen.

On the other hand, for tired men holding pitchforks and lacking any idea how to articulate their demands, the sheer size of Riffield was enough to strike elation dead.

Sir Maurice Dyer stood beside a window in the gallery which ran the full length of the first floor. He felt pleasantly excited by the prospect of a lark, and since, once stripped of fashionable languor, his character was more courageous than imaginative, this excitement remained unspoilt by any sense of fear, or of pity for the idiots capering in his courtyard.

He saw a figure detach itself from the mob, run up the steps and beat on his front door.

'What would you wish me to order the footmen to do, Sir Maurice?' His butler appeared at his elbow.

'Nothing.'

'Very good, sir.' The butler retired, his master's unflustered demeanour helping him to maintain a similar poise.

More thunderous knockings on the door, and a distant tinkle of glass. 'In, in, in!' A chant beginning too, but uncertainly. There must be fewer than a hundred men out there.

'Damn,' said Maurice Dyer aloud. He didn't mind a few trampled flower-beds, but a mob marauding through his salons was a different matter altogether. 'Crittle, tell the men to get ready.'

'Aye, Sir Maurice. No sign of the dragoons.'

'From what I hear of events elsewhere, they've never yet

arrived until everything is over. I can't afford to wait any longer, so we'll just have to leave that particular trap unsprung.'

Riffield's grooms and gamekeepers alone numbered some forty-five able-bodied men, all of them familiar with firearms of a kind; fowling-pieces, shotguns and coaching pistols.

While Davey was hammering at the porticoed front door every eye was on him, and at his biddng half a dozen men set their shoulders to the panels. The wood soon began to give way with great satisfying cracks, and not until someone shouted did Davey become aware of the file of men appearing through the stable arch behind his back, most of them holding guns.

'Christ, just look at the whoresons, we'll be bloody shot to pieces!' yelled Robin Butler.

'No more of them than there are of us, come on!' Davey raced down the steps, and fairly clawed his way through the crowd. God curse all Dyers for sneaking up behind a man.

'Stay where you are and no one will be hurt. Come one pace nearer and I shall give the order to fire.' Everyone recognized Maurice Dyer's voice, a man who possessed more power over their lives than the whole king's government put together.

'Stand, you blockhead, or you'll get us all killed,' Jim Huggett grabbed Davey's arm.

'It's too late to stop,' sobbed Davey, struggling. 'Don't you see? If he won't give us our rights, then it's too late to go tamely home again! We have to take them.'

'We can't do aught against guns, can us?'

'We can! We can! If we're quick.' Davey snatched Bert Wicks's knife, saw Robin Butler out of the corner of his eye. 'Rob, you rally your men and I'll do the same for us!'

Dyer's voice cut again across the babble of consternation. He was standing in the stable archway now, his men forming a solid block either side. 'I can see that only a few hotheads are leading you astray. Go home, and leave them to their rantings.'

'We want our rights,' yelled Davey. 'Give us our

rights and then we'll go. Come on, and we'll make him—'

He never saw whose fist clouted him, but one moment he was on his feet shouting defiance and the next sprawled, head spinning, on Riffield's gravel drive. Robin Butler, too, was thrust aside as, without even consulting his neighbour, everyone began melting away from that menacing line of guns and into the darkness.

'If we'd gone on, the bastard would have blown us apart,' Ted Sleech said apologetically, as he and Huggett dragged Davey away with them, his senses still only loosely grasped. 'We couldn't reach him nohow, could we? And he weren't going to give us nothing, nor stand watching while we took what we wanted. I've five children depending on my wage, though after taking an axe to Locock's thresher I'll be finished on the ridge.'

'Did you see how those Wadhurst men ran first? If we hadn't followed we'd have been left to face those curst guns alone.' A different voice this time, hysterical in the mist.

'Don't you dare blame anyone except ourselves for this, we're big enough fools as it is,' answered Davey, weeping.

Everyone tripping and swearing as they ran, comrades in a cause no longer but bitterly railing at each other. Running through wisps of fog caught under the oak branches of the Dyers's avenue, past the shut doors of Riffield's cottages. Back through soaked woods on leaden exhausted legs, to part from Robin Butler with no more than a hand-clasp by Tisbury Hill.

'Too late for snivelling now,' said Ted Sleech, nudging Davey's heaving ribs.

'Too late for everything.' He had stopped weeping long before but his breath kept coming in hard gulps and he slapped his hands on tree trunks as he passed in an agony of humiliation. 'Christ, how could we lose so easily when the cause is just?'

'How could we have been such fools as to finish ourselves to no purpose?' came back the bitter echo, although Davey never knew who spoke.

* * *

All through that long day Furnace Green street was empty of people, while everyone left behind stayed indoors to wait for what might happen next. As soon as the men moved away from the Meeting Oak it was known that they were going to break up Locock's thresher, and the smell of burning soon told its own story of success. A ripple ran through the village then. Doors opened, shapes slipped from one backyard to another, whispering, fearing, delighting over what must have happened.

At Greenview House the doors stayed locked, though none of the servants there ran off to join in the fun, as happened at Danesdell House. Akehurst again spoke for them all when he observed, quite simply, that General Braybon would mislike it if they did. Special constables they would not be, but a well-liked master ruled the rest of their lives.

'A good excuse to keep their skins safe whichever way the matter finishes,' commented the general, although he was not entirely displeased by this compromise. All morning he had prowled restlessly from hall to conservatory and out on the front door step, straining his ears for anything out of the ordinary in this most exceptional of days. No matter what sympathy he might feel for swindled paupers, he longed to ride out and discover what was happening, to defend threshing-machines with his sword and scatter rioters into the woods, yet he dared not leave his house undefended.

'I ought to discover if Locock needs help,' he exclaimed, as he had every few minutes since the smell of smoke first wafted through the mist.

'I forbid you to leave us alone with servants who cannot be trusted,' Mrs Braybon answered automatically; she knew he would not go. 'Hark, what is that?'

The general threw open a window and raw air swept in, bringing with it the sound of hobnails tramping past their wall. 'They're back. Some of them only by the sound of it, not more than twenty there I fancy. I wonder where the rest have gone?'

'For heaven's sake shut that window, unless you want me to die of cold!'

The general slammed it down irritably and went out, for a moment stood irresolutely in the hallway, then, with a guilty look over his shoulder, he slipped back the front-door bolt and went out.

Mist lay thicker on the ridge than anywhere else, the rain which later would wash it away not yet begun. Sounds were muffled by damp air: voices calling in the street and once a shout which carried '. . . tell him it's the end of tithes as well!'

The general unbolted a door in the garden wall which led to the stable yard. This in its turn was closed off by outer double gates, which ought also to have been bolted. Instead, they were ajar. General Braybon immediately forgot caution and marched indignantly over to the figure he could see, an eye set to the opening between the gates.

'What the devil do you mean by opening up my house to ruffians?' he grasped the figure by the shoulder and spun it round. 'Liddy!'

Liddy gasped with shock, and also pain since the general's grip was far from gentle.

'Well, miss? If you would be so good as to explain yourself.' He stood back, tapping his cane on brickwork.

'I wanted . . . I—I had to know—' Her voice trailed away.

'You would do best to tell me without shuffling. Otherwise I shall have no choice but to dismiss you for disobedience, and I do not often retreat from a judgement.'

Liddy lifted her eyes from her employer's waistcoat to his face. Moisture had gathered in droplets on his eyebrows and whiskers, and that tapping cane made her feel he could scarcely wait to beat her. 'Oh, sir, I could not wait any longer in the kitchen without trying to hear what was happening to Davey. I know he'll lead the rest and be the one who's took, unless—'

'Well?'

'Unless the rest get what they want quick, and refuse to

follow him further into trouble. If burning a thresher was enough, then Davey might stay safe. I had to know, you see, once I heard some of them were back.'

'Hm.' The general tapped his cane on his teeth instead of the wall. 'Thank you for that explanation. I myself found it hard to wait in ignorance much longer. Under the circumstances I think we might venture a little further. Now the nature of our troubles is becoming clearer, like Akehurst I find it hard to believe that the storming of Greenview House is imminent.'

'I think they plan to go to the vicarage next, but I didn't hear Davey among them.' Liddy couldn't believe her good fortune in discovering such an ally.

'Well, let us bring succour to Parson Dyer then, but if anything untoward should happen you are to run back as fast as you can.' General Braybon stepped out of the gate as if he was leading a troop of Sikhs.

By that time the street had again filled with figures running through the murk. Only the bolder spirits had gone to Locock's but now Mark Smith had led some of those back in triumph, more left their cottages to join in the excitement.

When Liddy and her employer arrived at the vicarage gate they saw a considerable crowd gathered and shouting about tithes, not by the house but outside the shed where Parson Dyer conducted his experiments. Davey isn't there, thought Liddy feverishly. Could he have been hurt during the attack on Locock's? On such a day as this he would never willingly stay away from wherever trouble was; even as she watched, the crowd surged forward to jostle the vicar in the entry to his shed.

'I perceive that it must be our duty to assist the good vicar to be heard above the hubbub and discover what kind of a showing he makes then,' announced the general with a chuckle, and marched through the crowd, cane sloped over his shoulder, until he reached the circle of lamplight thrown through the open shed door. 'Well, Reverend. These people have come to ask a favour from you, I believe.'

'They have come to threaten and will leave to face the consequences,' answered Dyer, pale with anger.

'Ah, I am glad that your time in the army left you a better soldier than a parson. God, indeed, is not a battery of guns kept in reserve to hold a breach.' The general turned. 'What is your purpose here, sirs?'

Mark Smith rubbed his face; as an ex-sergeant he found it infinitely harder to face General Braybon than a squitty captain like the reverend. 'It's like this, sir. Us smallholders can't pay tithe as well as a living wage to our labourers. We reckoned the church could get by easier without it than poor men.'

The general turned back to Dyer. 'I am but holding the ring for these discussions. Do you have a point you wish to make in response to Mr Smith?'

'Certainly not, except to say that most faces here are known to me and I intend in due course to furnish the dragoons with the direction of each man I recognize.'

'I trust you may think better of such a threat, since they would then have nothing to lose should they decide to treat you more rudely than has hitherto been the case.' A muttering spread as this patent truth dawned on everyone gathered there. 'Well, if I can no longer assist by enabling some accommodation to take place, I shall withdraw,' the general added blandly.

'You cannot simply go and leave me to a mob! Good God, Braybon, my family are within the vicarage and I keep only female servants,' said Dyer furiously.

'I do not think these men have any quarrel with your wife or children, and certainly not with your female servants, but I am happy to succour your family at Greenview House if they wish.'

'My wife would not leave me!'

'Excellent. Then the choice remains with you, does it not?'

'By God, sir, you are inciting a mob to attack my house, did you know that?'

'I am, of course, a sinner, but not I fancy in the way you

suggest. Mr Smith would not dream of alarming women and children, would you, sir? And where we are standing, we must all conduct ourselves with particular prudence, there being gunpowder stored in this shed.' He paused to let this sink in before turning back to Mark Smith. 'A padre of course does not sin, so you may trust Mr Dyer's word when he agrees no longer to collect tithe.'

'Do you swear?' Smith demanded eagerly. Not until he faced the vicar had he realized, as Davey was to realize when he reached Riffield, that unless victory was tamely yielded then the only alternative to defeat was pillage, like an army run amok. This he had seen in the Peninsular War, but his experiences there made such scenes harder, instead of easier, to visualise in Sussex. Already, Mark remembered that he was late for the evening milking. But, as General Braybon's words reminded him, perhaps deliberately, gunpowder was stored in the shed. Not much of it, but accidents happened easily to explosives.

'I shall never swear,' snapped Dyer, and folded his arms.

Ex-Sergeant Smith of the 35th Foot pulled out his pipe. 'Then if you'll allow me, sir, I'll just come in out of the mist to light up. Since it looks as if we're going to have a long discussion, like.' Without seeking any further permission, Smith pushed past into the shed; when the vicar tried to haul him back someone shoved him so hard that both he and the general staggered.

'Don't you dare strike a flint in there!' shouted Dyer. 'Good God, man, you've been a soldier and know how dangerous it would be. There's black powder loose on the bench, ready for an experiment.'

'Nay, I'll use your lamp instead. I'm a more reasonable man with a pipe in my mouth; once it's drawing I might listen to an offer of only half of your tithes left uncollected.'

Dyer cast an anguished glance to where a lamp flickered behind a glass screen for safety, and then along the shelves of notebooks either side. Only two months ago he had been elected a fellow of the Royal Society. If he lost his notes he would look uncommonly foolish when his experiments came up for discussion.

Smith twisted a piece of paper into a spill, before lifting the lamp from behind its safety screen and flicking open the mantle to uncover a flame.

'For God's sake—' Dyer cried again, as the spill caught fire.

Mark did not need telling how careful he had to be, cupping flame between his palms as he moved it closer to marbled notebook covers. 'You said something, Reverend?'

The smell of singeing leather drifted into the mist as the back of a notebook began to char, its pages to blacken and curl. 'God damn you,' said Dyer in a shaking voice. 'Half of the tithes then.'

'You swear it?'

'I have said so, have I not?'

Disregarding the heat, Smith pinched out flame and deftly caught a charred flake of paper when it would have fallen on a bench gritty with black powder. He smiled. 'Then if General Braybon will witness that we parted in friendship after discussing our troubles together, I'll smoke my pipe elsewhere.'

General Braybon and the vicar were left standing side by side when Smith left, herding the crowd of villagers in front of him. 'I'll never forgive you for this, never,' said Dyer.

'I thought my presence helped preserve everyone from harm. You, your family, and the hard-working but wretched people of Furnace Green alike. If you will be so good as to replace the glass in front of your lamp, then we can be sure of it, I fancy.'

'The church has been harmed! Nay, humbled by a mob of louts!' All the same, Dyer made haste to replace the glass.

'The church stands where it did, and will be the more honoured for a wise concession to its poor.' The general left with a flourish, sweeping up Liddy on his way. 'Well, girl? Did you discover what you wished?'

‘Oh, sir, he has gone off to Riffield,’ cried Liddy, wringing her hands.

‘On his own? For what purpose?’

‘About thirty went with him, or so they say. As for the purpose, there will never be an end to Davey’s purposes. Today he means to take his rights from off the castle wall.’

The general gave a great hoot of laughter, thereby showing himself no less human than the other inhabitants of Furnace Green, who were laughing and shoving each other in delight all the way down the street, made boisterous by the thought of how cleverly their half-victory had been won. ‘Then he’ll soon be home with his tail between his legs. Run back to the kitchen now, there’s a good girl, and don’t let me find you outside again.’

Liddy was glad to go, at a loss over what further she could do now Davey was gone off to Riffield. Surely he would never get into a great castle set on its hill, to find his rights or anything else. And if he did, then like as not he’d be marked out as the leader of a riot, for the dragoons to seize as soon afterwards as they could. Oh Davey, Davey, how could you be so wilfully, hopelessly brave? So foolish, if truth was to be told.

Events in Furnace Green itself had not yet run their course, however. Once Mark Smith had left to walk back to his farm at Pigpasture, most of the other smallholders and craftsmen left too, well satisfied with a result which suited them so well and already totting up in their minds how much they would save in tithe during the coming year. Once this sober element was removed the atmosphere in the street changed into a more reckless mood, and Charlie Twort soon had the idea of running to Wyses and harnessing old Miss Brown’s pony to her trap. When she screeched and threw a bucket of slops at him from her bedroom window it only made the joke seem better. Once Charlie had the trap out in the street he whipped the staid old pony into a canter, scattering everyone into the fog. ‘We’ll get Hooke now! Whoa, you beauty!’ he yelled.

Oaths changed to a roar of approval and half a dozen younger men began thumping on the weatherboard walls of Hooke's cottage.

'Come out! Come out!' A bellowing like the sound of penned bulls brought more people running, although by then not many remained aloof from the tumult. In the tap-room of the Dyer Arms, Walter Keyes began nervously to offer free beer in an attempt to divert ill will away from his affairs, and the effects of his generosity soon spilled into the street. Men who had only ever drunk small quantities of weak ale became swiftly bemused by Keyes's Best Ordinary, jostling more roughly and giggling in front of their indignant wives.

The whole front wall of Hooke's cottage was by now lifting to repeated blows, tufts of thatch slithering down on the heads of the crowd below. Charlie Twort jumped down from Widow Brown's trap to join them, and began to kick like a madman at Hooke's barricaded door. 'Ho!' he shouted. 'Ho, ho!'

At this, the crowd yelled and waved their fists more fiercely than ever; to them, like Charlie, noise had become more important than words.

'What's that?' cried Jack Paley, a labourer at the vicar's Church Farm. Out of the corner of his eye he had caught sight of movement at the school entrance, at the far side of Hooke's cottage. 'By God, 'tis him trying to sneak away! Now we'll have some sport!'

His cry ended in a grunt as Tom Rabbit's wife shot out a fist which caught him instead of Hooke, and by the time his wits returned Sarah Rabbit had grasped Hooke to her bosom as if she intended to gobble him up bones and all for supper.

'My Tom will never work again!' she screeched. 'You —you rascal, you, I'll teach you to make him beg at your window!'

And she hurled Hooke into the swarm of faces behind her, where he was thrust from one rough grasp to another, twirling in mockery from hand to hand without ever being allowed to fall; round and round, his face turning green then yellow. Tiring of that at last, Jack Paley tied him by the wrists to the tail of Miss Brown's trap. 'Whip him away, Charlie!'

But when Charlie Twort tried to climb back on the whipster's bench, he found himself tumbled peremptorily over the further side to sprawl in the mud beyond. Spitting like a cat, Sarah Rabbit hauled herself up in his place. ''Tis my place to run him out.'

The men gaped at her, then someone clouted Miss Brown's pony on the rump with a piece of wood and it bolted, Sarah shrieking and hauling at the reins, the trap lurching and bounding into the air while Samuel Hooke ran for his life at a rope's end.

Fortunately for Hooke, neither the terrified pony nor its driver was capable of negotiating the right-angle turn at the end of the street. The pony swerved but the trap hit the churchyard wall with a crash, polished wood flew in every direction, wheels buckled and the pony careered out of sight, a few fragments of wood jouncing at its heels. Sarah Rabbit was left sitting dazed on the ground while Hooke, realizing with commendable speed that he was attached to nothing more than a two-foot plank, took to his heels and vanished into the mist.

'I haven't laughed so much for years.' Jack Paley wiped his eyes.

'I were well out of that and no mistake,' agreed Charlie Twort. 'Where's that skinflint Keyes pouring this free beer, then? I haven't tasted so much as a drop of it yet.'

And, quite quickly, the crowd drifted away from the street and down to the Dyer Arms. As if by alchemist's magic, laughter had lanced the poison out of fury; and satisfaction too, because Hooke was run off at last.

Only his battered cottage was left to tell of what had happened, and Sarah Rabbit coming groggily to her feet by the churchyard wall. At first a kind of laughter swelled in her throat, too: how splendid it had been to watch Hooke bobbing at a rope's end and then scuttle out of sight, with only a plank to show out of all his gains in Furnace Green.

Then laughter rose into her mouth and she vomited.

What truck had she with laughter?

One of Farmer Locock's sons had brought Tom home earlier in the evening; his face sweating pain and his arm bundled in linen to the elbow.

'Here, take your man,' the boy had said insolently, dropping Tom off his crupper. 'I'd have left him to bleed on the midden but my father said no, bandage him and lift him home. But take it from me, he needn't ask for work around our place again.'

'What happened to him?' cried Sarah.

'Our thresher took revenge before it burned,' the boy answered, and laughed as he reined aside.

Tom with a maimed right arm! Tom, whose traps and snares kept her and the children eating when there wasn't any work! 'How will we manage?' she said aloud, as she supported Tom's dragging weight into their hut, and knew they couldn't manage. In winter, the old sometimes filled their bellies with straw and chaff hoping by such means to keep out of the poor-barn, but children died from such rubbishing fare.

Tom mumbled something, but was scarcely conscious, moaning and tossing as his arm swelled, once she had him bedded down. Mrs Locock had spread goose-grease under the linen bandage but when Sarah looked at Tom's torn and dirty flesh, she knew he would be lucky if he lived.

Luckier still if he died quickly without depleting their few winter stores, since once these were eaten they would be forced on the parish, where Hooke counted every crust. It was this despairing certainty which had driven Sarah to join the throng in the street as it grew noisier. Tomorrow she, not Tom, must beg at Hooke's window for relief, knowing before she began that this time the most cringing humility would gain her nothing. The law said that outdoor relief was only paid to bring an insufficient wage up to subsistence. Those incapable of earning any wage at all received nothing, unless they went as the living dead into the parish poor-barn: their meagre possessions lost, their homes tumbled down within weeks, since only endless patching kept such hovels upright.

At least it had been she who drove Hooke out. Sarah didn't expect his disappearance to change anything; nothing ever changed for the destitute, but she would cherish the memory of Hooke at a rope-end during the years ahead. Now, the first thing she must do was knock Tom's useless dog on the head while his master still muttered in a fever; the creature never caught enough to feed itself. One less mouth might add as much as another month to the time before they were forced into the barn.

Still dizzy after her crash and with her face lifted to the first spatters of rain, so not even she could have said whether or not she wept, Sarah Rabbit walked away zigzag up the street.

Davey Portnell returned to Furnace Green in the small hours of the night, by which time the village was sleeping off the effects of strong beer and excitement. He was soaked and utterly exhausted, his hands so numb he clattered the latch on their cottage door, when he had hoped to creep in without waking his mother.

He need not have worried; she was sitting fully dressed at the kitchen table, although dozing until he came.

'Davey,' she cried, blinking. 'They said you'd gone to Riffield Castle, but that can't have been right, can it?'

He slumped down at the table. 'It was right.'

'But you thought better of it and came back.' She was begging for reassurance.

'Yes, I came back.' He knew he ought never to have come back; the magistrates would soon learn the names of riot-leaders, wherever these had appeared. Locock, for instance, knew who had burned his thresher, even if no one at Riffield Castle was likely to have recognized an unknown from Furnace Green.

Yet, instinctively, Davey discounted the witness of Farmer Locock. He was both too hard a man and too good a neighbour to relish fighting his battles in front of alien judges; he would keep his mouth shut, and exact his own punishment by never again employing anyone who had come riotously to his farm.

So, tonight, Davey believed he could sleep safely in his own bed, and decide tomorrow what next to do. He lifted his head. 'We failed.'

'Bless my soul, failed at what? All I know is you'll catch your death gallivanting around the countryside in soaked clothes with naught in your belly.' His mother ladled broth as she spoke.

Davey gave a hiccuping laugh. 'I thought we'd take a meal out of the castle kitchens as part of our bargain.'

Her jaw dropped. 'You never went a-threatening Sir Maurice, like Mark Smith went after the vicar here?'

He nodded, ravenously gulping broth.

'Mind your manners, Davey, do,' she scolded, but absently. 'Whatever made you do such a madcap thing? No one saw you, did they, away in Riffield?'

'Not me more than the rest,' he lied.

'Word gets around terrible fast in the Weald. Oh, Davey, you'll have to go right away for a while, and then what will I do?'

'There's sure to be plenty of building work in London. No one will know me there and I'll send you money once I'm settled. You'll be all right, I promise.'

She shrugged. If he believed that, then better to leave it so. 'There's been doings here as well, and Sam Hooke was run off.'

'Good,' said Davey, momentarily cheering up.

'Aye, but the law will ride in as soon as word reaches outside, and Hooke escaped, remember. Oh, dearie me, how could everyone be struck moon-mad all in a heap?'

'They won't come looking for me over doings at Furnace Green, because I wasn't here. Unless Locock squeals, that is, and I don't think he will. He's a ridge-man, after all. I'll go tomorrow night. It'll be safer after dark and I must see Liddy first. I'm safe till then, I reckon.' He stood, a huge yawn cracking his jaw. 'God, I'm tired.'

'You stay out of sight, then, and I'll say you haven't come back. Now just strip off every stitch and I'll wash your clothes while you sleep.'

He touched her arm. 'Thank you for waiting up for me.'

'As if I wouldn't!' She dabbed at her eyes. After tonight she would have no one left to wait up for.

Davey nearly fell on the stair, he was so tired. Unwillingly, he had a vision of his mother crawling up these same steep treads with more difficulty every year; old, cold and alone.

Well, what else could I have done? he thought, enraged. If no one ever fought, we'd all be slaves for ever.

The upstairs landing was scarcely bigger than a cupboard, two tiny rooms leading off it. Exhausted though he was, Davey stood for a moment listening to the old boards creak. Last time, last time, they said. When he pushed open his bedroom door, the damp familiar smell made his head spin with relief. He fumbled open the window and leaned on the sill: perhaps the dawn air would make him feel less defeated. Below him lay the street, and beyond the cottage roofs he could glimpse ploughed fields and distant wooded hills all softly silver under a paling sky.

This is my home, he thought, which tomorrow I shall have left. Maybe it won't be safe to return for years, and then it will never be the same.

It did not occur to him that he would never come back.

He reached up to touch the evil little carving he had tucked out of sight behind a rafter. Almost jokingly, he had thought of its ugliness as the wrongs of Furnace Green, and intended ceremonially to throw it away when his part in righting them was done. Now, he'd take it with him when he went.

Meanwhile he left it hidden, not fancying that baleful stare on him while he slept; mustn't forget it, mustn't . . . he fell half-fainting on his bed. As his filthy boots on the coverlet faded out of view, he only just had time to think: Ma will be after me with her broomstick for dirtying everything up. Then he was wonderfully, mercifully asleep.

* * *

When the dragoons arrived at Riffield some hours after the rioters dispersed, Mr Aitchison, smarting from the inglorious part he had played in the previous day's events, immediately offered to ride with them to Furnace Green.

'That is your business, as magistrate of a damned disorderly place,' answered Sir Maurice coldly.

'I recognized three of those leading the mob, and if they have been foolish enough to return there, I can tell the soldiers where to find them,' explained Aitchison. 'The sooner we have the ringleaders punished, the sooner the countryside will settle down. A quick lesson is sharper than a slow one, my father used to say.'

'You will also feel safer riding back escorted by dragoons,' Sir Maurice replied derisively. All he wanted was to be rid of an uncongenial guest. Tipstaff's work was no employment for a gentleman but it had to be done; if Aitchison would take himself off and do it, then he was doubly in luck.

So it was that, soon after Davey fell into exhausted sleep, some twenty dragoons drew rein beside the pool. There, while tired horses drank and men scooped water over their faces, Samuel Hooke appeared out of the mist and whispered another name; then the file divided, half the men riding to where a lane branched off from the highway to the church, the rest moving past Greenview House to block the near end of the village.

Liddy was on her knees kindling the drawing-room fire when she heard harness jingle past the garden wall, a couple of hours before the gentry were awake. She raced to the passage window but by then all she could see were scarlet backs and rain-dark horseflesh. Dear have mercy, soldiers in Furnace Green! Gathering her skirts Liddy hurtled down the back staircase, to find Akehurst standing by the kitchen door. 'Who have they come for?'

He gripped her arm. 'Steady.'

'I won't . . . Has anyone been taken yet?'

'Nay, they've only just come. But they know who they're looking for all right. That pig's bladder Aitchison was riding at their head, as pleased with himself as you could reckon.'

'Let me go!'

'Nay,' he said again, and did not wince when she struck out at him. Grey whiskers, shrivelled face and polished gaiters might have been designed not to show emotion. He just spread his feet wider as he might to hold an unbroken colt, and took no further notice of her at all.

So all Liddy heard was shouts, one quite loud and the others distant. Running footsteps, once a bellowed order, then the orderly beat of hoofs again.

'They will have taken Davey,' she cried.

'He hadn't come back, not that I heard,' replied Akehurst, thereby revealing that he had visited the Dyer Arms the previous night.

Billy Rabbit's face appeared at the scullery window. 'The soldiers have taken Ted Sleech, Davey Portnell and Wicks the butcher. They caught Charlie Twort, too, sleeping off last night's ale in Wicks's kitchen. They say they'll lock them all up in the cells beneath the Bear!'

'They have?' said Akehurst slowly, and rubbed his face.

'Aye, and once they've baited their horses they're taking them off to Lewes gaol.'

'No one else?'

'Aren't four enough for you, mister?' said Billy cheekily.

Two strides took Akehurst to the scullery window and Billy howled as a cuff on the ear jarred his cheek against the jamb. By then Liddy was away, pulling the back-door bolts, running across the stable yard and down the slope which led to the Dyer Arms, the Bear as it remained to Billy and most others.

Trapped, she thought feverishly, and meant herself not Davey. Ever since she heard he had gone to Riffield her mind had been made up: she would tell Davey to go his own way and leave her in peace to travel hers. Anyone foolish enough to do what he had done deserved to stew in his own concerns. She had been almost relieved to have decision forced on her. Liddy knew she would always feel for Davey, never walk down Edenham lane without remembering their first kiss. Remember above all how splendid a first love was, how warm were lips and soft the strongest fingers.

Because that was what she had determined Davey would become: a first love. Her life was not for him to take, and then leave in a mean cottage with a skirtful of children, while he ran off preaching hopeless causes.

But now, before she had been able to tell him, he had got himself arrested. The injustice of it burned at her. As she ran headlong to the Dyer Arms Liddy simply felt a furious exasperation that he had been daft enough to return where the dragoons could take him easily. Even so, she could not let him be taken away without so much as a smile to remember, when men died so easily in gaol. There, a will to live might make all the difference, and the least Liddy could do was be whatever memory Davey needed in the hard time ahead. Once he was free again, she would explain how she had decided to travel a different way from him.

The taproom of the Dyer Arms was full, the bright colours of the soldiers' uniforms dazzling at close quarters, and Liddy hesitated in the doorway, too preoccupied with her own concerns to feel afraid, but puzzled over how she might manage to see Davey. If she entered boldly there was bound to be someone who would say she couldn't; on the other hand, if she waited tamely in the yard the dragoons might easily guard Davey so closely that when they took him away he wouldn't so much as lay eyes on her.

The cells built long ago by the Dyers beneath the inn could only be reached by stairs from behind the taproom bar; yet, so greatly had custom changed in the past fifty years, it was now considered shocking for women to enter a tavern tap. Liddy bit her lip. Cells under the taproom would be dank, dark and cramped for four men thrust in anyhow. As she hesitated in the doorway, one of the dragoons looked up and smacked his lips. 'Look who we have here.'

'You mind your tongue,' snapped Liddy; characteristically, indecision evaporated the moment her plans hit a snag. 'I want to see one of your prisoners, please.'

'He'd like to see you, too, I'm sure. But prisoners is prisoners, see? Locked away from pretty wenches until they're put in front of a beak. You'd do better to drink ale with us, wouldn't she, lads?' His tone was disrespectful but not unkind.

Why, dragoons weren't bad at all, thought Liddy, accepting a mug of small ale from a disapproving Walter Keyes. 'I can't stay above a few moments. I left the fires unlit in the house where I work and I've been in enough trouble already for running off when told to stay indoors. It's Davey, you see. I wanted to stop him getting into trouble, but I couldn't. Now he's arrested and will be taken off to Lewes—please let me see him before he goes! You can watch all the time if you want.'

'Well, I dunno.' The dragoon scratched his head. 'What do you think, George?'

'Dunno neither,' answered his friend laconically, and drank deeply through his whiskers.

'She could ask the sarge,' suggested a voice.

'Ask old fart-face? Do better wi' the lieutenant than wi' him, she would.' They spoke in a sharp-edged drawl which made them difficult to understand, especially once they began to argue among themselves.

'What's your name?' asked the first dragoon, turning back to her at length.

'Liddy.'

'Liddy? I never heard that before.'

'Not everyone has common names,' she answered pertly, feeling keyed up and excited, conscious she was attempting something very daring.

The dragoon laughed. 'I like it anyways. I'm called Jogger 'cos everyone says I ride like a sack. See here, I can take you to the lieutenant if you like. The sarge now, he's in the stable somewheres but even if we did ask him . . . Well, we don't think you'd like him much. Proper bastard, if you understand me.'

'You—you couldn't just take me down to the cells yourself, could you? I'd be ever so quick.'

'No. Pretty you may be, Liddy, but you aren't worth a flogging.'

Liddy accepted this as reasonable. 'All right. I've come so far, I might as well chance this lieutenant as well.'

All the same, her heart beat fast with apprehension when Jogger took her through to the parlour. This was the old public tap and the larger of the inn's two rooms, the stained panelling which had seen smugglers' carousings, the death of Giles Dyer and Bart and Rose's blasphemous marriage cursorily painted over.

A very young officer lounged with his boots on the hearth, before a hastily kindled fire.

'A woman to see you, sir,' said Jogger and withdrew, winking encouragingly as he went.

Liddy curtsied, determined not to let a boy little older than herself see how afraid she felt. 'I came to ask a favour, sir.'

He looked her over approvingly. 'Come and sit beside me then. I like granting favours to pretty maids.'

'No . . . Please sir, I want to see one of your prisoners, David Portnell.'

He pulled at soft young whiskers. 'It's against regulations once a man's been taken.'

'But, surely—would it matter if one of your men stood by?'

'It's still against regulations.'

Liddy took a deep breath. Well, she had tried. 'Please sir, what will they do to Davey?'

'That's not my business.' But he was frowning at his boots now, instead of staring at her bosom, so she could tell he felt uncomfortable about rousting unarmed men out of their homes. 'I take prisoners to Lewes and that's the end of it so far as I'm concerned. He'll be tried according to whatever he has done.'

'Would I be able to see him if I walked to Lewes, then?'

'I shouldn't think so. The gaols everywhere are overflowing at the moment.'

'Then this is my last chance! It's naught to you but—but when he's crowded into one of those stinking places it could be all the world to him!' Liddy did not know why she was so certain this was so, except that anyone so filled with sentiment as Davey was bound to use memory as a lifeline.

'I'm sorry, I'd like to help you but I can't.' He called to Jogger, who was waiting outside the door. 'Where the devil is my breakfast? Morrison—'

'Yessir?'

'Have you offered this woman any refreshment?'

'Mug of ale, sir.'

'Well, since she is somewhat distressed I suggest you take her down and draw off a jug at my expense for her to carry home. The 5th aren't niggardly over hospitality like some regiments I could name. Don't dawdle too long about it though.'

'Aye, sir,' said Jogger, grinning. He shut the door carefully behind Liddy. 'Now who's a lucky wench?'

'He meant it like that?' cried Liddy joyfully. 'He really meant you to take me down and not draw from the tap?'

'You heard what he said. Regulations is regulations but the 5th Dragoons are mighty proud of their good fellowship, and even Sergeant Bloody Milton can't say as we're doing aught but keep up with our good name.' He went behind the tap and heaved up a trapdoor cut in the floor while the other soldiers shouted jokes that Liddy couldn't grasp.

'Mind you don't trip over your skirts,' said Jogger, watching unashamedly from below.

There was a close cold reek to the cellar, made up of sour beer, wet walls and confined humanity. A flickering dip set on a ledge was the only lighting and most of the space taken up by kegs of beer. Only a tiny square of floor was left, where she and Jogger Morrison could stand to peer behind the ladder, his hand resting altogether too familiarly on her buttock. But there was Davey; him and Ted Sleech, Charlie Twort and Bert Wicks. Four pallid faces pressed against bars set in the wall, two crammed into each minute cell.

Liddy gulped; pity, horror and a dreadful kind of anger all stirred up together so she couldn't speak.

'Hurry up,' said Jogger brusquely, and turned his back.

'They only let me come for a moment.' Her voice sounded unnaturally loud, the whole situation so monstrous that words snapped like wolves between them.

Davey tried to say her name but no sound came, his body pressed hard enough against the bars to make him gasp for air. Bert Wicks, with whom he shared a niche five feet high by three feet either way, was very solidly built.

And, quite suddenly, the words she needed came. 'Davey, I had to see you. The lieutenant says they're taking you to Lewes and once you're there I'd never be allowed to see you. Until after the trial, anyway. But you just remember I'm thinking of you all the time. Don't give up. Never give up and you'll come through. You haven't done aught they'd hang you for, have you?' She added in sudden panic.

He shook his head. He did not know, but wanted very much to please her.

She touched his thick brown hair where it fell like a tassel through the bars. 'It'll be all right, you see if it isn't. When all the gaols of Sussex are full to bursting, they can't keep anyone locked up for long.'

'Oh, Liddy!' he whispered, and some of the tension ebbed out of him. 'No, of course they can't.'

'You'll be back in six months at most. Do you remember when old Jem Downes was taken up for poaching and in the end they couldn't prove a thing against him? Him with deer smoking over half a dozen fires in the forest, as we well knew. You only marched to Riffield and back, a judge might even let you off.' She, too, instinctively assumed that the Lococks wouldn't witness against a neighbour.

'Perhaps,' he said shamefacedly, any comfort infinitely precious now.

'Do you think so?' interrupted Charlie Twort. The other three until now had pretended not to listen, although their faces were so close together that Liddy could hear their lungs pumping for breath. 'Christ, Liddy, do you really think so?'

'So long as you make sure to tell them that all you did was take a day away from work! And you're your own man, after all,' she answered, smiling. Charlie's family would have to abandon his smallholding if he wasn't there to do the heaviest labour.

'I'm afraid of death,' muttered Wicks. ''Tis the dark when all's said and done.'

'It's glory to the Saviour,' answered Ted Sleech stoutly. He walked every Sunday to an evangelist tabernacle near Ockham.

'Don't start thinking of death, for mercy's sake,' cried Liddy. 'A few months' gaol is what you've got to fear, so keep up your spirits and think instead of the day you'll come back to Furnace Green. Why, you'll be treated to Keyes's Best Ordinary right overhead from here, and no small alc to follow!'

'I'll think of you, Liddy,' said Davey simply. 'I've no regrets over what I did, except we failed. Next time must be different now we've learned more how to go about it. You'll wait for me, won't you?'

Trooper Morrison turned, suddenly impatient. 'A few words you said, not jabber-jabber half the day! Bite your tongues, will you, and finish. I've my breakfast to eat.' He thrust a jug of ale into Liddy's hands. 'Here. Take this and go.'

Liddy tilted the jug against each of four months in turn, and because they could not reach between the bars a great deal ran down their jerkins.

Davey drank last, and as he did so she kissed his fingers curled in hers.

'I'll remember that,' he said, and his eyes were on her lips, not ale.

Her last glimpse of him was those same eyes glinting in the light of a guttering wick as Jogger shoved her up the ladder with a kind of regretful haste. I never promised Davey I'd wait, thought Liddy. She would have promised if she'd had to, and broken her promise once he was free, but was glad it hadn't been necessary all the same. Given any luck at all, he ought to survive a few months in gaol without too much harm, now he was sustained by hope and love as well as by his own more furious passions.

As Liddy emerged into the taproom again she felt quite dazed by loud voices, laughter and the scrape of boots. Keyes mumbled something disagreeable about light-skirted trollops as she went past, then a sour-faced sergeant collided with her in the doorway and shoved her off the step.

She had done what she could for Davey. All that remained was to sneak back into Greenview House without the Braybons seeing her.

Liddy was clearing breakfast dishes when four blue-faced prisoners were hauled up from the cells some two hours later, nor did a single soul in Furnace Green run to stare when they were driven ignominiously away in Berk Wicks's own butcher's cart.

The East Sussex special winter assizes opened in Lewes on the 20th December 1830, where charges of machine-breaking, incendiarism, riot and conspiracy were brought against fifty-two men and women from all parts of the county. Meanwhile, the disturbances which were to become known by the name of Captain Swing—a fictitious personality so far as Sussex was concerned, since, where the name appeared at all, it was used only to disguise the identity of local leaders—had reached most parts of the country, eventually bringing some two thousand persons into the dock in places as far apart as Whitstable, Penzance and Carlisle.

The judges went swiftly about their task, although evidence of good character and circumstances was admitted. John Locock, farmer, and General Braybon, late of the Honourable East India Company's Army, swore between them that those arraigned from the parish of Furnace Green were hitherto known as diligent men of good character, whom they had not seen take part in any violence.

This testimony, which contradicted that offered by Henry Aitchison, magistrate, caused some of the charges against them to be dropped, once acrimonious wrangling among the witnesses threatened to confuse the court. Generally speaking, however, men of property everywhere had been given such a thorough-going fright that inconsistent evidence was considered less important than teaching disaffected labourers an exemplary lesson.

Edward Sleech, a cowman resident in Furnace Green, was sentenced to two years imprisonment for riot.

Charles Twort, a freeholder of Furnace Green, was sentenced to six months imprisonment for uttering threats with menaces.

David Portnell, apprentice mason of Furnace Green, was sentenced to transportation for a period of fourteen years to the colony of New South Wales, Australia, for instigating a riot which led to the destruction of property, to wit: iron gates, flower-beds, grass, windows and door panels at Riffield Castle.

Albert Wicks, a butcher of Furnace Green, was sentenced to hard labour for seven years for carrying a weapon, namely a knife, with the intention to endanger life.

When Farmer Locock brought back news of the sentences, at first there was an outcry. Until then, few had believed that punishment for an affair which had fizzled out so easily would be harsh, especially after Locock and General Braybon put their heads together and decided what to swear on behalf of the accused. Anxious women with children at their skirts gathered around Locock when he dismounted in the street, and read the sentences from a paper.

'Hard labour!' shouted Bert Wicks's wife, aghast. 'Why, Bert's been his own master since he was a lad! He'll never live through seven years of breaking stones!'

'Fourteen years in the wilderness for my Davey, just because he marched to Riffield!' Mrs Portnell's hands were wringing in her apron. 'Master, did the judge understand that Davey were short of twenty years old, and only went marching in the rain?'

'He understood,' answered Locock. He felt no particular pity for idiots who had gone out looking for trouble, and had only forsworn himself because he knew the disaster their dependants faced.

Annie Sleech simply wept and asked no questions. Two years was not so long a time that her Ted might not come home again, but how could she manage until then? She with five children surviving under nine years old and another in her belly! Ted had been a good husband, seldom out of a hiring and kindly with the children; after being kept two years in a pit he might return like a ravening beast.

Only Charlie Twort's wife stayed silent, her mind calculating busily. If she sold their old horse and she and her eldest son, aged eight, harnessed themselves to the plough this winter, while Meg pulled roots in Mark Smith's fields at twopence the sack, they might just manage until spring brought Charlie home again. Meg was six, and ought to be able to gather forty sacks a week if baby Frank was sent to help her. Six months—five perhaps because Charlie wouldn't misbehave—it could have been worse. Much worse. Mercy, but she'd give him the edge of her tongue when he returned, for being such a numbskull.

Because General Braybon had stayed a night on his way back from Lewes, Liddy did not hear the sentences until Akehurst came home from driving the mistress out on her calls.

'Transportation?' she said blankly. '*Fourteen years?*'

'Aye, and the prisoners from Lewes are already on their way to Portsmouth, so John Locock says. There's fever in the gaol and they're better away in God's good air.'

'Fourteen years in Australia!' she said, not listening. 'Dear have mercy, that's a lifetime. Tell me, did Farmer Locock say how Davey seemed?'

Akehurst smiled sourly. 'Angry enough to tear out the judge's throat, so Locock said. Which helped get him all those years, I suppose. Sleech is naught but a simpleton and Charlie used to doing what his good wife says, they wouldn't seem worth too much. But Bert had a knife and Davey his rage to brandish, so they were done down proper.'

'I'm glad he did brandish it,' cried Liddy. 'I'm glad, d'you hear? Davey would sooner take his rage with him in one piece than grovel in the hope of mercy.'

She looked out of the kitchen window to where a January wind drove off the shoulder of the ridge, shaking branches as it went. Men fresh out of Lewes gaol would have a hard march to Portsmouth and a rough old journey to the far side of the world, but Davey would survive. She knew it. With this certainty came a kind of relief; she had done as much as she could for Davey, and now would be spared that task of explaining how she wanted to go her own way after all, no matter what he said.

But, in spite of this half-guilty sense of relief, Liddy couldn't help trying to picture the cruel buffetings which must be testing Davey's endurance every day of that journey. If she woke to hear wind shrilling around Greenview House eaves, she would wonder how seaworthy a prison ship might be; when snow piled deep in February and the kitchen seemed even snugger than usual, somehow she couldn't chatter as easily as before for thinking how terrifying it must be, locked into a dank, dark hold while the sea beat all around, trying to find some weakness in the timbers.

As the cuckoos began to shout in spring, Liddy took another important step towards bettering herself. Ellen, who had replaced philandering Annie as upstairs-maid, left unexpectedly to be married and Mrs Braybon gave her place to Liddy rather than have another upheaval among the staff. An upstairs-maid after less than a year of service! It was unheard-of to take such rapid steps through tortuous household rankings.

But Davey . . . Davey. One day, General Braybon had shown Liddy Australia on his globe, half the world away from Sussex and upside down as well.

'Use your brain, girl,' he had answered irritably when she sought more information on this point. 'If there was the least difficulty about the world being round, do you not think we ourselves would stand on our heads each night? But I never heard you or Cook rumbling around my ceilings, and your young man will do so only on board ship. Which, God knows, may be achieved as well in the English Channel as anywhere.'

It must have been after this that Liddy finally managed to convince herself that, truly, she need not worry any more, because sometimes a week would go by without her thinking about Davey at all. Even so, she would still occasionally measure distances with her thumb on General Braybon's globe, wondering where Davey could have reached. By April she thought he must have turned the sharp pink end of Africa, in May be racing along the Roaring Forties, so labelled in straggling gothic print.

Ultimately, perhaps the void into which he vanished made it easiest to forget. Once Liddy's imagination could only manage a small sunlit picture of Davey released at last from his convict ship into God's good air, the weeks when she only occasionally thought about him gradually became months.

Two years slipped past, by which time Liddy was beset by quite different worries. The Braybons, well liked as employers, seemed to keep their staff for ever, and after that one slice of luck which had brought her from 'tweenmaid to housemaid with a rush, there seemed no prospect of bettering herself any further. Mrs Braybon ordered her own menus, instructed her servants and threw china at those who showed signs of becoming slack; no matter how hard Liddy tried to become indispensable, in reality the household ran nearly as well without as with her.

Then the Boyds came home from Canada and advertised for staff to open up Hill House again. On her next Sunday off Liddy walked to their shuttered house beyond the church and was hired as head housemaid. It was a wrench to leave Greenview House, but she had become convinced that only by entering a quite different style of household might her ambition to become a housekeeper with a whole establishment depending on her skill ever be fulfilled.

Nothing, indeed, could have been more different from her previous experience in service than the circumstances at Hill House. All the Boyds came home sick after living rough in Canada, and poor Mrs Boyd was tearfully thankful when her new head housemaid proved a rock of strength. Though Liddy missed the companionship of Greenview House kitchen and the Braybons' unconventional behaviour, never could she have imagined how well her hopes would be served by a move from one end of Furnace Green to the other. Both Major and Mrs Boyd died within the year and their two unchaperoned daughters were snapped up soon after by fortune-hunters, even though they looked frail enough to blow away. Martha died two weeks before she wed, Matilda married a penniless younger son twenty years her senior, whose attentions any parent would instantly have discouraged. Actually, Percival Dersingham was not unkindly, simply an ageing roué anxious to secure some comfortable means before it was too late. Once Matilda became sole heir to her mother's wealth, it had not taken him long to decide to overlook the regrettable fact that her father had been no more than a Lambeth waterman's son who could build canals.

As soon as they were married, modest Hill House was progressively torn down and rebuilt as a gothic chunk of masonry, henceforward to be called Hill Grange. Since Percival Dersingham continued to invite whoever he chose to visit at all hours, in the resulting chaos most of the trained servants left. Then Liddy became the one fixture in a long nightmare for newly wed Mrs Dersingham, once she had, perforce, to manage with others less well recommended. She was promoted to dining room maid in time for Christmas and saw the spring in as head parlour-maid.

An outward sign of this dizzy success was the flattering way in which Akehurst, General Braybon's groom, treated her almost as an equal when he brought her a much folded page torn out of a ledger, superscribed to Liddy Larkworthy, at Greenview House, Furnace Green, England.

'The master said it came all the way from Australia, so you deserved to receive it before Sunday.' He feigned disinterest but Liddy could see he was as sharp and curious as a polecat.

'Australia!' She stared at scraggly writing. 'Davey!'

'I daresay,' agreed Akehurst. 'He's never writ before, has he? Though his ma heard once, I'm told.'

Liddy shook her head, her fingers fairly twitching with impatience to unstick the gummed wafer holding that single sheet tucked up together. All the same, Davey had written to her, not Akehurst's cronies at the Dyer Arms. 'Thank you for bringing it over, Mr Akehurst.'

'Be good news, I hope.'

'I hope so.'

'Mistress Dersingham keeping well?'

'As well as can be expected, thank you.' Of course she ought to ask Akehurst in for a mug of ale, her repute and that of Hill Grange diminished because she practically slammed the door on his inquisitive nose, but all she could think of was how to get away and read Davey's letter all alone.

She fairly raced up the five flights of stairs to the attic, where her new position had brought the unprecedented luxury of a room to herself, and stood with her back to the shut door, breathing hard, but gripped now by a strange reluctance. If I had any sense, I'd run straight back down again and throw this in the kitchen range, she thought. For her the years of success had healed the past; Davey, why can't you leave me alone to follow the way I want?

Parramatta May 1833

Dear Liddy,

I writ hoping to find you well as this leaves me at present thank God. This is a hard place but I ham glad Devil Hooke taut me to writ becos I ham sometimes imploy'd inside on reckerings. My master promis'd to send this by the nex ship. Liddy you did not replie to the other letter I sent. Please writ to this one. I love you still.

DAVEY

But for two long weeks Liddy fought against replying. If she wrote to Davey now, heaven knew what he might start thinking. Instead, she fairly drove her mind at her work, scurrying up and down Hill Grange's gloomy staircases, whirling in and out of red plush reception rooms as if a single speck of dust was an insult. Yet in the end, how could she bear not to reply, when clear as clear Davey was wretched in the hard place where he was trapped, and longing for a soft word from home?

Hill Grange November 1833

Dear Davey,

I was pleas'd to hear you are well. I am well and working for the daughter of Maj. Boyd who died. She is sick too. I am Parlourmaid now but this place always in a bustle. My da and ma are in London and well I hope. Your ma is well and sends her love. Pete is come back as he hates London. He works for General Braybon on Corndown Fields.

Yrs LIDDY

Liddy read through this latest of several attempts doubtfully. Surely even Davey couldn't read more than bare civility into those few, carefully measured lines. Before she could decide to tear this one up like the rest, she put on her best starched apron and went down to the drawing room to ask if she might run over to slip it in the postbag at the Dyer Arms, without waiting for her afternoon off.

Mrs Dersingham was lying on the sofa, as pale as curd with her first pregnancy, and exclaimed at once, 'Oh Liddy, there you are! Wherever have you been? Mr Dersingham is bringing Mr Rice and Mr Holden home with him, and Cook tells me we haven't anything in the larder fit to eat!'

'Then may I suggest, mam, that I run down to Mr

Wicks's for a cut of meat, and on my way I can ask the shop to send up whatever else we need?' In Liddy's opinion Cook was quite as idle and inconsiderate as Mr Dersingham, which meant just about as tiresome as it was possible to be.

Mrs Dersingham sighed. 'I knew you could arrange it. I don't suppose you could also think of something to make me even a little bit better?'

'You will feel well again as soon as your babe is born,' she answered soothingly. 'Now you let me send for a heated brick and a posset, then if you lean on my arm perhaps you will fancy a walk in the garden when I come back from Mr Wicks's.'

And on my way I can call in at the coaching stable and leave my letter without so much as needing to ask leave, thought Liddy delightedly.

That winter Liddy was busier than ever. Mrs Dersingham had a miscarriage just as the last pinnacle was added to gleaming new Hill Grange, and, once snow threatened, Mr Dersingham invited half a dozen acquaintances to stay for as long as they wanted, so that, together, they might drink and gamble the dull weeks of winter away. This made an enormous amount of extra work, and trouble as well, when upstairs-maids needed to take care not to be caught in dark passages by guests Liddy would have hesitated to describe as gentlemen. If she also spent at least part of every morning surreptitiously watching for the boy who brought up the Hill Grange letters, then no one else noticed it.

Davey's next letter did not in fact arrive—and of course she hadn't really wanted him to write again—until the following autumn, five months being an average voyage by sailing ship to New South Wales.

Parramatta April 1834

Dear Liddy,

I was so pleas'd you wrat I read your letter so often I c'd tell every word. I ham tiyed to a Mr Garret at Parramatta. I do not lik being tiyed but he is fair. The land is not lik Sussex but dry and hard and hot most of the time. I do not nowe how long more I ham tiyed. Liddy w'd you come here if I asked.

Yr loving DAVEY

No! thought Liddy, panic-stricken. No. Never. I belong in Sussex, not in a hard dry country where Davey is tied to a place with a heathen name. She went over to her bedroom window and stared out at familiar cool spaces of windy air, the flash of brass furnishings on horses turning rich furrows in the earth. This was the inheritance she knew, the setting she wanted for her life. What a fool she had been ever to reply to that first letter Davey wrote, no matter how unhappy he had seemed. Well, she wouldn't answer him again, not if he sent a dozen times to ask.

Parramatta May 1836

Dear Liddy,

I writ to tell you I will be free'd from Bond soon. I told you last year we were lik to be pardon'd and the Governor has alredy relees'd some of us saying we be decint men. I ham tiyed to Mr Garret til then but not long now. Liddy it is so long since I heared from you. I think a ship must have sunk.

This is not an easy land but there are places without aney rich men where we c'd settle. The Governor says if aney of us sent out after the riots want our wives or promis'd women to come the govt will paye the fare, the land needing respektible women. I sayed you still waited for me tho' the years were long and me not wishful to go Home. Tho' I hev not forgot the best-brewed you promis'd at the Bear when I was free! So your name is wrat down for a passage. Dear Liddy I ham tiered of Travelling the World alone. Please come. I sweer we can be wed the moment you are here and no wagging tonges. I hev my Craft and will not rest til you hev a fine Home of your own.

Is the Street the same and the Pool and the Oak. Too bad bloody Aitchison werent a decint man lik Locock and we man and wife in a cottage there. This is good sheep countray I will lik it when I ham free you too I hope. Please Liddy come.

Yr loving DAVEY

If you come bring Cloth and Needles w'ch is hard to come by here. Please give my love to Mother and all Inquirin frens and to your Dearself of coarse.

'Mrs Larkworthy? Mam, the mistress asks you to attend her in the withdrawing room. 'Tis urgent, so she said.'

Liddy looked up from this latest of Davey's letters, written doggedly at six-monthly intervals over the past two years regardless of her failure to reply. A 'tweenmaid was curtseying nervously in the doorway. 'Very well, Liza. I will be down immediately.'

She stood and smoothed rustling black silk skirts, glanced in the mirror at her hair under its starched lace cap. Not a wisp out of place, and her dress ruched and buttoned from neck to waist to denote her status. Two months earlier, Liddy had ceased to be senior parlour maid and become Mrs Larkworthy, housekeeper of Hill Grange, when her mistress had finally given up the struggle to manage increasingly untrained and insolent servants for herself. 'I just can't worry along any more on my own, Liddy, when I feel so dreadfully ill and worrying makes my head ache worse than ever. Mr Dersingham has said I must take care now I am expecting again, but really I cannot, when I never know how many people he is going to bring home next. Sometimes this house seems so large I quite expect it to swallow me up! In Canada we lived in little better than a cabin, you know, and though it was dreadfully stuffy and made us all cough in the winter, I remember best how cosy it was together.' She sighed. 'But I would like to have this baby and Doctor Purslow says I will lose it unless I rest. Oh Liddy, would you really be able to see to everything for me?'

'If I am given the authority to do so, yes, certainly, madam,' said Liddy firmly. She wanted to dance a jig on the hideous red Turkey carpet instead of keeping her face all primmed up.

'Oh, yes! A keyring, black silk dress and anything else you would wish!' exclaimed Mrs Dersingham, clapping her hands. 'Dear Liddy—I can still call you Liddy when we're alone, can't I?—I knew you would be the one to manage.'

And from that day on, Liddy had been the one to manage. New servants were engaged who had never known her as a housemaid, the silk dresses ordered and a sitting room set aside where she might labour on menus and reckonings. Time now to agree with Davey that Samuel Hooke had been a good teacher of those who desired to learn, whatever his other failings. An attorney's clerk in Maidstone he was nowadays, so rumour said.

I wager he manages to squeeze plenty of sovereigns for himself in that trade, mused Liddy. How Davey would rage if he knew!

She jerked her mind back irritably, but even walking down the front staircase to the withdrawing room—only menials used the breakneck back staircase—she remained conscious of Davey's letter in her pocket. Surely she couldn't be such a chuckhead as to entertain for an instant the notion of going off to a place like Australia and marrying Davey. See what Canada had done to the Boyds, and never a word from Alec since he'd decided to strike out further west. Not that Alec had ever been a great one for writing.

As for herself, she had achieved the hardest part of what she wanted, and when the mistress died . . . God knew she had the look of death. Once Mrs Dersingham died, Liddy could in conscience apply for the kind of position she really craved, in a household—well, perhaps not quite as large as Riffield Castle, but better regarded than Hill Grange.

That would show them. Little Liddy Larkworthy, whose family had been turned out of Edenham Mill for dishonesty, as grand as a ladyship with half a hundred servants scurrying to do her bidding.

'Yes, mam?' she said to wan Mrs Dersingham, poor mite.

'Liddy, do you know, that dreadful Mrs Aitchison has only this moment gone, imagine it! You don't know how long it seems since I was enjoyed a good coze with a caller I felt pleased to welcome. Do you think they have all quite decided I can only lie on a couch and moan? I don't mean to, really I don't.'

'How can you say such a thing, when everyone with the least sensitivity is afraid of tiring you until after your babe is safely born?' Liddy lied. The ladies of Furnace Green conscientiously visited Mrs Dersingham, but between her ill health and their dislike of her husband, relations between Hill Grange and other nearby households remained strictly formal.

Instead Liddy herself would often chat for hours to keep up her mistress's spirits, and set out now to make her laugh aloud by wicked mimicry of starched-up Mrs Aitchison; so much so that half an hour later Mrs Dersingham looked quite cheerful again. 'If I mulled a glass of wine to my own particular recipe, do you think you could drink it and then doze before supper?' she asked at last. Heaven knew, there were a hundred things waiting for her attention.

'Oh yes! Dear Liddy, you always make me feel so much better. What I should do without you I don't know.'

I'm sure I don't know either, thought Liddy. She felt uncharacteristically depressed herself, as much by the gloomy atmosphere at Hill Grange as by a growing sense of entanglement in oppressive, unwanted obligations.

'Oh . . . Liddy—' Mr Dersingham stopped her on her way to the kitchen.

Liddy inclined her head, hands folded in her stiff black skirts. 'Good afternoon, sir. If you recall, sir, now I am housekeeper here, the name is Mrs Larkworthy.'

'By Jove, yes, I keep forgetting! Liddy . . . Mrs Larkworthy, I expect six for dinner tonight and with the roads in such a state I daresay some will stay the night.'

'I will see that bedrooms are prepared. Should I instruct

the footman to serve claret or burgundy in your library beforehand?'

After a decision in favour of burgundy Liddy swept on, chuckling to herself. The master certainly disliked her as much as she did him, but his comfort was most excellently served by capable Mrs Larkworthy; in consequence, she had rapidly established a position of cool ascendancy.

Very late that evening, after her final visit to Mrs Dersingham, tucked up in bed, Liddy read Davey's letter again. *Dear Liddy I ham tiered of Travelling the World alone.* Heavens, how often she, too, was tired alone. How her body yearned for comfort when she lay awake, listening to the sounds of night and wondering about the might-have-been. The might-have-been for Davey too; though he had served only six years of a sentence which sent him so far away, he seemed changed from the old Davey spoiling for a fight. *Me not wishful to go Home*, he had also written; yet plainly he still hankered for Furnace Green. The only answer to that riddle, that he could no longer face squandering the remainder of his life in hopeless battles.

Nowadays Liddy had few reasons to walk down the lane to Edenham, but not long ago she had gone that way with Pete, on a Sunday afternoon when he had a fancy to see how the old house was faring. When Pete was ten years old, Da had given him three sovereigns and allowed him to choose: apprenticeship in a London craft, return to Sussex, or a passage out to Alec in Canada. There was never any doubt about his choice and when Liddy asked, General Braybon agreed to employ him at Corndown. There Pete remained and would remain all his life, entirely content so long as he laboured on the ridge. It was after this that they never heard from Alec again, so perhaps he only stopped writing in disgust.

As for Edenham, it was dying as a mill, so everyone said. 'I don't want to see it. You walk on and tell me what you find.' Unexpectedly, Liddy had felt unable to go on when she and Pete reached the last bend in the lane.

He shrugged and went off, whistling. Pete liked fields

better than any dirty mill; he was curious to see what had happened to his home but unworried by its ruin. Left alone, Liddy had sat on the bank and looked around her. The autumn sun shone; on just such a day as this Davey had first kissed her. She touched a rut with her toe: they had stood exactly there.

She had always known that particular memory would refuse to die, but hadn't expected it to remain as fresh as if he had kissed her yesterday. Perhaps this was because, for her, there had never been anyone else. No one she fancied after that dreadful time when Davey was in gaol, then suffering all the way to Australia; and once she began to better herself, she had needed to keep her distance from the other servants. Living-in staff usually lost their positions if they married, so, although there were dozens of young grooms and footmen and gardeners in the larger houses around Furnace Green, they weren't often thinking about a wedding. As for the other young village men, after that wild year of Captain Swing the name of Larkworthy had put them off for a while. When one or two did start asking to walk out with her, it wasn't long before she found fault with each in turn. Dick French seemed horribly dull, although as a farmer's son he was an excellent catch; George Parlben she considered a lazy, charming scoundrel, and Roger Locock's smug insensitivity soon irritated her almost beyond civility. Indeed, for the last year or so Liddy had behaved more like an old maid than an unwed girl in her twenties, using her day off as often as not to call on May and Cook at Greenview House, or after a solitary stroll taking tea with her cousin, Amy Sleech.

Mrs Dersingham's second baby was prematurely born in November 1836, with Liddy holding her mistress's hands while the doctor saved her life. Afterwards Liddy took the pitiful unmoving scrap and wrapped it ready to join the other unnamed casket in the churchyard; a boy this time, clenching tiny perfect hands, its face as unreal as crumpled paper.

Sighing, she laid the tiny bundle aside, and as she did so a fiercely possessive desire reached out of nowhere to splinter her composure: a passionate wish, as unexpected as it was sudden, to hold a child of her own. Instantly, she thrust it away again. Yet once it had come it refused to leave her, as if Davey's latest letter uttered urgings of its own. Only seconds later and almost subconsciously, she decided that not one but several healthy brats would suit her best, who would tumble joyfully together as she remembered doing on the banks of Edenham's stream. Times had never been so hard that they hadn't all laughed together.

'I'll speak to the vicar on my way home,' the doctor said wearily. 'Mind you get some sleep soon, Mrs Larkworthy.'

'I will sir, thank you. Would you care for a glass of port before you leave?' Efficient, unflustered Mrs Larkworthy, wed to someone else's household. Mrs Larkworthy the cheat, who had pretended to Davey more affection than she felt, cold-bloodedly offering hope to help keep a frightened boy alive.

The same Mrs Larkworthy who had wanted so much to better herself that she was glad when brutal justice excused her from the need for explanation. Could she really have felt that half-guilty gladness when Davey was transported? Because what she felt now was shame, when he still hoped against hope that faithfulness rather than ambition had kept her an old maid of twenty-four.

Although she was dreadfully tired after the wasted struggle to save Mrs Dersingham's baby, when Liddy was eventually free to retire to bed she found she couldn't sleep. Her fire had been lit as a matter of course and the room was pleasantly warm; she had only to ring, and a tray of tea would be brought up to her. The bed was soft, the room full of solidly polished furniture. How close she had come to what she'd always wanted.

Outside, it was raining. Rain which came straight down in sheets and filled the silence of her solitary room with its forlorn and desolate sigh. Alone, alone, said the rain. Alone, thought Liddy, though blood and heart and instinct suddenly all shout together how very far I feel from being an old maid, at only twenty-four. I've bettered myself, and here I am alone.

Furnace Green December 1836

Dear Davey,

I am pleased to hear you will soon be free. I cannot leave Hill Grange now as my Mistress is sick and Depends on me for everything. The Doctor says she cannot see the winter through so come next Spring I will find a Ship to bring me to Parramatta. Is Parramatta a port and is there really land we can have of our own? The Street and the Pool and the Oak are the same and the low wages too. The new Overseer is to board some of the paupers out so they may earn pence cutting firewood. Workhouse barn is too small for the numbers now. Your mother sends her love.

Yr. affect. LIDDY

Please send the Governor's chitty for the passage.

Goulburn June 1837

Dear Liddy,

I ham free and land is there for the taking but not easy land lik I said before. Now you will soon come I ham looking for a good place to settle. Liddy I will try to make you happy but I ham not the same fellow you knew. I hev brown wiskers and drink to much. I will not drink when you come. I remember how I was druv out of Sussex but with you this will be our home.

yr. very loving DAVEY

London December 1837

Dear Davey,

As you see I am on my way. My poor Mistress died two months ago and I am spending a few weeks with Ma and Da before I sail next month. I will be on the Francis Charlotte *to Sydney. Da has done well in a Bell Foundry in Whitechapel wch is very hard but the Wage is good. They rent a cottage in a row all to themselves wch not many folk have but everything so dirty I am glad Pete is out of it. Da looks old and Dick died three years ago but Freddie is earning at the Foundry now. Kate went off with a swell she met and is no more spoke of.*

Davey you wont drink will you once I come. I am worried when you say how you have changed. The day I left Furnace Green it looked beautiful and the ploughteams were in the fields. The harvest is good this year thank God. What will we grow in Australia I wonder.

Yr. affect. LIDDY

Six weeks later Liddy stood on the deck of the *Francis Charlotte* watching the shadow of England dip beneath the horizon. Devon, the sailors said it was. Two nights earlier when they had sailed close in to the Sussex shore she had seen nothing in the dark, an unreasonably bitter disappointment.

Dear God, what a fool she was to start from the beginning again, just when she could have applied for a position in some of the best households in Sussex, and with a drunken convict for a husband, too.

Except that Davey didn't sound as bad as that in his letters, not yet anyway, although for the life of her she had been unable to infuse real warmth into her replies.

Perhaps everyone has something they cannot lie about, mused Liddy, and she couldn't bring herself to lie twice to Davey about her feelings for him. Instead she had chosen, and this time chosen quite dispassionately, recognizing her choice for the enormous gamble it was. Davey, too, must be left with a choice when they met again, to accept or reject a woman who had come to him across the world for reasons of her own. Romantic dreams would not help with a harsh new Davey nursing bitter disillusion, nor make it easier for self-confident Mrs Larkworthy to adjust to the life of a settler's wife. Their best chance of happiness was to accept each other for what they were, and then build on what they found.

Liddy turned her back on the haze which was the last she would ever see of England, and lifted her face to wind driving out of the west.

. . . THE WITNESS

At five o'clock this morning a strange thing happened: I woke feeling strong and well. Whereas yesterday I was as nearly blind as usual, this morning I could see the sun rising in a smother of pink and gold, the green haze of spring on the trees. Everything a little blurred at the edges to be sure, but light striking through my own secret coils of mist only made the dawn seem finer. I got out of bed and dressed, moving more easily than for years, went downstairs and opened Edenham's front door.

Birds were singing with the kind of wild rejoicing I remember in my youth, too early yet for traffic on the road. As if to complete the illusion of an older, more spacious England from the past, I even thought I saw a flower-faced owl fly swiftly by, caught unaware by the dawn.

I walked through wet grass to where the cold dark water of Edenham's brook was beginning to glint silver as the sun rose higher. The cobwebs between unfolding bracken fronds were glinting too—on the ridge, bracken soon comes creeping back wherever man ceases to cultivate the soil. As the light strengthened I no longer saw so clearly but I walked on eagerly, my head turning to greet the places and people I knew so well. The women smiled in reply and the men raised a hand, everyone glad to see me, or so it seemed. In the fields were others I recognized, and animals too. I wanted to greet them all, except there were so many.

After a while I climbed up to the road and walked, more slowly now, towards Furnace Green. An early commuter hooted angrily and swerved with a squeal of tyres, but as soon as he passed I had forgotten him again. By then my early vigour was fading fast and I was intent only on reaching the seat on the green before I was forced to rest on a dew-soaked bank. Exhaustion settling like sediment into my blood, that seat a haven I needed my last shred of strength to reach.

Hardly had I sat down before a pedlar came to sit beside me. He had the brown complexion which comes from a lifetime on the road and immediately began to look about him with bright inquisitive eyes. 'You're out early,' he said.

'I woke and felt young enough to walk for ever,' I answered.

He sniffed the morning air, joyfully, like a hound on a tail-high scent. 'In spring everyone feels young again.'

'A feeling which unfortunately does not last, at eighty-one years old.'

'Oh . . . it lasts, my friend, when you have achieved what your heart desires.'

I stayed silent, thinking of Chris. Without her, I lacked for always what my heart desired.

'You have this,' he spoke as if answering my thought. 'And, like me, you are a teller of tales, are you not?' He was laughing, head thrown back. Rico, an earlier chronicler of the ridge, acknowledging a companion who knew as he did the heady elation which comes at the end of a long and splendid story truly told.

'Last night I felt triumphant,' I said slowly. 'I sat beside Edenham's hearth and thought: it's finished. Forty years since I returned to Furnace Green, two since I decided its story must be written down. During those two years, how often have I wondered whether I would ever finish. It's the hell of a task for a half-blind man to write and dictate a million words. I woke feeling triumphant still. Now, only the emptiness of finishing is left.'

'Your lifetime has joined the rest, after eighty years you lived as best you could,' answered Rico easily. 'What more could anyone ask?'

I thought of the greetings I had sensed about me that morning as I walked, and felt comforted. Good fellowship is precious, after all. As to what more there is, I'm still not sure, perhaps that's part of the trouble. Would one of Furnace Green's past priests, whether saint or scoundrel, be a better companion at the lonely end of life than the man in whose footsteps I have followed?

I would trade them all for Chris, as they are wise enough to know. But, for what it is worth, here at last is my lifetime to join and mingle with the rest.

4

The Long Flight of an Arrow

1906–1987

I was born the last surviving child of Albert and Eliza Smith, in the cottage next to Furnace Green's grocery shop. Both these belonged to my uncle, Mr Portnell, who worked with his wife and only daughter in the shop; we children were for ever pestering him to send us on errands, since the reward was a trumpet-shaped twist of thick blue paper filled with raisins, or tea, or sugar, and a gob-stopper for ourselves. Uncle and Aunt Portnell usually contrived to seem pleased to see us, but probably they were relieved when their siege was lifted and we moved a little further away to join my grandmother at Edenham.

This was in February of 1913, when I was six. My grandfather had just died and grandmother decided to offer us houseroom. To be more exact, she had no intention of looking after a farmyard full of pigs and hens herself when we could do it for her. It must have seemed a clever idea to have the work at Edenham done for nothing, but later, the inconvenience of seven extra people squeezed into a fairly small house was a constant irritant.

I wept for my grandfather when he died, but soon forgot my grief in the excitement of going to live in what seemed to me somewhere quite enormous. The reality turned out somewhat differently. Edenham was smoky-dark and made uncertain by my grandmother's temper, we children put to work in whatever time was left over from school or paid errands. My grandfather had struggled for years to keep the place going as a smallholding while prices dropped relentlessly, but even before he died the struggle had been lost. A paddock, some pigs, an orchard and a barn full of hens were all that remained, although I can just remember Edenham's last ox. He was called Cheerful, a vast dark-red creature with soft eyes and a nudging nose. By then most fieldwork was done by horses, but my grandfather had said he could never remember a time when there hadn't been an ox called Cheerful on one of the ridge farms, and that his grandfather had told him the same. When our Cheerful had to go to the butcher's, my sister, Sally, and I rode there on his back and Mr Twort was forced to knock us sprawling when we arrived at his slaughter-yard, because we clung to Cheerful's horns refusing to get off. We stood in a huddle, howling, as poor Cheerful was led out of sight.

Many years passed before I discovered that our Cheerful was last in a line which stretched back as far as curiosity would reach, the pattern of cultivation on the ridge as much theirs as ours.

But as I was saying, work filled most of our days at Edenham. My elder sister Florence was already in service, but before six o'clock in the morning I would be pulled out of bed and sent to feed the pigs, while my other sister Sally coped with the chickens and older brothers Mark and David chopped wood and drew water before walking with my father to work at Locócks Farm. My mother scrubbed at Hill Grange and after we had all left for work or school, my grandmother would dart like a pike around the house all day, looking for tasks to give us in the evening. How I hated those pigs! We had five sows and their litters, sometimes as many as forty little ones. Although they were meant to stay in the barn they wandered everywhere, grunting and rootling in the undergrowth, turning everything into swamp; it was impossible to make them stay anywhere for long. Since I was meant to keep track of them I received a great many cuffs for failing in what seemed to me a hopeless task.

In addition to the trouble the pigs caused around the place, there was the business of keeping their sties clean. I did my best but at farrowing time particularly, the sows sensed my fear and dislike of them and became more aggressive than before. Then my grandmother, who had a mania for inspecting everything, became even freer with her slaps and pinchings.

Those terrible winters after we first came to Edenham! Come rain and wind, snow and frost, out I had to go at six o'clock into the yard. Within minutes I was plastered in stinking mud, my breeches soaked, which meant I had to wash in freezing water before setting out to walk to school with Sally. When people look back now on a past they imagine was better than today, they should think instead what it was like to work in such conditions.

But in several ways I was lucky, and knew it. Lucky, too, in one particular way, and only later realized my good fortune.

This particular way first. I was born at the very last moment when I could have grown up in a pattern of life which stretched back all the way to the first settlement on the ridge, so that, later, I understood instinctively a great many things about my ancestors which others would have needed to puzzle over.

The year after we came to Edenham the First War began, though at first it made little difference. All the same, it sent a ripple through the parish and some of the young men hurried to join up, including my brother David. Soon, the war was everywhere. Soldiers trained in the Dyers' deer park, Hill Grange became a military hospital and most of the village women worked there, for which they were paid more than they had ever dreamed of being paid before. As a consequence a few luxuries found their way into the cottages; better clothes and food, some gaudy china pots. The old men in the tap of the Dyer Arms spent their evenings arguing over stories they read in illustrated magazines, where cavalry dashed gallantly after beaten Huns. Those magazines cost money, but the old 'uns no longer grudged a penny each out of their weekly allowance, doled out by their wives for beer and tobacco.

That first year of the war started like a bubble of colour in our lives, but then the first casualties came home and names of the village dead began to be read out at Sunday service. The excitement went out of the war after that, leaving only the changes behind. Changes coming faster than we could comprehend, faster and faster until a few years later we suddenly realized the old life was gone without our ever noticing. The ancient tale-telling by winter firesides, the long ridge mornings and summer junketings, the rhythms of certainty, the quiet. When I look back to my boyhood now, it is the quiet which strikes me as extraordinary. Until a year or so after the war ended, the sounds on the ridge were mostly those there had always been: the sounds of wind in the trees and dogs barking, a shepherd's whistle perhaps or the song of a ploughman walking alone behind his beast. It was this quiet world which vanished, and took with it the simple, deeply savoured pleasures which are the reward of unremitting work.

My brother David was killed on the Somme in 1916.

Both the Twort boys were killed within a few months of each other, and a name which grew out of the beginnings of the ridge died with them.

By the end of the war forty-two Furnace Green men were dead, ten more would never work again. In 1918 I was twelve years old, an age at which village schooling often petered away no matter what the law said, and a lifetime of work began.

'Mr Pomfret said I ought to sit for the Grammar School exam,' I said one day to Chris, who even then I considered my particular friend. It must have been Easter 1918; I know I had one more term at the village school.

'Why don't you, then?' she answered carelessly.

'I couldn't.'

'Of course you can, silly.' My memory reminds me that on this sunny afternoon Chris wore her white school pinafore tied with a sash over a pale-coloured frock. Out of all the village girls, only she ever dared to belt her pinafore, usually with some dashing bow slung low about her hips. Already Chris skipped, slid and danced her own way, heedless of criticism.

'Only farmers' and tradesmen's sons go to grammar

school,' I answered, but tentatively, as if by telling her my dreams somehow they might come true.

'Of course I know that.' She jumped over some horse-droppings in the street.

'I'm not a tradesman's or a farmer's son.'

'Oh, lumme,' she said elegantly, this being the expression most favoured in Furnace Green that year. 'What a fraidy cat you are, to be sure, Mister Smith.'

'I'm not!'

'You are. Fraidy cat, fraidy cat! Anyway, who wants to go to fusty old grammar school?'

I did. I wanted to go to grammar school so badly that it hurt. I knew I should hate drudging for the rest of my life on someone else's farm; worse still, I should never be any good at it. But the choice wasn't as simple as that. The grammar school was six miles away and I should need a bicycle to reach it. Even if I won a scholarship, I would be told to buy special clothes we couldn't afford, as well as a satchel and a cap with an enamel badge in front. The other boys would buy dinner each day, have money in their pockets for the extras needed there, whereas I should have to take a dinner basket and wear hobnailed boots. I felt noble because I hadn't mentioned the grammar school idea at home, but fear of derision as much as awareness of the sacrifices the rest of the family would have to make if I went kept me silent.

Still, the idea stabbed and swirled and rankled in my mind all that last summer at school, making me miserable. Worse still, I began to despise my contemporaries in the village with whom until then I had been moderately friendly.

'You're just an old grump,' said Chris, with the candour only found in childhood friends. 'I don't like you any more.'

'Then I don't like you either.' Stupid, infantile reflex; of course I liked her and always had.

'Oh yes, you do. Everyone likes me,' she answered complacently. 'I'm off to play at Maisie Small's, are you?

Later on, everyone is asked to our make-believe party by the pool.'

I shrugged. 'Not everyone, 'cos I'm not.'

'You're always moping around your old books, so I expect she thought you wouldn't want to come. What's the point of so much reading, I'd like to know? Everyone will think you want to be a parson.' She paused, and then added doubtfully, 'Or a schoolteacher, I suppose.'

'Of course I don't want to be a parson or a schoolteacher.'

'Then why bother about reading all the time? Even Sandy Huggett said he'd join in, and you know how grand he is about going where there's girls. It's going to be a very special make-believe party.'

I swallowed. 'I'd come if you asked me.'

'Why should I?' She ricocheted gleefully from one foot to the other, little puffs of dust rising from the roadway.

'All right, I'll come on my own. The pool's on the green, anyone can go there.'

'Not today. It's private and ever so secret.'

'I tell you, I'm coming!' My misery suddenly became passionate rage, an agony of frustration. I can feel it still. Only yesterday I walked past the place where it happened, and my suffering over what seems such a trifle still hovered in the air. And how old fashioned were the figures I saw in my mind's eye: Chris in plaits and pinafore and me bundled into handed-down serge shorts which reached below my knees. Behind us, a few older men in the street were still wearing smocks, their corduroys tied with string below the knee. Children clattered to play in enormous hobnailed boots and bowled iron hoops—you can still see the chips in the churchyard wall where we used to hurl them down the street in such a way that, with luck, they would leap clean over the wall. The women in aprons and dark dresses long enough to brush the dust, tuckered bonnets tied under their chins at harvest time.

Yet to us, even after everything began to change, it all seemed so permanent. Like my anguish when I wasn't asked to the make-believe party; although I tried to stop them, my lips began to tremble.

Chris saw this at once. 'Cry-baby!'

'I'm not crying.'

'Yes, you are. Fancy a boy your age crying.'

'You often cry, I've seen you.'

'Girls are allowed to cry and boys aren't.' Chris was walking backwards away from me. 'Johnnie Smith's a cry-baby, cry-baby! A cowardy-custard too, I shouldn't wonder. Cowardy, cowardy-custard, afraid of his mother's mustard.'

Her mockery stirred up such blind anger in me that I ran after her across the green, arms flailing while she dodged, laughing, and sent the sheep which grazed there scampering. 'Look at you! Lumme, just look at Johnnie Smith in a bait!'

'Stop it!' I shouted. 'I'll kill you if you don't.'

'You wouldn't dare.' She tossed her plaits in the air.

Burning with the lust to hurt, I tucked in my scrawny elbows and somehow caught her next time she swerved. Crooked my arm around her neck and fairly threw her down on the grass. Mud and sheep-droppings splattered over us both, although my rage evaporated almost at once, as I realized for the first time in my life how warmly different a girl felt from a boy. The surprise of it took me unaware.

Not so Chris. She always had an exceedingly low boiling point, and never more so than when she was young. As she struggled against my grip her hair broke from its plaits and whipped into my eyes, her fury and my surprise combined so she was able to throw me off.

We scrambled to our feet and stood staring at each other, while a group of interested children gathered around us.

'I hate you,' she shouted, hair snapping in the wind like a battle flag. 'You said you wanted to kill me but I'd like to *murder* you.'

'It's the same,' I said feebly.

'Oh no, it isn't. Murder's worse than anything, and that's what I'd like to do to you. I'm sheep all over everywhere. Father will be furious and come after you with a stick.'

'My dad whipped me when I kicked my sister, and Chris isn't even your sister,' announced Vic Hawkins, out of the crowd. 'He said it was cowardly to kick a girl.'

Chris pounced. 'I told you so. Cowardy, cowardy-custard, Johnnie's afraid of his mother's mustard. Kicks the girls and runs from the boys till we all fall down!'

Everyone laughed. My whole world filled with white teeth and crimson mocking mouths, while I stood wishing I was dead.

Nevertheless, looking back, I know that this was the day I fell in love with Chris.

I loathed her at the time of course, and walked home alone; excluded and unhappy. A little afraid as well, because my father was strict about behaviour and might easily whip me, too, if he heard I had disgraced him by attacking Chris.

Chris's full name was Christian Portnell; she was my cousin and the only child of Uncle and Aunt Portnell who kept the shop. It never occurred to me then to wonder whether she was pretty and afterwards it didn't matter whether she was or not. Certainly, she was all fire and movement. Long limbs and fair flying plaits, brilliant brown eyes and taunting mouth, made all the more infuriating by unusually full and well-shaped lips. Her moods were as changeable as clouds swept across a brisk spring sky: you never knew what was coming next. She also possessed a capacity to hurt like no other woman I have ever known, perhaps because I cared so much for what she thought of me.

As soon as I reached home I climbed as far away as I could from everybody and huddled on the corner of the bed I shared with Mark, awash with self-pity and pretending to read a book.

Books were difficult to find in Furnace Green. We

possessed a Bible of course and I loved its splendid words, but other books were scarce. At school we had only some readers and a set of unbelievably dreary Moral Tales. Once my mother found a book tossed in the grate at Hill Grange; presumably its contents had annoyed irascible Mr Jay, who bought the place when the wartime hospital closed. Mum brought this charred trophy home in some trepidation, in case whatever had annoyed him was sufficiently serious to corrupt me; alas, the book was in Latin, although I kept it and later was glad I had.

Sunday school prizes looked fine but were usually unreadable. Otherwise only the occasional rummage sale remained as a source of supply, where tattered books of all kinds might be picked up for a penny. I had fourteen of these by the time I sat on my bed after my fight with Chris, of which *Treasure Island* and *Ivanhoe* stand out in my mind. The Edenham back bedroom then was almost entirely filled by this sagging old four-poster, which became all kinds of pretend places whenever my brother David had condescended to play with me. But David died on the Somme and Mark was so much older that we seldom exchanged more than grunts. Mark's collection of birds' eggs stood on the boards one side of the room, my books on the other. As I looked at them that day, I knew beyond doubt there would be no grammar school for me. Instead I should become like Mark and my father, a contrivance for bending, lifting and shovelling, trudging about from day to day until I was old.

After a while I wiped my face and went downstairs, sulkily stupid and casting a gloom over everything. No wonder my family lost patience with me sometimes. I marvel now that all I remember is kindly anxiety, a desire to help overlaid by the certainty that the best thing for me was to accept farm work as my future. Everyone else did; really, they found it difficult to see what all the fuss was about.

Of course life wasn't all gloom. There were concerts at Christmas, cricket in the summer, sing-songs in the Dyer

Arms, a reassuring neighbourliness in our lives. A smartness, too, which I miss in this age of dishevelment. My mother starched and ironed as if her life depended on it, as in a way it did. The Dyers' horses gleamed and their harness glittered in the sun; the few cars had bright brass radiators. Even poor men wore hats which weren't quite bowlers nor yet homburgs but something in between, and stiff collars on Sundays. The women possessed one best bonnet and kept a clean apron handy in case visitors dropped by. Because we had so little we hankered above all for self-respect; a best suit or single pot on a windowsill the mark of managing well. Pride was cherished and scrupulously respected, any disgrace bitterly felt.

My next sharp memory is again of Chris, this time glibly reciting 'The Charge of the Light Brigade' at a Christmas party while Vic Hawkins and I invisibly drummed our heels on the floor in imitation of Lord Cardigan's doomed squadrons.

'Bravo, bravo!' called the vicar, Mr Bond, when she finished and everyone clapped while Chris curtsied, not in the least embarrassed by being the centre of attention. 'Gosh!' she said as she flicked behind the curtain to make way for the Misses Hawkins to play a piano duet, 'Gosh! Did you notice when I left out a whole chunk?'

We assured her that we hadn't.

'Good. I thought everyone was bound to, but I daresay they're too full of plum cake to care. Johnnie dear, would you come with me to Granny Paley's? Mother made me promise I would take her a share of the tea, but I forgot and now it's dark.'

I didn't find this request strange. Granny Paley lived in a tumbledown hovel by the pool and the green was creepy in the dark. Besides, Granny Paley was well known as a witch.

We walked hand in hand, I carrying a basket of left-overs from the tea and Chris a small jug of ale: Granny derided the modern habit of coddling entrails with tea. The green was powdered with snow, rushes standing like upright icicles in the pool. Lately the water level had unaccountably begun to drop and the previous summer it had been nearly dry.

Chris did not speak, her hand clenched tightly on mine. I knew this for a delicious fear of the eerily moonlit ridge, but I had never been so happy. She had chosen me instead of Vic Hawkins to go with her in the dark, knowing that she would want to hold my hand. I glanced to where the moon lit the curve of her mouth and wished . . . Well, I don't know what I wished. In that unsophisticated age I was still far too young to understand what I would eventually want from Chris.

Really, she had chosen me because she knew I didn't mind Granny Paley being a witch, so long as she told good stories. Granny lived close to a great fallen oak by the pool, from where the parish council had tried several times to evict her, saying that no one had the right to live on the green. But Granny knew too much easily to be thrown off, and dared the council to prove that poor folks hadn't an immemorial right to live by the pool. 'In rich years they might choose a drier place and good fortune on them,' she would say. 'But come bad times and back my generations came.'

Granny's generations were her ancestors, a cloud of witness who could make themselves excessively disagreeable if they found any fault with the tales she told. Which is why I did not mind too much that Granny Paley was a witch. To me her tremendous tellings were enhanced by the terrors I had to brave before I heard them, stench and spells and an ancient gleaming stare the setting they required.

Chris and I knocked on Granny's door experiencing our usual trepidation: Chris did not much care about hearing Granny's tales, it was the daring of visiting a witch that she enjoyed. The moment we opened the hovel door, reek swept out to meet us; I can smell it now. Acrid, vaporous and throat-catching; dirt overlaid by smouldering herbs.

'Gosh,' whispered Chris. 'I forget each time how awful she smells.'

'At least it's warm,' I whispered back, trembling quite as much as she.

Granny was sitting by the hearth, her skin shining like oiled leather in the glow. 'Who is it? Who is it?' she called.

'We've brought your share of the party.' Chris stayed by the door.

'Who is it, I said. Come where I can see you!' A hand moved out of darkness and set a twig in the ash until it flared and showed us shivering by the door. 'Ah. Christian and John. You've been a long time coming.'

'How did you know we'd come?' I suppose it was clear enough that someone would come on Christmas party night.

'Maybe I could see you holding hands on the green, eh? Here, give me what you brought.' She seized my basket and burrowed through it, while Chris laid her jug on the hearth and hastily stepped back.

'Granny—' I hesitated.

'There's not much here, and poor stuff too,' she said querulously. 'What do I want with vittles fit for pigs?'

'I put in some of Mother's best plum cake to please you,' exclaimed Chris, annoyed.

'Plum cake? Good meat keeps my teeth in their gums.' She pounced on a packet at the bottom of the basket, discovered bread layered with beef and began cramming the slices into her mouth.

'Let's go,' whispered Chris, tugging at my hand.

But I shook my head, and after a while Granny stopped eating and began to cackle. 'You want your tale, don't you, boy? Well, 'tis Christmas, so this time I'll call up Rico the Silver-Tongued, and tell a tale you won't forget.'

'What a lovely name,' breathed Chris. 'I'm sure I'd like anyone called by a name like that.'

'Which shows you up as a minikin fool, miss. Rico wasn't to be trusted, as Meg the Harlot found. He fathered a brat on her, didn't he? And went off next day, never to return again. Granny Paley the witch, you call me, but 'twas Rico made me so. Fringe folk my generations been, but now 'tis finished. No more Paleys after me, nor folk to remember the ridge's tales.' She threw a handful of herbs on the hearth and the embers flared up immediately, rolling smoke into air already so thick with stench and fumes it could scarcely take any more.

Chris and I stood with our limbs so loosed with fear that we did not even think of bolting, while out of sight behind the smoke Granny began to chant. Gradually her voice became more confident, as if she was not old at all. The hut, which had been hot, suddenly seemed clammy cold and though I knew there was no one there except ourselves, my sense of another presence grew so strong that I kept glancing behind my back. Then Granny's voice changed again and spoke as a man would, but liltingly, so I scarcely recognized the words as hers.

That feeling of someone behind my back strengthened, strengthened, all the time. Granny's voice speaking and swooping, until it seemed to coil into others all around. Then the air quivered and I was coughing; Chris coughing too, beside me. As I live, I am telling exactly what happened, a mile from where I am writing now and less than seventy years ago.

'Stand straight, John Smith, and listen,' said Granny. 'You wanted a story and now I shall tell it. Once upon a time . . .'

Once upon a time. The invariable words with which most old 'uns in the village signified their willingness to begin fingering through the centuries, a tocsin and open sesame to inherited memory.

Quite why Granny chose to tell that particular tale with such trappings of awe I cannot say, but perhaps the last of the Parleybens recognized yearning when she saw it. Of course, nearly everyone in the village enjoyed winter storytellings, but they also took them for granted. Whereas for me, the ridge's past already held a fascination which would only grow stronger as time passed. Now she wanted to begin passing on her tales in ways which might ensure that I didn't forget them, once she was dead.

As Granny told it then, Rico's tale came with him sitting at the hearth beside us, and all twined about with names I did not yet know: Sim and Greg Wyse, Benedict, Alice and John the Carver. She paused when she reached John, and drank some ale. 'You mind the clump of nettles between here and the pool?'

'I stung my hand on them in the dark,' said Chris.

'Not in winter, you didn't, girl. You keep from putting yourself forward. You marked the nettles, John?'

I nodded. Sheep grazed the green, but because it was no one's business to dig out its rough places, a patch of nettles persisted in a hollow near the pool.

'That is where John the Carver lies buried, killed by his kin for the evil he carried in his heart. The church of Furnace Green, which his craft could have made renowned, instead was cursed and fell down, as you know.'

My heart thumped so loudly Granny must have heard it. 'Once . . . I found a carving in the cottage where I was born, number twenty-six. It was hidden behind a beam in the front bedroom, a piece of stone—' I clenched my fist —'like that. One side broken, the other—'

'It was evil?' asked Granny, matter-of-factly.

'Yes,' I answered, as simply. 'It was also marvellously carved. My mother threw it away when I showed her and I wasn't sorry, but—but I didn't want to lose it. I buried it for safety and since have added to it the other things I've found.'

'What other things?' she screeched, bolt upright.

'S-some slag I liked the shape of, and an old billhead which said reckonings would be settled the last day of the month, at the Black Bear in Furnace Green. It's a better name than the Dyer Arms.'

Granny laughed scornfully. 'So say we all. But in the end, who's lasted longer on the ridge I'd like to know, the Dyers or the Parleybens? Them Dyers tired of our turned backs soon enough, and sold out to incomers when they could. Davey Portnell now, he lived in the cottage where you were born, and worked a-pulling down the old cursed church. Maybe he found your carving. But beware, whatever John the Carver made, he cursed. Davey were took and sent away, John got himself killed and good riddance.'

Not long ago I traced Granny Paley's birthdate in the parish register. In that Christmas of 1918 she was eighty-two years old and yet she remembered and remembered . . . also mingled time and distance into a single whole which was the life of the ridge itself. Neither she nor her ancestors had any interest in chronology but each generation had preserved their own particular tale and passed it on to the next, as often as not inextricably tangled into knots. I, on the other hand, suffered from the modern desire for provable detail. Even as a boy I asked what the true name of a monk called Benedict might be and when exactly he lived, wondered why our church should ignominiously fall down when it had been built by such a remarkable man. Researches which ultimately led me to fit Bruiser Bywood and the death of Tobias Hosmer into their respective places, and back . . . and back until in the distances of time there lived another monk called Theobald.

By that winter of 1918 I had already started work, and to begin with it wasn't at all bad. It was early July when I first pulled on working boots and clumped off up the lane to Newhouse Farm; Loc0cks, where Mark and my father worked, had no need of a boy, although in that last summer of the war it seemed as if the fighting, and consequently farming prosperity, would last for ever. Newhouse was a smallish holding of flattish, poorish land, which wartime shortages had brought back from semi-dereliction. The house had been repaired, although there was no trace of the tower which Granny informed me had been there in Parson Syke's day, and Mr French the farmer used his new prosperity to replant hedges and generally bring things up to scratch, as the government urged. He felt deeply about his land and had suffered with it during the long years of depression; now he strode about, small and dark and bright-eyed, looking as foreign as his ancestors must have looked when they first came to Furnace Green as Huguenot refugees. I considered I was lucky to have him as a master, compared to those who had endured the Parson Syke of Granny's tales: all the same, I enjoyed imagining him stamping about the cobbled yard at New-house, roaring damnation on all idleness.

Not that Mr French was easy on idleness, far from it. But he had a way with him, a pride in good husbandry which made him easy to serve. My job was to help the drover who managed one of Mr French's two teams of horses. I brought him whatever he wanted since he was too grand to fetch anything for himself, raked swathes away from the cutter when he mowed, loaded carts and so on. Those first weeks of my labour were shot through by a great sense of relief. The sun shone, insects whirred, warm breezes blew. It was pleasant to be in shirtsleeves earning money, although a boy wasn't worth much, agree-able to listen to the steady clatter of the mower, the clop of hoofs. The cut crops were a delight in themselves, heavy with wild flowers at the butt and tapering into a delicate tracery if they were oats or barley, a firm fretwork if wheat. Uncut fields bent to accept the wind and, no matter where we worked, all around were wooded hills, deeply green and peaceful. The contrast with the slaughter in France helped us to savour our lives, however hard: on the Downs they had heard the guns when the Germans advanced to Amiens in the spring.

As the summer continued I was not just relieved to be rid of my fear of farmwork, I was actually happy in a new experience. However exhausted I might feel by evening, the time did not seem long, and while I worked words formed in my mind, offering a quite different pleasure. Whole paragraphs and conversations were born out of Granny Paley's stories about past generations on the ridge, since everything I touched was theirs; cleared ground, hedges, bricks, worn paths. The landscape belonged to them as much as it did to us, or to nature itself. Our thoughts mirrored theirs, our customs and even our jokes repeated what had gone before.

At harvest time the tempo quickened and men worked harder than their beasts. When cutting finished the horses were rubbed down and stabled through the heat of the day, while we began turning the swathes cut yesterday or stooking shocked corn. Late in the afternoon the horses would be brought out again and carting began; then we would split into teams, two to pitch, one to load, another to cart. Mile after mile, acre after acre, backwards and forwards, plodding on. Weariness gathering into a daze, boots as heavy as iron pigs, arms and legs trembling. Sometimes the church clock struck ten across the fields before pitchforks were leaned against the barn wall, the horses turned away for the night, a tarpaulin pulled over any part-finished stacks in case of rain.

Weeks went by without my opening a book, without time to see Chris. My muscles were so sore I wondered whether they would ever harden, my feet swollen like a gaffer's, the palms of my hands hard and shiny from the friction of rake and pitchfork handles, and yet there was a satisfaction from watching the harvest come in, the fruit of my labour helping to sustain the earth.

Then came winter. In November, the armistice brought the war to an end at last; the village hung out flags which dated from Queen Victoria's Diamond Jubilee and the vicar organised a tea, but it wasn't a joyful celebration. Of course we were glad the war was over, but it was our losses we remembered. Forty-two names waited to be carved on the village war memorial, among them my brother, David Smith. There was also Harry Wicks to remind us that some things are worse than getting killed. Harry had played cricket and football for the village, and was just out of his apprenticeship as a saddler when the war began. At the armistice party he sat drooling while his mother tried to feed him, half-crazed and as near paralysed as made no difference.

In December, the Christmas party was merrier. We wanted to put the war behind us and the village was full of children who could not remain depressed for long. This was the party when Chris and I went across the green to Granny Paley's, and by then my worst fears about work had been fulfilled.

The bleak discomfort of labouring on the ridge in winter at a time when nearly everything still depended on brute muscle, was indescribable. Others seemed to adjust to it but I never did, although I toughened up. The fact is, I did not want to become accustomed to it. I wanted to write poetry, design buildings, be a scholar, anything rather than that. It did not matter that I had no talent for poetry, and probably precious little for designing buildings either; I thirsted to stretch my mind and did not know how to begin. So I imagined I might become a poet.

Chris became very impatient with me, but we didn't quarrel in any final way until nearly two years had passed and I was dreading the onset of my third winter labouring at Newhouse Farm. We were on our way to Riffield Fair, pushing borrowed bikes up the shoulder of Tisbury Hill. Except during harvest, Saturday afternoons were free, so Chris and I usually went somewhere together. By Locock wagon to Tunbridge Wells, or maybe for a walk to Park Lake. Best of all were fairdays. There was a market in Riffield every Saturday, but four times a year this developed into a fair which went on all day. Young people from all around would gather there, watching quickfire bargainings, eating toffee apples or hot potatoes, drinking beer and trying their hand at the sideshows.

On this occasion, I was thinking about winter coming round yet again with nothing changed when Chris suddenly exclaimed, 'You used to be fun, Johnnie, and now you're just a sulky bear. I wish I'd gone with Vic Hawkins instead of you.'

'If that's how you feel, then I wish you had,' I snapped.

'Gosh, that just shows how touchy you've become! I

didn't because I wanted to come with you, but all you've done is gloom.'

'I haven't.'

'Oh yes, you have. At least Vic would take trouble to see I'm enjoying myself, *and* he makes me laugh.'

'Anything else he's good at? Let's hear some more about how wonderful Vic Hawkins is.' I knew damned well it was my fault the day was going wrong. Vic was two years older than I, splendidly male and with a temper to match.

'All right, I will. He's wonderful at cricket and at Saturday night hops in the schoolroom. All the girls simply swoon if he asks them to dance.'

'Including you.' I had thought Chris enjoyed coming to the hops with me.

'Of course including me.'

'What do you mean by that?'

'What should I mean? Except I'm sick of you mooning about, saying you don't want to be a farm labourer! You are one, aren't you? So why not get on with it like the rest, and then have fun when you've finished work?'

'I want to have fun, only—'

She squeezed my arm with one of those sudden changes of mood which made her so endearing. 'Don't, Johnnie. Don't be unhappy. I hate to see you unhappy.'

It was then, when I should have accepted her eager generosity and been thankful, that the real quarrel came. Point-blank, I asked her: 'Chris, do you like me? Really, I mean.' I was fourteen years old, which I suppose is some excuse.

She didn't answer at once, and that hurt. When she did she meant to be flippant, but her words ruptured all my ridiculous pride. 'What I really like is watching Vic's face when I go with you instead of him. All the other girls come running if he so much as snaps his fingers.'

'Then perhaps that's what you'd better do, too.'

'Oh, I don't want to!' she answered blithely, but the damage was done. After that, the space between our bicycles widened with each step we took up the hill.

I saw Vic as soon as we arrived at Riffield, hurling coconuts and surrounded by his cronies. 'There he is if you want to go.'

'Oh, Johnnie, you are difficult. I only prefer Vic if you sulk all the time. If you would only enjoy yourself then I shall too. Is that so hard?'

I tried, I really tried to recover from the self-pity into which I had plunged myself, because I knew the causes of it had nothing to do with her. But I failed. With our arms no longer linked, we wandered speechless through the raucous fair until, inevitably, we came face to face with Vic.

'Hullo, Chris,' he said, black hair curling and eyes spoiling for a fight.

'Hullo,' she answered and tossed her plaits in the way she did when she was pleased or angry. This time she was pleased.

'Enjoying yourself?'

'Of course. I love fairs, don't you?'

His teeth flashed. 'I think I'm going to enjoy this one.'

'Vic won a shilling wrestling with a pig,' chipped in Tim Huggett.

'Gosh, Vic, you must be strong.' Chris squeezed his arm, laughing, while he struck an attitude, biceps bulging beneath his coat.

'There's a tug of war soon, and Furnace Green is taking on all comers, aren't we, you fellows?' Vic's grin took in everyone except me.

Chris clapped. 'We'll come and cheer! Where is it to be?'

As brazen as the Devil, Vic took her hand and tucked it under his arm. 'Of course you're coming. We wouldn't win if you weren't there.'

I stood like a ninny while they all swept away together through the throng, laughing and shoving and leaving a great many angry looks behind them. Chris glanced over her shoulder once, laughing too, and waved. Later she said she was telling me to follow, but that wasn't how it looked. A gesture rather, of loyalty transferred.

I don't know how long I stared after her, thinking about all the impossible ways in which I would show her I was better than Vic. Eventually so many people barged into me that I began to wander in search of somewhere I could skulk unseen. If I returned home early I should only have to face questions I didn't care to answer.

At the far end of the fair there was a row of seedy stalls with scarcely anyone about them. Chris loved bustle, so we had never gone so far when we were together. I turned irresolutely, and as I did so glimpsed what looked like a heap of furniture. Never dreaming that the next few paces would be the most important of my life, I strolled over to look at whatever was there, more out of a desire to stay away from crowds than any particular curiosity. The heap was indeed furniture, but behind the cupboards and chairs was a pile of books. I spread some of these out on a table, feeling excitement begin to flow. I had never seen books like these before, thick volumes in tooled leather bindings, though spotted with mildew and curled by damp.

A board announced that these were threepence and fourpence each: I counted eightpence into the stallkeeper's hand, with which I had intended to treat Chris to porter and hot chestnuts before we went home, grabbed two fourpenny volumes and fled.

I stopped under a napptha flare to inspect what I had bought: a complete poems of Keats and something in Latin, I discovered. I hesitated over whether I dared go back and ask to change this last for an author I could understand, but decided against it. It was something to buy a book in Latin, after all.

All that week I was drunk on Keats and work passed in a blur. By Friday, the only thing I could think of was whether that stall came each week to Riffield or only once a quarter to the fair.

Looking back, my mood seems very strange. I refused to think of Chris at all, books taking over the space which previously she had occupied in my imaginings. I would have been excited over finding so many books if we could have gone together to inspect them; as it was, all my desires were poured into impatience for a return to that stall each week.

The next Saturday I fairly raced home to sluice off by the pump, and within minutes was riding Mark's bicycle like a maniac for Riffield.

The stall was there. Mr Grace, the owner, nodded when I spread the books out again. 'You look as if you like reading those old things.'

I assured him fervently that I did.

'Well, I don't. I've a good mind to burn the lot.'

'Oh, I wouldn't do that,' I said anxiously. 'Anyone would want to read books like these.'

'They don't, and that's a fact. I'll make a bonfire of them one day, you see if I don't.' He glanced at the three I had chosen with this week's shilling, all I possessed after paying the other seven over to my mother. 'You're just wasting your money, young shaver.'

'I'll be back next week. You don't really mean to burn them, do you?'

He grinned. 'I clear out houses, see? Sometimes I have to take books if I'm to get the pieces I want, but take my word for it, books is hell to sell. These came in that cupboard over there, and a damned bad buy it was, too. But I daresay I won't burn them yet awhile.'

The following Saturday I was back again and this time selected four threepenny volumes entitled *Great Authors of the World*. They were falling to pieces but inside was a vast range of writing. Chaucer, for instance, of whom I had never heard. It was out of these volumes that I learned for the first time that behind the great English writers lay an endless procession of others, all the way back to Greece and Rome. I fingered the Latin book I had bought and the other my mother rescued from Hill Grange hearth; I had never thought the Romans might actually have written things I would find interesting.

I read and read that winter, dilapidated old books spread flat on the kitchen table to catch a gleam from the lamp, fingers stuffed in my ears. I scarcely went into Furnace Green any more, whether to avoid Chris or keep from squandering precious pence I am not sure. My mind obstinately closed to Chris, although I could quite well have read what I wanted and also walked out with her on a Sunday afternoon. One day I would show her and Vic and everyone . . . There my dreams stopped short. I did not know what I could show them, and so stayed shut up in my books.

Mr Grace continued to go to sales, usually returning with a cartload of junk. He never minded my grubbing among chipped china and kitchen pans; long before the next spring came we were quite friendly even though he thought me barmy over books.

One Saturday I was rummaging through an old chest and came on a mouldy satchel. Inside were some old school books, in Latin. There was a dictionary, some prose and poetry, a child's history of Rome, and a grammar. All were scribbled over with tags and gobbets of translation, as if Latin had given the original owner a great deal of trouble. The grammar was the most dog-eared of the lot, its end-boards missing, all the exercises scrawled with notes. Everything except the binding seemed to be there, though, and I turned the browned pages in rising excitement. Scholars knew Latin; real scholars, like the masters at the grammar school where I'd wanted so much to go. To know Latin would be a huge step towards the shining heights of knowledge which I sensed were all around me, if only I could see them. It was this sense of frustration which had turned me into such an impossible companion. Certainly I loved books and always would, but my ostentatious reading was, above all, a symbol of ambition.

I learned *mensa* by heart that very night and felt too excited to sleep afterwards. Instead I lay and whispered it again and again to the room, while Mark snored beside me. I had mastered the first declension! Nobody in Furnace Green, except perhaps the vicar, now knew as much Latin as I did. Here I felt a qualm and considered the people inhabiting Greenview House and Hill Grange. Some of them might know Latin. But I soon cheered up; big-house people didn't really count.

After that I began praying for a late spring. Once I had to work twelve or fourteen hours a day I would be too tired to learn anything after my tea. But even when the spring work started, I toiled slowly on: repeating declensions and conjugations to the rhythm of the crops and in the evenings attempting paragraphs of translation. Often I felt very close to my bewildered predecessor and blessed his crib-notes in the margin, but now my yearnings were harnessed to something definite, time ceased to seem meaningless. Instead my self-respect began positively to glow, which must have been quite as tiresome as my previous gloom.

'What are you going to do with this stuffy old rubbish, I'd like to know?' demanded my sister Florence perhaps eighteen months later, on her Sunday out from service at Greenview House.

'I do it because I want to,' I answered grandly. 'It's what scholars learn.'

'But why? Why frowst over some language you'll never speak, when you could be playing cricket or ferreting like the rest?'

'Because I have to start somewhere,' I shouted, goaded. 'I suppose you're another who thinks I ought to be content to follow a horse down a furrow day after day and sleep like a log at night?' Which was horribly rude, considering that was exactly what Mark and my father did.

'Better things to do at night than sleep,' Mark observed.

'You'll wash your mouth out with soap same as you did at ten years old, if you go hinting dirty things,' my mother said sharply. 'Why shouldn't John learn Latin if he wants? He's not doing any harm that I can see, and it keeps him out of trouble.'

Mark had been taken up by the constable for being drunk two weeks before. 'Call it keeping out of trouble if you like, but they're saying John's moonstruck down in the village. Close as a miser with his pence and talking out loud to himself in the fields. If you had his interests straight, you'd order him into the Dyer's Arms come Saturday night.'

'I'm sure I don't want any brother of mine driven off in an asylum cart.' Florence was sharp in everything: nose, words and starched bodice.

'What a horrible, untrue thing to say!' My other sister, Sally, grabbed my hand. Sally was closest to me in age and could be relied on to see such virtues as I possessed. 'I think he should come and ask Mr Bond's advice.'

'Why?'

'Because he's a scholar too. You never saw so many books as he has in his study. It takes all morning to dust just half of them.' Sally was in service at the vicarage.

'I'm sure the reverend would just love to bandy scholar talk with Mr French's farmboy,' scoffed Mark. 'Besides, John really reads his books. Vicar looks as if he'd be happiest with a handkerchief over his face.'

Actually, even Florence was quite proud that I read so many books, and Mark amazingly good-tempered over the clutter in our room. In Furnace Green at that time a family's worth was weighed in two ways: by respectability, and by their ability to keep other people's noses out of their affairs. Naturally, everyone tried hard to poke them in, as you did into theirs, the game played all the more earnestly because it was so difficult to keep anything really private. So on the one hand my family swanked discreetly about my learning, on the other they protected my activities as best they could from prying eyes, a proceeding which invested a perfectly ordinary desire for knowledge with the trappings of necromancy.

'Well, does the vicar ever open his books?' I asked after a pause. I dearly wanted someone to tell me whether my studies were futile; scribbled notes were all very well for helping with the easy stuff, but I had now embarked on the book I had bought which was written in Latin, and was finding it difficult indeed.

'Of course he does! Sometimes he stays hours and hours

in his study all alone.' Like everyone else, Sally enjoyed boasting about her employers if she could.

'Like I said, I reckon he's asleep,' said Mark sceptically. 'He certainly isn't writing sermons.'

We all laughed, although Mum pretended to look shocked. Mr Bond gave short pithy sermons on such matters as manners, not swearing, and polishing your boots. I daresay he was afraid of preaching over the heads of a rustic congregation, but we got the impression that providing we took our caps off promptly to God, there was no serious obstacle to entering Heaven.

'I don't know,' Mum said thoughtfully. 'Is it worth a try, do you think, Sal?'

'Anything you want enough is worth a try,' answered Sally promptly.

I pushed back my chair. 'I'm not a prize bull to be exhibited to the vicar.'

'Well, Father?' My mother ignored me.

Dad rasped his thumbs along his jaw. 'Aye, Mother. You'll know what to do for the best, I daresay.'

Which was perfectly true, so while he went off to his evening milking, Mum and Sally put their heads together and the upshot of it was that Sally would choose a favourable moment to consult the vicar about my Latin.

'What is Sally going to say?' I asked uneasily.

'He's the vicar, isn't he? Put in a vicarage especially to help people like the Good Book says? Well, you've worked and worked at that dratted old Latin and I'd be a poor mother if I didn't make a push to get you a chance to ask whether there's an ounce of good to be had out of it,' answered Mum inexorably.

'What good can come out of addling brains?' Florence settled her cloak on her shoulders in quick angry swipes.

Mum and I exchanged glances, and I was the one who looked away. Some weeks before she had asked much the same question, but gently. And I had answered that I supposed there wasn't any good in it, except the little I could achieve for myself. Boys who left village schools even earlier than the legal age had no chance of trying for a university, although I thought some scholarships existed.

University.

It had slipped out without my thinking, the dream of my heart. I knew it for a dream, but had seen Mum grow instantly thoughtful as she began to plan. Mum was the ultimate connoisseur of plans; no effort spared to achieve the unlikely, a lifetime devoted to fixing the impossible. Sometimes she planned things for pure fun, more often out of necessity. It had taken her half a year to trap Harry Field, the builder, into repairing our roof at Edenham in return for half a pig.

It didn't matter that Mum was uncertain precisely what going to university meant; she perceived that this was what I desired so much that I scarcely dared to put my longing into words. Considering it afterwards, I was almost sure she had arranged beforehand with Sally what she must say that night at tea; Sally was warm-hearted but would not herself have realized that the vicar's books might help me.

The next Sunday when Sally came home, she was bursting with news. 'Mr Bond says you may go to see him tomorrow night at eight o'clock sharp, John. When I said you were trying to learn Latin and had become somewhat stuck—'

'I'm not stuck!'

'If you aren't, why do you want to see him?'

'It wasn't my idea to go crawling off to anyone, vicar or not,' I said, very much put out.

'It must have been difficult for Sally to explain anything properly when she was meant to be getting on with her work,' Mum interrupted firmly. 'I hope you said John could come any evening which suited the reverend.'

If the visit had been arranged by anyone less strong-willed than my mother I wouldn't have gone, because going to the vicar felt to me like begging, but Mum wouldn't let me off the hook she had baited. Mark lent me a jacket which was newer than mine but fitted nowhere, Mum starched my best shirt until it crackled, Sally rubbed my cap with breadcrumbs and stuffed the peak with newspaper before she went back that night. Between them all, I lost the chance to refuse to go.

All day Monday I was in trouble. I don't blame Mr French for being angry, the wonder is he didn't sack me on the spot. Crop prices were plummeting and his anxious care for the farm during the prosperous war years was beginning to run to waste again, and there was I, harnessing the horses wrong and leaving as much as a pint in each udder at evening milking! But I couldn't think of anything except eight o'clock in the vicarage, although what I hoped for I'm not sure.

Evening came at last and in plenty of time for me to wash and change, with the season drawing on towards winter again. I remember my mother and father standing in Edenham doorway, silently watching me walk off up the lane: I don't know what they hoped for either.

When I reached the street there were quite a few people about, it being the time when women went to sit by each other's firesides and the men walked down to the Dyer Arms. I had become such a stranger there that several of them stopped to ask questions, but I was good at the game of keeping curiosity unsatisfied and they didn't get anything out of me.

Then I walked smack into Chris at the corner by the shop, where I needed to cross to the vicarage gate. 'Johnnie! Wherever have you been hiding? I haven't seen you for an age.'

'You could have, if you'd come any evening to Edenham.'

'As if I would, without being asked! I kept thinking you'd come up the street to call, but you never did.'

'I expect you did better on your own with Vic,' I answered nastily. She looked more grown up, but nothing else had changed. She still wrung my heart just by standing there looking joyful.

'Oh, Johnnie, you are a–a *snake* sometimes! Why shouldn't I walk out with Vic or anyone else if I choose?'

'No reason at all.'

'There you are then. Let's be friends again and I'll walk out with you as well. I've missed you. There, what an admission! I went to Granny Paley's last week and she seemed awfully cross you hadn't been to see her either. Spoke of whipping black hounds after the scent your spirit left, which sounds perfectly horrid.'

'Why did you go?' I interrupted, hoping very much she'd gone on the offchance of finding me there.

'Mother heard she'd been ill and sent me with a basket of groceries from the shop. And do you know, Johnnie, she wasn't in the least bit grateful! Just kept mumbling on about black hounds and having more to tell you before she died. Though if you ask me, she's lucky she hasn't suffocated already in the stink she keeps in that hut.'

I shrugged, bitterly disappointed. 'She won't die before she wants to. As it is, she makes me trudge up there a dozen times before I can piece together a single fragment of what really happened here long ago. She could easily say it straight out in a single telling.'

'I expect she's lonely.'

Time had been so lacking for me for so long, my eyes often closing as Latin and interest in the ridge's past fought exhaustion after work, that it had simply never occurred to me that a witch could be lonely.

Chris and I stared at each other in light spilled from the shop's lamps, thinking about loneliness.

'Gosh, Johnnie, you're pale. Is anything the matter?'

It was on the tip of my tongue to tell her the momentous reason why I had come up to the village, the feeling that tonight anything might happen, but I didn't. 'No, of course not. What could there be?'

'Well, I don't know. I just thought there might be something.' She linked her arm in mine. 'This is a stupid conversation, isn't it? Why don't you come in for a while? We're putting up the shutters any time now. Did you know

I was going to be apprenticed to a milliner in Tunbridge Wells, and live in with the family all week?'

I shook my head.

'It's a tremendous chance for me, because my aunt in London says milliners are ever so well paid up there. When I'm trained, I can lodge with her and earn a fortune making hats for swells. I'll be famous and all the gentlemen will make clandestine appointments to meet their ladyloves in my shop.' She pirouetted on tiptoe button boots.

It was perhaps typical of my priggishness that my first reaction should be to reflect that the only books Chris read must be penny novelettes, and it showed. My second was no less disastrous, because I took her by the shoulders and shook her. 'Don't you dare talk like—like—'

'Yes?' she said, all stiff in my hands. 'Like what, exactly?'

'A conniving madam,' I answered proudly. I had recently been reading Thackeray and the phrase rolled agreeably off my tongue.

'Oh!' Two angry spots of colour burned in her cheeks. 'You don't need to tell me what that means because I can guess. I'm not a green girl any longer.'

'After such a long time walking out with Vic, I never supposed you were.'

'Go away! I'll never, never forgive you for saying such hateful things. As it happens, Vic plans to train as a mechanic and then enlist in the Air Force, so put that in your pipe and smoke it. He really means to amount to something. I'll enjoy walking out with a handsome airman in a year or so.'

'Oh, I'm going,' I said, feeling sick. Not only because everything I'd said was unforgivable, but because I'd remembered the vicar. God knew how far after eight o'clock it must be by now. 'I'm not interested in competing with swells in a milliner's shop, nor with Vic for that matter. I'm following my own way. One day—' I hesitated: one day, next day, some time, never. All my earlier hopes had vanished; I couldn't see my way heading very far, nor many chances along it to outbid Airman Vic.

Chris tossed her head. 'You go where you like. I'm sure I don't care if I never see you again.'

'Thanks very much for telling me.' Dignity trembled but stayed in its place until after I had scuttled away, the church clock striking the half hour as I passed. But, late or not, I had to stop and scrub my eyes on Mark's jacket sleeve before I was in any state to knock on the vicarage back door.

Sally opened it. 'Wherever have you been? Mr Bond's as angry as can be at being kept waiting.'

She did not wait for an answer, fairly racing me up stairs and through baize doors until we reached the vicar's study.

'Enter!' he bellowed in answer to Sally's knock, and she thrust me inside. What with Chris and the first big house I had ever stepped inside, my wits by then were completely scattered.

Mr Bond was a heavy man with greying hair and fierce features, usually made more forbidding by an inquisitorial stare. He reminded me of an engraving in my Latin grammar of one of the later Roman emperors.

'You're late!' he shouted, before the door had shut behind me. 'Take off your cap!'

I whipped it off. 'I'm very sorry, sir. I thought I left home in plenty of time.'

'Think? Think? What's the use of that? You need to be sure, don't you?'

'Yes, sir.' I was damned if I was going to explain.

'Well, never mind that now. I've wasted enough time this evening. Tell me what it is you want.'

It was not a tone of voice which suggested willingness to listen to anything I said, but I possessed a temper too. If he had been kind, probably I would only have managed some routine questions about the more baffling aspects of Latin grammar. As it was, awed by the size of the vicarage, torn by anger and desperation over Chris, I asked him point-blank whether there was any way a boy of my background might reach university.

'What makes you think you merit a place at a university?'

'I don't know whether I do or not. I want to try if it is possible.'

We stared at each other across a polished circular table like duellists measuring blades, then he took his pipe from his mouth and tapped out the dottle in the grate. 'Well, now. Tell me why you think trying would be worthwhile.'

I wasn't sure whether he meant what hope had I of getting in, or what possible use could a university be to the likes of me. 'I don't know anything about it except that universities are there, and I would give anything to go.'

Would I give up Chris? I wondered fleetingly. But she was no longer mine to set in the balance.

'Hm. Sally told me some mish-mash about you reading books, some of them in Latin. Is that true?'

'Yes, sir.'

He thumped the table with a roar. 'Don't dare play games with me! What good is yes sir, may I ask? Inform me, pray, about the books you read.'

So I plunged into telling him about the books I'd found at Riffield market, although I couldn't have begun to describe what finding them had meant to me. I was also nervous about naming which ones I liked best in case I revealed poor judgement, but when I mentioned Chaucer he interrupted fast enough. 'You've read Chaucer in the original?'

'I think so, sir,' I said cautiously. I read Chaucer how he was in the book, some of whose rhythms were not too different from Granny Paley's sing-song.

'You understand it?'

I bit on the retort that I wouldn't waste time on it if I didn't. 'Mostly, sir.'

He got up to fetch a copy of the *Canterbury Tales*, and asked me to read a passage as if it was modern English. When I finished, he started questioning me about the Latin, looking very sceptical when I said I'd learned as much as I could from an old grammar I'd found among some junk.

His questions were simple at first, and since I had learned that one book of grammar practically by heart I answered them fluently enough. Then he wrote some sentences and sat me down at the table to translate them. He was definitely interested by now and I could feel my heart begin to beat like a kettledrum in hope. His face looked meditative rather than fierce while he read what I'd written and paused, pipestem tapping his teeth.

Now, I thought. The real test is coming.

He went to the bookshelves again and took down a volume while I watched every movement. Books covered three walls of the study and I believed Sally now, when she said that Mr Bond was a scholar. He flicked over a few pages before deciding on a passage. 'There is some Caesar in this grammar of yours, you say. See what you can make of this.'

It was the passage in which Caesar tells how he crossed the Rubicon and so settled his future for ever. I think Mr Bond fancied using it as my Rubicon, too; if I could do this, he would take me seriously.

Between one breath and the next, the seed of hope within me put out shoots, tendrils, a jungle of green leaves. All I had to do was convince him that I had accomplished something and possessed the capacity to do more. Then he would help me. Suddenly I was so excited that sentences were impossible to form, my translation horribly bald and crude. In my eagerness to impress, everything came out wrong.

'Take it quietly, there's no hurry.' His voice was cool but for the first time I felt he actually wanted me to succeed.

Gradually, gradually I fumbled my words into some kind of order, until I finished the paragraph.

He made no comment but stood for a while looking first at the Caesar and then at what I had written. The lamp on his desk lit the two of us, the book in his hand and a section of table. It is sixty years ago now, but I remember tooled leather, polished wood, the blue veins on Mr Bond's hands, as if it was last week.

He sighed. 'I owe you an apology, John. I thought you were boasting to gain attention, but I was wrong. Sit down again and let us see where we can go from here.'

My fate had changed.

I left the vicarage with every thought in my head shaken loose and rearranged.

I was to leave my job at Newhouse Farm and come to work in the vicarage garden. This was so that I should have money to take home, yet be on hand whenever Mr Bond had time to tutor me. He also said I could use an old saddlery room for study once I had finished whatever wanted doing in the garden. 'Mind you don't skimp the carrots for Catullus, nor Catullus for carousing,' were his parting words to me. 'It will be slavery for the next two or three years if you are to succeed.'

As if I cared!

Mr Bond had attended Durham University and he knew of some scholarships there which were open to all comers. I would have to master Greek as well as Latin and a great deal else, but if I possessed the gift for classics he professed to perceive in me, then in two years' time I could be ready to sit for one of these.

Perhaps the best way to describe my state of mind is to say that I passed Portnell's shop on my way home without thinking of Chris. The golden city of Hope had appeared at my feet with all its gates wide open, and briefly I could see nothing else.

Back at Edenham I faced a fusillade of questions.

'I'm going to work for Mr Bond,' I announced, as nonchalantly as I could.

'Is that all?' Mum looked so disappointed that I relented, nor could I have kept the grin off my face much longer. 'He's going to tutor me when he has time, and in two or three years he thinks I could try for a scholarship to Durham University.'

'Why, little brother,' drawled Mark, and punched me in the ribs. 'Now you'll be able to take a whole day instead of just an evening over deciding which line a word should go in.'

'And the next whole day to change the order back again,' I retorted, and punched him back, laughing.

That was how it was from then on.

I no longer gloomed or sulked, and almost ran to work in the morning. The job in the vicarage garden was quite hard because Mrs Bond liked everything just so, but the vicar coached me for at least two hours every day and to the devil with the flower-beds.

For the first time in my life I had a room of my own to study in and a goal I desired with all my heart. Even so, there was so much I did not know, which other scholarship boys would have learned by instinct, that I only stopped working when the lamp-oil ran out. To tell the truth, I didn't like Greek much and even Latin lost some of its lure once it became only one of many things I possessed of my own. But if Latin and Greek were the keys to university, then a classicist I would be. Naturally I never asked him, but I suspect that Mr Bond could not have tutored me to a sufficient standard in anything else. To him, the classics were all and he spared no effort once he believed he had discovered a reflection of his zeal in me. He charged nothing for his tutoring, and paid me more than I was worth as gardener's boy. I owe him more than I can say.

Chris soon vanished to her apprenticeship in Tunbridge Wells and only returned home on Sundays, when it wasn't too difficult to avoid each other in church. In many ways I was relieved about this. Realistically, I could not compete for her affections while I lacked even an hour to call my own, when more often than not I was exhausted. I did not want to quarrel, nor be defeated by Vic Hawkins again, so I put her on one side until I might be better placed. But because in all of that two years I never walked out with another girl, Chris seemed more desirable than ever to me.

Granny Paley was a different matter. For a while I

completely forgot her. Then, it must have been about nine months after I started work at the vicarage, Miss Wicks, the parish busybody, stopped me on my way home. 'Granny Paley is asking for you. She's taken mortal bad, so you'd better haste off quickly unless you want to be ill-wished.'

'She's been taken bad every winter since I can remember.' I felt pretty ashamed about neglecting her all the same—I'd been hungry enough for her tales when I needed them.

'She's a deader this time,' answered Miss Wicks with relish. 'I've seen a-plenty like her in my time and mark my words, she won't last another week.'

I decided to go straight away, Chris's comment that Granny had been lonely rather than a witch scraping away at the back of my mind. Her hut stank even worse than I remembered, the atmosphere enough to kill an ox, let alone a frail old woman. There was no fire and Granny lay under a single blanket on a dirty feather mattress. She had nothing. Nothing at all, except that mattress and blanket, some bread and an empty bowl in which someone had brought her some soup. Nowadays it's difficult for even the poorest of us to imagine owning nothing.

'Hullo, Granny,' I said awkwardly.

'Ah, the Smith boy at last,' she said with satisfaction.

'Have you got an axe? I'll go and find some dry wood for kindling.'

'Nay, you stay where you are. I got things to tell you which won't wait.'

'I'd come back—'

'Stay where you are, I said!' Her voice was thick, but strong. 'My black hounds had trouble hunting you down, you were that took up wi' quibbling things. Now you've come they'll take your soul between their teeth and not let go until I say.'

I can't describe how she said it, conjuring dread out of darkness, stench and ancient mysteries. Though my brain had become overstuffed with classical rationality my blood still answered hers, our kin had lived too long together on the ridge for it to be otherwise. Somewhere, somewhen, her ancestors would have lain with mine. Larkworthy, Sleech, Wyse, Fawkner, Laffam, Carpenter, Smith and Parleyben. The old 'uns of the ridge were a single breed, and because of it Granny could curse me if she wished.

She cackled. 'Come where I can see you.'

I knelt beside her mattress.

'You've been fair addled by them books, haven't you? I can't read books. Never could. I don't hold with 'em.'

'Your memory is like a book,' I said.

'Aye, once get addled by writings and you don't have a memory no more. Not so it stretches back and back until things your great grandma said were as if you'd done 'em yourself. You like them books of yours?'

'I like the doors they open, as your tales open others.'

'Aye, open doors if you must, but beware of what you find inside. But there, you won't shake off your generations as easy as you think.'

No, I haven't shaken off the ridge, nor wanted to. Here I am, standing in Edenham kitchen by the same oak table where I learned my first declension, dictating this book which is Granny Paley's as much as mine. My own memory also much improved because, like her, I now must speak instead of write.

'Nosey Wicks said you wanted to see me,' I ventured, when Granny seemed about to doze.

She gave a gasping laugh. 'Ratty Wicks we called her ma, a-burrowing and a-craftying where she weren't wanted. Aye, I wanted to see you, when tomorrow I'll be done. 'Tis strange to be nearly dead when my memory's as alive as ever was. But now I must hand it on to you, because there's no one else. I had a son once, did you know?'

I shook my head.

'I can't remember who fathered him, but I loved him

and he went. Lots of us Parleybens went off but others always stayed. Now I'm the last, so there it is. Are you listening?'

And while I knelt in mud with my bones turning cold, Granny used the last of her strength to tell me everything she thought she might have forgotten to say before. No striving this time for effect, no sly tricks, no tantalising breaks. She hadn't long to go and spent each breath telling such truth as she knew. Only when she spoke about the Hosmers did I interrupt. 'The vicar has a fine map of Sussex in his hall, signed by a Joseph Hosmer.'

'Poor diddly Joe,' she snuffled a laugh. 'He wed a gurt besom of a wife after he were near-blinded by the smugglers. Yes, midear; no, midear; three bags full, midear. His life weren't his own no more. So he sat in a corner all good as gold at Danesdell, and fancied-up maps line by line, a-squinnying out of a good corner in his eye. Fine stuff they were, the few he finished.'

The map which Mr Bond had in his vicarage then, now hangs on my wall, those later Hosmer maps so beautifully engraved that they are much sought by collectors. Joseph, I suppose, is Furnace Green's most famous son, if such an idea has any meaning, but at the time when Granny first told me about him all I could find to ask about was the church. Joseph had marked each village with a tiny sketch and Furnace Green, naturally, was the most lovingly drawn of all. And its church had a spire instead of the tower I knew.

'Aye, a fine vainglorious spire we had and no mistake,' she answered unhesitatingly. 'The monk who built it were a vainglorious man, who tried but failed to kill his pride. Me, I like a man with pride. And he fought for them as needed to be fought for.'

As in his way Mr Bond was fighting for me, I reflected: I was and was not a believer, am and am not a Christian. Granny wasn't religious at all, although on acrimoniously familiar terms with a great many spirits. Nevertheless, her tales were filled with the church's many-sided gifts and oppressions, because without them the ridge would have been an unimaginably different place.

'Rest for a while and finish later,' I said when her breath began to rattle.

'Nay . . . nay, there's a long cold rest a-waiting for me, and I'm not hasting to meet it. Tell me, what make of day is it?'

'It's night. The kind of moonlit night where the stars lie close above the ridge.'

'Ah, I'd a-liked to see it all once more,' she whispered.

'I could carry you out, but—'

'What do I care if it kills me? Go out good, that's what I'd like. A lusty young fellow a-holding me in his arms and . . . the promise of spring a-leaping in my blood.' She wheezed laughter through stumps of teeth.

Her brittle bones seemed little heavier than a plough-horse's nosebag when I picked her up, stooped through the doorway and stood beside the pool while she lay with her grey hair snaking across my shoulder. A half moon soared between bright edged clouds, everything below part-dim, part-silver. Houses huddled colourless, the rutted road trying to shine, heaped shadows making familiarity strange.

'The oak is down,' said Granny.

'It's been down as long as I can remember, and not much left before it fell.'

Her head moved against my shoulder. 'Be naught but ill-wishing, once the ridge is left without its oak.'

I thought of forty-two names on our war memorial; of Mr French at Newhouse already ruined by plunging prices, as most farmers were as soon as England no longer needed them. Since the oak fell perhaps the ridge hadn't known much luck.

'The pool . . . what's happened to the pool?'

Was it really so long since she'd left her hut, or had her mind reached so far into the past that she'd forgotten the changes during her lifetime? 'It seems to be leaking, I don't know why. They're talking of running a drain from the road to top it up.'

Her lips puckered as if she wanted to spit, but almost immediately her eyes wandered and she gazed and gazed out over the gulf beyond the ridge, where our splendid sweep of windy country rolled away into the night.

I was just beginning to think she was heavier than I had thought, when suddenly she shifted, flung wide an arm. 'They've gone, they've gone! Cocks will lay eggs afore my hounds come back again.' She grunted at the look on my face. 'Lucky for you I told 'em to ease their teeth out of your spirit afore they went. They'll find another mistress, never fear, while there's witches still in Sussex.'

And though of course I didn't believe in witches, I felt the skin roach up along my spine, as if black hounds still loitered very close.

''Tis beautiful. Real beautiful, but I'm cold without my hounds,' she added dreamily. 'I'd like to jump and run over the green like I used to, that I would.' And in my arms her breathing changed into the long gasps broken by full stops and commas I remembered from the time my Aunt Daisy died.

It's a good way to die, remembering how you jumped and ran as a child. I was glad that at her end, this was what seemed most important to Granny Paley, not the black hounds of loneliness.

My only other memory of those years belongs to the time just before I was due to sit for my scholarship. I had been studying late at the kitchen table while my father dozed by the hearth. Mark had recently married and my mother was out by the bedside of a woman in long labour. My eyes kept closing; only three weeks to go. I could not imagine the enormous spaces in my life when the need for helter-skelter study in every spare moment was gone. Tawny light from a late June sunset splashed high on the wall above my head, a gauze of dust-motes dancing in its rays. I sat back, sighing. I could not make sense of any more Greek tonight.

'Time we went up,' said Dad, bones creaking as he stood. Dad didn't talk much. He was a provider, and he was kind. He got up at half past four every morning instead of a quarter to five, so he could make up the fire for us before he left, and never in my life did I hear him say a malicious or ungenerous thing. He dug the garden after he came home from working a thirteen-hour day, and now, at nearly sixty years old, he had only rheumatics and a tiny pension to look forward to. I was the youngest of eight children, six of whom had lived past infancy, and between us we had sucked every spare penny from his wage.

I stood too. 'If I get a scholarship . . . Afterwards I should be able to get a good job and see you and Mum all right.'

'I'll look forward to that.' He smiled, but I knew I'd be lucky to slip much help past his pride.

We were not a demonstrative family, but that night I felt the need to go over and stand close to him, and I'm glad.

'Promise me one thing,' he said suddenly.

'If I can.'

'If you get this scholarship, don't ever feel too grand to use your hands. I know farmwork is not for you, but if I could choose again I'd say, Give me the fields of Ferenthe Ridge and let me tend the creatures there.'

'I hope I shall feel as content as you do when the time comes for me to look back,' I answered. Even then, I understood that doubt would never be far away once I lived a different life from my kin, whereas my father accepted certainty as his birthright.

'Aye, well, to my way of thinking there's always a catch in good fortune somewhere. But so long as it's what you want,' he hesitated. 'You won't feel awkward out there, will you, John? Suppose you're always one on your own, what then?'

'Why should I care? They study at a university, and I

want to study. I can get on by myself if I have to.' After all, my life at Furnace Green hadn't exactly been full of friends. 'Don't worry, Dad. I shall find my way by one means or another now.'

'Good,' he said and went up to bed, his mind at rest. He had felt worried and liked having things out straight. Now he was satisfied that my choice had not been blinkered, whatever I did was all right by him. This was the other way I was lucky and knew it, as I said earlier. I grew up in a family which loved and cared, but also let you be.

I stayed standing by the hearth, almost too tired to drag myself upstairs. Dad was shrewd but belonged to a different world to the one I had already begun to inhabit, willy-nilly, whether I won my scholarship or not. What did it matter if people reached out by different roads? There was no reason why we should dislike each other on that account. In Furnace Green class was seldom mentioned, its constraints too obvious for remark, our community sufficiently faceted by the centuries that in practice there was little strain. Even the Dyers were considered useful, now they had sold most of the land they used to own on the ridge. We did our job and they did theirs; there were differences but little sense of inferiority when we met. The reverse in fact; we enjoyed beating them at cricket if we could. Ever since I left home I have heard more nonsense on the subject of class than on any other; I thought then, and still think now, that inferiority is in your own mind, or not, as the case may be. It wasn't going to be in mine. If others wanted to stick their noses in the air, they could. It wouldn't bother me.

I suppose I must have been more keyed up than I realized, thinking about my father's words and deciding how I felt. My toe tapping on the hearth, hands spread on the beam above, fingers drumming at fissured oak, my nail picking irritably at something I felt there; click, click; click, click. Absently, I ran my thumb across the place, feeling an edge beneath a rime of dirt. Without thinking, I picked the breadknife off the dresser and ran its point along the crack, coiling out a worm of grime. Half way along, it struck the edge I'd felt.

My attention caught, carefully I began to clear the fissure out. The oak was as hard as steel, the fissure a result of using green timber long ago. Several times I nearly gave up but whatever was in there kept shifting slightly, as if it had been taken from its hiding place before. Eventually, I had it clear: a flake of iron perhaps two and a half inches long. I rubbed it gingerly, the dirt covering it greasy rather than corroded.

As I did so I felt excitement rise, the kind of gut-twisting thrill anyone is lucky to experience once in a lifetime. I held an arrowhead. An arrowhead so old I couldn't begin to guess its age. The point was flattened, the edges crinkled and in places so thin that specks of iron stuck to my palm when I turned it. I licked my thumb and rubbed cautiously; preserved by sappy timber and subsequent grease were scratchings which might have been a maker's mark. A beast of some sort, I thought; a deer perhaps. I stared and stared at that fragment, which must already have been old when Edenham was built. Old, very old when the tree which held it was cut down to become part of this new millhouse. Old when it was shot into a sapling which grew through the centuries until a block of its timber was adzed to span a hearth.

Once upon a time . . . No, not yet. There's still a while to wait before explanations make much sense.

In the summer of my eighteenth year, I simply stood gazing at that arrowhead and felt the immensity of time through which it had already flown.

Eventually I heard my mother returning up the lane, and without hesitation slipped my find back into its hiding place, covering the marks I'd made with lamp-black. Then I snuffed the lamp and went upstairs to bed, but tired as I was I slept poorly that night, my imagination roaming as far afield as Granny's black hounds.

* * *

Three weeks later I went to sit my scholarship.

Greg Locock had started a carrier's business during the war, and he gave me a lift as far as Tunbridge Wells railway station. As shrewd as most Locks, Greg had rightly reckoned that farming would be in the dumps again as soon as the war ended; now he was prospering and not as mean with it as some other Locks I could name.

I had saved up thirteen shillings for my journey, and Mr Bond gave me five pounds out of the Braybon Fund. I think I mentioned that this was an endowment left by a former resident, to help deserving boys and girls with tools for apprenticeship and so on. 'Should General Braybon wish to argue the toss with me when we meet, he can,' said Mr Bond, looking as if he relished a duel outside the Pearly Gates. 'Meanwhile, I'm trustee of his fund and if I say university is an apprenticeship then it is, and five pounds you shall have for your fare and lodging. Times change, and I daresay Braybon would be the last man to try to hold improvement back.'

I had never seen so much money in one place before, let alone in my pocket, and kept hold of it most of the way to Durham.

This was the year 1925. Greg Locock had already given up his horses and ran three solid-tyred lorries, which rattled at a great rate along still soft-surfaced roads. I missed the slow horse pace which let you see what was going on behind the hedges as you passed, the gossipy chatter of a drover's bench, and as we swooped in minutes off the ridge I thought of all the slow toilings that steep slope had seen. Greg Locock's lorries spelled the end of old Furnace Green more surely than the war.

At first the countryside we passed in the train looked comfortingly familiar. London I found quite terrifying, and the instructions Mr Bond had written out became a lifeline from one policeman to the next. Then it was the train again and more country reeling past, flatter than the Weald until we reached Yorkshire, where everything changed at once. Although I had never previously been there, the idea of London was familiar and so I had not been surprised by its alien hugeness. I could never have imagined the industrial north, the ruin of beauty it represented. Here and there craggy hills or a stream wandering between ancient banks but choked by filth, its water black, gave some measure of vanished loveliness. As for the rest, the train steamed through a cankerous wasteland, past endless grimy rows of houses, foul drains, gaunt winding gear, heaps of spoil.

Once, these had been villages like mine, each with its own history, its individual arrow curving from then to now. Yet, however often I told myself this must be so, I found it impossible to grasp. The shock was extraordinary as within a single day I journeyed from England's ancient heritage into a world with which I had no point of contact. Many of these tenements might not necessarily be damper or darker than the cottage where I was born, what seemed so unimaginable was the desolation of spirit wrought by a prospect of unremitting squalor.

By the time the train reached York the landscape had changed again, but I was too disturbed by what I had seen to feel comforted. Then we came out of a cutting and on to a long viaduct, and there was Durham Cathedral towering above the curve of a river with a castle just beyond. I was back in a continuity I understood.

I shall not describe the kindness I found in Durham, the quadrangles and halls of its university. I was surprised not to find myself more anxious when I sat to take the examinations, considering how much was at stake. I think I believed that having come so far, I could not fail. All the blundering effort, the dreaming, and above all a handsome slice of luck, had led me here; somehow the result was in other hands than mine.

As I said before, I am and am not religious. I was also very tired, and that is how I felt.

At the end of a week I went home. Only as the train pulled out of Durham station did I begin to panic and suddenly believed I had no chance at all. How foolish to imagine that a raw South Country farmboy learning Greek and Latin on his own could compete against fellows who took education for granted! Probably I knew too little even to sense that what I wrote was wrong.

My job at the vicarage was finished. It had never been more than a way to give me time to study, and when I went off to Durham I am sure Mrs Bond was delighted by an excuse to engage someone more useful in her garden. However, harvesting was at its height and I was able to get temporary work, although the farmers were shedding permanent labour and laying down fields to pasture as depression tightened its grip.

On days when harvesting was impossible I hung about at home, time a chasm at my feet. I thought once or twice about going to search out Chris but lacked the heart for it, until word came from Durham. Perhaps people who failed scholarships never heard anything at all. Then I would have to tramp off looking for a job in a factory like those I had seen on my way north; so many chimneys must need a great many hands to stoke their fires.

At last a letter came and Mum rushed out with it to where I was helping bring in the barley. Everyone stopped work when they saw her and then went on faster than before, determined to pretend that this time they didn't intend to pry. Of course they were still watching, covertly between each pitched stook.

Mum made no such pretence, she knew how much that letter meant to me.

And so, with the scent of harvest all around, I opened the envelope and read that I had won a scholarship. Not the best, but one I could live on if I was careful. I had done it. I had broken away from the ridge, and just for a moment in Corndown's harvest field I did not know whether to be glad or forlorn. The old Furnace Green I had been born into, which had existed in many ways unchanged since Saxon times, was finished. Greg Locock's lorries and my ambitions were both part of the same grey storm-wave of change, piling higher and higher above the horizon, which soon would sweep the life we had known away. I was lucky to have lived it while its vigour remained, luckier still to have escaped circumstances to which I, John Smith of Edenham, was so unsuited.

One hand clenched on my pitchfork and the other on a letter from Durham University, the long slow curve of triumph took me by the throat.

University term began in October and meanwhile I needed to earn every penny I could, which left a single Sunday between the end of the grain harvest and the beginning of hop-picking for me to go in search of Chris.

By then she had finished her apprenticeship and become an assistant in an exclusive London milliner's. Aunt Portnell at the shop gave me the address of her lodgings, looking wistfully at the paper as she wrote; it was hard on them that she came home so seldom, since she was their only child.

I felt very knowing to be taking a Sunday excursion ticket to London just as if it was an everyday matter, and had written to Chris that I would call at her lodgings about eleven o'clock. I would have liked to surprise her but with only one day at my disposal, decided that it was foolish not to make sure she was at home. Chris must have a great many friends after living nearly a year in London. Really, it was surprising she hadn't married.

This thought had occurred to me many times before, but on that fine September Sunday jealousy began to loom closer and I spent most of the journey to London wriggling on third-class plush, thinking violently about Chris surrounded by amorous swells. Not to mention Vic Hawkins in his Air Force uniform. Considering how desperately I wanted Chris to like me, it was strange that towards her I should invariably display my least attractive traits.

The address Aunt Portnell had given me was in Tulip Street, Clapham, which took a long time to find. When I reached number thirty-one at last, I heaved at the bell-plunger like a drowning man, my heart shaking as I heard shuffling steps approach from the basement. I had hoped Chris would be on the lookout for me.

After a fear-filled pause the door opened to show a woman in her fifties, hair scraped into a bun, false teeth set into artificial gums which threatened to jump out of her mouth.

'Does a Miss Portnell lodge here?' My voice was trembling.

'That's right.' Her eyes shifted from my face to my boots and back again.

'Miss Christian Portnell?'

'Cripes, mister, it ain't such a common name as all that! Yerse, name o' Chris I 'ear blokes call 'er.'

I swallowed. 'Who call her?'

Her face crinkled in derision; she must have seen a great many lovesick youths in her life. ''Er pals. You're one of 'em, aincher? So what d'you call 'er then?'

There seemed no answer to that. 'Can I see her? I wrote . . . she ought to be expecting me.'

'Ah, mebbe she was an' mebbe she wasn't. She's gorn out, see? I thought she was waiting for summat this morning, but—' she laughed, keeking back on her heels. ''Tis too fine a day for a young leddy to spend indoors.'

'Will she be back today, do you think? This afternoon, perhaps?'

'I dunno, do I? She might and she mightn't. I'll tell 'er you called if you like.'

I left the step with such dignity as I could, crushed by disappointment. If Chris cared for me at all, surely she would have waited longer? Of course, it had taken me ages to find Tulip Street. I didn't own a watch, but it must be after midday.

I paced up and down that dingy road like a madman, hearing the quarters strike on a distant clock. One, two o'clock, and still Chris had not reappeared. A woman walked past selling roses and I bought six: I still had several harvest shillings in my pocket. I had planned to treat Chris to a hot pie in the park, to ride together in an omnibus perhaps.

Then, quite unexpectedly, she was there.

I would have known her walk anywhere; her feet always seemed to dance impatience from the time she was a child in pigtails.

'Johnnie!' she called as soon as she saw me.

'Why didn't you wait in for me? Didn't you get my letter?'

'Oh, don't be a crosspatch on such a gorgeous day! I waited and waited until I simply had to go out. Oh Johnnie, how lovely to see you again!' She stood tiptoe and kissed my nose.

Of course I forgave her instantly, presented my roses and kissed her fervently back. Not on the nose, either.

'You are a dear.' She breathed scent from the roses. 'How long have you got?'

'The last train's eleven-fifty. I can always walk home from Tunbridge Wells.'

She laughed, pirouetting in her achingly familiar way, and clapped her hands. She was wearing a smart grey coat cut daringly short and a hat which seemed to be constructed entirely out of feathers. 'Where shall we go? I can't tell you how glad I am to see you! What are you doing? Did you pass your stuffy old examination? Mother wrote you were gone somewhere in the north to take it, but that can't be right, can it?'

Her fusillade of questions peeled back my reserve, at first leaving little space for me to answer. It didn't matter. She kissed me even more warmly when I told her of my success, seeming really glad in a way I had not dared expect. Nor did she give a tinker's curse that I clumped by her side in country boots and brook-washed corduroys, while she looked as pretty as a princess.

We caught an omnibus just as I had planned and chattered all the way to Kensington Gardens; I might never have known what awkwardness or jealousy meant, and when we strolled with the other couples in the sunshine it wasn't long before her fingers linked lightly into mine. I suppose everyone cherishes one day in their lives which remains illuminated by a soft romantic glow, each detail clear. It makes no difference if subsequent events should mock romance, nor if we would prefer to remember more momentous happenings. These others fade, the fleeting instants of romance do not.

I remember that half day I spent in London with Chris as if it was yesterday. Above us the sky was a gentle autumnal blue, the crowds appeared as happy as we, even the city colours seemed soft to the touch.

'Let's go on the Serpentine,' Chris said suddenly, and we ran over the grass hand in hand, laughing when she tripped in her pale strap shoes, all the fashion then.

I had never been in a boat, and of course made a great hash of rowing while Chris tackled the hopeless task of steering. 'If you could only row both oars at once it would help,' she observed after we had described two complete circles. 'Just look at the tut-tuttery you're raising on the bank.'

I glanced to where old gentlemen sat in green deckchairs, one or two of whom were indeed beginning to regard us with derision, and missed another stroke. 'It's your fault for putting me off. How can I row when you sit there looking like—like—'

Chris crowed. 'I love really juicy compliments. Like what, exactly?'

I opened my mouth to make some clever classical allusion, but changed my mind. 'Like Chris. To me there'll never be any dearer compliment than that.'

Her eyes widened as if for the first time she considered the implications of my feelings for her. Really considered them, I mean. She had taken Johnnie Smith's admiration for granted for so long that she had ceased to think about it, even before she left Furnace Green. 'It seems an age since we went together to hear Granny Paley's tales,' she said after a pause.

'Did you know Granny had died?'

'Mother told me when she wrote, I think. I forget. I've changed, Johnnie. You'll change too, once you get away to Durham and Furnace Green doesn't matter any more.'

'I think it will always matter however far I go away.'

'But it won't! Why should it?'

I reflected, and nearly went head over heels, missing another stroke. 'Being in Durham won't change what Furnace Green made of me, only what I make of myself.'

'You wait and see. In three or four years, when you go back there for a visit, you'll look at Mark and think: gosh, I would have been like that if I hadn't got away. You'll know then that so far as you're concerned, Furnace Green is just the place where you grew up.'

'Is that how you think when you come back: gosh, look at the yokels chewing straws?'

She flushed. 'Of course not.'

'Your parents miss you.'

'And you, Johnnie, do you miss me?' she teased, trailing her fingers in the water.

But quite suddenly I was embarrassingly incapable of thinking of anything except how round and smooth were her arms, how supple the curve of back and breast; a kind of breathless fantasy uncoiling inside my brain, which prevented me from answering.

She smiled, well satisfied. 'I do try to go home if I can. The trouble is, I feel horrid before I go, because I can't help thinking of a Sunday wasted. Then, when the time comes for me to leave, they keep asking how long until I come again, which makes me feel even worse. My life is here now, and that's all there is to it.'

I rowed under a bridge, beginning to master the art of keeping my strokes together. Here willows crowded closer to the water and some ducks swam alongside. Chris flicked water at them, and then at me. 'You're getting too good at rowing already. I like to see you doing badly at something.'

'Me?' I exclaimed, astonished. 'There isn't anyone in Furnace Green worse than me at nearly everything.'

'Oh, farming,' she said dismissively. 'Who cares about trudging through mud? I mean, things that matter.'

But, oddly, though I ought to have felt proud that Chris thought me good at things that mattered, instead I was irritated that she should so easily pitch aside the whole web of complex skills whereby, after several thousand years of effort, men prospered sufficiently here and there on the globe to spare a small surplus for millinery.

Irritation did not last. As I watched her dreaming in the sunlight, eyes narrowed against reflections from the water and lips quirked in contemplation, desire, fantasy and joy fused into a single whole. I loved Chris. There would never be anyone else for me. She was self-centred and bobbed like a wren from one thing to another, but to me that was part of her charm. I loved her because I understood her, and no one else would ever understand her half so well.

'We've had our hour,' I said reluctantly at last, looking over my shoulder at the tin clock by the landing stage.

'Oh, it's so lovely here. Let's have another,' she begged.

'But if you'd like some tea—'

'Hang tea! I'm happy. Your train doesn't go till late, let's eat this evening.'

I hesitated. It had seemed to me I brought a great deal of money with me to London, but between my fare and our omnibus ride, the roses and boat hire, if we took another hour on the Serpentine then I didn't think I should have enough left to take Chris back to Clapham, let alone offer supper on the way. But I hated to admit poverty. 'This hour has been so perfect, I'd hate to spoil it. Let's go while you're happy, and before you begin to be polite.'

'Oh, I'll promise never to be polite,' she said.

'In that case I won't risk you becoming disagreeable once it gets chilly.' I pulled towards the bank while she still glowered over not winning her way, but my powers of dissimilation proved less successful than I hoped, because as soon as we were away from the landing stage, Chris invited me back to her lodgings for supper.

'Mrs Agg lets us help ourselves on Sunday,' she explained. 'She's a decent old thing and doesn't mind us entertaining.'

'I thought you might like a pie somewhere.'

'Oh no! Let's talk and be comfortable. Minnie and Edith—they lodge with me, you know—will very likely be late back and even if they aren't, you'll find them quite agreeable.'

'I can afford two pies,' I said in her ear.

She jumped. 'Oh Johnnie, I thought you'd be taken in and I could raid the larder while Mother Agg's back was turned!'

I drew her arm through mine. 'I know you too well, Chris. As you knew immediately when I tried to lie about why we shouldn't stay longer in the boat.'

'If you're such a thought-reader, what am I thinking now, then?' she demanded.

I pretended to consider. 'You're thinking about what I'm thinking you might be thinking about.'

She gurgled with laughter, mouth and lips tantalisingly close. Her hair shone like wheatstraw, brown eyes sparked amber. 'You old cheat. What was I thinking in the boat, then?'

I remembered her pensive look as she stared across the water. 'About some wonderful future when you're—' I bit my lip. Chris's dreams wouldn't be about success in millinery, but of marrying some dashing swell who could pour furs and diamonds in her lap. '—When you're married.' I finished lamely.

'That's rather clever of you, Johnnie. As a matter of fact I *was* thinking it would be lovely married to someone nice.'

'Anyone particular?' Impossible to keep my tone light.

'Oh no! I don't know who at all. Just someone terribly attractive, but down on their luck perhaps. A little sad, you know. He'd need me to help him make the best out of things.'

'A situation you would manage perfectly?'

'I think so. Because I'm not in the least shy or sad, so thanks to me he'd soon become successful. The wedding—'

She gave a little skip. 'It would be dreadfully grand and I'd be frightened; nice frightened, of course. Afterwards I'd learn where to buy the best clothes and become famous as a hostess.'

She was joking, of course. Entering into the stupid game I had begun, so as to help me forget I hadn't been able to afford a second hour on the Serpentine. All the same . . . 'None of your plans includes me.'

'You?'

'It will be years before I can afford to marry.'

'Gosh, yes! Scholars are horribly poor, aren't they? But you'll be ever so happy up in Durham, Johnnie. It's just what you've always wanted, all day long with nothing to do except bury your nose in a book.'

I didn't answer. Afterwards, I often asked myself whether it would have made any difference if I'd said straight out: I love you. Without you, even books might lose their power to comfort and inspire. I doubt whether it would, but I'm not sure. Chris had many faults but she was not deceitful; if I had spoken and if she had agreed to wait, then at least she would have told me as soon as she decided something different.

As it was, we walked on, arm in arm, and eventually I thrust hurt out of sight. Chris was such a merry companion and on that September afternoon all I wanted was to enjoy myself completely. So, as usual with blinkered wantings, I succeeded in my ambition.

'You are nice,' exclaimed Chris, when we reached her Clapham doorstep and I gave her a twopenny bag of humbugs as my parting gift. 'I shall improve of course, but at the moment you're much, much nicer than me.'

Greatly daring, I kissed her on the mouth and she kissed me back, whispering, 'You are slow! Don't you think you could answer that I'm very nearly as nice as you?'

'Much, much nicer,' I said, fervently but uninventively. 'Oh Chris, I have enjoyed today. Can I take you out again on my way to Durham in October?'

'I'm only off on Sundays. You'll have to press your nose

to the shop window if you come through in the week.' She kissed me again and I remember being faintly shocked that she should so clearly feel as eagerly passionate as myself. Consequently, I was almost as much relieved as disappointed when she broke away from my arms, saying cheerfully, 'I'm not quite sure I'm behaving well. Heavens, whatever would Ma say if she saw me?'

I fingered the stucco balustrade. 'Chris . . . do you ever see Vic Hawkins?'

'Vic? Not for ages. He's a mechanic in the Air Force now, and sent off somewhere. Africa or Turkey, I forget. He sends a card occasionally.'

'There—there aren't any others who want to kiss you, are there?' Dear God, how foolish are nineteen-year-old boys.

'Well . . .' She fingered the stucco too.

'Are there?'

'Oh Johnnie, don't be such a baby. Of course there are, but they're not in the least clever and amusing or full of such lovely ideas as you.'

'Good-looking?'

'Oh . . . some of them, I suppose.'

'But you don't really like any of them?'

'I like them, of course I do. But I don't love them, if that's what you want to know. How could I, when I've quite decided not to love anyone until my grand passion comes along?'

'Me too,' I said eagerly. 'Only . . . only . . . Chris, I'm not really a scholar. I love books and learning but I want to do more with my life than read. I ought to be able to make some money as well. It's bound to take time of course, but if—if you want things enough, why, anything can happen!'

'I hope it does for you.' She squeezed my arm, then ran up the steps into the house. I don't think I had bored her during the rest of the time we had together, but I'm sure she laughed at my desperate earnestness as soon as the door was safely shut.

* * *

In retrospect, the time I spent in the city and university of Durham was the only period in my life when choice was spread out for my pleasure. I would have preferred to study history rather than Classics for my degree, but this the terms of my scholarship prevented. However, it was a trifling constraint. Lectures, debates and libraries were open to everyone, formal courses of study a minor part of the kingdom of knowledge spread before me. If in the end I was secretly disappointed not to achieve a particularly good degree, I could not regret the reason, which was my indiscriminate and gluttonous feasting on the wisdom of other disciplines than my own.

I also made acquaintances from many walks of life and one very good friend, Jack Armstrong. The Sussex roughness softened but did not vanish from my voice and I acquired a new passion: flying. I suppose it was a lingering jealousy of Vic Hawkins which first turned my mind towards the university air squadron, an ignoble desire to swagger in front of Chris as a pilot when he was a mere mechanic. Quite soon, I was flying for the joy of it.

Really, you needed money to join the air squadron. None of us had any notion of learning to fly in order to fight: while I was at Durham the Kellogg Pact renounced war for ever and we cherished the ideal of a League of Nations which would make any pact at all unnecessary, ours the generation which accepted peace as its birthright. It was the fun and daring of flying we fancied, revelling in speed and the clean solitudes of the sky.

In the prevailing mood of pacifist optimism the RAF provided instruction for the unversity air squadrons and not much more, but at Durham there were two men up at the same time as myself whose fathers had profiteered out of the war, and when it finished bought huge quantities of surplus equipment at knockdown prices. We didn't mind about that, to us the war was irrelevant, but amongst this equipment had been aircraft, most long since sold off. Eight came to Durham and were kept in barns close to the moors.

They were a mixed bag: five two-seater Avros, a French Nieuport and two SE5's, the latter beat-up and unreliable.

Jack Armstrong and I drifted along to watch the flyers one day early in our second year, and found ourselves helping to hold an SE5 on the ground long enough for it to take off into one of the easterly gales which were Durham's speciality. After that, one thing merged into another, and we were in. I lived on bread and margarine for a month in order to afford RAFVR uniform, otherwise I paid for little except my share of the beer. So long as you loved flying and didn't shirk stripping those damned SE5 engines in a draughty barn, most of the squadron were rich enough not to worry if John Smith couldn't cough up his share of the funds each year. Even Jack Armstrong was a distant cousin of the Armstrong Whitworth engine family, although himself the son of a parson and studying theology. 'Flying has to be considered a professional necessity for me,' he explained. 'Dammit, I shan't get nearer to heaven than an SE5, shall I?'

'An Avro goes higher and the engine doesn't conk out so often.'

'Ah, but it's also safer. You need faith as well in an SE.'

To go solo was what we longed for, to stunt and loop alone in the cold east coast skies, and, being a precarious and only semi-official outfit we did not have to wait as long as we should have done. One Sunday afternoon (when Jack, as a budding parson, refused to fly) I had been trundling around Tow Law with Flight Lieutenant Barnes, our instructor, doing left-hand circuits and some indifferent landings, when, after the last of these, he climbed out of the cockpit. 'The wind has dropped. You might as well go on your own while it lasts.'

A void appeared where a perfectly good stomach had been only seconds before. Of course I wanted to go solo, but . . . 'I've only had eleven hours dual, sir.'

'Christ, how much more do you want? I had five in 1916.'

I wanted to say that it wasn't necessary to cut corners in 1927 as it had been then, but lacked the courage.

'Remember to take plenty of room and look out for gusts,' he yelled from the ground.

I nodded, alone in the Avro cockpit. Gusts were the devil below Ushaw Moor, where we used some sheep pasture as an airfield.

Taxi slowly. Try the controls. Rudder, elevator, ailerons. God, why had I ever wanted to fly? The Avro was a biplane; engine, struts and wings seemed entirely to block the view. No good waiting. Heart pumping, breath held, I opened the throttle. Too tentatively, we were barely moving. Close your eyes and thrust it forward, why doesn't the tail lift? Bounce . . . bounce . . . she's lifting! Bloody hell, why can't I keep her straight? Stuttering and yawing we climbed above the moor, skidding in gusts hurtling in from the sea. Now, what about a turn? A thousand feet. That ought to be safe enough. No, let's make it two in case she slips. Avros were treacherous on a bank.

My hand must have hesitated on that first turn, because the wing came up like a punch on the ear. And so around Tow Law, gaining confidence, until I began to wonder how the devil I was going to get down. I hated putting that nose down again as if I meant it; without Flight Lieutenant Barnes to yell at me, I should have landed twenty feet above the ground several times this week. Nose up a bit; no, down. Down, for Christ's sake, DOWN! God Almighty, there goes a clump of pines. Hold your breath. Ease her, ease her. You're flying into the ground! Up! Pull her up! Now . . . where's the ground vanished to? Why don't we land? We're stalling. Engine, quick. An enormous thump snapped my tongue between my teeth, a rumble like stones caught in a thresher and we were down. I haven't crashed! I've done it, DONE IT! Come on, Johnnie, pull yourself together and taxi over to that swine Barnes as if you landed solo every day. I've really done it. Switch off. Thank God.

'That was a bloody heavy landing,' said Barnes.

'I haven't damaged anything, have I?' Because I couldn't pay, I was terrified of damaging something a spanner wouldn't repair. Which perhaps explained my habit of landing twenty feet above the airfield.

'God, no. Avros'll stand anything, even louts with hippopotamus hands.'

'D'you know what I'd like to do, Jack?'

'Invent indiarubber undercarriages for SE5's,' Jack answered promptly. The week before I had finally bent one of the squadron's aircraft, after nearly two years of blameless flying.

'Idiot. No, I meant really, once I finish here.'

It was our final term at Durham, and we were lying in the sun by the River Wear when we ought to have been working.

He took his pipe out of his mouth and squinted at the sky. 'I wondered sometimes whether you wouldn't try for a late commission in the RAF.'

Jack was shrewd; not because I'd ever considered the RAF, but because he'd seen my indecent desire to show off in uniform. 'No, although I was flying when I discovered what I really wanted. At least, I may have had something of the sort in mind ever since I came north to take my scholarship, but couldn't see how to manage it. I want to help clear up slums and give people decent homes.'

'Who wouldn't? But how, dear boy?'

'Well,' I said slowly, 'if it was easy, it would have been done, I suppose. I know I shall need to learn a great many different things to what I've learned at Durham if I'm to succeed. Building, law, making and begging for money; I'm not sure how to begin. I'm not even certain I care what means I use. But one day I mean to look down from a cockpit and say: Look, I changed that. I helped to build one row, two rows, more if I'm lucky, of decent houses where people lived like rats not long ago.'

'I'd like it if you began where I'm to be vicar,' Jack said dryly. 'But John, care a little about the means you use, all right? Do it crooked, and you won't enjoy that view from the cockpit as much as you expect.'

'Why should my enjoyment matter?' I said fiercely. 'Don't you see, Jack? I'm starting from scratch. I'll have to cut corners somewhere, or end up with nothing done.'

He laughed. 'You wouldn't know where to begin. How often have you looped the Nieuport fifty feet up?'

'Never.'

'Derek Harrison does.'

'Derek's a damned lunatic in a cockpit.'

'That's what I mean.'

I thought about Jack's meaning that night, between bouts of Aeschylus, whom I did not care for. Damn Jack, who had a habit of sound judgement. It wasn't so much that I would shirk being a crook if it was the only way to rebuild slums, but, as he saw, I lacked the knife-edge nerve, the reckless disregard of risk which might enable a nobody like me to learn how to become a successful crook.

I flew once more before I left Durham. Examinations over, we were all packing up to go and flinging parties in our rooms before facing outside reality, where conditions everywhere looked threatening.

It was July, 1929.

I took the remaining SE5 high above Durham City, marking the curve of the Wear around cathedral, castle and heaped-up houses. Further again and coal dust almost immediately dimmed the sprawl below: Houghton-le-Spring, Consett, Sunderland, Newcastle; all softened by grime suspended in summer sunshine. It didn't matter that I could not see the dingy streets and pitheads, the warm enduring people who lived there. Let grime perform one service: to hide squalor this last time.

Today was for joy, flying alone in silver air.

Next to my love for Chris, I never knew such sureness as the moment I decided what I wanted to do with my life: a year before, flying in dirty weather above South Shields. I knew it again on that final Durham flight, and even as I looked down from the cockpit the landscape changed, which I saw as a kind of promise. Industrial wasteland was replaced by the Northumberland fells and Hexham in its valley, the line of Hadrian's Wall beyond. I am unsentimental about country living, having experienced the drudgery it exacts, but that wall, the moors, snug Hexham and close-by industrial sprawl, all laid together beneath the SE5's wings, made me think again about the Weald. Such different country this, so many layers from the Roman Empire to SE5's, yet each grew out of the one before and were part of each other.

Of all my dippings into knowledge at university, I loved and read history most; Granny Paley's tales might be flesh and blood, but I knew they lacked the bone structure of painstaking study and research. This I had begun at Durham, but, while I continued to read and think and juggle the pieces of puzzle Granny had left me whenever I had time, it was on that flight above Hadrian's Wall when my instincts first moved to the rhythm of what I'd learned.

Once upon a time . . .

I rolled the SE5 and as I did so the sinking sun shot a beam high into space, where it turned a layer of cirrus into gold. Below, shadow crept across the earth until beauty lingered only in the sky; I turned for home and throttled down, all my attention now on finding a single grass field in the dusk.

The cirrus turned to copper, pink and mauve; mist drifted shroud-like off the North Sea. At five hundred feet I spotted barns and field, gunned the engine to clear the plugs and touched down with the easy rumble which means a perfect landing. Farewell, Durham.

Next day I left for London.

My youth was over.

I came down from university with twelve and eightpence in my pocket. There was nothing for it but to go back to Furnace Green for the summer, and earn enough to pay for a London suit and lodgings while I looked for a job. At first I had thought I might learn what I needed by working for a building contractor, but decided that knowledge of how houses were built would not help me to pull down slums, where money must be the crucial factor. A clerk's job in a local council promised to be equally dead-end: councils were already doing what they could, which wasn't much. Profits, sites, financing, these were the skills I needed to learn. A whole new world, of which I was utterly ignorant.

Meanwhile, Furnace Green received me back. No prodigal rejoiced more than I did at the feel of a pitchfork in his hand, the familiar sweep of country, known cadences of speech. The ridge was no longer a prison but, quite simply, home. A welcome pause before beginning again, and full of the dreamless sleep which comes from physical rather than mental exhaustion.

Nothing much had changed, although change was there. After years of whist drives and fêtes, as well as some healthy contributions from the richer families round about, a hall had been built on one corner of the green as a memorial to our forty-two dead in the war. Producing plays and getting up dances were now all the rage, rivalling cricket and football in popularity. There had never been such a cheerful winter as the last, so everyone said. Isolation was going, going while you watched, and a good thing too; except the old 'uns wondered where it would all end. No one guessed it wouldn't end until every shred of the life they'd known had vanished, good and bad together.

In London and Durham all the highways were long since metalled, not so in Furnace Green. There, the women still fought their immemorial battle against dust and mud, but the steam-rollers and tar-gangs were expected soon. Some cottages had been painted too, testimony to a brief interval of prosperity and hope which would finish with the economic crash, only weeks away.

Edenham had not changed at all. No paint there; some dirt, not much. Rag rugs beaten every day; just enough food for no one to feel exactly hungry. My mother scrubbing,

scrubbing; skimping, cheerful, settled. The arrowhead still hidden in its place above the hearth. Dad creaking more slowly to work but following the same routine as in my childhood, which Mark followed too. That unchanging framework of past times! How impossible now to imagine a life where nothing changed except the seasons.

I went every other Sunday to see Chris in London. I hated to explain that at the age of twenty-three I still couldn't afford to come each week if I was to save enough during a single harvest to support myself while I looked for a job. 'Soon I'll be living up here too,' I said. 'I can't wait to take you out to the theatre, or a music hall if you'd prefer it.'

London had pleasures for every taste, gallery seats only one and sixpence then.

'That will be fun!' She did a few dancing steps on the paving stones. Every time I saw her she wrapped tendrils tighter around my heart; her gaiety, her enchanting figure, her increasingly elegant clothes a challenge I longed to accept. And because I could not yet accept it, a matter also of some fear.

This fear began to shoulder everything else aside when a scribbled note came which said she would not be in London the next Sunday I planned to see her. I wrote back at once, but received no answer. When I went to Portnell's shop Chris's mother said proudly that they had received a postcard of strange-looking houses; infuriatingly, they did not know where these were and refused to notice my hints that I would like to see their card.

'So nice for her to have the chance of a few days' holiday.' Aunt Portnell could only just see over her glass jars of sherbet and aniseed balls. 'Last year Chris looked real peaky when she came to see us after the summer finished. Why don't you come home for a few days, I said, but no, she wouldn't. It's the Season, you see, garden parties and the like, when grand ladies want hats as big as cartwheels. They refuse to wait a day, even if you're rushed off your feet, but take their custom elsewhere without so much as by your leave. I'm right glad this year she's been able to get away, I can tell you.'

Aunt Portnell wasn't usually so forthcoming; I could tell she was worried too.

I wrote again, but probably Chris was still away. Anyway, no answer came. The soft September days lagged past, and I wrote to say I was coming up next Sunday whether she replied or not.

By then fear had gathered into an abscess which only a quarrel could lance. I turned into grey Tulip Street as the clock struck nine and there she was, tripping along the pavement for all the world as if virtuously on the way to church. Which, being Chris, she certainly wasn't.

The wind whipped a strand of hair across her cheek, her eyes sparkled and, though I suspected she was taken aback to see me so early, she ran to hug me, laughing. 'Whatever time did you leave Edenham to reach Clapham at this hour?'

'Half past five. Chris, I couldn't wait. Why didn't you answer when I wrote?'

'Oh, I know I'm dreadful but it takes hours and hours for me just to *decide* to write! I wanted to, but really you were lucky I remembered to tell you I was going away.'

'Perhaps you felt you owed me that. To stop me from coming up and finding no one here.'

'Well, now you've come there isn't any need for letters, so why worry? Sometimes you're a dreadful worrier, Johnnie.'

'I can't help worrying about you.'

'In that case I shall just have to put up with it, I suppose,' she said cheerfully. 'Let's go for a walk and be happy, shall we? I hate glum faces.'

So off we walked together, she holding my arm and chattering, I answering very much at random. The abscess remained unlanced, my thoughts chasing like badly trained sheepdogs after scampering jealousies. I also wondered where she had been going, a scant hour before the earliest time she expected me to arrive.

'You are fusty today,' she exclaimed at last. 'What's the

matter, or has going back to Furnace Green made you think of nothing but stooks of hay?'

'Corn.'

'Hay or corn, what does it matter? Johnnie, sometimes I could shake you.'

'And sometimes you need a damned good spanking,' I said furiously. 'You know as well as I do which crops are stooked and which are not, but no! Madam has to pretend she's a society lady too languid to set pen to paper, and without the wit to tell wheat from oats. As it happens, I'd sooner know the worst. Where have you been these last ten days and where were you off to so merrily, to make sure you were away when I arrived?'

'What business is it of yours?'

'Every business. I love you. You know perfectly well that one day I intend to ask you to marry me.' There, it was out.

She stopped, and her hand on my arm turned me to face her. We were half way up the Wandsworth Road, not a romantic area. 'My dear . . . my dear. Of course it would have been sweet if you'd asked me to marry you—'

'Would have been?'

'Johnnie, I know you'll be splendidly happy with someone as different from me as possible. It's just—well, I've known you for ever, haven't I? And I suppose it'll be for ever before you can marry anyway.'

'Five years at least.'

'There you are, you see.' She sounded relieved. 'I don't expect you to understand this, but I've been in London five years already and I can tell you: five years is a long time.'

'I might be able to earn enough to marry sooner, if you didn't mind managing on next to nothing for a year or two.'

She didn't answer at once, which hurt me. When she did, it was clear that her mind was made up. Had been made up for some time. 'Johnnie, I do love you, you know I do. But—'

'There aren't any buts in love. You have everything there is of me, and always will.'

'What a dear you are! But I'm absolutely the wrong person for you. I'm extravagant, and I adore parties where no one knows the difference between wheat and oats. You might not mind waiting years to get married when there's so much else you want to do . . . You say I've got everything there is of you, but it isn't true. How often recently have you told me about your splendid plans for slums and things? All I've got is hats, hats, hats.'

'And someone who's willing to take you away from hats.'

She met my eyes, half apologetic, half triumphant. 'Yes. Someone nice who's willing to take me away from hats.'

'Do you love him?'

'Part of me loves him. I'm honest, you see. The rest of me just wants to enjoy itself away from hats. But that doesn't matter, because I mean to be an awfully good wife.'

'The kind of wife a terribly attractive, but sad, man needs if he's to make the best of himself,' I said nastily.

'You're horrid sometimes,' she answered without heat. 'As it happens, he isn't in the least that sort. He's the most exciting person I've ever met, who's able to get whatever he wants for himself. I can't believe that includes me, but it does. I finished at the shop three weeks ago and I've just come back from being with him in Paris.'

'You're married already?'

'Oh, Johnnie! That's exactly what I meant when I said five years in London could be an age. No, I'm not married.'

I felt blood rush into my face. 'Chris—'

'I'm not going to listen to any more. I'm happy, and I never did see the point of waiting for things you wanted if they were there for the taking. So will you go? Now. Because I shall always love you too, and in a different way from anyone else.'

I went. There seemed nothing else to do. And as I went I heard her footsteps running after me, the eager lightness

I would have known anywhere. I turned and she flung her arms round my neck, kissed me on the mouth. 'Goodbye, goodbye. I couldn't bear you to go without a kiss.'

I held her fiercely, oblivious of smirking passers-by. 'It isn't too late. Change your mind now and I won't care what's happened in the past.'

'No, no, I can't change. Be happy, Johnnie. I want you to be happy.' An omnibus was slowing alongside where we stood and she jumped on the step, stood there waving and smiling until she was hidden by the traffic. Chris always enjoyed drama wherever she could find it.

As for me, I travelled all the way from Wandsworth to Edenham without seeing a single thing on the way.

Three weeks later, when the hop-harvest ended, I packed clothes in a carpet bag and left the ridge for London to make my fortune.

I took a room on the top floor of a Bethnal Green lodging house, which was sufficiently close to the City to save pennies by walking there each morning in search of employment. Mrs Clegg, my landlady, was also a holy terror for cleanliness. In Bethnal Green conditions varied from appalling to modestly prosperous, but inside Mrs Clegg's there were no concessions; dirt was vanquished daily by her mops and pails.

At first I walked all day. From Bethnal Green to the City, then around streets populated by bankers, brokers and dealers, gawping at brass plates. I was so ignorant of the world of business that I hadn't the remotest idea what kind of a job would suit my purposes, supposing I could find it. Occasionally a longing for flight back to the ridge would seize me; always there remained the pain of Chris, which I defeated how and where I could.

After a week of hesitant loitering, I decided that a surveyor's office might suit me best. Bankers were too grand, stockbrokers too marginal, lawyers too detached for my purposes. Slums were property and surveyors traded in this commodity which, I hoped, made them not too far removed from more familiar shopkeepers. After a great deal of inexpert thought, I had already decided that fringe deals in land perhaps offered my best chance of making money.

After less than a week in employment, I began to cherish serious doubts about my judgement in this matter. In 1929, the City surveyors were an upright bunch of charming gentlemen who wouldn't have known how to recognize a fringe deal if they saw one. On my very first day as office dogsbody in Mathwick & Taylor, the senior partner took off his hat to me when we met in the street, just as if I was a client: at the time I didn't know whether to be more astounded by his civility or his knowledge of my name, but afterwards doubts crept in. Fortunes were unlikely to be made in commerce by genuinely delightful gentlemen.

'Mr Mathwick knows everyone who works here,' said Dobbs, the chief clerk and a far more awesome personality than any of the partners. 'So you mind your manners outside the building as well as in it, Smith. We wouldn't expect to be let down by a clerk seen purchasing a second half-pint for his lunch, any more than by ill-written accounts.'

'That's one in the eye for me,' confided the man on the stool beside mine. 'I swear old Dobbs pays other chief clerks to tip him off if they see us buying second rounds at lunch.'

'And you do?'

'Invariably. God, how would I last through the day without a full pint? Two would be better, of course.'

Soon after I took up my appointment with Mathwick & Taylor, the 1929 stock market crash began. We were lucky not to be directly affected, since most of our fees were earned by routine management of property, but inevitably business contracted. If I had delayed seeking work for two more weeks I should not have found it anywhere in the City, but fortunately once Mathwick & Taylor took on a man, he was regarded as in The Firm for life. Unless he himself wanted to leave, of course, which was considered both disloyal and indicative of moral flightiness. In some ways the City's attitudes were not as different from those of Furnace Green as might have been expected.

I worked hard, driven by my demons and determined not to remain a clerk for a moment longer than necessary, but progress was agonisingly slow. 1929 became 1930, then 1931, and business remained flatter than ever. There was only one refuge and that was books, but now my studies were strictly utilitarian. Often my spare time was spent looking at sites whose particulars passed across Mathwick & Taylor's desks, trying to figure out the kind of coup which no one else seemed interested in imagining.

One day in November 1932 I found the first possibility and, after a night of flustered calculation, I requested an interview with Mr Mathwick.

'Why should the likes of you bother the senior partner? I'm responsible for the clerks.' Dobbs regarded me with his usual horned-toad stare.

'It isn't to do with my regular work as a clerk, and I should like to see Mr Mathwick personally.'

'You can't, and that's that. A fine kettle of fish it would be if every jackanapes who fancied a grievance could worry the partners with it! You go back to your duties, Smith, or we'll all be staying late to finish.'

Fortunately, the partners never tidied themselves into their offices as resolutely as Dobbs would have liked, and I had little difficulty in encountering Mr Mathwick on the stairs.

'A moment of my time, Mr Smith? Why, of course. I am always pleased to help any of our people in a scrape. This way, my boy, this way.'

Dobbs's face mottled alarmingly as we swept past; even his throat swelled like a toad's.

'Now, my boy.' Mr Mathwick flung an assortment of plans and cups off his desk. 'What is the trouble?'

'No trouble, sir. I wanted to ask about the Coleman Court tenants.'

'Coleman Court? I'm afraid I don't know anything about

it. If you are in difficulties over collecting rents you should consult Mr Kane. He is the partner responsible for management, as you must know by now.'

'Yes, sir. The block is condemned and the tenants have notice to quit.'

'What is the difficulty then?' He hauled an old half-hunter out of his waistcoat pocket.

'Sir, Coleman Court is just around the corner from Guildhall. It is too good a site to remain as cheap tenements.'

'Tut, tut, Mr Smith. When you have been in the City as long as I have, you will know there isn't a single reputable firm which would consider a Coleman Court address for an instant. Near Guildhall it may be, but everyone knows it as a disreputable alley.'

'Moorgate is a good address. Not the very best perhaps, but good.'

'What is that to the matter, pray? Coleman Court is around two corners from Moorgate, which makes it not at all the same. No, no, Mr Smith. I appreciate your zeal but I must ask you to attend to your own work.'

'There is a small building for sale in Moorgate at the moment. The agents are Pace & Tremlett. Because it's small the price is lower than you would expect, but part of its back wall adjoins Coleman Court. Look, sir.' I put a map on the desk in front of him. 'There's only a twenty-foot frontage to Moorgate but that doesn't matter. If Coleman Court was pulled down and rebuilt as offices, it could be joined to that frontage by a narrow section here, and the whole have a Moorgate address. Because of the size of such a development both properties would have many times their present value.'

Slowly Mr Mathwick pulled out his pince-nez. This hung on a thin gold chain from a spring-loaded button, into which they retracted whenever he wasn't using them. 'Pace & Tremlett are the agents, you say?'

'For the Moorgate office, yes, sir, but they haven't thought to enquire from us about Coleman Court. The junction between the two is not, of course, particularly obvious.'

'Hm. Perhaps it might be possible to interest them in finding a purchaser for both. Our clients would be pleased. Tenants in a place like Coleman Court are a poor investment.'

'But . . . should we not seek to buy the Moorgate property from Pace & Tremlett?'

'Really, Mr Smith, I am surprised at you. We are a professional firm and never buy on our own account.'

'No, of course not, sir. But couldn't we work up a scheme and approach a client who might be interested in buying and rebuilding both? In confidence, before Pace & Tremlett should think of such a possibility for themselves? Then we could expect fees for managing the whole afterwards, as well as for buying and developing an important site.'

Mr Mathwick stared at me with a mixture of horror and meditative interest, then wrinkled his nose so the pince-nez fell off and retracted with a snap. 'Well now, Mr Smith. And where did you get such unscrupulous ideas from, may I ask?'

'I don't see why they should be thought unscrupulous,' I said doggedly. 'All we have to do is go a few steps further than simply offering property for sale. Put one site together with another, approach some banks for finance, work the whole thing out to show a tempting rate of return before we pick a likely client. Take the initiative instead of waiting for clients to come to us, as has been the custom. Trade is beginning to improve, why—' A new idea hit me. 'A purchaser might be able to sell at a profit even before the foundations are put in, simply by being able to advertise Coleman Court as Moorgate.'

This relatively simple technique for developing property, where a professional firm supplied the expertise which could assemble sites in such a way as to command speculative investment capital, often without the actual developer contributing a penny of his own, later became commonplace. In 1932 it was a dubious novelty, provoking many shaken heads. But it was profitable. Upright, gentlemanly Mathwick & Taylor cleared the equivalent of two years' earnings on the Coleman Court deal, and also became known as a firm which knew what was what in development. Which, of course, it didn't.

The Moorgate–Coleman Court block was blitzed in 1941 and the site swallowed up in later, more grandiose postwar rebuildings. Even so, I still think kindly of the place because it was there I began to make my fortune.

Not at once, needless to say. That wasn't how Mathwick & Taylor operated. Immediately, my wages were increased from twenty-five to forty-two shillings a week, and at Christmas Mr Mathwick somewhat shyly gave me a cheque for twenty pounds. Nevertheless, after that a new kind of client began to come to Mathwick & Taylor, whom the firm found it difficult to satisfy. Mr Mathwick, particularly, dealt with them splendidly, of course; the rawest developer warmed to his charm and also his shrewdness in established practice. It was the art of recognizing a quite different set of possibilities to any that had previously occurred to him which he found alien. An art best practised by those who lacked fixed notions.

Like me.

By the summer of 1935 I had become modestly prosperous, the possibility of a junior partnership occasionally mentioned. Except that I would have to become qualified first. More examinations, more study in the small hours of the night: my days had now become full of interest but the apparently endless succession of toiling nights were a different matter. Jaded and alone, I sometimes fell asleep across my books and it was then the dreams of Chris began. Terrible dreams of her trapped by vultures, in black ooze, under twisted metal; dreams in which I heard myself cry aloud, without being able to wake until the last dreadful moment of her agony wrenched me to my feet, wild-eyed and trembling. Then I would know I dared not sleep again that night.

This was my state of mind when I met Audrey. Her father was a financier called Colestock, and I went to his house one evening with plans of a possible site assembly scheme in the West End. We talked for about an hour and as I was leaving, his daughter came into the room. Colestock presented me to her absently. I always received the impression that his mind did not engage fully with anything except business. 'Audrey, my dear. This is John Smith of Mathwick & Taylor. He talks sense about property, so you'd better give him a cocktail and find out if he talks sense about anything else.'

'Do you like cocktails, Mr Smith?' she enquired, acid-sweet.

'At the end of a long day, yes, very much.' She was attractive, as well as excellently dressed and groomed. I was finished with love, of course I was, but women were a different matter. Women were release from loneliness, from stress and punishing dreams; yet I had already discovered that for me, casual desire was quickly sated. I was so busy, my acquaintance more or less limited to those I met on business: since I worked in London I had encountered few women whom I cared whether I met again or not.

Almost immediately, I knew Audrey was different. So poised and perfumed she shook the blood in my veins, and, quite as important, intelligent as well. Her hair was even fairer than Chris's, pale silk in texture. From that very first cocktail I wanted to run my fingers through the smooth flow of it. Grey eyes and delicately shaped bones offered an impression of fragility; in fact, as I soon discovered, she was physically and intellectually tough. Too late, I also found out that emotionally she was as frail as her looks suggested.

'Tell me, Mr Smith, do you eat, sleep and dream property as my father does?' she asked, sipping gin.

I was annoyed to feel myself flush, her remark a trifle too close a hit. 'Any business is difficult at the moment, although some aspects are beginning to ease at last.'

'Which means you do, I suppose. Why?'

I considered. 'When I first began I could have answered easily enough. The trouble is, when you're working hard, really hard, I mean, it's easy to forget the reason why.'

'I imagine that's true. In which case it might be simpler to explain what you had in mind when you first began to work hard, really hard, I mean.'

I fiddled with my glass, thinking. She was mocking me, but the cocktail was excellent; nor was I over-eager to return to Bethnal Green. 'When I came down from university I wanted to clear slums. I went into property to learn how it might be done, also to make money so I might begin to do it.'

'And how many slums have you cleared, Mr Smith?' She looked at me out of grey unfathomable eyes.

'None.'

'Why not?'

What could she know about how hard it was to begin from nothing? How difficult to hold on to an ideal while the daily millrace swept you along. As soon as I had earned the kind of money slum clearance needed, I would honour the vow I had made in the sky above Durham.

Truthfully, I could have begun to honour it already. Even if modernising a single terrace cleaned out all my savings, it would have helped to keep my purpose bright. 'I hope to begin soon,' I said at length. 'Next year I shall be qualified as a surveyor, and in a better position to see which way to go.'

She inclined her head, smiling slightly. 'I know I have been an interfering bitch, but you don't know how lucky you are to be able to decide the direction of your life. It makes me furious just to watch men drift, when most women can't do anything interesting at all.'

I was still unsophisticated enough to dislike hearing her use the word bitch, but also unable to resist her appeal. 'If that is so, then I quite agree.'

'You know it's so, of course it is! But I want so much to do something worthwhile with my life! I have some money of my own in addition to what Father gives me. He'd stop that, you know, if he didn't approve of what I did. I shouldn't care, of course, if only I knew what I really wanted. Sometimes I wish there were still suffragettes, except politics aren't very interesting, do you think? Worst of all, I went to school in one of those places for young ladies where you don't learn any of the things you really need. Then wasted simply months coming out.'

'I expect you enjoyed it all the same.' She seemed terribly young under all that expensive grooming.

'Yes, I'm afraid I did, but now the only thing anyone expects of me is to get married.'

I murmured some idiocy about girls and marriage, and she said, 'Of course I shall want to, but not only get married, if you see what I mean. You never wanted only to marry, did you? You've had this idea of clearing slums, I should have thought you might understand a little of how I feel.'

Did I compare her to Chris?

Of course I did; all the time. In some ways they were similar, which was one reason why I was drawn to her. Both were thrusting and impulsive; both in quite different ways able to charm my senses. But where Chris was direct, Audrey only seemed so. Chris never minded admitting she was wrong or ill-tempered, cheerfully begged forgiveness and then did the same again; nor had she ever pretended that she loved me. Audrey was too proud to beg for anything, even forgiveness, and hated to admit she could be wrong. She also fell romantically in love with the man she imagined I must be, without considering that the bargain might prove one-sided as well as self-deceiving.

Audrey and I saw a good deal of each other that autumn, and I bought my first-ever suit of evening clothes to squire her to parties, which I admit I enjoyed. Even so, I continued to live at Mrs Clegg's in Bethnal Green, the contrast laughable between my dawn homecomings and the Park Lane ballrooms where I danced through the night. By then Audrey's every movement revealed her love, and my self-esteem was further increased by the knowledge that other men envied me the woman on my arm. For a while it seemed like a game: social minefields and elaborate décor one moment, Bethnal Green and a mad scramble to make up for lost time the next.

Then, one December evening, I took her home and it was snowing. We ran up the steps together and into the shelter of the portico, Audrey laughing and shaking her hair loose. 'I love snow. Everyone else hates it, but I imagine all kinds of secret happenings behind the flakes.'

I kissed her, the first time I had done so unless you count the polite kissings well-brought-up girls expected. It was a bad mistake, because I immediately became aware of how intensely I desired her. I had known before, but, mesmerised by the game we played, refused to face the implications. I released her more quickly than she wanted, pulled the bell and fairly thrust her into the butler's arms.

Back in my room in Bethnal Green, I cursed myself for an idiot, stripped off ridiculous evening clothes and drank enough black coffee to keep me awake until I finished some work I had neglected. My final examinations at the Surveyors' Institution were only three months off.

Next day I wrote to Audrey, saying that unfortunately I must work most evenings for the rest of the winter. I wished her well, but was forced to decline any further invitations she might be kind enough to obtain on my behalf.

I thought Mrs Clegg looked at me queerly when I came home the following evening, but she always was a clacking biddy. I knew I looked awful, tense and grey-faced with tiredness: that day Mr Mathwick had pointed out, with extreme civility, several errors in my calculations. He might be little use at developing new business but remained a stickler for accurate procedures, and a good job too, if my brains were about to addle.

Audrey was waiting beside my gas fire.

She jumped up when I entered, one gloved finger to her

lip, more like a child than a débutante. 'I had to come.'

'I told you, I haven't time for parties now.' I was furious she had somehow discovered where I lived, had seen for herself the ludicrous gulf between our circumstances.

'I came about you, not parties. John, I know you have to work. I don't mind waiting until after your examinations.'

'It isn't a case of examinations, but of a different life. What would your father say if he knew you were here now?'

She laughed. 'He'd have a fit. Not about you, but because I was in Bethnal Green. I don't care. I told you before, I intend to lead my own life—' She broke off. 'I mean, I intend to decide what I want for myself, John dear.'

It was the first time she had called me dear, the change of wording making her meaning completely clear. Her cheeks were flushed and she looked at me very steadily, willing me to understand.

'I'll take you home,' I said dully. Had she not loved me I would have bedded her there and then, as she so plainly wished.

'No. I came because I thought you might have some stupid notion about my money, and now I see you have. Whatever does it matter? I haven't earned a penny of it for myself, and you . . . Well, one day I'm sure you'll have heaps, all earned yourself.' She stopped, looking very hot and self-conscious.

I came as close as I ever did to loving her then, proud Audrey reduced to pleading because she wanted to make me the purpose in her life. She was beautiful; warm colour relieving her usual pale hauteur, that accursed smooth hair a maddening invitation. What indeed did money matter, now I was nearly on my way? I was sure old Colestock had been a rascal in his time. Audrey would bring me instant acceptance in business, allow me to take a great many difficult corners fast, provoke envy wherever I took her as my wife. Anyhow, she wasn't impossibly rich if her father disapproved of the match, merely sufficiently wealthy to allow me to embark at once on clearing slums.

What did love matter, if I couldn't marry Chris? Especially when marrying Audrey would show Chris I didn't care; if we should ever meet, what triumph I should feel at having such an elegant wife by my side. Like gathering clouds these desires and excuses ran together into one enormous storm of temptation, and the most powerful desire of all was the hunger to show Chris what a fine fellow I had become without her.

'Audrey, are you sure?' My throat felt tough, like hide.

'I am sure, I am sure, I am sure.' She came close, lifted her face to mine.

Her kiss was so sweet, I came stupidly close to tears. Chris, Chris, were your lips ever as sweet as this?

For a few moments longer I fought the knowledge that it was a crime to take her—far more, to marry her—when I had so little of myself to give, this the cut corner Jack Armstrong had warned me against, which would prevent me from looking out of my cockpit with enjoyment, no matter what I might achieve. But emotions are seldom as softly convenient as we would like them to be; soon my struggles ceased and I accepted what was so eagerly offered me.

My position now was completely reversed from what it had been with Chris, Audrey as in love with dreams as ever I had been as a boy. I could lead her anywhere, which, immediately, meant away from Bethnal Green. At least I wasn't quite such a cheat as to make love to her during that time of her first great foolishness. Probably what I did was worse, but it made me feel better that for four months she had every chance to retract from marriage.

She never showed any sign of wavering, however, and we were married at St George's, Hanover Square, the following April, just after her twenty-first birthday since Colestock refused his consent while she was under age. He was furious and I don't blame him, although I was surprised he kept up his opposition for so long. I had thought he cared deeply only for business, and Audrey would eventually obtain whatever indulgence she wanted while he thought of something else; this overlooked the fact that he considered her as property. With his money and her graceful looks Audrey could have married anyone, and she married John Smith of Furnace Green. His colourless but ambitious wife shared his disappointment but the formalities were observed: when Audrey proved adamant, her wedding, brideclothes and their gifts to us were all suffocatingly expensive. Only afterwards did rage thaw into tepid acceptance as her father and I met over various business deals. Audrey was their only daughter, and Colestock and I profited too much from each other's abilities for estrangement to be worth while.

I took her to Edenham once, but the visit was not a success. Her bandbox appearance made the old house look unkempt, although I knew every cranny would have been scrubbed before we came, and my parents sat each side of the hearth with work-gnarled hands tight on their knees, wondering what on earth to say. To them Audrey looked infinitely more exotic than Lady Dyer of Riffield, who wore old hats and tweeds with uneven hems.

Mark did not appear at all and I was unsure whether to be glad or sorry, as one after another Audrey's gallant attempts to set everyone at ease fizzled into nothing.

Only as we were leaving did Mum kiss me and whisper, 'If you're happy, we are.'

'I am.' Be happy, Chris had said. 'Johnnie, I want you to be happy.'

Mum looked at me searchingly, she and Audrey as unlike each other as two members of the same species could be. 'Will you do something for me?'

'You know I'd love to. What is it?' I suppose I expected some shamefaced request for money, although I ought to have known better.

Mum touched my cheek. 'Walk through the village before you leave, instead of puffing past in that gurt car of yours. I doubt you'll be back for a while.'

I think my mother always believed the starting handle on a car served a kind of boiler under the bonnet. 'Of course we'll be back. By Christmas at the latest.'

'I haven't asked much from you these last years, I want you to do this for me,' she said obstinately.

Put like that I couldn't refuse, though I was damned if I wanted to parade Audrey like a prize heifer down the street. Oddly enough, the one thing I would very much have liked to do was dig the old arrowhead out of its hiding place and feel it in my palm, which was mere foolishness amid a flurry of goodbyes.

At the corner of the green I set my foot on the brake of our old Sunbeam. 'Would you like to get out for a stroll?'

Audrey shivered. 'No, thanks. The wind feels as if there isn't anything between here and Siberia. Oh, all right, if you really want to freeze.' She climbed out and slammed the door.

That unwillingly slammed door stirred me unexpectedly. Audrey tried so hard to please, so eagerly and unstintingly offered her love. I tucked my hand under her arm. 'I wish sometimes you were less sweet than you are. Then I shouldn't feel such a boor.'

'But you aren't, how can you say such a thing! I love you so very much, my dearest.'

'And I love you with all my heart,' I lied, since she deserved whatever I could give. We had reached the pool and stood close to where Granny Paley's hovel had crumbled into the earth. Wind blew ripples among the reeds which now almost choked the surface of the water, a rime of mud where generations of boys and maids had come seeking omens of fertility and love.

Audrey sighed contentedly. 'How I've longed for you to say it. Now, I'm glad you waited until we were in your own place before you did.'

'Audrey, my dear. I hope I never fail you.'

'Oh, I'm not afraid of that. Not now I know you love me. You see, I wasn't sure before.'

I drew her against me, soft silk hair blowing across my

lips as we kissed; and as we did so, perhaps because I knew this pool had uncovered so many hidden longings over the centuries, my heart nearly broke for love of Chris.

'You're shivering,' Audrey said. 'Let's walk down to the church and you can show me your ancestors' tombstones going back to the year dot.'

I was glad to turn away. 'My favourite is Great Grandfather Mark, who fought under Wellington and was lucky not to go to gaol for inciting a riot. But all the inscription says is "Here lies Mark Smith Who argued with The Vicar. Died 18 August 1861".'

Audrey laughed delightedly. 'I must see that. John, I do like your village, you mustn't think I don't. And now it will always be the place where you said you loved me.'

The Portnells had given up the shop two years before; a name I didn't recognize was painted above the door. I was glad when we were past, the church and the decorative iron slabs with which the old ironmasters had marked their graves admired. I had never thought of Furnace Green as a museum to be stared at and didn't relish the experience; the only moments of pleasure came when a pack of children cascaded out of the school and two Locock lorries clashed bumper to bumper at the awkward corner by the churchyard. Trust Lococks to use changing circumstances to their advantage: as we drove past the Dyer Arms, I saw they had set up a petrol station in the old coaching yard.

Be damned to museums, the ridge was still alive.

Audrey and I bought a small terrace house in a not too fashionable part of Hampstead. It was pleasantly uncrowded there and, compared to what Audrey was used to, inexpensive, although at first the bills and bank loan terrified me. Audrey seemed delighted with it and never once compared our small rooms and sparse furnishings to her father's house in Park Place. I, too, I must confess, felt pleasure as piece by piece we purchased furniture we liked, laid carpets, hired a second maid; my pleasure all the keener once I became a junior partner in Mathwick &

Taylor and began to earn enough not to feel beholden.

By the end of that first year of marriage we had settled into an agreeably companionable relationship, Audrey was expecting our first child, and I had purchased a terrace of run-down slum housing in Middlesbrough.

'Why not in London?' demanded Audrey. 'Heaven knows I saw some dreadful places when I came to you in Bethnal Green.'

'That part of the East End is prosperous, compared to some.' I added up some figures in the account book we kept together, as a means of laying money methodically aside. The sums were tiny, but, nine years after I left Durham, at last we had begun on what both of us wanted to achieve, even if the means came more from her allowance than my earnings.

'Then why Middlesbrough?'

'Because a friend of mine, Jack Armstrong, is vicar there, and prices are a quarter those in London. Even slums have value, at five bob a week for a decaying hutch. After years of depression in the shipyards the local council is desperate, and Jack has arranged that they will rehouse free of charge while we modernise.'

'We aren't in this for the money,' said Audrey sharply.

'We can't afford to spend unnecessarily, or we'll come to a dead end before we've properly begun.'

'I hate to hear you talking development language over something we planned to do for—for . . .'

'We want to do it because people deserve decent homes. God, I remember enough leaky roofs along the street when I was a boy, and Edenham will fall down soon unless someone spends money on it.'

'Why don't you?' she said tightly.

'Because Mum and Dad wouldn't let me. They take a pound a week from me because they'd be on the parish if they refused, now Dad can't work. They won't accept a penny more and I can't force charity down their throats.'

'It seems so silly . . . I'm sorry. But why should they refuse a few extra shillings we wouldn't notice?'

I shrugged. I remembered very clearly the old village attitudes on accepting charity, as distinct from neighbourly help, the desperate craving for pride in a world which allowed farm labourers almost nothing of their own. I doubted whether I could explain it. They took my pound a week because Dad wasn't old enough to draw his Lloyd George shillings—as Furnace Green still called the old age pension. Next year when he became seventy, they would refuse it. In this year of grace 1938 the terror of destitution still raped the pride of the country poor, the prospect of being able to reject unwanted help once they received a pension which was theirs by right most eagerly awaited.

Audrey poked the fire which a fickle April made welcome. 'I oughtn't to, I know, but I can't help wondering whether you chose Middlesbrough because it's too far away for me to interfere. I did want so much that this one thing should be both of us together dreaming dreams. But you're not like that, are you? You're kind, indulgent even, willing to let me think I'm helping; it's only recently I've realized the decisions are yours alone. Then, if I should disagree, you're so wretched over quarrelling you can't sleep, and I feel a brute even if the quarrel wasn't my fault. But, all I want is to share a little more of you.'

'You have all of me,' I said, taken aback. 'Audrey, I don't remember a single quarrel that anyone would call a quarrel since we married.'

'Because each time I've given in. As I'm about to now. Again. Buy your terrace in Middlesbrough, I'll come up by train to look at it when you've finished.'

'We might even fly up together if you'd enjoy to try it. I'm thinking of reviving my licence if I can.'

'You see? You don't even listen to what I'm saying! John, please. Before it's too late, let me be the kind of partner I thought you wanted when we married.'

'My dear, you are the kind of partner I wanted. Why, I couldn't have got anywhere in the time without you. Hostess, adviser, sympathetic listener to botched-up deals; you are my refuge and so much else besides.' I pulled her to her feet and tilted her chin gently until she had to look at me. 'I am so proud of you, so happy, so grateful for everything—'

'You said once that you loved me. Was it a lie? I've wondered sometimes lately.'

'I love you, I love you, how could you doubt it,' I said steadily; oh, the effort, the disciplined effort of repeating the words which any woman craves, even one so poised as Audrey. At night desire sparked easily between us; by day, I still found it enormously difficult to infuse passion with sincerity.

In truth, I did not understand myself. I remembered all Chris's bad points quite clearly even while her features began to blur in my mind. Almost certainly she would have made the devil of a wife; yet I could not shake loose from her. Like the old 'uns of Furnace Green I continued to hanker for an imperfect past, while all around me a better future beckoned.

'I have bought the terrace in Middlesbrough now, promised the people there I would rebuild their homes,' I said after a pause, while Audrey stood close to me in my arms. 'I don't think you would want me to disappoint them. Next time I'll buy in London.'

'We'll buy.' Her grey eyes were unreadable.

I cursed myself. 'We'll buy, and you will be far better than I am at making the tenants understand what we propose. The moment they hear their homes have been bought by a developer, they're afraid. It's an infuriating waste of time just to get them to listen to what you've got to say. Which isn't surprising. Slum tenants have no reason to trust their landlord.'

'I should try to do my best.'

Her tone was flat, although whether this was because she realized for the first time the rough nature of such work, I wasn't sure. Audrey was enthused by the idea of giving people decent homes but quite unsuited to brawling neighbourhoods awash with the kind of life she had never experienced. In her own home she was invariably immaculate, with that inborn facility for keeping every fold in place no matter what the circumstances: in backstreet slums her desire to help would simply provoke anger and mockery. She had no training, precious little education nor desire to improve what she had, no knowledge of business beyond the faint contempt of someone born to wealth. I could not imagine how I might turn her enthusiasm and undoubted intelligence to practical use, lacked time to explain the simplest essentials of the developer's art. Which would not anyway have interested her.

Christ, what a trap temptation had fastened about me when I married a woman I liked but could not love, whose money my pride detested spending. And yet, I needed Audrey. I respected and was fond of her, looked forward to the passion we enjoyed together, to returning to our quiet well-ordered home after a difficult day.

That night when we lay together after love, she said out of nowhere, 'Why have you suddenly decided to revive your licence?'

'Licence?' I mumbled drowsily. 'What licence?'

'You said you thought you might see if you could revive your flying licence. I wish you wouldn't, I see you too seldom as it is; and a tired man must make a bad pilot.'

'It was just a thought. It's been so long since I've flown . . . I expect I'd have to start from scratch again.'

'Then please leave it as a thought. I'd much prefer to take the train to Middlesbrough.'

I stared into the dark, wide awake now. How easy to agree, and offer the concession she needed to put what else we'd said today behind her. 'I haven't worried about anything except my own affairs for years, then since we married—well, happiness is selfish, I suppose. I'm not political, as you know. Now I'm very much afraid there's going to be another war.'

'John, no! There couldn't be! Why, there's just been a meeting here in London, settling things.'

'Let's hope so, but I doubt whether elderly diplomats telling the Czechs to be nice to Hitler will settle much for long. I've never put two thoughts together on Herr Hitler before the past few weeks, but now he's got away with taking Austria, I believe he'll decide he can get away with taking Czechoslovakia too. And after that anywhere else he fancies, until in the end the French and ourselves will be forced to show him it isn't so. Which means war. By then he won't stop for less.'

'You said you weren't political.'

I smiled against her hair. 'I'm not, but the property world attracts all kinds, including sharks. I can recognize greed when I see it. Also a—a kind of mania I can't describe, although I could name a few names you'd recognize. Men who can't stop once they've smelt success, who want more and more long after they've forgotten why they want it.'

'Father?'

'No, of course not.' Old Colestock was a middling ruthless operator, who made money precisely because he understood that some limits are desirable if a business is to prosper.

'John—' she shifted in my arms. 'You can't be thinking of fighting as a pilot if there is a war.'

'Why not?'

'I should have thought it was obvious. You haven't flown for years and you're too old to begin again on the kind of planes they fly now.'

'I'm thirty-two this summer,' I said, annoyed, and then was amused by my own annoyance that Audrey thought me old. 'If I could get crocked-up SE5's off a sheep pasture in an east coast gale, I ought to be able to do circuits and bumps over Surrey in a Tiger Moth.'

'You've been already to find out if they'll take you.' Audrey's voice accusing in the dark.

'Yes,' I said, as gently as I could. After some hesitation the RAF had stretched a line over my age, because I had flown before.

'So nothing I say will make any difference.'

I hesitated, and then shrugged.

'Not even if I remind you that our child will be born while you're risking your neck playing airboys in—in—'

'A Tiger Moth. My dear, that least of all. I wouldn't want a child of ours to grow up a Nazi, and nor would you. You remember Peter Fielden, who came to dinner last week? He's a Jew, which never entered your head and why should it, when he made you laugh. In Germany he'd be lucky if they let him stay alive, after they'd stripped him of everything he possessed.'

'There you go again,' she said, and turned away from me in the bed. 'I told you earlier, you always make up your mind before you tell me anything. Then if I disagree you set out to make me feel a selfish bitch.'

'I hate it when you try to shock me.'

'Good. I hate it when you treat me like a whore.'

'When have I ever done such a thing?' She had succeeded in shocking me this time, bumpkin that I was.

'Every time you forget I'm part of your life, not just a woman to be visited when you happen to spare the time. Between Middlesbrough and Tiger Moths in Surrey,' she added sweetly.

I heard the springs twang as she wriggled into a more comfortable position, and to myself swore good old-fashioned Sussex oaths I hadn't used for years. In many ways I deserved every harsh word she chose to fling at me, but in this I felt myself to be entirely in the right.

We patched up that particular quarrel but, looking back, I'm not sure our lives ever settled easily together again.

I was accepted into the City of London Training Unit of the RAFVR in May 1938, on the same day the Czech ambassador was assured by Hitler that Germany had no aggressive designs on his country. The newspapers were cock-a-hoop and I felt several kinds of fool, wasting time I couldn't afford learning to form fours in a drill hall off Moorfields. Needless to say, Durham University Air Squadron had not considered its young gentlemen needed to learn such mundane things as drill and, eleven years on, I remained unconvinced. I had not taken the decision to join the RAFVR lightly, in fact 1938 was an infernally inconvenient time to divert energy away from home and business; only occasionally could I see the wry joke of wasting a commodity I was so catastrophically short of, stamping about in a drill hall. I was just beginning to make my way in the property world, might soon be offered my first directorship. Within another year, if all went well, I ought to have begun earning the kind of money which really counted for something.

In June our son was born, and named Robert Larkworthy Smith. I would have liked to give him Paley as a second name but recoiled from explaining why to Audrey, so settled for my mother's maiden name instead. Robert was Colestock's name so everyone was happy. Or nearly so. Like my superstitious ancestors, I had felt that though Robert was unlikely ever to live on the ridge, Granny Paley was more likely to instruct her tame spirits to look after him if he bore her name. Still, ever since Liddy's brother Pete returned to the ridge the Larkworthys had become well and truly twined into Furnace Green's past; one day the very oddity of the name might start Robert wondering about his heritage if I was no longer around to tell him.

Because, as the months passed, I became sure again that war was coming, and soon. A new kind of war which as a pilot I would be lucky to survive. Too late now to write down the tales Granny had entrusted to me, even had it been possible to distil the brew of legend, enchantment, hearsay and experience which were my birthright as well as hers. One day I had intended to attempt it . . . One day, one day, the story of my life. If I was killed then Robert could be as curious about his heritage as he liked, but most of his questions would remain unanswered.

Still, it was no good worrying. I snatched what minutes I could to play with him, whirled in and out of the house in the hope I might seem to be there more often than I was, studied navigation in taxis between appointments. By then the RAF had decided that flying was more important than drill, and three times a week and every other weekend

I reported to a grass airfield near Woking which possessed an excellent bar, some very long-suffering Tiger Moths and a gully. This gully stretched right across the airfield and it required tough nerves to take off into any wind stronger than a breeze, since the Moth's power was barely sufficient to drive it at a decent speed up the further slope. The slightest miscalculation resulted in an undignified ground-loop. Fortunately, the little biplane was tough and light, a great many ham-handed pilots saved by its forgiving nature.

I was delighted to find that, once learned, biplane flying was an art not easily forgotten. I did indeed have to start again at the beginning with everyone else, but flew solo after only four hours' instruction.

By then, flying had become a deadly serious business.

Two days before I flew solo, Chamberlain returned to Croydon aerodrome with the Munich Agreement in his pocket, which gave Hitler the Czech Sudetenland. Peace in our time, he called it, but the RAF no longer appeared to think so. The hours of our training grew longer, my difficulties in continuing to earn a living increased. The Middlesborough houses were only half-renovated, and unless finishing them was to wait into an indefinite future I must swallow my pride and ask Audrey to pay the bills. Since I wanted to feel something was completed before Hitler knocked it down again, and pride anyway had ceased to seem so important, I asked her after only token hesitation. She paid without comment and neither of us was able to go and see the result. Jack told me the tenants were quite pleased.

Worst of all, I began to have dreams again. Since my marriage and the generally good physical relationship between Audrey and myself (and, it is fair to say, our happiness that first year of marriage) these had vanished. Now they returned in even more horrific forms. Great black nightmares left me sweating and exhausted, humiliated too when Audrey had to comfort me like a child squalling in a thunderstorm.

'You're doing too much,' she said at first, with which I had to agree. The RAF would solve that particular problem by calling me up soon, anyway.

I went the next week to see Audrey's father, detesting my beggar's role.

'You think you will be called up permanently?' Colestock considered me with detachment. Rich men recognize those who come asking for favours.

'As soon as the winter is over, yes. Flying's very limited at the present, the RAF at full stretch taking new machines into squadron service, but with the spring they'll need to train us full time. Some of the newer designs take a great deal of flying.' We had gone for a weekend to a regular base at Tangmere, and I had been appalled by glimpses into the cockpits of Blenheims, Defiants and Hurricanes.

'What have you settled with Audrey?'

'Nothing yet, but I shan't be able to keep up the Hampstead house on a pilot officer's pay. I wondered whether you would invite her and Robert to live here for a while.' I was fixing things behind her back again, I realized.

He nodded. 'Of course.'

'Thank you, sir.'

'We shall enjoy to have her home again.' He meant it too, being fond of Audrey and delighted by a grandson. The cold ungenerous tone merely signalled that he despised any man, no matter what the circumstances, who could not support his own wife and child.

That night I dreamed again of Chris. She was strapped into the passenger seat of my Tiger Moth, the engine gunning in loud angry bursts as I tried to increase speed sufficiently for take-off. Nothing I did made any difference, my limbs like lead, the Moth careering out of control between huts, up gullies, and helter-skelter through crowds of screeching people. Though I was the pilot I was also watching, forced to watch Chris's mouth gape in terror, her futile struggles to escape as the Moth flew straight at a wall. The flash of flame set her flesh bubbling in its heat.

I remember shouting, 'Chris . . . Chris,' and then Audrey woke me. Usually on these occasions she cradled me until fright receded, murmuring endearments; I suspect she was not too displeased to find me jellified occasionally. It was only when, this time, she turned away while I still trembled that I began to wonder what else I might have shouted.

Next morning I came downstairs to find her seated behind the teapot, gazing vacantly at nothing. Her eyes focused as I sat down. 'Who is Chris?'

I was tired. Physically exhausted and also very tired of lying. 'A girl I loved when I was young.'

'How much do you love her now?'

'My dear, I haven't seen her in nearly ten years.'

'That wasn't what I asked you.'

I bit my lip, already wishing I could call back that moment of cruel truth.

Audrey nodded as the silence lengthened. 'Last night you called her your love. And—and your wife.'

'I had a nightmare. You know what stupid dreams I have sometimes, they don't mean a thing.'

'Usually. You've just convinced me this one meant something, although in the past I've always tried to think: Poor John, he's over-strained. God knows that's true. The mistake I made was thinking the strain came from work or flying, when all the time the cause was living lies with me.'

I fiddled with my teaspoon, listening to Robert yell upstairs. Then I nodded.

I was defeated.

Audrey put her face in her hands. 'You haven't seen her for ten years you say, and you still love her enough to call her your wife. Why, oh, why can't you forget her?'

'I don't know. I've asked myself the same question a hundred times and never found an answer.'

When she lifted her face it was the first time I had seen

her look unkempt; lipstick smeared, hair in damp coils. 'Will you tell me one thing, quite truthfully?'

'If I can,' I said, like an imbecile.

'Did you love me at all when you married me?'

'My dear, of course.'

'Did I come first with you, at least at the beginning?'

I stared at her, hesitated, and was lost.

'I see,' she answered quietly. 'What was it you wanted, my money?'

'No.'

'Not after we married, no. You've hated it then, haven't you? Before, money must have been part of it.'

'Yes,' I said reluctantly. 'Yes, I'm afraid it must, although I'd forgotten. But, Audrey—I was fond of you, admired you . . . you gave me confidence. A great many people aren't in love when they marry . . . I loved you in my way and we were happy. Surely that counts for something.'

But she was no longer listening, leaped to her feet and stared through the window at February frost. February 1939; if only we could have lasted a few months more, the war might finally have driven us together. But then again, as things turned out, perhaps it was just as well we didn't.

'Audrey, dear—'

'I should have liked to be loved. I wanted to do such splendid things with my life, and then you came. I loved you so much, John. If you'd mattered less to me, I might never have suspected there was anything wrong between us. But as you've just said, dreams are often stupid, aren't they?' She turned, tears on her cheeks. 'All kinds of dreams, the wonderful ones as well as nightmares.'

Because I couldn't answer I went over and held her hand, which somehow seemed easier than before. We stood quite still and close, offering comfort to each other. At last Audrey looked up and tried to smile. 'Listen to Robert howl, Nanny must be bathing him. Well, my dear, what next? Do you want to go?'

'I shall be off into the Air Force soon, anyway. I think

it is for you to say what you want.' My heart was wrung by her gallantry.

'I want Robert to have a father, and I don't want to be pitied. If you promise not to tell anyone what has happened then I'd sooner you stayed. So long—so long as—'

'I won't be seeing Chris, if that's what you mean. I told you, we lost touch years ago.'

'Then I'd like you to stay, but I can't be a wife to you ever again.' Her self-possession was astounding, my sense of guilt so oppressive that I mumbled the kind of thanks one offers a reluctant hostess and escaped from the room, without immediately considering the kind of the bargain we had struck.

When I did, I scarcely knew whether to laugh or feel enraged. With myself, with her, for being such fools. How could we live as strangers in the same house, when sex was the one uncomplicated relationship we enjoyed? Of course I had injured her, emotional deceit the most crass of marital offences, but if she meant what she said—and knowing Audrey I was nearly sure of it—then she was behaving like a child. If we were to remain together as she wished, then we had to re-establish our relationship in the best way we could manage. Punishment for its own sake would not help. Hurt and anger, yes. I wouldn't have minded if she had screamed and slapped my face, understood only too well that hurt might make it impossible for her to accept me for a while, but ungenerous pride which refused to salvage the good things of our marriage would swiftly undo the remaining ties between us.

However, for the moment I felt too remorseful not to try and expiate my sins, the uncertain future another reason for holding on to home and family. Robert was a joy; the idea of him growing up in another man's house quite detestable.

Six weeks after our estrangement I returned home late one night to find my call-up papers on the silver salver in the hall. Hitler had just taken over the rump of Czechoslovakia without a shot being fired, and I was to report in ten days' time to an OCTU unit near York for advanced flying training.

A clock struck eleven. Audrey was already upstairs but her light was on, the door ajar. All at once I felt certain this was deliberate. She must have guessed what that buff envelope contained and chose this easiest of moments to bury the past.

I went up the stairs like a young man on his wedding night; I had never been physically unfaithful to my marriage and this last six weeks of estrangement had been very trying.

She was lying back on pillows, reading. 'Darling,' I said, and sat on the edge of her bed.

She smiled. 'Long day?'

'Yes, very. All right now, though.' I picked up her hand and kissed it, my touch showing how much more I desired.

She pulled away, almost shuddering. 'No!'

'My dear,' I said as reasonably as I could. 'I know you've felt bitterly towards me these past weeks, but we must begin again sometime if our marriage is ever to seem worthwhile.'

'It won't,' she said drearily. 'I thought you knew. Marriages aren't like your property deals, to be renegotiated when they hit a snag.'

'Perhaps they are more like business than you realize. Either they get bigger and better, or smaller and worse. I think you have to choose.'

'I don't want a divorce.'

'Neither do I, if it can be avoided. Perhaps it can't, for very much longer.'

'I don't see why. You promised you'd stay, or isn't your word to be trusted either?'

I consider myself slow to anger, but I was becoming angry. Be careful, I thought. I might be dead inside a year and Robert hear only harsh things about his father, unless I stayed a little longer. What did it matter, after all, when in ten days' time I should be away at an airfield outside

York? 'I said it was for you to choose what you wanted, and was prepared to stay while you needed me. I'm no longer sure you do. Sometimes things don't seem as simple to me as they do to you.'

'Really?' She looked faintly interested.

'All right, I still hankered for Chris when I married you, but I hadn't seen her for years and I haven't seen her since. A great many people must hanker after youthful loves, without it meaning anything particular. I simply don't understand how you can wreck a good marriage just because you forced me to admit something I knew you would prefer not to know.'

'That's your trouble. Only reason makes sense to you.'

'No,' I said, thinking of many things. 'No, that isn't true.'

'Oh? Then it just shows how little I know you, doesn't it?' Her fingers fumbled blindly with the pages of her book. 'I married a dream and thought it was real, while all the time this Chris of yours held everything I thought was mine. Even my marriage; you made love to me and pretended I was her.'

She was dry-eyed but I heard the desolation in her voice. This was what she found impossible to forgive: that my unhinged babblings had named Chris as my wife. Because I wanted to comfort her, I put my hand to cup the curve of her breast. It fitted as it always had, softly into my hold.

'Don't!' she said sharply.

I put my head in my hands, I couldn't think what else to do. 'I'm going away in ten days' time. My call-up papers were downstairs. Your parents are expecting you and Robert to live with them while I'm away, as you know, so I suggest we leave this now. If nothing has changed by the time I come back on leave, then I think you have to realize we can't go on like this.'

'I don't want a divorce.'

I stood up. 'Goodnight.'

'Sometimes I wonder if I'm fair to you, John.'

I laughed, since otherwise I might weep. 'Think about

it before I come on leave. I'd like to find you waiting for me, making an effort to be fair.'

By the door, I hesitated. I could get her back if I ignored squeamishness about forcing my wife against her will. Afterwards, she might even be grateful. The question was, did I want Audrey back for more lasting reasons than winning this night's quarrel? The answer, yes, I did. For several reasons, but for Robert most of all. Which meant that if reconciliation was to work we had to achieve some kind of understanding. A truce in bed was valueless.

I slept alone that night and for the remaining time before I left, dreaming sometimes. The dreams were bad but contained fewer horrors than before; possibly one advantage of a celibate bed, I thought: alone, the horrors appear to be less.

Thorn Hill RAF Station was five miles outside York, a small airfield still under construction. The weather remained cold right into June, the food was atrocious, our quarters leaked and we all found flying Hawker Harts difficult to master: I can't remember ever being happier in my life.

Suddenly, after juggling a dozen different deals while Mathwick & Taylor, my home life and air force training squabbled over the remnants of my time, I shared one purpose only with companions I found congenial. Most of us were older than the average trainee pilot and we shared many interests, above all a determination to prove we weren't too old to fight in a cause we had come to believe was just. We also realized we had very little time in which to learn the things we had to know: tactics, gunnery, navigation, flying, flying, flying. We talked, joked and thought aircraft, looked forward to and also feared converting soon from the Hart to modern monoplanes. I had pushed through as much professional work as possible in my last frantic year as a civilian, collected fees ruthlessly, hoarded cash; with luck there would be enough for Robert not to be brought up entirely on his grandfather's bounty.

But now, all that was past. I don't remember thinking once about money in that whole summer of 1939.

In the time left over from flying we marched all over the Yorkshire moors, singing songs I would have blushed to sing a few weeks before. We whistled at girls, gulped illicit beer if we halted in a village for a breather, and nearly blew up from the consequences a couple of miles further on. When we turned out of bed in the morning an appalling old sergeant-major, borrowed by the RAF for the purpose, drove us into doing physical jerks all over the airfield; in the evenings we were expected to have energy to spare for playing football or cricket.

I slept dreamlessly from the moment I fell into my hard bed until reveille, recovered my old ecstasy flying in air as clear as a draught of spring water. The England I looked down on was quite different from the industrial slums which had so shocked me when I first travelled away from the Weald: almost completely flat but as tranquilly green as my own South Country. Within the triangle formed by York Minster, the Humber and Lincoln Cathedral we flew, careering all over the sky in mock dogfights or terrifying ourselves by attempting to navigate at night. And as we flew I believe each of us felt a new deep love for the land beneath, although we never spoke of it.

We worked so hard that in the whole time between April and September I received only two seventy-two-hour passes, when I went dutifully to London. Nothing changed. Audrey remained unreconciled and time was too short for quarrels, decisions, lawyers. I played with Robert, went with Audrey to places where company helped us through any awkward pauses, and slept as far apart as a double bed would allow. 'Mother and Father would be dreadfully shocked if I asked for two singles,' Audrey explained, apparently unbothered by anything except awkward explanations.

I let it go, but was glad to return to Yorkshire. There were several accommodating girls around the airfield, and after my first futile leave I accepted the inevitable. I simply couldn't make the effort to break with Audrey at the moment, and for Robert's sake did not want to break with her when war had come so close. All the same, I never managed to fight off a sense of furtive guilt over breaking my marriage vows.

By August it was clear that war was coming within days, and I received my second weekend pass.

'What will you fly when you go back?' Audrey asked on the second morning after breakfast, looking up from black headlines in the newspaper.

'Lysanders,' I said ruefully. Older pilots got all the rubbish. 'A single-engined artillery spotter, God help me. Top speed two hundred miles an hour.'

'I'm so glad,' she said gently. 'I'd hate to think of you actually fighting.'

Since I couldn't imagine anything I'd less like to fly in a war than an ambling, almost unarmed artillery-spotter, I changed the subject. 'Where shall we go today?'

'Would you like to take Robert to the sea?'

It seemed a good idea and we went, after arranging to ring up at midday in case a recall came for me. Even the air felt unsettled, hot and thundery, and lines were beginning to form at the petrol pumps as if people expected rationing the moment war was declared. Only Robert remained untouched by it all, bounding up and down on his nanny's lap in the back seat of Colestock's Daimler, delighted by everything.

'He looks like you,' said Audrey, glancing back.

'Somewhat rounder, perhaps.' Secretly, I was pleased.

She laughed. 'How far from here to Furnace Green?'

'You must be a thought-reader. Would you mind? It isn't very far out of our way.' Ever since she had suggested a trip to the sea, I'd been wondering how to propose a detour. Now I began to plot ways of sneaking into the shop without her, so I could ask the present owners if they knew where the Portnells lived. Then, providing Chris's parents were still alive, they could tell me where she was.

I felt the same tug of emotion as I'd felt when flying as

we reached the hill which led to the ridge, the turn to the church where steep banks closed in on either side. If Hitler thought he was coming here, he'd taste his own blood very soon.

I pulled up opposite the shop so Nanny could take Robert off for a romp, since she had rigid ideas about the behaviour of young gentlemen and wanted to work off his fidgets before we went on to Edenham. He was too young to be shown the many things I would have liked to show him, but I watched with enormous satisfaction as he stood uncertainly in the middle of the street, before setting off at a great rate on his hands and knees, leaving Nanny panting and scolding in his wake. Crawling in a dusty roadway was another thing which didn't fit her ideas, Smith, Larkworthy and Paley dust though it might be.

At this point fortune played into my hands. Audrey loathed the earth privy at Edenham, and left me alone while she walked down to the Dyer Arms.

I crossed the street and went into the shop. The same sacks and jars inside, the same fusty smell. An unfamiliar face behind the counter: middle-aged, male and bald. I bought sweets for Robert and Nanny, two pounds of China tea in a tin for Audrey; when war came she would be glad of a few luxuries put away.

'Do you remember the people who kept the shop before you?' I asked, trying to sound off-hand.

'Aye, they'd let the trade run down summat terrible.'

'You're Yorkshire, aren't you? I'm training near York at the moment.'

He was as delighted as if I'd brought some of his native soil in my pocket, agreed that he had the Portnell address somewhere and then stayed talking while I fretted, wondering how much longer Audrey would be away.

Eventually he went to look for it, but came back shaking his head. 'The wife might know where it is, but she's off visiting. I'll send it on if you're gone before she's back.'

I scribbled my address and fairly bolted out of the shop. God knows why I felt ashamed, Audrey had made it abundantly clear that she had no intention of changing her mind about anything.

We wandered around the churchyard and called on the vicar, but Mr Bond had retired the year before. The whole place felt eerily unfamiliar, and yet that same strong love for it clenched ever tighter in my heart. The street was empty but then it always was, at midday in harvest time. All over Europe there would be village streets like this, emptied of life while everyone laboured in the fields, hoping that if they turned their backs on it the war would go away. Instead, this particular storm was building higher and higher above the horizon, the rumble of thunder blowing in on the wind.

'They've changed the name of the pub,' Audrey remarked, somewhat at random as my silence lengthened.

'What?'

'It's called the Black Bear now. Rather nice, I think.'

I laughed, and she looked relieved. She knew I was odd about Furnace Green and hadn't been sure how I would take the change. 'Most people called it that anyway, when I was a boy.'

'Oh? When I asked the landlord why he'd changed, he said a Dyer on the bench had fined him for watering his beer and he was damned begging your pardon ma'am if he'd have his inn called after a nosey-parkering bag o' bones what didn't know good beer when he drank it anyways the kids love that bloody bear begging your pardon ma'am so it brings in extra trade.' She paused for breath.

I laughed again, the sun hot on my back and the smell of her perfume in my nostrils. When Audrey was often such good value, why couldn't we have managed our lives better? 'That sounds exactly like old Dick Locock, the most sanctimonious windbag for miles around. Don't tell me the Lococks have got their hands on the pub as well.'

We went to look and there alongside a very merry black bear was the legend: *Richard Locock, licensed to sell spirits, wines, beer and tobacco.* He came bounding out as soon as he saw me. 'Why, if it isn't young John Smith come back.'

We shook hands circumspectly, Smiths having been much condescended to by Lococks in the past. 'I see you've put the bear up in his place again,' I observed.

He said something exceptionally rude and Sussex about the Dyers, which Audrey pretended not to understand, and offered free pints all round. So we went inside, since it was an event when a Locock offered anything free, although I don't think Audrey had ever been inside a public bar before. A few old men emerged bashfully from behind their pints and greeted us; the beer was awful, wet and thin, the bar utterly unchanged.

I looked and looked at scuffed panelling and oak beams, thinking: I remember. I remember the first pint I was allowed to drink here, which in village life marked acceptance into manhood. I remember the tales Granny told of the many Black Bear happenings.

Once upon a time, on the very day my grandsir, Rico, came to Furnace Green, all weren't well with England nor the Weald, said Granny Paley. Rogues and Frenchmen threatened everywheres and we never been a folk to take threats lightly. So Rico told them the tale of Agincourt, there in Wat Apps's tap. How Englishmen like themselves beat ten times as many French, and then taunted them to charge again if they a-wanted more. When Rico finished, even fat Wat Apps set off to defeat the wicked, so his wife hung up the Black Bear sign while he were away. But why? I had asked, and Granny's spittle sizzled on the hearth. 'Twas the Scovell sign, one o' them Norman bastards what killed their way to power. But that Scovell were English, see? By then his kind and our kind were in some things together, like happened at Agincourt. Wat's wife reckoned a gurt lord's sign might keep the hangman out of her tap, and, when Wat came back, I heard mayhap it did.

The tale of Agincourt: as good a gift as any to take away with me from Furnace Green in this last week of peace.

'I hate beer,' said Audrey, burping delicately when at length we extricated ourselves from good wishes.

'He'll get fined again if he isn't careful. Trust Lococks to make money by selling watered beer.'

We walked back to the car, arms linked and feeling no strain at all. The shopkeeper bobbed out as we passed, waving a piece of paper. 'My wife found the address you wanted. Mr Portnell died a while back, but his missus lives in London with her daughter.' My heart slammed so hard into gassy beer, I was nearly sick. I don't remember whether I thanked him or not, the paper with Chris's address on it pleated into smaller and smaller folds between my fingers as I stood like a lunatic between church and shop, fighting a desire to bolt instantly to London.

Audrey withdrew her arm abruptly. She is acute over nearly everything, except what is better left unsaid. 'It's Chris, isn't it?'

I nodded, flattened out the paper and read: one hundred and twenty-six Upper Regent's Park Road. Very nice too. Lucky Chris.

At that moment Robert and Nanny came back with a rush, and we drove on to Edenham. I glanced once at Audrey. Bright spots of colour patched each cheek and she stared at the dog mascot on the Daimler's bonnet much as Balaam must have looked at his ass. More in disbelief than outrage.

'I'm not coming in,' she said when we reached Edenham in no time at all, twenty minutes down the lane for generations of heavy-footed people now three or less in a car, according to the driver's mood.

I got out and jerked open her door. 'You must. None of this is my mother's fault, and I don't suppose you will ever have to come again.'

She came then; Audrey behaving well. Her husband behaving like God knew what, only scraps of his mind to spare away from Chris. I understood, vaguely, how discourteous and unreasonable I was being but could no longer help it. This very night I would go to find Chris, and discover whether my most painful love bore any relation to reality at all.

My father had died the year before, and the day after his funeral Mum gave up drudging to sit by the fire and doze. She wore her Sunday bonnet and best cross-over shawl every day, hummed little tunes beneath her breath and in between cat-naps strolled along the ridge's lanes. It was not that she became senile, but she simply saw no point in wearing herself out any longer. She made no demands on Mark and his wife, ate whatever was put in front of her and enjoyed the first leisure of her life. Nearly everyone on the ridge believed that old people should creep about trying to be useful until they dropped, and was deeply shocked in consequence. I admired her willpower, which kept her aloof from everything which might spoil this short time of pleasure.

Robert had come to Edenham once before and remembered his Gran with enthusiasm, scrambling on her lap at once. The two of them spent our whole visit mumbling very quietly together, two self-absorbed and kindred spirits. Audrey and Nanny disapproved of this, as if Mum suffered from some contagious disease, but both sensed I was in an awkward mood and let well alone.

'My Ted has volunteered for the regiment and is training away in Norfolk,' Mark said, puffing his pipe and looking very like Dad. In Furnace Green the regiment meant the Royal Sussex; the West Kents, which in the old days also recruited from the Weald, the only other military formation worth considering.

'Our other two boys will soon be old enough to join as well, if this dratted war goes on long.' Mark's wife, Kate, threw up her hands. 'They can't wait, of course.'

'What do you think, John? Will it last like t'other one which took David?' Mark tapped out his pipe, and he and Kate stared at me as if living away from Furnace Green made me privy to Hitler's secrets.

'I don't know.' Privately, I thought the bigger the war, the longer it might last. And this one was beginning to look menacingly big.

'You'll be flying, you say?'

I nodded.

'Ever come across Vic Hawkins? He's a gurt thug of a

flight-sergeant now, the terror of any mechanic, I'd say.'

'In that case, I hope I do come across him. I like mechanics kept up to the mark,' I replied easily. No doubt Vic would think it a huge joke to discover that he was indirectly responsible for me flying Lysanders in a war.

Mark sighed. 'It seems strange to me, my little brother who couldn't take his nose out of a book, up on one of them planes with the birds.'

'It seems strange to me sometimes.' A whole generation lay between Mark and myself.

'Ah well, at least prices will be better on the farms.'

''Tis terrible it takes a war to bring a decent living to the land,' Kate said hotly. She was a bustling body, as quick-moving as Mark was slow.

Mark shrugged. Better times would be welcome, the two decades since the Great War so bitterly hard for farm labourers that often he was at his wits' end how to manage, my payment for Mum's keep grudgingly accepted. And yet they seemed content. Happy and comfortable together, Kate's sharp chivvying painlessly absorbed by Mark's calm. Their boys looked healthy and uncomplicated, Edenham's kitchen spotlessly clean. But bare. One rug, the same oak settles and scrubbed table; the fireback I'd gazed at through countless evenings grinding away at Latin and Greek; Mark's rush-seated chair which had been my father's, and grandfather's before him; the dresser which must have seen the house built around it, since it could never have come in through the door.

I stood up and went over to the hearth. 'Should I show you something?'

'You always were a lad for showing,' answered Mark, smiling.

'I really think we ought to be going, or we'll never get to the sea and back by Robert's bedtime.' Audrey stood too.

'It won't take long.' I opened a penknife and cleared out the crack I remembered so well, felt the same click of metal on metal. Carefully I levered out the arrowhead, held it in my palm. 'There you are, boys. An arrow lost in sapwood long before this house was built, and, if I'm any judge, already many centuries old when it was shot there.' I flicked it over so my nephews could see the scratched mark on the other side, which just might be a deer.

Once upon a time . . . I could feel the arrow's power where it lay in my palm, the quiver of senses which told me how many of my blood had lived and died while this scrap of metal watched.

Mark came over to look too. 'When did you find it?'

'Oh, years ago, one night when I'd been sitting here alone with Dad.'

'You ought to take it up in your plane as a mascot,' Tom, my youngest nephew, said eagerly. 'I'm sure it would bring you luck.'

'Shoot down Huns with your bow and arrow.' Geoff, his brother, grinned.

'I shan't be shooting down Huns in a Lysander.' I inserted the arrow back in its crack. I had a disagreeable feeling about flying Lysanders in wartime, and preferred not to lose the ridge's arrow in a futile attempt to bolster up my courage. I would have liked it as a mascot all the same, had sat there thinking: maybe it can make me a survivor, too. And so I had been driven to hold it one more time, my pretext that someone besides myself ought to know where an interesting curio lay.

Mark put his hand on my shoulder as we stood together in parting. 'You'll be all right, I reckon.'

I nodded. 'Tell Ted good luck from me when you see him next.'

'Aye. I'm glad your boy is out of it, this time around at least.' He hesitated. 'Feelings is strange, they don't mean nothing. You'd be too young to remember, but that last time David came home from France, he and me got drunk together in the Bear. He told me he knew he'd come back but lose a leg. I wonder which one it'll be, he said, kicking out first one then t'other. Bloody useless at farmwork I'll be, without a leg. He were killed by a bullet clean through the head, his officer's letter said, so it goes to show there's no such thing as feelings, don't it?'

I said it did indeed and we shook hands solemnly on this grisly little anecdote. Mark realized I had shown him the arrow after all these years because I was afraid, but I can't say I found his choice of comfort particularly encouraging.

Ah, what the hell. Tonight I would see Chris.

We never did get to the sea; when I rang the Colestocks' from a phone box, the butler said a telegram had arrived, recalling me to York.

Everyone on the road seemed to have the same idea at once, to get back home. Some would have telegrams waiting for them there, others expect letters which would send them to ships and camps all over Britain in the next few days. The rest just sensed that it looked like the real thing at last, and home was the place to be.

When we reached the Colestocks' I went up at once to pack, which was easy since I had only been back two days. Audrey didn't appear, so I went alone to the nursery to kiss Robert farewell. He gave me a sleepy hug, smelling delightfully of bathwater and powder, damp hair brushed up into a spiky comb.

'We'll look forward to seeing you again soon, sir,' said Nanny, in the kind of voice which wanted an end to goings-on in her nursery.

I replied suitably, thinking harder than ever about Chris. Chris my bolt-hole away from fright, doom-bells ringing ever louder in my mind, warning that I should not see my son again.

Audrey was standing beside her parents in the drawing room, stiffly unsmiling. 'I expect the trains will be all over the place,' said Colestock awkwardly into the silence.

'Well, it's early yet.' I looked at my watch. 'Plenty of time to reach York tonight, I hope.'

'Good luck, my boy. Give me a ring if you have any business worries.'

I assured him I would, although it seemed unlikely I should be troubled by property contracts for a while, which shows how wrong you can be.

Mrs Colestock kissed me more warmly than her daughter, my wife, did. All my fault, of course. Or was it? God knew. Anyway, it didn't matter any more.

As soon as my taxi was round Park Place corner, I tapped on the glass. 'Take me to Upper Regent's Park Road, will you?'

'Blimey, guv. The war come and gorn, 'as it? You wanted King's Cross a moment ago.'

I laughed and said I'd just decided the war could get on without me until tomorrow, at which he looked very knowing. Satisfied, too, a leer of fellow-feeling on his face.

A hundred and twenty-six Upper Regent's Park Road was not quite as fashionable as I expected, a corner block with its entrance in the mews. The ornate stucco looked impressive though. An unexpected snag emerged when I discovered the eight flats were all occupied by males or married couples: I couldn't ring every bell and demand if a woman called Chris lived there. After some deliberation I retired to a florist's and bought a large bunch of roses. *To Chris with love*. No signature.

The messenger boy taking the flowers was quite a long time inside, but came out whistling. 'All right?' I said.

'Cor, you made me jump. Yah, I found 'er in the end. Please sir, do you fly fighters?'

'No, Lysanders. Pipsqueak single-engined greenhouses. I'm sorry if you had trouble. I said third floor back.'

'Then they didn't write it on the label and it'd bin wrong if they 'ad. But I found a biddy wot knows everything in the block, they're 'andy sometimes. Not often, mind.' He thumbed his nose. 'The only Chris is fourth floor front. Thank *you*, sir.' He scooped my half-crown into his pocket.

I heeded his warning about the biddy, and chose the stairs rather than a creaking lift. Gritty marble landings, ornamental grillwork, solid polished doors; the atmosphere was anonymous rather than rich. The card above the fourth floor front bellpush announced that Mr & Mrs Raymond Carlisle lived within, and an intimidatingly respectable maid answered my ring. 'Yes, sir?'

'Is Mrs Carlisle at home?'

'No, sir.' She began to close the door.

'I think she is. Will you tell her John Smith has called, please?' I don't know how I sensed Chris was there, holding my roses and wondering.

'Madam would never receive gentlemen who give false names.' There was a smirk behind that dour exterior somewhere.

It wasn't worth explaining that my name really was John Smith, so I shoved my shoulder against the door and walked in. 'Then you'd better tell her to come and see who it is for herself.'

A door across the tiny hallway snapped open and Chris came out with a rush. 'Johnnie! How lovely, lovely to see you again! You clever old thing, how ever did you find me here? Wow, don't you look exciting behind wings and braid!'

'Just like an angel,' I agreed. 'Except they have aerodynamic problems with the braid.'

Chris shouted with laughter in the way I remember her doing as a child, then rounded on the maid. 'You just take that disagreeable look off your face, Bailey. Johnnie and I have known each other for an age.'

'So I perceive, madam,' she said frigidly, and withdrew through a baize door.

'Horrid old hag, but she's sometimes very useful, you know. Johnnie, dear, don't stand there holding your bag, come and pull the cork out of some champagne. I always find it odd how men never get wet opening bubbly and women do.' Chris bounded ahead of me into a chintzy sitting room which offered no evidence for Mr Carlisle's existence.

'I'll get wet this time.' I held up my hands so she could see them shaking. 'Chris—'

She was older than me, but no longer looked it. Or I

looked older than my years while she now possessed the comfortable plumpness which accepts time easily. Her legs and arms retained their sinuous grace, her lips and eyes their invitation.

She blew a kiss with her own entirely steady fingers. 'Gosh, Johnnie, you look as if you'd swallowed a bad oyster.'

'It's stupid. I've thought for eleven years about this moment and now I don't know what to say.'

'What a waste of eleven years.' She looked pleased all the same. 'But Mum still hears from gossips in Furnace Green, and they said you were married.'

'Yes. Is Mrs Portnell here?'

Chris nodded, eyes dancing. 'She's bedridden and a bit deaf. Don't worry.'

I went over and kissed her lightly, softly on the lips, feeling the same instant knowledge of Chris I had always felt. Nothing had changed; I did not pause to consider whether nothing changing was entirely good news for me.

'Have you really thought of me all those years?' she asked against my cheek.

'What the devil do you think?'

She kissed me perfunctorily and plumped down on a sofa. 'There! Look at the reality of a fat old frump.'

I laughed. 'Still Chris.'

'You might at least pretend I'm not really fat. I do try dreadfully hard to be good over diets, but it seems so horribly rude always to pick at treats people have taken trouble to choose especially so I'll like them.'

'Still Chris,' I repeated, and sat down beside her. 'You were always saying how you would improve, when all I wanted was to love you how you were. If only you would have let me.'

I remember . . . Do you remember? Yes, we both remembered.

'Chris,' I said. 'Oh Chris, Chris. Everything spoilt because I wanted you so.'

She raised her eyebrows. 'Was I really as bad as that? Poor Johnnie.'

'No, of course not bad, but I love you, you see. Even today I thought if only I could come—'

'Hair of the dog?' she suggested. Where feelings are concerned, Chris is very quick.

'In a way . . . yes, I suppose so. If I could only have you at last I might get you out of my system. How disgustingly crude it sounds, my dear. You see, I've treated my wife and son so badly I was desperate for a cure, but of course I was still lying to myself. As soon as you came through that door I knew some kinds of love are never cured.'

'You make me sound like a tumbler of quinine. Hold your nose and gulp me down.' She stood up and held out her hand. 'Come then, and enjoy yourself for once.'

As easy as that.

Be happy Johnnie, I want you to be happy.

We lay together all evening; loving, laughing, remembering, even occasionally dozing in each other's arms.

'I've decided you're nicer than quinine,' I said; by then it must have been ten o'clock.

'Oh, good. I'm ravenous, aren't you? Do you think you're brave enough to wheedle Bailey into giving us something to eat?'

I didn't give a damn for Bailey, in fact I thoroughly approved of her trying to keep men out of Chris's flat. Jealousy stirring out of nowhere as it had with Chris before.

'Champagne!' she exclaimed, when I carried a loaded tray back into the bedroom. 'Johnnie, you're a marvel. Was Bailey dreadfully cross?'

'I didn't notice.'

'Heavens, don't start being stuffy after the lovely time we've had! Here, nip in again.' She patted the bedclothes.

I nipped, and, propped up by pillows, we ate chicken in aspic and drank champagne, giggling like naughty children. By now I ought to have reached York, and be waiting for transport out to the airfield.

'It's lovely you still like me now I'm all faded and baggy.' Chris licked her fingers complacently.

'I'd be surprised if you aren't still the devil of a girl at seventy. Chris, will you marry me? Not at once of course, I need a divorce. But as soon as ever we can.'

'Marry? Johnnie, really! No, of course I couldn't. Why, you were as proud as a peacock when you told me you'd got a son, and nearly everyone in Furnace Green must have written to tell Mother your wife is lovely.'

'Yes, she is. Perhaps if things had been different we might have been happy, but I threw away any chance we had because I still loved you. Not even Robert can bring it back. And this evening surely you have loved me a little, too. No, listen to me. Doesn't how we've been together mean anything at all to you, once we're out of bed?'

'Vulgar pig. Yes, of course it does. You know jolly well I'd have to love you too for us to have enjoyed ourselves so much.'

Delight shot upward in a shower of tingling sparks. Chris loved me. If I survived my Lysander, then we'd live together always. 'Darling, oh, my darling. God, what fools we've been to waste eleven years.'

I don't know what she answered because she was again as eager as I for love. A splendour of love together, which this time I understood to seal our bargain.

'I'm happy,' Chris said some time in the middle of the night, joyous echo of her earlier wish for me. 'Put that among your rememberings as well. John Smith made me happy in August 1939.'

I laid my head between her shoulder and breast, smelling her perfume and also the scent of desire, hot and unashamed. 'Why did you try to say no when I asked you to marry me?'

'I still say no, and will go on saying no. Why not admit you're simply being conventional, and don't really want to marry someone like me at all?'

'But I do! I've never wanted anything else. I suppose I thought . . . Well, before tonight I did wonder . . . how I would feel if we met again. Now, I know. I love you more than ever I could all those years ago, when I adored you like a goddess.'

Chris gurgled with laughter. 'Oh, Johnnie, and how I adore you too. Gosh, I never dreamed people really said things like that. But don't you see? If we married, you'd be as suspicious as a Locock sheepdog inside a week, and I—'

'Yes. Perhaps it is time you told me how you really feel,' I said evenly.

She rustled bedclothes, thinking. 'Cross. I'm sure I'd feel cross. I hate jealous men glowering at me. Then I'd probably feel bored and boredom's always so dreadfully dreary. Why, there's a war coming! How could I shut myself up like a nun just when everything's starting to get exciting?'

'You have a very odd notion of how I'd treat my wife.'

'You'd expect her to be faithful,' she answered candidly. 'I bet you were to Audrey, whether you loved her or not, until she was so silly.'

I got out of bed, feeling sick. What a narrow stuffy cell she made love seem. 'If we married I shouldn't find it a burden loving only you. I simply wouldn't be interested in other women any more.'

Chris blew me a kiss. 'What a gorgeous prig you are. The trouble is, I think you mean it.'

'Of course I do.'

'I thought so. But, Johnnie, I'm so different! I never have the guts to do a thorough job on anything. I don't know how it is, but I have this knack of forgetting things two moments after they're past. Sometimes it's convenient, sometimes not.' She laughed. 'So there you are; I'd make the hell of a wife. I learned that once.'

'You don't forget everything then,' I said tightly. 'Mr Carlisle?'

'Oh no, he was a poppet. So was my husband, really. A big dark rotter who sometimes gave me a lot of fun. I don't like my men too good.' She looked my sandy nondescription over critically, before slipping her hand into mine. 'I don't like them too bad, either. I love you, Johnnie, in a way I shan't love anyone else. Let's leave it at that, shall we?'

We left it.

The first six months of the war were unlike anything I had imagined: routine and anticlimactic, my doom-bells proved ludicrously wrong. At first our squadron kept together, annoying the citizens of York with low flying by day and rowdiness at night. Then, just before being granted Christmas leave, we were told that in the future each of our twelve Lysanders would be attached individually to artillery regiments for spotting and co-operation duties, in my case to a newly formed outfit under training in Scotland. This meant the end of the squadron as a unit and my last memory of it is the binge we had in York before that Christmas leave.

A binge which also marks the place where my memory begins to play tricks on me, where distance and time start flowing together. Even now, sometimes I wake in terror and do not know whether the flames which scorch me come from earlier hauntings of Edenham millhouse, or my own. Those are the nights when I am grateful for an empty bed beside me, and even more grateful when Mrs Sleech comes trudging down the lane to mark the end of another lonely vigil.

On good days my old man's dozings by the hearth conjure Granny Paley out of the void where more recent memory is lost: then my head doesn't nod in drowsiness but in eager greeting to old friends. My hand lifts to touch Cheerful's muzzle, the ox I loved as a child, and perhaps in amused acknowledgement to Liddy Larkworthy, who also greeted ghosts beside this same hearth. I wish Laffams good hunting (which neatly covers a multitude of sins), stand again beneath a mighty Meeting Oak where a great many things began.

And when I wake to warmth glowing on chequered

brick, often I am not sure how much I dreamed, how much I shared with others before me on the ridge.

On bad days . . . no. I shall not speak of what happens on my bad days. God knows, they come too often without being summoned up. Then the only defence I have is to turn, this time quite consciously, and beg old friends to help me keep hold on sanity. Old, old friends, since I have few others now; meals-on-wheels and village neighbours come to call but I cannot talk to them as I should. Old friends are best, who see behind appearances.

So what are dreams, forgetfulness or remembering? How much of what I understand belongs to the years I have lived as a recluse, passing the time in study and reflection? How much is owed to my own ridge blood, to Granny Paley and gut-knowing buried in the past?

But . . . What was I saying? Yes, back to the party in York.

. . . Twelve pilots and their observers going off on leave. I remember, do you remember? Within seven months scarcely any of them would be left to remember anything.

By nine-thirty we were all noisily drunk and singing the less printable of our songs. Most other diners in the restaurant began to leave, the war not yet sufficiently bloody for civilians to feel indulgent towards rowdy servicemen.

Cliff Masters, my observer, climbed on a table and from there conducted the final ritual chorus of the squadron's war-cry:

'Is it one two three?'

'No!'

'Is it four five six?'

'Siiix!'

'Seven?'

'Seeeven!'

'Eight?'

'No!'

'Nine?'

'Niiine!'

'Six Seven Nine Squadron, Roooyal Air Foorrce?'
'Six Seven Nine!'

At that point someone remembered the London train and we all surged out of the door, carrying several waiters' trays with us, while Cliff wore the chef's cap. We raced each other, tripping and laughing, ricocheting off pedestrians, all the way to the station, dodging across a siding when we glimpsed an avenging patrol of military police. Keith Parker-Duff, the caricature of an English gentleman when drunk, commandeered an electric luggage trolley into which we all piled and then drove it like a fairground dodge'em along a platform crowded with passengers, his thumb on the warning bell.

The stationmaster was summoned and appeared wearing a braided cap which Desmond Knight deftly removed, for, as he said, it was an admiral's cap and you couldn't have an admiral commanding a railway station. Whistles. Final arrival of the MPs. Pilots on Christmas leave? Put 'em in the bloody luggage van, it's all they're fit for, an' the guard'll shovel 'em out at King's Cross in the morning.

Fortunately, we possessed young men's digestions as well as their high spirits, and slept instantly, sprawled all over the mailbags.

Most of that Christmas leave has vanished altogether from my mind. Cleared out like unwanted jumble among the many other things I somehow must forget. I remember wanting Chris and staying with Audrey. Robert running all over the house, unwrapping more presents than were good for him, his arms round my neck as I raced him piggy-back up the stairs.

'Tittermatorter! Tittermatorter!' he yelled at the top of his voice, thudding soft heels into my ribs, for I had told him this village word for see-saw rides. I'm glad the last time I saw him, he was laughing.

Audrey looked lovelier than ever, remote snow-queen loveliness which kept each soft hair in place. She also talked cleverly to hide a great many awkward moments, and nothing had changed at all.

Chris . . .

'Gosh, Johnnie. I hope you're as fast with aeroplanes as you are with me.'

'Sorry.' I wasn't sorry.

'Oh, I like it.' So I kissed her again with a passion which was always new, our bodies quickly and strongly joined together in Christmas celebration.

Then memory is turned out into the street again, tramping dark wartime pavements because the day after Boxing Day Chris didn't answer her bell. If she had gone to a party then she hadn't warned me; if not, it was better to walk than stand watching darkened windows. You should have told me you'd be back for Christmas, she had said. Until she failed to answer her bell I had chosen not to wonder what she meant.

And so a new year came in, and still nothing happened in the war. People began to expect it simply to fizzle out. Shook their heads wisely and declared that Hitler had taken all he wanted. He knew he couldn't get away with taking more. Bet you it's peace this year.

In Scotland, this new year of 1940 roared in like ten thousand devils, the weather so atrocious that during January and February we scarcely flew. I was, however, becoming attached to my Lysander. Now the squadron was dispersed C Charlie became my own machine, and a lousy one at that. On take-off she swung like hell and once in the air flew with one wing low. The controls were stiff and Cliff and I nearly died of cold every time we went up. But the Bristol Perseus engine was reliable and in a single-engined machine that counted for a lot. She would land and take off from almost anywhere if we got lost—and once spring came we were lost nearly everywhere in central Scotland—and I loved her because she was mine.

Aircraft were simpler than women, any day.

In April, everything changed. The Germans invaded Norway and Denmark, then Holland, Belgium and France. Hitler hadn't yet taken all he wanted, but it was too late for collecting bets.

The regiment of artillery to which I had been attached was sent haring south for emergency embarkation, but by the time we reached Hampshire the Germans were motoring almost unopposed through France, having cut off most of the British army on their way, and we were set to dig trenches outside Winchester instead. Winchester, where I went to collect stores one day and in the high street passed a splendid statue of Alfred the Great, hand on his sword and still standing guard over England. I thought we might have need of another Alfred before we finished.

At the end of May, by which time the Belgians had surrendered and half the British army was stranded on the beaches of Dunkirk, Cliff and I received orders to fly to Hawkinge, in Kent.

I can't remember what we thought about a lone Lysander being summoned to fight the Luftwaffe, but, almost unarmed and lumberingly slow, we were on our way to war at last. My green South Country edged slowly past the duck-egg blue of our fuselage as we flew quite low from Winchester to Kent. A glorious clear day in which to say farewell. A bloody bad kind of day for thinking about enemies hiding in the sun.

Soon, I saw the Weald coming up ahead. A flecked maze of woods and heaths, minute villages, confusing roads, an undramatic harmony like nowhere else on earth. Ashdown, Ashurst, Hartfield; Crowborough Hill, Tisbury Hill, Brightling Beacon; Mayfield, Riffield, Furnace Green.

As gracefully as a Lysander could, I put C Charlie into a roll. Once, twice. A spark struck in the sunlit air between myself and my ridge, lying all green and soft summer brown below. There was the wandering road which led from Tisbury Hill with its Iron Age camp on the summit, to the ancient, almost dry pool. Here our village green curving beneath my wings, Danesdell and Locock's to one side, Bywood's smithy on the other; the yew where Bart's bones had been hung up replaced by a red phone box. Figures stared upward in the street, the same white dots as Tobias Hosmer saw when he fell from the steeple. Then, flying less than a hundred feet above the cottages, I saw a most extraordinary sight: a ditched rectangle as sharp-cut as on the day the ridge-people were forced to dig it, nearly a thousand years before. Granny Paley had said the cottages there were built inside the line of Fawkner's palisade, but on the ground there was no sign of this. Now, as I banked around the church tower, not only ditch and bank, but the marks of vanished barns, a well and an entry gate were clearly etched by the westering sun.

Edenham passed swiftly below as I opened the throttle wider. More shadows in the grass there: the tracks, vanished mills and furnaces of the great days of Wealden iron. I glimpsed a figure which might be Mark, shading his eyes beside a herd of cows, and waggled my wings.

Twenty minutes later we landed at Hawkinge.

We took off again the following morning for a small emergency airfield near Dover. The Channel was hazy with heat but as we landed we could see the eastern horizon stained with smoke, the shuttle of ships crawling across glittering water.

Two hundred thousand men had already been snatched from the beaches of Dunkirk. Another hundred and thirty thousand still waited patiently under an onslaught of bombs and shells, and the word had gone out: somehow get the men, though every weapon must be left behind. Only get the men and they can be rearmed. Then, between us, we'll save a nation. Even, perhaps, a civilisation.

The advance airfield was disconcertingly close to the cliffs, and tiny. Two Lysanders were parked under some netting, from their identifying letters Des Knight's and Taff Jones's. A burned-out Spitfire and a shattered Lysander had been pushed aside into a ditch to keep the grass take-off strip clear: no Spitfire could have got down on that small field in one piece.

'That's Keith's Lysander,' said Cliff, jumping down.

'The wrecked one?'

'Yes. M Mother.' Keith had had a ruder word for M.

A tent served as dispersal and we met Taff and Des there. 'Keith?' I asked.

Taff shrugged. 'He came in shot to bits and crashed. He was killed, his observer died after we pulled him out.'

'Where did they get him? Have the Jerries started strafing over here already?'

Taff and Des exchanged glances, and it was Des who answered. 'We've lost half the squadron in two days. We're taking turns to orbit over Belgium and spot the Jerry raids coming in. Our fighters have to fly from Kent now their French bases are lost, and unless they get a few minutes' warning of the German raids coming in, our squadrons arrive too late over Dunkirk beaches. Jerry has dropped his eggs and gone. But if they scramble too soon, they're out of fuel and on their way back to base before the Jerry bombers turn up.'

Whatever I had expected, it wasn't this. 'You radio a warning in clear?'

'It's the only way. Dodge the Jerry fighters and circle as long as you can. Radio as soon as you see a raid coming in, then get the hell out.' Des looked at his watch. 'Peter Mason is over there now, and I relieve him. You after me. Taff got away with two trips yesterday, God knows how, but his Lys is crocked. They're working on it now.'

We sat on deckchairs, waiting.

Keith had apparently survived one trip unscathed before he was shot down, the other five Lysanders were all lost first time. Cliff and I went to see the controller but he added little to what Taff and Des had said, information as scarce as everything else. 'Orbit close to Ypres at between fifteen and twenty thousand feet. The German fighters seem mostly to be keeping lower, to strafe our troops probably, and the bombers so far have rendezvoused in that area today.' We bent over the map, eyes following his finger. 'They're concentrating just east of Ypres, here, to wait for stragglers, tighten formation and pick up their fighter escort, probably. Providing we have a spotter in position, our fighters get between five and six minutes' warning of a raid. Which is just enough to scramble them to reach Dunkirk with a maximum load of fuel. Don't break radio silence for Jerry fighters, hide from them if you can. It's warning of the bombers we want.'

'Any cloud?' asked Cliff.

'Very little. Some smoke and haze.'

'Oh sure, we'll see a bloody lot of Heinkels if we stay dodging about in smoke at two hundred feet,' snapped Cliff.

The controller nodded. 'That's the snag. But we need those reports in time to get the fighters up. About three-quarters of our entire army is surrounded on those beaches and only the navy can get them out. The pongoes have scarcely any anti-aircraft cover and very little machine-gun ammunition left. There's hundreds of ships stopped in the shallows trying to take men off. The Jerries are sending in waves of fifty or more bombers at a time. It's murder each time they get through without our fighters up.'

The sharp staccato of Des's engine announced his time to go. We watched as his Lysander taxied to the end of the field, swung slightly as he tested the controls and took off without even a wave in our direction.

'When's Peter due back?' I asked.

'When his fuel runs dry, unless a raid comes in first. Say twenty, twenty-five minutes.' A Lysander carried fuel to last perhaps two hundred minutes airborne, less if it had to dodge fast or often. An hour for it to grind slowly to Dunkirk and back, two hours in which to try somehow to stay alive over German-occupied Belgium while watching for bombers rendezvousing around Ypres.

'Any contact?'

'No.'

The minutes dragged past while we stood on cliffside turf, straining our ears for the distinctive Lysander drone. The sound of gunfire travelled quite clearly across fifty miles of water, and the distant stain of black smoke hung higher in the sky.

Twenty minutes. Twenty-two. Twenty-eight.

I don't remember sitting in my deckchair again, sun lancing into my skull and sweat cold on my back, because by then we were waiting for Des.

I remember the field telephone's ring and Taff answering it.

'Des?' I asked.

'Indeed, no. It's the exception if they come back, you know. I was lucky twice and Keith once, if you call it luck.' He jerked his head at the wreck of M Mother. 'Usually it's a question of whether you have time to bale out or not.' He tilted his face to the sun and closed his eyes. 'My Lys will be ready in time to follow after you.'

'And then there were none.'

'The other two are due in tonight. Gerry from Cornwall and Crowdie from Northern Ireland. They'll take over tomorrow, and upon my soul the navy cannot have much longer to get the army out.' Taff was chapel Welsh; he said things like that, and meant them. His body was never found after his Lysander was shot down the following day; his observer parachuted safely and spent the rest of the war behind wire.

I suppose it must have been mid-afternoon by the time we were airborne, but this is another blank. I recall looking down on a Channel filled with ships, two of them burning and several trailing slicks of oil. Destroyers, yachts, old paddle-steamers; from the air, unseaworthy wallowings and packed khaki decks were brutally clear. It's murder if the bombers reach the beaches without warning, the controller had said, a massacre surely if they reached these overloaded and defenceless ships with their scant few inches of freeboard.

'They must have taken off the hell of a lot of men today,' Cliff shouted.

'A good few more to come,' I answered as Dunkirk lifted out of the smoke ahead. A hundred and thirty thousand more, the controller had said, which was more than the motley armada of ships we saw could lift off bombed beaches in a day. Soon, away to our left, we could see dark waiting lines of soldiers etched against yellow dunes, red and yellow explosions, black smoke, blue cloudless glare. Men and more men on an open beach, waiting to be taken home. Burning ships, and in the countryside beyond the beaches, gunflashes frighteningly close.

We dropped lower as we crossed the coast, jinking to take advantage of such hiding places as I could find: a row of poplars, a hillock, a blessed dark green wood. Although sedately slow, the Lysander was probably as safe as any other British aircraft in these hostile skies so long as we could hug the ground. Willing, manoeuvrable C Charlie was difficult for faster aircraft to pick out from among the contours. Our cockpit, too, was so high above the fuselage that there were scarcely any blind spots, which was more than could be said for fighters.

Cliff kept yelling directions over the intercom as we navigated almost from one crossroads to the next. Once a wood directly ahead unexpectedly spewed flame and dust, which must have been a German battery shelling the beaches, otherwise I retain an impression of lanes full of vehicles, all German, the thud of rifle bullets into fabric, of squeezing between two houses with a roar which spilled a motor cyclist into a ditch.

Then I remember climbing in laborious spirals as, far too soon, the time came when we couldn't hedge-hop any longer. We flattened out at about eighteen thousand feet and began to circle, keeping position by the pall of smoke above Dunkirk, nearly forty miles to the north.

That awful curdling of the stomach muscles as I craned my neck like a madman! Look back, up, forward; squint at the blazing sun. An ache began at the back of my head and settled behind my eyes as glare struck into the cockpit. I kept glancing at the fuel gauge, willing it to drop towards empty so we could with honour sneak away.

'Aircraft five o'clock below,' Cliff said softly, as if afraid the enemy might hear.

Instantly I was drenched in sweat, my weight hanging

on the controls so the Lysander shimmied like a startled blonde. Twelve glinting blobs were outlined against ground haze, a meticulous formation looking every inch the part of conquerors. Messerschmitt 110's. Hardly daring to breathe, we watched them dwindle and disappear, then did not speak of them again in case they came hurtling back.

The fuel counter dropping slowly, slowly; the sun even more slowly in the summer sky. Oil pressure and temperature, normal. Wind, calm. No other aircraft in sight. Reckoning carefully, I decided that in another twenty minutes we could turn for home. Twenty-five at the very most, to make sure I never had a twinge of conscience afterwards over leaving early.

Perhaps the Germans wouldn't send in another raid today.

'Surely someone will report we're here,' said Cliff.

With the whole countryside below crawling with victorious Germans, Christ knew how many AA spotters must already have radioed that another lone Lysander was circling Ypres. I was surprised they hadn't taken some pot-shots at us, but perhaps the Germans, too, were having their problems with supply. For different reasons from ourselves, of course.

The sky was vast and blue and clear, no way of making things more difficult for the fighters. If I circled Maastricht or Bruges or Lille the Lysander would be just as easy to see, and besides, the Jerry bombers were assembling over Ypres today. Or so the controller thought.

Sweat gathered inside my gloves, the right one absolutely sodden. The roar of the Lysander increased my sense of isolation, so monotonous it became a kind of silence. Cliff and I turning, turning in our seats; the Lysander circling, sun and earth dipping and circling too. If only we could spot some bombers gathering before the fighters came for us, we could report them and get out, without waiting for that damned fuel gauge to drop towards the red. Longingly, I glanced down to where mist-green trees and valleys were almost hidden under haze. I felt completely alert and yet oddly dazed, dreaming with my eyes wide open and spine turning, turning: Chris, my Chris. Chris, with her store of grins and different-coloured kisses. Why must some sticky residue of pride prevent me from accepting her as she was? How could she be everything I'd ever wanted, yet refuse me the one thing I really wanted?

'Chris?'

'Mm?' We had walked last leave along the Chelsea Embankment.

'You look quite beautiful.'

She tilted her head and laughed. 'I told you, I'm a hag.'

'Chris?'

'What?'

'Nothing.'

'Yes, there was.'

My head light and spinning, hands and feet heavy. I hadn't dared ask her again to marry me, since another refusal must mean final defeat, now she knew how good we were together. But, quite suddenly, I had to try once more. 'Chris, you must marry me. I can't . . . I hate it like this.'

'Oh, Johnnie, you are difficult!'

'I've always been difficult over you. I can't help it. You know I love you. Too much to share.' A night for me, a night for him, a night for someone else.

She frowned. 'Not quinine this time, but an ice-cream cornet to be hoarded.'

'I meant it.'

'I've always known you did. That's why I'll always say no, my dear. In spite of what you think I'm not particularly fast, but somehow you'd never quite believe it. I do like enjoying myself, and I'm not sure I would enjoy myself with you.'

'But I love you! Why couldn't—'

'Oh, don't be such a bore! It has nothing to do with bed.

There! What an admission! Why, now I'm fat and lazy I might even *enjoy* being a virtuous wife, but—'

'But?'

'Shall I tell you something terrible? You said you meant what you said, well, so do I. I love you in a way I won't love anyone else, but I'm miserable unless I can be empty-headed if I feel like it, encourage men who think I'm nice. With you I'm pretty sure there'd be an awful lot of times when I'd never enjoy myself at all. I bet your Audrey is all the things I'm not. You go back to her and be happy.'

'I can't.' Oh, the pain of understanding at last that to your love you're nothing more than an earnest bore. We didn't speak all the way back to her flat.

'Take care.'

'Yes, and you.'

'Phone me when you're due for leave again.'

'Yes, I will.'

She closed the door, and outside it was drizzling.

. . . 'Three, no, four gaggles gathering, one o'clock high.' Cliff's voice crackled in the intercom, making me jump. Could I really have been dreaming?

Almost immediately I spotted some con-trails, very high. 'No! There, there!' Cliff yelled, and suddenly I saw them. Black swarming Jerries converging on us from the south and east.

Bombers, so many had to be bombers.

I opened the throttle and began to climb again. The manufacturers swore a Lysander would reach twenty-five thousand feet, although none of us ever managed it. But I had to make sure that what we saw was really bombers before reporting back, no matter how great the risk. Scramble our few remaining combat squadrons to meet a Jerry fighter sweep and they would be out of fuel by the time the bombers came, lose aircraft we could not afford.

Above our heads a different pattern was beginning to

form and I recognized the slender silhouettes of Messerschmitt 109's. 'They must see us,' I whispered. My throat contracted, toes curled in my boots.

'For Christ's sake,' shouted Cliff. 'Radio base and get down on the deck.'

'Not yet.' We had to be sure, the swarm in the east still too far away for positive recognition. Get the men, get the men. It's murder on the beaches unless we intercept the bombers coming in. If all those dots were bombers, this raid would be the bloodiest yet. Chris, come closer to me now.

The Lysander stuck at twenty-two thousand feet and we levelled out. Not far above, the Messerschmitts sailed along, apparently blind.

Head swivelling frantically, I saw even more black specks boiling away to the east, before everything suddenly changed shape. The fighters overhead wheeled, wings glinting in the sun; the formations we had been struggling to recognize became rapidly larger. 'Heinkel 111's and Dornier 17's,' Cliff shouted.

Now, I too could see glittering glass noses and the distinctive shape of Dorniers. I flipped the switch on my radio. 'Hullo Buster, Hullo Buster. Mike three calling. Two hundred plus bandits ready to run. Repeat, two hundred plus, ready to run. Mike three in position Zona. Two hundred plus bandits range six to twelve thousand yards. Fighters overhead.'

The second I finished, I kicked the rudder bar and broke for the ground, a hell of a long way below. Not fast enough. Red tracers danced past the propeller, then a Messerschmitt was right in front of me, black crosses, yellow spinner and all. He had overshot a slow Lysander and his wings quivered as he pulled up out of sight, trying to get back for more.

Incoherent pictures are superimposed on the chaos of my memory. Chris, leaning back against a Chelsea parapet, shaking damp hair out of her eyes. Three Messerschmitts waggling their wings at each other, tracers criss-crossing, dirty grey trails from exhausts. My trusty C Charlie grinding like a steam-roller, wind howling past the wing-struts as I dived faster than its frame was ever designed to bear. If we could only reach trees, hills, mist, the faintest chance remained.

Another Messerschmitt raced past us, I could see the pilot leaning forward in the cockpit before it flicked out of sight. I squeezed a burst from the guns fixed above Charlie's wheel-spats but I'm sure they went nowhere near. Behind, I could hear the rattle of Cliff firing his Lewis: only ninety-seven rounds before he had to change the drum.

Where had the other Messerschmitts gone? Beware, beware the Hun you cannot see. I began to panic, the ground seemed as far away as ever, each second an eternity.

A sudden series of crashes overhead tore daylight through the wing, the sound of more behind. Freezing air ripped into the cockpit as I half rolled to the left, and for a moment thought fuselage and wing were about to split apart. A sharp explosion under the engine cowling, oil splashing on the windshield, wisps of smoke joining the ferocious draughts in the cockpit. I don't know what speed we were doing by then, but it must have been bloody fast for a Lysander and the smoke almost immediately seemed to blow itself out.

'Bale out, Cliff,' I yelled, and heaved on the stick with all my strength, hoping to pull up long enough to give us the chance to get out. We were getting low by then, but there was still height enough if we were very, very quick.

No answer.

'Cliff!'

For an instant we were flying almost level, smoke drifting up again between my feet. Oil on hot metal probably, not a proper fire. Yet. I snatched a glance over my shoulder. Cliff was hunched against his harness, moaning. 'Cliff!'

No answer. I could see his eyes flicker, but he looked in a bad way.

Some instinct made me jam the controls into another

roll, too late. A dazzling shower of tracer flashed past, the Lysander shuddered and dropped like a lead pig. Dazed by shock, paralysed by fear, the kind of dreadful fear which liquefies your guts and fills your mouth with vomit, I felt my muscles lock. Saw a high tension cable flash past alongside, a river only feet below. An appalling crash suggested that the fixed undercarriage had fouled a branch: only our forward momentum prevented us from plunging into a hillock just beyond.

As it was, we were still flying. The engine spitting, a section torn clean out of the fuselage by my left ankle through which I could see an almost detached wheel and a snatch of ground, but still flying.

Timidly, I tried the controls. Ailerons as stiff as hell, the skin on the wings flapping above my head. Jammed trimming cables weighed on the stick and the cockpit cover was oiling up. Between that oil on the windshield and smoke again eddying into the cockpit, I had already lost all forward visibility, the thought of attempting to land quite horrifying. Normally I could have put down into any medium-sized field, now the only ground I could see was a hurtling patch beside my ankle, and Lysander cockpits wouldn't jettison whole. Further back, Cliff ought to be able to see something, guide me down perhaps. Between the two of us was a large fuel tank and a great deal of clutter, there was no way I could reach him. He seemed conscious, his eyes flickering and teeth grimacing against his lips, but didn't respond to my shouts and I dared not turn for more than seconds. Trees, telephone wires, cows, all tearing past that hole, almost level with the dangling wheel.

My heart failed me then, and I lost courage for staying low. To hell with Messerschmitts, like this I would fly into the next row of poplars. I pulled gently on the stick and the engine cut out, coughed, caught raggedly again.

We wallowed up a couple of hundred feet and levelled out when the engine showed signs of failing altogether. I cowered in my seat expecting more bullets at any second but nothing happened; probably the Messerschmitts were on their way to Dunkirk beach by now.

Above my head a narrow section of cockpit cover was still clear of oil and I could see, well over to the right, the black smoke above Dunkirk towering higher than ever. So I had a choice. Steer by that smoke and hope to reach the sea, where if we pancaked or baled out there was a chance of being picked up and taken home. Or put down now, completely blind, and risk that bloody petrol tank between us catching fire.

I twisted in my seat, screaming at Cliff. No good. He moaned a little but did not move. And I was selfish enough to wish him dead, anything rather than a helpless passenger. Because, even if I could gain enough height to bale out myself, I killed him if I jumped.

No choice, really. No choice so long as the engine lasted. Oh, Johnnie, shall I tell you something terrible? I'm not sure I would enjoy myself with you. Johnnie the bore. Johnnie the earnest dreamer, with nothing beside a very little money to show for all his wantings. Cliff, old son, do you find me a bore, trying to fly you home in a Lysander full of holes?

The cockpit was becoming very hot, the smoke definitely thicker. My mouth getting dryer and dryer, my body tiring from the effort of flying an aeroplane which yearned to fall out of the sky.

The black Dunkirk pyre was pulling slowly astern, I must be over sea by now. I craned my neck, trying to see through the hole and nearly hit the water before I saw it glitter.

Should I pancake immediately and hope against hope to get Cliff out, support him until a ship came? But I was bound to land so heavily that shot-up C Charlie would sink within seconds. At the best of times it was a struggle for the observer to get out past the petrol tank and Lewis gun. Cliff would certainly drown, quite possibly I would too.

To this day I do not know whether I decided to make

for Kent because by then our fuel would be used up, the risk of fire on landing less, or because I funked crashing in water I couldn't see. I glanced at my watch and found to my surprise that it was broken. For the first time felt my left arm ache; it couldn't be anything serious or I would have noticed it before. But once I began to feel it, the ache became steadily worse and blood seeped slowly on to my knee.

I started to pray. I am somewhat ashamed of this since in my safe years I had never prayed; now I was back in Furnace Green church. Moist cool stone against my forehead, a drone of entreaty in my ears.

My flying boots were beginning to smoulder; as soon as I realized what was happening I pulled them back in a panic and the Lysander lost a hundred feet before I could face jamming them back again. I forget how much longer after that it was before I saw dunes and bright green marsh grass through my friendly hole. Kent? Or had I flown in a circle and was back again in France?

Here everything finally chars together in my mind, as my face began to crinkle and reek of its own fat, scarlet light to explode behind my eyes. I heard myself gasping and straining at the controls, speaking and answering too, my lips bleeding as I chewed them to hold back the agony of roasting feet I must somehow keep on the controls. The ground was there, THERE.

We touched, leapt high and bucketed at an appalling speed across ground I couldn't see. I remember my blood frying among the broken gauges, the stench of cooked meat; then, when I thought we must go over and burn in a pyre like Dunkirk, the tail came down with a crash and we stopped.

I couldn't move.

Surely I couldn't move.

I was trying to move. Trying. Slowly my fingers fumbled out the pin of my harness, fumbled, fumbled with parachute straps. Pure terror bringing strength back now as I struggled with the cockpit cover. It was stuck. Jammed!

Forgetting pain, I put both feet against the instrument panel and heaved with all my might, and felt it move. I strained again, screaming now as flame licked out of the engine towards my eyes, and it flew open with a jerk. I dragged myself out anyhow, reached back to free the harness holding Cliff. A bastard of a distance to reach past a petrol tank turned into a timebomb by heated fumes, to haul out dead weight and down on the grass with Cliff.

A touch faster on landing and we would have pitched into a drain. A fraction harder into the ground and I wouldn't have lived to roll screaming in a ditch and hear my own flesh sizzle.

A little less or more of this or that. What the hell. I was just lucky.

Or so they said.

I never imagined such pain, although doubtless others have.

We had reached Kent, which was something.

Cliff had an armour-piercing bullet against his spine, paralysing him until it was removed, but he would recover, which was another thing.

Audrey came, very nice of her of course, but a bad thing altogether.

I lay wrapped in wet dressings from scalp to the soles of my feet while Dunkirk ended, the Battle of Britain came and went. I couldn't see, I could scarcely move, I was bitterly hurtful to Audrey. I wanted her to go and in the end she went. The prospect that pity might force her into offering a lifetime of spurious affection was quite intolerable.

As for Chris, the old bore never phoned her next time his leave was due.

That was the year my friends came to keep me sane, not always sanity as others would define it. When they took turns to sit by my bed and spin their tales, which were and were not the piecemeal tales I had heard from Granny Paley. This the time when time lost its meaning, pain and more pain the only change I knew. When the only bolt-hole left to a blind and tethered man was to set every instinct burrowing into the sediments of his mind. And there, instead of madness, I found the ridge waiting for me. Its tales and instincts, my half-forgotten Durham beginnings of research, the rhythms of my childhood. These I clung to frenziedly as my last defence, until they seemed to come alive and speak beside my bed. Scholarship, folk memory and experience like drops of rain on glass, each running into the other until they made a whole.

Once upon a time . . .

In the autumn of 1941, more than a year after I crashed, I was discharged from hospital. I would return again and again as plastic surgeons learned new skills from the horrific injuries of war, but for the moment I needed time for recuperation while they decided which part of me to tackle next.

I had become used to wandering around the hospital grounds, more painfully grown used to loneliness as, with a measure of recovery, my friends from the past stepped back to watch. The doctors were pleased when my mind steadied along with the rest of me; I found it chilling to turn or try to sleep and find no one waiting for me there.

A different aloneness altogether opened up when I returned to the workaday world. A woman with a kindly voice had interviewed me some time before. She knew I was estranged from my wife and did not probe. 'If you have nowhere to go, the RAF has rehabilitation centres where some of our patients prefer to lodge.'

'I think I have to go out, even if only for a few weeks. If not now, then I might never make it.'

'Certainly it would be better if you did. So where can you go? Parents? Friends?' She understood that brisk impersonality was easiest to bear.

'My parents are both dead and I never had time to make the kind of friends who wouldn't mind housing an incinerated face.' Jack Armstrong wouldn't have minded, but I had neglected him for years and meanwhile he'd fathered three little girls.

'Family?'

I considered Mark and Edenham, but flinched from returning where I was known until some better patching had been attempted. Then I thought of my sister Florence. Matter-of-fact, pinned-bun Florence, housekeeper to an elderly widower in South London. Perhaps she wouldn't mind a mess hidden away in her back room.

Although the RAF was fighting a world war, it cared for its own. Letters were written, Florence interviewed and prepared, a car laid on. Otherwise I would have panicked at the last moment and bolted into a rehabilitation centre, probably never to reappear.

Florence and I hadn't met for years, which eased matters slightly. I could tell from her voice that the sight of me made her retch but revulsion was such a natural reaction I accepted it more easily than false jollity; once she became used to me, she behaved naturally in other ways as well. Like her employer, I was bullied for my own good and set to such tasks as I could manage. Although previously I had considered household potterings a waste of time, by then I was quite extraordinarily bored and found each small achievement enjoyable. I was not completely blind, but sunlight had turned grey and everything vanished into mist six feet from my nose. When I wanted to sleep I had to put a black cloth across my face, since they hadn't figured out yet how to graft on eyelids. Eventually it became a matter of pride not just to potter but to discover how much I could do. Once I had taken the decision to come out of hospital I hated more than ever the idea of being an object of pity for the rest of my life. Of course if people saw me they were revolted, then grovellingly sorry; the only answer was to avoid going out by day. And if most daylight hours would be solitary from now on, then the more I managed for myself the better.

Compassion would not help, nor easy indulgences. Only toughness.

I could read for short periods, and valued reading as never before. I spent hours anticipating and deciding on what I would read during the half hour or so before my sight blurred over; more hours considering, analysing, savouring afterwards.

I developed low cunning to maximise sight and movement: my left arm was stiff but usable, my legs very awkward after the cooking they had received. Still, I could walk, and because I always walked at night to avoid pitying curiosity, I fed greedily on blackout sounds, picturing life in South London in the blitz.

Inevitably, I wasn't good company and the first thing I made sure of was that the hospital covered my tracks from any second thoughts Audrey might have. Chris's mother, who kept in touch with Furnace Green gossips, had died the previous March: with luck, Chris ought never to learn what had happened, which was a comfort. Though she said she loved me, and probably did love me a little, I never doubted that when I failed to call again she would simply assume that I accepted our affair as hopeless.

Actually, I preferred to be alone, even Florence's prosaic care beginning to grate on my nerves.

One wet night I discovered how to make my old profession work for me again. It must have been November by then. An air-raid had been going on for some time, and the ground shook from the blast of bombs, the crack of guns. I liked raids. I ought not to have done, but I did. Death held no fear for me and I was in a state of mind where, for the moment, I was unable to take account of other people's suffering. I'm not proud of it, but it's true. Raids made me forget myself, their violence so elemental that exhilaration took the place of absent fear.

That night much of South London seemed to be tumbling into shattered brick and as I looked at smeared crimson, which was all I could see of earth and sky, I thought. The Jerries are making a better job than I did of clearing slums.

Then I thought, bombed property must be going cheap.

It was November 1941, remember. The Russians were in the war but practically defeated, America smugly neutral. No end to war in sight, nor any conception of a time after war.

We knew we'd win, of course, none of us had any doubts we'd win; it was the how and when which had become unimaginable.

But as I stood there I began for the first time to imagine it, and next day wrote to old Colestock under seal of secrecy not to let Audrey know where I was, asking him to act for me in buying blitzed property. I had a little money saved from that last frantic prewar year and borrowed a great deal more, on his guarantee. I think he was so relieved I really did mean it when I said I wanted nothing more to do with Audrey or my son, that a chance to exchange cash for conscience was truly welcome.

I am being unfair. He did everything I asked, and more, while working a ten-hour day at the Ministry of Supply. He kept my wife and son, and at the end of the war he and I owned between us sites in half the blitzed cities of Britain. As time went on I did a good deal of the work myself, learned to type, dealt on the telephone with solicitors, war damage assessors and so on. Property prices remained low for several years although never again so ridiculously cheap as in that winter of 1941, and both Colestock and I had an eye for development potential. We did not attempt to buy large sites, could not have afforded them out of our own resources, only the keys which would unlock large sites in the future. One day, a great many developers would find they had to buy out Messrs Colestock and Smith before they proceeded with their projects.

It was the nineteen-fifties before the great rebuilding boom took off; fortunately both Colestock and I believed in patience where land development was concerned. Eventually I became quite rich, and to a man in my situation money provided the chance to work interestingly out of sight. At last I had the means and leisure to clear slums; I am glad, looking back, that I left local councils to go crazy over tower blocks and stuck with small-scale refurbishments, where each scheme contributed something to the next. I understood the kind of homes villagers liked, and reckoned industrial workers were villagers at heart. My only regret is that I could not do more. I enjoyed the nineteen-sixties particularly, when the old oak table at Edenham was strewn with plans, the telephone rang often and I needed every capacity I retained in order to keep so many negotiations on the move; often, when my eyes played up, by memory alone.

I also used these years to discover more about the ridge. Once I could afford it, I also occasionally employed a researcher to chase after some of the queries thrown up by my own recollections and more amateurish incursions into the past, the infinite queries raised by Granny Paley's tales. Tales which, no matter how fantastic, proved each time to have some leavening of truth. Of course, an infinite amount still remains to be discovered and wondered about.

Really, that is the end of what I have to tell. I prefer tidy details, or I would have finished on the day my Lysander crashed. For me, the last forty years of my life have been more eventful than I could have dared expect, and in them I found a kind of peace, at Edenham.

In 1967 my son Robert came to visit me. He was then in his late twenties and it was only when his grandfather Colestock died that he discovered I was still alive. Audrey had married again, and he had always understood his own father was killed in 1940. At first, I had an absurd desire to hide when he said who he was, later, I was glad he came. After he got over his shock, I think he was too. We've become easy friends, although by the time he came my sight was too poor to be certain what he looked like. I believe he is well regarded in the oil industry and, strangest of all, his company is now drilling an exploratory well on Corndown. Oil on the ridge. I bet the Laffams would have devised a way of profiting out of that.

When my land-dealings produced their first surplus, in

1954, I bought Mark out of Edenham, which gave him enough to buy a cottage in the street and raise prize vegetables, as well as the first leisure of his life in which to play bowls and smoke his pipe on the bench outside the Black Bear. All three of his boys survived the war but none came back to live in the village, which is the tale of villages nowadays.

By then the surgeons had decided they couldn't do much more for me; I had eyelids, a nose and (more or less) lips again. The bits between looked moderate, as, at that time, was my sight. The Weald, my Weald, beckoned. I could not see its hills, but Edenham welcomed me home as its child. Each creaking board was familiar, the brook's spate in spring, the tap of creeper in a storm. Brick underfoot in the kitchen, worn into hollows by Rabbits, Wyses, Larkworthys. The snap of embers on the chequered brick hearth, a cat on my knees in place of Cheerful in his stall, and a sense which only grows with the years of having many unseen friends around me. The tiny, toiling figures cast by the first Master of Edenham into his splendid sixteenth-century fireback seem almost to move whenever I throw a fresh log on glowing ash.

Once upon a time . . . One day not long ago I was on the green at dusk, the time I still prefer for walking out. A young couple were there, standing beside their car studying a map.

'I wish I knew where the hell we are,' the boy said plaintively.

'Nowhere, really,' answered the girl. 'Come on, there'll be a road sign further on and then we'll see how to reach a motorway.'

They kissed and got back in the car, young and in love enough to kiss most times they touched. I heard them drive off to join the traffic racing along the ridge, three minutes or less before they passed Tisbury Hill. Tiw's Hill as it had long ago been called, when, through many centuries, men's entrails melted in awe as they watched its sacrificial pyres burn redly in the night.

Nowhere, really. A chance remark or did it warn of a deeper heedlessness?

I walked back to Edenham, slowly, needing a stick these days, and stood in the kitchen with its memories, laid my hand on the old dresser where I kept my haphazard collection from the ridge's past: the evil little figure I found as a child behind a rafter in number twenty-six, the street; a piece of slag whose shape I liked, and an old glass seal which probably came from a smuggled keg of spirits. On the wall I'd hung a Joseph Hosmer map, given me by Parson Bond when he heard I was coming to live at Edenham again. He was as old and doddery then as I am now, but a kindly well-wisher praying for my soul.

On the other side of the dresser from Joseph's map was a small framed cutting: *In Memoriam PORTNELL David, Lieutenant Royal Australian Navy, DSC. Killed in action, North Atlantic May 1943. Never Forgotten, Jimmy, Joy and Pete. Taree NSW.* Someone had seen it in the paper a year or so ago and Mrs Sleech brought it along, knowing I was interested in the ridge's history.

'There used to be Portnells in the shop, if you remember, Mr Smith. It isn't a common name, so perhaps this one might be some relation,' she said.

I had never once entered the shop since that last day of peace in August 1939, although now I know how it came there, I should have liked to touch the fine iron lockpiece I remember on the parlour door.

'I remember the Portnells who kept the shop,' I said, replying to Mrs Sleech. I remember, do you remember? Do we both remember still, oh Chris, my love? Some things are never easier with the years.

'Australian, though, just think of that. I wonder how Portnells got all the way to Australia, don't you?'

Well, there is Davey's letter, I could have said. One of my researchers found it among a collection of papers on early farmsteaders along the Manning River, New South Wales: *Dear Liddy . . . I remember how I was druv out of Sussex but with you this will be our home, Yr. very loving DAVEY.*

All things considered, I felt that Furnace Green owed a debt to this particular Australian who had come to help us and died in the North Atlantic, so I had framed the cutting.

And yet, despite so much of England's past sharing a single stretch of wall, in all the years since I came back to live at Edenham I had never taken the arrow from its hiding place above the hearth. That evening, after hearing those youngsters on the green, I did so.

The ridge, Tiw's Hill, the Weald, existed long before the arrow, but here in my palm lies the beginning of my tale. My son, Robert, has often said I ought to set down all I know about Furnace Green before it is too late, but always before I have resisted his suggestion. I am old and nearly blind, by most reckonings more than a little strange. But I know what I know, have learned, studied, discovered more, and this evening that snippet of overheard conversation finally convinced me he was right. The modern young hurtling between their motorways need a heritage too. Why? . . . I could reply that in my own extremity, this in the end was what upheld my courage and helped me to survive. Others might call on love, or rage, or hate to sustain them. Which is why I prefer to answer that fresh leaves only unfold each spring because sap rises up to reach them. And sap comes from roots and soil which have been a long time in the making.

As I stand by Edenham's hearth with Brac's arrow in my hand, I begin to realize just how formidable a work I am undertaking so late in life. But then, a task I can really get my teeth into is just what I most enjoy.

Once upon a time . . .

. . . THE WITNESS

The Coroner's inquest opened at 2.30 pm on Thursday 23rd April 1987. The first witness was Mrs Rosina Sleech of Furnace Green, who agreed that she went in twice a week to clean for the deceased, John Smith of Edenham Millhouse. Although the house was that full of bits and pieces you couldn't hardly call it cleaning, and Mr Smith got upset if you moved anything. Well, perhaps a blind man did need to know where to put his hand on what he wanted. Then there was that pert minx Sandra Hemmings with her dratted computer, printing out snakes of paper everywhere. Yes, Mr Smith was seen sitting on a seat on the green quite early last Friday morning but no one had approached him until later . . . About ten o'clock, she thought. Yes, he often walked some distance at night but seldom during the day. Poor gentleman, he was terribly burned in the war and people couldn't help staring, although really he was as nice and harmless as anyone could wish.

A gushing and irrelevant witness.

Victor Hawkins was called next, who stated that he had approached the deceased at about ten a.m. to ask if he wanted help to return home. Yes, they had known each other as kids. No, he wouldn't say they had ever been friendly. Yes, of course he had seen at once that Johnnie Smith was dead. No, he wasn't surprised. If he'd been burned like that he'd have shoved his head in a gas oven years ago.

A reticent witness.

The deceased's son, Robert, said that he had last visited his father two weeks before his death. Yes, he seemed cheerful enough, but then he always contrived to be cheerful no matter how difficult the circumstances of his life. In answer to a question, Robert Smith agreed that he was fond of his father and in recent years particularly they always got on well together. He added that his father had been engaged in writing a book, which because he was nearly blind and had become somewhat forgetful, frequently left him very strung up by evening. Although he would by then be very tired, he often walked too far in the dark, and in unsuitable weather.

But on this occasion he broke his usual custom and walked out in daylight?

The bed had certainly been slept in.

Can you suggest any reason for this?

I think so, yes. When I tried his tape-recorder I discovered that he had come to the end of what he wanted to say in his book. He loved Furnace Green and needed the daylight to say goodbye to it.

You are an oil company executive, Mr Smith?

The witness laughed . . . Even oil executives are sometimes capable of using their imagination, Mr Coroner.

An affectionate and unusual witness.

A verdict of death by natural causes was recorded on John Smith of Edenham Millhouse in the county of East Sussex, and three days later his body was buried in Furnace Green churchyard, where it lay between the dust of two ancestors: Mark Smith, one-time sergeant in Wellington's army, and Rose Oxley.